KT-433-414

Realm

The Armada is Coming

JAMES JACKSON

JOHN MURRAY

First published in Great Britain in 2010 by John Murray (Publishers)
An Hachette UK Company

2

© James Jackson 2010

The right of James Jackson to be identified as the Author of the
Work has been asserted by him in accordance with the Copyright,
Designs and Patents Act 1988.

All rights reserved. Apart from any use permitted under UK
copyright law no part of this publication may be reproduced, stored
in a retrieval system, or transmitted, in any form or by any means
without the prior written permission of the publisher, nor be
otherwise circulated in any form of binding or cover other than that
in which it is published and without a similar condition being
imposed on the subsequent purchaser.

All characters in this publication – other than the obvious historical
figures – are fictitious and any resemblance to real persons, living or
dead, is purely coincidental.

A CIP catalogue record for this title is
available from the British Library

Hardback ISBN 978-1-84854-001-9
Trade paperback ISBN 978-1-84854-002-6

Typeset in Monotype Bembo by
Servis Filmsetting Ltd, Stockport, Cheshire

Printed and bound by Clays Ltd, St Ives plc

John Murray policy is to use papers that are natural, renewable and
recyclable products and made from wood grown in sustainable
forests. The logging and manufacturing processes are expected to
conform to the environmental regulations of the country of origin.

John Murray (Publishers)
338 Euston Road
London NW1 3BH

www.johnmurray.co.uk

For my godchildren –
in the hope that they will be alive to history
and history come alive for them

1588, and England faces one of the gravest threats in her history. Some will triumph. Many will die . . .

Nought shall make us rue
If England to itself do rest but true.

William Shakespeare

ELIZABETHAN LONDON

Palace of
St James

Richmond
Palace

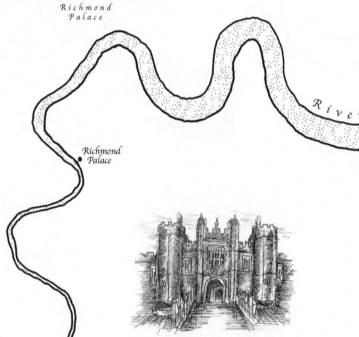

River

Richmond
Palace

Hampton Court
Palace

Hampton
Court
Palace

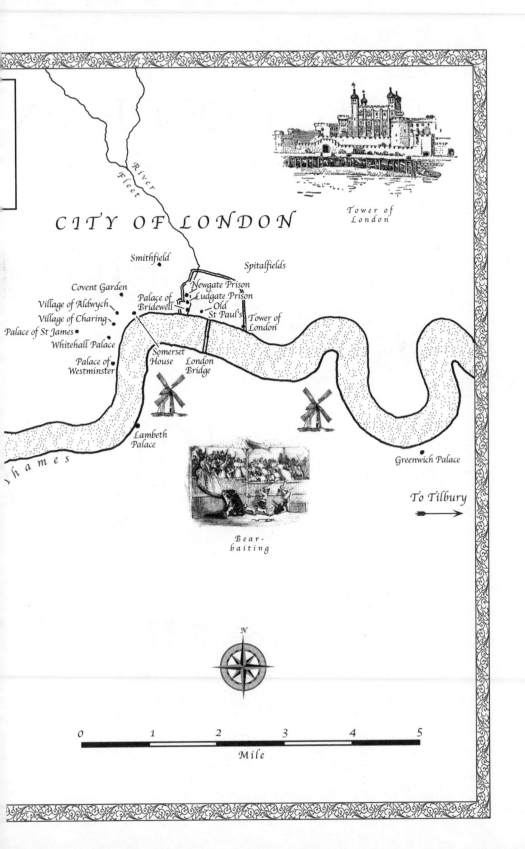

River Fleet

Tower of
London

CITY OF LONDON

Smithfield

Spitalfields

Covent Garden

Newgate Prison

Village of Aldwych

Palace of
Bridewell

Ludgate Prison

Village of Charing

Old
St Paul's

Tower of
London

Palace of St James

Whitehall Palace

Somerset
House

London
Bridge

Palace of
Westminster

Lambeth
Palace

Greenwich Palace

Thames

Bear-
baiting

To Tilbury

N

0   1   2   3   4   5

Mile

Beginning

Martyrdom had its own rituals and rhythm. She had asked for more time, another day or two in which to pray and prepare and make her peace. But the stone-faced nobles of Elizabeth had sneered the more, had reminded her they were present merely to announce her execution for the following morn. That morn was come.

Only a few hours since delivery of their news: a few hours for her to write last letters and final testament, to speak and dwell upon the words of the Old Religion. As she had lain upon her bed in the quiet hours, her ladies had gathered round and read to her stories from the times of Christ. He had died for her. Now she was to die for Him. There was no greater privilege or comfort. She would show how a true heir to the English Crown could meet her end: with dignified calm, with the strength and certitude of a Roman Catholic. No bastard offspring of the whore Anne Boleyn, no heretic usurper, would wrest the glory from her. Approaching six o'clock, drawing near to the appointed hour. The concluding act in the life and death of Mary Stuart, Queen of Scots.

Fotheringhay Castle, a grim and forbidding place set bleak upon its motte. Her own personal Calvary. In the hearth, the weak fire did little to chase off the pre-dawn chill. It mattered

I

little. She would not shiver or show fear. Her mind was on higher things, and her fingers clasped around a gold crucifix on which the Lamb of God was fixed. What honour to shed her blood for the cause, to be a rallying beacon for the coming war. Those who had tormented her, those who had entrapped her, would one day lose their humour as they in turn were forced to mount the scaffold. She felt a visceral rush of excitement at such prospect. As God was her judge, it would happen.

'Your Majesty.'

She lifted her arms while her ladies-in-waiting busied themselves in respectful grief to fasten the jet acorn-buttons of her black satin gown. Much care had been taken in choosing her wardrobe for this moment. Set with pearls and trimmed in mourning-velvet, and with sleeves slashed in imperial purple, it would add presence and regality to the event. *Your Majesty.* She was indeed a queen – a queen wronged, a queen betrayed, a queen denied her rightful place upon the throne of England. Instead, her neck was to be rested on the block and her head struck from her body. By order of her own kinswoman and cousin Elizabeth. Yet vengeance was so close, and these murderers so blind.

For a moment she thought she could hear the hammering of carpenters at work in the great hall below. But the sounds were simply imaginings of her mind, the residual echo of a night through which artisans had laboured to create the stage for her passing. Each dull thud of a mallet or rasp of a saw, every nail-booted step of the guards outside, had made the outcome more solid and her destiny assured. Their efforts were as nothing to the great enterprise under way in Lisbon, to the provisioning and preparation of ships and the mustering of troops. King Philip II of Spain was embarking upon holy crusade against England. And she knew, had read of it in the secret communiqués smuggled to her by friends and loyalists.

A pity she would not live to see the ancient faith restored, or to witness the conquering Spanish enter London. A pity too those secret messages had been intercepted, those friends and loyalists compromised, caught, and turned. Walsingham had brought her to this point.

That name, that dark eminence. Sir Francis Walsingham. The spymaster of Elizabeth had sent so many to the rack and scaffold, had placed so many agents, had revealed so many plots. She had been wrong to believe she could outwit him, foolish in thinking there was any sanctuary from his reach. Ever austere and always watchful, with the patience of a serpent, it was Walsingham who had uncovered her scheming and pursued her to the end. His henchmen would be secreted among the gathered audience, would soon report on her destruction. Perhaps he would raise a smile, a toast. She had other concerns. Besides, there was scant advantage in regret.

Her women fastened the girdle at her waist and attached a rosary, placed a pomander-chain and *Agnus Dei* about her neck. The finishing touches. She was forty-four years of age, and in her nineteenth year of captivity in England.

She reached and lightly brushed the tear-patterned cheek of her favourite servant. 'No weeping, my sweet Jane. I beg it of you.'

'Forgive me, my lady.' The eyes and voice were hollowed in sadness. 'It is too much to bear to see you mistreated.'

'Mistreated? I am raised up, chosen by God to do His bidding.'

'We lose you, my lady.'

'Nothing is lost save the frailties of flesh and the burden of existing. Be happy for me. I have prayed for this moment, for relief from my suffering. Now it is upon me.'

'May we not mourn for you, my lady?'

Mary smiled in gentle admonition. 'I forbid it. For I go resolved and willing as penitent sinner to my fate.'

'You leave us behind, my lady.'

'To rejoice and to well remember and to keep alive the name of Mary Stuart, Queen of Scots.'

'I could not forget, my lady.' The voice of the lady-in-waiting constricted between sobs.

Drawing her women close, Mary comforted them, her words soothing, her arms embracing. For long years they had been her companions and confidantes. No secrets were left; nothing remained to be done.

In turn, she kissed them. 'For your service I thank you. For your friendship I thank the Lord. Be strong. Our parting is but a temporary thing.'

Another servant wailed. 'You are our mistress and our very reason, my lady.'

'Even as dust I will continue to be so.' Mary stepped back. 'Now fetch the men so that I may say my farewell.'

They processed in — her surgeon and apothecary, her steward, her porter, her groom, all stooping to press their lips to her proffered hand, each burdened with a private anguish. Then she took a few morsels of bread soaked in wine, the better to sustain her in the desolate drama ahead, and withdrew alone to her oratory. The Last Supper followed by Gethsemane. Her attendants waited.

Dawn brightened into day, the sharp February sunlight glancing between embroidered drapes and presaging a promised spring. New beginnings. Mary prayed on in silence and seclusion before a wooden cross. Doubtless her Protestant slayers would claim such clement weather reflected divine benediction on their efforts. They could suppose what they liked. Past eight o'clock.

'*Open in the name of Queen Elizabeth! Attendance is called! Make haste!*'

Interruption was rude but expected, arrived with urgent

4

shouts and a flurry of loud impacts on the oaken door to the bedchamber. The ceremonial escort was outside. Access was given, and a man officious and ill-tempered in his duties marched through. Mayhap he thought the prisoner was flown, perchance he suspected the traitorous Catholics would pull one final trick. He would take no chances.

Kneeling and composed, Mary glanced up at him. 'Why, if it is not the Sheriff of Northampton.'

'You are required, madam.'

'Solely by God my saviour.'

'Your appointment is with the block. Let us away to it.'

'Is there such hurry?'

'There is engagement to keep and a delegation at the door.'

'Fain would I have them wait.' She raised herself to face him, and scrutinized him further. The man was of a type she recognized, raw ambition wrapped in finery and a ruff. 'Each to our business, my lord sheriff.'

'We shall maintain it as such.'

'I will not protest.'

She turned and kissed the foot of the wooden cross before following him, pausing only while her ladies fitted her veil. It was a dressing of finest lawn edged in bone-lace, attached with silver wire to her caul, and falling in delicate train down her back. She was ready. Tenderly, with the frozen emotion of departure, her ladies completed their task and curtsied low. The door opened, and Mary Stuart made her exit.

Familiar and unsmiling faces greeted her. The dour countenance of her jailer Sir Amyas Paulet, the kindlier visage of the Fotheringhay castellan Sir William Fitzwilliam; there too the regretful expression of the Earl of Shrewsbury and the choleric-hued eyes of the Earl of Kent.

The latter noble was spokesman. 'Events undo you, madam.'

'I remain unbowed, and the Spirit of the Lord is with me.'

'Your composure does you credit. It will be needed, for you go to mount the scaffold unaided by your servants.'

'That is not the custom.'

'It is the order of my queen.'

'Am I not her cousin? Am I not anointed queen of Scotland?'

'To us you are mere traitor.'

'While to others I am but sacrifice and victim.' She peered in turn at the assembled. 'Is it not desirable the manner of my death should be observed and reported by those who know me? Is it not right that some dignity and rank be accorded me even as I face the axe?'

Quick looks were exchanged and agreement reached. Kent nodded. 'Very well, madam. Your steward and three manservants may join the foregathered in silence and obedience; two ladies may help disrobe you. That is all.'

'What of my priest?'

Anger emerged as a scowl. 'I am not so mutable and persuaded as the Duke of Norfolk, madam.'

Indeed, he was not. The old duke had been a fool, had fallen prey to her coquettish and calculating ways, had served sentence in the Tower for his misjudgement. Kent was of a different humour.

He leaned forward. 'Servants you may have; popish comforts you may not. Put aside your crucifix and carry instead your blasphemous faith in your heart.'

'Shame on you, sir.'

'No shame exists in what I do. It is my instruction.'

'Instruction will save none of you. England is for the fiery pit. Those Protestant lords who this day condemn me shall themselves be condemned. Those who believe themselves architects of my damnation will one day prove themselves draughtsmen of their own.'

'Be silent or be bound.'

'I will be bound by nothing save my religion.' She smiled benignly at the discomfort caused. 'My noble lords and sirs, today it is my reckoning. Tomorrow it is yours.'

'So let us dwell on the present.'

Mary kept her gaze steady and resisting. 'I lift my eyes to heaven. Now you shall see how Mary Stuart gladly meets her long expected end.'

Journey to the site of execution could begin.

Black canvas draped the scaffold. Set near the centre of the great hall, it was a simple structure some twelve feet square and raised two feet from the ground. Upon it, surrounded by quantities of scattered straw, and itself standing two-foot proud, was the grim focus of the piece, the block. And lying close on a fold of dark cloth was the sharp and wide-bladed axe. A stark scene for a portentous drama – one lit by the leaking sunlight, by the rows of tallow lamps hanging in their brackets, and by the warmer glow cast by a roaring blaze in the fireplace. Still the coldness clung.

An audience of three hundred had assembled. Behind a row of drawn-up soldiers, lords and notables were seated. To their rear, standing or settled on trestle benches, were others. Local worthies and churchmen, the invited burghers and the curious – all had been brought together by prospect of historic and defining act. Expectation and low murmur filled the room, a festiveness that mingled oddly with drab unease. The weight of the moment could ever dampen the pleasure. It had passed the hour of nine.

A stirring, a craning of necks and swivelling of eyes, and whispers eddied through the crowd. It had begun. Members of the retinue took their places, and principal actors approached the stage. Here, the Dean of Peterborough, severe in his ecclesiastical gown; there, the executioner and his assistant, anonymous in their leather hoods and tight-fitting jerkins.

'*The prisoner arrives.*'

They rose in unison – not in respect for the condemned, but in deference to their queen who had signed the death warrant. Somewhere a drum beat a funereal tattoo. Then, preceded by the Sheriff of Northampton, Mary Stuart, Queen of Scots, entered her arena.

Shocked and collective silence fell upon the whole. She was not what they anticipated – not the alluring demon of their nightmares, nor the devious papist siren who had served as talisman and rallying-point for rebellion against the Crown. Just a stooped figure, made stouter through imprisonment and moving slowly for the raised platform. Yet there was something undimmed in her manner, a majesty and serenity that transfixed. Beneath the veil a half-smile played, and the famed auburn hair marked her steady passage through the crowd. Truly a royal presence.

With the aid of her two ladies, she climbed the three steps to the scaffold and halted to listen as the words of the commission for her execution were read.

Standing below her, the Dean of Peterborough began his address. 'It is not too late to renounce your sin, never too late to reject Catholic heresy and vile superstition and adopt the Protestant faith of this nation and our sovereign queen.'

'I am settled in my religion, Mr Dean. And I am here to shed my blood for it.'

'Then you will surely suffer the torments of hell.'

'On the contrary, I escape the torments of this world for the wonders of everlasting life.'

'Unburden yourself and become a child of Christ.'

'He shall receive me at this hour and at the moment of my death.'

'Be reconciled to our cause, my daughter.'

'Do not trouble yourself, for I rejoice in my own.'

The Protestant minister knelt at the base of the steps to pray in loud and sonorous tones. But Mary turned her back and prayed louder, her voice rising strong and her words in Latin echoing through the hall. Spectators shifted uneasily at the sound of the forbidden rites. They had not heard such utterance for many years. Undaunted on her podium, Mary stood her ground.

As the churchman finished, Mary knelt and clasped her hands, changing to the English tongue for her plea of intercession.

'O, Lord, in Your mercy, wash free our cares, banish the afflictions of the English Catholic faith, have pity upon my son, and allow Elizabeth my cousin to serve You in years to come. May the saints intercede for me, may the good citizens of this kingdom return to the path of righteousness, and may God avert His wrath from our beloved England.' She kissed her rosary, crossed herself, and spread wide her arms. 'As Christ suffered and died upon the Cross, so too must I stretch out my arms and be received into Your embrace. Forgive my sins, O God, and take me from this world of travail.'

She rose, the creak of her Spanish shoe-leather loud against the muted backdrop. The pageant was inching towards finale. It was the turn of the axeman and his aide to beg forgiveness, a formal act lent trembling intensity on the stage. They lowered themselves before her.

'Will you pardon us for what we must do, my lady?'

'Willingly and with all my heart, for now it is you I hope who will end my troubles.' She murmured closer in the ear of the executioner. 'Should you perform with the skill and quickness of the carpenters on this scaffold, you shall have from me no complaint.'

There was convention to observe, the need to undress. Calmly, she seated herself on a padded stool and surveyed the throng as her ladies moved to her side. One removed her veil, the other the ornaments from around her neck.

'I confess I have never before put off my clothing in such company.' Hands loosened her girdle; fingers that had so recently fastened the buttons began to unpick them.

'Majesty . . .' Desolate anguish spilled from her servant.

'Reserve your sorrow for those without faith, dear Jane.' She returned to her feet, permitted her ladies to fuss round.

'May God go with you, my lady.'

'And always be with you.' Whispered conversation broke off as the Queen of Scots cast a warning look at the encroaching executioner. 'Touch me not, good man. You are no groom of mine.'

He ignored her and pulled free her gown. She had wanted dramatic effect, was counting on its impact. The audience gasped, its breath held in three hundred throats. In front of them, a slash of colour in the blackness, Mary was revealed in crimson satin bodice and velvet petticoat of brightest scarlet. The symbol of blood and of Catholic martyrdom. None could ignore its meaning or duck the visual shock-wave.

Mary exchanged glances with her servant standing wretched with a silken scarf in her hands. '*Ne cries pas pour moi. Ne cries pas.*' The blindfold was tied about her eyes.

Mumbling their prayers, her weeping ladies were ushered away. On the bleak scaffold, the Earls of Kent and Shrewsbury had assumed their places on low stools and the execution team was ready and flexing. Beheading was a performance art. For a few seconds Mary was alone in thought at the threshold. This was her life, her purpose, her consummate act. Let all see, and let the heart of Walsingham quake. Fulfilment and ecstasy bathed her bound and upward-tilted face. She found the cushion at her feet, and sank to it before the block.

'*In Te Domine confido, non me confundat in aeternum* . . .' In You, Lord, is my trust; let me never be confounded.

Carefully she reached out, her fingertips touching and tracing the contours of the wood. She was a pilgrim at the start of a journey, a supplicant at the altar. Leaning forwards, she positioned her chin in the groove and held wide her arms.

'*In manus Tuas Domine commendamo spiritum meum.*' Into Your hands, O Lord, I commend my spirit. Four times she called out. The assistant to the executioner placed a steadying hand on her body, and the axe swung.

The blade bit deep, its contact thudding hollow and startling and ballooning into the shivering atmosphere. Yet it was no clean strike, and steel had embedded in the back of the head. A messy undertaking. The mouth leached an involuntary groan. Cursing to himself, the executioner prised metal from bone and arced the weapon again into the descent. Accurate and almost through. Bending to his labour, the axeman worked the edge and severed the remaining sinew. Butchery was done, and the head fell away.

Sudden violence gave way to a dread and unsettled stillness. It was a pall beneath which people blinked stupefied or clenched tight their eyes, balled their fists, muttered oaths or prayers. Ten o'clock. On the dais, blood coursed and collected in rivulets.

'*God save the Queen!*' The executioner held aloft his detached and battered prize.

The Dean of Peterborough joined him in rousing cry. '*So perish all the enemies of the Queen!*'

'*Amen to it!*' Parading near the slumped torso, the Earl of Kent gleefully entered the chorus. '*Such be the end of the enemies of our Queen and Gospels! May they all share this bloody fate!'*

But few seemed to listen. They were concentrating on the ashen face of the deceased, on the lips that parted and closed and which seemed to curse them all. Surely wrong had been done. With still less dignity, the head dropped from its wig and bounced hard on the boards, its aged features twisting, its hair cropped and grey, its mouth continuing in secret monologue. The axeman bent to retrieve it. Close by, the Earl of Shrewsbury retched and wept.

There was more horror. In the aftermath, as spectators were herded dumb and troubled from the hall and the executioners worked to strip their carcass, a muffled whine sounded on the platform. From the deep folds of the petticoat in which it had been hiding, a small Skye terrier, treasured companion to the departed Mary, emerged cringing. It sniffed and whimpered, recognizing the scent, disturbed at the strangeness, and crawled through the thickening slick to cower forlorn below the headless shoulders. The creature would not be leaving its mistress.

Accompanied by a small retinue, the Earl of Shrewsbury rode hard and south along the Roman road for London. With luck, fair weather and the aid of fresh horses stabled on their route, they would cover the distance in good time and bring their news to the Queen. Behind them at Fotheringhay the scaffold would be dismantled, the blood sluiced, the vital organs removed and burned, and the corpse sealed in a lead casket. All signs, any relics or tokens of remembrance, were to be expunged. As though Mary had never lived.

Beyond sight of the riding-party, far ahead, was another horseman. He too was making the journey of some eighty miles; he too had witnessed the grisly spectacle in the great hall. But his destination was different. He carried his report to the orchestrator of that day, the spy chief and Principal Secretary of State Sir Francis Walsingham.

Chapter 1

EARLY JANUARY 1588

'Haste, my brothers.'
The voice carried urgency; and a light Scots brogue came from a man who paced fretfully at the wharfside. He had cause to sweat and fear, motive to curse the wind and check constantly the tide. On enemy soil, conjuring escape was ever part of the plan. He glanced once more to the east, followed the trailing rays of the sun across the immense vista-sweep of the river Tagus. Out there were galleons and hulks, the silhouttes of a fleet that seemed larger by each day. He had watched it grow, had visited warehouses and boatyards and counted the guns, had prowled the mansions of the Bairro Alto and listened to a thousand conversations in the street-warrens of Alfama. Spying could make faint-hearts of the bravest. *Haste, my brothers.*

A wine-barrel was rolled past, and he bent to assist. All hands were needed, every wit and sinew required to maintain the deceit. They were Scottish merchants, committed neutrals and dedicated traders unfettered by hostilities between England and Spain. It allowed them to voyage at will, and won them precious and unchallenged entry to harbours and ports the length of Europe. Lisbon was merely the latest waypoint on an unremarkable run. Nothing to draw the eye.

He back-swiped the perspiration from his brow and muttered another prayer. Soon they would be beating out to sea, conducting their retreat. Not a moment to waste. He knew things – secrets gleaned from numberless sources, mysteries unearthed, encrypted and stored for clandestine delivery to receptive hands. Such information could see him killed. He had heard tell of agents eliminated by a stiletto-blade to the back, of others choking their last on subtle blends of poison or kicking vainly against the strangulating grip of a ligature. There were too the covert ferrets vanished or silenced during public fiesta or sudden street melee. The life-cycle of a Protestant spy for England had tended to be shorter of late.

Along the length of the Baixa, hoists delivered goods to the holds of barques and freighters, crews hollered, and lighters moved with purpose among the weathered hulls of larger craft. An industrious scene. The ships would take advantage of a break in the Atlantic storms, would sail with their sacks of spice, their silks and leather, their salted fish and strips of cork, to offload and resupply in the berths of northern Europe. Yet some were heading nowhere.

'Do I intrude on your time, Señor Hunter?'

They were English words without malice or anger, were akin to a sentence of death. The Scotsman was staring. Into his vision-field had stepped a figure of darkness, a tall and gaunt man in the black soutane of a Jesuit. With him were Spanish soldiers, pikemen and musketeers wearing steel morions and fanning out to encircle and impede. Inquisitor Garza had arrived, and he was methodical in his approach.

The captain muttered softly to his crew. 'Steady, brothers. Rash move will have you killed.'

They were unlikely to attempt a breakout. The paralysis of shock had rooted them where they were, their labours abandoned, their expressions fixed dull with awareness of their plight. Their captain spoke for them.

He folded his arms, a merchant-mariner wronged. 'I did not suppose my affairs the concern of the Inquisition.'

'Temporal or spiritual, all things are matters for our scrutiny.' Garza moved closer. 'Such scrutiny informs and leads. Such scrutiny brings you to capture.'

'This is affront to the very name and dignity of King James of Scotland.'

'On the contrary, it is the netting of spies.'

'Spies? We bring naught save friendship to Portugal and Spain.'

'A friendship I do not desire.'

Bluster and lie would not preserve the Scotsman, the Inquisitor reflected. He had observed it before, experienced the pleading and beseeching cries of men, women and children unmasked as heretics and base Protestant enemies of the state. Spain was a force for revelation and good, he the executor of its Catholic will. He took no selfish pleasure in it. Humility was too important. It was the dry duty of his faith and the manifestation of his life-calling. That calling had urged him on long journey, had seen him consign thousands to the galley-oar, the garrotte or purification by fire at the stake. Throughout Spain he had brought terror, in the Low Countries had sat on the Blood Council and crushed revolt with determined zeal. King Philip of Spain could rely on him. It was why he was appointed to become Inquisitor-General of a conquered England.

He sensed the controlled desperation in the speech of the merchant.

'Our wares are not the stuff of intrigue. See, we carry items for trade, the usual objects of our business.'

'Yet you dwell too much in ours.'

16

'I am wedded to commerce alone.'

'You are in league with Satan and England, a servant of Francis Walsingham.'

'I serve none but myself. Examine our papers, our cargo.'

'We shall.' Garza peered unpityingly at the trapped man. 'We will further inspect what is borne within your mind and heart.'

The pale Scots complexion had acquired a greyer underlay. 'I am a true Catholic, a believer in the ancient faith.'

'Reciting the catechism, possessing a rosary, renders you dissembler rather than devout.'

'We are innocent men.'

'There is none innocent in the sight of God, no truth that may not be determined by the rack.'

'As He is our judge, we do no wrong.' Stuttering protestation tumbled fast.

'I shall be your judge before the greater trial.' Without turning, Garza directed a command to his cohorts. 'Begin.'

They obeyed in disciplined order, advancing to dismantle and tear open every article within their grasp. Ropes were sliced, casks split, the contents of hemp sacks and wooden chests tipped and sifted. In mute wonderment and fear, the crew looked on. Even their shoes were taken and the soles cut away. Nothing would be left unprobed. At the centre, a still presence among the bustle of destruction, the Inquisitor stood motionless. His face showed only the barren detachment of one accustomed to inflicting suffering and whose soul was bled of feeling. The features of the merchant-captain were more mobile. Garza marked time, stroked the plain wood crucifix about his neck.

Discovery was made. A shout as a keg ruptured and a Spaniard rummaged among the splinters and soft release of brined cheese. His hand emerged clutching a greased inner receptacle that was quickly slashed wide. Reality arrived in a thin sheaf of papers.

'Drawings of ships and description of guns; tabulation of troops and crews.' Garza received and cursorily perused the pages. 'Is this your meaning of commerce? Of innocence? Of belief in the ancient faith? Of friendship?'

'My men have no part in it.' The truculence of the damned.

'Unhappily, they find themselves ensnared.' Inquisitor Garza gave a new order. 'Take them.'

Protest was noted then ignored, the captain and his coterie bound roughly and dragged away. To be scared was their sole remaining right. The search continued. Garza picked his way through the working throng to a corner in which a man sat apart. There were few distinguishing characteristics. He was dressed as any local in jerkin and hose, wore a cap pulled low above his eyes. Most would overlook him. Not the Inquisitor. The seated observer of events was privy to conspiracy, essential to the task. Indeed, he would prove himself more useful, more powerful, more critical in this year of 1588 than an entire army of Spain. And he was English.

The renegade nodded to Garza, addressing him in the Spanish tongue. 'Holy conflict devours another.'

'A single arrest leads ever to the next; the slightest rumour brings us irresistibly to the door of further perfidy.'

'Do not misjudge the guile and endurance of our foe.'

'I embrace it.' The Jesuit tracked the gaze of the Englishman out to the dark forms of the fleet. 'We are a force your country cannot thwart.'

Eyes narrowed. 'My country? It is the country of Elizabeth, a country stolen, a country seized by Protestant robbers who poison minds and punish our faith.'

'Have no fear, we shall return it to the path. Reckoning is soon.'

18

'Soon is too easy a word. The Marquis of Santa Cruz sits idle and aloof, his Armada builds too slow.'

Garza tendered a warning frown. 'Let the commanders to their purpose and we to ours.'

'Each day we tarry, Elizabeth prepares.'

'She stalls, holds tight her purse, sends emissaries forth to sue for peace. These are not the signs of strength.' The Inquisitor tugged at the cincture of his robe. 'Meantime, we blind Walsingham, silence his agents, sever the rapacious tentacles of his office.'

'There will be more.'

'All of as little consequence as the rest. Be still, friend. Our moment is close. England may build alarm-beacons throughout the nation. Yet her people will not guess of the fires we will start, of the pyres we shall set in every town and village and into which each heretic and traitor will be cast.'

Nor would they comprehend their queen would be killed before a single Spanish soldier put foot upon their soil. The Inquisitor was right, the renegade mused. He should be patient, could afford to wait. An old Iberian proverb counselled that a man who bided long enough at his gate would in time see the corpse of his enemy carried past on a bier. He had bided for years, was well practised in the craft of killing. The Spanish needed him; the Spanish called him by his code-name *Reino*. In English it meant Realm. It was the body of *Gloriana*, Queen Elizabeth of England, he would witness being ferried to the grave.

~

Seers and soothsayers had prophesied disaster, had foretold a year beset with woe and rent by destruction upon fair England. Porpoises had been observed cavorting in the river before the watergate to Greenwich Palace, and stranger happenings sighted in the evening sky. All the signs could be interpreted, any interpretation feed prediction and rumour. The populace had reason to dread. Spain was readying. That knowledge and foreboding clung as toxic as the sulphur-stench of burning sea-coal in the frost night air.

Midnight. On the south bank of the Thames, people did their best to forget. From Lambeth to Southwark they swarmed, noble and commoner dancing and drinking, gaming and whoring. Along the entire stretch, the world was at play with a frenzied compulsion that lit up the darkness. There were jugglers and fire-eaters, acrobats and freak-shows. There were games of dice, cups and cards, matches of quoits, bowls and irons, the ad-hoc entertainment of bodies being flung dead or alive from taverns. And all brightness had its contrary shadow. In the alleyways, brawls and knife-fights erupted and subsided and ignited again; among the fields and pleasure-gardens, ha'penny-fucks and sodomites coupled with abandon beneath the trees; around the baiting-pits and whipping-posts, spectators gathered to lay bets as dogs tore badgers, horses or each other to pieces. Close by the church of St Saviour, bigger spectacle entertained: another shift had ended, and the mauled carcasses of bulls and bears were dragged from the gabled arenas. Heaven or hell. Anything could be had; anyone could be taken.

And everywhere noise, the pulsing shouts and screams of crowding humanity. The hollering of tapsters and patterers crying their wares; the call of doxies; the snatches of song from wandering balladeers. Boisterous times.

'*Who will see this bound dwarf lowered in a barrel to pull from it live eels with his teeth?*'

'*Do any seek a cure to the ague?*'

'*What will you have? What do you want? A pie? A cut of venison? A piece of fowl?*'

'*Oars! Oars!*' The sated were calling for river-craft to carry them home.

Trade was bountiful and brisk, the stalls and booths thronged. Bowls of wine and punch, bottles of ale and liquorice-spirit fuelled the raucous merriment. Even the cut-purses who preyed on the unwary, the prancers and priggers who robbed and pilfered in hordes were enjoying themselves. If this were the end of days, there was impulse to commit to revelry. One evening in the reign of Good Queen Bess.

On a crude and sawdusted stage lit by burning torches, a fencing-master demonstrated his artistry with rapier and dagger. Men and women had flocked to see. They had been drawn by the wildfire-talk of others, had drifted from nearby cockfights and wrestling-bouts, from cookshops and bawdy-houses, to marvel at the prowess of this young warrior-god. Their applause was rewarded with virtuoso display. Candles were snuffed with the flick of a steel tip, weapons were spun, thrown and caught; multiple foes were disarmed and sent tumbling in mock and acrobatic duel. Spectators cheered and whistled the more. Christian Hardy acknowledged them with a bow.

He stood, light on his feet and with a smile on his face, a youthful and commanding presence who could steal a show and at will appropriate female hearts. Yet there was no arrogance or conceit. He might have been a courtly gallant, but for the hardness of the soldier in his build and the practised ease of the veteran in his manner. Not for him the costumed swagger and peacock pretence of nobility.

His audience studied him, pleased at what they saw, enraptured by the body-alchemy of athleticism and fine looks. There was the way in which he held himself, in which he filled his hose, his felt boots and his brigantine jacket of armoured blue velvet. There was the tautness of line, the subtle assertiveness of cheekbone and chin, the ultramarine of eyes set below light-brown hair. Something of more southern latitude might have sat exotic in his blood. He in turn looked back at them.

They who had travelled short distance to this place would not have conceived how far he had journeyed. Born to an English adventurer and noble Maltese mother, he was product of love and war, the offspring of a union made and blessed during the brutal months of the Great Siege of Malta some twenty-two years before. His father had been a hero, a celebrated fighter who had manned the ramparts and refused to yield against an Ottoman foe and overwhelming odds. It was a miracle he had survived the siege, a tragedy he had succumbed to the pistol-shot of a traitor. That traitor met his own bloody end, as did others who had sought to destroy the daring boy from Albion. A Prior Garza was among them. He had been killed by crossbow-bolt fired by Fra Roberto, the rebellious priest and friend to the English warrior, the humane and roguish giant whom Inquisitor Garza had voyaged eventually to hunt down. Revenge rarely came colder than in the calculating twin of the late prior. By then, Fra Roberto was an old and spent force, had put up no resistance as the Spaniards pulled him from his hermit seclusion and hanged him on gallows set above the gates of the walled city of Mdina. The child Hardy had watched.

Time did not heal, but merely clawed wide existing wounds. For a while he had remained and grown on the Mediterranean island, learning the skills of sailing and combat, nurturing contempt for the imperious and pitiless ways of the garrisoning Spaniards. Contempt evolved to hatred. One night he had heard a scream, had stumbled from sleep to find his mother fighting for life and virtue and a Spanish captain of the guard manhandling her to the ground. He could not stand by. With youthful fury and a drawn blade, he had attacked, the officer attempting in vain to ward off the blows. The result was foregone. A body lay bleeding and a culprit was sought. By darkness, aided by friends and persuaded by his mother, the fifteen-year-old boy stole away.

His was an odyssey that took him through Italy and France, that led into countless incident and taught harsh lessons of survival and endurance. He thrived. Contacts were made, missions performed, and always the urge lingered to harm the interests of King Philip of Spain and subvert the servants of his dominion. Eventually he reached England, land of his forebears. Now he was twenty-one, a linguist and fixer, a dealer and chancer, a swordsman of renown, a seafarer, a spy. Of use to the state.

He flicked up a wooden sword with his booted toe, expertly caught it, and dipped its blunted end in a leather pail of chalk. 'Who is man enough to face me in mortal combat?'

Raucous whoops replied, and a hesitant volunteer was propelled forward to gleeful acclaim. The joke was already evident. He was bandy-legged and hollow of chest, a fall-guy with a feather in his hat and a grimace on his face. Perhaps he would make a stab, take a run at it. Hardy hauled him to the stage.

'Your rapier, sir.' The fencing-master pressed the facsimile weapon into the sweating palm, took up a matching instrument. 'Assume your guard.'

The man obeyed, a comic turn palsy-quaking in his fright. His supporters yelled their approval. Christian Hardy surveyed him.

'Think of me as the Spaniard, as the devil who would seize all that you cherish, who will steal your family, your home, your soul and your life.'

'You shall have none of them, sir.' The stammering reply seemed to surprise even its deliverer.

'Is this so?'

'I will stand against whosoever come to take England.'

'A fine answer.' Hardy nodded in salute. 'Yet will you fight well? Will you prevail?'

'You shall find me willing to die in my effort.'

'May Saint George smile on you.'

Saint George probably laughed. Emboldened by his status as newfound champion of the weak, the man rushed forward in attack. An error. Sticks collided, the blow was parried, and with effortless grace a counter-strike was planted home.

Both the fellow and his feathered cap emerged in sorrier state, and a white mark was scored on the front of his doublet. No harm caused, except to dignity. There were jeers and catcalls, the good-natured banter of a crowd well satisfied.

Hardy addressed them. 'Here, a white spot. On the field of battle, a blood-red stain. Practise your skills, my brothers. Follow each parry with instant blow, be quick with your mind and sound on your feet. And never extend beyond your balance.'

Demonstration was done. Yet as his victim retired sheepish from the stage, another recruit pushed his way through the mob. A very different prospect. Hardy rested on his makeshift sword. The newcomer was young and handsome, perhaps his own age, had the dress and bearing of an aristocrat. Friends and flatterers attended. There was sport to be had, face and reputation to uphold. Always hazardous.

From his vantage, Hardy waited. He recognized the strutting bravado, anticipated the challenge. The starched and goffered ruff, the satin splendour of the doublet with its pinking and peascod belly, the brocaded richness of the mandilion jacket slung across wide shoulders. A vision of privilege, a picture of baiting hostility.

Gripping the edge of the platform with pigskin-gloved

hands, the arrival peered up. 'You defeat a jester. Do you dare cross blades with your better?'

'Should I find one, I shall face him.'

'He is present.' With a single bound, the man vaulted to meet him. 'Now he is opposite.'

'Is this offer of fight?'

'It is promise of a memorable incident, a pledge to knock you from the plinth.'

'I have heard tell of men whose tongue speaks louder than the weapon in their hose or held at their side.'

A hand rested on the hilt of a rapier. 'Why talk of the sword when you may draw it?'

'My tutoring is complete for the night.'

'Mine is not.' Liquor and aggressive intent flushed in the noble features.

'Step away, stranger.'

'Concede to me first, knave.'

'Knave?' Hardy considered him. 'What argument is it you have with me?'

'One I shall win.'

'I have no wish to cause you mischief.'

'Yet I have urge to bring you wound.'

Mood and conditions had changed. The warmth of the crowd had ebbed to glacial quiet, nervousness replacing the previous gaiety. They expected a kill. It was a contest that intrigued, competition that would be one-sided.

Hardy paced slowly, exploring the ground, feeling his way. 'You are no soldier, stranger.'

'Test me.' The man freed his rapier. 'Choose your second weapon. Buckler or *main-gauche*?'

For a bully and braggart, the young noble was certainly committed. Buckler or *main-gauche*, the Tudor or the modern way of duelling. Hardy opted for the buckler. A small round shield fashioned from hardened cowhide, no more than twelve inches across, it would cause less hurt than the dagger. The contestants armed themselves.

Raising his shield high, Hardy squinted over its rim. His opponent was swaying, gauging. 'You would be safer elsewhere, stranger.'

'I would be less content.'

'A rope-dancer or ventriloquist provides ample delight.'

'Not as this.' The man lunged.

There was space to play awhile. Blades and hilts clashed, the rapiers pitching and rising in busy exhibition. Hardy worked his arm, tipped and circled his wrist, his breathing steady, his feet adroit in their advance and retreat. He kept moving. Inertia was for novices and the dead. His buckler blocked, his right hand thrust. He could hear the grunts of his rival, see the calculation in his eyes and the tremor of exertion in his limbs. The man had been taught well, had like many devoured the texts of the master Morozze. It would not alter the outcome.

Point scored. A tear had opened in the trunk hose of the stranger. Second strike. The padding was leaking, its bran, cotton and horsehair contents spilling through the vent. A third hit and the filling was cascading and scattering on the crowd. The hose had lost volume, its owner any semblance of respect. Uproar and hilarity were assured. In frenzied desperation, his face reddening to the colour of his hair, the noble fought back. His rage paralleled the general joy. Someone would be injured.

Patience was spent. Switching position, feinting and drawing back, Hardy pivoted and leaped again with the point of the steel extended. A clumsy manoeuvre, intended to be. The shield of his rival swept hard, swatting aside the immediate threat, leaving exposed a face that registered belated

26

knowledge and alarm. A rapier flailed. But Hardy was inside it, his buckler now a weapon and its rivet-heads driving full into cheek, nose and teeth. Blood sprayed with the onward velocity, and the young noble dropped shrieking.

The victor crouched low beside him, his breath unhurried and misting in the chill. 'A fool and jester after all. Digest well the teachings of this night.'

Response was muted.

With that, Hardy rolled his beaten adversary from the stage.

Early hours saw Hardy returning by wherry across the Thames. Around him the cries of boatmen scudded fitfully on the black water and the spreading skeins of ice. None cursed louder or more rudely than these folk. An eel-boat rode close, its proximity igniting an oath-laden exchange. Old habits and London custom. Hardy ignored them, sitting low in the stern and pulling tight his cloak against the gathering breeze. Catching the gusts and the flickering bonfire-light, the sails of windmills turned above the departed shore. They prompted reminiscence of the past, of stories told about the Great Siege, of the arms on the windmills of Senglea afire and rotating to disintegration. Another memento of the father he had not known.

The wherryman spat overboard and did not ease his stroke. 'Mark me, sir. When summer comes and the sun smiles, the Spaniard will come.'

'We shall do for him.'

'I would glad gut wide any foreigner with my knife. Yet it is said their army is large, and their fleet of ships with it.'

'Drake singed them once, will have at them again.'

'I pray God you are right, sir. Who knows what we may face?'

There was one who might have fair idea. Hardy did not reply.

A lantern in his hand, he alighted from the bow platform to the landing-stage and negotiated the rimed planking to the lower end of Temple Lane. Before him, the dirt track climbed the elevation to Fleet Street, its short and unlit stretch passing the halls and church, slumbering residences and smoke-infested inns. He had walked it many times, had doubtless encountered before the same black rat that now careened past on secret quest. Each to his own trade.

He emerged on to Fleet Street, the noise of the thorough-fare loud and its illumination strong after the brief peacefulness of the gloom. But it was quietening for the night. A couple of guards manned the gateway to the Bar, two more stood bored beside a corpse still hanging from its gallows erected near St Dunstan-in-the-West. Few would cast a second glance. In the morning, the remains would be quartered and dispatched for exhibit in varied parts of the metropolis. By then, scavenging kites would have rummaged out the eyes and tongue. The authorities liked to reinforce a message.

Dodging the wheels of a late dray, Hardy crossed the rutted track and slipped into the passageway of Fetter Lane. Darkness again. He paced on, impatient to be home, anxious to see Emma and to climb to the warmth beside her. She would be awake. There was scarcely a moment she did not worry for him, never a day he did not count his blessings or give thanks to God for her. She was an unassuming country girl with beauty, warm eyes and gentle ways, a soul of strength and sweetness who understood without too much talk. A lover and friend, a woman who had near-tamed him; a wife and haven to whom he hurried, a mother to their sole child, Adam. She did not care for London, preferred instead the freedom of the coast and fields of Dorset where once they had met and courted. Yet she stayed by him, would do so unto death.

To the left and right, orchards and market gardens rolled out around the half-timbered houses and tenements. He knew the landscape as well by instinct as by sight. Their cottage behind Plough Court was a simple affair, had been costly too in so popular a locale. Everyone wished to be here. Not Emma. He smiled to himself, drawing close to the turn, his lantern casting its weak beam ahead. Another brace of buildings was under construction, dwellings he could well afford. It was fortunate he had inherited not only the sins of his father but also his Ottoman gemstones, battle-trophies sewn into the clothes of the son and used as currency and insurance as he passaged through Europe. On occasion they had bought him his life or a favour, had allowed him to corrupt the highest to the low. Prize-money of his own had since supplemented his wealth. At twenty-one, he was close to the age at which his father perished. Luck ran in families, sometimes ran out.

Shadow within shadow, a footfall that disturbed. Over the years, he had learned to trust and tune his instinct. Briefly, he paused – long enough to detect the hard shuffle of feet and discreet snap of a winter twig, to feel the prickle-warning of his nerve-ends. More than two spectres followed him. They had increased their stride, were confident but careful, had plainly taken the decision to commit. No characters fallen drunk from a local tavern these, no casual ruffians stumbling opportune upon a victim. Too purposeful for that. They had been assigned. At least they would be carrying daggers for close-in slaughter, were not likely to risk the unpredictability or clamour of powder and shot. Distance was narrowing. He raised the lantern, the better to be seen, the easier to coax them in. But his eyes were averted, adjusting to the dimness.

Three men were in pursuit, had readily identified their target as they idled at their charcoal brazier in Fleet Street while he passed them by. The setting provided sufficient cover for their role. A quick and wet job, a rapid escape, a welcome payment. Few complications existed. Of course, they had been advised of the sly nature of their prey and the quality of his skills. In previous nights they had witnessed for themselves his embellished demonstrations. But clever swordsmanship was no match for surprise and brute force. Nice to be on the move, to ease numbed hands and feet back into life, to earn a killing wage.

The lantern glimmered at the edge of an alleyway and disappeared, its light re-emerging glow-worm soft among the trees. A short-cut, an opening. The men went forward. Ahead, the outline of the cloak indicated position, the sound of water passing described the scene. Their victim was taking a piss, would have his hands full. They drew their blades and struck.

'Eventful and bloody night for us all.'

They had recognized their error, had spun from the draped cloak and the water-butt with its streaming tap to confront the voice behind. Hardy had chosen his killing-ground with care. One man raised his knife, entangled it in an apple-branch, and died with a single exhalation and a rapier through his abdomen. The next went low, crouching and jabbing blindly in his fear. He too fell, his wrist broken with a downward snap of the blade, his eye pierced with a solid thrust that penetrated brain and skull. Hardy kicked off the weight and deployed for the third. The assailant was blundering terror-stricken in his flight.

Escape lasted fifteen paces, culminated in a grunt and impaling to the cross-guard of a different sword. Hardy recovered his cloak and lantern and moved towards the late arrivals.

About him, firebrands blossomed in the hands of armed men.

'As flies to honey do they seek you out, Hardy.'

Isaiah Payne lowered the body to the ground and daintily wiped clean his blade before handing the soiled cloth to a companion.

'You come late to the feast, Payne.'

'Solely that I may more enjoy your scraps.'

He produced a falsetto laugh that conveyed little humour. Jest only made him the more unsettling. Dressed in high-crowned hat and current fashion, he was an emaciated figure with protruding eyes and full lips, a composite grotesque of effete flamboyance and nervous tic. Several of the fresher heads on spikes atop London Bridge owed their lofty position to his intervention. Isaiah Payne, the perfumed bloodhound. He was a thief-taker mutated to hunter of Catholic seminarists and recusant priests, a Searcher, a vital accessory in defence of the realm. The costume and fripperies were mere dressing. He was a dangerous and fastidiously sadistic man. Walsingham found employ for many kinds.

Taking a spluttering torch, Payne stooped to examine the corpse. 'Cropped ears, Hardy. Little more than a common thief and hireling.'

'Thus his readiness to flee instead of fight.'

'There is scarce fight in him now.' A foot turned the prone head. 'A week past, I vouch, he was content to sup with other swill in the sewer-dens of the Savoy. Yet the promise of easy game and wage lured him out.'

'All to the advantage of our tally.'

'What are three among a popish infestation of thousands? They are as lice, Hardy. We crush them here, they breed there. We scrape them from the body of London, they gather and cluster in darker recess.'

He carried his inspection to the remaining dead, identifying one as a low-level denizen of Bridewell and admiring the eye-wound inflicted to the other.

'Regard, Hardy. Soft and unsullied hands more used to working a rosary than a knife.' He gestured to his men. 'Search him.'

They found nothing. Payne accepted their news as though his suspicion were now confirmed.

Hardy kept his distance. 'You know him?'

'Of him. A recruiter of rough and mercenary ruffians sent to execute the wishes of the Spanish and to slay the upper ranks of our intelligencers.'

'I am flattered by such attention.'

'He is less enamoured of it.' Payne lifted the head to study the exit wound to its rear. He released his hold and straightened. 'A lively night, Hardy.'

'One I am happy to bring to swift close. I bid you well, Payne.'

'We are not yet completed.'

'I give you performance across the Thames and bodies in this garden. That is completion.'

'The master awaits.'

'He may continue to wait until I am slept.'

'Do so in the saddle. You ride.'

Refusal was no genuine option. Grudgingly, with the shiver-fatigue of skirmish and exertion, Hardy accompanied four of the company to their horses. In silence they mounted up and trotted out, threading their way past Aldwych and along the bridleway of the Strand. To either side were the palace-mansions of the grandees and courtiers – of Leicester and Burghley, of Raleigh, of Worcester and Bedford. Men who jockeyed and feuded for power and privilege. For sure they slumbered through the winter night. They would neither appreciate what was done for them nor fully comprehend what was undertaken in the name of their queen. Hardy pressed on. It would be Emma who was kept waiting.

Chapter 2

Plot and threat were everywhere. So the bosom-viper Mary Stuart, 'Queen of Scots', was gone. It made no difference. England was crowded by the forces of Spain and the insidious menace of the Catholic Church in Rome. Yet she could fight, would still confound her enemies. The figure rested from his papers and wearily rubbed his brow. Late night or early morning, there could be little pause in his toil, but limited relief for one immersed in the affairs of a state in mortal danger. Bad tidings were about. He closed his deep-set eyes to contemplate, his body motionless and severe in its cladding of black doublet and starched white ruff. In this dark and panelled room, for this broodingly intense and fiercely brilliant man, there was no allowance for frivolous comforts and no concession to the cancer that clawed him from within. Sir Francis Walsingham was in residence.

From every corner the messages came, always the same, confirming the gathering might of the foe, revealing the next attempt on the life of his queen or the identity of another Jesuit sent to subvert. He could not allow his guard to slip or his vigilance to wane. England depended on him. It was why one of his agents had blackmailed a gentleman-of-the-chamber to Pope Sixtus V and gained access to a letter from King Philip II of Spain detailing the entire battle-plans for his intended invasion. It was why he had a Flemish spy inserted in the

Lisbon household of the Marquis of Santa Cruz, commander of that venture. And it was why he had over fifty high-level sources planted in the royal courts of Europe, hundreds more scattered under cover in ports and towns from the Black Sea to the Baltic. Their every report was sifted and logged, each paper read by him and signed with his personal trefoil cipher. The greatest espionage network in history. An extraordinary and terrible burden.

The Armada. Inexorably it grew; inevitably by the summer it would sail. He had done his utmost to delay it, more than most to divert the coming thrust. Through his endeavour, a mercenary force had been assigned to France to fight the Spanish-backed Duke of Guise; with his persuasion, Elizabeth had conceded an armed assault against the Duke of Parma and his Spanish army in the Low Countries. Neither venture was successful. At least there was Drake, his friend and fellow Puritan, who in previous year had led his flotilla to Cadiz and run riot amongst the ponderous Spaniards. Pressure-points existed to be pushed. But it was not enough.

Outside, among the knot-gardens and sunken walkways, his guards patrolled. It was not beyond the bounds of possibility or reality the enemy might try to strike him here. Even in the seclusion of Barnes, cloistered in the privacy of his Barn Elm manor, he was not far from their reach or the river Thames. What prize it would be to take the head of the guardian of England, to murder with poison or dagger the finest spymaster of his age. From this place he surveyed everything and con-trolled all; from this place he sent out his couriers and intelligencers on countless mission. Seventy horses were main-tained in his stables, their riders waiting on his command and sealed letter. A vast web, a most meticulous spider.

Vibration on the diamond-patterned panes, the suggestion of hooves on compacted earth, roused him from his thoughts.

His invitation had been accepted and his visitor was arrived. They would be in conference for a while.

Doors opened and closed, hushed voices and rapid footfall intruded nearer, and Christian Hardy stood before him. Walsingham continued to read. Eventually, when satisfied, he put the paper to a candle-flame and rose to drop its burning remnants in the hearth.

'You survive ambush and escapade, Mr Hardy.'

'My cloak is the worse for it, your honour.'

'Small price for your life.' The Secretary of State gestured Hardy to be seated and poured him a goblet of wine. 'The tempo and gusto of their assaults are stronger by each day, Mr Hardy. I am the wind-gauge, and the wind turns foul.'

'There is news, your honour?'

'None that may improve the mood of the Queen or of her council. We know King Philip directs himself to our oblivion, know too the number of his ships and men and disposition of his barges. Yet we cannot appraise where his army will make land nor the matter of its timing.'

'We may send further expedition against him in his harbours. It is already shown successful.'

'Her Majesty disallows it. She believes it wasteful of our resource, considers our navy better used close to our shores where the men view clearer the land for which they fight.'

The voice lapsed to introspective silence, leaving Hardy to savour the wine and guess at motive and intent. It was leading somewhere, but the route would be circuitous. The dark eyes of Walsingham emitted nothing.

'For whom do you fight, Mr Hardy?' An opaque and calculating question.

'I wage war to protect my wife and child.'

'Or to earn the acclaim of your father from his grave.' Walsingham nodded in confirmation of his own answer.

'Were the older Christian Hardy alive, he would salute a fellow soldier, would envy your intrepid endeavour in our cause.'

'I thank you, your honour.'

'As we in turn owe debt to you. Was it not you who sailed with Drake to Cadiz this April past and burned or captured near forty Spanish ships? Was it not you who saved the life of Drake in storming the fort set high above Cape Sagres? And was it not you who was first to board and take the Portuguese carrack *São Felipe* off the coast of the Azores?'

'It was privilege to play some part.'

'A part that has enriched our state and diverted for a moment the thunderbolt of Spain.'

That moment was plainly gone. Hardy was aware of the labyrinthine climb to revelation, felt himself manipulated to its course. Flattery before the fall. He let his gaze catch on the peripheral glimmer across the room, detected the reflection of candles on a polished steel cuirass.

Walsingham observed the shift in his attention. 'New armour for my person from the Dutch. There may come the day when we all must don breastplate and helmet and do battle in the field.'

'Many sound men prepare for it, your honour.'

'There is yet less visible contest in which we must engage, and for which you show an equal gift.'

Espionage and soldiering, Walsingham and Drake, the flip sides of the same lethal coinage. For the English admiral Hardy had sailed and plundered, had thrown himself into dangers that made lesser souls retreat. For the English spymaster he had run errand and gauntlet, had bribed and blackmailed, had sub-orned and dispatched. Each hierarch claimed ownership of his talents and possession of his soul. He accepted such demands with proficiency and cheer.

The shrouded countenance and measured voice were unchanged. 'I recall your excursion to France to attempt for me the kidnap of the papal legate.'

'It failed.'

'Other exploit did not. In league with our City merchants, you cajoled and persuaded the gold exchanges and banking houses of north Italy to deny credit to the Spanish Treasury. Madrid was starved of funds, its Armada of supply.'

'Fortune lent me connection with the financiers Corsini.'

'And deeper connection with their daughter, who was but sixteen years of age.'

Hardy squinted at him. 'Duty calls me to many parts, your honour.'

'From some of which you scarce escape.' No beat was missed, no expression flickered. 'For some, providence is more unkind. We lose agents, intelligencers whose word I covet and whose repository of detail may yet help turn the blood-tide of the foe.'

'You have one in mind, your honour?'

'A merchant, a trusty by name of Hunter, whose dozen ships ply the seas from Naples to north Europe. He sees things, espies the flow of hostile vessels gathering on the Tagus. Now he is taken.'

'You desire his return?'

'That or his infinite silence.' The eyelids lowered a fraction.

'It will be arduous, your honour.'

'Perchance impossible. Yet he is the kernel who must not crack, the core that must stay remote from the probing of his captors.'

So that was it: a prisoner requiring saving from the enemy or himself. For the greater good. Hardy breathed deep, let scenario and implication wash across his brain. Walsingham would not tell him all, was too far ahead to bother with elaboration. He needed a job done. There was no bombast or embellishment, no reminder of office or rank. Just the quiet forcefulness of his manner and cold energy of his eyes. Choice that was never a true choice.

Hardy drained the goblet and placed it down. 'My ship is ready?'

'The *Black Crow* anchors at Margate. You will receive under sail the remainder of your instruction.'

'I would ask your honour to permit me my full complement of cut-throats.'

'You may carry two of the three. The third, your Maltese knave, resides in Newgate under sentence to hang. His error was to steal the mount of the Lord Dudley, Earl of Leicester.' If there was jest, it stayed covert. 'Your graver mistake this night was to beat senseless to the boards the beloved stepson of that noble lord, the young buck and gallant and favourite to the Queen. The Earl of Essex himself.'

'My apologies if I cause offence.'

'You will garner instead the regard of the court, who tire of the impudent and vainglorious pup.'

Hardy dipped his head in acceptance. 'Are there matters else, your honour?'

'None that may not wait. You will be aided by Portuguese patriots loyal to their own Crown and chafing at the Spanish yoke. Use them, deploy them to advantage, find our man to discover what he learns. And should you choose to bring brimstone and fire upon Lisbon, you shall not see me oppose it.'

Conversation was over. Hardy stood to take his leave, aware of past audiences he had here attended, the perils and trials to which they had brought him. History was forged and destruction meted from this twilight chamber. He wondered how many bodies were hid behind its stained panels.

39

Concluding word went to Walsingham. 'Of some curiosity, perchance, Mr Hardy. The man Hunter is held in shackles by one with the title and name of Inquisitor Garza.'

In the monastic stillness of the house, Walsingham resumed his labours. Before him were bills of lading, the paper-trail of trade and diplomacy that might yet stay the poised fist of King Philip II of Spain. Twenty-five thousand bars of tin, thousands of tons of oak and cast iron, all to be shipped gratis to the Ottomans. From the tin the Turks could make musket-balls; from the bell-metal of destroyed religious orders they could produce cannon and shot; from the seasoned timber of English forests they could build sturdy hulls and oared galleys. Anything to please the Sultan, to persuade him to send force against the soft and southern underbelly of Catholic Europe. Again the pressure-point, the indirect approach.

He gasped, rode out the surge of pain and bit hard into a leather strap. Had to concentrate, had to keep alive for the sake of his queen. Too much opiate would merely serve to dull his instinct. Panting, shuffling grey and sweat-streaked to the fire, he bent and stoked the blaze back into semblance of combustion. His bones and gut ached, his soul felt heavier than its fifty-six years. For the last fourteen of those, as head of foreign and domestic intelligence, he had sacrificed his health and being to the continued existence of the Protestant nation. The project was almost complete.

Flame stirred memories. He sensed the heat, heard the echo-cries, of St Bartholomew's Day 1572. What ghostly sights, what haunting sounds. On that day of 24 August, the Catholics of Paris had risen up and butchered the Huguenots, had provoked wider murder of defenceless Protestants across the whole of France. White crosses were daubed on the doors of targeted dwellings. Slaughter then ensued. He had been there, as English ambassador, had sought to protect as many cowering innocents as he could. They were pitifully few. He would not forget. And the Pope in Rome had struck a medal commemorating great victory. Walsingham gazed further into the flame. Perhaps it was recollection, or maybe it was portent.

~

'Again.'

At his command, his men held the head of the bound and seated prisoner, tilting back his chin, prising wide his mouth and forcing once again the rag between his teeth. The shouts became grunts as the tongue and teeth resisted, as breathing laboured through a mucus-filled nose. Inquisitor Garza sat close and considered the subject.

'There are ways to avoid such pain, Señor Hunter. There are means to attain understanding between us.' With fully comprehending eyes, the Scotsman stared back. 'Tell me what you know, Señor Hunter. Advise me of your sources here in Lisbon, where they are secreted and the nature of their findings.'

Response was disappointing, came with a stubborn shudder of the head. A definite no. But Garza was patient, had been *Inquisidor* long enough to appreciate the pulse and nuance of the torture-chamber. Should the Scotsman endure, there were other practices to which he would be inducted. *Garrucha* or strapping, in which the victim was hoisted aloft with weights attached to his feet, could dislocate every human joint; *potro*, the rack, could lengthen the body and shorten the life of any within its grasp. They might yet be called upon. Garza always broke through in the end.

Anticipation before the deluge. Today was for *toca*, the subtle art of introducing water into the mouth and lungs to

41

induce the sensation of drowning. Outside these dim-lit dungeons of the Estaus Palace, the populace of Lisbon milled and thronged around the Rossio and went about their daily lives. A few paces distant, hidden behind the unadorned frontage, an alternative existence had been created. It was one of question and answer, of punishment and reward, of a ceaseless attempt to enforce the writ of King Philip of Spain and ensure the supremacy of his Church. Effort and diligence were required.

A pail tipped and water sluiced across the gaping lips to drench the embedded rag. The fight for survival could be strenuous. Rearing, choking, his eyes straining wild in their sockets, the Scotsman emitted hard gargling sounds. His hands would be flailing, clutching at his throat, had they not been tied. It gave Garza pause for thought. Most merchants were rogues, men who would sell their wives or mothers should a profit be assured. Not Mr Hunter. He protected his knowledge with a bravery and foolhardiness that suggested the high value of his secrets. Condemned by his very struggle. More water went in.

'Hear me, Señor Hunter.' Garza leaned close to the blackening features. 'Ease your suffering. What can be more important than your life? Are the machinations of Walsingham worth all this? Will he come to your rescue? Does the bastard queen of England care one ducat for a lone and cast-off Scot?'

He saw the dying of the light, the fading tremors in a torso whose movements pulsed less frenzied and extreme. With a sharp tug, he released the gag and let the water surge. It erupted in vomit-cascade as though soul and bowels came with it, the heaving back and retching throat projecting liquid over flagstoned floor. Air worked its way in; grating and contorted sobs forced their way out. Slowly, the body clawed its way back. An ugly sight, with accompanying noise.

'Well may you groan, Señor Hunter. We have your plans, your ship, your crew. You have so little left.'

A voice that was ragged and waterlogged. 'I have my God.'

'A cold and valueless thing. Like your chief, Walsingham, He is nowhere here and is unexercised by your fate.'

'I am a merchant.'

'Then conduct your trade. I offer you relief from torment in return for your collaboration.'

The man still gulped for air, his voice rasping. 'You discover what you need.'

'There is more. You are condemned, a soul whose days draw soon to close. Ease your travails, confess to me.'

'I tell you all.'

'You reveal nothing. And nothing begets horrors and torture of deeper hue.' Garza sat back and lightly held his crucifix. 'Today you drown. Tomorrow, who may guess? I pray you may save yourself this plight.'

'Pray as you wish, priest.' The Scots brogue slurred wet.

'You inform your masters of our design, notify them that our guns fire high and in main are cast of iron. You advise them too of rumour in our ranks, of the quintals of powder and weight of shot, of the stores we set aside.'

'Any among us might have inserted such message.'

'Yet it was you who did so. Identify to me the names of your agents.'

'I have none.'

'You have a wife? A son? A daughter?' The voice of Garza was insistent. 'One future day they shall receive a cask, a barrel overflowed with your cured remains.'

'My concerns are not of your jurisdiction.'

'They are brought to my attention. Am I so different from your Francis Walsingham? Are we not engaged in equal and deadly pursuit? Are we not each inspired by our fervent conviction?'

Again the excuse. 'I am a merchant.'

'And I your Inquisitor.'

Garza had flayed so many to their core, had shone light into the darkest recess of traitorous minds. The Scotsman was tough. Yet he would be taken apart, piece by piece, pared back until his spirits and skin lay bleeding on the ground. The Jesuit thought of other times, of his assignment to the Inquisition tribunal of Granada in the wake of the uprising by Arab Moriscos. Brutality had quickly suppressed the revolt. Each victim now had resonance with the past, every situation equated to similar results he had before achieved. Same words, same defiance, same capitulation. From Granada he had moved on with his questing intellect and busy hands.

Without ceremony or announcement, he left his seat and walked for the doorway. A guard stiffened to attention as another swung wide the studded portal. There were more prisoners to visit, letters to write to the Suprema in Madrid, the renegade Englishman with whom to confer. At least the Scotsman was held. Whatever he had gleaned would never reach London; whatever annihilation was planned for heretic England and its queen would avoid disclosure to Sir Francis. Garza strode through, listened to the squeal of hinges and the crash of the latch. Behind him, the drumming heels and bubbling cries of Mr Hunter were resuming.

In another place, in a different jail, misery also prevailed. If several kinds of scream existed, none came more varied than in Newgate Prison. There was the pained and strangulated shriek of a captive flogged at the post, the screech of those going mad, the hopeless calls of men protesting innocence or beseeching pity. The jailers were as impervious as the walls.

Only the inmates who drank themselves to a stupor in the below-ground shebeen seemed content. They were half dead anyway, were already in the underworld.

Accompanied by a seasoned team of warders bearing cudgels and lanterns, Christian Hardy picked his way across the open sewer for firmer ground. The brown flow coursed foul and sluggish through the central enclosure, infected the air with its corrosive stench. Treacherous terrain. And the far side was no improvement. The path to hell was scattered with primrose, passage here marked by the eggshell-crackle of lice and roaches crushed underfoot. All scavenged for survival in Newgate.

They went deeper, their lights crawling faint into alcoves and corridors and guiding them down the steep switchback stairs. Pale faces stared from the darkness, eyes and expressions dulled. Humanity was in chains. The visitors splashed on through the puddled labyrinth, turning to descend a last flight of steps and arriving before a heavy-set door placed low in the dripping wall. It would take a man on hands and knees to enter, a miracle for one ever to get out. Bolts were shot, the door lifted, and Hardy took a lantern and crawled in.

'You take your time, Christian.'

'This tavern is not one I frequent.'

He was a swarthy and thickset man, mid-thirties in age, his back resting against a corner and his shackled legs stretched out in relaxation. A study in nonchalant repose. Neither circumstance nor surroundings appeared to disturb him. On his lips was a smile, in his eyes amusement, and the laconic greeting in Italian reflected only ease at privation and hardship. The orphan-boy who had once killed with knife and slingshot scores of enemy Turk, who had befriended on Malta the earlier Hardy, had grown to manhood and become asset or inconvenience to Christian Hardy the son. Luqa had reached London, and was in trouble.

45

'Is Luqa come to this?' Hardy crouched and raised the lamp. 'You were a saltpetre-man, were tasked with collecting the piss of horses. Instead, you take the favourite mount of the noble Earl of Leicester.'

Luqa shrugged. 'I lacked adventure.'

'You have it now. A hanging awaits you.'

'I do not complain.'

'In three days you go to the waiting-cell, and then to the gallows.'

'What of it?'

'I tire of such antics, Luqa.'

'So you come to release me? To return me to the light?'

'I am here to bid you farewell.'

The news was accepted without rancour or reproach. Good tidings or bad were to be treated or dismissed with the indifference common to a risk-taker. If a wound did not slay a man, the plague might; if sweating fever did not bring him low, there were plenty forms of flux and pestilence that could usher the Reaper to his door. Luqa was well beyond the age to which many survived. He was blessed. But blessings were finite, in this stinking hollow had reached their end.

Luqa yawned. 'This week past, a Catholic priest was starved to death in the cell beside me.'

'They create room for others captured.'

'Your Walsingham is busy in his work, Christian.'

'Threat rises and he must meet it. He sends me on mission, Luqa.'

'With Hawkhead and Black Jack?'

Hardy nodded. 'We sail from Margate within the week.'

'And you leave me behind.' The inmate sniffed, unconcerned and casual. 'You need me, Christian.'

'It is over.'

'Over?' The head of tight black curls was cocked to one

side. 'When is it ever over, Christian? When have I not stood by you? When have I not guarded your back or parried the blow as I did for your father?'

'I am powerless in this instance.'

'Your words bring such comfort.'

They laughed, the exasperation of Hardy dissolving against the comradely insouciance of his friend. He had learned from Luqa the alley-skills of a fighter, had absorbed the feral tricks and insights of an islander who grew to manhood with a whirling sling in his hand and a tally of dead to his name. The bond was secured, the loyalty total.

A head ducked through the opening, the scowling face of a guard appearing in the feeble glow.

'Come away from the prisoner. Greeting is done.'

'We have more to say.'

'Keep it for the seconds before he swings.' The man spat a nugget of phlegm against the wall. 'Many reserve their best for the last moments.'

Luqa sighed. 'Quick, a nosegay for me, Christian. The plague enters my home.'

'As a lash may cut your skin.' The threat communicated intent.

'I expect no less.'

Luqa stared him out, willing him to confrontation. Hostility was mutual and meant. There might come an hour when the challenge was accepted, when the custodian dragged his obdurate prisoner to the pressing-room reserved for crushing confession from a victim with weights. It would provide amusing diversion for the guard.

But Hardy intervened, his tone placating. 'Good man, I heed you and withdraw. I ask solely the chance to take from this wretch my brotherly leave.'

'Make your parting swift.'

47

Hands clasped, glances were exchanged, and Hardy backed out to join the grudging warden. Inside the cell, Luqa began to whistle a little tune. He was killing time, was prepared to slaughter anyone.

~

Further goodbyes were necessary. In a limewashed room in their house off Fetter Lane, Hardy held Emma and stroked a tear from her eye. He could feel her tremble, sense the quiet and aching grief that came always with his departure. It was the anguish of every potential widow. And he cursed himself for inflicting such hurt, blamed himself for so routinely bringing sorrow to his home. Yet his wife would forgive. It made it the harder to leave, encouraged part of him to want to stay and another to wish to sail fast and avoid regret. So he clung to her and kissed her face and said kind things.

'Be brave, my sweet. Be strong.'

'How may I find strength without my husband?'

'You are never without me.' He touched her face and caressed her hair. 'As I am never without you.'

'I saw your cloak, Christian. I placed my fingers where the sword-thrusts came.'

'A mere and merry incident.'

'Would that it were so. Would that you were named Tarlton and were jester to the Queen.'

'My work is of more grave and great import.'

'Than your wife? Than your son?'

'I am called by my commanders, Emma.'

'No, Christian.' She shook her head and gazed in his eyes. 'You are guided by your nature, drawn by adventure, by the darkness of your trade, by the edict of Walsingham.'

'Should other men go in my place? Would it be right I ignore the call to arms?'

She understood duty. But it would not assuage the misery or quench her fear and doubt. He rocked her tenderly in his arms. How many times he had done this, had whispered encouragement in her ear and sworn he would return. There were occasions when he had strayed, when events and rash urge had led him to the bedchambers of ladies or wenches. There were too events when a sword-blade or musket-ball brushed close to his cheek and grazed his existence. It made him who he was, allowed him to come alive. Emma would be waiting, accepting, ready to salve and bind the wounds and conscience of her beloved man. He belonged to her, and her possession was assured.

'I will be safe, my Emma.'

'You know this?'

'Always.' He pressed his lips against hers. 'Have I ever failed to come back?'

'No.'

'Have I carried injury that could not be healed?'

'None I have observed.'

'So be still in your soul and be close this night with me.'

Grateful to forget, wanting to commit, she yielded to the pressure of his body and insisting movement of his hands. Clothes peeled, fingers travelling and coaxing, talk subsiding into tongues. They swayed gently, their breath deepening. Craving and temperature grew. Fluid embrace acquired the clumsiness of roused and profounder passion, sighs becoming groans, inhalation and exhalation shuddering to staccato gasps. Man and woman had met. Skin warmed on skin, building the moment, riding the shock-wave, sliding together as bodies tumbled indiscriminate to the bed. A force of nature; a form of madness.

She drew up her knees, let him inside with panting urgency and visceral need. Emotion and physicality fused – desire and despair, celebration and mourning, all emerging in bucking limbs and the arc and fall of labouring backs. Hardy felt the bite of her teeth and the tracing mark of her fingernails, tasted her sweat and love and the intensity of the act. He was out of his body and into hers, was creating a creature only they could make. It had a spirit and energy, a sound of its own. Something else.

An unburdening, an enfolding, a rapture and release. Emma moaned, her husband cried out. The heightened state ebbed, and the two were left spent and entangled on the spread of twisted linen. Exhaustion fell leaden upon them. In the stillness of the aftermath, Hardy cradled her in his arms, just clasping and being, listening to the easing beat of her heart and steadying pulse of her breath. So comforting and known. He was sacrificing it for the menacing and the strange.

He woke and rose early, fumbling in the dawn gloom to light a taper from the fire-embers and transfer its flame to a candle. Emma slept on. Rapidly he dressed, splashed with water the sleep from his eyes and ate bread and dried meat for the journey ahead. He was almost ready. Noiseless, he crept through to the room in which Adam slumbered, placing down the light, kneeling beside the cot to take leave of his child. May God bless and preserve him. Hardy put his ear close. The small breaths of the two year-old were barely audible yet could wring the heart; the little hand still wrapped itself instinctively about his finger as he reached to touch the palm. With a prayer and a racking sadness in his throat, he leaned and kissed the powder-soft curls. It was the practised gesture of an absenting father.

The wood shutters cracked soft to the sound of a tossed pebble. They had arrived. Hardy was in position, seated and waiting in the downstairs parlour. He crossed to the window and threw wide its cover, the cold air inrushing and the shapes of two men framed and silhouetted against the morning frost. Hawkhead and Black Jack were present, two-thirds of his team.

No words were exchanged. Without pause or backward glance, Hardy vaulted through the opening and joined his companions. The crossing was made.

Further east, where London Bridge reached the north bank of the Thames, a pair of waterwheels turned in the current and pumped water along lead sluices to the City. As light glimmered in the sky, a corpse floated unobserved into the course of the wheels and was pulped on their broad paddle-blades. Isaiah Payne had disposed of his trio of bodies in the Fleet, and the ebb tide had done the rest. In death as in life, things often went full circle.

Chapter 3

'Wake, you cur.' The prison guard yelled through the low opening. 'Even slops are wasted on your miserable belly.'

There was no answer from the cell, not a sound to indicate habitation. The guard was unconcerned. If the prisoner had died in the night, so be it. That was the lot of many in Newgate. But this inmate had been in rude health, appeared to relish surroundings and sojourn that drove other men to despair or lunacy. A difficult one, this foreign knave. His insolence, his self-assuredness, his banter, all provoked. Nothing a whip or noose would not cure.

He called again. 'Make movement, you dog. Shake a leg. Show me you live or I shall give you cause to regret you do.'

The chamber stayed silent. Cursing aloud, vowing to make the chains rattle and their incumbent bounce, the warder placed down the bowl of gruel and with his lantern wormed his way through. Argument would be brief. He had cracked enough skulls, fractured sufficient bones, to instil fear around the prison and confidence within himself. A sound beating could banish most ills. The captive had to learn, was probably a detestable Catholic as well as mere horse-thief.

He looked about him, caught instantly his breath and a glimpse of a scenario he had not imagined. Not here, in the putrid cellars of the damned. An escape. His was scarcely the quickest of minds, yet it could register a threadbare blanket knotted and climbing to a high window whose oak bars were split. And it could process the likely route taken and the implications of a breakout. Sweet Jesus! They had been too kind to the wretch, had too easily accepted the bribe to provide a horsehair cover against the winter chill. Someone would now pay a dearer price.

Rumination was cut short. A length of improvised rope looped itself about his neck and jerked tight, strong hands applying pressure, accented English hissing soft into his ear.

'Resist and you will die. Slowly. You understand?' Yes, the jailer understood. 'Take off your keys and drop your cudgel. Step forward a pace.'

Each instruction was obeyed, every move accompanied with a persuasive tightening of the cord. Swaying inverted above the man, his feet hooked into ceiling brackets, Luqa kept stranglehold of his prey. A childhood spent climbing cliffs and scaling walls had left him accustomed to such situation. After the fury of a narcotic-crazed Iayalar or cold professionalism of an Ottoman Janissary, a slow and dimwitted guard posed little challenge.

'Remove your jerkin.' Luqa swung composed and threatening. 'Be willing.'

'You shall not escape.'

'Yet a guard with clothes and certain swagger may.'

'They will hunt you.'

'And I shall evade. Come, man.' Luqa had the upper hand.

The guard stripped, his fear overcoming his reluctance, until he stood cowed and waiting for the next unpredictable move. It was so much more pleasant to dwell at the other end of the leash. Luqa jumped down, knocking him forward and pinning him to the ground. Boots and hose were wrenched free. Then shackles clamped tight about the ankles.

'Unbind me, foreigner.'

'This foreigner will not.' Luqa fastened the protesting arms and rolled the victim on his back. 'This foreigner will give you taste of days imprisoned.'

'Vengeance is a sin.'

'Then I am a sinner.'

Luqa was dressing, donning the garb and tools of his former captor. With luck and a sense of direction, he would find a way out, with measured stride and mind of purpose he would join Christian Hardy and his crew. He had welcomed the visit by his friend. Brothers-in-arms could be relied upon. So they had talked, and thus had a steel pin changed ownership as their hands met in final parting. A veteran of conflict and subterfuge could do much with a sharp metal object.

Malevolence flared in the eyes of the guard. 'Mark my word. You will be back in Newgate before day is ended.'

'Abandon the hope. I shall not be missed and nor shall you. We are ants forgotten in this gutter.'

'I will not forget.'

'I am moved by it, mistress.' Luqa delivered a hard and playful slap. 'A pity I must go.'

He affixed a gag in the mouth of the dazed and lolling form, rising to appreciate his craft. Others appeared to enjoy it less. With care, he edged to the opening, inching through, venturing to peer into the blackness before drawing back. In the lantern-light, the eyes of the guard widened as Luqa approached with the bowl of gruel. Deliberately, the Maltese islander stooped and ground its contents in the face of the hapless detainee. It was important to experience all aspects of Newgate.

'One final thought.' The boot went in with feeling.

In an environment of such sordid desolation, few had noticed and none had asked. Walk with certainty, and a stranger could venture anywhere. So Luqa had progressed, a spectre among other spectres, a lantern passing through, perhaps a lone guard journeying to deliver meagre rations or harsh chastisement. That was his prerogative and business. Keys unlocked, barriers lifted, and he slid towards the daylight. Near the main gate he had loitered awhile in the shadow, gauging the tempo and choosing occasion. There was no margin for error, no scope for the kind of rash misjudgement that had brought him here. Discovery would mean summary execution. He need not have worried. The door-keepers had been drunk, were concerned more with taxing the riches of visitors than studying the identity of the departing. Unknown, staying low, Luqa had slipped out and crossed the river Fleet.

Later, beyond the Bars and bounds of the City, he made it to the area of Clerkenwell. An army would not follow him here. Among its mud-spattered alleyways and wild scrubland, hidden in its stewhouses and dens of thieves, people could disappear. Often they did. It was the land of the outlaw and the pariah, site of hovel-dwellings and the deepest of secrets. The perfect refuge for a wanted man. Luqa watched from the undergrowth. An aged beggar shuffled by, searching for discarded apple-cores to feed himself or the bears caged for baiting. A group of drunken youths headed noisily for Cock Alley to sate themselves and catch syphilis in the passing. A rogue fought another, lost his argument and footing, and pitched headlong in the cesspit river. No one cared. It suited Luqa fine.

Sundown, and the ranks of waterwheels along Turnmill Street creaked and pounded in endless industry. By now, Hardy and his two companions would be well towards Kent and Margate and waiting on the wind. The escaped prisoner flexed his stiffening limbs and blew warmth back into his hands. He could not allow Hawkhead and Black Jack the glory, could not permit adventure in which he played no part. To stand beside Christian was his right and his inheritance. He crawled forward, his eyes adjusted to the darkening hour, his senses attuned for possible challenge. And at the rear of the tavern known as the Baker's House he found the low-built wall. His fingers worked along its length, probing and testing, connecting with a loose stone and prising it away. The contents were safe.

Those gentry who gambolled and played at archery and bowls in the grounds of Islington, those perfumed dandies who strolled and took the springs in Notting Hill, could rest easy at their pastime. Luqa would not be preying on their purses or steeds. This night his priority differed. He reached into the cavity and withdrew a knife, a sling and canvas bag of shot, a silver crucifix he placed about his neck. Small objects: relics of his past and totems of his present. He was almost complete.

One long whistle starting low and soaring high. He counted seconds and repeated. There was a light footfall, a scampering that carried excitement, and Fearnot the dog bounded over the wall and threw himself in heedless delight upon his master. Luqa buried his face against the warm and broken-haired coat. He had won the canine in bare-knuckle fight with a crewman of the Irish pirate-queen Grainne O'Malley, had carried his bundled trophy in triumph from her remote fortress on Clare Island. From that moment, owner and plain brown terrier pup were twinned. The Maltese islander held the beast close. It was good to be free and reunited. He and his charge were again going to war.

~

A bronze culverin cannon swung high above the deck of the four-masted caravel and was winched in slow descent to nestle in its cradle. Another gun emplaced. On the riverfront of Lisbon, where the Tagus widened into the lagoon-like Bay of Nau and Sea of Straw, the sights and actions were repeated a hundredfold. The effort was tireless and the pace sustained. Even at night, by the flickering light of numberless lanterns, the sweat-streaked torsos of seamen and labourers continued to struggle at their task. Capstans and windlasses were turned, ropes coiled, cables attached to bitts, and anchors chained to their cat-heads. Everywhere frenetic energy. There was a schedule to keep, a summer wind to catch. Each day brought the event closer and made the defeat of England the more immediate.

Against a smoke-grained backdrop, a replacement mast was elevated to the vertical on a waiting and wide-beamed taforeia transport. The haze came from the smithies and from the slaughter-sheds on the foreshore to which bellowing cattle were driven to be butchered and dismembered and their meat dried and salted for long journey. Detail was all. In the sail-houses and roping-halls, men and women stitched and tempered, hunched in rows at the bidding of King Philip II of Spain. It seemed as though most of the city populace of over one hundred and twenty thousand were directed to a single venture. Holy crusade demanded such sacrifice.

Set apart from such activities, cocooned in a waterfront palace off Onion Square, the luncheon guests sat in formal array about the marble-inlaid table. There was a certain strain in their manner, a tension that communicated in occasional glance, word and gesture. Enmities were to be expected, Inquisitor Garza mused. They could prove creative or destructive, were bound to flare when the senior commanders were gathered in a single place. Armada was no small undertaking.

While it had surely taken its toll of the weathered Marquis

of Santa Cruz, Captain-General of the Navy and Admiral of the Ocean, it had commensurately favoured the urbane and rich landowning noble the Duke of Medina Sidonia. One a doughty veteran of sea-battle from the Mediterranean to the Indies, the other a diplomat and administrator tasked with building the fleet. Santa Cruz was fallen from grace, a plain-speaker resented for his truths and excuses for delay; Medina Sidonia was acclaimed by the King and had shifted blame from himself on to the Admiral. A fascinating if uneasy match. Separated by age and character and an expanse of golden table-ware, each man faced the other. Garza presided.

He intoned the blessing in Latin, let his gaze rove among the others present. Some met his eye, but most averted their faces and found engagement in inner contemplation or the minutiae of their fingernails. Just like his earliest days in Lisbon, when he had arrived as iron fist of King Philip and assistant to his viceroy and had read the Edict of Grace in the cathedral of the city. The calling-card of the Inquisition. They feared him, and that was to the positive.

Broth of fish was brought, wine was poured, and conversation filtered to the fore. The Portuguese hosts rarely stinted on expense. It was one way to show loyalty. Perhaps it was a front.

Garza unfolded a document and held it up. 'What is it you see before you?'

'A pamphlet.'

'Indeed so, my noble lord.' The Jesuit nodded to the Marquis of Santa Cruz. 'A pamphlet printed in Paris, carried hither in the holds of enemy ships, designed to vex and frustrate our plans for the enterprise of England.'

A Spanish general snorted in derision. 'How may a mere scrap of paper thwart our invasion and ambition?'

'Through the simple device of propaganda and false truth,

of spreading disquiet among our men. In this single page are the lies of soothsayers, counterfeit prophecies that speak of disaster for our ships and divine deflection of our aim.'

'None would believe it.'

'Many do.' Garza stared at the officer. 'These untruths are peddled in the army camps, infest as lice the furthest lodgings of our seamen. Men mutiny and desert, or fail at all to report for muster.'

Santa Cruz gruffly concurred. 'The Inquisitor is right. Reports reach me of dozens scurrying away by night, of spirit and confidence waning beneath the weight of such insidious assault.'

'Who spreads this vile and seditious canker?' The general was more intrigued than persuaded.

'Sir Francis Walsingham. It is ever Walsingham.'

Garza sat back and observed their faces, gauging reaction, measuring the mood. He often had questions of people, generally extracted answer. Those who betrayed the name and service of the King, even the insignificant who slipped away from their posts, would be tracked and brought to justice. His justice. There was ample capacity in the cells of the Estaus Palace and in the Poço dos Negros, the rotting-pit reserved for the corpses of slaves.

He turned the paper in his hand. 'This evidence was discovered on board the vessel of the imprisoned Scotsman. It leads to London, incriminates the English Secretary of State.'

'You capture his agent. He is not impregnable.'

Nor is his Queen. Garza eyed a naval captain who spoke between gulps of his soup. 'Impregnable, no. Yet do not underestimate Sir Francis. He is as persistent as the plague, and twice as dangerous. His spies lurk in the boatyards and in your homes, ride on your carriages, and work in your kitchens. They poison the minds of men and purchase their hearts. Be wary.'

'I am forever suspicious.' Medina Sidonia rested his spoon and threw a sardonic glance towards Santa Cruz. 'Suspicious that Walsingham will provide yet further defence for delay in our readiness.'

Santa Cruz bridled, his ruddy features deepening to an angrier hue. He had the experience of sixty-one years against the thirty-eight of a courtly opportunist. His grandfather had taken part in the conquest of Granada, his father in the capture of Tunis. A venerable name and an unsullied lineage. He himself, a member of His Majesty's council and the most senior of naval commanders, was survivor and hero of count-less battle. Cannon-shot and splinter were more deadly than the barbs of a pampered and land-hugging bureaucrat. But these could still provoke. Confrontation was imminent and assured.

The ageing admiral scowled. 'Keep to your affairs and I shall stay with mine, your grace.'

'The Armada is my concern.'

'You are better spent in dealings with your land.'

'And miss the confusion that erupts in Lisbon? Allow lassi-tude and disorder to impede our plan?' Medina Sidonia shook his head. 'His Majesty commands me to hasten and encourage our endeavour.'

'Instead you hinder.'

'It is not the opinion of the court.'

'Always the court, your grace. Your ambition will see you undone.'

'As your failings will see you disgraced.'

Soup spilled as the fist of Santa Cruz crashed furious on the marble. 'Remember to whom you preach, Sidonia. It is I who saved the Christian fleet when I attacked the galleys of Uluj Ali at Lepanto. It is I who chased the Portuguese pretender and his mercenary fleet from the Azores at the Battle of Ponta

Delgada. And it is I who persuaded His Majesty these five years past to proceed with invasion of England.'

'Talk has since replaced your urgency.'

'How may I sail without the ships? How may I fight without the men, the artillery, the shot?'

'In Madrid, such questioning is oft construed as treason.'

'You would dare make accusation of me?' Santa Cruz glowered threateningly at his younger rival.

His grizzled rage made little impression on the finessed restraint of the Duke. Lazy eyelids slid downwards as Medina Sidonia resumed eating. Point made, strike scored.

A female voice intruded. 'I have heard much of Walsingham and more of your intentions to vanquish England. Yet you do not speak of *El Draque*.'

Innocent remark or intention to goad. The routine-hardened eyes of Garza slewed their attention to the young woman seated at the distant reach of the table. Constança Menezes, twenty-year-old chatelaine of the palace, smiled with the beguiling sweetness of her nature and proud confidence of position. Well she might. She was an aristocrat, a sculpted and privileged beauty of Lisbon with intelligent eyes and tumbling dark tresses, with wit and fire and charm. Rich nobles courted her; the trappings and gemstones of the Discoveries surrounded her. Yet the Inquisitor was immune, could resist the irresistible. For she was the offspring of a man who had defied the occupation of Portugal by King Philip of Spain eight years before and who had perished on the battlefield for his country's cause. Rebellion could run in the blood, a strong spirit prove itself wayward. Garza noted the warning and insistent look of her brother. Neither of the pair was to be trusted.

It was that brother who responded hastily to her remark. 'I am certain our fleet is equal measure to Drake.'

'Equal?' Santa Cruz raised an eyebrow, happy for diversion from his feuding with Sidonia. 'We are superior in every way. Our ships are larger and heavier, carry more men and ordnance than ever the vessels of England.'

'Does it not make the enemy more fleet of foot, my lord admiral?' The question from Constança was soft and unthreatening.

Beguiled, the old mariner wrinkled his face. 'We shall be as a bull trampling a peasant. Ask your brother Salvador here. He is to serve aboard the galleon *San Mateo*.'

Salvador beamed. 'It is both my duty and my pleasure.'

'How may any take pleasure in embarking on war?' Constança summoned a light frown. 'Fighting consumes and does not create. We are the nation of da Gama, a land of discovery and learning.'

'This year we unearth England, my lady.' Santa Cruz twinkled paternally, pleased at his own joke.

'I trust it is at cost well spent.'

'Faith is priceless, and its reward beyond imagine.'

'Then I shall pray with all my heart for swift conclusion.'

Medina Sidonia rejoined the conversation. 'You will find swiftness and our Admiral of the Ocean are not close acquainted, my lady.'

Argument reignited. Inquisitor Garza let them to it, his sight resting on the twin lateen sails of a small *falua* proceeding on the Tagus, his mind wandering to other and darker places. There was his strategy for the liquidation of Queen Elizabeth to consider, his wider project for the subsequent uprising in England and arrest of the Protestant hierarchs to arrange. The renegade code-named Realm had the former well in hand.

They were a dispirited and shuffling band, sixty men driven on by the curses and occasional blows of their guards. An unhappy situation. It was not their fault that their cover was blown, hardly of their choosing that they were kept in a dungeon and fed on slops. Now, at least, they could see the sky and taste the salt on the ocean breeze, look down to the broad expanse of the Tagus and the low hills beyond. Of their captain, the Scotsman Mr Hunter, they had heard nothing. His misfortune was their capture, and for it they would blame him. Yet their new masters seemed to have a plan, appeared to have assigned them to a work detail. Hope sprang vigorous in those who craved a positive outcome.

Around them, dominating the highest point of Lisbon, the solid mass of St George's Castle threw a long and heavy shadow. They were drawn in, herded through the outer gates, corralled into passageways and courtyards lined with rampart-cannon and planted with olive and cork. Then the Fernandina, the wide esplanade atop the defensive buttresses, the dog-leg route past killing-zones built by Moor and crusader and furnished with arrow-slits and channels for burning pitch. The least welcoming of places. Men muttered prayers or swapped opinions in whispered asides, their eyes straining for a sign, their ears listening for any suggestion of their fate. Before them, its sloped walls rising stark and threatening on the far side of a moat, was the inner bastion, the citadel. The prisoners were about to be inducted on a training exercise.

For a while they stood, uncertain, at the threshold. No tools had been provided for their labours, no instruction as to the nature of their task. They shifted uneasily, aware of their vulnerability and the overlapping nature of the surrounding arcs of fire. A sailor belonged at sea; an unarmed convict suited anywhere but here. The castellations loomed.

'I bid you welcome to the Castle of St George.'

It was an English voice that echoed in the stone-grey stillness, the figure speaking framed small in a tower embrasure.

Even at a distance, his tone was harsh with derision. A fellow countryman, and yet no friend in this moment of need. His captive audience instinctively closed ranks against the threat. They knew him for what he was: a turncoat, a traitor, a Catholic.

He laughed at their fearfulness. 'Such trepidation in those so stout-hearted. Where is the resolve of the soldier, the happy countenance of the pilgrim?'

'We are no pilgrims, but captives.' The shout was one of defiance.

'That you are.' He gazed down upon the trapped ensemble. 'Fateful is it not how St George is patron saint both·of England and of Portugal?'

'It is plain to us whom you assist.'

'As it is clear to me why you must die.'

Revelation was without fanfare or embellishment, for it was important they understood. To appreciate the odds was to create better sport. At first they seemed confused, jostled with the caged energy and nervous anticipation of the condemned. Reactions would always vary. Some searched for invisible peril, turning, calculating. Others cowered docile, their expressions fixed in apprehension. All would be tested, and none would survive.

Leaning from his vantage, the man code-named Realm delivered his instruction. 'Regard these walls. Contained within are twinned courtyards, an east and a west bailey. Pass through the gate before you, cross the bridge, and enter the portal.'

'For what purpose?'

'Diversion and amusement.' The renegade surveyed the gaggle. 'To live, you must reach the roof of the Tower of St Lawrence on the far side of this edifice. Should you tarry, you shall be killed. Should you plead, you shall be killed. Should you seek refuge or fail in your journey, you shall be killed.'

Incredulity that was yet believing. 'A game?' 'Some mon-strous trick?' The crowd cried its response.

'No trick, but certain fact.'

'Give us weapons and we will show you fight.'

'Alas, you will depend on your wits and speed alone.' Realm raised his hand, to either silence or salute. 'You had one former use, and now you find other. Go to it.'

Encouragement was required. The hand dropped and a shot cracked, the aim true and the musket-ball removing the back of a head. Stampede began. Bellowing and ungainly, the seamen rushed the bridge and crowded the narrow opening. Whatever they faced, they had no desire to fall behind, no appetite for lingering or mounting a rearguard action. One down, fifty-nine to go. Race was on.

Disorientated, they tumbled to the interior, their shouts and scrabbling feet reverberating in the maze. Blind alleys and false doorways confronted them. More confusion, rising terror. They charged on, emerging into the east ward, running for shelter and for their lives. High battlements encircled them, pressing in, closing down, their crenellations punctuated by hardpoints and watchtowers. Such detail was lost on the pulsing throng. Men tripped and were helped onward, divided to spread the risk, conferred in breathless panic. It was of little value. Around them, dark forms emerged, sharpshooters secure in their eyries. Every man for himself, every downed crew member a prize for his assassin. The trap was set. Fire opened.

Ordinary marksmen they were not. Captured in numerous encounter and skirmish with the Spanish, re-educated and redirected under the rigorous tutelage of the Inquisition, the killers had once belonged to the elite corps of Janissary shock-troops of the Ottoman Empire. Born to Christian families, they were consigned to the service of the all-conquering

Sultan, had been forged as Islamic praetorians to slaughter in his name. Now they again were Christian, dedicated with renewed fanaticism, maintained for special duties to the Spanish throne. And they could still drop a moving target with an arquebus at four hundred strides.

They rarely missed. Their quarry was fast but aimless, scampering in urgent migration, attempting to dodge the winnowing puffs of smoke and whining trajectory of lead. A gun-muzzle flared, its report lost amid the rest. Impact was in the chest, the arms flung up, the head snapped back, the smock spattered bright with blood. A result. Scattered around, corpses lay and the wounded screamed or called. The world had diminished to one of chaos, to a girded enclosure in which the ground pitted and threw up dust and where smears of red erupted to add colour to the drabness.

Maddened with fright, a young sailor was pursued and cornered in the cistern tower. He was quickly subdued and thrown headlong and screeching down the well. A different kind of sound. Realm, the traitor *Reino*, absorbed the scene. His countrymen below could scarce have imagined the nature of their employment or contribution to the fine-tuning of skills. Vengeance was a dish best served with such sights and noise and drama. As a boy, he had marched with his parents in the great Northern Revolt of 1569, had accompanied the earls of Westmorland and Northumberland in their campaign against Elizabeth. The uprising had been short-lived. For sure they had seized Durham and its cathedral, had burned the English Bible and Prayer Book, had travelled for Staffordshire with hope in their hearts and Catholic fire in their veins. Their ranks swelled, farmers and peasants emboldened to join in popular crusade, until over seven thousand souls trudged southward in holy unison. Tutbury Castle was their goal, site of incarceration for Mary, Queen of Scots. There they would liberate her, proclaim her their rightful queen, sweep aside the hateful and illegal reign of the bastard Protestant witch. They had failed. In the reprisals that followed, some ten per cent of the insurgents had been executed – seven hundred and fifty rebels selected to act as example and warning. His mother and father were among them. Almost twenty years on, he was returning the compliment. Experience could scar a man, render him unmoved.

Their numbers diminished, survivors broke through to the far side of the bisecting wall and the next stage of their ordeal. The western courtyard. From its seven surrounding towers, arquebus-volleys cascaded into the open space. More fell; more spun and clutched reflexively at faces; more choked and crawled and ceased to move. Bodies littered the flagstones in bloody dis-array. Yet a determined few had managed to reach their initial objective, were making headway in the storm to climb and claw in painful ascent to the top of the ramparts. Realm wanted to applaud them. He observed their desperate progress, watched as they threw themselves with frenzied relief down the long and narrow sweep to the jutting roof of the St Lawrence Tower. It was a voyage of one hundred and forty-nine steps, a crazed and slithering journey peppered with shot and plummeting dead and the shrieks of the mortally injured. A firestorm erupted and a group of men vanished pell-mell in the orange-black flame. Only one emerged, tottering aflame and haphazard before he tripped and took others. The Janissaries had resorted to fire-grenades.

Quite a score. A mere handful of the original merchant crew sat exhausted and dazed in the aftermath, a three-hundred-foot drop below them. Congratulations were in order. Realm picked his way through the battered interior of the citadel, inspecting the destruction and pausing occasionally to deliver a *coup de grâce*. A throat slit, a heart pierced – all were mercy-killings, each brought solace to his soul and conjured thought of what would be. His Janissaries would soon embark on more difficult mission and unfinished event.

He knelt beside a prone and groaning man, reached to close his eyes. 'Go in peace to your God.' The knife went deep.

Perhaps he had been wrong to suggest longevity to those who attained the summit of the St Lawrence Tower. They were already being dispatched. The training-exercise was complete.

~

'Into what dismal venture do you lead us, Christian?'

'One that will lose you limb or life.'

'I expect no less under your command.'

Hawkhead grimaced and spat a tobacco-quid at a loitering seagull. The bird danced away and he scowled some more. Perched on a water-keg lashed to the main deck, he was a sparse man with grudging manner and elusive smile, the very essence of discontent. Hardy took comfort from it. When Hawkhead complained, the man was happy; when he affected sourness, exploit was afoot and his spirit brimmed with joy. It was why he sat stropping his falchion-blade on a whetstone, why a bandolier of throwing-knives was festooned across his chest, and why his wiry frame was encased in the fur-trimmed garb of a natural pirate. A reliable friend.

Wiping the salt air from his eye, easing into the rhythmic wallow of the ship, Hardy scanned the harbour. Margate was a grim location in winter. Within the protective compass of its bay, a meagre scattering of vessels nudged at anchor or sidled in position alongside jetties. A brace of galleons fitting out for spring or summer fight, a trading-hulk, a gathering of ketches, a solitary pinnace. Beyond them, the cloud-laden sky and blacker waters. Neither a season of cheer nor a time for invasion. Random ships might chance a voyage, could depart on a prayer or seek shelter from the tempest. But no admiral would lead his fleet in full sail from Europe. Not yet.

A gentle cooing pulled his attention back on board. The sound came from for'ard, issued from holding-boxes containing a flight of carrier-pigeons. The stuff of long–distance communication and of espionage. Each bird might bear a communiqué or secret; all were trained to fly homeward at speed and land on a welcoming and familiar perch. Their owner was Walsingham. Every item and effort on the *Black Crow* was directed to his purpose. Her appearance was that of a conventional barque, while her role was wholly exceptional; her crew possessed the calloused hands and lined features of common seamen, and numbered cartographers, hydrographers and linguists, able to map and navigate the tightest shallows, to land by night a raiding-party or pluck an agent from the shore. Even the lobster-pots clustered near the stern had use. They were for dropping clandestine message to fishermen and smugglers off hostile coasts. Stealth and deception kept her afloat.

'The *Bonaventura*, Christian.' Hawkhead pointed to the warship. 'One year we sail proud with her to bring death to Cadiz and the Azores. The next we skulk aboard this spectre ship and hope to go unseen.'

'It is the business we choose.'

'Where is choice? I am hauled where on a whim you go.'

'You would rather rot with Luqa in Newgate?'

'There is too much pleasure to think on him there alone.' A thumb jerked towards Black Jack. 'Methinks he too would profit through strict confinement.'

The slow and towering Negro took no notice. He was in a trance, stamping his feet and grunting, rolling his eyes, casting dried lavender, heather and pomander scents to the sea and to its vain goddess Lemanja. An African slave taken by Drake from a Portuguese transport on passage from Brazil, his mother had been a *cabeza feita,* a shaven-headed witch-shaman who scattered and read blood and bones and made intercession with the dark *orixa* deities. Black Jack had inherited her skills. Yet his daily trade was as sailmaker, and at his belt were hung a heavy serving-mallet and a carved bullock horn with tallow for holding a collection of long roping-needles. His chosen tools; his favoured weapons of contact. Hardy owed much to the fighting talents and sixth sense of the big African who rarely spoke.

Hawkhead wrinkled his nose. 'We battle the Catholic and allow Black Jack every heresy and pagan rite. It makes no sense.'

'Did conflict ever make sense?'

'I like to know for what I strive, Christian.'

'For fellowship and for England.'

'Walsingham and Drake.' Hawkhead pulled a cynical face and fished in a canvas pouch for more chewing baccy. 'I vouch Isaiah Payne and his Searchers should cast their gaze upon our black devil here.'

'They will be busy in their energies hunting other game.'

A smile of recognition widened on his features as he rose to lean and stare. The backdrop had changed, contained the travelling image of a small craft heading their way, of a broad back bending to oars, and of the dog Fearnot standing alert at the prow with his eyes bright, ears cocked, and a tail upright and quivering with enthusiasm. Hardy let out his breath in slow relief. His full complement was in place.

Chapter 4

Someone else was visiting Margate. A longboat with invitation had come to the *Black Crow*, carried Hardy towards the *Bonaventura* by return. He studied the familiar and graceful lines of the warship, the lowered castles and flush deck, the closed gun-ports, the canvas-wrapped spars. From beak to stern lantern, she was the model of English design, her narrow mackerel-keel able to outsail and outpace any lumbering Spanish galleon. Piratical flair rendered in wood form. A comforting sight.

He grabbed for the rope-ladder and scaled to the half-deck, his mind awash with memory, his head lifting above the gunwales until he faced the lopsided grin of a bosun.

'How fare you, Mr Hardy?'

'I live and breathe, and that suffices.' He hauled himself over and jumped down. 'It is good to feel again this deck beneath my feet.'

'Though I see you desert us for lowlier craft.'

Hardy laughed and clapped the man on his shoulder. 'It seems I am not alone in it. Where is your crew?'

'Unpaid and ashore, while I pace here and act the ghost. We are stood down for the present.'

'When the weather warms and waters clear, they once more will be called.'

'It is ever our lot.' Resignedly, the sailor tilted his head aft. 'You will find him in the roundhouse.'

Hardy left him to his labours and the polishing of a falconet and worked his way to the stern. He could not take lightly his summons, would never presume to dismiss as ordinary an audience of this kind. The presence of greatness could be wrapped in the most everyday of guises.

He ducked at the entrance to the cabin, encountered the reek of tallow and the pungent bite of tobacco-smoke. His host awaited him. In the subdued light, Sir Francis Drake puffed contentedly at the long stem of a clay pipe, stroked a lodestone across the magnetic points of a compass. Around him were strewn the objects of his trade, his articles of faith: astrolabes, shadow instruments, dividers and charts. A workshop as much as a place of respite. Sir Francis, mariner and legend, was in his element.

That mariner favoured brotherhood over ceremony. He rose delighted, and holding his arms and clay pipe wide embraced Hardy in fraternal greeting.

'Rumour reaches me in Plymouth, Christian. It is past six months since last we met.'

'A handful more till we are reacquainted.'

'Ah, Walsingham has call on you before me.' There was regret in the light Devonian burr.

Drake gestured to a barrel-chair and both men sat, senior commander and his junior collaborator bound in a circle of smoke and fond camaraderie. The older man remained unchanged. Scourge of the Spanish Main and bogeyman to Catholic Europe, privateer, circumnavigator, merchant and adventurer, contradictions rested easily on his short and stocky frame. The eyes of green-brown were wide and full of mischievous intent; the full face with its red-flamed hair lightening at the beard was jovial and bluff. Yet behind the bonhomie was steel, and behind the steel was a will driven by patriotism and Puritan faith. His life was dedicated to vanquishing the Spanish foe. If

72

he did so while enriching himself and exalting his queen, there was no shame. The churlish might resent him, the envious decry his shimmering flamboyance and charismatic showmanship. He would be forgiven by his sovereign, was beloved by his nation. *El Draque*, the sea dragon, was untouchable.

'So you passage for the Tagus.' The seafarer chewed contemplatively on his pipe stem. 'I vouch we shall be dancing *la volta* with Santa Cruz ere the autumn is come.'

'We shall see how high he jumps, sir.'

'Or how hard he falls.'

'On journey to Kent, I have witnessed our defences build and our regiments form. Everywhere, we prepare.'

A sigh. 'Yet we are unready. The Queen, in her divine wisdom and with customary thrift, guards her purse and husbands our resource. The fleet is mobilized then decommissioned, the ships made idle and men dispersed. Meantime, I am prevented by her royal stricture from my desire and duty to assail the Spaniard in his harbours.'

'I shall try myself to attack them.'

'You will not disappoint.' There was a smile of reminiscence. 'You recall the fort at Cape Sagres?'

'Such adventure I could not forget, sir.'

'Nor should you, Christian. At my side, you stormed those heights. With me, and beset by musket-fire, you laid brushwood and pitch against its gates, created blaze and effected surrender.'

'The enemy is perplexed by our English ways.'

'He has reason for it.' Drake jabbed the air with the clenched bowl of his pipe. 'From our clifftop perch and domination of St Vincent, we summoned down havoc, captured in that single month of May last one hundred Spanish ships.'

They were vessels that had been destined for Lisbon – galleons and transports not yet armed and sailing straight into the English trap. The gain for Drake was delay and grievous loss for the gathering Armada and the Spanish Crown. Queen Elizabeth had won respite, her subjects breathing-space for another year. Her little corsair had done well.

Eager for revenge, smarting at the destruction of near forty ships in Cadiz and the greater tally off St Vincent, Admiral Santa Cruz had led a hunting expedition against the foreign pirate at his stolen southern base. The reputation of Drake had alone kept the flotilla at bay. By the time he returned home at June-end 1587, ten thousand tons of Spanish shipping existed no more.

Hardy nodded. 'We are certain to have earned the wrath of the Admiral of the Ocean.'

'Let him come and renew his friendship. It is time we brought matters to conclusion.' The mariner knocked the tobacco embers into a sand-pail. 'When he sails within our grasp, you shall stand beside me, Christian.'

'I put myself at your service, sir.'

'As you have done on much occasion. I will show Walsingham you are owned by the sea and not by his devilish intrigues.'

'He yet has claim upon my efforts.'

Drake turned the lodestone in his fingers. 'While I, like this elemental stone upon a compass, will ever return you to true course.'

This provoked a grin of acknowledgement from his visitor. Shared danger and expedition forged a rare tie. The plundering of the Americas in 1586, the later raids on Spain itself. Memorable forays. Hardy could not compare himself with the hero of England and of the hour, still barely believed he could sit and converse in idle ease with the titan of his age. But in the forty-seven-year-old he perceived a chancer, and treasure-seeker, a natural leader and committed warrior, a shadow-trace of his own late father. Perhaps too Drake saw something of himself reflected in the younger form. A burden as well as an honour.

Above the leather mantle of his winter-doublet, the open face of the seafarer exuded confidence. 'A race begins, Christian. We build eleven new ships, the foe builds twenty. We call to arms our peasants and yeomen, and the Duke of Parma prepares against us his seasoned forces in the Low Countries.'

'Who will win this race?'

'Doubt not it shall be we.' Eyes quicksilver-gleamed with pleasure.

The cool reserve of Walsingham versus the earthy animation of Drake, and he was prisoner or servant to them both. Hardy felt a barbed pang of remorse. He was miles and a lifetime from his Emma, had bounded from the window of their home to an old and compelling existence. His baby son Adam would not know of the world in which his father dwelt, might grow to manhood without memory of him. Such was the price and the risk. Hardy glanced at Drake and could believe it was worthwhile. *Doubt not it shall be we.* He was settled in his unsettled fate, was entering the territory of Inquisitor Garza.

As, towards sundown, the *Black Crow* slipped her mooring and bore out on a northerly breeze, a different journey was under way. Inland, heading for London from the port of Dover, a train of ox-drawn wagons negotiated the rutted Watling Street trackway that would take them to the capital. Progress was slow and mud-spattered. Piled high on the laden carts were goods brought from France: silks and perfumes, tapestries and ornaments, the finest of things still produced in time of upheaval and civil war. Their value accounted for the presence of armed guards riding in close attendance.

There were books too: religious tracts and political treatises, leather volumes sealed in canvas and placed in crates for onward passage. In an era of English Protestantism, there was appetite for the latest translations of beleaguered and like-minded Catholic brethren abroad. So the caravan proceeded, whips sounding, shouts echoing, on the route through the dank orchards and shadowed downs of Kent. Soon they would reach Faversham, could put up for the night. A circuitous trek, one that bypassed the more obvious and convenient Pool of London. But coastal lighters and barques were costly in this chill season, and merchants were rarely particular in the manner of delivery.

Interception was swift. Riders had appeared, halting the less-than-stately progress, their authority clear and their menacing presence reinforced with drawn swords and pistols. There was consternation in the column. Even the armed guards seemed cowed. Well they should be, for the intruders were government men who bellowed orders that demanded instant compliance.

There was purpose in the interruption. Flaming brands held high, a pair of horsemen trotted to the third cart and reached to throw aside its cover. Their inspection was brief, their information evidently correct. They found the package. With a warning to the fearful drivers and their escort, and promise they would return, the outriders wheeled and galloped away. Left behind, mute in their residual shock, the wagon-men collected themselves and picked up their reins. They had been commanded to silence, were in no mood to discuss the incident among themselves. It had started to drizzle as their journey resumed. An uncomfortable night, a strange affair.

It was to become stranger. Carrying the oilskin parcel in a saddlebag, the group of riders made their way fast for the metropolis. The same two who had recovered the hidden bundle later reached Rotherhithe, journeying west along the river and taking boat at Greenwich for fresh mounts and onward ride to London. It was close to midnight when they found their destination. Hooves clattered loud on cobbles, equine sweat steamed, and the messengers halted and dismounted before a fine City mansion on Seething Lane. The residence was a few hundred yards north of the Tower of London. A well-situated and unobtrusive place, discreet enough to absorb the comings and goings of many types, large enough to contain the staff of secret servants to the Crown. Sir Francis Walsingham had chosen well for his London headquarters.

Without delay, handover was effected. Behind the lowered drapes, candles had been lit and the specialists assembled. They were masters of their varied crafts – forgers and engravers, printers and tricksters, all with criminal or expert minds, and each dedicated to the defence of England and the outwitting of her multitudinous foes. Skilled hands took the package, turning it for examination. A charcoal rubbing of the seal was made, then an imprint in softer tallow and lard. These were borne away. Next the seal was broken, the bundle unwrapped, the drying-salts put aside, and the books contained within laid out in a row. As expected, and as revealed by a source within the entourage of the Spanish ambassador to Paris, the tome was where it should be. *Discourse of the Subtill Practises of Devilles by Witches and Sorcerers.* An unremarkable offering by Puritan essayist and preacher George Gifford. Such English works were common enough, would go unnoticed in any collection. Señor Bernadino de Mendoza had been industrious, was proving as underhand and meddlesome as he had been during his undiplomatic sojourn as ambassador in London; Señor Bernadino de Mendoza was in league with Inquisitor Garza. The book was not as it seemed.

Fingers caressed it, held its spine above a steaming implement that softened the adhesive gum until the leather could be

peeled back. Only a small opening was created. It was sufficient for the insertion of a small pair of tweezers, the extraction
of a delicate piece of hemp paper. Part of the binding and
nothing more. Yet the process was not ended. Carefully
unfolding the blank scrap, the chief interceptor put it close to
the candle-flame and peered intently as the heat worked its
alchemy and the invisible became seen. Letters and numbers
appeared, the ink of alum transforming brown and faint. It was
a code, its substitution and transposition keys inscribed in lines
and waiting for translation. The paper was handed to a confi-
dential secretary and a facsimile made with invisible ink for
replacement in the book. After an hour, the reverse effort was
complete, the spine fastened, the volume repacked, and
sealing-wax dripped on to the ribbon-cord. With an experienced eye, a faked seal was applied and the ruse inspected. Just
in time to return the stolen item.

The following morning, as the carts resumed their plodding
travel, a horseman delivered a seemingly untouched parcel
back into the care of its guardian. Exchange was performed
without question or answer. None the wiser, the carter was to
conduct his deliveries in orderly fashion to a series of book-
shops established in Holborn. Now it was the turn of Isaiah
Payne and his Searchers to be patient and to watch. There
would come a day when the book was collected, when the
collector was trailed, and when the trail led to a cipher.
Without that cipher, there could be no decryption of the
certain threat contained in the camouflaged message. Secretary
of State Walsingham needed to know.

~

'It is rare you smile of late, Constança.'
    She did not turn to greet her brother, but continued to stare

out across the Tagus. There was much on her mind, too many cares and thoughts to permit her levity. Before her, spread out, were the gathering shapes of the Armada, their masts pricking the sky and puncturing her ease. They were a portent of things to come, of glorious venture that would lead only to inglorious heaps of drowned and broken dead. Yet drums rolled and fanfares sounded, banners were waved and soldiers marched. It was difficult to feign eagerness when her soul wept and her heart was heavy.

'I see nothing that pleases me, Salvador. It is a tableau of folly, a picture rendered in spars and rigging that speaks solely of destruction.'

He shook his head and stepped forward to take gently her arm and stand beside her. 'A mighty venture is no mere folly.'

'Matchless error is no mere venture.'

'There, the mighty flagship *San Martin*.' He pointed. 'And there, *La Regazona* and *Santa María Encoronada*.'

'They fail to lift my spirit.'

'You are not moved, sweet sister? By the majesty, the strength, the garnering of will?'

'Their will is not mine.'

'Though your brother is destined to join them.' He laughed lightly and craned to view the distance. 'You observe her, Constança? You see my ship, the *San Mateo*?'

'How to divide one wooden vessel from another?'

His sigh was at once playful and reproachful, the exasperation of a boy whose zeal was burdened with the doubts of others. She did not blame him. At eighteen years old, he had every right to prove himself as man and noble, every instinct to reburnish the tainted family name. Salvador Menezes would make his mark, would return from campaign as victor and hero. That was his intent. There was little she could do to protect him from himself or the vagaries of fate, nothing she could do to prevent him from going to war. Two years his senior, she was no longer his guardian and guide. It was to be expected. Yet she felt she betrayed him.

'Our family is too small to lose you, Salvador.'

'Its standing is too diminished to survive without my embarkation.' He looked at her. 'The Spanish do not forget our disgraced father fought and fell against them when they occupied the throne.'

'Their bruised sensibilities are no concern of mine.'

'They should in every aspect be. King Philip is our sovereign master, Constança.'

'He does not rule by dint of right, divine or other.'

'Our nobles accept him, our people applaud him. His court was no despised and alien beast when it lodged here in Lisbon.'

'Why then did he land an army, Salvador? Why then did our father perish?' She had no enthusiasm for King Philip II of Spain, since crowned King Philip I of Portugal. 'It seems I alone possess reason.'

'Hush such dark and disloyal thought.'

Her eyes were pitying. 'So you might sit and sup at ease in their presence? So you may be held more esteemed in their regard? My beloved Salvador, our father taught us to be true to ourselves.'

'He is dead and condemned as traitor.'

'Yet he was a great man.'

'No, Constança. He was unwise.'

'You would instead serve Inquisitor Garza? Medina Sidonia? Admiral Santa Cruz?'

A resigned motion of the head. 'To the victor go the spoils.'

'But not the souls of men.' Her comment cut deep, and she regretted it.

'What must I do, Constança? Should I stay, I would be branded coward and breaker of earnest promise. Should I fulfil my duty to the fleet, I would restore position to our house and pride and dignity to our estate.'

'I will love you whatever is your choice.'

With the warmth of an older sister, she let her arm circle his waist and leaned her body against his own. What friendship they had always possessed, what happiness they had enjoyed and sorrows shared together. Their mother died young, their father was to follow when he attempted in vain to rally fleeing Portuguese troops at the Battle of Alcântara. It would have been easier to concede gracefully to the invading Spanish force. His loss meant shame and ignominy for his children. Proposals of marriage fell away; others high-born turned their backs. But they endured, Constança ever yearning for her father, Salvador ever trying to forget. They buoyed each other, confided much, were each critical to their joined existence. She feared it was soon to end.

Salvador interrupted the silent reflection. 'Beware the Inquisitor, Constança.'

'I am not frightened by the likes of Garza.'

'You would be wise and well counselled to be. He earns repute for sound reason. It is of a restless and savage bent, of the coldest of insights and most merciless of ways.'

'Shall he drag me to the stake? Or constrain me in a dungeon at the Estaus?'

'Do not jest.' His young brow furrowed with concern. 'I saw when we dined how you pricked the characters of our masters, how you did so with delight. I saw too how Garza appraised us.'

'There is no harm in pleasant pastime.'

'Who may know where harm may fall? Take care, my sweetest sister. Guard well your words and deeds.'

She kissed him softly on the cheek. 'Now it is you who loses ability to smile.'

Brother and sister stood on the palace balcony above the broad river expanse and watched the small craft navigate passage and the larger hulls idle at their anchors. One day the high stern- and forecastles would be crowded with soldiers; one day the sails would unfurl and drop, the canvas fill, and the Armada set out to sea. Constança would observe it alone. Men-of-war, and the wars of men. A kettledrum sounded, ringing hollow and rhythmic on the water as a galleass paced by in practice manoeuvre. She was vast, a bloated and giant hybrid, part-galleon, part-galley, her bulk propelled by the dip and pull of fifty banks of oars and the sweat and bend of three hundred toiling souls. Constança and Salvador followed her progress, mesmerized by the glistening pulse of her blood-red blades. The rate of the drumbeat appeared to be increasing.

~

Fearnot, the dog, had discovered and killed a rat, was parading it with aplomb and to cheers along the length of the main deck. He was a skilled assassin, could dispatch rodents with a single and virtuoso toss of his head. Now he displayed his prize with the upbeat insistence of a true performer, growled and pranced his way across the planks. The crew shared in his delight. Early February, and the *Black Crow* had spent three weeks at sea negotiating the variable winds and treacherous waves of the Bay of Biscay. The enemy shoreline was close. There was nothing to do but prepare and watch Fearnot catch rats.

Presented with the corpse, a crewman stooped to tug it free and dance it by the tail. The dog pounced in mock ferocity and re-enacted the encounter.

Hardy swayed in the scramble nets. 'A sea-dog with tenaciousness and tricks. He is an Irish fellow to watch.'

82

'I would as soon skin a Spaniard as a rat.' Hawkhead scowled in concentration at the leather jerkin on which he worked.

'Apply yourself to your costume, for that moment near approaches.'

'Not with speed enough, Christian.' The piercing-tool went in. 'My favoured words in the Spanish tongue are those pleading mercy or screeching hurt.'

'You have a bloody appetite, my brother.'

'Name one among us who does not. Even the hound savours the kill.'

Leaning on a folded bale of canvas, Luqa could not resist the chance to goad. 'You have yet to catch a rat in your mouth, Hawkhead.'

'While you may taste my fist in yours.'

'What vicious threat from one with hands so soft.' Luqa folded his arms. 'Are you seamstress or fighter, Hawkhead?'

'You know me well for what I am.'

'A sweet-natured friend who finds happiness in his own simplicity.'

'I would gain contentment were you to fall from this ship.'

'Yet your smile betrayed joy when I stepped aboard.'

'It widenened when you were cast into Newgate.' The spare little man punched a deeper hole in the leather. 'Lowborn I am, but I share with the noble Earl of Leicester his intent to see you hanged.'

'Come, Hawkhead. Let us argue with the Spaniard.'

'You think I have not strength to face both King Philip and a wretched Maltese knave?'

'I think a blind and aged beggar or my dog alone could best you.'

'Is it so?'

Hawkhead put down his tools and rose with measured slowness to his feet. Disagreement with his comrade generally ended this way, with positions taken and knives drawn, with words exchanged for crowd-pleasing scrap. They were friends of sort, but it was friendship taut with contradiction and tainted by rivalry. Blood might be spilled.

To murmurs of disappointment, Hardy swung himself down on to the deck. He would not let fruitful tension abrade to outright hostility. That would be foolish so near to this coast. Peace-keeping was an art, a necessity with Luqa and Hawkhead. He had become adept. Commanding in his brigantine jacket, a short Katzbalger brawling-sword in a scabbard at his side, he filled the space as referee between them.

'Are you no more than snivel-nosed schoolboys?' Hardy drew the Katzbalger and circled it in open challenge. 'Confront one and you shall confront me.'

Luqa was offended. 'There is but one way to solve dispute, Christian.'

'Speaks a man whose instincts have led him to prison.'

'Your tongue is cruel.'

'My sword sharp. Put up your temper or prepare for its consequence.'

'You would inflict wound on a friend and brother?'

'I will rain a thousand blows on any who defy.' He flicked a glance to Hawkhead. 'Do not play the fair and innocent maiden.'

Luqa shouted across, 'He is too bald and misshapen a gargoyle to be innocent or fair.'

The taunt provoked, but the forward motion of the angry Hawkhead was checked with a blade held steady towards his throat. Fearnot growled in mild defence of his Maltese master, though it was unlikely the threat would ever break through.

Thwarted, Hawkhead fumed. 'What justice exists when you band against me, allow his insult, and preserve his worthless foreign pelt?'

'This foreign pelt guards your back.'

'More oft he stabs it.'

'I weep at so anguished a tale.' Sheathing his sword, Hardy called out to the assembled crew, 'Fetch me an emptied clay pot and make it quick.'

'Your eye carries demonic gleam, Christian. You have a plan.' It was an observation from Luqa rather than a question.

'I create diversion.'

'Should it engage in towing Hawkhead beneath the keel, I will join in it.'

'Regard.'

A clay jar was found and tossed to Hardy, the young man sauntering to the bulkhead step of the mizzen to stand square-on and face his audience. The crew were accustomed to his tricks and feats of daring, marvelled at his prowess with a sword and acrobatic ease among the halyards and rigging. He could scale the tops faster than any man, could outpace a dropping mainsail in descent. Yet he could still surprise.

He turned the object in his hand. 'To either side of me a stout wood stanchion. On my crown will rest this crude and basic vessel.'

'For what you intend, it is not so empty as your head.'

'I teach you a lesson, Hawkhead.' Hardy lifted the pot into place.

'Are we to watch a simple act of balance?'

'When my arms drop, you will direct a knife as near to me as you may while Luqa addresses his whirling sling to this jar. Fail and I will suffer. Prevail and you are rewarded with my thanks and an end to your petty squabble.'

Argument ceased. They knew Hardy to be serious, comprehended that honour, trust, life and mission were at stake. It could concentrate a mind, focus competition in unexplored direction. As the deck cleared, the two contenders tested their weapons, flexing fingers, eyeing the sight-lines and trajectory of travel. Burying the hatchet was laudable, so long as it was not planted in the twenty-one-year-old form of their chief. A near-miss could prove a fatal one.

Hardy stretched out his arms, surveyed his two companions. Behind them, Black Jack was immersed in activity of his own and Fearnot was sprawled with a lazy eye upon proceedings. Challenge was under way. Bracketed by the chosen targets, Hardy kept his torso rigid and his gaze unwavering. He could sense the charge of expectation, view detached the vehemence of Hawkhead and sleight-of-hand of Luqa. An unconventional match. They were assessing positions, adjusting their stance. His arms fell.

Impact was shattering, the explosion of clay and heavy strike on wood cascading about him. He shook the powdered debris from his hair and stepped across scattered fragments to view the aftermath. Embedded close was a knife, lying at a distance was the single ricocheted slingshot.

'I see you perfect the skills practised with my father, Luqa.'

'He would not forgive me had I misjudged.'

'And you, Hawkhead.' Hardy turned to the small and wiry man. 'I do not lose so much as an ear.'

'A poor result when I aim for your eye.'

There were jeers and laughter from crewmen, a staccato whistle from Luqa that sent Fearnot racing to retrieve the stone. Once it was delivered, the islander gave two short yips. The canine spun and accelerated for the mast, leaping high, clenching the haft of the knife between his jaws and using his weight to drag it free. Successful, he brought it to his master.

Luqa flipped the blade in his hand and proffered it to Hawkhead. 'We are better combined than apart.'

'Though it be a union forged in hell.' The peace token was grudgingly accepted.

Final word went to their leader. 'Our theatre is done. Look to yourselves and to each other, make your peace and your plans. The morrow or the next, we step ashore to Portugal.'

Order had been restored.

In the misted light of evening, a fishing-boat had appeared. She was of a type common to Iberian waters, a sturdy and net-festooned vessel capable of weathering Atlantic storm and with a crew able to handle themselves. Out here, there would be no interruption, no chance encounter with a roving Spanish ship. The optimum state of affairs. Her lantern flickered the code paroles. There could be no doubt she was a friendly, was on time and at location, was seemingly engaged in guileless sortie from her coastal village of Ericeira. Sea-folk were rarely inno-cent. Some twenty-five miles north-west of Lisbon, beyond the hills of Sintra, the inhabitants of the fishing port bore no love for their remote and ageing overlord in Madrid. They were loyal to Dom António, prior of Crato, exiled claimant to the Portuguese throne; were taxed by the Spanish and sub-orned by Walsingham. For the while, their cooperation was assured. Tonight would see a different catch.

Her nose to wind, the *Black Crow* allowed the fishing-boat to come alongside. Grapples were thrown, hawsers exchanged, and with a farewell wave and Hawkhead, Black Jack and Luqa behind, Hardy sprang lightly across. Transfer achieved, trans-formation complete. Without word, the lines were returned and the hulls parted, yet not before Fearnot had bounded joyfully to his new home. Luqa crouched and embraced him as his companions steadied themselves against the swell and looked back at the departing barque. She represented assur-ance and solidity, a physical bond with England. The link was cut.

As the sky dimmed, the crew took up their places and their

passengers grouped to confer in low and murmured tones. At dawn they would make landing, would avoid the garrison at the Milreu fortress and travel by donkey and on foot and with new identity towards their goal of Lisbon. There was much to discuss. At any waypoint they might be challenged, at any stage could be betrayed. The clifftop windmills, the terraced vineyards, the groves of lemon and orange, the stubble fields of wheat – all could hide an ambush, conceal a posse fore-warned of their approach. Hardy put it from his mind. He had been tasked with leading in his men, with tracing an agent and determining secrets. That he would do. Drake and Walsingham were far distant, his wife Emma and son Adam further still. This was life, what made him alive. In his blood and sinew was the experience of constant quest and perilous endeavour; in his brain and marrow were the nature and calling of his father. And in the burlap carried on his back was a coiled length of fuse-cord. A day might arise when distraction was required, when situation demanded fire or explosion to throw off pursuit and confound the foe. He did not doubt the moment would come.

Fearnot sniffed the air and gave a gentle whine. The *Black Crow* receded to the dusk.

Chapter 5

He was old, sick and wearied, carried the weight of sixty-one years as though they were a hundred. It was a thankless task to be Admiral of the Ocean. Santa Cruz laboured heavily up the ornate staircase to his apartments. At least here he could find refuge from the politics and machinations of his foes, earn respite in the simple surroundings that any mariner would favour. His limbs ached, his head pulsed with the pressure-pain of worry. From Madrid each day came the insults and fretful questions of his king; from the Viceroy and Medina Sidonia in Lisbon came spiteful asides and careful positioning. Everyone wished for reward; all searched for a whipping-boy.

Guards came to attention. He ignored them, failing to acknowledge the fawning presence and knowing gaze of the palace acolytes, and proceeded alone into his chambers. The Devil take each one of His Majesty's ungrateful subjects. Santa Cruz scanned his evening room, noted the lit candles, the flagon of wine, the covered dishes of bread, cheese and salted meats. Simple repast for an uncomplicated man. This man was taking a rest.

With a groan, he eased himself on to a low couch and stared in semi-trance at the shadowed ceiling. Sleep rarely came to him, was often ambushed and defeated by rogue thought and recurrent nightmare. The Armada must succeed. His adult life had been devoted to the service of God, Spain and her king, his entire being dedicated to the cause of guarding and enriching Philip and extending his domain. How he had built up the treasure-fleets to carry wealth from Mexico and the New World to Cadiz; how he had hunted Drake and attempted to defend the gains that had been made. Yes, Your Majesty. It can be done, Your Majesty. Anything, Your Majesty. Except His Majesty no longer listened, no longer cared. The contemptuous old ruler in Madrid now favoured others.

Curse those others. Santa Cruz swallowed the bile in his throat and pondered on Medina Sidonia. It provoked an involuntary and scornful grunt. The man spoke figures without knowing fact, joined in the Machiavellian chorus of complaint without offering solution. And to think he was merely captain-general of the Andalusian galleys, a ducal landowner and bureaucrat whose privilege ensured he had never made it to sea. Even a fool would comprehend the impossibility of taking, holding and ruling a hostile nation without sufficient forces. Medina Sidonia, apparently not. Nor the Duke of Parma, the blood-stained general waiting in the Low Countries with his barges and an army diminished by disease. Once the Armada had sailed from Lisbon and progressed up the Channel to anchor off Calais, embarkation and assault upon England could begin. In theory, on the lips and charts of the courtly elite, so easy; in practice, it was no less than mad and reckless gamble.

The Admiral exhaled, his indignation rising at memory of the slights he had suffered, of the way in which his reasoned argument and well-grounded plans had been dismissed. Career over, reputation traduced. King Philip II would regret such folly. Rather than agree to the proposal by his loyal Santa Cruz for five hundred ships and a landing of almost one hundred thousand men in Ireland for staggered incursion into England, he preferred instead to scale back and reap the whirlwind of his parsimony. Santa Cruz was the past, an anachronism and embarrassment.

Yet he would strive in his duty. He swung his feet to the floor and rose to inspect the meagre fare set out by his personal steward. A commander was obliged to sustain himself into the small hours in order to study and refine the latest details of flawed preparation. It did not help that, in his sortie to St Vincent and the Azores, Drake had destroyed the entire stock of seasoned-oak stays for Spanish storage-casks. A clever and far-sighted move. The Armada would depart on campaign with its victuals and water carried in barrels made of green wood. Leakage would ensue, and spoiling result. Another problem, a further headache pounding in his temples.

He decanted wine to a goblet and drained it fast. A second glass followed, a third. He felt better already. Maybe he should anticipate with greater relish the opportunity to redeem himself, to beat *El Draque* in pitched sea-battle and return as darling of the country and restored confidant to the King. It would certainly wipe the supercilious half-smiles from the faces of Medina Sidonia, Inquisitor Garza and the rest. He was no has-been, no buffoon to be intimidated or trifled with.

His eyelids began to flutter with nervous animation. He was tired, and the odd spasmodic tic could be explained. But not his hand. It was jumping as he reached to cut a slice of cheese, continued to flex and jerk as he brought it level with his eyes. A curious exhibit, becoming stranger. He peered in fascination, his vision blurring and clearing and fading again. It made no sense. He shook his head, angry at the unfamiliarity of the situation, leaning heavily on a chair as dizziness crept in. Soon he was seated, his breath labouring, a sweat breaking on his brow. It would pass.

Confused and faint, he pressed his face into his palms, felt his chest tighten and the perspiration flood between his fingers. He should have cried out, should have called for his servants and physician. But his brain would not permit it. Matters were beyond his control. Without warning, his body jolted upright on a sudden cramp. He caught sight of himself in a mirror, saw reflected only damp sickness and spectral grey. Plainly, he was not himself. The other presence stared back, communicating something, unable to articulate. Santa Cruz attempted to decipher the mouthed gestures and wide and pleading eyes. No luck. His consternation and bewilderment grew. There must be cause and explanation, for there was certainly effect. The grogginess had increased, taking hold, pressing down.

Another stage interrupted, the warmth of the wine turning to ice-chill and spreading numb from his gut to his larynx. He could not shrug it off. It gripped him, possessed him, squeezed out his breath and hung leaden on his bowel. He defecated. Christ have mercy. He crossed himself, bubbled a prayer from a gaping mouth. Heedless of command, his limbs had joined his hands in twitching dissent. Briefly, the mist lifted. He understood perfectly, grasped with the clarity of one presented with religious vision what the stranger in the mirror had tried to tell. He was about to die.

Propelled by revelation and residual strength, the mariner staggered upward and moved directionless for escape. He was Methuselah wading through raging tempest, a titan blundering wounded from the fray. And he was Álvaro de Bazán, 1st Marquis of Santa Cruz, weakening with every step. He fell, clawing onward and dragging his weight behind.

Saxitoxin was an unforgiving poison. Found in contaminated shellfish, it could quickly strip a victim of dignity and life, was guaranteed a kill. The human nervous system was its target. Interface between brain and muscle would be disrupted, paralysis would widen, respiratory failure would follow. It was why assassins favoured such method. There was no known cure.

The Admiral was too occupied to concern himself with the detail. He was vomiting, groping blindly forward, his body rearing and shaking as though fighting with itself. Closing down. He rolled, clutching at his throat, and recovered momentum, rage and instinct driving him on. Progress was erratic and halting. Somehow he had to warn, had to raise the alarm. A last surge and he had reached a wall, his hands travelling and pulling him upward in mindless and wasted struggle. Collapse came. With a thin wail he crumpled back, wrenched a tapestry from the wall in his flailing descent. The embroidered shroud covered him. Beneath it, he continued to tremble and writhe and make the faintest of sounds. His tongue flickered. Finally it ceased movement and lolled swollen from the blackened face. Heart and breathing had stopped. The ninth of February 1588. Admiral Santa Cruz, commander of the Spanish Armada, was deceased.

A manservant found him some hours later, was quick to send word to Inquisitor Garza. After all, it was the Jesuit who paid him. There would be no call-out of the guard, no general pursuit or hue and cry. An old man had died and that was that. For sure, he was captain-general of the fleet, a celebrated leader and sometime naval champion. Yet he was also in frail health, had felt the pressures of his office and command. A poisoned chalice. The King would understand, indeed might breathe sigh of relief that a constant complainer and impediment to future success had so convincingly been removed. Upkeep of morale required investigation to be brief and its conclusions preordained. Inquisitor Garza would arrange it.

Garza stood motionless and alone in the centre of the room,

his vision flickering across every contour and recess. The death-trail of the Admiral was all too obvious, its culmination displayed in a tangle of ripped tapestry and a jutting pair of well-heeled shoes. What a foolish old devil. Without emotion, Garza bent and pulled back the covering. It was hardly a pleasant sight, presented him with the image and accompanying odour of a man frozen in the throes of agonizing demise. Undoubtedly a murder. The suspect would be long gone, perhaps a member of the household staff who had bided his time and struck when opportunity arose. But the real organizer, the instigator of foul deed, was further afield. Garza was sure of it. If proof were needed, he would discover it within minutes and a few short steps.

Pausing only to sniff fleetingly at the half-emptied flask of wine, he moved with a lighted candle to a second chamber. Smaller than the previous, it had served as library and study and was bestrewn with the nautical and literary scavengings of a lifetime spent at sea. Armillary spheres, military decorations, a crucifix fashioned from the timber of a galleon. Santa Cruz had achieved much, was yet nothing more than a corpse in awkward pose with outlandish expression on his face. Every war had its fatalities.

Garza searched in a fold of his dark vestment and extracted a key. It was important to know the thoughts of men, advantageous to gain access to the correspondence and jottings of courtiers and chief officers alike. The King relied on it. How else to control and preserve, to be alert to conspiracy and disaffection. In his dotage, Santa Cruz had proved unreliable, had earned repute as aged prevaricator and recalcitrant. No problem had been so large that he could not make it worse, no delay in preparation for Armada he could not summon excuse for. This small key had been invaluable. The Inquisitor approached a heavy writing-desk and felt for the hidden compartment; the metal entered, the lock turned, the drawer slid wide. Emptiness presented itself.

There was scant surprise in such result. He had simply uncovered the confirmation he sought. Within the vacant space had once rested two ledgers, the carefully assembled research of those committed to cleansing England of its heresies. In one book was a register of leading Protestants destined for the gallows or stake, in the other a compendium of Catholics and secret allies likely to aid the holy Spanish cause. Twin sides of the same campaign. As Captain-General of the Armada, Santa Cruz had served as keeper of the lists, a guardian of the flame that would consume every privy counsellor and lickspittle noble and gentleman of Albion. Death was too good for them, slow killing not enough. The Admiral of the Ocean had been derelict in his custodianship.

'Walsingham?' Realm, the renegade Englishman, was unobtrusive in his entry.

The Inquisitor closed the drawer. 'It is none other than he, no person else with power or reach so great.'

'A reach that slays our high commander.'

'No matter.' Garza returned the key to its pouch. 'Santa Cruz was tired and blown, was ripe to fall from the tree.'

'He is poisoned?'

'To the world, he succumbs to the frailties and random act of age, to the anxieties of his office.'

'Some may surmise.'

'While the King will applaud and Medina Sidonia benefit. In the heat of preparation for the enterprise of England, little shall be recalled of this day, of how the redoubtable Santa Cruz encountered his sad ending.'

Realm narrowed his eyes. 'Walsingham will recall. Walsingham will have possession of the contents of this desk.'

'And I have their full copy, *Reino*.'

At ease with the situation, Garza began to collect up papers, to sift and gather articles of interest to investigation. The Inquisition had right of ownership. When satisfied, he returned with his items to the previous room for final observation of the corpse. Realm trailed him.

'Many will mourn the old dog, Inquisitor.'

'They shall give thanks he lived so long and died at peace.' Garza placed down his bundle. 'His sacrifices for his king will be example to the rest; his legacy will raise spirits and spur every Catholic to continued endeavour against England.'

'Thus even a bloated cadaver will have its use.'

'It is not Sir Francis Walsingham alone who may turn tragedy to advantage. He will believe he has here succeeded, will lull himself with self-congratulation that he undermines us and throws us from our course. That is to our profit. He will not expect a counter-strike, cannot imagine how the hourglass seeps towards moment when his queen is plucked from him and the nation ripped from his careful grasp.'

In his role as victim, Santa Cruz appeared to grin with accord. Yet there was no boastfulness in the tone of Garza, merely the dry precision of a priest, state servant and canonical lawyer who understood the price of a life and the true value of a death. The eternal conflict between the Roman Church and English heresy would always throw up setback and casualty. Strategic gain was what counted. Things would come to pass, Garza reflected. He would be conducting the severest of interviews with Mr Hunter, his obdurate Scottish captive.

~

'*Domine, ut placatus accipias, diesque nostros in Tua pace disponas, atque ab aeterna damnatione . . .*'

Just words, but words in Latin that could see them tortured, dragged face down by horse-drawn hurdle to be hanged, castrated, eviscerated and quartered. A further strand in the eternal conflict. In a room of this modest Oxfordshire manor, as the recusant priest raised his arms above the consecrated Host, treachery was under way. It was a quiet act of faith, a symbol of devotion to the old religion. But the old was forbidden, the rites of the Catholic Mass banned, and the Searchers of Walsingham ever able to hunt down dissenters and root out aberrant belief. England threatened was no place for a Catholic.

They prayed fervently and hard, beseeched the Lord to hear them, to guard them in life and preserve them from final damnation, to count them among His chosen. God would wish them to be steadfast. Only through courage would they prevail; solely with patience could they wait for the day when the true faith was restored. They knew the risks. Anyone might be an informer, any random twist of fate betray their presence and their business. Yet Christ had suffered and died for them, the Holy Spirit was with them, and the mystery of the Eucharist had transformed the sacrament to the flesh and blood of the Son of God. That was worth the sacrifice.

The priest was barely out of the seminary, a young man aged by experience and the hazardous nature of his calling. Hiding out, moving on, staying one step ahead and a priesthole away from capture, he was briefly in the area. To stay longer was to draw attention and invite pursuit. But for a while he could inspire and comfort his flock, bring solace to them in their hour of darkness. Before him were the linen corporal, the silver paten of unleavened bread, the holy chalice of wine. The signs of commitment. What honour it was to provide the sacred Host to those who crept in secret to his side; what fortitude it took to make the journey. He raised his eyes heavenward.

A bell rang. It was not the gentle sound that symbolized the presence of the Holy Ghost, nor the signature tinkle showing progress of cattle and sheep grazing on the sweeping winter pasture. The worshippers knew, understood the menace presaged by the rough metallic clanging. Visitors were at the front. A child cried, men and women scrambled for escape, and the words of the priest imploring calm and pleading for deliverance sank faint against the background din. They were undone. *Pursuivants, pursuivants, pursuivants . . .* Shouts, screams, the splintering of wood and explosion of movement, and armed men entered the room. Somewhere, there was blood, the crash of toppling furniture. Then stillness. Within a circle of steel and raised swords, faces that had expressed such hope now cowered in bleak trepidation.

Isaiah Payne stepped into the space, a wizened gnome sporting a colourful feather in his hat and impish brutality on his features.

'I will be sure to convey your felicitations to Sir Francis Walsingham.'

The priest stirred. 'State your business here.'

'Is it not as clear as your own?' Payne circled lightly on his feet. 'You are condemned by the very trinkets and baubles of your superstition.'

'Christ is with us.'

'You will find He is not.'

With theatrical flourish, the Catholic-hunter whipped away the linen cloth and sent the sacrament tumbling. The priest cried out, was silenced with a blade pressed close at his throat.

Payne smiled, watching reaction as he ground the bread beneath his foot. 'Do you not learn the folly of resistance and traitorous belief? Are you not instructed by the foolhardiness and fate of the sometime Mary Stuart, Queen of Scots?'

'We draw inspiration from her death.' Speech came soft from a woman cradling an infant.

'And you shall discover precedent in her misfortune.' The chief Searcher reached and touched her face. 'You sweat much for one confident in her assertion.'

'Unhand me, sir.'

'I treat you more gently than will any future jailer.'

'You cannot threaten, cannot bring low my spirit, cannot imprison my faith.'

'Pretty words from one so fair and with so delicate an off-spring.' He waggled his tongue before dancing teasingly away to address the whole. 'Who else is willing to be entered in the Catholic martyrology? Who among you has skin that may crackle like a hog when put to the flame?'

The priest managed a croaked retort. 'One day soon the Armada will come, our persecutors shall be the condemned.'

'Not yet, papist.'

'As the Israelites returned to the Promised Land, so shall we regain England.'

'The ground you shall inhabit, I promise, is a cell in which you will be chained.'

'Do as you will, servant of Satan.'

'I shall as I may.'

He was well pleased at his effect and the sing-song terror he had brought. Glory and stature might belong to the likes of Christian Hardy, women swoon and men grow envious at the panache and skill of the young soldier-spy. But it was he, Isaiah Payne, whose diligence and detection consigned hundreds to a burial plot. And it was he who devoted his skewed and corrupted being to the guarding of Her Majesty. That was no small feat.

With glee he surveyed his catch, stinking popish fiends each one of them. They would be processed and tortured, of course, would be crushed or stretched until every last gasp of information was extracted. A single good turn deserved another. The priest was right to quake and pale. He faced either a racking at the Tower or long sojourn and eventual passing in a dank and forgotten dungeon. The internment camp at Wisbech Castle was a notoriously vindictive institution.

'What is to become of us?' Tremulous words stuttered from an old man. 'What are you to do with us?'

'Be at peace, uncle. You shall be well cared for.'

Gently, Payne took the quivering face in his hands and planted a Judas kiss upon the forehead. It might calm him for a while. Then, with a shriek, his mood changed and Payne started to belabour the ancient with a metal-studded cudgel. Accustomed to such demonstration, his lieutenants waited on. The blows grew glutinous, the body limp, the cries faded to silence. Panting slightly, flecked in blood, the Searcher inspected the lumpen pile at his feet. He enjoyed leaving his mark. These unrepentant beasts needed to learn, would gain from re-education at the hands of their masters. In any case, suffering was at the heart of their creed. Perhaps they could revive the old man with holy water taken from a bowl sited near the door. It would be true miracle.

Laughing at an unshared joke, Isaiah Payne moved to depart. Another house raided, a further cabal of dissenters rounded up and neutralized in accordance with the diktat of the Privy Council. Meanwhile, the book with its coded message from the enemy abroad had not left its drop at the shop in Holborn. Things were in train; anything might happen.

What a rabble. The Spanish sergeant glowered with undisguised contempt at the throng of soldiers. They could barely stand up straight let alone form into ranks, were as handy with a pike as an aged leper in a skiff. Yet he would bully and punish them into shape, would not pause in this military camp north of Lisbon until every man knew his place and duty and was a well-drilled part of a fighting whole. Some were veterans, slack with the arrogance of experience in duelling the Turk. Others were mere novices, eager but callow, liable to faint or flee at the sight of human matter falling in their laps. England was their aim. His orders, his divine obligation, was to prepare them. He was glutton for both tasks.

'Santa Cruz is dead. Yet you live. And while this is so you are in my charge. *Entendido?*'

'*Entendimos!*' They understood. A positive start.

'You are dogs. Indeed, you are the shit that drops from the arse of dogs. Yet that is what I am given to craft into a regiment, this is the burden I must carry to England.' He paused. 'Are we together in this venture?'

'We are!'

'Then listen as though your lives depend on it, train as if the hateful Protestant were climbing through the chamber window to ravish your women. I want to see sweat and pain, will flay any man with mercy in his eye. You hear me?'

'We hear!'

'Medina Sidonia is our new commander and Captain-General of Armada. King Philip places his trust in him, and we will serve wheresoever he directs.' The sergeant rested his hands on his hips. 'What is your desire?'

'To kill!'

'How shall we achieve?'

'With steel and shot!'

'Are you ready to grapple and board the enemy fleet?'

'We are! We are!'

'Which nation do we conquer?'

'*Inglaterra! Inglaterra! Inglaterra!*'

Cheers echoed, spirits lifting beneath the dull winter sky.

Having malingerers and shirkers hanged had plainly worked a transformational effect. There could be no doubt that intensity of marching and manoeuvre had quickened, that the tented military encampments spread ever wider on the plain. The mission demanded readiness and a Spanish force that could cut bloody swathe through the English resistance. Few could question the predicted outcome. Spain possessed a standing army, while England did not; Catholicism was advancing in France and the Low Countries, while Protestantism was in full retreat. Invasion of a small and troublesome island was simply the next logical step in counter-Reformation and the total cleansing of Europe. The sergeant looked about him at his men. He would yet make heroes of them.

His attention slewed upon a different sight, and he frowned. Before him was an image out of kilter and keeping with the rest, a jarring intrusion of four men at ease where ease was unacceptable. This was no occasion for a cookhouse get-together, no place for casual reunion and idle chat. He would have words. Better still, he would have these unschooled monkeys chewing mud without benefit of their teeth.

'Stand when I approach.'

'We choose to sit.' The young soldier examined him with striking blue eyes.

Temporarily disarmed by the palpable insolence, the sergeant loitered uncertain. His antagonist spoke with the accent of Italy, had the contained poise and level stare of one who had seen action and was prepared to puncture flesh or authority with either his bare hands or a knife. A good-looking boy, an obvious leader. Accompanying him were his crew, a motley gang of rogues comprised of a large Negro slave, a stocky Mediterranean seafarer, a short and bald corsair of unascertainable type. Somewhere too they had acquired a dog, a brown canine that crouched vigilant at their feet. The sergeant breathed out a perplexed and aggressive sigh. Discipline was forfeit, would need to be restored.

'I ask for soldiers. They send me pirates.'

'Would you favour soldiers who can dance over pirates who can fight?' Christian Hardy drew up a crate. 'We volunteer for the fray when your own men desert. So be of cheer and share drink with us, brother.'

'Brotherhood is earned.'

'It may be fashioned as much in talk as in battle.'

Antipathy had not evaporated. 'State from whence you hail.'

'Each of us is a wanderer and adventurer, a *mercenario*. Yet we are sons of Tuscany, come with the blessing of its duke, follow the scent of English blood and the generous spoils of war.'

'I encounter your kind at many a turn, find they are the first to break when their bluster is confronted by enemy charge.'

'You are a wise and practised man, sergeant. But, though younger, I too have steeped my sword in blood. I have challenged infidels and chased heretics, have stood my ground on burning decks.'

Maybe he spoke the truth; certainly he carried himself with engaging conviction. The Spaniard studied the rich brigantine jacket and Katzbalger sword, noticed the Turkish amulets hanging at the throat. Slowly, he sat.

'The dog?'

'He catches rats, entertains us as any travelling jester.'

'Your Negro?'

'Who else would carry our heavy loads?' Shared laughter at the knowing quip.

The sergeant relaxed. 'Fine trophies you acquire, boy.'

'When pay is short, the gemstones of the dead suffice.'

'You fight the Ottoman?'

'On occasion too numerable to mention.' Hardy removed a charm and presented it as gift. 'Such trifles are to be shared.'

Such trifles were to be accepted and turned in greedy fingers, were to be caressed and admired. Real emeralds. The sergeant cleared his throat in apologetic gratitude. He had misread the situation, had underestimated the strangers.

He beamed paternally. 'My grandfather fell in action against the Saracens at Tunis.'

'As my father perished against the Ottoman on Malta.'

'The Great Siege?' Eyes widened in admiration. 'We have not seen the likes of such valour since.'

'Until this day, brother.'

The Spaniard nodded. 'England will surely test us, will see butchery on grand scale.'

'May the best of us succeed.'

They could raise a beer to that. Comradeship was assured. Drawn in, animated in the company of the like-minded and the capable, the more senior soldier wallowed in reminiscence and swapped tales of the past. His audience seemed appreciative.

Then a trumpet-call, the stampede of feet and shouts of officers as the camp burst to action. Visitors were arriving. Accompanied by a squadron of cavalry, their carriages jolted over the rutted track and made their way through loose ranks of hastily formed-up men. Inspection was under way, the spot checks on loyalty and order beloved of a nervous Spanish state. In the window of his moving transport, the thin face and lightless eyes of Inquisitor Garza stared out. He had not changed, mused Hardy. It was the vision he remembered as a boy, the same emotionally barren countenance that had looked upon Fra Roberto as the old priest was hanged. Renewal of acquaintance might not be sweet, but it was long overdue.

'*Bastardo.*' A Portuguese soldier muttered an insult and spat in the mud.

It scarcely compared with the thoughts crawling through the mind of the Englishman beside him.

~

Along the Alfândega, the commercial street of Lisbon, bustle and trade were ceaseless. From the warehouses, the money-exchanges and the orange-brick dwellings of the merchants, business spilled and flowed in general murmur. Through it came a carriage, a handsome affair drawn by four horses and attended by a liveried coachman and a groom. People stepped from its path. The Spanish had brought change to the city, had imported arrogance and swagger and the prospect of Armada. They had also brought in carriages. An aristocrat was on the move.

Shielded by the lowered hangings, Constança discreetly viewed the passing street scene and swayed to the motion of the wheels. Somewhere, the spies of the Inquisition might be watching: crouched in an alleyway or lingering at a tavern, a snoop of Garza could be following with intent. She was ever careful. At least pomp and privilege afforded some camouflage, the illusion of display lent her space for private conscience. Today she made the short trip to the Church of the Conception, would enter its gloomy basilica to pray to the Blessed Virgin and light candles in accordance with her faith. One for the father she loved and missed; one for the lately deceased Marquis of Santa Cruz, whose bluff affability had warmed her so; and one for her young brother Salvador, who would yet depart on naval folly. May the saints intercede for them all.

She alighted outside the church and proceeded through its imposing portal, a noblewoman without concerns save piety and commitment to her religious duties. None would fault her. The hour passed to the next, the jostling din of the street fading through the grey walls to the quietness of worship. Constança knelt before the altar and clenched tight her hands in act of supplication. She required guidance, would need strength.

When observance was done, she rose and retraced her path to the waiting coach. Her attendants leaped to her service with the assiduousness of those caught idling or diverted. She would not chide them. They were her beloved servants, retainers who had seen her grow from girlhood to woman of fiery independence and warm compassion. Ideal guards and companions in the swarming conurbation.

She started at the presence, drew back from the indistinct figure of a priest occupying a shadowed corner of the carriage.

The muted laugh reassured. 'Blessings be upon you, my daughter.' Christian Hardy had achieved contact.

✛

Chapter 6

As the carriage rolled through the teeming streetscape, they talked. There was both comfort and vulnerability in their situation, the chance to reconnoitre, to make leisurely journey through hostile terrain. On the horses trotted. Nobility and prosperity lent confidence, and confidence afforded an interloper the right to roam unchecked. Everyone knew their place. It did not diminish the tension, could not banish thought of armed intervention by waiting horsemen or roving patrols. Hardy glanced through a fold in the drapes. Few were taking much notice. The transport trundled at a steady pace, the clop of hooves and rumble of wheels driving forward past Palace Square and on towards the Rossio. With over twenty churches sited close to the central market, a fugitive dressed as a priest should enjoy anonymity and some advantage.

He let the curtain fall back, allowed his gaze to refocus on the dim-lit features of Constança. There was an energy to the girl, the seductiveness of courage and an open heart. His beloved Emma was kind and gentle and constant, the essence of his life and guardian of his being. But this. He peered the short distance through the gloom. The young Portuguese noblewoman risked her life with a careless ease and passion that entranced. When on mission, he was neither husband nor father; he was a servant of England and hostage to circumstance. The girl and he shared common ground, were close in age, proximity and purpose. Poised at the edge.

She leaned forward and touched his thigh. 'The Secretary of State sends you far, señor.'

'Where he assigns me I will go, my lady.'

'What are you beneath the guise of a priest?'

'I travel with my crew, come here in masquerade as soldier of fortune and adventurer from Tuscany.'

'And below that?'

'A mere wanderer commanded to unearth the secrets of Armada, to sow confusion in its ranks, to spring the captive Mr Hunter from his dungeon.'

'You embrace the impossible, señor.'

'Yet you sit and listen and give succour to one embarked on such madness.'

'Madness may touch us all.'

Perhaps there was resignation or excitement in her voice, maybe a depth of motive he would never uncover. He had studied the documents aboard the *Black Crow* and had learned of her father and the indignities heaped upon her family since his death. There was little reason to pry. His attention was to be directed elsewhere, his orders to prise the Scotsman from the tight clutches of the Inquisition. That he would attempt with the aid of Constança. *Madness may touch us all.* He was simply grateful for her presence.

'I hear Santa Cruz dies, my lady.'

'Whether it was to natural cause or some darker act I know not. Yet he was an old man I liked well, a mariner worth ten of those he leaves behind.'

'Garza?' Hardy noted the involuntary shudder. 'It seems we both of us share enmity for the Jesuit.'

'He haunts my city and invades my dreams, brings chill dread wherever he roves. I fear for England should he step ashore.'

'Let us dwell instead in the present, my lady. He is but a man, and a man we shall delight in humbling and discomfiting.'

'Have you observed the ships gathering on the Tagus? Do you encounter the army collecting in the camps?'

'The taller the giant, the harder he falls.'

'Armada will not be diverted.'

'Nor shall we, my lady.'

She smiled, in spite of herself and because of him. 'You wear your assuredness with ease, señor.'

'For I have fair lady before me.'

The carriage rocked, and its occupants – an apparent priest and a blameless female – moved to its travelling rhythm. A different kind of confessional was under way. There was much to talk of, the sifting of rumour and evaluation of fact. Time and distance could pass in haste.

'Tell me all of what you hear, my lady. The smallest of fragment, the most fleeting of hearsay, may carry a truth or conceal a plot.'

'There is scheming aplenty, señor. I dine on occasion with Medina Sidonia and Inquisitor Garza, meet and converse with the viceroy of Portugal Archduke Cardinal Alberto himself.'

'Nephew to King Philip II.'

She inclined her head. 'To me, he is an ogre. To me, each one of these men is part of a kingdom that takes my brother Salvador on expedition from me, that is steeped with the blood of my late father.'

'It seems we are orphans of happenstance, my lady.'

'Yet I do not bow or shrink before it.' Resolve steeled her words. 'There is gossip sweeping Lisbon, tale of phantoms seen and muskets heard at the Castle of St George.'

'Is it so strange in a city preparing for campaign?'

'I repeat what is borne to my attention, señor.'

'And I am thankful you bring it to mine' Awareness entwined.

They had reached the Rossio, the carriage turning in a wide circuit of the square. Stalls and barrows filled the space, produce of every kind was heaped inviting, and traders called and citizens haggled in never-ending spate. It was, too, where information was bartered, where tittle-tattle became certainty and was handed on as truth. But the populace avoided the blank palace frontage on the north side of the plaza. There a stillness prevailed, and the only movement came from pikemen and musketeers in breastplates and sloping their arms.

'The Estaus.' Constança whispered from her window-seat. 'It is where they hold your Mr Hunter.'

'Have you news?'

'None of late. When the Inquisition takes a man, it is seldom he is seen again.'

Hardy followed the vista as the coach traversed. 'Perchance they are too confident in their state.'

'They have good reason. Observe their troops and the height and thickness of the walls; ponder the nature of the work performed within.'

'I see only opportunity.'

'As I perceive an Englishman carefree with his life.'

He reached and lifted her fingers to his lips. 'Is it not the mark of any true Englishman?'

'You play with me, señor.'

'I pay you tribute.'

The whip cracked, the wheels jolted, and the coach settled into its climb towards the higher ground of the Bairro Alto. Other transports manoeuvred by, conveying the titled and rich and those grown fat on the presence and proceeds of the Spanish. Hardy rested his head against the silken and shuddering lavishness of the couch, listened to the soft commentary of his guide. There was mutual attraction, the draw of like minds and compatible bodies. Stray and straying thoughts. She was a remarkable woman.

He distracted himself, hunched to view a further building as the carriage mounted and levelled over a rise. Another mansion, an additional city feature.

Constança was speaking. 'A dwelling built by my family, once owned and loved by my family.'

'You have your palace.'

'Yet not this building, señor. It was seized from us, taken as prize by the occupiers when my father fell and Portugal was cowed.'

'Who now resides here?'

'Garza, señor. It is the home of the Inquisitor.'

An excellent home it was, and one worth revisiting. It was a night with little moon and a sharp breeze across the Tagus, a time when even street-dogs slept and nightwatchmen dozed at the end of their rounds. Maybe the old man stationed in his shelter at the gates of the house slumbered too well. His lantern was extinguished, his sword and partisan rested at a distance, his snores wheezed noisily into an empty street. Boredom had persuaded him to share an earlier libation with a generous passer-by. The Samaritan stranger had been convivial enough, had offered him a full canteen of rough wine and the benefit of tales from the Spanish Main. Lisbon provided anchorage and abode for tens of thousands of such weathered seamen. Before he sank into deadening sleep, the watchman had reflected on his considerable luck.

The sleeping-draught had worked and Hawkhead had earned his bonus. From the murk, Christian Hardy edged his way along the contours of the building, keeping close, staying low. Occasionally he paused to listen and watch, then resumed his journey with the same sinuous flow. It was the unusual that people noticed, the grating note or jarring movement. Still the watchman snored. Hardy would do nothing to disturb his drugged repose. He crept silently on canvas soles, his clothes dark, his lantern shrouded, the scabbard of his Katzbalger strapped tight to his side. Any encounter would be violent, any challenge met with ferocity and steel. He could not allow a survivor to compromise the task.

Inching round, his breathing steady, he reached the target. It was a low and iron-studded door, its double thickness dead-nailed for strength, its action barred with a heavy lock. For the possessor of a key, that would pose no hindrance. In their haste to claim occupancy, the Spaniards had overlooked the original residents and forgotten to limit all access. A costly lapse, and one to the advantage of Constança Menezes. Her English visitor was the beneficiary. He applied the metal length, counted several beats, unlocked, and was through.

No alarm had been raised, no confrontation came. So far, so easy. He let more light filter into the space, allowed remembered description and his instinct to guide him forward. The young noblewoman had proved useful. Around him were bare walls and myriad recesses, the cluttered cellar-workplace of lowlier staff. He moved slowly through the labyrinth, sniffing the air, following the pungent scent of gesso, the odour-trail of chalk and treated wood, of oil-paint and cat-skin glue. Like the Spanish fleet itself, Inquisitor Garza was preparing for departure. Hardy entered a jumbled chamber and raised his lantern. What fascinating insight. There were the scattered tools of restoration, trays of gold leaf, brushes and flasks, pestles and crucibles, the smooth faces of burnishing-agate catching in the glow.

Hardy wrinkled his nose. A cat might have several lives, a black one act as familiar to a witch. Yet here it had a single purpose: to provide sealant and undercoat for fine paintings. He recognized the art, had seen such things in Italy. A Titian, a Bellini, beauty rendered on poplar and used for pleading and payment from Valencia to Antwerp. Blood-money, and Garza had won ownership. The crates told their own tale. Everything that would make a newly appointed Inquisitor General feel comfortable in his adopted home of England.

Stone stairs that led to higher landings, doorways that became more ornate and opened on to tiled and richly decorated passages and halls. The English agent ascended. There might be clues, could be items pointing to the fate of Mr Hunter or intentions of the Inquisition. It was chance balanced by potential reward, risk that might escalate to outright disaster. Hardy slid through the shadows cast by his own lamp. He was, after all, an intelligencer, had been assigned to seek and find and where necessary spread havoc. Sir Francis Walsingham expected result.

How fortunate the Inquisitor was in late conference on the far side of the city, his retinue of guards attending and his household dormant. For the while, with care and providence, the intruder would not be disturbed. He halted and cocked an ear, feeling his way, sensing the beat of the mansion and the pulse of his heart. Successful incursion required absorption and awareness. Satisfied, attuned, he pushed on. A further door, a second key. He lifted the latch and entered. The chamber was large, a panelled expanse hung with tapestries and religious works and littered with the administrative detritus of power and control. He gazed about, his eyes blinking and breath shallower with anticipation. This was what he lived and could die for, the essence and meaning of his trade. Papers everywhere. He began to rummage, searching randomly with intuition and intent for items he did not know existed. An instruction from the Suprema, a signed order from Garza, a pamphlet from Cardinal William Allen in Rome accusing Queen Elizabeth of engaging in unspeakable varieties of lust. Little wonder the Cardinal had been appointed by King Philip as Archbishop of Canterbury-in-waiting. The prelate would be forced to continue his wait. Hardy found writing-paper and wax, explored until the seal of the Inquisitor was in his hand and he was pressing his authority on to the page. An official stamp could open doors and loosen tongues.

He stopped, his senses tearing on an object caught in the glimmering light. It could not be. Yet there was no mistake, not a brushstroke out of place or a detail that was different. He was transfixed, numbed by incomprehension, was a small boy transported to stand before the same painting in his family palace-home tucked within the ancient walls of the Maltese city of Mdina. A rarity, a Giorgione. He reached and touched it, let his fingers trace its gilded circumference and his sight travel the delicate imagery. Before him, a Roman centurion was bathed in illumination by the Holy Spirit and knelt in awe and wonderment at the foot of the crucified Christ. Once, the picture had filled him with fascination. Now it contaminated him with cold dread. Exhilaration was gone. Garza possessed the painting, might as surely have driven a blade straight through his soul.

∼

Passing-out was under way, or at least a variation on its theme. At one end of the fortress esplanade, two men were tied to stakes with wire garrottes about their necks. Facing them, separated by a hundred-yard stretch of hurdles and selected obstacles, was an initial group of Janissaries. Sporting prowess would be on show. The intended victims were the prize, a reward for the fastest pair to reach the far posts. It would test skill and agility, combative ethos, commitment to the kill. Something of a festive occasion for the enclosed community of St George's Castle. From a window set high in the outer defences, Inquisitor Garza and Realm looked on.

A cymbal clashed and the race was started, a throng of competitors throwing themselves over the jumps and yipping and charging for the finish. They were cheered on their way. As mortality confronted them in a rush, the captives struggled helpless at their winning-posts. They had heard of the fate befalling their fellow sailors from the merchant vessel, had believed in little prospect for themselves. But reality was cruel, its dawning grim and beyond their immediate comprehension. The pack was closing. Wild eyes stared at terrified ones, the distance thinning, the howls and battle-cries ringing crazed above the castellations. The Janissaries had forgotten their religion; they had not abandoned their desire for blood. Leaders pulled in front.

It was over quickly, the eager shrieks of the winners punctuated by the harsher screams of the condemned. A turn of the screws, a tightening of the nooses, and a pair of heads were near-severed from their torsos.

Garza cleared his throat. 'It is as well they reach conclusion of their training. We expend most every one of the captive crew.'

'Such news would vex your Mr Hunter.'

'Our Scotsman is in no state to voice his protest.' The Inquisitor watched as the corpses were untied and borne away. 'You achieve much with your charges, *Reino*.'

'Victory will come only when the blood of the usurper queen flows on the very ground she steals.'

'To this end, the ship is ready. It will carry the assassins to

France, where they will board trading-vessels and voyage on to London.'

The renegade cast a glance at the Jesuit. 'What of the uprising?'

'All is prepared and hidden message sent. Those who would revolt against the Protestants wait on.'

'There will be bloody fight before we are done.'

'One we must relish as sacred and cleansing.' Garza continued to study the scene below. 'Doubt not it shall end more to our favour than your previous endeavours.'

'Then I was a child. We are near twenty years on.'

'Indeed we are. Elizabeth will be dead, the Armada set on its course, and the hot wind of our ancient faith sent howling through the land.'

Realm appeared content. 'I have waited long for it.' From the time he was a boy, from the moment his parents were martyred as conclusion to the Northern Revolt.

'A pity not all are so committed to our cause.' The Inquisitor waited as two more prisoners were brought out on parade. 'It seems the Lady Constança gives refuge to a priest in her carriage.'

'Is this so unusual?'

'Sufficiently strange for her groom to inform me. Remarkable enough that this supposed and unknown priest should engage with her in secret conference as they travel unseen throughout our city.'

'You are suspicious of it?'

'Of everyone, and of Constança Menezes above all other. She is loyal to the past and the sullied memory of her father, clings to the false notion of the Portuguese Crown.'

'Yet she is weak and a mere woman, commands no army or regiment of firebrands.'

Garza let his vision drift to the far shore of the Tagus.

116

'Perchance her sedition is of more subtle hue; mayhap she is in league with darker and formidable force. Lisbon is awash with spies, infested with elements who would do us harm.

'Many are caught.'

'And many remain.' The Jesuit returned to the activities below, regarded them with experienced eye. 'I will watch and follow the young Constança, shall see her burn before I am through.'

The course was set and the latest participants bound in position and left as ready as they would ever be. Again, the opening clash of the cymbal and the frenzied dash for the line. A winning pursuit, an unrivalled blood-sport. The group of Janissaries took it in their stride, leaping, scrambling, diving through hoops of fire and chasing up ropes and walls. There could be only one result. Inquisitor Garza studied the shuddering faces of the captives. They seemed so alone, so bereft of certainty and hope. That was the trouble with those of a heretical bent.

Triumphant shouts, and it was done. Elated in the aftermath, the Janissaries gathered below the window to listen to their supreme commander. For them it was a proud moment, culmination of a personal and military odyssey; for the Inquisitor it was opportunity to congratulate and to reveal their future path. He had persecuted enough late converts, had scourged and executed sufficient quantities of Mohammedans, to hold limited respect or affection for these men. But they had proved themselves adaptable and willing, and he would repay such dedication with the assignment of their lives.

Remote and unyielding, he began his address. 'You do well. You strive and attain; you maintain your discipline and your talents. That is to your benefit, and to be commended. Yet training itself is no end. Purpose lies ahead; reason exists for your lengthy sojourn in our charge.'

He assessed the upturned countenances, the martial set of the eyes and jaws. 'You are soldiers, superior warriors who vanquish all and bring fire and wrath wheresoever destiny and your leaders ordain. Once you were known as the Invincible Ones, the spearhead of your army. Today you are unleashed anew. Neither question nor disobey command. Embrace life and death as though they are one and indivisible, and prove yourselves worthy servants of Spain. You are ready.'

They cheered as men predestined to violent death so often did, with their fists raised high and their voices fervent. Garza and the Englishman known only as Realm stood above them to take the clamorous salute. A memorable event – one that future history might care to recall.

'Some haste, blackamoor.'

But the African proved impervious to the hissed entreaties of his Maltese comrade. Luqa stared at him, willing speed, wishing he had brought his rival Hawkhead in place of this stubborn Negro. The cathedral of Lisbon was no location for practising *macumba*, for prancing and moaning in front of a shrine. Black Jack did not seem concerned. He had already left as offering a dead chicken beneath a pentagram symbol in the Gothic cloister, had moved on to the apsidal chapels and was depositing a carved wax doll in the alcove of St Cosmas and St Damian. His companion prayed for patience. Yet, if they drew attention to themselves, few would dare confront the human colossus of a slave. That was something to be grateful for.

Rituals appeared complete. With a final grunt and shake of his head, Black Jack broke from his mystical reverie and the two men strolled unhurried and as innocents towards the great west door. A nun stared, a trio of priests conferred in whispers, a wealthy Spanish wife of a sea-captain scowled as she knelt over her rosary. Their expressions reflected their united thoughts. In these times of readiness and war, the city had thrown itself wide to the most undesirable of elements, to the ruffians and rogues who were drawn to serve in the army or the fleet. Once the Armada had sailed, life would be quieter and certainly less malodorous.

Outside, and with a quickening pace, Luqa and Black Jack negotiated the stepped alleyways and labyrinthine paths of the Alfama. Above them, the walls of St George's Castle rose sheer and unassailable. The fortress could repel a besieging army. Yet every defensive position had its entrance, any garrison required provisioning. Luqa took comfort from such things. It was fortunate that his commander and friend Christian had made contact with the Lady Constança, still more favourable she had found them a small dwelling among these twisting streets a mere five hundred paces from her palace. They were embedded and in play, as in their missions of old.

The vintner sized them with a sceptical eye. 'Is this who the Menezes family now send me for my troubles?'

'They purchase your wine, pay you well.' Luqa proffered a winning smile, was fluent in the local tongue. 'Are you not grateful the Lady Constança discovers labour for you at short moment?'

'Gratitude can wait until I find your mettle.'

'We are willing and industrious.'

'Words I have heard a thousand times before a barrel of my finest grape goes missing and the heaving shoulder behind it.'

'You have our pledge, the word of Lady Constança. We are not thieves.'

No man is, until he is revealed as such.' The wine-merchant wiped his hands on his apron. 'The Negro carries the tools of a sailmaker.'

'He has the backbone and hands of Atlas.'

'And you, my sturdy friend? You own the mouth of a jester and the manner of one accustomed to hazard.'

'Who is not acquainted with danger?'

A resigned sigh. 'It is true we are beset by peril. It is also true my sales climb each month.'

'So decide whether we are to leave or stay.'

'I have use for your muscle if not your lip.'

Luqa was counting on it, relying on the greed of his new master. He was not to be disappointed. There were many deliveries to taverns and inns that day, an endless and sweat-stained round of hoisting, rolling and transporting the casked lifeblood of the town. Demand was insatiable. Thirsty throats welcomed their arrival, focused stares followed their progress. In these quarters, people had been killed for less than a drink. The two labourers neither slackened nor complained. They were where they wished to be, a duo who merged with the crowd and emerged as diligent workers. The merchant could not fault them.

Later that day, after dispensing to a host of monasteries and mansions, the two men were directed to carry wine up to the castle. A difficult order to fill, for no horse and cart could happily travel the steep and restricted incline. It posed little challenge for Black Jack. Wordlessly, he hefted a barrel to his shoulder and mounted the steps in casual bounds. Luqa followed as foreman and herder, ever watchful, hurrying to keep stride. They were heading for their target.

'*Alto!*'

The shouted warning was expected and came from a guard idling at the outer gate. Luqa responded with a grin and cheery wave, his eyes registering openness and missing nothing. At this distance he was judging, counting, assessing the damage he could inflict with slingshot or knife. Beside him, Black Jack was heaving the cask across the cobbled and sloping approach.

The giant African would be undeterred by any hostility, would if necessary take on an entire garrison. Luqa hoped it would not come to that. He measured the man.

'Hail to you, brother.'

The stance was distrustful. 'Why do you come?'

'Is it not plain, brother?' Luqa gestured to the Negro. 'We bring wine for your table. See the brand of the merchant.'

'I do not know you.'

'What is one labourer from another? What threat may we pose to an entire castle?'

Another soldier had joined the first, a fleshy and aggressive soul in leather jerkin and clutching a sharp-tipped spear. He intended to menace.

'A Portuguese pig and his Barbary ape. It is rare to see such breeds gather at the castle gate.'

'We mean no ill.'

'Is it so?' The man jabbed a finger into his chest. 'Tell me then what you mean.'

'Our task is to deliver and to depart.'

'You do not enjoy our company?'

'I am scarce invited to share in it.'

'How may we be sure you are not present as spies? How may we restrain ourselves from running you through?'

'A pig and an ape are the unlikeliest of your enemies.'

The soldier nodded, aware he was failing to cause the slight-est hint of trepidation. There would be no sport today. Stifling his disappointment, making his decision, he jerked his head towards the entrance. They were in.

Escorted by a pair of guards called from the gatehouse, their cask now mounted on an iron-wheeled cart, Luqa and Black Jack progressed through the outer wards. For a castle whose royal court had transferred to the Tagus riverfront earlier in the century, it had signs of habitation and the maintained trappings of security. The place was certainly not disused. Luqa viewed his surroundings as he manoeuvred the barrel on its transport. This had been the command centre of Moorish rule in Portugal for over four hundred years; this was where Vasco da Gama had been received by King Manuel on his arrival home from India. New guests were less welcome. Ahead was the residence of the governor, a bland three-storeyed affair with iron balconies and ochre facade and set beside the inner gate. It was where the journey would end.

'Lay down the cask and leave.'

'We are willing to carry it further.'

A sharper command, the slap of a palm on a sword-pommel. 'Go or regret you came here.'

Luqa obliged, turning on his heel, pausing only briefly to listen and to scan the environs. Perhaps it was the discarded metal cauldron that caught his notice, the dry grains of rice scattered near its broken rim. Maybe it was the faint clash of a cymbal or acrid trace of burning pitch suggested on the wind. A trick of memory and his mind. Yet the hair rose at the nape of his neck, the blood pulsed quicker, the sweat sprang between his shoulders. He could not be wrong. The Ottomans, the enemies who had frequented the dreams and island siege of his youth, were here.

He shrugged, his eyes still searching, as he and Black Jack walked away.

～

Protected by the Moorish walls of their safe-house hidden deep within the Alfama, Hardy and his crew gathered to confer and to plan. On the flat roof above, the dog Fearnot prowled and watched the winding street. He would give good warning of a threat. And in the sparse room on the ground floor Black Jack and Luqa ate goat stew, Hawkhead whittled idly with a knife, and their young commander applied himself with a quill to the writing of a letter. Weapons were kept close. The men were far from safety, on enemy soil, and daunting task lay ahead. A domestic scene containing its own tensions.

Luqa placed down his spoon. 'So, Hawkhead. You put to sleep an old watchman with your mastery of the Portuguese tongue.'

'I shall put you to sleep with this blade should you goad me further.'

'Goad? I observe.'

'Then observe how through my effort Christian penetrated the dwelling of Inquisitor Garza. Observe too how your chief feat was to set down a barrel of wine at the entrance to a castle.'

'We carry wine, you drink it with an ancient.'

'An ancient whose doubts I overcame; an ancient who might have raised alarm and cry.'

'And an ancient without mind or teeth. The most ferocious of contests.'

'I would not shy from fight with an island native.'

The knife bit deeper and the slash-mouth of Hawkhead tightened to lose the rest of its lips. A bad sign. Luqa took another mouthful, waiting for an outburst, savouring the effect. There was method and amusement in the game, little else to do in the mud-brick confines of their lodgings.

He glanced at Hardy. 'Writing is the task of poets and not soldiers, Christian.'

'It is the measure of true men.' The Englishman did not look up.

'Has your sweet Constança your full measure?'

'She has my confidence as I have hers.'

'Is it your handsome face and fine frame she craves? Is it the blue wells of your eyes into which she sinks?'

123

'Better my blue eyes than the green of your envy.'

'I am wounded.' Luqa slumped in mock-injury. 'Yet who would not lust for her favours and charms?'

'Embrace instead the mission before you.' Hardy directed a fleeting look to his friend.

There was a rare seriousness to his tone that was barely disguised by a smile. Since incursion to the dwelling of Garza, a withdrawn and thoughtful quality had entered his demeanour. Neither Hawkhead nor Black Jack would notice. It was the natural reserve that kept officers separate from their men. But it was out of character. Something was troubling Christian.

Breaking off a piece of chestnut bread, Luqa returned to his supper. 'Are we secure in our house, Christian?'

'As safe as any foreigner in a foreign part.' The quill scratched on the paper. 'Yet work will be more perilous than mere service to a vintner.'

An accepting laugh. 'Why else do we visit Lisbon?'

Hardy turned to display the document he had created. 'Note the signature and seal. They give authority to their holder, show he acts in the interests of his lord the Inquisitor.'

'To what end, Christian?' Hawkhead had abandoned his wood-fashioning and peered intently and illiterate at the page.

'Luqa and Black Jack are no longer traders in wine alone. I send them for gunpowder to the arsenal.'

'We do battle?' Luqa was ever-hopeful.

'It may come to it.'

Hawkhead was not to be outshone. 'You and I, Christian?'

'Our moment is near.' Hardy surveyed the pugnacious little fighter. 'We are to visit the dungeons of the Inquisition.'

Distant from the conversation, Black Jack chewed slowly on his stew.

★

At about the same time in London, and in an isolated corner of her husband's thoughts, Emma Hardy sang a lullaby to her son Adam and gently kissed the small boy goodnight.

Chapter 7

None witnessed the first thrown punch; no one remembered in the cindered aftermath the argument that ignited a brawl that escalated to general melee. A stall pitched over, a trader was jostled, and tempers flared. Such things were to be expected in the bustling market-square of the Rossio. Hostilities were usually calmed and the parties mollified through reasoning and apology. Not today. The eruption was sudden and seemed to engulf the whole in a joyous rage that fed on tension and drew in others. Confusion created a simple equation, one of opportunity and crime. Scores could be settled, goods pilfered, the affluent robbed. So the fire was set.

'Hold back! Keep away or I shall run you through!'

A merchant had drawn his sword, screamed in scared frustration as his stall was picked clean. Few took any notice. He lashed out. Blood was spilled and mood and attention turned. The trader backed away, his escape blocked and folly apparent, his cries for clemency ignored as the crowd surged and he vanished shrieking beneath a welter of blows. The solid wave veered to a new trajectory. There was fresh bounty and added spillage, each casualty fuelling the excitement. It was an unstoppable force.

Scavengers arrived, the poor of Lisbon drawn by the noise and the promise of food. They committed themselves with gusto, sliding into the fray with knives drawn and eyes and hands seeking out a deal. Never before had the Rossio appeared so inviting.

'Help me. Please, help me.'

The wife of a draper sobbed wretchedly beside the slumped corpse of her husband. She wept tears smoked with the ash of a burning trestle, and clutched a eam of cloth for comfort to her bosom. The material was snatched away, then the front of her dress. In a frenzy of flailing limbs, her face staring upward without hope or comprehension, she sank beneath the tide. An ugly scene lost amid many as disturbing.

Someone had seen troops. The news failed to deter. After all, soldiers were not immune to the temptation of easy plunder, were as likely to carry off spoils as they were to attempt restoring order. And so it proved. Without their officers, infantrymen gladly joined the pillage. Lisbon was not their city, the outlying camps not to their liking. If King Philip wished them to die for a holy cause in England, they would obey his instruction with the taste of dainties and fine wines lingering in their throat and the gratitude of the doxies on whom they had lavished extravagances ringing in their ears. The more the merrier, violent and rapacious.

Hardy would thank his new-found friend, the sergeant from the camp. The man had been easily bought and persuaded. For a few trinkets and silver coins the bargain was struck, the jaundice-eyed veteran agreeing to vent apparent grievance against a trader in the market. The complaint of the young and blue-eyed Italian mercenary seemed genuine enough. He had been cheated by the stallholder, his name and his girl insulted. At the very least it deserved rebuke, a slapdown and a kicking. It was the way of the soldier and of comrades-in-arms. Yet confrontation had developed, the appetites of his companions lured to other fights, to tables heaped with leather-goods and expensive silks, to the wares of shoesmiths and tailors. A cheery and profitable afternoon was in store.

One for all. The sergeant would not be owning up to his involvement, appeared to have started a war. Hardy wiped the sting of the drifting haze from his eyes. Perhaps the smoke-screen created was more intense than he had imagined. But it served its purpose, would provide both diversion and time.

With Hawkhead beside him and in matching attire of steel breastplate and morion, they were merely infantry as leaderless as the rest, an ad-hoc pair of soldiers hard-pressed and pushed against the backdrop of the Estaus. At some stage the focus of riot changed, applied itself to a shouted hatred of taxation, of the Spanish, of the control exercised by Madrid. Given its head, a mob could lose its mind; given a nationalist spark, any-thing might happen. A dangerous situation was turning critical.

'Fall back!' A Spanish captain waved his sword. 'Take up position behind the gates!'

Dutifully, the guards obeyed, jostling and stampeding in their haste to retreat. Hardy and Hawkhead were among them, pushing their way between coughing and stumbling forms to regroup within the palace complex. Reinforcements would soon arrive, a regiment of royal guards march up from their station on Palace Square. In the meantime, it was the role of the resident and paltry force to hold the line and defend against attack. Suddenly, ceremonial duties and prisoner escort seemed the worst of postings. A musket discharged, its report abrupt and faint against the din, its ball cracking on stone and causing men to flinch. The diminished garrison was under siege. Luqa and Black Jack were doing well in the tumultuous crowd.

Scattering, the impostors rushed to the interior and joined

others in their flight to refuge. The stout walls of the palace could withstand an army. There was scant reason to expose oneself to the ire and random gunshots of the raging mob. Soldiers cowered and waited. Behind them, Hardy and his small and vicious companion issued down long passageways, testing doors and searching for descent. What they sought would be in the cellars. A state servant scurried by, pale and wide-eyed in fright at the sudden disorder and brutal twist of events. If push came to murder, the two Englishmen would drag the corpse from the building and dump it as random casualty in the chaos of the Rossio. For the moment, they went ignored.

Emergency rendered people myopic. They were too busy looking to themselves, peering horrified from hastily shuttered windows, to challenge the strangers wandering in their midst. The sight of soldiers could only reassure. Out there was a rampaging and dangerous horde baying for blood and capable of anything; in here was respite and the advantage of defence. But the sounds intruded and trepidation climbed.

'You.' Hardy jabbed a finger at a listless figure pacing near a suite of rooms complete with ranks of bookstands and ink-wells. 'Can you fight?'

'I am a secretary and no man of war.'

'This day you learn to be both, may find blood as well as ink staining those delicate hands. Come with us.'

'My place is with my papers.'

'While your obligation is to King Philip.'

Already thrown from his equilibrium, the man shook his head in nervous perplexity. 'I am of no use to you. My weapon is the quill and not the sword.'

'You are yet of service. Direct us to the prisoners of Inquisitor Garza. We are sent to reinforce the guard.'

Happy to accommodate, relieved at the chance to divest

responsibility, the secretary proffered an indication of the route. Further shouts and the mad dash of colleagues chasing past distracted him again. Hardy and Hawkhead tramped on. Like entry to the residence of Garza, there was artistry in the play-acting and method to the daring. Confidence and purpose could take an interloper far.

The Scotsman was not hard to find. He did not shy from the light of the lantern, did not speak or react or give indication of really being. Hardy stared at him through iron bars into a cell that seemed no more than a recess and ossuary hollowed into subterranean rock. A cruel place. Curled within it, foetal-prone in his own filth, the merchant captain Mr Hunter lay inert and spectral grey. If there were life, it was tentative and undecided. His breathing was shallow, the eyes opaque with suffering, the flesh torn and ragged over a brittle skeletal frame. The lack of response was unsurprising in the circumstance. Hardy removed his morion.

'I arrive from England, sir.' He delivered the words softly, not wishing to frighten or disturb. 'Sir Francis Walsingham bids me come.'

There was no movement in the body, no flicker of response or recognition in the bruised and swollen face. Yet the man listened, Hardy was sure of it. Somewhere, the heart beat and blood coursed; somewhere, energy was being conserved and directed to survival. Time lapsed and Hardy continued to crouch at the barred opening. He willed the Scotsman to live, would stay until strength and trust and confidence were exchanged between them both.

He tried once more. 'I am present with a comrade. We are here to break you free.'

'You are too late.'

The voice when it came was as broken and feeble as the figure itself. It was bled of force and hope, whispered in the thin and stilted monotone of the near-dead. Hardy swallowed back the lurch of pity in his throat. He needed to keep the man talking, had to haul him to the light from his well of despair. It would be a fragile dialogue.

'Mr Hunter, I am travelled far to see you, sail from Margate to bear you home.'

'My home is death.' It was said with hoarse certainty.

'Should I believe such thing, I would not pass guards and dodge the foe for your company.'

'What company do I provide?'

'That of a courageous man, of a servant to our Queen who sacrifices much in defence of the realm.' Hardy pressed himself closer. 'I pledge to you your liberty.'

'It is not yours to grant.'

'Such gift exists to steal.'

In the silence between them, fragments of sound spilled from the world above. There were outbursts of shouting, the directionless pounding of heavy soles on flagstones. At some point, at any moment, the panicked denizens of the Estaus would regain their composure and would start to search. Safety was fleeting. They had caught the waters in, would need to ride the breakers out. As Hawkhead stood guard, Hardy concentrated on his find. The man lay still. But there was change and process behind the mute exhaustion, the reflexive cunning of a wounded animal behind the dulled facade. Mr Hunter was alive and pondering, at once savouring the presence of purported friendship and suspicious of its meaning.

Voice followed thought with painful slowness. 'Are you devil or angel? Are you trick of my mind or of the light?'

'None of these, sir. I am of flesh as you.'

'See me. I have little flesh remaining.' The head tilted a fraction. 'They have killed my crew. They have exacted every savagery and punishment on me, beaten me, drowned me, starved me, racked me. Now you appear and create illusion of shelter and escape.'

'There is no illusion.'

'No? I remain locked inside a cell and you within a prison.'

'Have I not proved I enter Lisbon at will? Do I not show ability to intrude on this jail as I desire?'

'It confirms nothing save you are agent of damnation or of Garza himself.'

'I swear it to you I am neither.'

'In here we are in shadow where lies and truth co-mingle.' Growing intensity had crept into the battered countenance. 'I know the compact, comprehend the way of things.'

'Trust me.'

'Trust a man who may himself be captured? Put my faith in a stranger who soon might be condemned as I?'

'I take a risk for you.'

'Then you are a fool. For I am finished.'

'While I begin.' Hardy was insistent, would not let go. 'If you have belief in no other than yourself, listen to what your mind and spirit tell you.'

'That mind is seared by hot irons and that spirit wrecked by cudgels and the implements of torture.'

'Each will be restored.'

'Though not my crew. The Spaniards kill them all.'

Another wheezing pause, further seconds that lengthened to infinity in the tension of the moment. The Scotsman was summoning strength and corralling his wayward thoughts, an effort that caused the limbs to shake and the gaping mouth to pant. Somewhere, a veteran intelligencer was reclaiming his reason. A corpse was coming to life.

'Have you keys for these dungeons?'

'I find none to hand.'

'As I say, you are a fool.'

'A friend also. One who shall return to bear you from this pit.'

'I tarry more in resignation than in hope.'

'Whatever sustains you, my brother.' Hardy signalled to Hawkhead to make ready for departure. 'Do other prisoners dwell in these depths? Are there women held in such purgatory?'

'I am kept confined from humanity. Yet I hear their screams, absorb their nightmares as my own.'

'Such nightmares will ease.'

'They will never leave. For I hold secrets, clandestine things the Inquisitor torments me to reveal.' The words trailed, his lucidity fading.

'Things?'

A laboured rallying. 'Garza has bled confession from me, believes me enmeshed in the death of Santa Cruz.'

'You were not?'

'My secret goes deeper, my discovery is one I care not to confide to the demonic Garza.'

He moaned, his breath fractured, his head with its red stubble-hair shocked white lolling on the naked stone. Total fatigue had wrung him hollow. But he had achieved a victory of sorts, had confounded Garza and kept hidden the blackest intelligence and most guarded of thoughts. It had allowed him to endure. The young Englishman peered through, wanting to reach and take his hand and console. Instead he brought only a promise. He would be back, would do more than merely spring a sea-captain from his cell. Chaos and fire would be brought upon the heads of the enemy, a mass breakout would be arranged. Anything to occupy and disconcert the Spanish and their allies, to facilitate escape, to execute the wishes of the

English spymaster in his manor of Barn Elm. Reconnoitring was over.

Eyelids fluttered weakly, the undertow of despair vanishing for an instant. The prisoner gazed directly at his visitor.

'Garza and his henchmen. They plot to murder Queen Elizabeth.'

Order had been restored. Undemonstrative in his ire, Inquisitor Garza stood amid the wreckage of the market square. The Rossio was no longer the busy centre of trade for Lisbon's citizens and vendors. Rather, it had become a field of battle, a vision of charred and toppled stalls and of the strewn detritus left in the wake of untrammelled force. That force was now spent. Garza lightly coughed the soot from his throat and dabbed at his mouth with a linen kerchief. God surely worked in more unusual and mysterious ways than was customary. The Inquisitor narrowed his watering eyes, watched a vapour-trail of black smoke coil from a flaming cart. How fortunate he had led up a regiment of the royal guard from Palace Square, had with senior officers directed the capture of scores of miscreants and their consignment to the nearby Estaus. These thugs and opportunists would be interrogated in depth and beyond the limits of their pain. He doubted they could reveal much.

Nothing would explain it. Evidence was trampled or carried away, the initial spark long lost to greater conflagration, the perpetrators of sedition and discord hidden among the crowd. There must be reason. Coldly, he surveyed the blighted scene, saw a body lifted to a litter, studied an old woman howling in anguish where she sat. Behind them, burnt on the walls of the Estaus Palace and into his chill consciousness, were the scorch-marks denoting the sulphurous rage of the mob. They had been quick to temper and equally fast in taking up arms. The

Portuguese ingrates. Spain had brought harmony and civilization to these fisherfolk, had introduced the full majesty of her rule and consolidated and defended the bounds of their dual empires. This was how noblesse was repaid: with murder and looting, with arbitrary destruction and concerted acts of sabotage. They required a lesson in manners, a reminder of the advantage to be gained through loyalty and compliance. A taming was in order.

His fingers unconsciously touched the crucifix about his neck, his focus flitting and alighting on the dismal and the shattered. Connections could be made, suspicions realized, a thread linking apparent random incidents uncovered and examined. Devil was in the detail, and also perhaps the agents of Sir Francis Walsingham. The murder of Santa Cruz and the ruin of the Rossio. There was planning and purpose to the mayhem. The English were here. He could almost taste their presence in the burnt residue clinging to the roof of his mouth. Credit should be given for their dash and ingenuity. It would not save them, would not prevent him from tracking them as he had done the rebels of the Low Countries and the heretics in Spain; it would not halt the sailing of the Armada, the fist of the Lord from smiting the damned. In his dry and fervent way, Garza relished the challenge. Christ was ever testing him. Briefly, a vision of Constança Menezes in clandestine meeting with a bogus priest entered his thoughts and merged with other ruminations on matters of disguise and treachery. The English were sly and resourceful adversaries. They would pay for it.

~

An early-morning drizzle spattered the trackways of London, churning up the mud and gusting miserably by the mansions and tenements of the outskirts. Late February 1588, and the entire populace seemed to huddle against the dank chill. But few hankered for the spring. In years past they might have followed the natural course of things and celebrated the new season, enjoyed the rising of the temperature and sap, thrown themselves with gaiety and vigour into the prospect of the coming months. Yet it was the dead hand of winter that had been their safety. No longer was Spanish invasion to be postponed; no more could Drake summon luck and magic and mount raid to blow a hole in Catholic plans. As weather cleared and the winds died to a more settled state, the mighty fleet of King Philip II would cast off its moorings and sail from Lisbon. So too the infantry of the Duke of Parma would gather at their embarkation points to act as spear-thrust from the Netherlands. The citizens of London had every right to wonder if the Christmas Advent gone would be the last conducted in Protestant form.

On Holborn, rainwater guttered in the street and soaked the panes and shutters of the shopfronts. The beginnings of the day had brought the usual desultory traffic of laden wagons and barrows struggling along the road. Nothing to arouse doubt or prick the nerves. Keeping from the rain, dodging beneath the overhead jettying of the higher storeys, a tradesman pushed a handcart. He was unhurried in his pace, was more eager to stay dry than to reach his destination at speed. It allowed him to notice things, permitted him to pause and glance and survey the puddled landscape with the resigned air of an old and practised toiler. He did indeed work hard. As a Catholic, he was committed to the overthrow of Elizabeth and the restoration of the ancient faith; as an agent of Spain, he was in position to facilitate such event. The role carried a thousand dangers, was beset by constant risk of denunciation and discovery. He would persevere, would manoeuvre his cart as though nothing else mattered. Salvation depended on it.

He slowed below the overhang of the bookshop, registered no surprise and offered no reaction as a sealed packet dropped neatly in his pushcart. A deft flick of his hand and the parcel was submerged among the remainder of his wares. He had just become the incidental owner of a volume on witchcraft and sorcery by the author George Gifford. To lesser men, a daunting responsibility; to him, a joyous contribution to the secret struggle against the Protestant oppressors. Possession of the encrypted communiqué from the Spanish masters had passed.

One of those Protestant oppressors was himself making a journey several hours later. The weather had not improved, but Sir Francis Walsingham was glad to be travelling by river, grateful his cancer-racked body was not subjected to the rigours of the road. He sat on velvet cushions beneath an awning on his private barge, listened to the grunted stroke of the oarsmen, observed the approach of Richmond Palace. A nest of vipers rendered magnificent in stone. He stifled a grimace. It was a Tudor confection of towers and crenellations, of spires and chimney clusters, a royal seat of government and centre of the court where the favoured clung to status and patronage and jostled and plotted against each other. They also watched.

As the barge edged to the bank and a trumpet sounded his arrival, as the yeoman guard stiffened in salute, he imagined the whispers already chasing down the corridors and entering the halls. These people feared him. They disliked his inscrutability and incorruptible nature, were suspicious of his insights and omnipresent shadow. He could read their minds and private correspondence, delved into their pasts as effortlessly as he predicted their future intent. An uncomfortable figure to have close. That suited him well.

A liveried manservant assisted him to the landing-stage and

escorted him along the covered processional way to the grand entrance. In the forecourt, a sodden detachment of Lord Hunsdon's militia drilled and paraded and gamely wielded their banners. There were few onlookers. When invasion came and emergency struck, when a superior Spanish force marched against London, it would be these men who acted as final defence for the capital and last gasp for the Queen. They waved their flags prettily enough. Walsingham nodded in stately encouragement.

Beyond them was the overlaid sound of a morris dance, its merry tempo invoking the spring and called by royal command. An unseasonal intrusion, the spymaster mused. Yet reality and palace life were rarely and only fleetingly acquainted. Let them clash sticks and swap blows with pig-bladders, carouse and politic and indulge in fantasy and pretence. Real work was being done, genuine danger endured by those he had deployed in secret task. He thought of Christian Hardy and his devoted band, of the enemy fleet growing in Lisbon, of the Spanish command sent inside a book to unknown agents in England. The hidden warfront was long since opened, and he was certain Inquisitor Garza was no passive bystander.

He proceeded to the great hall and on into the inner sanctums frequented by the chosen and the charmed. His instincts were acute, his eyes sweeping the terrain for political trap and unexpected menace. Some stares were hostile, others ingratiating and placatory. All were ambitious, venal and untrustworthy. There, splendidly vain and returned to favour, was the old and sickly dolt Leicester; with him his stepson and future hope the impetuous young Earl of Essex. Across from them, another group, privy counsellors gathered around the ancient and cunning fox Burghley and Robert Cecil his pygmy-hunchback of an offspring. Old rivalries and entrenched factions. Behind them all, pacing fretfully and protecting his advancement, was the bedecked Sir Walter Raleigh. His ear was perpetually to the door of the royal bedchamber, his eye to its keyhole. Her Majesty was close.

Burghley, chief adviser to the Queen and Lord High Treasurer, inclined his head in greeting and approached. A key ally.

'How now, Walsingham? You would not suppose there is war afoot with the play and gossip of this perfumed sty.'

'What is the humour of Her Majesty?'

'If you come to seek additional monies, it is poor. Should you come to persuade her to hasten the pace of our defences, it shall be worse.'

'I tell the truth as I discern it.'

'It is why she distrusts you. You are too clever for her, too direct, too stern and puritanical in your bent.'

'Yet I remain the most loyal of her servants.'

'Without dispute, Sir Francis.' Burghley hitched at the lapel of his fur-trimmed robe. 'What she wishes to hear are soothing words that peace with Spain is possible, that room exists for further discussion and withdrawal from the brink.'

'There is no such possibility or room.'

A wearied sigh disguised by courtly correctness. 'I recognize it, as do you. But the Queen?' The voice sank to sotto voce. 'She sends Lords Derby and Cobham to discourse on talks with the enemy.'

'They will achieve and stave off nothing.'

'Then it is as well you control our land preparations, dig trenches and throw up breastworks on every threatened beach, place cannon on horse-drawn limber.'

'Still it will not suffice.'

Burghley grunted thoughtfully, the elder statesman at the height of his power and yet powerless to persuade his queen. He had grown more stooped of late, his sixty-seven years etched vivid in his features. Perhaps every courtier buckled eventually before the strain and contradiction of his office. Yet the cunning was still present, the razor-reflex that allowed Burghley to cut opponents to the bone or down to size.

'Look about you, Walsingham. They are content to be content, happy to prance and preen while the world is set to burn.'

'They do not know as we.'

'Nor are they aware of how Her Majesty so far prevaricates. She prevents our ordering the call-up of ships from the maritime towns. She restrains Drake from pre-emptive strike upon the Spaniard.'

'We must obey.'

'And we must ever bite our tongue.' The aged lord stared briefly at the orange fury of the blazing hearth. 'What latest news of the Armada?'

'I believe it will sail in the midst of May.'

'Our time is modest.'

'It shall be used well.'

An eyebrow arched into a question. 'I trust you have some conjuring that may vex and outwit our dangerous foe?'

'My lieutenants work hard at it.'

Without offering trace of explanation, the Secretary of State readied himself for his audience with *Gloriana*, Queen Elizabeth of England.

~

'What manner of request is this?'

'One that demands five kegs of powder.'

The captain of the ordnance store squinted at the official letter, scratched his head in perturbation. It was rare that a demand from so august a personage as Inquisitor Garza himself should be delivered straight to his hand. Strange too that a priest should require the tools for engaging in war. Yet the seal was genuine and the signature formal, the approach conducted by a swarthy Portuguese soldier in company with a Negro slave. The captain lifted his gaze from the page and studied his visitors. They had the casual certitude of men who had the weight of officialdom behind them, the crude hardness of those who had fought in both brawl and in battle. He was in no position to countermand their instruction, was merely assigned to count lists and inspect the guard, to while away days in this shit-hole posting in a depot at the fringes of the city. If Garza wished for gunpowder, he would have as much as his servants could place upon their handcart. They did say the Jesuits were the shock-troops of Christ.

He passed back the letter. 'The powder you demand is sufficient to destroy an entire street.'

'Ours is not to question the command of the Inquisitor.' Luqa took and folded the paper to insert into a canvas pouch. 'Nor is it yours.'

'I have served long enough to recognize my task.'

Putting his fingers between his lips, the officer whistled for attention and shouted orders to his men to retrieve barrels from the store. In the coming weeks, the powder-mills would be busy and the workers toil through the nights to generate supply and fulfil demand for the Armada sprawling on the Tagus. It would be an eventful period at the depot. Everyone was focused on departure and the glorious feats ahead.

Luqa stood calm and fluent in his deception, idling with the large African beside him and the dog Fearnot at his feet, watching as a parade of artillerymen hefted the explosive consignment to his barrow. With Black Jack stationed to its rear and himself manning its forward poles, they would make unhurried progress. It was the privilege of Christian to determine eventual application of the cache. At the very least, Lisbon might reverberate for a while. Garza was in for the shock-wave of his life. The thought pleased the Maltese islander, for the Inquisitor was as tall and austere as his twin brother, Prior Garza, had been sybaritic and fat. What a delight, over a span of near twenty-five years, to challenge a hateful pair of siblings.

Loading was complete. Offering his thanks and manning the cart, Luqa began to negotiate his burden on its way. A more rewarding game than hauling liquor. Fearnot ran ahead, checking alleyways and pressing his nose into the openings to hovel-dwellings, acting as scout to the lumbering cortège. They maintained a steady pace, Luqa straining and Black Jack pushing behind. It was an inelegant form of transportation.

A warning bark alerted them to the threat. Fearnot went low, his ears angling, his lip curling to bare white teeth. Four street toughs had detached themselves from the shadow of a screening wall, were ambling nonchalant and intimidating towards them. They were of a kind, their bodies synchronized in bullying swagger, their hostile stares set hard with intent. Luqa and Black Jack slackened speed and relaxed their grip. Pride and posturing would not allow the oncomers to retreat. An unavoidable inconvenience.

'Hail to you, strangers.' Luqa lifted a hand in familiar greeting.

'We are not the strangers.' The leader of the gang was quick to identify himself. 'What do you carry?'

'Items not for trade.'

'Perhaps they are for taking.' The newcomers spread out in a fighting-line.

Luqa folded his arms, comfortable with the direction of conversation and the odds that were presented. Minor tyrants always overreached themselves, tended to be blinded by the aura of their own local repute. Status was fragile, and could be reordered as easily as a face.

The man pressed in. 'You cross our territory.'

'We were unaware of it.'

'Now you are aware.' The chief glanced at his associates, sharing in the joke, enjoying his moment. Pain was about to be inflicted.

Luqa leaned against the cart, his palms depressed against its sides, a controlled and reassuring smile writ across his features. It seemed to disconcert the group. They had expected fear or blundering flight, had counted on a meaningless and garbled attempt at parley. Instead, the intended prey were unmoved by their antics. Their attention was on the shorter man.

'What is the value on your wares?'

'Your lives.'

It drew an unsubtle laugh, their mirth already dissolved to irritation. The nerveless interloper to their streets was standing his ground and frustrating their entertainment. Perhaps he was insane. Soon he would not stand at all, would be nursing a hundred shattered bones.

A finger prodded Luqa in the chest. 'Give us what we demand.'

'I would rather provide what you need.'

'For it you will suffer.'

'Because of it you shall die.'

He was as good as his word. Expertly, the thugs drew their knives; instinctively they turned at sudden knowledge of their error. They had overlooked the giant slave. He was to their flank, the tools of his sailmaking trade ready in his hands and his demeanour frighteningly placid even as he struck. The mallet arced. Its impact was direct and between the eyes, its force crushing bone and driving through to brain. No contest. The victim dropped as a colleague lunged hapless with a blade, the wrist of the seconder caught, turned and pinned hard through to a door before he had chance to emit

143

his first piercing scream. He gaped in bafflement at the roping-needle crucifying him to the wood, tugged fretfully at his arm. His friends would surely rescue him.

They were in no condition to intervene. Number three had experienced his collarbone breaking, a disabling precursor to limit defensive movement before he too succumbed to the defining impact of the hammer. Black Jack was methodical. Facing him, stripped of henchmen and bravado and half delirious in his panic, the former leader of the gang was stammering out his plea.

'I meant nothing of it. It was mere jest.'

The joke remained on him. Deliberate in his task, steady and unswayed in the face of such entreaty, Black Jack replaced his mallet and selected two further needles from the tallow-packed horn at his belt. His opponent vomited. There could be no misunderstanding of his mistake or the consequence to follow, no shutting-out of the pained shrieks from his held companion. He stared at the improvised weapons, iris-point to needle-tip. A double thrust, a small gasp, and the leader fell to his knees and pitched. Black Jack rolled the corpse and extracted his protruding stiletto-shanks from the eye-sockets.

There was precious little left to say, almost nothing left to hear. Fixed to the door, guarded by Fearnot, and bled of energy and the power of speech, the surviving accessory had possibly seen enough. It was Luqa who approached.

'You followed the wrong cause. Now you go to your God.'

He slipped his knife below the ribs and dug upward, putting the man from his agony and letting him hang single-handed in position.

From behind there was a quiet sob, the sound of a child shocked and terrorized by the carnage-strewn event. It pricked the senses, cut through the moment. Even Black Jack had paused in his labours. The boy stood still, quaking and unable to flee, a tear-streaked youngster transfixed by the horror. Luqa wiped and sheathed his blade and slowly paced to crouch before the witness.

'I am sorry you see it.' He rested his hand on the shoulder of the juvenile. 'Our argument is with these men. You will not come to harm.'

The boy ran.

Chapter 8

It was both celebration and affirmation, a magnificent reception held in the grand halls of the royal palace overlooking
the Lisbon waterfront. The great were come to review the
gathering fleet, princes and aristocrats and the ambassadors of
Europe mingling in happy communion to congratulate themselves and each other on the Catholic enterprise of England.
Beneath the plucked and floating notes of a vihuela, they
drank fine wine and gorged on silver platters of sweetmeats,
laughed and gossiped in joyous abandon. Here were like
minds and singular ambitions, the chance to outdo friend and
enemy in eagerness and visual statement. Opulence was essential, a flaring of excess and finery before the sober restraints of
Lent. Already, small boats had taken them on the Tagus to
marvel at the galleons and nod approvingly at the size of the
squadrons. Later, with darkness fallen, further spectacle was
promised. By invitation of the Viceroy.

Radiating little in the way of obvious gladness, Inquisitor
Garza surveyed the indulging throng. They were sinners to a
man. He wondered how many were bigamists or sodomites,
pondered who might be a crypto-Lutheran or harbour anti-
Spanish sentiment in his heart. It was probable that a number
had sold their souls and allegiance to the English. How foolhardy of them. In time, they would be unmasked; with effort
and the application of pliers, would reveal their hidden

thoughts and accomplices. Torture was a concomitant to progress and peace. He was merely a facilitator, was tasked to ensure there would be no embarrassment or stumble on the path to general enlightenment and continued dominance by Church and state. The incident in the Rossio had proved an unwelcome distraction. Yet it served to remind all of the precariousness of order, informed him once again of the nature of threat and the need for vigilance.

Someone had started that riot; someone had forged his seal and signature and through them obtained casks of gunpowder; someone had murdered four local ruffians with the savage professionalism of an assassin. He could not let it lie, would not be complacent. Just as well the Viceroy had granted his permission to hold an auto-da-fé, an act of faith, with multiple burnings at the stake to take place in Palace Square. The people required an occasional prompt. It had not taken long for the tribunal to choose its victims.

The drone of a tabor and stately beat of a psalterium announced the start of a pavane. Men and women formed into lines for the peacock dance, their hands touching and bodies moving in formal array through the choreographed series of ornamentations. A splendid sight. Garza followed their progress, picked out amid the swaying throng the noble countenance of Medina Sidonia and the sterner aspect of the Viceroy. There was much to see in this glittering chamber. He searched for and found the face of Salvador Menezes, young and keen in the candlelight. So desperate to restore his family name and fortune, so enthusiastic to embark upon Armada. Close by was Constança his sister, a passing image of dark-haired beauty and fiery resolve. The gaze of the Inquisitor trailed her. Perhaps her step was not quite as light as was her custom, her grace and vigour thrown by events and involvement in intrigue. He considered the matter as she was lost to view.

Pavane evolved into a galliard, the boisterous dance chasing along the length of the hall and its participants leaping and hopping in bejewelled and athletic display. The guests were enjoying themselves – deservedly so. Within months, England would be nothing more than a vassal state of the Spanish Empire, an occupied and subjugated island ruled by the daughter of King Philip II. He had legitimate claim of ownership, was descended from John of Gaunt, had been married to the Catholic Queen Mary of England. God smiled upon his endeavour; the Pope blessed it.

Merriment flowed as easily as the wine. Couples were reverencing and skipping, flirting and laughing. And Garza observed. With the Englishman *Reino* directing, his spies moved among them as footmen and serving-boys, offering food and drink, ever attentive, listening to tittle-tattle and waiting for indiscretion. A slight to the monarch, a sardonic jibe aimed at a prelate, a dissenting murmur on issues of faith. All were dangerous errors of judgement punishable by imprisonment, the galleys or death. Better still, they provided the Inquisitor with untold influence over the whole. He walked slowly in his circuit of the room.

'What fateful encounter, my lady.'

Momentarily troubled behind her eyes, Constança curtsied at his words. 'You do not dance, Inquisitor.'

'Faith and frivolity are rare companions.'

'Yet you attend.'

'Is it not the role of a priest to remind all of the fleetingness of pleasure?' His gaze narrowed. 'Is it not the task of the Inquisitor to reveal before Christ the earthly sin and corruption of man?'

'I am certain God watches over us.'

'Be sure also He assigns me as instrument of His Word.'

She smiled, had regained her composure. 'This eve we

forget our cares, abandon ourselves to dance and song and a thousand entertainments.'

'I neither forget nor overlook, but inform myself these lords and ladies disport themselves not five hundred feet from where perished the late Admiral Santa Cruz.'

'Mortality is our lot.'

'Treachery the affairs of many.' He saw the flicker of uncertainty in her face. 'It is why there is to be an auto-da-fé, the reason we must cleanse this city and its people of the stain of their own faults.'

A cloud of concern had descended on her features. 'A burning?'

'No finer or more godly way exists to champion righteousness or uproot heresy and subversion from our midst.'

She fell silent, her recovery and fluent lying stalled. Garza perused her, studying her correctness and control, analysing the shallow heaving of her chest. An interesting specimen this girl. It was while a human was under pressure that stress was magnified and weakness showed. She tried hard. Yet she was of a traitorous disposition, was immersed in activity he had every intent to expose.

'You seem vexed, my lady.'

'No more than any advised of barbarous practice to be meted on their fellow kind.'

He savoured her discomfort. 'Of what kind is that?'

'Men and women undeserving of such forfeit and penalty.'

'Do you question the authority of the Inquisition?'

'Solely its method, *Inquisidor.*'

He registered her flame of defiance, the light and heat that only the guilty could produce. So far he had toyed at the margins, was baiting and testing and feeling his way. Gently would he make his catch. It was the expertise that had allowed him to save so many souls, had dragged confession from numberless throats. She needed to be scared.

'In Lisbon, my lady, we fight ceaseless war against a dauntless foe. Truth is with us, and the Devil with them.'

She appeared pale. 'Then we have nothing to fear.'

'We must each of us fear the Day of Judgement.' He was measured in his tone, the more threatening for it. 'By the blast of God they perish, and by the breath of His nostrils are they consumed.'

'You are persuaded England will go that way?'

'The Almighty will answer our prayers.' He edged close. 'Yet who will answer my questions? Who will tell me why a Negro slave and his accomplice no doubt of English stock prowl and kill on our city streets? Who will reveal where the agents of Sir Francis Walsingham operate in our city?'

'Affairs of men and their base conspiracies are of little consequence.'

'They are everything to me.'

Solemn words, slowly enunciated. Her eyes widened with the shock of revelation, with the implication that she might be suspected. Another indicator of her perfidy. Around them, the music beat in double time, the figures whirled in frivolous rapture. Garza and Constança were immune to it. Their contest, their collision of wills, was more deadly and intense. He imagined her arraigned before his tribunal, pictured her tremulous defence before the prosecuting *fiscal* and the theological onslaught of the *calificador*. His officials could make a charge of heresy stick to a saint. Small wonder perspiration had sprung to her neck and cleavage.

'I find you, Constança.' Pleased at his discovery, Salvador pushed his way through. 'You miss the final measure and cadence.'

'Dance will ever lose to the art of conversation, sweet brother.'

150

He noticed and bowed to Garza, at once wary and youthfully enthused. 'I interrupt, Inquisitor?'

'No more than gaiety does in any private discourse.'

'My apology for such boldness.'

'It is the manner that shall earn you reward on campaign, which will see you returned as soldiering hero.'

Flattered, the boy smiled. 'I will not disappoint or forget my duty.'

'What example you provide your sister and country.'

Unaware of inference, diverted by the surrounding revelry, the eighteen year-old took his leave and pulled his older sister back to the partying melee. There could be no let-up in the pursuit of noble standing, no easing of the pressure to show willing and conform. A fresh dance was begun. It was a game called The Hunt, a cheerful pursuit of the appointed prey between the gathered lines. The most apt of titles, the Inquisitor mused.

The intervention was dramatic, and arrived with a ball of light and splintering roar that spilled across the Tagus. Excited, the palace revellers crowded through the doorways on to the riverside terrace, jostling for vantage to enjoy the full impact of the pyrotechnic scene. Whoever had conjured the show was a genius. Before them, a replica of a galleon had burst alight, the flames climbing from the orlop to the sterncastle and racing along the deck to ignite the masts and rigging. A glorious evocation of battle and ferment. Lords and ladies clapped and cheered, their shouts and laughter escalating to every billow of smoke and porthole eruption. They had not expected quite so great a feast for the senses. Another spasm of illumination, a further crash of timbers, and the tones of astonishment sharpened. Those were humans casting themselves into the water; those were genuine screams ratcheting through the widening din. An incendiary cloud mushroomed through a hatchway, vomited figures that rushed alight to tip overboard or topple in disarray. There was no illusion or pretence. On shore, appreciation had died to a confused and barren state of horror.

As the pyre raged, as the expressions of Medina Sidonia and the Viceroy were fixed grim and orange in the pulsing glow, it dawned on the guests they were witnessing catastrophe. Some women fainted or clung to their husbands; some men ran to commandeer boats and effect a rescue. Action of any kind would be to little avail. The sky seared bright and was raining debris, the disaster manifested in lapping fire that chased itself to the fighting-tops. An explosion, and the sides burst. The spectators were not to know the precise seat of the conflagration, would never have guessed at its cause or have suspected the two sailors manning the rowing-boat that loitered at the edges of their previous excursion. Luqa and Black Jack had been diligent in the application of their ill-gotten powder. They had ferried out a consignment in the happy tumult of oars and sails, had circled until the target vessel was chosen and opportunity arose when the light faded. The skeleton crew had failed to post lookouts, were anyway engaged in viewing the rich pageant ashore, and an open port close to the waterline had showed itself inviting. Maybe they had found the body of their comrade, a joiner who was working on repairs down below; perhaps someone stumbled on the lit fuse and had tried to raise alarm. By then it was too late. The intruders were gone, had left behind wreckage and inferno. In their wake, ships were hauling anchor and manoeuvring to get themselves from danger. As parties went, it had not been an unalloyed success.

～

Tension was to be expected, the increase in roving patrols a natural corollary to events on the Tagus. Citizens talked,

152

speculating on the source of such disaster, wondering at the portents. Already the authorities were rounding up deserters. There would be no concession to faint-hearts and doubters. Armada would proceed as planned, Medina Sidonia would take the command as captain-general of the fleet and architect of invasion. It was what King Philip of Spain desired, what the princes of Europe hailed as predestined. No death of Santa Cruz or unfortunate accident aboard a vessel could blunt the sharpness of purpose or change the direction of outcome. Old men died, ships could burn. That was the way of things. Yet such reasoning did not lessen anxiety and fretfulness on the streets.

Through those streets, hurrying into the thickening web of the Alfama, Constança pulled the dark hood closer about her face. She was merely another low-born moving anonymous in the rank murk of the alleyways, dodging from one lightless path to the next. Of course there were perils. She was unaccustomed to the plague-like stench, rarely stumbled into this world of predatory vagrants and angry suffering. Neither innocence nor innocents lasted long in the cruelty and random viciousness of the threading passages. Anything might happen, any corner or opening hide a cut-throat or give shelter to a gang of thieves or worse. Slipping unseen from her palace-mansion on Onion Square had posed the lesser challenge. Surviving, reaching the concealed destination, delivering her warning, these were the imperative.

She thought of Christian Hardy, of his laughter and his eyes, of the threat that prevailed and pushed in. And superimposed was a vision of Inquisitor Garza. The domed head, sunken face and hooded gaze; the measured tone that cloaked fanaticism; the expression of understanding that held only contempt. He had made his declaration. In the great reception-chamber of the royal palace, he had sought her out and presented his findings, had obliquely revealed the depth of his insight. He knew of the English agents. She in turn understood what she must do. So she pressed on, her footsteps echoing urgency, her mind fixed ahead on the news she would deliver.

Compulsion and fearfulness brought her near. The house was as squalid as the rest, was intended to nestle as unobtrusive hideout and safe haven. That function seemed compromised. She backed into the moon-shadow, listening for noise and straining to identify the subtleties of the night. A restless cockerel or scavenging rodent, a mewling baby or prowling cat, a jangling of a key or the jarring of her nerves. All could serve to trick or entrap.

A hand clamped over her mouth and tugged her into deeper blackness. She tried to struggle, wanted to scream, but the force was insistent and the strength immutable. An arm circled and grasped her tight.

'You are drawn to hazard, my lady.'

'Release your hold.' She resisted unsuccessfully, remained committed to escape. 'I am no common felon.'

'Soft now, Constança.'

She felt his breath on her cheek and his lips close, recognized the easy mirth that played in his whisper. It was Christian Hardy who so rudely pre-empted her arrival. Still she could not turn to face him. His grip was too muscular, his presence too commanding to allow for slightest movement. She was uncertain if the situation constituted violation or provided comfort.

He answered her private enquiry. 'I restrain you for sound reason, Constança.'

'From where I am, I see no reason.'

'You think me a knave?' He pressed against her. 'A rough miscreant who would handle you without cause?'

'I know you little.'

'Though sufficient to consider me a friend, to comprehend I would not dishonour you or let you come to harm.'

'Why then these actions, sir?'

'I am compelled to protect you, driven to save you from all manner of risk.'

'It is you who is in danger, Christian.' She blurted the words, wanting to confide. 'Garza identifies your men. He seeks you out, is aware of your method and the steps you take.'

'More so since a Spanish galleon burst to flame.'

'I do not jest, Christian.'

'Hush your fears.'

There was a quietness in his tone that quelled her doubt, a warmth and assuredness that saw capture flow to deeper embrace. She was aware that her breathing had altered to a pant, found herself twisting and leaning into the enfolding arms. At times before, when meeting in secret and in disguise, they had maintained decorum and a certain distance. Yet the nature of their work dictated a bond; the character of the moment and the manner and proximity of English adventurer and Portuguese noblewoman meant an inexorable slide to a different state. Temptation existed, opportunity with it. Her resistance had subsided to a low gasp and residual tremor.

Momentarily angry, she drew back. 'My faith does not permit it.'

'Your inclination will.'

They kissed, and she again made gesture of retreat. 'Such sinfulness is condemned.'

'I no longer play the priest.' He cupped her cheek, brushed her lips with his own. 'God would not deny us the chance he has delivered.'

'We will be undone, Christian.'

'The hardest part of any pleasure.' He brought her hand to his groin.

Communication receded to glottal sighs and random grunts, tenderness mingling with an energy that bordered on force. The pair annexed a wall. They were on waste ground, shared mutual pursuit, their bodies rocking and frenetic in the throes of their obsession. Lips met, tongues meshed. Nothing would interrupt. It was wrong, though in these strange minutes was everything they wanted; it carried an intensity that made all else worthless. Breeches lowered and petticoats lifted, the small of her back shunting higher on the brickwork as she rose to take him in. She stifled a scream. Chasteness was ending with a throaty whimper, with lolling heads and the damp animation of the rut. Limewash was friction-powdering from the wall.

Heedless, he pushed upward and worked himself deep, could hear the sharp intake of her breath and murmur of her voice. Marriage was another country, his wife and child and home in a separate place. He could not explain, could never justify. The instinct was too immediate, the burning within too uncontrolled. His true self remained loyal to Emma. It was a stranger who made love to this girl, an agent at bay, a foreigner whose fate might go unrecorded and sacrifice unthanked. He should be allowed his simple delights. The last wishes of a condemned man.

A juddering cry, the confusion of release, and they were done.

Hours had passed and late night had crawled into early morning. In the safe-house, Hardy and Hawkhead dozed, Black Jack stitched a canvas sack, and Luqa and his dog Fearnot kept vigil on the roof. Out on the river, the blackened hulk of the galleon had been towed to the wreckers for salvage and cannibalization. Its presence among the fleet was deemed to cast a woeful spell. Up here on higher ground people would keep their distance, absconders would hide out, and the shadows would hold their secrets.

It was Fearnot who heard it first. With a cautioning whine, the canine slithered down the narrow stairway and paced fast and low across the room. Luqa came behind, his knife drawn, his footfall summoning others to arms, and shapes tumbled silent from sleep to instant readiness. Black Jack shuttered the lantern and crouched behind a barrel. Whoever was outside would not catch them unprepared.

'Their number, Luqa?' Hardy hissed the question.

'I count one.'

'It would be improper to make him wait.'

His comment was as good as a command. Standing aside, reaching gingerly to loosen bolts and provide a clear arc of fire, the Mediterranean islander obeyed his friend. With a single flick of his blade he had flung wide the door and in a second and seamless move had overpowered the intruder and jerked him through the threshold. The door slammed shut.

They studied the stranger in the renewed light of the lantern. The shock of the moment, the rapid and negative turn of events, did not appear to unnerve him. He was a beggar, ill-nourished and scarcely clothed, his rags hanging filthy and limp, and his battered hat pulled deep and concealing on his brow. A contrivance. His demeanor alone suggested purpose, his steadiness indicated one acquainted with the darker arts of intrigue. He was no madman, no shuffling fool.

Hardy rose to greet him, kept to the Spanish tongue. 'Vagrants do not seek shelter or alms at such an hour.'

'It seems we each of us adopt a mask.'

'Yours more ragged and lowly than most. You are no true beggar.'

'While you are no mercenary soldiers come to find fortune in the pay of Spain.' Head and hat shifted as the stranger surveyed the whole. 'Yet our varied guise suits us well.'

'Identify yourself.'

'A wanderer and keeper of deep secrets.'

'Success is measured in how long you live.'

An accepting nod. 'I take my chance as you take yours. I presume I am in company with those who disturb the peace, upset the Viceroy, put flaming torch to a galleon resting before his palace.'

'Your imaginings are wild.'

'My instinct correct.'

There was an uncompromising sureness, a quickness and alertness that suggested authenticity. Hardy did not put up his sword. Accepting coincidence or swallowing half-truth, abandoning caution to gut feeling, had exposed and killed many an agent. He wanted to hear more. The accent was Flemish, the bearing that of a spy familiar with the terrain and willing to stand his ground. Recognizable traits. A brave man, or a doomed trickster.

'Let us regard your full visage, stranger.'

Carefully, without theatre or sudden movement, the visitor removed his hat. Revealed were steady eyes that peered through matted hair and heavy growth of beard. There was character present, an even temperament, a knowing candour that showed he did not lie.

The man spoke. 'You are not the sole practitioners of our craft who toil in Lisbon for Walsingham.'

'You are ally to the Secretary of State?'

'As God is my witness and as I stand before you.' He paused as Hardy absorbed the information. 'It was I who took the life of the Marquis of Santa Cruz.'

'Any soul could make such claim.'

'Not any soul served in the house of the Admiral or enjoyed his trust and confidence. Not any soul received orders of clandestine kind from London. Not any soul had skill enough to apply the dose of poison.'

'You have proof?'

In reply, the beggar-spy unhooked a cloth bag from within the torn folds of his garments and threw it to the ground. He had rehearsed each step, was master of his presentation.

Hardy stooped to retrieve the offering and withdrew from it the hidden contents. Two leather-bound volumes rested in his hand. In the gloaming beam of the lamp he began to turn their pages, checking one and then the other, glancing on occasion at the bearer of the gift.

'Regard them well, friend.' The visitor waited patiently for the verdict. 'They are lists of English names, of those the Spaniards believe they may rely upon, of those they deem necessary to capture and to silence. Should Albion and Queen Elizabeth fall, what is written herein will be enacted.'

'These you stole from Santa Cruz?'

'I liberated them at his death. They are the work of Garza at the behest of Satan, are his plan for the destruction of the Protestant faith. Armada is but one aspect of the coming inferno. This the other.'

This the other. His words resonated, his conclusions were fact. Hardy stared at the roll-call, each carefully inscribed name a vote of confidence or intended sentence of death, each separate register the Holy Grail for an intelligencer. The sheep and the goats. England would kill for such information – already had.

Yet the itinerant was not finished. 'If the Inquisitor searches for me, he also scours the city for you. I discover your lair, for you yourselves are near discovered. It was simple measure to trail the Lady Constança to these quarters, no great feat to observe the sly henchmen of Garza lurking close behind.'

'You jest, stranger.'

'I warn.'

'Constança betrays us?'

'Unwittingly she leads the enemy here. I was to divest on her these books and to look to save myself.' The Fleming regarded the four men. 'Instead I am obliged to caution and save others of my calling.'

'I see no friendly army at your shoulder.'

'Haste and action is your stronger companion. You must depart at once this town.'

'And miss occasion to further prick the Inquisition?' Hardy would not cede the argument. 'We have work remaining.'

'You are stubborn, friend.'

'It is why a captive Scotsman in his dungeon cell retains the light of hope.'

'Your effort is wasted. The seafarer Hunter will be already close to death.'

'Are not we all?'

The stranger sighed and returned his hat to its crowning station. 'Remain in Lisbon and Garza and his men will soon be here.'

'I would rather stay and bring war direct upon them.'

Decision was reached and assent provided with near-imperceptible blinks of the eyes. Hardy, Luqa, Hawkhead and Black Jack were not about to run.

~

To the superstitious people of Lisbon, the muffled clop of hooves and rumbling night-time passage of a dark and closed-up carriage was reason to cross themselves, to close their shutters or avert their fearful eyes. The Devil was abroad, some said. But most understood it was the Inquisition at work, that another poor wretch had been dragged from his slumber and was journey-bound for the dungeons of the Estaus. *El Papa Negro* the citizens grimly named the transport. There was an ironic truth to the moniker, for it was also the unofficial title applied to the

Superior General of the Jesuits and a Jesuit who exercised ultimate command of this prison wagon. Since arriving, Inquisitor Garza had proved unsparing in his use of the black pope.

Moving at trotting pace, the coach swept in uncontested fashion through the deserted city streets. It was always on time, ever kept to the hours of darkness. From raid to delivery of a captive might take only twenty minutes. The crew prided themselves on their efficiency, basked in the unsentimental process set in motion with the slamming of doors and the crack of a whip. Citizens trembled, and that was to be enjoyed. The coachman could expect the bleary-eyed thanks of the *alguacil*, the bailiff, would receive extra pay and a flagon of beer. On occasion, he might even be permitted to witness a session of torture. A clean catch and safe handover earned ample reward.

As he hunched above his reins this evening, the coachman had cause to lower his expectations. He and his companions had not anticipated the ambush, had never before suffered the injury and shame of their vehicle being seized. The blackguards who accosted them had scant comprehension of the forces with which they trifled. One moment there was routine and convention, the next there was enemy swarming on the bodywork. It challenged belief. Silent in his shock and misery, the driver concentrated on the road ahead. He would be patient, would do as he was asked, would applaud the reckoning when it came. Beside him on the box, Hawkhead clutched a sharp falchion blade and muttered orders in his ear.

Inside the conveyance, weakly illuminated by the glow of a hanging oil-lamp, Hardy and Luqa continued to prepare. Stacked around them were muskets and swords, horns of powder and boxes of shot, the materiel for fighting and instruments of escape. There could be no half-measure, would be no retreat.

Luqa tended to a crossbow. 'You break me from Newgate and now herd me to a prison.'

'You doubt my judgement?'

'I question our friendship.' The islander glanced up with a half-grin. 'What call have we to go to the Estaus?'

'The need for Mr Hunter.'

'We know Queen Elizabeth to be in peril, have too the ledgers from the Flemish agent. Our labour is over, Christian.'

'It is not ended while an intelligencer sits in an Inquisition cell.'

Luqa squinted along an ash quarrel, inspected its tail-flight, and fitted it to the groove. 'A noble and insane cause.'

'Are they not the best?'

'In my experience, they are the ones you favour.'

'Fine words for a horse-thief.'

'This horse-thief counsels cautions. This horse-thief knows when the gamble is too great.'

'You would abandon our sport?'

'Never.' Luqa cocked the weapon.

His commander turned away and prodded the tip of his Katzbalger through the frontal louvre. It would keep the coachman on point and guessing, would prevent him articulating a cry for help. The Estaus was close. If the ruse worked, they would achieve total surprise; should their plan be compromised, the carriage would become their private hearse. Luqa was right to question his wisdom. But there was more at stake than the well-being of an imprisoned Scotsman, more to do than merely start a prison riot. Doubt was unnecessary so advanced in the game.

A sharp tap on the roof indicated run-in had begun. Hardy braced himself and reached to snuff the lamp. As its flame died, he noted Luqa press his lips in fleeting and reverential kiss to the silver cross about his neck. Such a popish act would have drawn a scornful jibe from Hawkhead. Hardy did not comment. He would reserve his own prayers for later.

'*Salutations to you! Busy work?*'

'My usual load of dung.'

The nightwatch suspected nothing, the captain of the guard waving the coach and driver through with bored indifference and a swing of his lantern. There was no reason for alarm or delay. The vehicle was on schedule, its form unaltered, its pock-faced master and his helmeted sentinel perched visible and familiar to the fore. A reassuring sight. All was well with the delivery.

As *El Papa Negro* rolled to a halt in the yard, a bailiff and his lieutenants approached.

'What do you bring?'

'Sufficient to keep the interrogators toiling.'

A gruff laugh. 'The most committed heretic learns to love our ways.'

'It is God's work.'

'And it is necessary labour.' The bailiff placed his hand on the door of the transport and called through to its interior. 'Do not be coy, my children. This day you attain hell.'

He was to get there early. The bolt from the crossbow entered his mouth and departed the back of his skull in a distorted plume of brain. He had time neither to hear the plaintive cry from the driving-station nor to fully discern the nature of the hidden shapes within. His disfigured body dropped. In the same instant, Hawkhead wiped his blade across the throat of the coachman and slipped lightly to the ground. Already, Hardy and Luqa had launched themselves to the fray, overwhelming and cutting down in a directed flurry of blows.

Only the *alcaide*, the Inquisition jailer in charge of feeding prisoners, remained standing. Isolated among the littered dead, trembling in the voided contents of his own bowel, he was a wretched sight. Without ceremony, the visitors seized him. His temporary reprieve and involuntary odyssey were for a purpose. He had knowledge of every prisoner, possessed keys to their cells, would act as pliant guide for the unofficial tour.

'*What is such meaning?*'

The challenge was sharp as it was short-lived, a throwing-blade from Hawkhead punching into the chest and bringing down the guard. On the expedition flowed. Gates were opened, doors flung wide, irons and chains shorn off to ringing impact and the rising shouts and cheers of incarcerated souls. It was the first time hope had ever entered these chambers. Optimism was slow to take hold. Yet it grew, blossomed from the fear of cruel trick to realization that other prisoners walked free if stiffly from their bondage, that those who had been held appeared now to have ownership of swords and muskets. Clamour escalated, sweeping the rage and fervour of liberation along the subterranean parts. Through it came Hardy and his men.

A small posse of guards had mounted a rearguard fight, were surprised, outnumbered and then culled by a vengeful mob that left behind it little in the way of discernible human remains. The parade continued. Heads appeared on spikes and were carried high, severed hands were improvised as epaulettes, and a prisoner danced close and joyous with the dismembered torso of one of his tormentors. A necessary outpouring.

Hardy had expected to find this level, had known there was a floor sited deeper than the rest. He had left behind Luqa and Hawkhead to manage the exodus and bear the ailing Mr Hunter by stretcher to the carriage. It would take all their skill and mastery of chaos. His was a more specific imperative. He carried a lantern, casting its light about him, searching into empty hollows, edging along deserted corridors with dread and hope wrestling in his gut. Maybe he was the victim of his own hoax, a casualty of the fears accumulated through a boyhood and manhood misspent as warrior and spy. Memory could warp the senses and conjure demons. A painting could create false echo. He longed for it to be so.

'Christian . . .'

Through a narrow slit set five feet into a stone wall came his name and the voice of his mother. He tried to convince himself it was a phantom, attempted to cast it off as further trick of his restless mind, the light, or the resonance of this place. But she was real.

He put his mouth to the opening. 'Is it you? My mother?'

'As surely as you are my son.'

He struggled to speak, found his throat and thoughts near-frozen. 'How could you know?'

'Who else but you would journey to discover me? Who else but a mother would recognize the presence and footfall of her son?'

'I will free you, Mother.'

'It is beyond your strength or mine.' The disembodied voice floated whisper-soft to his ears. 'There is liberty enough in speech, divine freedom enough to touch another hand despite the confines of these walls.'

He leaned against the stonework, his tears dry-forming, his arm extended until his fingertips made connection. Everything was in the moment and focused at that single point. Happiness and blind grief, the mutual exchange of history and warmth and unconditional love, and the shuddering awareness of greeting and farewell. Hardy gasped for air, burrowed his forehead against the crude solidity of the wall. There was no deeper agony, no crueller intensity of despair. He was powerless.

Again his mother spoke, her fingers communicating with his. 'What made you search, Christian?'

'The Giorgione, the painting.' He swallowed the burning ache in his larynx, his emotions besieged. 'It is in the possession of Inquisitor Garza.'

Her stillness could be felt. 'How easily the devout become rapacious plunderers. Garza gathers trophies as surely as he collects innocents to his jail.'

'He captured you, mother?'

'One visit to Malta did not suffice. On hearing news of your affray and later escape, he found excuse to return and bring greater punishment on those who held his brother Prior Garza in contempt.'

'Was his execution of Fra Roberto not enough?'

'You are the son of Christian Hardy, hero of the Great Siege, and I his widow. It gives motive for his action.'

'Then I am sole cause for your plight.'

'Instead you are my bringer of joy.' She gently worked his fingers. 'That I should once more hold the hand of my beloved child will leave its imprint on my soul.'

'I have my own son, a strong and handsome boy you shall one day meet.'

'Not in this life, Christian. You must go.'

'I cannot betray you.'

'Betray?' Her voice seemed to drift mesmerizing in the fetid ether. 'You would betray me should you stay. You would betray your mission and the memory of your father should you allow yourself to be taken.'

'I care not what becomes of me.'

'Yet I care what becomes of my own. I have fought on the ramparts beside your father, might have died a hundred times against the Ottoman foe. My life is near through as yours begins. Be glad it is fulfilled.'

166

'Where is gladness?'

'That we speak and share time and may press together fingers, that you are of my flesh and womb.'

'Let me see you, Mother.'

'I am unused to the light, and you to an aged crone you would scarce recognize. Remember me as I remember you. Carry me as I once cradled you. Without your being, there is no memory of me and no father for your son. For us all, you must leave.'

'I will break down the wall, will discover an entrance. I shall call prisoners to attend.' He was frantic for deliverance, pummelled his fist against the surface.

'Heed me, my son.'

'There is a way, must be a path to freedom.'

'Passage to these chambers is by separate route, is denied to any but Garza himself.'

'For what reason?'

'Does the Inquisition of Spain or Portugal need reason?' Her hand was old and chill in his. 'What is the name of my grandson, Christian?'

'He is Adam.'

She repeated it in faint murmur. 'Adam. A sweet and worthy name, a foundation for each one of us. He will be waiting for his father.' Her hand withdrew.

'God help me, Mother.'

'He will bless and keep you, and His love and mine will for ever bear you on.'

For the moment it would crush him. Hardy slid to the ground and began to crawl and part-stagger away. He did not possess the will or spirit to rise and walk, did not own the right to conduct himself in any other manner. He was deserting his mother; acting in her name, was consigning her to the bottomless pit. Garza had done this. His creed, his methods, his dark-robed minions had created a world in which a kind and beautiful noblewoman could be transported as slave or prisoner and stowed in a vile dungeon. Maria was her name – a name lost on them, and a mother kept from him. There was no justice or mercy. It was why he fought, why he would drive the battle straight into the heart of the enemy. Retribution would arrive. In his numbed and desolate state, he permitted himself that late prayer.

Chapter 9

'Impenitents shall be consumed!'
    'Your flesh and sins will be as ash!'
'The Lord will ever punish heretics and apostates, will ever hew the tree of rotten fruit!'
'Repent or face the furnace!'
'Tremble and perish!'

Such were the insults hurled at those paraded on their way to execution at the stake. It was a festive occasion, rich in symbolism and fecund with the heady atmosphere of thousands come to taunt the victims in their final shuffling steps. Auto-da-fé was always a crowd-pleaser. Fifers and drummers played, honeyed pastries were sold, and the people of Lisbon thronged the route from the Church of São Domingos, around the Rossio, and down to Palace Square. A state occasion with a difference. For this closing act, the Inquisition had read aloud the charges and relinquished its prisoners to the care of the secular authorities. The Church itself could not be seen to draw blood or have tainted hands. And so the procession of the condemned began, clerics and nobles craning from windows, rumour and comment sweeping ahead. Nothing could match the excitement or dilute the enjoyment of such a malignant carnival.

Clasping small wooden crucifixes and reciting from the Gospels, two parallel lines of Jesuits walked in solemn show.

Between them were the captives, six men and women strangely attired in yellow penitential *san benito* robes and their heads crowned with pointed *corozas* jutting upwards a full three feet. As if not gaudy enough, the costumes were emblazoned with vivid depictions of demons and the fires of hell, reminders of what awaited a short distance hence. Yet the prisoners were unable to pass comment. Their mouths were gagged, bound fast to prevent utterance of oath or blasphemy against the religion that sent them to their deaths. Their hands too were tied. Only their eyes expressed something of the dumb horror and inner dread, strained wide at the enveloping scene or swivelled in shock at each new vista. They passed now the Carmelite monastery to the side of the Rossio, the friars and nuns in their white mantles crossing themselves and murmuring prayers. Plainly the condemned had chosen Baal over God. They were to be pitied.

To those looking down upon the whole, it appeared the entire city populace had converged upon a single point. Spring was promised in the warmer air of early March, great event was laid out in glittering Sunday tableau. Watching from a balcony of the Estaus, Inquisitor Garza could afford himself a degree of satisfaction. True, he had been thwarted by event and foreign plot, had seen his dungeon bastion penetrated and his prisoner Mr Hunter freed; true also he had failed to catch the perpetrators, had with difficulty doused the fires and put down revolt within the very building in which he stood. The path to glory was never easy.

It had posed a direct challenge and outrage to his authority. Through diligent questioning he had acquired descriptions of the suspects, one of whom matched the blue-eyed priest in secret meeting with the Lady Constança, two others those who had stolen gunpowder and engaged in the murder of local vagabonds. A commander, a swarthy lieutenant, a vicious knife-man and a Negro. Four men, all vanished. The trail laid by an unsuspecting Constança Menezes had run cold: the house in the Alfama raided by his troops had proved empty and hastily vacated. Should the enemy be on the move, they would be detected. Patrols were out, the roads to the coast guarded, the fishing-villages watched. While the citizens were diverted by public burnings, would applaud and gasp as fire-brands were first thrust in the screaming faces of the captives, he would continue in his search.

Below, processing onward to the travelling sounds of affirmation, the party of prisoners trooped miniature and comic in their garish apparel. There was not long to go for them. These fiends would die looking out to the Tagus, would see the invasion fleet that would bear to England the power and majesty of the faith. Today the devouring by flames of a few; tomorrow the vengeful incineration of thousands and the reclaiming of a nation. The group of Janissary assassins was already sailed. Then shall the righteous shine forth, Garza mused.

'My lord Inquisitor.'

He turned at the voice, acknowledged with chill correctness the presence and ingratiating bow of a trusty. 'You have news?'

'Of some import, Inquisitor.'

'Such claim is not yours to make.'

'Forgive my reckless zeal.' The underling again inclined his head. 'We find the foreign spies, Inquisitor.'

'Spies you contrived before to lose.'

'They were fleet of foot and alert to our approach, escaped their dwelling in advance of our assault.'

'I am informed of their action and aware of your excuse.'

'They are yet now cornered, Inquisitor. An agent of ours espied one of their company, the Negro, entering a house below the eastern parts of the castle.'

'One blackamoor is as like to another.'

'None similar in size or bearing to the instance reported.'

'Your man might be mistaken, our vile enemy flown.'

The officer shook his head. 'He begs you to send troops, Inquisitor.'

'So we may again chase phantoms and shadows? So you may once more stand before me and proffer news of your discomfiture?'

'Scavenging close to the dwelling is seen a small dog, Inquisitor. A beast near in each detail to that described by the boy who in his street witnessed killing of the four knaves.'

'A Negro, a dog. It is ephemera and not proof.'

'This hidden abode is well suited for refuge and defence. The walls are strong, the windows set high, the area within designed for stowage and safekeeping.'

'Its position?'

'Commanding.'

Unhurried in his manner, Garza re-entered the body of the room. He seemed oblivious to the noise beyond, ignored the messenger and even the faint and acrid trace of smoke from the damaged floors below as he paced in inner contemplation. The foe remained in Lisbon. Four men who had inflicted loss to property and life, who had engineered a prison breakout and might yet execute additional outrage. He did not require further evidence of their capability and daring. They had means and motive, and possessed gunpowder.

He swung on his heel. 'Send word to the camp. When auto-da-fé is complete and the light fades, then shall we send force against the resting adversary.'

It was a dream of sorts, a process in which she was the object of attention and yet almost entirely overlooked. Maria took another step, kept her gaze on the trembling head in front, narrowed her focus to her own breath and tread and the steeling of her nerve. Around her, the fervour of the crowd scarce intruded. Their jeers and shouts, the force-field of their jubilation, were not to impinge on those condemned to die. She was merely an anonymous female, with a shaven head and in clownish garb, chosen to sate a bloodlust and provide uplifting spectacle for the devout citizenry and rulers. The role was not a complicated one.

Ahead, the upright line of stakes hove stark into view. They had a simplicity of form and honesty of function that cut through religious lie and the false embellishments of pomp. She was to burn. Even as she had reached to touch on that blessed and desperate eve the hand of her own son Christian, she had known of her sentence and accelerated fate. Inquisitor Garza wanted example; Inquisitor Garza had long cherished thought of eradicating any associated by familial tie to the killing on Malta of his brother. This was the predictable conclusion to that event. She had not told her son, saw no advantage in deepening his grief or widening his sense of culpability. They had said their farewells. Perhaps it was a privilege to be forewarned of the precise moment and manner of her own passing.

She stared before her, bit into the knotted cloth that was fastened in her mouth. Some might weaken at the dark reality, might feel their knees buckle and their minds stray to the verge of lunacy in the shadow of impending doom. Not she. Her quiet faith would carry her through, the spirit of the Englishman who had made her his wife would comfort and embrace her even as she suffered. Flames could not vanquish memory or love. She thought of that bold adventurer who had once held her close and given her child, of the sight and sound and smell of war through which together they had travelled, of the brief time they had shared and the union they had forged. It had been a life rich in its fulfilment.

Urine spattered the earth, a cowed prisoner leaking his fright in the closing approach to Palace Square. The crowd roared its delight. Fever-pitch was reached, had been primed the previous night with grim dress-rehearsal and the elaborate ritual of the Procession of the Green Cross. Savagery was ever lent legitimacy by ceremonial. Let them have their entertainment. She turned her head, searching in the multitude, exploring the mass of leering faces for contact, for a glimmer of humanity or warmth. A small girl rubbed her eyes, a single tear trickling on her cheek in her distress. It was enough. Maria willed a smile to her, maintained her tender stare as a hand pushed her in the small of her back and directed her to a stage among the kindling. She had found her Calvary.

Everyone talked of the burnings, spoke excitedly of where they had stood and what they had witnessed. The show had proved an outstanding success. Yet darkness was now come. The pyres that had raged for several hours, that had been fuelled by turpentine and the incendiary qualities of human fat, had faded to embers and cooled to ash. Bodies once living, which had amused with their impromptu and contorted dance, were now little more than blackened fragments to be raked out and scattered. The crowd was gone, the noise abated, the carriages of the nobles dispersed to the mansions and palaces. Justice was done and morale well served by the events of the day.

Those events were not quite over. On the eastern edge of the castle district, a force of infantry stood armed and ready for assault. They were mustered below a long flight of steps that led to a squat stone building lodged between a jumble of similar kind. There was nothing remarkable in its construction. Yet it housed the enemy, acted as bolt-hole for spies from England who had inflicted grievous punishment on the authority of King Philip of Spain. A chance sighting had drawn attention and would prove to be their downfall.

'Ready yourselves.'

The sergeant whispered back to his men, cradled his sword in his hand, and knelt prepared behind a low buttress. His orders were to capture or kill, and he would most definitely opt to kill. A personal choice. The four men trapped inside the target structure corresponded in every detail to the Italian mercenaries he had met in the army camp. He and the quartet had struck up fraternal alliance, a link that could prove a liability. These fugitives could not be allowed to talk. In negotiating for their lives, they would doubtless reveal their contact with a certain sergeant they had persuaded to incite violent affray in the Rossio. That sergeant was mired by association and their perfidy, possessed gold coins and gem-set baubles presented by the young and blue-eyed leader of the group as token of his esteem. To think he had been outwitted. It could make an old soldier angry, determined and greedy. There would be opportunity for redress and further riches, a single occasion to close down the tired friendship. He braced himself for the ascent.

A sound that none expected disrupted the stillness, the bounce and roll of a heavy object as it gathered momentum on the slope. Its course was awkward, but its destination fixed by the downward channel of the steps. A barrel dislodged from its storage, perhaps. The sergeant peered cautiously from his shelter, squinted perplexed at the unexplained article lumbering solid and threatening for him. There was something menacing in its progress, something aimed and intended, something delivered with a fuse-string attached that sputtered and flickered in the dark. This was definitely no part of the plan. The sergeant gaped, unable to speak, powerless to process either image or outcome. Identification arrived. It occurred at the precise instant of detonation, emerged with a scream of alarm that was buried in explosion. Hardy and his cohorts had designed the bomb well. Iron nails, musket-balls and scrap metal lining the body of the powder-keg blew outward, tearing off limbs, cleaving heads, propelling human remains in a blurt of flesh and rubble. Of thirty troops who had waited to charge, a handful remained alive. They were in no state to accomplish their task, would barely be able to crawl away.

Firing began from the house, developed into a brisk exchange of shots with other soldiers advancing from a different quarter. Battle was joined. In a blind rush, Spanish infantrymen stormed forward and were driven back by ripple-volleys across a pooling field of blood and splintered scaling-ladders. They tried again. Clay pots arced from the windows and shattered below, flaring in oily blooms of wildfire that caught many in their reach. Sulphur, nitre, resin and naphtha made for a deadly blaze. It clung to flesh and clothing, burnt through leather, roasted men in their armour as they stumbled or ran. The defenders could hold off an army.

Inside the building, Hardy discharged an arquebus, rolled to a second opening and let loose with another weapon. On he moved, ducking as a shutter fractured, catching a firearm thrown by Black Jack and rising to unleash the shot. The shrieks and the flames assisted his aim.

'We are ready, Christian.' The voice of Luqa eddied through the smoke.

'Then we pay last respect to the Spaniards and vanish from their sight.'

Speed and illusion would be their salvation. As a musket-ball impacted and flattened close, Hardy exchanged a glance with the giant African. The former slave was content among the powdering walls and enveloping debris of war, his large hands skilfully loading and rodding the muskets. He enjoyed a fight as much as he found solace and reward in repairing a sail.

His appetite would be more than catered for. Each knew the odds, understood that retreat needed to be covered. Hardy left him to his duties.

Escape was staggered, advanced in bursts across planks arranged between the rooftops and over the alleyways of the castle environs. Noise pursued them. In grudging cooperation, Luqa and Hawkhead manhandled a stretcher on which the Scotsman Mr Hunter lay. The merchant captain was in no condition to walk, scarcely remained alive. Fearnot the dog trotted behind, doubtful at first and then nimbly embracing the skyline adventure. Hardy followed. They had wreaked their worst on Lisbon, had sunk a galleon and broken wide a jail, had discovered secrets and caused infinite distress to Garza and the Spanish state. Even Walsingham might indicate emotion or approval. The young Englishman negotiated the span to the next edifice. It was good to move, to slough off the sullen guilt and leaden sorrow weighing heavy since encounter with his mother.

He paused, watching the dim shadows of his men, listening to the receding noise of skirmish. Black Jack was maintaining the deception. He clambered forward, found his knee pressing on something detached and warm and thrown there by explosion. He flinched, and brushed away the severed hand.

They had reached the ground, hauling themselves down to a dirt track winding to the north. If the city were awakened to the squall-disturbance of conflict, at least here the inhabitants chose to leave the armed parties to their own device and devilment. Elsewhere, axes and pitchforks would be seized and hue and cry raised. It would add to the chaos, create more favourable conditions for flight. The Flemish agent too had promised to play his part, had busied himself with laying false trails and abandoning a fishing-boat on the far side of the Tagus to draw pursuit southward. Moment was brief.

Panting through exertion, Hawkhead whispered fiercely from the gloom. 'I thought prison would render this Scotsman lighter, Christian.'

'I believed challenge would make you complain less.' Hardy drew his Katzbalger and knelt beside the wall. 'Proceed to the cart and make ready for departure. I shall await Black Jack.'

'Is it not right the Maltese should stay in your place?'

Luqa laughed at the pointed proposal. 'I would not risk you abandoning me to the Spaniards, Hawkhead.'

'A wise decision.'

'Enough words.' Hardy silenced the exchange. 'Put haste in your minds and stealth in your feet. And go.'

They obeyed, running low and fast, bearing their cargo in the direction of the hidden wagon. Hardy loitered, imagining the source of every sound and the battle he could not see. The African would be unable to hold the enemy for ever. With a final fusillade, he would put taper to fuse and bolt for the roof, would traverse the overhead walkways and ditch them in his wake. Hardy had confidence in his sailmaker.

More immediate concerns breached his thoughts, split the false calm and the air around his head with the close release of a pistol. He tasted the powder residue. The shot had travelled wide. With reflexive fury he charged the threat, was parrying and thrusting with his blade at the flitting reach of a rapier. His assailant had made an error in allowing him to live, and error created chance. Hardy would exploit it. The Katzbalger was quick in his hand, made up for its lack of radius with its merits as a street-sword. Essential in a scrap. He worked his way in, beating back the stranger, would outclass and outfight him with brute force and unrelenting drive. Steel sparked; steel cut through leather and flesh, and the man cursed loud. His tongue was English.

'A son of England?' Hardy pushed forward. 'You traitorous dog.'

The voice was tight with pain. 'Who but an Englishman would read your mind as I? Who other might predict your method or thwart your piratical intent?'

'It is you who is countered.' Hardy hacked away the incoming blade and lunged.

A counter-stroke and immediate retreat. 'Walsingham soundly trains his beasts, I see.'

'He tutors us to kill.'

'You are no match for our cause.' Realm circled his rapier and edged for a new vantage. 'You and your rabble will perish here.'

'Yet we alone draw blood.'

In the murk-light that waned and waxed, they struggled for position and conclusive blow. Hardy detected a weakening in the effort. His opponent was losing blood and concentration, was throwing his all into angry and final act of desperation. He was no natural swordsman.

Hardy delivered a kick to the knee and the duellist screeched and tumbled to a limp recovery. But the young soldier was on him, would break and butcher him for the wife and child in England he protected and for the mother he had deserted. It would pass the time, would be a sweet lesson in vengeance.

'You adopt the wrong masters, renegade.'

That renegade answered through bloody lips. 'Spain will be the saviour of England.'

'As she proves to be your downfall.'

'Your Protestant queen will die, her heretic servants with her.' Realm was scrabbling for purchase as he backed against a stone projection. 'We shall prevail.'

'For it you must keep your poise.'

A savage sweep of the Katzbalger, a glancing strike on the

shadow form, and the stranger lost footing and plunged backwards to the drop. The fall was ragged, the impact hard. Above, the victor had vaulted to a loose block to assess conditions for the follow-on slaughter. He would climb down for a clean finish. But circumstance again altered, surged on the distant thud of eruption and the brief discoloration of the night. Black Jack had obliterated both house and pursuers.

Hardy peered at the sprawled and groaning shape of the Englishman below. 'Pray to your God we do not soon renew acquaintance.'

Such event appeared unlikely. The stranger had been spared by coincidence and timing, was free to bleed and drag himself away. Christian Hardy too was set to leave the area.

The African former-slave would not be joining him in the exodus. Wounded in the chest and shoulder, his head lacerated, he had committed himself to the spirit world and waited patiently for the decisive scene. Eventually they came for him, Spanish and Portuguese troops trampling over the bodies of their slain and stampeding through in number to put an end to the stubborn resistance. They had not expected to discover a large and injured Negro with a smile on his face and a lighted brand in his fist. Still less did they anticipate his greeting them with a blissful howl and the thrusting of the torch direct into a nearby keg of gunpowder. It was the most effective of diversionary tactics. This was freedom, a parting gift to his companions. Black Jack called to his gods and his ancestors and was gone.

~

Immortal struggle had many dimensions. In the county of Derbyshire, perched on a hill overlooking a tranquil landscape of oak-woods and bracken moors, the farmhouse provided an unlikely setting for intrigue. Sheep were the main business of the area. Yet it was to this location that a horseman had ridden before dawn, skirting the village of Beeley below and pausing long enough only to hurl a padded sack through an open window. For nights past, the visit had been expected. Then the rider and horse departed, leaving by a different route, galloping fast and jinxing across countryside in order to evade detection. On enemy terrain, the danger could be anywhere. Calm settled, morning broke, and the locals rose to their daily tasks undisturbed and none the wiser. After two months of feint and manoeuvre, the encrypted message from Europe had finally reached its objective.

A hearth-fire had been lit, its smoke drifting from a chimney and hanging lacklustre on the damp morn air. It would be a busy day. There were wool merchants to contact, shepherds and farmhands to direct, and the early lambs to inspect and count. And in a small upper chamber of the house the Catholic cipher-bearer pored over the slip of paper he had extracted from the spine of a common book on witchcraft. Lives had been risked to get the note to him. It was his ordained role and sacred duty to decode and translate, to ensure that the contents of the message were disseminated among believers and to those who planned usurpation of the Crown. From here, the world would collapse about the satin-sheathed feet of Queen Elizabeth of England; from here, a great army would emerge to strike Protestantism in the back as it turned to face the Spanish invasion. History was often determined in such forgotten places. The cipher-carrier again read the words and committed them to memory before putting the paper to the grate. He had glad tidings to deliver.

At the back door he sniffed the air and listened to the unfolding tempo of the day. For the while, he was safe. Strangers would be noticed and challenged, local militia sighted at a distance of miles and discreet alarm raised. Luck and a fair walk would permit him to reach the tavern by noon. From there he would travel on, spread the word, passing the flame of rebellion to seminarists and recusants and to the noble families and secret adherents who awaited call to arms. The ancient faith was poised to return.

He was fifty strides into the field when the bark of a dog reached his ear and he turned. Something glinted from a coppice; something made the rooks call loud. He stared, trying to catch the subtleties of movement, straining to discern form within the thicket. Light glanced off metal. For a man conditioned to suspect the merest discordance, it was sufficient. The cipher-carrier bolted. He veered from the danger, charging down a slope, slithering into a gully that funnelled between trees and led him gasping to a lower ridge. There was no time to think or pause. Distance was the priority. He threw himself into the descent, scattering sheep and clumsily mounting a stile. Had to keep moving, had to get away. Ahead lay another wood. He could hide himself and lose pursuit, could refill his aching lungs and pacify his shocked nerves. Surely the enemy could not have trailed him.

Options were ended by a sudden rattle of musketry. There were multiple hits. Propelled backwards, his chest and abdomen ruptured, the man slumped dead. It had been all too easy to channel him into the zone and towards its predictable outcome. An unusual figure dressed vividly in lilac finery detached itself from an emerging group of sharpshooters and went to examine the prone body. Isaiah Payne could congratulate himself on his patience and resilience and rejoice at this singular affirmation of his ability and place at the head of the Searchers. A further Catholic pig was consigned to oblivion. He leaned above the shivering corpse and rummaged in a cloth pouch at its side before extracting a small leather notebook. Possession of the cipher had transferred. Reward went indeed to those who waited, in a thicket. Sir Francis Walsingham would gain fresh insight to the mind and method of the Spanish foe.

Tension had risen on the streets of London. There were the shouts of sergeants and the beat of drums, the rattle of gun-carriages behind teams of horses, and the constant din and drill of mustered men. No one conversed without first cursing King Philip of Spain and his damnable intent. Patriotic songs were sung and poems read, pamphlets distributed with chill detail of Catholic brutishness, and everywhere was exhortation to save the kingdom and defend Good Queen Bess. Perhaps the Armada had sailed, the invasion force of the Duke of Parma already sat embarked and waiting on barges in the Low Countries. Many questions were asked and few answers provided. Yet all knew that battle was close.

In the house behind Fetter Lane, Emma laughed and played with her small son Adam. Every day he asked of his father, and every day she told him the same. Christian would be back soon. It was said in the street that Queen Elizabeth would lead her own army; it was rumoured Drake was preparing to strike pre-emptively at the Spanish fleet. Such things were of little interest to her. She wanted her husband home, wanted to hold him, wanted to see him step from the dark affairs of state across the threshold to his family. For two months now he was vanished – two months filled by lonely wondering and the empty desperation of fear. She could have taken Adam south to her kinsfolk in Dorset. But her place was here, her duty to abide and to prepare for the day when her husband returned. *Soon.* It was the cruellest word in the English tongue.

She watched as the two-year-old contented himself with building a tower of wood bricks. He had the smile and vivid blue eyes of his father, the indefatigability and determination, the mischievous cheer that warmed all who met him. May he never in his life draw a sword or fight as Christian did; may God in His mercy protect and preserve him and keep him from harm. Adam set an Ottoman jewel atop the structure and looked up at his mother. She tried to staunch her tears, was pretending happiness even as she sank to the floor and the little boy, his face wrinkling in concern, tottered fast to comfort her. Her weeping dropped to a silent and deeper grief.

~

'Did I not counsel you to leave me at the Estaus?'

Mr Hunter was dying. He lay on his litter in the woods behind the cliffs, a merchant captain reduced to a pitiful and lingering state. There was no hope for him. Yet he had outlived his own crew, had survived long enough to be carried from his dungeon as a freed man. Hardy knelt beside him and gently put a flask of spring-water to his lips. The Scotsman turned his head away.

'I do not revive, boy.' It was nothing but the truth. 'Why such endeavour for a heap of broken bone?'

'To save a life for a second is to live oneself.' That too was the truth.

'Is it much recompense, boy?'

'Confounding Garza is reward enough.'

'You endanger yourselves. You remained in Lisbon longer than you ought, and lost a good companion in the Negro.'

'Black Jack embraced and welcomed jeopardy.'

'No more or less than you.' The eyes were glazing with an opaque film. 'I must thank you each for my liberty.'

'No praise is due. It is you who uncovered rumour of plot against our Queen. It is you who placed your ship and crew in the service of Walsingham.'

The Scotsman repeated the name on a stuttering breath. 'Walsingham. He exacts a heavy price with our toil.'

'Would you have it other way?'

'I would not, boy.'

They rested in stillness for a while and let the sound of the wind and ocean wash through the screening trees. Luqa and Hawkhead kept stag, and Fearnot prowled close. Their journey to this point had been circuitous, aided by miracle and trickery and the application of fuse-cord and gunpowder to further confuse the enemy. An army camp had caught ablaze, several houses and a grain-store joining it. The Flemish agent had taken naturally to his destructive spree. *A heavy price for our toil.* Mr Hunter was right, reflected Hardy. But there could be no regret, for they had struck hard and learned much and brought living souls from the jail twilight of the Inquisition. And no value could be placed on the blind and fleeting encounter with his mother.

'You have a wife, boy?'

Hardy nodded. 'A son also.'

'Then they are braver than we. For we choose our part and delight in its danger. They instead are burdened with our calling.'

Another truth he cared not to consider. When the *Black Crow* appeared, he would divest himself of certain events in Lisbon and prepare himself for homecoming. Memories of Constança would be stripped out, images and feelings abandoned, the unhelpful past offloaded for lighter travel. It was for the best, and it was for Sir Francis Walsingham. The spy-chief would invite him to conference, would listen with quietness and courtesy while he divulged every relevant step and told of an English traitor met violently in the night.

A hand gripped his, insistent with sudden strength. 'Dispose of my body at sea, Christian.'

'I shall.'

'Tell Sir Francis we laboured for him, boy. Tell him that sound and true men died for his regard.'

'He will be aware of your sacrifice.'

'Stay with me.'

'I am with you.'

'No more the struggle, no longer the torture and the pain.'

Hardy felt the fingers tremble. 'Hark to the sea, my friend.'

'You have brought it to me, Christian. You deliver me home.'

The hand fell away, the wisp of breath carried to a single gasp, and the Scots mariner was no more. For minutes, Hardy kept vigil beside the corpse. He had travelled far to save this man, had risked everything to pull him from his cell. A result of sorts had been achieved. He was left with a cooling body, with the pride and privilege of witnessing departure, and with a renewed sense of urgency. Armada was close behind.

Chapter 10

On 25 April 1588 a great parade took place through the crowded streets of Lisbon. It followed the same route as the auto-da-fé a month before, moving in grave pageant from the cathedral to the waterfront of Palace Square, and was in its own fashion an act of faith. At the head of the procession were the Viceroy and Medina Sidonia. Behind them came marching bands of drummers and trumpeters, serried ranks of infantry, the colourfully robed and hooded members of the guilds. There was much to celebrate, every reason why banners should hang from buildings and the people cheer and whistle. For the Captain-General of the Navy it was vindication of his effort and affirmation of his role as the bearer of the sword of judgement and the spear-point of the Catholic faith. After setback and delay, having endured attacks by Drake and the dark subterfuge of Walsingham, the Armada at last was arranged.

Medina Sidonia presented a stern and noble sight as he paced on his way. To be part of history and of divine conflict demanded concentration. His responsibilities did not allow for levity or expression of delight. Yet he thrilled to the applause, revelled in the honour bestowed upon him. That old bastard Santa Cruz would have choked to witness such things. Indeed he had choked – had vomited his last in his private apartments, and ensured the task and credit for invasion went to a younger noble. The Captain-General traced with his eyes the line of flags ahead. If the city populace was so enthused now, its emotion at his future return from conquest would surely be uncontained. He could not decry the excitement. It was infectious, heartfelt; it would carry him along this roadway and in a few short steps take him to a grand display of victory in the streets of London itself. No small achievement. To reach so far he had bullied and cajoled, threatened and imprisoned, beseeched his King and berated his underlings. The size of the march-past alone banished all doubt.

A fanfare sounded, its notes curling bright and optimistic above the sun-washed scene. Happy faces reflected the glad and portentous times. God bless you! the people cried. And that was what the Lord had done – had bestowed the Armada with one hundred and thirty ships and filled the hearts of men with pride, courage and single purpose. Medina Sidonia walked on, took it in his stride. The chain of office felt comfortable about his neck, the fur-trimmed cloak of supreme naval commander sat easy on his shoulders, and all was right with his world.

In Palace Square, there would be a holy service of thanksgiving and commitment. On that very spot where heretics and traitors had recently writhed in the flames, where the cracked and blackened flagstones had been scrubbed clean, an altar was erected for the occasion. The Viceroy and the Admiral, the senior captains and the local dignitaries, would eat the flesh of Christ and drink His blood. A culmination and a beginning. In front of them were the vessels of Spain and Portugal, navies united, galleons dressed in silk pennants and streamers and fitted out for war. There could be no turning back, no deviation from what had been ordained.

Constança preferred to keep her distance and her counsel. At the open window she heard the dull echo of festivities and the saluting boom of guns, shuddered at each upbeat permutation of the day. It was no event for her. She did not share the sentiment of the crowd, and desolation prevailed where others discovered gladness. She had failed to prevent the imminent sailing of the Armada, had failed to sway her young brother from the recklessness of participation, had failed to weaken the detestable influence of Spain upon her land. What was left were bitterness of defeat and regret at loss.

Yet she had tried. More than that, she had aided English intelligencers in Lisbon and abetted their destructive work. Without her, there would have been little prospect of breaking the Scots mariner from his prison and scant chance of their surviving as they did. Christian Hardy had introduced her to life and danger, and for it she was thankful. She had sullied her virtue for him, would do so again; she had given herself to him as cheaply as a whore because of love and need and the shared fervour of a moment. That in itself was an act of defiance. It was worth it. She would not forget the minutes stolen in darkness against the wall, the addiction and forcefulness, the gasping ache of pain and rapture. Hardy was escaped to England. Left behind was a young Portuguese noblewoman standing at her window and a farewell note delivered by an unseen hand.

'*Constança!*'

She was aware of his rage before she turned to face him, had heard it in the crash of the doors and the thunderous tread of his approach and in the single shout of her name. Salvador stood before her, his face pale and suffused with anguish, his body shivering in wrath. The eighteen-year-old knew.

'What is it, dear brother?' She tried to be placatory, recognized in that instant they would never again make light of things.

'Betrayer.' He spat the accusation. 'Deceiver most foul, besmircher of our name, destroyer of our family honour.'

'You lay pernicious slander.'

'Would you deny it? Would you seek to lie and hide now you are uncovered?'

'Am I to endure such charge, my brother?'

'Your brother is gone and I remain.' The eyes of the young man glistened to tears of anger and incomprehension. 'I was raised with you. I trusted and loved you. I held you in esteem, hid no secret from you. And all the while you dissemble and disguise yourself from me.'

'I may explain.'

'There is no rhyme or cause for what you do.'

'My motive is pure, Salvador.'

'Its execution corrupt.' Her brother stared, his face knotted in contempt. 'You consort and conspire with the foe, undermine our endeavour, weaken our faith and the foundation of alliance.'

'Your endeavour is not mine.'

'Witch. Sorceress. Devil.'

'Salvador, my brother . . .'

'*Silence!*'

He made as though to strike her, his fist balled and voice quaking fierce, his breath panting on the emotional charge. There was a distance between them she had never encountered. Instinctively, she reached out her hand to comfort him.

Salvador recoiled. 'I will not fall for your tricks. I will not bend to your false manner.'

'There is no falseness, Salvador. Our father . . .'

'He is dead, as are you.' The words were cut with spite. 'I have laboured to preserve our title, striven to redeem the rank and station squandered by the man we called our father. Do not conjure him to your defence.'

'We share blood, Salvador.'

'No, Constança. We share nothing.'

'Where is honour when you sell yourself to Spain? Where is reason when you march bewitched to the beat of the drum of war?'

'Spain is our master, King Philip our sovereign.'

'Each is worthless without the sanction of our hearts.'

'Halt your serpent tongue.' He had his hand on the pommel of his sword, paced threatening and confused. 'Would that I had not seen this day, had not heard tell of your wickedness.'

She pointed to the window. 'Against a massed fleet and prospect of battle, am I so wicked?'

'How easily you are purchased.'

'And for what price do you offer yourself to Spain? Your soul? Your birthright? Your nation?'

'Traitor.'

'Perchance it is you who is traitor, Salvador.'

The rapier was part drawn from his belt, the effect of a mind bewildered and intention half formed. He despised and hated her as she pitied him, had impulse to end uncertainty with a single lunge. She dared him to it. Better to die proud at the hand of her beloved brother than wretched in the clutches of the Spaniards. It was not to be.

'Why, Constança?' His fury had dissipated to a questioning sob. 'Why?'

Salvador fled before she answered, his presence replaced by the gaunt and black-garbed spectre of a Jesuit. She had expected the moment. Yet her preparation did little to douse her fear.

Inquisitor Garza studied her. 'To the victor come the spoils and the captured opponent.'

'I see sadness and no triumph.'

'Walsingham loses a servant and England shall lose a war. Both are occasion to celebrate.'

'Conceit is ever the failing of the Inquisition.'

'Foolhardiness ever the flaw in a countess.' Garza stepped closer. 'Did you believe we would not expose your crimes? Did you suppose we would not discover your dark association with the forces of the enemy?'

'I willingly choose my path.'

'Wheresoever it may lead? Whatever consequence may befall you?'

'You could not prevent the burning of a galleon. You failed to safeguard the dungeons of the Estaus. You were too late to seize those who pricked you.'

'No matter, my lady.'

'Matter enough that you should come hither.'

'All these acts condemn you.' It was said quietly and without rancour. 'The foe acquired my seal and signature, obtained gunpowder from a store, through gaining entry to my home. It was you who enabled. Again, it was you who hired a dwelling in the Alfama to offer safe haven, and you who gave warning my men were on the scent.'

'Your diligence is to be commended, Inquisitor.'

'While your misjudgement should be condemned.' There was no pity in his eye, no emotion upon his face. The Jesuit merely wished to scrutinize. Constança Menezes was an embarrassment.

He plucked a scrap of paper from the folds of his cassock and held it up before her.

'We search your private chamber, my lady.'

'To what avail?' The breath had tightened in her throat.

'A keepsake provides evidence as if it were the blade of a knife stained in blood. A note written in parting and sweet sorrow by a lover and English spy is akin to a sentence of death.'

'It holds no fear for me. I already lose Salvador my brother.'

'You shall have your time to dwell on it. The Viceroy

decrees your trial and judgement should be delayed, your intended death put off. At such hour of mortal reckoning with the heretic English queen, it is no moment for public purge of the high-born of this nation.'

'I am glad to stand as symbol before my people.'

'And be forgotten as your father.' Garza eyed her with the aloof coolness of the winner. 'When Armada is done and England vanquished, then your neck will meet the sword at the site of execution.'

She laughed. 'England will not fall, nor Portugal submit for ever to the weight of Spain and her Inquisition.'

'Take care, my lady.'

'Or you shall have me cast into hellfire? I am beyond your reach, Inquisitor. I am as free of your chains as Christian Hardy, the writer of this letter, the valiant who led your doltish men a merry dance.'

The Jesuit did not reply. At once she regretted her comment – not for its indiscretion, but for the stab of memory and sting of yearning it provoked. Garza seemed to look directly into her. Perhaps there was a hint of recognition, a knowingness of things she did not comprehend. It was fleeting. She thanked God that Christian was safely away, prayed without hope her own fate might come to a rapid conclusion.

~

'You live, and thus I must obey the compact and surrender your service to Drake.'

There was a restrained warmth in the voice of Sir Francis Walsingham, relief that his protégé was returned from foray overseas. Across the sculpted gardens of his Barnes manor, the sun cast its warming glow. But here, in the dark-panelled study, coolness and shadow prevailed and matters of state and intrigue ensured neither light nor prying eyes fell upon the whole. A private retreat for a secretive head of espionage. Christian Hardy sat opposite and waited. He would reserve judgement as to whether it was of benefit to be home.

The spy-chief regarded him. 'You conducted yourself with spirit. You carried out your mission with skill and daring.'

'It is no more than my duty, your honour.'

'Would that every Englishman possessed such sense of obligation. The Queen herself takes note.'

'We lost good men in her cause.'

'And yet gained much for their sacrifice.' Walsingham allowed controlled sentiment to reach his words. 'Whether Mr Hunter or your Negro, both are to be praised and remembered for their peerless feats.'

'I value it, your honour.'

'As we in turn value the intelligence they made possible.' The Secretary of State rested a hand on the leather volume before him.

'Lisbon was rich in surprise, your honour.'

Walsingham began to turn the pages. 'Indeed so. I see the names of Protestants, of privy counsellors and myself, of those the Spaniards would arraign for posing threat to their new order.'

'Your Flemish agent prised them from the grasp and chattels of the dead Admiral Santa Cruz.'

'What of further revelation? A second ledger?' The gaze of the spymaster flicked questioning and calm. 'What of the book which holds the names of Catholics, which lists the perfidious knaves who would conspire in demonic union with invading Spaniards?'

'I know nothing of such things, your honour.'

'To know and not reveal is treason, Mr Hardy.'

'It is fortunate I prove myself a loyal subject of the Crown.'

He met and countered the appraising stare, felt the mind of Walsingham attempt to open wide his own. The spy-chief was searching, assessing him for weakness and untruth, would explore any path and every gesture. Hardy would be careful, would remember that with the raising of a quill or casual shuttering of an eye friendship could turn to enmity and privilege transform to sojourn in the Tower.

Threat and incident passed as Walsingham altered subject. 'You speak of an Englishman in Lisbon. Tell me of this renegade who accosted you with sword and gun.'

'I left him wounded in my escape.'

'We would rather you had run him through. It would be one less creeping insect on which to tread.'

'He is of little consequence, your honour.'

'It is often the creature ignored or dismissed that later bites with most venom and force.'

'Do we not have more pressing concern?'

'Perhaps.' Walsingham clasped his hands in thought. 'As the traitorous Englishman shows, attack of whatever kind may trip us at any step.'

'We shall defeat it, your honour.'

'I trust it is so. Yet my faithful Mr Hunter discerned before his death the outline of a truth. There exists an insidious plot to kill Her Majesty.'

'Are there not many of such kind?'

'None I fear more than those born in Lisbon and Madrid, conceived in the mind of Inquisitor Garza.'

Hardy nodded in understanding, though he was instead closer to indifference at the subtle shades of intrigue. He was tired, wished to forget, and wanted to sleep with Emma in his arms. The Secretary of State might chafe at releasing him to Sir Francis Drake, but there was an honesty in the sea and wind and a directness to the art of soldiering that the clandestine life did not possess.

Walsingham raised the lid to a wooden box and withdrew a

sheet of paper. He offered it for perusal. 'Your insight, Mr Hardy.'

'A coded message requiring decipher.'

'Such message is exact copy of a dispatch sent by the Spaniards some three months past. We followed it to Derbyshire and thence to the guardian of the malevolent flame, the den of the cipher-carrier himself.'

Hardy returned the page. 'Isaiah Payne and his Searchers would slaver for such a kill.'

'They attained it. And we, by turn, gain a communication showing conspiracy more deadly than any posed by Armada and invasion alone.' He extracted a second page and handed it to Hardy, looked on as his young lieutenant studied the text. 'You see it?'

Hardy did. Before him were words transcribed by the code-breakers of Seething Lane, a riddle whose bearer was dead, a note that promised murder and intended to inspire revolt: *When the blood-red light of a sickle moon casts deadly spell upon the river waters, and when the bastard throne is toppled, arise and claim vengeance upon the unjust foe. God is with you.*

Some forty buildings clung to the nine-hundred-foot span of London Bridge, contributed to a feature considered a marvel of civilization and the city. Above the nineteen arches and the twenty great supporting piers set within their rubble-filled starlings, the houses projected over the water and dominated a river glutted with trading-craft of every kind. A spectacular vista. Visitors travelled far to view the scene, gawping at the magnificent constructions of Stonegate House, Nonsuch House and the House of Windows, at the vessels negotiating the rapids of Chapel Lock or Long Entry, and at the severed heads of traitors mutating on the central spikes. Sightseers were rarely disappointed.

The Catholic agent did not look upward as he crossed from the south bank. He needed no reminding of the risk he took or the fate he might share one day with his fellow believers. It was a matter of time. Maybe the dark servants of Walsingham already followed him; maybe he was marked for capture, would be seized on this very bridge as its ten-foot width narrowed from a traversing cart. He would banish such discouraging thought. The Lord stood with him; the Catholics of England depended on his initiative and nerve. It was that nerve which brought him here, that initiative which had persuaded a prosperous merchant to let his shop and dwelling on the bridge to a trader recommended by a host of wealthy nobles. Praise Jesus for the treacherous high-born who bet each way on the coming invasion. They could not know that he had made his selection on the basis of its view down to the Tower and its possession of an overhead *hautpas* gallery connecting it to a building opposite. Eastern and western approaches were covered.

He entered the building and locked the door behind him, stood awhile to let his breath and tension subside and his eyes grow accustomed to the shadow. The house provided a temporary refuge. A shallow interior, a floor hatch for the lowering of pails and baskets to boats below, a steep and narrow ladder-stairway rising to the upper storeys. Everything prepared and as it should be. He moved to the rear, unlatched and threw wide the shutters, and gazed out across the Pool of London. There, Billingsgate and its foul-mouthed and bareknuckle-fighting fishwives; there, the proud Norman features of the White Tower and its grey surrounding walls. The Catholic dropped his gaze, searched among the clustered barques and freighters for the strangers in their midst. He found them.

They were in position, not yet laden, moored adjacent to the main channel and on opposing sides. Their crews moved in the unhurried way that shore-time often dictated, with a deliberation that would draw neither comment nor suspicion. Queen Elizabeth herself had given dispensation for their presence, was advised of the need to promote relations with the Ottoman Sultan and sweeten him into military assault on the Mediterranean interests of Spain. Turkish ships. It had been the plan of Sir Francis Walsingham to hinder the Armada and divert King Philip; it had been the plan of Sir Francis Walsingham that was intercepted and was turned now back upon the English. The supposed Turk vessels in fact had sailed from Rochefort in France. Their crews were not comprised of ordinary merchant seaman, were trained to levels and in skills undreamed of by others labouring nearby. In the holds were barrels of gunpowder and shot and wrapped bundles of arquebuses, firearms which in the hands of specialists could take down a target at several hundred paces. The Janissaries had made it to London.

These were days of foreboding that forced their way into early May, days to be cherished as though they presaged the end. Hardy spent them with Emma and their young son Adam. He immersed himself in the pretence of normality, tried to forget where he had been and where he was destined. Domesticity constrained as much as it gave succour. Yet it allowed him to bury his grief and to love his wife, to dwell again in the light and laughter of his family. He could not speak of the deaths of Black Jack and Mr Hunter, of the blind and piteous meeting with his mother, of the time spent with Constança. So many secrets, and so few words with which to convey all that he felt. He was now twenty-two years old, the age at which his father perished.

It was early evening. They had strolled to the playhouse in the old monastery of Blackfriars, had dined in a threepenny cookhouse and watched jugglers and fire-eaters outside

Bridewell Palace. There was a desperate cheer in the mood of the crowd, a need to believe that nothing would change. One man in their midst had seen what would come.

'You will waken the maid, Christian.' Emma made little effort to push him away, let her token protest slide to submission.

He kissed and held her. 'What do I care of maids? What do I care of anything save my wife?'

'Your wife sets great store by the calm manner of her household.'

'Not so her husband.' He caressed her head and pressed it close against his chest. 'I have missed you, Emma.'

'And I you.'

She said it with a soft earnestness that carried an echo of the solitude of past weeks and the residual ache of separation. He knew she had wept tears, recognized too she had suffered with the stoic dignity of a country girl who did not question circumstance or ever bend before it. He was grateful she was mother of his son.

He ran his fingers through her hair. 'In these months past, Adam is grown.'

'He will be strong and tall as his father.'

'I pray he owns more sense than to abandon those he holds precious.'

'Adventure already courses in his blood.'

'Then we are doomed.' He spoke lightly and felt the pressure from her fingers tighten.

'Are we doomed, Christian?'

'We do not yet die of plague, are not yet burned by invading Spaniards at the stake.'

'The Spaniards will sail.'

'And we shall resist.' He touched her face, gently stroked her lips and cheek. 'You and I and our son will outlive any danger and stand against all foe.'

'Swear it.'

'I swear it.'

He wished it were true, hoped it was not merely a further lie to heap upon the rest.

Commotion outside fractured the peace and the moment, brought oaths and yells spilling through the window. The present always crashed in. Hardy had reached into a cedar chest and retrieved his oiled Katzbalger, was already through the opening and running for the sound.

He should not have been surprised, had long ceased to be alarmed by the actions and thinking of Luqa. His Maltese friend faced off a posse of armed men, was holding them at bay with a wicked grin and the simple expedient of pinioning with his forearm a hostage by the throat. Even in the ungenerous light of firebrands, it was possible to identify the captive as Isaiah Payne. The disproportioned head, the twisted profile, the gaudy clothing draped ill-fitting on the spare frame, all indicated the chief of the Searchers. His switch from hunter to prey was not a comfortable one. Nor was it improved by the exultancy of Luqa or the knife pushed crude and hard against his neck. The eyes of Payne bulged more pronounced than usual, the nervous tic had developed to near-spasm, and the teeth were bared in fixed and wary smile. Isaiah Payne was unhappy. In the no-man's-land between opposing camps, the dog Fearnot snarled and barked and joined in the theatre.

'Call off your base savage, Hardy.'

'Order back your own.'

'He compounds his sin, adds to the crimes of horse-theft and flight from Newgate for which he is meant to hang.'

'One more offence of sticking you through will make scant difference.'

'You trifle at your peril, Hardy.'

'I have meddled with worse.'

'Do not create an enemy of me.'

'Or you shall force me to submission? Frighten me to retreat? Scare me to foul my hose?' Hardy swung the Katzbalger at his side. 'It is you who has a dagger to his neck.'

'Unhand me or face penalty of the law.'

'Luqa would not take you without reason.'

'A dog has no reason.' Payne winced as the knife-edge bit close.

His captor was relaxed. 'He pries and probes around your home, Christian. He digs, searches, sniffs at every cranny and hollow.'

'To what purpose, Payne?' Hardy studied the prisoner.

'I am on official business of Walsingham.'

'Business?' The young Englishman was not about to relent. 'You have no business here.'

'His honour desires a book, a ledger with the names of Catholic traitors willing to aid the cause of Spain, a list he believes you acquire in Lisbon.'

'So do you steal in like a thief by night.'

'Deny us and you ally yourself to treason itself.'

'How quickly does a man fall from champion to outlaw.' He nodded to Luqa, who loosened his grasp. 'Take message to Sir Francis. Tell him should he again deploy you and your rodents he will discover not a leather-bound volume but your dismembered corpse.'

Fidgeting with relief, his face distorted and enraged, Payne danced free from the choking embrace. Where he had lost authority, he replaced it with waspish menace.

'You shall suffer for such insult, Hardy.'

'For the while I am content.'

'It will not last. There is room in the Tower for traitors, ample means to correct an errant spirit.'

'While you don perfumed clothes to hound priests and

women and children, I draw blood on the battlefield. What England is this that places you higher?'

'An England that demands allegiance and punishes dissent.'

'The country for which my companions die is not the same as yours.'

Payne stepped nearer, his confidence steeled by the proximity of his henchmen. The tone was jeering.

'Heed my words, young warrior. Your handsome looks and gallant ways shall count for nothing when judgement calls.'

Hardy meted his own sentence, delivered it with a balled fist that struck fast and connected with teeth, cartilage and bone. With a shriek, Payne fell away. He was still weeping and spitting blood, clutching his broken face, as his disciples ushered him from the arena. From the house, Emma watched them go and bided until the crab-walking figure at their centre had fully disappeared. Part of the external life of Christian had intruded to her own. It left her with premonition and a hollow sense of dread.

As the torches departed and the light died, Fearnot was chasing his tail in a victory jig.

~

There was energy in the air, a pace and excitement that showed in the lighters ferrying their final stores, in the sailors crowding the yards and rigging, in the soldiers mustering on board. Across the Tagus, the vast array had come alive. Officers paced their poop-decks, bosuns called and whistles blew, and the people of Lisbon gathered along the banks of the river to view the spectacle and bid farewell, to rejoice and pray, to weep for husbands and lovers and sons who embarked on high adventure and religious crusade. With the steel glint of infantry cuirasses and the towering fore- and aft-castles of the galleons, it seemed as though the very forts of Catholic Europe were on the move. A formidable sight and inexorable force.

The formations were in position: the titanic galleasses of Italy; the Portuguese flotilla; the Biscayan, Andalucian and Guipúzcoan squadrons; the armed freighters and merchant hulks; the naos, taforeias and caravels. And at their head the mighty one-thousand-ton flagship of Medina Sidonia, the *San Martin*. Over twenty-one thousand troops and nine thousand seamen, all told. It was 18 May 1588, and in a fury of colour and on waters glittering beneath a brilliant sun the Armada was readying to sail.

In his cramped rooms on the Baixa, the renegade Englishman known as Realm kissed a rosary and placed it on the Bible beside his bed. Where he was headed, he could carry no item betraying his faith or his intent. Success depended on his merging with the whole, on moving unhindered and unobserved through the feckless ranks of his so-called countrymen. They would be organizing frantically to repel invasion. He wondered how ready they would be to counter the kind of raid that he introduced. Such promise. He shouldered a sturdy canvas knapsack and went to the door. These modest quarters had never been true home, had merely served as temporary dwelling and refuge from the theological storm in England. Conditions had changed. By now his trained Janissary sharp-shooters would be in place; by now the raw wound to his face and injury to his leg inflicted by one Christian Hardy were healed; by now the chaos of impending war would favour his arrival. He took a final look at the abandoned space. Should he return, it would be as avenged hero.

Others too thought of epic deed. Aboard the Portuguese galleon *San Mateo*, Salvador Menezes, brother of Constança, watched the pilot boats scurrying between the warships and the oars of longboats rise and fall as their crews laboured to swing about the larger ships. All was activity. He smelled the air, let it cleanse his head and erase any memory of his sister.

The future was one of glory, of triumph for Spain and her allies, of restoration to power and influence of a title inherited and tarnished by his late father. He was only eighteen years of age, but he could fight; he was only a novice in matters of politics and war, but could win the admiration and respect of veterans and commanders twice his age. Much rested on him. Yet he would prove himself and banish doubt, would stand again as equal with the nobles of the Order of Christ and the ancient names of Portugal. Let his companions and foes see of what he was made, and let England quake.

Before a crucifix in the chapter house of the Monastery of Jerónimos, Inquisitor Garza prayed alone. Soon he would be joining his collection of relics and precious artefacts aboard the great transport hulk *El Gran Grin*. He would climb the ladder to a destiny ordained by God and blessed and guided by His hand. The Lord would stiffen his resolve and inspire him for the onerous venture. It would require his full devotion and attention to drive heathen belief from England, to brand the authority of Spain and the ways of the old Church deep into the obdurate souls of the conquered. He was confident of success. Everything before this day had been rehearsal; every body he had broken and community he had rent wide was but a marker-stone to his appointment as Inquisitor General of Albion. The wind blew and the ships were waiting. Even he would permit the enthusiasm of the moment to enter his frigid core.

Also in solitary contemplation in the gilded confines of the monastery was the Duke of Medina Sidonia. Prostrate in front of the high altar, surrounded by the tombs of the brave and the statues of the saints, he flung himself at the feet of Christ. Parading through the streets of Lisbon had constituted the easy part. What he attempted was the near-impossible; what he faced were infinite hazard and a trial of strength with the

English fleet. No Armada ship or master would be found wanting. Yet they needed fortune to smile, the sea to stay calm, the army of the Duke of Parma in the Low Countries to be ready for invasion. An operation shot through with uncertainty and employing the vaguest of detail. But King Philip II commanded. Slowly he rose to his feet, bowed to the Cross, and proceeded to the antechapel to pay passing homage to the tomb of Vasco da Gama. At least in death there was no burden to carry. The Captain-General thought of his predecessor Santa Cruz, of how the old sea-dog would have loved to lead the charge. Instead it was he, Medina Sidonia, who was accorded the honour, who would pit himself against the ocean gales and coastal shallows, who would encounter the elated wrath of Drake. He would not, could not, fail his King. With a delicate incline of his head, he put his lips to the white marble and took his leave of its famed incumbent. From the traveller of today to the voyager of yore. Then he turned, paced to the south door, and descended the steps beneath its immense and yawning portico. To his front were the lead formations of the fleet, a host of vessels riding on the Tagus and awaiting his orders. He stepped into a small boat and seated himself for the short passage to his flagship. Expedition could commence.

For two days the ships of the Armada manoeuvred past the Tower of Belém and streamed from the mouth of the estuary into the Atlantic. In the van, the *San Martin* flew the pennant of Medina Sidonia and hoisted the sacred banner adorned with a crucifix and the figures of the Blessed Virgin and Mary Magdelene. With her came the behemoths of the age, the four muscular galleasses, the bloated transports, the preening galleons, all filling their sails on the south-westerly and bearing northward for the Scillies and the English Channel. It was a proud and stirring spectacle. As they rounded Cabo Raso and spread out towards Cabo da Roca, the headland was lined with well-wishers eager to bear witness to history. At the Capuccine convent a short distance inland, the Franciscan inhabitants left their cork-lined cells to watch; on the heights of Sintra, at the Convent of Our Lady of Pena, the monks abandoned their inner reflection to cluster in awe at the panoramic scene. The ocean was seeded white with unfurled canvas, spotted with the moving prows of ships throwing off spume and tracking in unison for the glimmering horizon. Sharper eyes could make out flags bearing the crossed keys of St Peter, the legend *Jesu Cristo*, the armillary sphere, the clenched fist of wrath. There could be no wavering, for holy war was under way.

Chapter 11

Events and the wind conspired against them, a storm blowing in from the north and scattering the Armada across a violent expanse. What had started in proud and stately review ended with raging seas and haphazard retreat. The Atlantic was an unforgiving ocean. Masts and yards were sprung, canvas torn, and ships battered into splintering flight as they chased pell-mell for shelter. Vessels limping into the exposed bay of Corunna in northern Spain over the following weeks scarcely resembled the previous majesty of a holy cause. They were damaged and the men sick, the detritus of the voyage and the bodies of the dead littering the foreshore as work-gangs toiled to expedite recovery and reinvigorate campaign. June would be a long and arduous month.

The imperative remained. Medina Sidonia had not sailed in pomp from Lisbon in order to cower at temporary anchorage; King Philip II had not committed his forces to sacred quest only to have them stalled by unfortunate occasion. The path to glory and eradicating heresy was never smooth. So it was that boats were dispatched from Corunna to scavenge wood and provisions from neighbouring ports and soldiers were deployed into surrounding areas to round-up local *tiros* and make good depleted crews. Urgency prevailed over mercy. Too many seamen had deserted or fallen prey to disease for the Captain-General to show selectiveness in their replacement. Too many casks had leaked and their contents spoiled for him to show concern or constraint in foraging for supplies in nearby towns and villages. Ruthlessness on every front was the key to defeating England.

'We have over two thousand convicts chained as rowers at the oars of our galleys and galleasses. Volunteer for the fleet and you shall not find yourselves among them.'

Garza stared at the villagers, his gaze ominously neutral and his message clear. Yet they appeared not to comprehend, carried the dumb insolence of fisherfolk and the rank hostility of apostates that could land them in trouble and would see them damned. He waited a beat or two. Once fear had percolated and the consequence of their stubbornness became apparent, they would come running and begging to volunteer. It always took a while to convert the stupid. For the present they found themselves caught between a rock and a hard troop of infantry, clustered in the bedraggled state that innocents so often acquired when their lives or livelihoods were threatened. He had not come this far to show clemency, had not spent days confined to a rolling cabin, praying before his portable altar and heaving up his guts, to listen to excuse. The King wanted the able-bodied, and Garza would provide.

'Do you know who I am?' Their mute response suggested they did not. 'Inquisitor Garza is my name. I am tasked with saving souls and preserving the dignity and faith of our state.'

'We are simple fishermen.'

'As were the apostles Simon and Peter, and as Jesus was a fisher of men. Your humble calling will be transformed to glory, your mortal duty directed to immortal ends.'

'Let us in peace.'

'War does not provide for it.' He raised the wood crucifix on its cord about his neck. 'Regard the Cross. The Lamb of

208

God died to save you. Now it is your turn to repay such debt.'

'What of our village?'

'Indeed, what of it? Your dwellings and your trade have no meaning when set against the new Jerusalem and the promise of the Kingdom of Heaven.'

'While there remain fish in the sea, our task lies here.'

'Even as there is a fleet to man and the demands of a king to oblige, you will accompany me to the ships.

There was the shake of a head. 'Our families will starve.'

'Disobey and they shall hang.'

Unfriendly mutterings came, the mutinous glances of villagers trapped by circumstance and unwelcome visitation. The Inquisitor did not care. It felt good to stretch his legs and to carry out the will of God. These immovable and dull-witted creatures would soon bend to his argument, if necessary would be driven on by whips.

He regarded them with blank indifference. 'Five men are all I require.'

'It is too many.'

'In the eyes of God it is but few.' Garza appraised the latest to speak out, a sturdy youth with open face and honest eyes. 'Your name?'

'Juan.'

'You worship the Lord, Juan?'

'With my heart.'

'You serve the King?'

'I do.'

'Then step forward. You are first to join our ranks.'

The boy edged to the fore, reluctant to commit and yet unwilling to refuse. There was something in the empty tone and unwavering manner of this priest that unsettled and commanded and promised grim chastisement. Beside the Jesuit, the soldiers stood ready with their swords. It was a strong negotiating stance.

An older man raised his arm to block the transfer. 'I have more experience at sea. Take me in his place.'

'A selfless act from one so crude and plain. We shall use you both.' The Inquisitor pointed to another. 'You too are chosen.'

The subject quivered. 'I am no seafarer.'

'Chance arrives to learn new skill.'

'There are others more able, others stronger in frame and build.'

'It is you I pick.'

'You are mistaken. Can you not see I am ill-matched to your need?' Sweat shimmered on the mobile features as the victim backed away in search of a decoy. 'He repairs nets and is expert with the needle. And he is a carpenter who restores our boats.'

'Yet I come to you before them.'

'I am of no value to you.'

'Perchance solely as example.'

Terrorizing a village was in his character, enforcing the directive of the King a priority. He listened to the bleating of the man and dismissed it. Individual complaint could not affect the whole. From the oak-laden slopes above, the sporadic discharge of muskets crackled distant through the trees. Troops might be hunting game, could be flushing out deserters. All contributed to the overarching aim of the Armada.

He indicated his assent and a rope was thrown across a branch. While the noose was fashioned and its slip-knot tied, the man was plucked from the group and dragged kicking and bucking towards the intended site of summary execution. None rushed to save him. It seemed there was an airless space around the captive, a distance between the dead and the still living, a vacuum he filled with distressed moans and imploring sobs. As though it made a difference. Garza had looked upon such scenes a hundred or a thousand times.

Without delay, accompanied only by the swallowed howls and protest of the prisoner, the rope was slipped about the neck and its length pulled taut. Toes scraped and stretched and the body lifted. He put up a fight as the soldiers strained against his weight, the noise from his throat cutting short, his torso and legs dancing in wild enthusiasm and erratic rhythm. It took minutes for the eyes to glaze and the tongue to flicker its last, for the gyrations to ease through tremor into stillness and the mottled face to blacken to its final state. The point had been made.

Inquisitor Garza addressed his rapt gathering. 'Who shall remember this wretch? Will you be counted with him and cast to the bottomless pit, or will you be numbered among the divine?'

'*We are with you and the King!*' It was shouted with ragged gusto and drew supporting cheers.

'Fate blows the Armada to this shore as circumstance now throws you on my mercy.' The Jesuit took time to study each face in turn. 'For the obstinacy of your companion, I raise to ten those from this village I embark on campaign.'

They trudged as defeated men trudged, walked with their heads lowered and their fortunes altered. Sorrow created its own particular shapes. There were no waving crowds, no good citizens to wish them well. Pressed into service with the blessing of their sovereign, pulled from lives centred on small boats and fishing, they shuffled in the wake of the tall priest in black as though attending their own funeral. Behind them, the lone body remained aloft at the edge of the clearing. It would act as a reminder, would spread word throughout the area that every true Spaniard was a Catholic, each Catholic a resource, and all resource committed to the war effort.

As tracks converged, some of the marching prisoners glimpsed a figure emerging from the higher slopes. He might have been a woodsman engaged in routine clearance, but for the single detail that the bundled load he dragged was a corpse and not felled timber. The fishermen quickly averted their eyes. Resting temporarily from his exertions, Realm let them pass. The forests and hollows of the region had provided ample diversion, allowed him to refine techniques and sharpen instincts that might otherwise have been blunted by days shipbound and by unwelcome delay. He did not do it lightly or for pleasure. To kill one man was to practise for the next; to hunt a man and peer into his eyes, to smell his sour-sweet fear, was a test of nerve and an exercise in steadiness of hand. There was no substitute for experience. He would need it where he was headed.

Almost reflexively, the English renegade lifted his fingers to the livid scar across his cheek and followed it to the mutilated section of his ear. Beard growth had done much to hide the worst. Yet he recalled every detail of the night he met Christian Hardy, retained the incident in his memory as vividly as he did the events of near-twenty years before when his parents had marched against Queen Elizabeth and were murdered for their effort. A multitude of wrongs required to be set right. He returned to his trophy and leaned into the harness.

Lame and injured horses were being slaughtered on the beach, their cries and whinnies insistent and the water clouding red. Joints were sectioned, flesh stripped, bones washed and piled in cauldrons for reduction into glue. And everywhere the stench of rendered carcasses and summer putrefaction, the billow of oily smoke and the haze of attendant flies. Sailors cursed at their task. An animal broke loose. Its ears flattened and mouth foaming, it galloped screaming and ungainly from the slaughter, dashing along the foreshore and upward for a shingle berm before rearing and falling back in terrified death. Men crossed themselves or spat in disgust. First the storm and now this. They had not expected disappointment so soon, had not anticipated burying their dead, finding their victuals rotten and fresh water drained, discovering their invincible Armada already challenged. None volunteered to bring back the splayed remains of the escaped beast.

Salvador had witnessed the event. With a crew detail from the *San Mateo*, the eighteen year-old was working to man-handle a foremast on to a lighter for transfer to his ship. At least it kept him busy. He embraced the toil, welcomed distraction from the vexing sights of wreckage and disrepair that mirrored his confusion. The ocean gale had holed his previous confidence and conviction as surely as it had damaged the fleet. He would admit to no one, could scarce confess it to himself, that he had been in mortal terror. It was more profound than fear or any emotion he had known. To think he had accused his father of treachery and cowardice. He instead was the coward. Should the men about him read his trembling thoughts, they would see him hanged from the broken yardarm. Best to stay quiet, to maintain poise and pretence, to play the dutiful young noble enthused with cause and country. He told himself things would be all right, assured himself that given space and chance he would prove himself proficient and worthy of the family name. A faltering start was not unusual in a warrior.

'You daydream, boy. Put your shoulder to it.' The seaman clapped him roughly on the back.

'I remind you who is the officer.'

'Believe as you may. But it is sailors as I who will carry and guard your scented hide from Corunna to the ends of hell.'

'Rebellious talk.'

'Experienced words.' The grizzled sailor winked and indi-cated a Portuguese galley foundered on the shoreline. 'A fine vessel, and one I vouch is turned to firewood by a noble and an officer.'

'Let us see if you lift as well as you complain.' Salvador made to raise the length of wood.

'Have you spied a man cut through by cannon-shot? Have you seen a comrade as close as a brother weep to contain his entrails with his fingers? Have you been spattered with the brain-matter of your captain?'

'You goad me, sailor.'

A hand reached to grip his and the voice dropped low. 'We each of us is fearful, boy. There is no shame to it.'

Irked, his authority tested, Salvador shrugged away the gesture. He needed neither counsel nor jesting words of a fool to face his demons and his doubts. The crusade against England was just, and that would be his compass. He would dwell on it and nothing else, would squeeze his trepidation into a tight ball and lodge it deep within a recess of his soul. Constança, his sister, was already banished there.

'I stand with you, boy.'

'Keep such concern for yourself.'

The man shrugged. 'You will need your brothers when fire rains and judgement comes.'

Salvador turned away. On this fetid shore, peace and silence were what he craved.

~

'You believe Spain is the enemy?' Walsingham kept his murmur low. 'View this royal court, for true danger lies here.'

If there was humour to his words it was tempered by gravitas and inscrutability. Hardy did as he was commanded, noted the haughty air and predatory glances of the ladies, the cool aloofness of the men. There were shifting signals and the glint of jealousy, the chequerboard moves of those positioning and seeking influence or favour. He studied them as they observed him. A new figure arrived at Richmond could mean hazard or opportunity; a young and handsome blade in company with the Secretary of State suggested a thousand possibilities for intrigue and gossip.

They perambulated through the tapestry-clad chambers, the spy-chief pausing on occasion to exchange a nod or a word. Even when ailing he exerted the magnetic influence of the powerful. A man who watched over three and a half million English subjects, who defended his queen and the realm, who ruthlessly suppressed all threat at home and abroad, created his own restrained drama. Stares trailed them. Hardy felt their curiosity and pricking unease. He was part of the ritual, an element in the complex display of authority.

Walsingham guided him to a window-lined gallery. 'The nation mobilizes, men are called to the flag, and yet our pomandered nobles are loath to surrender their recreation and carousing.'

'Is not the Armada delayed?'

'Where there is will there is impulse, Mr Hardy. We already reach June, a summertime when they must either voyage or turn back. Disease and shortage will not long keep them in northern Spain.'

'They weaken as we find strength.'

'You shall not discover it here. Court is where prevarication is made art, where venal pettiness and self-regard become the most pursued of fashions.'

'To a stranger as I it creates fine spectacle, your honour.'

'While for a seasoned counsellor as myself it wearies the heart.' Walsingham halted beneath a cluster of stag trophies. 'There are better and wiser heads mounted on this wall than perched on goffered ruffs in the Palace of Richmond.'

'All smile and give warm greeting, your honour.'

'What is in a smile, Mr Hardy? A lie? A trick? A fawning aspect? A diverting sunbeam?'

'They seem as your friends.'

'As deer do not befriend the huntsman, so courtiers do not forge bond with one who may cause their downfall. They smile for they mistrust. They greet for they fear.'

'Are their wits not then quicker than you imagine?'

The spymaster gave no answer. He had avoided mention of Isaiah Payne and the night-time incident off Fetter Lane. Hardy would not press him. He was in little doubt there would be a fresh attempt, understood well enough the machinations of the world in which he moved. In the questing mind and persistent imagination of Sir Francis Walsingham, where connections were made and conclusions sought, where an ally today was potential opponent tomorrow, everyone was suspect. This neat and obsessive man dressed in dark garb and sickening unto death wanted the secret ledger of Catholics.

For the moment he pretended otherwise. 'Great honour is bestowed on you by your summons from the Queen. Answer straight and answer true and you will find in her an attentive listener.'

'Is there matter she prefers to hear?'

'There are most certain matters I would care to reach her ear.' The hooded eyes narrowed. 'She is the mistress of curiosity and learning. Feed her appetite, do not spare her in the telling.'

'In this is there riddle or method, your honour?'

'She will ask and you shall reply. Speak of Lisbon and of the Spaniards, of the mighty fleet on the Tagus which you observed, of things only one who has seen with his own eyes may swear.'

Hardy nodded his understanding. 'You intend for me to serve as weapon of persuasion.'

'As swayer of her mood. A vital task for exceptional

conditions. Even at this late hour, the Queen believes there is hope for peace and sends emissaries to the Duke of Parma. She must know it is fruitless. She must be told we are in a bleak and irresistible state of war.'

His briefing given, Walsingham ushered on his charge. They were approaching the carved and gilded doors to the presence chamber, moved solemnly through the resplendent ranks of yeoman guards and gentlemen-at-arms. Hardy stared ahead and remembered to breathe, stepped through the portal as though entering a dream.

He found himself in the orchestrated presence of greatness, and knelt to kiss the proffered and bejewelled hand of Queen Elizabeth of England. She had already waved away her attendants and banished her Secretary of State to a distant corner of the hall. Alone before her, the young soldier bowed his head and waited. He had never in his twenty-two years witnessed magnificence of this kind. She stood above him, glorious in an overgown of cloth of gold, her raiments gem-set and patterned with roses and pansies, her stomacher, kirtle and underskirt richly embroidered, her silver-gauze collar raised high. About her neck was a sapphire pendant; crowning her bewigged head of flame-red hair was a diadem of pearls. An extraordinary vision. His queen, his totem, his cause.

'Arise, young Mr Hardy.'

A narrow bodice and voluminous farthingale petticoat could stage-present the most ageing of monarchs; a whitening mask of alum, egg-white, poppy-seed and borax could hide the years on the most ravaged of faces. Yet she was more than the sum of her smoothed and restored parts. There was an energy present, a spirit, a steel will and restless intellect that shone in the eyes and declared in the voice. She had survived countless plot, and her nation had prospered for it. And she spoke to him, conversed as though discoursing with a friend.

'You are as becoming and fine as reported, Mr Hardy.'

'I thank you, Your Majesty.'

'It is we and the nation that are in your debt. We hear of your deeds on our behalf.'

'A feat is no feat when it is done for love of England and her Queen.'

'Noble sentiment, Mr Hardy.' A partial and flirtatious smile ghosted on her features. 'We are told the Spanish king dubs his Armada invincible.'

'I have seen sufficient galleons burn to know little is unconquerable, madam.'

'Shall we be conquered?' A painted eyebrow might have arched.

'The enemy is confident, and that is his weakness. His ships are vast and towering, and that is their chief failing.'

'Describe to us these vessels you observe.'

'They sit high in the water, each a thousand tons and more, each with up to fifty guns. The flagship of Medina Sidonia the *San Martin*, the Portuguese *São João* and *De Florencia*, the Andalusians and Castilians, the Biscayans, Levantines and Guipúzcoans, the merchant hulks and the great Neapolitan galleasses.'

'It seems they possess both means and intent.'

'One without the other would make mockery of their endeavour.'

'Are we to be cowed by such things, Mr Hardy?'

'I believe Your Majesty would be unfrightened by the Devil.'

The blackened teeth again gaped briefly from the splendour. 'Yet our own Privy Council deems us a fragile woman unversed in battle, wedded to peace, without stomach for the fray.'

'We shall all be tested, madam.'

'So long as none should break.'

Perhaps she studied him or withdrew into thought, her expression fixed by its cosmetic veneer. But her composure radiated. Whatever fate decreed, she would accept; however the Spanish came, she would respond. There was something human behind her regality, a warmth that eased the chill, a resolve that gave assurance. Hardy was proud to serve.

'Where do you now travel, Mr Hardy?'

'I join Drake in Plymouth, madam.'

'Our little corsair.' A veiled joke, privately enjoyed. 'Should any put the fear of God in Spain, it shall be he.'

'The Armada will scarce survive his interest, madam.'

'Were it to sail through his fire and bring its army to bear upon these shores, it would discover against it a force led by a Queen.'

Hardy bowed his head. 'I would give my life to serve in that force.'

'All life is in the gift of our Redeemer.' *Gloriana*, Elizabeth of England, let her focus drift to the distance. 'Advise your sovereign of plot you uncover in Lisbon to commit foul murder against her.'

Audience was through and Hardy stood alone in a corner of the palace. Matters of state and the urgency of the moment had quickly forced pace and attention to other business. Her Majesty was in conference. Hardy loitered, would watch the flow of messengers and the arcane practices of court, would absorb the sights and murmurings surrounding. There was much to record. Luqa and Hawkhead would contrive to mock him for soft and mannered ways; Emma would gently smile at the tales he related. He had met his monarch, and it was worth any jibe from his companions.

Meeting of a different hue confronted him. With the casual arrogance and swagger of a favourite, the Earl of Essex hove into view. He was a young nobleman secure in position and at home in these quarters, a handsome buck easily slighted and fast to find offence. The same strong build, the same insolent poise, the same redness to his hair and beard as encountered on that January night on the fencing-stage in Southwark. It was unlikely to be a polite or pleasant meeting.

Essex stopped to challenge. 'I do not recall when last I spied a knave and commoner trespassing on this royal ground.'

'Is it more rare than a noble earl face down and whimpering in defeat at the point of my sword?'

'Then it was midwinter and I was drunk. Now it is summer and I am sober.' Essex eyed him balefully. 'Circumstance may change.'

'Your lack of skill with a rapier will not.'

'You try me, fool.'

'Anywhere is fair site for blood-letting and sport.'

Essex flushed the colour of his beard, his rage prickling at the insouciance of a lesser rival, at present and remembered insult. 'Take care, Christian Hardy. The Queen fetes you and applauds your imagined acts of daring. I do not.'

'Envy most oft arises in those estranged from feat of arms.' Hardy ventured closer, goading. 'I see you restuff and patch your pierced hose, Essex.'

'I would willingly cross swords with you again, dog.'

'A dog will bite, a braggart fall.'

Adversaries, divided by hostility, rank and concentrated tension, were moving toe to toe. Essex would not be first in retreat, Hardy would not withdraw. The rage of the young lord grew.

'Be aware of your station, Hardy.'

'Crawl away to yours.'

'Pit yourself on me and you will die.'

'Better to die than submit to the will of a dullard, Essex.'

'Do you know with whom you deal?'

'A simple hothead, an empty poltroon, a braying ass.'

There was movement from beyond the circle, a hurried intervention that arrived in the footfall and presence of Sir Francis Walsingham. His expression was grave. He understood more than any the complexities of court and the implications of a quarrel. His timing was matchless.

'Enough of your argument, sirs.'

'Why, if it is not our Principal Secretary of State.' The Earl was venomous in his greeting. 'Your pleasure in soldiers and favour for strong-thighed boys is well known, Sir Francis.'

'Your lack of courtesy also, my lord. Quell your passions and rash impulse. Her Majesty will not suffer the violent affray of a fighting-cock.'

'Yet she seems to bear the company of one who causes me offence.'

'Mr Hardy is a welcome guest to court. Be mindful of it.'

'I am wise to how you conspire against me, how you and Burghley and his dwarfish spawn Cecil scheme to oust me in the regard of the Queen.'

'You damage yourself, my lord.'

'My desire and delight is to injure you.'

Walsingham did not flinch. 'Take care in what you seek, my lord.'

'Keep watch on what you own.'

With a last glance directed at both men, the nobleman turned and stalked from sight. The day was proving full of theatre and incident, Hardy mused. Beside him, Sir Francis Walsingham peered after the vacated space.

'Let us turn our eye and thought to the small matter of Armada.'

Far downriver, east of the City of London, a barrier formed of one hundred and twenty ship-masts was being laid across the Thames. Its purpose was simple, was aimed at preventing ingress by enemy invasion barges direct into the heart of the capital. An unintended and hidden consequence was that, with the river now sealed, the contingents of Janissaries waiting aboard their vessels close by London Bridge would not soon be casting off.

~

That small matter of Armada was too the subject of debate in a room of the gubernatorial mansion in Corunna. It was an uncomfortable meeting. Medina Sidonia sat across from a private secretary sent by the King, was parrying questions and defending his judgement with a patience and dignity that were sore beginning to fray. He was aware of malicious talk in Madrid, alert to the fate of his doughty predecessor. Santa Cruz would have laughed at the irony.

'His Majesty notes the Armada sits idle while July is close upon us.' The emissary did not spare the caustic remark.

'You observe for yourself our industry, Don Andreas. There is here little idleness.'

'No?' The man leaned forward. 'For four weeks you remain at anchor. For four weeks you let the heretic queen of England strengthen and prepare on sea and land.'

'There was a storm.'

'I care not, your grace.'

'Our crews are winnowed by sickness and need replacing; our stores are spoiled and demand replenishment.'

'Again you offer cause without true reason.'

Medina Sidonia gripped the arms of his chair, his knuckles whitening. 'Have you experience of arranging a fleet, Don Andreas? Have you attempted to equip ships and conjure troops in a place so crude and discouraging as Corunna?'

'Similar complaint was proffered by the Marquis of Santa Cruz regarding Lisbon and the river Tagus.'

'We departed that city, were scattered by tempest, stripped of masts, rigging, men and victuals. What would you have us do?'

'Sail, your grace.' The royal secretary was enjoying pressing the bruise.

'You intend for success?'

'The King demands it.'

'And His Majesty places his trust in me.' The Admiral rose stiff and piqued from his seat. I am the Duke of Medina Sidonia and captain-general of our fleet. You are mere messenger.'

'A messenger with the ear and confidence of the King, who rides to deliver his word. A messenger for whom you will be seated.'

'I shall not be directed in such a manner.'

'Yet you will heed, your grace. Gird yourself and gather your force, increase the pace of your repair. The King is in an unforgiving mood.'

'I know my duty.'

'So execute it, before disgrace and other form of ending comes.'

'You would threaten me?' Astonishment came as a whisper.

The private secretary watched with satisfaction. 'I choose rather to remind. The enterprise of England is the determination of God, of His Catholic Majesty and of Spain. Those who falter or show waning zeal shall be for ever damned.'

Medina Sidonia slowly lowered himself to face the underling from Madrid. 'My soul and life are bent to the Armada.'

'Be sure they are not wasted.'

Whatever the risk, however daunting the prospect, the Admiral would drive his navy on and force events to a conclusion. The menace behind was at least as great as the jeopardy in front. It could make a commander determined.

★

Along the street, in a small basement bordello, Salvador achieved sexual congress with a whore. In her arms he could forget past mistake and future horror; between her thighs he could distance himself from feeling. Here were cold-bloodedness and heated passion, the art of swordsmanship, the illusion of fearlessness. He would be brave, could be strong. To be able to kill, a part of oneself had first to die.

On the heights of Santa Lucia, looking down upon the walls of Corunna and the shallow sweep of the bay, Realm sat alone and still and watched the sunlight ebb and the shadows deepen. Evening was a time for reflection. He could see the untidy rows of ships, the miniaturized forms of sailors hauling on capstans and windlasses, the trail of longboats ferrying orders or supplies. All to a single end. On one side was the bulked mass of the *Gran Grin* on which Inquisitor Garza sailed, on the other the distinctive shape of the four galleasses *Zúniga*, *Girona*, *Napolitana* and his chosen vessel *San Lorenzo*. To be an outsider and to crouch on a hilltop provided a different perspective. The Armada might be delayed, but vengeance was rarely stalled for long.

On 12 July 1588, some six weeks after gathering at Corunna, the Armada resumed its journey.

Chapter 12

Idling in the shade of a spreading Somerset elm, drinking sack from leather gourds, the three companions had found excuse to rest their horses and wet their dust-clogged throats. The scene rarely changed and the traditions never varied. It seemed strange to consider that threat existed, that the villages and towns through which they rode might yet play host to Spanish troops and the black-garbed enforcers of the Inquisition. Portugal was an age past and several hundred miles distant, the figures populating the Lisbon mission merely players who had wandered on and off the stage. Sprawled in this summer-heated meadow, it was easy to forget what had been and what might come.

The whirr of a sling, the acceleration of a stone, and at twenty paces the emptied canteen was struck from its improvised plinth. Another victory for Luqa.

Hawkhead was unmoved. 'A single Spanish musket-ball would soon make end to your display.'

'Not before another brings down a shaven-headed goblin dancing with his knife.'

'My blade will ever outmatch a pebble.'

'A thought shared by many Ottoman before they fell.' With a sharp whistle, the islander ordered the dog Fearnot to retrieve. 'Proud Janissaries, baying Iayalars, plumed Spahis. All are dead from the kiss of my slingshot.'

'The kiss of a poxed whore would be more deadly to a Spaniard.'

'Though he must first die of mirth at your antics on a horse.'

Hawkhead scowled. 'I am a sailor and no horseman. I have not as you thieved sufficient mounts to learn the vital art.' Both his bones and his pride had suffered through his falls.

Stretched out against his saddle-pack, Hardy part-listened to the argument and the gentle sounds from the hedgerows. Again he had departed his home, had bade farewell to his wife and child. He had lost Black Jack on the last expedition. Perhaps on present assignment he would see Luqa or Hawkhead die, could himself fail to return. Whether in the service of Walsingham or the employ of Drake, anything might happen. He remembered Emma clinging to him as though in final embrace.

'God send Spanish chain-shot to remove your quarrelling heads.' He flicked open an eye. 'We have scarce covered a mile where you do not find cause for difference.'

'It is the stuff of fellowship, Christian.' Hawkhead played hurt.

Luqa concurred. 'Dogs may scrap and yet stay friends.'

'Are you so mannered since your visit to court?' The small and wiry seaman tilted his ridicule to a new target. 'Do you crave the elegant tongue and graceful airs of lords and ladies?'

The brawny Maltese native bowed with a flourish. 'Is this what you like, Christian?'

'Or do you prefer lower?' Hawkhead swept his head close to the ground.

'Yes, your honour. Yes, your grace. Yes, Your Majesty.' Luqa stooped to kiss the upturned rear of his comrade. 'I must ever be respectful, must always treat as holy relics the shit-holes of my betters.'

They paraded for a while, their rivalry discarded and their

226

enjoyment all-consuming. Hardy smiled. It was a moment to appreciate, a calm to remember. Fearnot had dropped his stone and cocked his head bemused.

'You frighten your own hound, Luqa.' Hardy moved to sit upright. 'We shall see how you both jape when Drake sends you scurrying to the topgallants.'

Hawkhead snorted. 'I will do anything to leave behind that horse.'

'Savour your time here. It will be no easier toiling for one Sir Francis than the other.'

'We may grow richer for it.' Luqa gave a knowing grin. 'What we did not earn with Walsingham we will surely win as prize with Drake.'

'And whoever we did not slay in Lisbon we shall finish off at sea.' Hawkhead relished the prospect.

Their young commander had every confidence in them. 'Black Jack would envy us our task.'

'Each blow I strike will be revenge for him, Christian.'

'The Maltese speaks as I.' Hawkhead had drawn a knife from his bandolier and tapped it in his palm. 'I would expend a thousand enemy in honour to his memory.'

'There will be tens of thousands more.'

Two of their number – Inquisitor Garza and an unknown English traitor – Hardy would dearly wish to again encounter. No fleeting glimpses on Portuguese soil, no fragmentary duel in darkness with its unsatisfactory result. Just a straight contest in which he held the advantage and a battle-rapier in his hand.

Luqa crouched before him. 'Garza will be yours, Christian.'

'He imprisoned my mother, tortured a merchant captain, butchered an English crew.'

'If you do not claim him, the Devil shall.'

'The Jesuit sets a plot in motion, Luqa. Our Queen is in peril of Catholic assassin.'

'Has she ever not faced such hazard?'

'Something changes. The skies darken and the mood grows bleak.' The young soldier stared at his friend. 'I felt it in Lisbon; again I sensed it in the royal halls of Richmond.'

'Let Walsingham meet this danger.'

'He fights blind as we.'

Luqa reached and patted his shoulder. 'We alone saw the might of the enemy, witnessed the preparation. Your bad humours are stirred by it.'

'My instinct is sharpened.'

'Our duty is to join Drake, to put cipher and dagger aside. Our calling is battle.'

'And I will answer.'

There was a glint of silver at the throat of the older man, a glimpse of the small crucifix. The Mediterranean had doubtless purloined it, added it to the valuables collected on his journeys. As souvenir it was modest enough. *Our calling is battle.* Luqa spoke the truth, had the mind and temperament of one happiest with the simplicities of life. Adventurers and soldiers could learn much from him.

With an abrupt flurry of speed, Hawkhead spun round and sent his blade travelling fast into the tree-stump vacated by the tin canteen. A second and third knife followed, each joining the other in dull impact and close grouping. A semblance of pleasure flitted on the tight little features of the marksman.

'Regard how to conquer a foe.'

Luqa nodded. 'A dead tree is no match for you, Hawkhead. The enemy must quake.'

'So speaks a Mediterranean savage, a pirate who discovered only a cracked rice-pot when he ventured to spy on the Castle of St George.'

'I stole gunpowder and set ablaze a galleon.'

'Would that you had directed the slow match to yourself.'

A growl from Fearnot cut short the threatened altercation, both men pausing to listen and turn in the direction of a sunken lane. Cavalry was approaching. In a clatter of hooves and armour they trotted by, the gleam of their helmets and tips of their lances parading above the bordering thickets. They were heading for the coast.

'Mules commanded by asses.' Hawkhead sent his insult after them. 'With the Earl of Leicester their general, we may expect the Spaniard soon to be in London.'

Hardy was on his feet and gathering up his pack. 'More the reason we should get with speed to Plymouth.'

The Armada would not wait.

In the coastal Hampshire town of Lymington another traveller was on the closing leg of his journey. He also was instructed to a mission. The Catholic agent who had rented a dwelling on London Bridge was accustomed to obeying the diverse commands of his foreign masters. It was pleasant to be free of the threat and claustrophobia of the city. He could congratulate himself on staying alive, was thankful for the miracle of remaining ahead of Walsingham and his coteries of Searchers. Every hour was a blessing. It allowed him to continue in his plan, to reconnoitre the ground ahead and stage horses on the road behind. If only these Protestants knew.

Along the quay, fishing-boats rubbed sides with pinks and hoys and the paraphernalia of warfare. The English were preparing a last-ditch defence. It provoked a flutter of amusement in the heart of the agent, for neither ditch nor defence could save the country. Out towards the Solent, where the mouth of the Lymington river widened through the salt marsh, a parade of small boats was shuttling out supplies. Its destination was the Isle of Wight. Conventional wisdom had it the Armada might attempt a landing there and Medina Sidonia shelter in its bays until ready to join the veteran army of the Duke of Parma. Anything was possible.

So it was that vessels laden with cannon and shot or with troops for the garrison and labourers to build entrenchments worked their way across the water. Urgency could sow confusion that in turn favoured the opportunist. To be one among a throng of hundreds was to find the perfect camouflage; to be a volunteer in time of trouble was to find welcome as a brother. If he were challenged, he would employ bluff. Should bluff fail, he would kill. Danger had made the Catholic resourceful.

'Hail, friend.' The soldier greeted him with innocent cheer from his temporary seat on a barrel of salted pork. 'You join us for the fight?'

'I do as God demands.'

'Or as our good Queen decrees. It is our misfortune Leicester commands us.'

'The noble general is not liked?'

A shrug from the man. 'I served him in the Netherlands this year past. An unhappy venture.'

'Now you ready again to meet the Spaniard.'

'That I do, and with complaint on my lips and devotion in my heart.'

It was nice to be trusted, the Catholic thought. He enjoyed conversation at cross-purpose and with differing belief, had hoodwinked so many with common ruse. From tavern-keepers to farmers, from merchants to lawyers and blacksmiths to infantrymen, none suspected. They were no match for the forces of righteousness.

The soldier squinted towards the distant island mass. 'You are brave to go hither with us, friend. It may yet be our grave.'

'One piece of soil is like to another.'

'True words for a warrior.' The soldier let his fingers drift across the musket on his knee. 'So long as there is blast of gunfire to my ear and sting of powder in my eye I am in the company of angels.'

'Stout hearts and steel will overcome the most zealous of our foes.'

'None come more deadly than the papist.'

The Catholic nodded his accord. 'We must be forever vigilant.'

'There are but two kinds I embrace. Those hanged and drawn and those soon to be hanged and quartered.'

'A most particular form of friendship.'

They laughed as instant acquaintances often did, sharing the joke and finding common ground. Around them, pikemen and musketeers milled and chatted, awaiting their turn for embarkation, chasing off fears with casual banter. Expectation created its own anxieties. There were rumours of what the popish demons did to prisoners, tales of how they butchered children and raped and tortured women. The gospel truth according to wise saws and old hands. None could say if a hostile landing on the Isle of Wight was certain. Mere possibility became fact in the minds of nervous men.

A young soldier vomited discreetly beside a heap of lobster-pots, a second squatted and voided his bowels beneath a cart. Tension affected everyone. Manoeuvring into position at a jetty, a small pinnace disgorged a rich lady and her scampering offspring. They were retreating from the island, moving inland with their retinue and other refugees and escaping a scenario in which they might be trapped. Well might they flee, the Catholic mused.

His new-found comrade grunted. 'Are they the rats which recognize what comes, or are we the goats who go blind to slaughter?'

'Each one of us decides the time and nature of our stand.'

'Then we choose no better moment.' The trooper slapped him heartily on the knee. 'Your name, friend?'

He plucked it from an imagined list and offered it as genuine. Like much else in his daily existence, it was a lie.

~

It was as he remembered it, the stately conversion of a Cistercian monastery into the elegant abode of a merchant prince or pirate king. Some had benefited greatly from the destruction and dissolution of Church power. Hardy wandered down the gentle escarpment, followed the path around the imposing barn and through the teased and geometric formality of the gardens. Buckland Abbey, the home of Sir Francis Drake. Here extraordinary deeds and adventure had been plotted; here the nave and apse, the squat central tower, the ecclesiastical stones that had once protected holy brothers in prayer and contemplation now housed an occupant of more rumbustious bent. Yet in this quiet Devon hollow, some nine miles from the sea, there remained an atmosphere of solace and mystic calm. Hardy approached the main door. The prodigal was returned.

Acclimatization from the sunlight to the embracing gloom of the great hall took several moments. He blinked and looked about him, absorbed emerging images redolent of past visit. There were the welcoming flames boisterous in the magnificent stone fireplace, the plaster frieze of the tree of life surrounded by dark wood panelling, the triangular-patterned flagstones of red and white. And seated on benches or clustered in dialogue were local worthies and captains of ships, the followers and retainers of a local boy made rich. The supreme seafarer of his age was the most convivial of hosts.

A steward drew near and bowed. 'Our greetings, Mr Hardy. You ride swift.'

'Occasion demands it. But I hail chance to smell again the sea.'

'You will not find the master too different in his leaning.' The servant smiled and motioned to an inner doorway. 'He bids me take you to him on the higher deck.'

They progressed through the house, a sortie through chambers and corridors decked with tapestries and replete with the trophies of trade and war. Oil-lamps burned, casting their soft light across glinting treasures and exotic woods, on carved masks and feathered headdress, on precious stones and colourful shells, on things exchanged and finery seized. Drake was not immune to the impulse for display. Yet few of his visitors required prompting on the character of the legend. He was a law unto himself, and the last hope for England.

'My young and blue-eyed princeling drags himself from court.' The mariner beamed as he strode to meet him. 'You gain powerful friends and patrons, Christian.'

'The Earl of Essex is not among them, sir.'

'Pay no heed. He is a jealous and impetuous knave.'

'A knave I care not to own as my enemy.'

'Your allies are stronger.' The embrace was fraternal and heartfelt. 'It seems you are none the worse for your sojourn in Lisbon.'

'Fresh challenge arises to replace the old.'

'That it does. Walsingham hurts to lose you.'

'I served his honour as well I could, sir.'

'And punished the enemy beside. We shall yet give you further combat, Christian.' The sailor shepherded his junior through.

As the study of Walsingham at Barn Elm manor was the hub of English espionage, this modest chamber at Buckland Abbey sat at the heart of maritime strategy. Charts covered the central table; globes and navigation instruments were strewn about the periphery. Presiding over them, divining the portents and searching for advantage, eager at the prospect of coming affray, *El Draque* appeared already transported to his warship. He crossed to an arched window and pointed.

'Regard my longboat fastened ready on the Tavy. At any instant, with the call of a petard or signal beacon, it will carry me down to the Tamar and on to Plymouth.'

'I have witnessed many sights of preparation.'

'We are far from set, Christian. The captains argue, the government keeps us short of powder and ball, the Lord Admiral is scarce acquainted with the distinction between fore and aft of a ship.'

'Will he not defer to you, sir?'

A shrewd and wicked glint sparked in the eye. 'Lord Howard of Effingham is cousin to the Queen, has nobility and rank, possesses right to his command and the flagship *Ark Royal*.'

'You will submit to his authority?' Hardy was disbelieving.

'As vice admiral, I must. Yet war is a confusion, the sea a fickle environ for passing and obtaining message. I shall doubtless be forced to obey my spirit.'

'A spirit that will scatter the Spaniard to the wind.'

'Pray it is so, Christian.' Drake bent and scrolled out a map of the southern coast of England, weighing down its corners with polished stones. 'Our battleground, as viewed from the sky by a circling albatross. Sir Richard Grenville and his ships off Ireland provide a screen to the west. Sir Henry Seymour guards the eastern end in the narrow seas. And we sit ready here.' He traced the positions.

'What stratagem and device do you plan for the enemy, sir?'

'First ask what it is the enemy seeks. He intends to destroy us prior to a landing by the army of the Duke of Parma.'

'He creates for himself an arduous task.'

'We shall make it the harder.' Enthusiasm glowed in the wind-scoured face. 'The method of the foe is his undoing. He will desire to grapple and board us, to sweep aside our resistance with his embarked weight of troops.'

'How do we answer, sir?'

'By denying him the chance. He sails close, we pull away. He lunges, we dart quicker. He attempts to dominate the whole, we stand off to worry him with ceaseless broadside and volley.'

'You have rare insight to the mind of Medina Sidonia.'

'His is the most ordinary of instruments. He thinks as a landlubber, and I shall have him for it. But still there is risk.' Drake jabbed his forefinger at the map. 'The Spaniard may surprise with sudden foray and catch our squadrons idling at Plymouth. He could invest harbours from Portsmouth to Southampton, build positions at Spithead until joining the forces sailing from the Low Countries.'

'Is there enemy aim we have most to fear?

The finger again thrust down. 'The Isle of Wight. Should he so choose, the Spanish captain-general may turn into the Solent and find refuge and muster-point for later assault.'

'He has opportunity the length of England.'

'Thus we must pursue and harry, drive him on to rocks or send him pell-mell across the Channel. We cannot permit him to think or settle.' The hand slapped blanketing on the parchment. 'If this is to be our Day of Judgement, I want the Satan Spaniard fighting blind, rudderless and disarrayed.'

Satan would find his match in Drake. The commander and privateer had confounded with daring and skill the naval might of Europe. On the Spanish Main, he had disguised his warship as a laden merchantmen, had slowed the vessel by shortening sail and dragging water-butts behind. It had attracted the attention of hostiles seeking easy prey, and had added once more to the tally of the Englishman. Another victory for the master, the sea-dragon. He alone would best the Armada. Hardy was confident of it.

He studied the face lost to concentration above the charts. 'May we not attack the Armada at Corunna, sir?'

'We are unsure he remains where last we heard.' The head lifted and turned. 'A wind that forced my skirmish line back may also have encouraged the Spaniard to depart. Lord Admiral Howard will try again to lead a squadron out, yet the Queen is anxious and prefers to wait.'

'Patience is a virtue as irksome as a curse.'

Drake nodded. 'We will have our moment, Christian. Now stay and dine here at Buckland before we step aboard *Revenge*.'

'You honour me, sir.'

'While by your presence you bear witness of the times of blood and glory we shared off Cadiz and the Azores. A servant prepares your chamber.'

'I am attended by my companions, would better ready for privation and harsh battle through sleeping in the barn.'

'So be it, though you remain my guest and friend.' Drake cocked his head in wry acceptance. 'Practise hard your rapier, Christian. I smell our adversary on the breeze.'

That same breeze which blew along the Tavy valley and rustled the oaks and poplars of Buckland Abbey also washed across the grass downs and fields of the Isle of Wight. The Catholic agent paused and wiped the beading perspiration from his brow. Carrying a pack and trudging on foot for the gently sloping southern edge of the island was no pleasant undertaking. Mistake or ill fortune, a random cavalry sweep or the loose tongue of a local peasant might yet see him condemned. Happily, focus of the Protestants was on the northern side, where the Armada might be expected to divert from its Channel progress and swing into the eastern approach of the Solent. While eyes were trained, he would prepare.

He listened to the distant reverberation of cannon. Sir George Carey, governor of the island, was doing all in his power to bolster the defence and test the readiness of his men. Yet every echoing rumble was illustration of deficiency and confirmation of their weakness. They faced the wrong way. The agent gazed across the tussocks towards the coastal sky and resumed his stride. Within the hour he should reach the small hamlet and find lodgings among its whitewashed houses. A heavy purse and profound commitment had brought him far.

A thought came to him, cued by a memory of others too who resided on occasion in the area. Through a second marriage, Sir Francis Walsingham himself owned the fine manor of Appuldurcombe. The place was steeped in tragedy, had been the site of conflagration at its gatehouse where stored gunpowder exploded and the two young stepsons of the spy-chief died. Over twenty years had passed since the incident. Perhaps irony grew only the sweeter, the Catholic reflected; perhaps the head of English espionage would be still more disconcerted by a new spark catching and setting blaze on his blessed Isle of Wight.

A fleet was at prayer. On board the one hundred and twenty-five remaining Armada ships that had sailed from Corunna, men bowed their heads and listened to their chaplains. Hope and fear were in their hearts, and they crossed themselves with fervour. It was an interlude before battle, an occasion to reflect, a time to distance themselves from who they had been and prepare for what they might become. Almost thirty thousand holy warriors were gathered beneath the fluttering pennants, stood or knelt on decks gently rolling in the swell. The hour was come and Christ was with them. *Amen*, they said. *Amen*, they whispered.

On board the flagship *San Martin*, a conference was in session. Medina Sidonia had called together his senior captains and squadron heads and was rehearsing each role and position for forthcoming event. Control and command were all. In the cramped day quarters of the Captain-General, surrounded by the creak of timbers and bathed in the glow of a solitary lamp, the leaders of the expedition protested and discussed. Their concerns showed. To a man, they were more experienced than their chief in matters of seamanship; to a man, they were weathered veterans accustomed to hold opinion. But the Duke was appointed by the Spanish king, and his judgement would prevail. Looking on, ensuring it was so, Inquisitor Garza sat silent in the background. His presence alone could taint debate.

'What if the Protestant fleet should escape to sea? What if it is more practised than we imagine?' The Biscayan captain was exercised in his thoughts.

Medina Sidonia was dismissive. 'Look upon the power of our formation, count the number of our sail and guns. We are a match for any.'

'For *El Draque*, your grace?'

'He is a brigand and privateer, a heretic versed in mischief and trickery. Our cannon will soon quiet him.' There were several murmurs of agreement.

Another voice spoke. 'Have you faced him in anger, your grace? I boast that honour.'

'Such experience renders you timid.'

'It makes me wise.' The officer glared at his commander. 'We shall reap only anguish if we meet him on open water.'

'I will suffer no distraction, will brook no deviation from our path.'

'Wheresoever it may lead, your grace?' A third captain offered his dissent.

They were interrupted by Admiral Leiva, a naval pure-bred whose views carried influence and whose status was unassailable. He was the chosen successor to Medina Sidonia, a better man kept in waiting. It would not prevent him from making observation.

He leaned on the table. 'Forgive my lack of tact, your grace. Like these brother captains, my motive is honourable and my desire to see through the enterprise to victory.'

'Then speak, Don Alonso.'

'Would it not be prudent to catch Drake and his vipers at anchor, to attack Plymouth and smoke the nest before they bite?'

'They are more akin to mosquitoes than serpents.'

'I have seldom encountered a mosquito with the savage tenacity of the English, your grace.' Uncertain laughter stuttered at the retort.

'Would you be sore pressed to recognize loyalty?' The eyes were half closed, the anger obvious. 'In Lisbon the people cheered, for we had purpose in our hearts and sure aim to our eye.'

'They will weep tears of bitterness should we return ragged in defeat.'

'Dare any talk of defeat when we are poised for triumph?'

Medina Sidonia trembled a little, his irritation pricked and insecurities wakened in the dim confines of the cabin. His senior officers compared him to the late Santa Cruz. Worse, they found him wanting. But he would show them how a privileged landowner might too create a legend as seafarer and conqueror. He was their captain-general and they his minions. Lest they forget.

'The pattern is decided and the placing of your ships

confirmed.' He swept them with a challenging eye. 'I will take the centre with the main body of our warships. To our rear will be the transports. Projecting forward on our flanks, with twenty galleons apiece, will be the defensive horns of admirals Leiva and Recalde.'

Juan Martínez de Recalde, the veteran commander, appeared unconvinced. 'We sail on the turbulent waters of the Channel, your grace. We have charge of galleons and not galleys, face the quicksilver wits of the English and not the plodding Ottoman.'

'More is the reason to be in close arrangement.'

'You tie our hands, your grace.'

'I create order and implant discipline. I keep the enemy at bay.' The chin was locked firm. 'Calais and rendezvous with the Duke of Parma is our concern, and safe passage its agent.'

'Yet it will not defeat *El Draque*, your grace.'

'Nor shall he defeat us.'

Questions and proposals surfaced fast. '*How may you speak of safety when my men already feed on rats?*'

'*We should revictual on the Isle of Wight, your grace.*'

'*Or seize it for our anchorage.*'

'*I would take Ireland and wait for stronger force.*'

'*How do we know the Duke of Parma is prepared, your grace?*'

The dry cough silenced them, swung their attention to the dark cassock and pale face of the Inquisitor. Seafarers rarely welcomed the presence of religious men. They preferred cursing and drinking, the hardiness of their own fraternity to the judgemental ways of a berobed brotherhood. Jesuits were the worst. Few came more unsettling than Garza.

He greeted them without obvious interest. 'Sacred duty requires no discourse. We are pledged to follow the command of the King and through him the will of God. To deny is sacrilege, to disobey is to commit a heresy. None of you here present will venture on selfish frolic of your own. Not a single admiral or captain has authority to dispute what is ordained. Go forward with ferocity and zeal or be for ever damned.'

They could be under no misapprehension: he would be the instrument of that damnation. Their retreat was instantaneous, nervous proclamations of devotion spilling from their mouths. Direction had been restored.

Raising his goblet, Medina Sidonia offered a libation. 'The rocks of the Scillies approach, gentlemen. Beyond them, England and our destiny. We at last have chance to right wrongs, to avenge the burning of Cadiz and the seizing of our treasure-ships, to return the Religion to this demonic island. Let us to war.'

Officers drained their glasses and stood. Their longboats were waiting, their ships lying close with shortened sail and their crews conducting final preparation. Cannon were rodded and grapple-hooks positioned, sword-blades sharpened on a thousand whetstones. Posterity would be the judge of such preparation.

Such a blunt instrument, mused Realm as from the deck of the galleass *San Lorenzo* he watched the lines of ships and their measured progress. The Spanish intended to drive the English from the Channel as precursor to invasion. So long as it kept both sides engaged, so long as it permitted him to complete his more discreet campaign uninterrupted and without fear of exposure. These men would have their day in battle. Yet beyond the clash of arms and roar of cannon, far from a naval trial of strength, was London. The Queen would be in council at Richmond, would in time be persuaded to move closer to the city. Each step was designed to further her security, and each step would bring her closer to demise. It was a comforting thought on such propitious occasion.

~

'Ships ahoy! Five sail to windward!'

The master trusted his lookout: he had depended in the past on his eye and instinct to forewarn of innumerable threat. Captain Thomas Fleming clambered on to the roped mound of salt sacks and peered into the horizon. The vagaries of summer weather could play havoc with the imagination. He blinked and stared. On a routine outing he would be bearing his cargo to the ports of France; on an exceptional outing the few small cannon he carried on board allowed him to indulge in small acts of piracy. His fifty-ton barque, *Golden Hind*, was a versatile lady and her crew a resourceful breed. Together they had endured storms and cracked skulls, had plundered and pilfered their share of booty. But today was not as any other.

He strained to see. 'Any else of you thieves spy this vision?'

'Aye, Captain.' A seaman jumped up beside him and pointed. 'There, as clear as the stones of Purbeck.'

'My sense is dulled by too long at this trade.'

Wiping brine from his eye, he cupped his face against the brightening mist and tried once more. Perhaps he had found something. He shook his head. Spots danced to his front and vanished, emerging and fading before materializing into definite form. There were puffs of white that transformed into canvas, dark smudges that turned into hulls.

'Spanish men-of-war, Captain. They wait on.'

'We do not.' The mariner leaped from his vantage and shouted to the wheelman. 'Hard about! Hard about! We make speed for Plymouth!'

The vessel swung, and her crew raced to haul sheets and lengthen sail. They would work as though the Devil were on their backs, would if necessary jettison their load. There could be no doubt as to what they witnessed, for the shape of the vessels and the size of their castles told one legend. But the Devil did not pursue. The Scillies were merely a gathering-point, a venue at which the lead elements would point to wind and bide time for the rest. Early morning, Friday 19 July 1588. A week after leaving Corunna, the Armada had arrived off England.

Chapter 13

Dank haze crawled over Plymouth harbour, cobwebbing yards and mastheads and merging the ships into spectral shadow. Summer had been banished. Yet within the smeared and pallid scene there was activity, the hollering of seamen and the rattle of cables, the frantic energy of a nation organizing for campaign. There were scores of vessels riding at anchor, each revered, all made legend by ambitious captains and assiduous pamphleteering. England expected; England had no choice.

Moored along the Cattewater, secured beside the causeway or at the trading-wharves of the family Hawkins, were names to be evoked and cheered. The *Mary Rose* and the *Victory*, *Dreadnought* and *Warspite*, *Golden Lion* and *White Bear*, *Defiance* and *Advantage*, and *Triumph* and *Hope*. Gliding back among them, nursed by a gaggle of hoys and lighters, were the flagship *Ark Royal* and her escorting squadron. Lord Howard of Effingham had sailed out for Corunna in order to confront the Spanish, but the strong south-westerly had forced him to retire and run for port. They would sit and wait and see what the wind blew in.

Hawkhead pulled a face. 'Methinks we will soon be in action, Christian.'

'I would favour battle above tarrying.' Hardy scanned the mired view. 'A further day to while, another hour to pace and stare.'

'I will find a dog and throw stones for it as Luqa.'

'Or you may pray as does Sir Francis.'

The hard little man grimaced. 'Dry baccy and a damp harlot are more to my liking, Christian.'

'Enjoy them both. We move nowhere for the present.'

'It is probable I will die of boredom before a musket-ball ever takes me.'

'Bloodshed shall come to those who wait.'

Turning from the eastern elevation of the Hoe, they retraced their path along the ridgeline. It was a circuit they had performed on numerous occasion, a leisurely stroll paralleling the Sound and passing the familiar waypoints of windmill, chapel and bowling-green. The pace and noise of the waterfront rarely intruded to the higher ground. Up here there was the occasional click of a wooden *boule* and the accompanying shouts of captains, the creak of rotating mill-sails, and the sporadic report of a welcoming cannon. There were too the excitable barks of Fearnot as he rushed to retrieve or engaged in feats of agility and speed. People talked or stayed aloof. All kept a weather-eye on the sea.

The door to the Chapel of St Catherine swung wide and Drake emerged fastening a sea-cloak at his throat. Not a frown of concern nor a trace of impending ordeal burdened his features. He was a vice admiral who wore his duty lightly, a man at ease and assured in his belief, a seafarer too experienced to be daunted. His certainty was contagious.

He raised a hand in greeting. 'How fare you, Christian?'

'I attend on your word, sir.'

'As that word waits upon Armada.' The Admiral gestured to the grey stone of the chapel. 'For centuries English kings have here knelt before the Cross and asked God to grant them victory. For centuries English mariners have prostrated themselves at this altar and begged the Lord to deliver them safe from evil. Each time He has answered. He will not now abandon us.'

'He steadies every soul mustered, sir.'

'Then, as their commander, I am blessed. Are you glad to once more be a sailor rather than a spy, Christian?'

'The sea-boots fit and the blade is sharp, sir.'

'Be comfortable with both, for I swear the *Revenge* will be in the thick of it.' It was a promise delivered as statement of fact. 'I see you keep your brutes-at-arms close.'

'I would not be without them.'

'Nor I, Christian. Small in number you are, but you prove yourselves at my side as potent as a regiment.'

'Black Jack would dear wish to be among us.'

'Your Negro died as we all must, was given place to meet his Maker with a shout on his lips and a firebrand in his fist. It is the fate to which we each aspire.'

'I sought to complete more in Lisbon, to wreak havoc on Armada.'

'Fortune provides you second chance.' He clapped Hardy on the shoulder. 'A day, a week or a month past is by now already history. Current event is our affair.'

There was a brotherhood of shared value and danger confirmed between commander and younger man. Walsingham was a courtier and Drake a fighter, a buccaneer whose world was forged of gunsmoke and mayhem and splintering wood. To be touched by his hand was to be chosen; to be regarded as friend was to become anointed. Hardy would stand by the admiral-adventurer until the end.

In a spatter of earth and cloud of shouts, horsemen appeared at a gallop and reined to a halt beside them. As they climbed from their mounts, Drake stood tranquil amid the commotion, surveyed them with narrowed eyes and a tilt of his head. He had recognized his chief visitor.

'Thomas Fleming climbs to the Hoe.' His welcome carried an edge of threat. 'A rare sight so far from your ship.'

'Events propel me, Sir Francis. This morning off St Mary's I espied the van of the Spaniard, a number of sail stood out to sea.'

'A number?'

'They arrive on the sou'westerly, Sir Francis. No drink or trick of light informs me. The hated foe is off our shore. Indeed, it may at any step surge past Rame Head to invest the Sound itself.'

'This is your opinion as master of a barque?'

'I attest to it, Sir Francis.'

'On your life as a robber and knave? On your word as a blood-sated louse who raids and costs dear my business in Mill Bay?'

The captain shifted uneasily. 'I voyage to warn and not to quarrel.'

'And you are fortunate to discover me in the aftermath of prayer.' Drake found a silver coin and tossed it to the messenger. 'Spend it well in New Street. The next penny you take from me, you shall hang.'

Rewarded and rebuked, the master of the *Golden Hind* withdrew. Drake laughed and turned to Hardy. 'The quarry arrives and our sport commences. Each to his destiny, Christian.'

He began to walk along the Hoe, his purposeful stride and controlled urgency gathering others in his wake. Imminence of combat had quickened the pulse. There were commands to give, dispatches to send, requests to make. Senior officers broke from their idleness to gaze or to question.

A bowling-ball was proffered. 'Time yet remains to finish play, Sir Francis.'

'My inclination is for a different game.' He waved the man

away. 'Henceforth, it will be rounded shot of iron we hurl at the target.'

'The tide still flows, Sir Francis.'

'We position ourselves to ride it on the ebb.' His attention swung to a courier attending with a horse. 'Mount up and ride hard for Richmond. Advise the Queen and her council the Armada arrives and we engage.' The herald bowed and Drake moved on. 'Instruct the quartermaster to break out the stores. Inform the merchants to give over their cherished ships and cosseted crews.'

'Should they refuse?'

'There is ever the sword-point, the noose, the oar of our four galleys to encourage their assent.' He led his assembly forward. 'Muster the men and hoist the colours. Draw every captain and able body from stewhouse and tavern and send them on board.'

'Aye, Sir Francis.'

His orders flowed and his subordinates raced to comply. Hardy stayed close, caught up in the pace, a witness to history. He did not forget that this showman and chancer, brilliant tactician and pious rogue, had nailed to the mast the hands of those caught stealing hard biscuit. Few were tempted to oppose Sir Francis.

The Vice Admiral paused above the harbour, looked down upon the crumbling bastion and the dimmed outline of the vessels beyond. He had made his decision.

'Our moment is now! Warp the ships!'

Beneath the immense limestone visages of Gog and Magog carved into the sloping hillside, the English navy started to manoeuvre. Longboats rowed out ahead and dropped ships' anchors, deck crews winching the great hulls forward before the anchors were raised and the process repeated. Warping was a laborious test of patience and sinew. Slowly the warships

248

edged towards the harbour mouth, moving against the current, preparing to catch the wind and slip into Plymouth Sound. They could not afford to be caught by the Spanish. It was imperative they sail, critical they should find the weather-gauge and reach to windward of the enemy. From there they would enjoy advantage of motion and attack. And the two Cornish giants stared down, mythological demon-creatures and talismans, to whom since time immemorial seafarers had turned for courage and luck. They would be needing both.

Through that day and into the night of Friday 19 July 1588 the Armada swept closer. The wind brought it past Wolf Rock and the Lizard, carried it by the fearsome shoal of the Manacles, and eased it across the mouth of the Fal estuary towards Dodman Point and the Bellows. To the fore were the small xebecs and agile pinnaces, specialist craft bearing pilots to navigate safe passage. The lookouts stayed vigilant. A flaring brightness appeared to speckle the high ground, a creeping orange glow that leaped from clifftop to headland and seemed to herald the advance. It came from the alarm beacons of a nation, a signal that travelled fast and wide until in hours every corner of the land was touched and its citizens knew the meaning. Families embraced and said their prayers. On the water, the splash of weighted lines and shouts in Spanish and Portuguese invaded the darkness. Along the shore, the defenders too were readying.

~

Daybreak on Saturday 20 July 1588 and, led by Drake on his *Revenge* and Lord Howard aboard the flagship *Ark Royal*, some fifty-four English sail were bearing out to the Sound. They made slow progress. Clawing against the prevailing wind and pushing through the drizzle-murk, the vessels straggled past

Wembury Point and headed south-south-west for the Eddystone Rocks some fourteen miles beyond. It was not till the afternoon they caught sight of the adversary: they had never witnessed such an ominous and awesome display. To the west, in the damp and shifting light, a vast crescent-formation of enemy ships had emerged. From tip to tip its concave front measured two miles across, an impregnable Armada of swelling canvas and towering hulls. It had the weather-gauge and possessed the numbers. As evening again closed, Drake studied the waves and wind and measured his foe. Unless he could outmanoeuvre the Spaniard, until he had threaded his squadrons out to sea, Medina Sidonia would crush him to leeward. Small wonder the English crews muttered and prayed and peered uneasy at the view. A threatening situation. A context in which Sir Francis Drake always thrived.

'Let havoc fly! Let the will of England prevail!'

The shout rang across the deck of the *Revenge*, echoed and directed the gathering pace. Gun-ports were opened, hammocks stowed, weapons bundled and placed to repel enemy boarders. The Spanish no longer enjoyed the lead, they would certainly take no pleasure in the approaching encounter. For Drake had used the hours of darkness well. During the night he had slipped ahead and south of the oncoming Armada, had gathered his ships to sit and wait on. Now, at dawn on Sunday 21 July 1588, it was the lumbering Spanish in the lee, and their right flank under the great Portuguese seafarer Admiral Recalde that lay exposed. *El Draque* would be the man to exploit it.

He stood on the poop, calling out orders, occasionally striding to gauge the trim and check the sails.

'See how they position to attack our laggards out of Plymouth, Christian.' Drake swept his arm across the vista. 'We shall have them while they are turned.'

'They are slow enough for it, sir.'

'Though armed suitably to cause us hazard. Distinct from our victories at Cadiz and Juan de Ulúa, they are not disarrayed or confined to harbour.'

'We may even so strike them well, sir.'

'It is my intent.' The Admiral added caveat with a grin. 'If the wind should hold with us and Frobisher not plunge his stiletto in my back.'

Hardy nodded, amused at the abiding resentment of a Yorkshireman for his Devonian superior. Drake was richer, more famed and lionized. It rankled with some captains – with Frobisher in particular. Yet the latter's magnificent ship *Triumph* shadowed the Vice Admiral, lending her support or jealously safeguarding expected prize.

'We are formed and rallied for battle, sir.'

'Then it would be churlish to deny it.' Drake raised his voice, directed his instruction to the wheel. 'Make straight for the enemy. Full sail.'

Santa Ana, flagship of Recalde, was the target. Break the strongest link and the entire chain might fracture. So *Revenge* and her cohorts moved in, riding the long swell, chasing through the swirling rain. It was a time for reflection, a state of suspension between decision and contact. Hardy thought of Emma and their two-year-old son, pondered on Garza and the renegade Englishman he had cut with a sword. *In extremis*, the mind commingled infinite themes. He had to focus.

High in the rigging, a sailor cried out. 'The *Santa Ana* swings to greet us!'

'I expect no less of herself and her admiral.' Drake leaned against the rail. 'She is as a bear pawing at the baiting-dog.'

'The pit is opened, sir.'

'Thus animals meet and melee commences.' He gave the

defining order. 'Tend to the whistle. Come close to the wind and give her taste of our broadside.'

Engagement began, the low and sleek English hulls sliding past and standing off to deliver cannon-shot against their rivals. Flame spewed and smoke poured, iron balls spinning and ricocheting around the foreign ship.

'We sever a spar and forestay, sir.' Hardy yelled against the noise.

His commander was unmoved. 'I would wish to carry off her mast.'

'Others seek to dissuade us, sir.'

The young soldier spat the bitter residue of powder from his mouth, steadied himself on the shuddering deck. Below, gun-carriages were rolling back and fresh rounds rammed home. The Armada was too unwieldy and slow to respond, to feint or to thrust. Yet the Biscayans could not leave one of theirs to stand alone. Medina Sidonia might press on, but his second-in-command had courage to face about and fight, could act as catalyst and encourager to the rest. Vessels swayed to meet the threat.

One of those vessels was the *Gran Grin*. Although a transport, she carried twenty-eight guns and could add weight to the resistance. With several galleons accompanying she joined the fray, separating from the main body and rolling on to a different tack. Her sides shivered as her rows of cannon opened up. Now it was the turn of the English to fall back, to veer beyond the grasping radius of the enemy. The *Santa Ana* had some powerful friends. Gradually they gathered close, a moving shield glimpsed through patches of downpour and flame. Shot skittered along the wavetops or dropped in plumes about the heaving men-of-war. Whatever the tactics or odds, the English were being tenacious.

Pacing aft, Inquisitor Garza mounted the steps to the

sterncastle and encountered the captain and his entourage. What a handsome array they made; what imbecilic fools they were. They might wish to indulge in rash foray, but his priority, his reason, was to continue and see conquest through. *Thy will be done.* He had not prepared for years, had not nurtured and tutored the English traitor Realm, merely to abandon his plans on the vainglorious whim of a naval man. There would be a confrontation.

He stepped on to the raised deck. 'Do you not heed the command of Medina Sidonia? Do you not hark to his counsel to proceed with haste?'

'I do as my conscience demands, Inquisitor.'

'Your conscience is folly and caprice against the edict of King Philip and demand of our captain-general.'

'Impulse of war takes precedent.'

'The will of God surpasses all.' Garza stared coldly at the man. 'You have no right to disobey, no authority to break formation and indulge in petty act.'

'Is saving the *Santa Ana* so petty? Is aiding our brave Admiral Recalde beyond the wit of a reasoned man?'

'You put at risk our mission, Captain.'

'Sailing is risk, Inquisitor. Armada is risk. Combat is risk.'

'Needless combat more so.' Garza did not shift his ground or gaze.

Nor was the captain about to retreat. 'Return to your quarters, Inquisitor. Battle provides no place for discourse.'

'We carry on board troops and materiel for the war on land, the sacred relics and artefacts that will bring peace and succour to the citizens of England. With rash care you set them in the path of harm.'

'I am Captain of the *Gran Grin*.'

'While I am to be Inquisitor General of a vanquished nation.'

'Until that time you are a Jesuit, a priest and passenger on my vessel.'

'Treason adopts many a guise, Captain.'

'Arrogance and conceit also.'

The arcing scream of a cannonball intervened, its trajectory catapulting the missile high into the gut of a soldier stationed on the fo'c's'le. Viscera were blown from the man as the sullied metal voyaged on. The body fell. A second ball careened into the foremast, deflecting in a random pattern that scattered limbs and fragmented wood. Strange figures lacking arms or faces wandered aimless in the aftermath.

Garza returned to the commander. 'You leave the pack and suffer consequence.'

'A flesh wound, Inquisitor.'

'Our force is misdirected, our strength drained for no avail.'

'I vouch where you have trod the slaughter is greater.'

'Be wise to it, Captain.' The eyes were passive and uncommunicative.

Around them the officers were nervous and bemused, unwilling to commit lest one party achieved submission of the other. It seemed Garza was in the ascendant. But the wind had altered west–north–west, its unpredictability reducing the scurrying English raids and providing chance of disengagement. *Santa Ana* was drawn back to the line and the Armada resumed its brutish momentum. On board the *Gran Grin*, the officers were transfixed by the sight of a severed head tumbling awkward on the planking.

Advance or retreat could prove a shattering affair. In their lazy haste to return Admiral Recalde to the fold, and in the deepening swell, several ships collided. With a crash of spars and impact of hulls, it was the large Andalusian nao *Nuestra Señora del Rosario* that ended as main casualty. At over a thousand tons and carrying fifty-two cannon and four hundred and fifty crew, she was a leviathan. Minus her foremast, she was a giant beyond either control or salvation. Perhaps Medina Sidonia, captain-general of the Armada, heard the four signal blasts of her guns; maybe he noticed the distress-pennants fluttering on her mizzen. He chose to ignore them and on a strengthening breeze led his fleet eastward along the Channel. First blood had been shed.

An explosion occurred, a powder-magazine aboard the Guipúzcoan galleon *San Salvador* igniting to a stray spark and blowing outward in catastrophic eruption. The fireball was immense. As the pressure-wave raced from the epicentre, wreckage and body parts avalanched through the blackened air and littered the waters in hailing shards of flame. Through the smoke and incendiary belch of lesser detonations, the vessel had suffered change. Her masts were shorn away, her decks were ripped apart, her stern was gone. In place of a proud ship of twenty-five guns was a drifting and open ruin populated by corpses.

There was little to be done. Yet bucking its way through the smouldering meadow of debris came a flotilla of small craft launched from ships of the line and looking for survivors.

'Bend to your oars. We must hurry.'

In the prow of his longboat, Salvador shouted back instruction and exhorted his crew to their labours. He had volunteered for the task, had willingly stepped in where others demurred. It was with a grim fatalism bordering on contentment that he made this journey, a private recognition he confronted his own mortality and weakness. Today these burnt remains; tomorrow his own. As a funeral-pyre, the galleon had only partially performed its role. Men still screamed, men still groaned, men still thrashed wild and drowning in the sea. He coaxed the boat on.

A crewman cursed, his oar striking without intention the head of a floundering victim.

'Back! Back!' Salvador hissed his orders.

Gently he reached and lifted the sailor beneath his arms, found him surprisingly light. He recoiled as the load surfaced, dropping it appalled when the lack of any body below the waist became apparent. The package disappeared.

A further distraction, a hand clawing at the gunwale and a quiet voice pleading for attention. 'For the love of Jesus Christ, kill me. I beg you to kill me.'

Salvador stared into the eyes, was paralysed by the intensity of their despair. He wanted to look away, to undo his stupidity, to retreat to the sanctuary of the *San Mateo*. Instead, he gazed mute at the creature, at the hand clamped over the stomach wound and at the floating broth of entrails. It was the bosun who finished the job with a cosh.

For fifteen minutes they trawled the scene, their boat nudging a passage through, their company dispatching or saving as they could. Charred timbers and waterlogged bodies made similar sound when striking on the sides. Finally the rowing-boats were recalled. The English were closing, their prowling galleons nipping at the rear and sending out sporadic volleys. Medina Sidonia would wait for no one. As his long-boat pulled away, Salvador tried to obliterate the images from his mind, sought to expunge the aromas of overcooked flesh from his nostrils. They persisted. The eighteen-year-old retched and wiped the spittle-bile from his mouth. He watched the flotsam recede and the ravaged skeletal form of the *San Salvador*, his namesake, dip and rise helpless on the tide. And he knew with absolute certainty he would not outlive the venture.

~

'Mama, the boats. Mama, the boats . . .'

Adam jigged excitedly, a two-year-old absorbed and enquiring of the watercraft on the Thames. Emma crouched beside him and pointed. She had brought her son to London Bridge as much to entertain him as to divert herself, found it comforting to laugh and play and count the wherries and trace the slow repeating progress of the windmill sails on the opposite bank. Her beloved Christian seemed present by his very absence. A splash of oars, the flapping of canvas – each reminded her of what he faced and what she missed. He would be in danger as he always was, would perform his labours with light in his eye and Hawkhead, Luqa and Fearnot close at his side. She had as companions only her child and her fears.

She stood and looked about her. Whether imagined or real, she felt on occasion the proximity of Searchers and their eyes like a heat-source hunting her through the crowd. Since Christian had chased off Isaiah Payne, an uneasy truce appeared to exist. They would bide their time and keep their vigil. It was possible she worried too much, probable the tension that affected all had permeated to her own resolve. Everyone was anxious; everybody waited on the news. The barrier of ship-masts erected downriver was meant for their protection, but served instead to stifle trade and increase the state of siege. Anger and restless energy needed to be harnessed.

'See the dwellings on the bridge, Adam.' She put her cheek to his and directed him to the edifice. 'Such building is named the House of Windows.'

His attention was elsewhere. He had been drawn by a shout, by the beginnings of an altercation that spluttered into life at a wharf. A gang of drunken apprentices had wandered to the riverside seeking sport and, making trouble, had singled out a sailor to whose presence they objected. The man was trapped.

Apprentices deserved their repute for intimidation and violence, administered beatings or stabbings with casual aplomb. A strange fellow with foreign eyes posed little challenge. Except that he moved fast, sidestepped their plodding brutishness with astonishing speed, and drove the hard edge of his hand straight into a windpipe. His assailant dropped lifeless. A second apprentice staggered blind and shrieking from the group, his eyes removed by the simple flick of thumbs, his hands clamped over leaking hollows. Behind him, the sailor had broken free and was running.

Emma lifted Adam close and shrank back protectively, the small boy burying his face from the outside menace. The murderous stranger was darting their way. There were oaths and shouts, the noise of pursuit, the toppling of goods and people as a mob gave chase. Londoners were an unforgiving breed. Armed with blades and cudgels, with improvised weapons that came to hand, they rushed in full cry along the riverbank. Anything to enliven the day. Eventually, when the man tripped, felled by a barrel rolled in his path, they had him cornered. He did not cower, did not implore, did not trouble to utter a single word. Rather, he eyed his opponents with the indifference of one who had already reached decision.

A fish-gutting knife poked towards him. 'You shall hang, you devil!'

'Your severed head will rest atop this bridge.'

'Not before you suffer the tortures of Newgate or the Tower.'

'Vermin! Beast! Knave!' A woman spat, and her phlegm trickled on his face.

'We will fetch the constable. Then you shall see.'

'Or do you ask to taste our own justice?' The pitchfork waved before his face. 'You care to have your scruple pricked?'

'Speak, you maddened dog.'

He remained silent and unswayed by their hostility. They had expected a response, were not expecting the answer he chose. In a single fluid move, a thin stiletto-blade sprang instant to his hand and thrust upward to lodge itself deep in his throat. A conversation-stopper. As the visitor bucked and died, as the horde stepped back in untidy shock, Emma fled with her son from the horror. Had she stayed, she might have noticed a Turkish amulet similar to examples owned by her husband. None of the citizens present were to know the deceased creature was one of many, had been a trained soldier, an assassin, a former Janissary of the Ottoman Empire sent by Spain with special sanction to kill the English queen.

Night had fallen at the end of the first day of naval engagement. The result had been inconclusive, more skirmish than pitched battle, but the threat to Plymouth was averted and the Armada had sailed by. Behind the Spanish ships the English maintained a wary pursuit, choosing to shadow and refusing to close. They lacked the weight of soldiers to grapple and board, were too limited in their stores of ordnance to effect a decisive outcome. All were at sea. Start Point and the fifty-mile-wide bite of Lyme Bay lay invisible to their north. The Armada would not risk becoming caught to leeward between the cliffs and a defending fleet. Darkness provided cover and relief until the morrow, pending the next hostile encounter.

Keeping pace was the *Revenge*. Her stern lantern aglow to mark the way, she forged on in the van, a leading light that left most others for behind. The Vice Admiral was not inclined to cede position, had little intention to forgo the prospect of future spoils and glory. He would play his part, but would get there first. The law of the sea and the outlook of Sir Francis Drake.

Bearing a shuttered candle, Hardy made his way aft. He had spent the eve forward with Luqa and Hawkhead, had discussed the bruising events of the day and communed with a crew resting from toil. A gust of wind billowed in the tops, and the ship surged.

'How fare my men, Christian?' It was Drake on the quarter-deck, always close to the wheel, ever attentive to detail.

Hardy lowered his light. 'They are glad to be aboard, confounded by their failing to scratch the foe.'

'I am wounded as they.' There was phlegmatic humour in the voice. '*Santa Ana* survives so that we may later take her. Medina Sidonia too on board his flagship *San Martin* will keep. We shall catch the Spaniard yet.'

'Their ships are of old acquaintance since I met them in Lisbon.'

'Now they are among us, and we amid them.'

He beckoned Hardy to follow and climbed the shallow stairs to the poop. From here he could survey the blanketing gloom, could finesse his tactics and maintain his guard. Just as he trailed the Spanish, so he kept cautious watch for any fellow commander who might seek to overtake or challenge his advantage. The *Revenge* was pre-eminent, and would continue that way.

Drake leaned on the carved balustrade, more at ease on his ship than in the study of his manor. 'I desire the Spanish to know we are near, to tremble and take fright, to discern us as we snap and bark and cut across their tail.'

'Is not our task to observe their fleet and guide our own, sir?'

'There are many ways to lead, varied means to fight.' The Vice Admiral was not one for conforming. 'We must harry and bleed them, weary them, excise the weakest from the herd.'

'Perchance they do not bleed enough.'

'Thank the Queen and her council for their parsimony and refusal to provide sufficient powder or shot. Instead we use guile and illusion, deploy every vestige of luck.'

'Fortune lies with us, sir.'

'I pray she does not tire. We drive the foe from Plymouth and press on for future reckoning.'

'However the end, I stand at your command.'

'Of my lieutenants, you are the most fierce and tenacious, Christian.'

The vessel dipped on a trough and Drake gave orders to spill wind. It was a balancing-act between pursuit and evasion. Ahead, perhaps surrounding, was the Armada.

'*Light to south and windward!*' The watch called out, a disembodied voice cracking with excitement.

Drake was silent for the space of several breaths. 'Threat shifts and we have duty to move with it.'

Against previous agreement with Lord Admiral Howard, possibly sailing into a trap, *Revenge* snuffed out her stern-lantern and with two pinnaces accompanying shuffled to a different course.

Chapter 14

S he was immense, a floating leviathan of soaring castles and vertical sides blistered with gun-ports and dwarfing the *Revenge*. In open contest, the *Nuestra Señora del Rosario* could outgun any in the English fleet. But she was a wounded giant, a nao unable to manoeuvre or maintain her pace and abandoned to the winds by her smaller escorts and by an Armada that could not stay. Cold calculation and the exigencies of war ensured the *Rosario* would play no further part in the invasion of England. She would either founder or be captured. For the moment she stumbled graceless on the waves, silent and battened down and unwilling to commit. It was her misfortune on this timid dawn of Monday 22 July 1588 that Sir Francis Drake had hove into view.

'We uncover the flagship of the Andalusians.' The English vice admiral scanned her structure with obvious approval. 'What think you, Christian?'

Hardy balanced against the swing of the deck. 'She rolls as a drunken boxer, sir.'

'One who may choose to land a blow. One who is undeclared and undecided on her path.'

'Submission is her only course.'

'And yet she has twenty guns more than we, and two hundred crew over us.'

'You intend to stand off and await her terms, sir?'

'I mean to prick her and to goad.' Drake looked mischievously at his young lieutenant. 'I wager it will prove of worth to have doused our lamp and wandered from our bearing.'

'Lord Admiral Howard would censure it, sir.'

'Our esteemed noble is nowhere about. Now is the hour to act, Christian, to carry across your villainous crew to be instrument of my urging.'

Hardy dipped his head in acceptance 'There is nothing which would cheer us so much as to board a ship of Spain.'

'Go to it, and deliver to me the prize.'

A skiff was launched, its spray-washed route taking it in a narrowing ellipse about the enemy vessel. Unerring instinct and a nose for riches had brought Drake to this patch of sea. He could sniff out gold or profit at a hundred leagues, had studied the risk and snatched reward in numberless confrontation. A distressed transport would never go ignored. It did not make it the more comfortable to steer an open boat beneath the shuttered maw of Spanish cannon. The guns of the *Rosario* might be loaded with grapeshot, could be discharged in an instant to atomize all within range. Christian Hardy, his coxswain, and his companions Luqa and Hawkhead were inside the kill-zone.

Hawkhead pulled in his already short neck. 'Sir Francis is a dragon to the Spaniard. To me he is a fool and menace to our lives.'

'I will thank this fool should your complaining head be removed by Spanish iron.' Luqa appeared unsympathetic.

'Your dog Fearnot would make better fighting comrade than you, Maltese.' The sparse little man peered up at the looming hull. 'At the least he is unable to give voice.'

'Though he will sink his teeth in any worthless arse.'

Quarrelling passed the time and diffused the tension. Another circuit was completed, the reconnaissance tightening into a grazing loop that drew no response from the closed-up foe. They would need encouragement. Hardy had made his decision, crouched in the bow with a grapple-line in his hand and a rapier and dagger strapped at his side, whispered the orders to commit. It helped that he had practised such antics as a boy, had with Luqa as his older guide boarded by stealth the Spanish galleons and galleys at rest in the grand harbour of Valletta. Back then it was for the challenge and occasional trophy, for the thrill of exploration and competing feats of daring. He had put aside childish things and taken up more dangerous pursuit.

The steel hook flew, caught on the forward anchor hanging near the prow, and drew the knot-full rope taut behind. Connection was made. At the bottom of the umbilical, made miniature in the shadow of the dark and glistening sides, the skiff was offloading a passenger. It did not take long for Hardy to gain purchase on the cliff. He swung on the rope, using the anchor as pivot, running and kicking his way in an upward arc until his trajectory offered him a grab-hold. The outsider wanted in. Panting against the calloused surface, his body clamped precarious and crab-like and his hands and feet questing for grip, he strained to crawl higher. Behind, the *Revenge* covered him from a distance; below, his companions waited to assist. Every nerve and moment anticipated discovery and the velocity of shot; every pore added to the slick of sweat. Caught in the crossfire that was yet to come. He did not look back.

Another fingertip-hold, a gradual and worming ascent on to the reinforced frame of a gun-port, and he had found his ledge. He worked quickly now. In seconds he had tugged open the bottom of a canvas bag, allowed a rope-ladder to fall suspended as he cast its metal claw the final feet to the main deck above. The climb was prepared.

'Christian! On your right shoulder!'

Hardy had seen the threat, had flattened himself to the hull even as Luqa cried out a warning. The Spanish soldier was picking his way along the edge, studiously maintaining his balance and intent on causing harm. In his hand was a musket, and on his face an expression of unalloyed pleasure. Crippled the *Rosario* might be, but she could still punish the impudent and the rash. The young Englishman dangled before him. It was too easy to resist, too tempting an opportunity to avoid planting a round direct into one of those wide blue eyes. Hardy watched the preparation, the checking of the wheel-lock, the caressing of the trigger. He wondered if his father had ever clung to so unenviable a position.

Situation altered in a puff of smoke and a travelling crack of sound, with the strike of arquebus-lead into the body mass of the Spaniard. The crew of the vessel had misjudged the aim of their visitors, had predicted reconnaissance instead of a raid. What they were about to receive was a lesson in brute force and the application of tactics carried from a siege on a small Mediterranean island almost quarter of a century before. And they would be less than truly grateful.

In normal conditions, the arquebus ball that penetrated the torso of the enemy soldier would have splintered bone and pulped internal organs. This it did, but not before the pig fat in which it was coated had ignited on impact and coughed flame across the stumbling and dying form. A further trick acquired by Luqa from his early mentors, the pirate Knights of St John. Fire engulfed the corpse, and it flipped in a blazing trail for the sea. Boarding was commenced.

Scrambling upward, propelled by rivalry and a basic instinct to conquer, Hawkhead and Luqa swarmed into the fray. In front of them flew their *sacchetti* grenades, their fuses lit and their explosive loads detonating on planks and stanchions and creating a fragment storm. Flesh tore and men screamed. Already the three raiders were among them, hacking and lunging, easing their way in widening swathes along the deck in a ceaseless flow of combat.

'I have him, Hawkhead.'

'You would steal from me?' Blood flecked his shaved head and aggressive features as Hawkhead cut down an opponent. 'Acquire your own.'

They mixed with the sparse population before them, ever moving and slashing and pushing forward, the harder for an enemy to think or recover, to gain a clean shot or sweep of a blade. Hardy jabbed, his shortened rapier glancing off a cuirass, the Spaniard countering with sure-footed attack. A classic response and a terrible error. In a parrying blur, an English dagger blocked and hooked aside the enemy sword and let the leaping thrust bear the assailant straight on to a steel point. Sword-swallowing was an untidy affair. Hardy lowered his rapier and stomped the pierced head free. There were other targets oncoming, surging into view.

A slingshot brought one down, a second defender sliding on the smeared planks and floundering on his back until the edge of a falchion-knife traced its line across his throat. The smile opened and brightened. Hawkhead looked down at the corpse, scarcely flinching as a pebble achieved concussive impact on an armed and encroaching sailor. He cast an angry glance at Luqa. There would be no thanks for the island native who saved his life.

One bound forward, two steps back, a pommel reversed into the bared teeth of an officer and the assault followed through to terminal conclusion. The immediate area had been cleared and grisly order wrenched from chaos.

'I commend you for your tenacity.' The voice was clear and proud, came from the richly dressed figure alone on the poop. 'My name is Don Pedro de Valdés, flagship commander of the Andalusians.'

Hardy bent in greeting. 'Your rank and high renown travel before you, sir. From my company, I am Christian Hardy and these my sergeants and brother soldiers.'

'Many warned me of the savage madness of the English.'

'This day you witness it yourself.'

'You are but three men, and we a crew of over four hundred.'

'We are mere messengers from the *Revenge*, harbingers of that which Admiral Drake intends should you fail to strike your colours and cede to him your ship.'

'He offers terms?'

'Sir Francis tenders his word you shall be treated as befits a noble and your men permitted their lives. There is not time for parley.'

Though he allowed pause for thought. A frown creased the brow of Don Pedro as he considered the scene. Maybe he weighed the possibilities, was reluctant to choose. Brazen intervention by a trio of cut-throats had clearly forced the pace. Hardy measured time, counted the likely outcomes.

'Christian, we strike gold.' Hawkhead was scavenging through the dead and had chanced upon a coin. 'A ducat, no less.' He spat on it, rubbed its bloodied sides, and tossed it to his chief.

The young soldier caught it in flight and raised it gently between his thumb and forefinger. 'Manna of the Spanish Main.'

'It is possession of His Catholic Majesty and of Spain.' Don Pedro trembled slightly as he spoke.

'How quickly it becomes property of Her Majesty and of England.' Hardy conjured it to invisibility. 'What is yours converts well to ours. Your guns, your nao, your crew, your gold.'

'We carry grain and provisions, the essential materiel of

war.' Perhaps the commander of the *Rosario* was too eager in his argument.

'Am I to believe a lowly crewman is true guardian of such keepsake? Am I to accept a solitary ducat rests alone within this ship?'

'We demand terms for our surrender.'

'You have them. Five minutes or there will be no quarter given. Lower your standard and give up your gold.'

Hardy led his companions back along the deck, withdrawing to the raised fo'c's'le and rotating a light swivel-cannon to dominate the space. With its two-inch calibre and its brass cartridges filled with scrap and grapeshot, and with Hawkhead and a slow-match standing by, they would repel all comers. The five minutes had started.

'Do we bargain or do we kill?' Luqa had a distinct preference for the latter.

'Patience, my brother.'

'It is tested where there is treasure aboard. We sit here while riches lie below.'

'As with any mine, we must force them to the surface.' Hardy viewed the Spaniard distant on the sterncastle. 'A stink-pot to the lower decks should bring us what we ask.'

His friend did not stint, moved cheerfully about the ship depositing smoke-bombs through hatchways and grates with the flair of a performer. A vessel that had seemed near-deserted, sealed against the uncertain progress of events, burst to life in a choking stench of sulphur. Clawing at their eyes, their mouths gaping for air, the crew erupted to the open. With them came wood chests and canvas bags, the snatched possessions and pilfered artefacts of sailors fleeing their senses and long preparing to abandon ship. Their priorities were noteworthy. Through the tumult and cascading human forms wandering the yellow-tinged clouds of smoke, the keen concentration of Hardy observed the heaviness of loads, the rupturing of crude seams, the accidental spill and glint of precious metal. He had discovered the vein. At the far end of the *Rosario*, Don Pedro de Valdés was reaching his decision.

Capitulation was inevitable, was sealed on the deck of the *Revenge* with a kiss delivered by the defeated commander to the hand of Sir Francis Drake. There was no value in resisting, no dishonour in yielding to the legendary English seafarer. After all, Medina Sidonia had abandoned the giant nao to the winds and cruel fortune and had no further use for her. Slaughter was averted, a new destiny ordained. *El Draque* would keep his word. He would also earn reward – a prize beyond anything imagined, a treasure trove amounting to almost one-third of the entire monies carried by the Armada. The perfect heist.

Now the tens of thousands of ducats were being transferred by longboat to his galleon, his sailors inspired by greed and the splendour of their catch. There were cheers and whistles, the bonhomie of plundering, the sight of men filling sacks and stowing booty and engaged in private pillage. Occasionally a thief would lose his balance and topple to the water, the hidden weight ensuring he did not surface. Hardy and his squad collected their trove and returned in the overladen skiff to the mother ship. It had been a successful morning, one of episode and surprise. Yet it had not changed things, had not slowed the Armada, had not altered the lingering prospect of a murder attempt by agents unknown against the Queen.

~

On pain of being hanged from their own yardarms, the captains of the Armada were commanded by Medina Sidonia into tight formations rear and forward. The Captain-General was in no mood to lose further stragglers or capital ships to the predatory thrusts of the English. Any who placed boldness before duty, who deviated from his rigid battle-order, would die. His Majesty dictated it, and he would execute. Mercifully the English were in disarray and low on shot, their pursuing galleons streaming miles behind, their commanders blown from the scent by the errant and avaricious ways of Drake. In snuffing his stern-light, Sir Francis had afforded the Spaniards a brief respite. They took advantage of it, coursing past Berry Head and Hope's Nose, leaving in their wake the enemy to bicker over profits and bring as prize the *Rosario* to Torbay. As evening drew in at the close of that day, the two defensive blocks of the Armada were paralleling the ragged Dorset clifftops, their impetus sustained. The morrow would bring fresh event.

At last Medina Sidonia had the weather-gauge and his chance. In the grained early light of Tuesday 23 July 1588 – four days since first sighting of the Spanish – the English navy royal had misjudged. Observing the wind swerve north-east, and eager to resume attack, Lord Admiral Howard had moved to lead his ships on an inner tack close to shore. A manoeuvre predicted by the foe. With booming cannon and show of force, Medina Sidonia organized to head them off. He needed to break and bloody them, reduce their strength, apply his firepower to gain mastery and free passage of the Channel. There was every possibility he might crush the irksome Protestants against the majestic rock projection of Portland Bill or strew their wreckage the pebbled length of Chesil Beach.

Again the prey were nimble, sliding by on the races and leaving the cumbersome Spaniards astern. But some proved slower. Among them was Frobisher aboard his one-thousand-ton *Triumph*, the largest vessel in the English fleet and now prevented from escape. A tempting objective for the Spanish, and worthy redress for the *Rosario* and *San Salvador* and the misfortunes already suffered. No matter the Armada hung in the lee. Assets existed to exploit such moment and improve the odds, to bring overwhelming arms to bear upon vulnerable English oak. Medina Sidonia ordered up his galleasses.

Stationed on the stern platform of the *San Lorenzo*, the English renegade Realm delighted to the sonorous beat of the kettle-drum and heavy sweep of the banks of oars. It was inspiring and sensual, an experience to savour and remember. Abreast were the three sister craft, the *Zúñiga*, the *Girona,* the *Napolitana,* two hundred guns in all closing with each stroke on the English laggards. A fine sight, an unrivalled feeling. He had waited so long for a time as this, had dreamed of vengeance and battle against the hateful sinners of his homeland. A swift assault on a trapped detachment of the arch-enemy would scarce affect his ultimate goal.

'Increase the rate.' Hugo de Moncada, commander of the galleasses, called out his orders and heard them echo-repeated by the officers below. 'Stand to your guns.'

The boat heaved as three hundred oarsmen strained on their benches in response to the lash and the powering tempo. In any sprint, there were always casualties. Elsewhere the crew were racing to prepare, fetching up powder and lifting the ports, running out their fifty cannon.

'We snare them well. The *Triumph, Merchant Royal, Quittance* and *Advantage.* All to be ground between our guns and the shore.' Moncada paced about in nervous vigour.

His English guest seemed more restrained. 'Should we not stay celebration until the act is done?'

'Our foe is cornered and we sit in the vanguard of attack. Is it not cause to smile, *Reino*?'

'It is reason for both thankfulness and care.'

'You are no mariner, *Reino*.'

'As Frobisher is no coward or drip-nosed schoolboy.' Realm directed a contained glance towards the commander. 'Yet I would dear wish to see him bleed to a round-shot or a straight-edged blade.'

'Then we are in accord.'

Triumph interrupted their discourse, her broadside aimed low and raking the moving tier of oars. A simple countermeasure that forced the galleasses to instant backstroke and chaotic retreat. It was a temporary setback. They circled warily, waiting as Medina Sidonia chased through with the heaviest of his galleons. An end would be brought to the rude resistance.

Realm examined a yard-length of splinter jutting from a capstan. 'Your endeavour is outfoxed, Captain.'

'We lick our wounds, but these English will soon enough eat their own entrails. The Duke shall see to it.' The convulsing noise and pall of smoke encompassing the *Triumph* appeared confirmation of his prophecy.

'For myself, I prefer more subtle duel.'

'So speaks our chosen one, a man anointed, a shadow agent impressed on us by Garza.'

'You doubt my worth?'

'Weighed against the might of Armada, I question your effect and the wisdom of a Jesuit.' Hugo de Moncada slapped his hand on the breech of a stern-saker. 'A man without true name is no more than a mystery or wraith, *Reino*.'

'I am happy to dwell in such domain.'

'And I am obliged to fulfil my task.'

'Once more we are in accord.' Realm regarded his host, his casualness conveying seniority, his lack of obvious rank allowing him control.

Moncada had paled. Yet it was not the frightened acquiescence of a junior. His stare was roving from the topsails to the land and out to sea. He had detected change, the delicate rotation of the wind south–south–west and the weather-gauge for assault flowing back to the main body of the English fleet. Shapes formed on the horizon. In line-astern and with full sail, Drake, Howard and a vast division were bearing down upon the Spanish.

So far, all was to the good. But there was no time for complacency, no place in this role or life to participate in early jubilation and relief. Sir Francis Walsingham stood with a coterie of his private secretaries in the shade of a coppice on the Richmond heathlands and looked out across the scattered herds of red and fallow deer. For the Queen this season there would be no carousing or joyous indulgence in the hunt. Her days, her hours, were instead filled with meetings of her council and decisions of war and state. Elizabeth was remarkably composed in the circumstance. The Channel seemed far off; the clash of ships and roared exchange of culverins dwelt in a dimension separate from that inhabited by court. Drake had matters in hand and was driving the Spaniards on.

The spy-chief tracked a solitary cloud riding high and northward on the vaster blue. Factors always emerged to sully the picture. He thought of the encrypted message sent by the enemy and intercepted by his agents. *When the blood-red light of a sickle moon casts deadly spell upon the river waters, and when the bastard throne is toppled, arise and claim vengeance upon the unjust foe.* It would not have been written without intention to launch revolt and foretell the slaying of Her Majesty. Much was clear. The Armada had arrived in crescent formation, as a sickle moon, was proceeding in harried fashion for the Isle of White and the mouth of the river Solent. To date, the riddle made sense. But there was scant indication of likely treachery, no chatter from the northern and most Catholic shires pointing to insurrection and the raising of armies. Conceivably the coded letter was no more than a fervent wish. He had deployed scores of his Searchers into the field to guarantee it did not mature to a dark reality. Something remained, however: the toppling of the 'bastard throne'. Mr Hunter, the Scots merchant-mariner captured and since deceased in Lisbon, had warned as much. Assassin or assassins were out there.

A flash of colour caught his attention. Isaiah Payne was ever punctual, approached in the oblique and fidgeting manner that defined him from other men. It provoked no obvious response in Walsingham. He was accustomed to the vicious eccentricities of his chief Searcher, relied on his methods and excess to remove the canker of popery from the living tissue of England. Personal taste had no relevance.

Payne presented himself with an ingratiating flourish. 'Such restful and wondrous idyll, your honour.'

'To be abandoned when Her Majesty removes for her safety to the walled confines of St James.'

'You journey there soon, your honour?'

'Within days and when the Queen is minded.'

'In time, no doubt, for glorious celebration and triumphal parade.'

'Business in the Channel is not yet complete. Our own is elsewhere.' The hooded eyes of Walsingham scrutinized his underling. 'My elf has been diligent?'

'I labour in your service each hour of day and night, your honour.'

'To what result? Have you found for me the ledger of Catholic names, that list of suspected traitors and Hispaniolates I know Christian Hardy will have borne from his foray to Lisbon?'

'We search his haunts, your honour. We delve in orchards and pleasure-gardens, in his favoured taverns from the Plough to the Bear. We even gain entry to his home.'

'Yet you discover nothing.'

'You train him well, your honour.'

'His conscience is his own. There lies the rub.'

It grieved him to distrust his young warrior–agent Hardy. But to be spymaster was a singular and unsentimental vocation. His priority was greater than the individual, outweighed friendship or rank, loyalty or feeling, or the longevity of life. Such principle had brought to the scaffold a cousin to the Queen. He would baulk at little in preserving the English Crown.

He turned to different matters. 'What gossip from the provinces, Mr Payne?'

'Scarce any item to vex or disconcert, your honour.' Isaiah Payne bobbed in anxious reflex. 'Every papist who poses threat is held captive. Any papist who covets his existence swears allegiance to the throne.'

'Until the "bastard throne" is toppled.' Walsingham repeated beneath his breath the words of the secret Spanish communiqué.

'All is as still as the grave at night, your honour.'

'It is the worms and insects we do not see, the very stillness we must fear.' He paused to think, dwelling briefly on his own imminent passage to the tomb. 'No word of revolt?'

'None, your honour.'

'Of plot to kill Her Majesty?'

'Likewise, naught to arouse our suspicion or concern.'

'Is there recent event or passing crime to cause alarm? An unexpected incident in London to draw our eye?'

Isaiah Payne shifted in his vivid clothing. 'Occasional murder and the random acts of knaves, harlots and cut-throats. The city is the city, your honour.'

'Some would deem it the sewer.'

'It being so, one of its rats these two days past saw fit to slay his baying persecutor, an apprentice.'

'The rodent is held?'

'He is dead, your honour.' The chief Searcher introduced a metal object to his palm and surrendered it for examination. 'Butchered by his own hand and with this knife.'

Walsingham turned the bone-trimmed haft between his fingers, engaged the catch and released a sprung stiletto. An item of beauty and workmanship.

'I have encountered these things in the ports of Italy, Mr Payne. A device from Constantinople.'

'They say the corpse was that of an Ottoman, your honour.'

'An Ottoman so afraid of our retribution he takes his life.' Walsingham retracted the blade and passed it to a secretary. 'Perchance terror drives a man to such. Perhaps many dwell within this realm who would drive such blade in me.'

Mirth arose and the meeting was ended, the different parties going their way.

Out at sea, Drake and his cohorts pounded the stately Spanish galleons; on land at Tilbury, the Earl of Leicester as commander of the Queen's army assembled a force some four thousand strong to guard the eastern approaches to London. *Naught to arouse our suspicion or concern.* Sir Francis Walsingham was neither convinced nor cheered by the news. For news could be partial and misleading, wrongly confirming or wholly confusing, as accurate as a guess or as deceiving as a lie. He was unlikely to be fooled.

~

'Over fifty thousand golden ducats, Don Pedro.' Drake beamed and refilled the goblet of his captive Spanish guest. 'Your *Rosario* is a fine gift of King Philip.'

'I would be more shamed to have surrendered her to other Englishman, *El Draque*.'

'You honour me, Don Pedro.'

'I recognize the worth of an adversary.'

'Adversary, Don Pedro? We are fellow mariners and friends.'

The Spaniard was content to agree and to converse in his mother tongue. It had been a dramatic two days since the seizing of his vessel, a time spent being entertained by Drake and watching from temporary incarceration aboard the pinnace *Roebuck* as the legendary English sailor rejoined battle off Portland Bill. Now he sat with his subordinate Captain Alvarez in the main cabin of the *Revenge* and again enjoyed the hearty largesse of Sir Francis. The wine they tasted was familiar and of Spanish grape. It came from supplies liberated by the Englishman a year before in his attack upon Cadiz. Everything went full circle.

Nodding at the irony, Don Pedro de Valdés raised his cup in salute towards Hardy. 'If there is one to whom I owe my present fate, it is this young and vengeful demon, *El Draque*.'

'He is the best on board my ship, Don Pedro.'

'Would that he was on mine.' The Spanish admiral leaned across the table. 'It was a daring and splendid display, señor.'

Hardy acknowledged with a smile. 'There were good friends and providence to guide me, sir.'

'And speed of blade and quickness of skill to cow my entire crew.'

Drake busied himself with a quid of baccy. 'You lose your vessel yet retain your honour, Don Pedro. For such, I will return to you, your captain and your gentlemen your personal treasure of several thousand reals.'

'Your kindness deserves praise, *El Draque*.'

'It shall not lessen the bounty placed by your king on my pirate head.'

'His Majesty is not your truest admirer.'

'Though he remains the greatest source of my wealth.' The

Englishman chewed amused on his tobacco. 'He would take less pleasure to see the punishment we mete his fleet.'

'Do you break us, *El Draque*? Do you sink a single one of our ships? Do you halt or divert for one heartbeat Medina Sidonia from his task?'

'Our Channel is long and our force not yet spent.'

'Then there is much left to play for.' Don Pedro drank from his cup.

Hardy matched him and placed down his vessel. 'What game does the Jesuit priest Garza play, sir?'

'That of future Inquisitor General of England.'

'He will find himself waiting.' Hardy maintained his gaze.

'You know of him?'

'I do. Is he with the fleet?'

'Aboard *El Gran Grin*, and content as any cleric may be in a storm.'

Hosts and guests laughed in camaraderie, their differences forgotten and their humanity shared. The rigours of naval warfare forged a common bond. Politics and religion might be debated, could even provoke heated exchange, but mutual courtesy and respect and a well-laid table provided ample reason for joviality.

'You enjoy our music, Don Pedro?' Drake tilted his head towards the sound of horn and drums.

'It surpasses in its delights the noise of battle.'

'Something to soothe the thought and calm the soul. I take my musicians wheresoever I voyage.'

'They must travel wide.'

'Indeed they do, Don Pedro. Such beat is the pulsing heart of England. There is not a man in our nation to resist its call.'

At least one exception was alive and at large. High on the western downs of the Isle of Wight, the Catholic agent who had travelled from London watched as the sun dipped and cast a softening hue across the Needles. A moment of splendour and reflection. Advancing on his position, still hidden beyond view, would be the ships of the Armada and the chasing English fleet. They were drawing near. He could read it in the wind, in the rumours and tension, in the galleons loading and tacking out to stiffen the defensive screen. How desperately the Protestants fought. He would maintain his vigil and hold his nerve, for patience and conviction were demanded by the Lord. Not long to go. In a while, and when least expected, what had been planned would come to be and what the English most feared would strike at their core. He was looking forward to the rendezvous.

Chapter 15

It had been a ferocious rearguard action, Drake ever worrying the slowest and weakest, and the Spanish responding with the sluggish predictability that their size and the nature of their commander dictated. The little corsair of Queen Elizabeth had the weather-gauge, and he would use it. At one point he almost cut a prized and armed merchantman from the solid formation, clawing near to deliver repeated broadsides and winnow the enemy crew. He had learned from previous engagements, and the adversary suffered for it. Double-shot at close range could inflict a deadly punishment. What saved *El Gran Grifon* was a failing of the wind that drove the English back and stayed their hand. The Spaniard shambled on. But between her decks was a dim and curious scene lit by the lanterns of her work-details: the sight of teeth and bone lodged in ceilings, of blood coagulating on every surface, and of hair and flesh and brain scattered randomly all about. The morning of Wednesday 24 July 1588, five days since the Armada was first seen. With the Isle of Wight in view, the risk had not been higher.

Day fell into night, and the opposing parts could once more disentangle and find succour among their own. There was every chance Medina Sidonia would attempt to seize the island, would on the following day gain the eastern approach of the Solent and swing round to make his stand. The English prepared. They needed to be alert, needed to organize, needed to put aside their jealousies and selfish greed. Out in the darkness, an object was moving.

She came in slow, one of the four oared galleasses moving ahead while the ships of sail in the Armada lay becalmed to her stern. The *San Lorenzo* had a most particular assignment. It was as though she searched for something, picking her way along the southern edge of the island, stealing by without illumination or any noise save the dip and pull of wooden blades. Her commander was not expecting interruption, though was ready for such occurrence. His gun-crews stood by with grapeshot loaded, his lookouts scanned both coast and sea, his wheelman and pilot sensed every tone of the current and slap of a wave. There would be no allowance for failure.

'We have them. Three lanterns. A red, a white, a green.'

'You are certain?'

'They are there on the beach, Admiral. I have no doubt.'

'Lower the boat.'

Hugo de Moncada, flagship commander of the galleasses, controlled his voice and the relief that flooded into it. He had not quite shaken off the embarrassment of Portland Bill, the indignity of being forced from the action by a few low and well-aimed shots from Frobisher and the *Triumph*. Redemption came in many forms. No ordinary vessel could perform this task, no other commander undertake so daring a mission. He was honoured and eager to assist as bearer of bad tidings to Albion. Beside him, the Englishman code-named Realm checked a sword-buckle and adjusted his leather jerkin. Quite the local soldier.

'You return to your native soil, *Reino*.'

'As avenger and not as friend.'

'Perchance we shall again meet when invasion is done and the writ of King Philip prevails.'

'We shall have some tales to share.'

'There will be more yet to tell.' Hugo de Moncada proffered his hand. 'I bid you fair travel and good fortune.'

'Each is in the hand of God.'

Farewell was over, and Realm made his way forward to the small cluster of sailors and the ladder they had hooked into place. There was no turning from the plan, had never been any doubt. He breathed deep and savoured the security of the deck. A mere two hundred yards divided him from the shore, the narrowest expanse representing the most challenging of steps. Anything could happen. His contact might be captured or dead, the landing compromised, the sand-shingle and the fields beyond crawling with the armed response of Sir Francis Walsingham. Only the naive underestimated the reach of the Principal Secretary of State. Yet honour and portent lay in this moment, advantage with those who dared. Without further word, he clambered over and descended to the open boat. The long-cherished dream of Inquisitor Garza was emerging to reality.

His crew did well, rowing him to land with unwavering nerve and a steady stroke. He was alone again, waiting for encounter, his feet planted wide and his heartbeat rising. There was nothing quite like the opening phase. Around him were the smell of seaweed and stagnant brine, the flow and suck of water. Extraordinary things could occur in an unremarkable setting. It was nice to be home.

'You come far, brother.' The voice was low and from beyond the cramped flare of the lanterns.

'How long do you wait for me?'

'A lifetime and more.'

'So approach and give me greeting.' Realm held wide his arms as the Catholic moved forward, with a rapid sidestep turned embrace into a stranglehold. 'You would harm me?'

'I would not.'

'Betray me?'

'Never.' The response was forced through a constricted throat and clenched teeth. 'On the life of my mother and the Word of the Holy Book.'

'Do you take them in vain?'

'I risk all to aid you.'

Realm slackened his grip. 'For it, I give you my thanks.'

'I am loath to suffer your scorn.' The agent massaged his neck and swallowed saliva back into his bruised throat.

There were tasks to perform, the dousing of the signal-lamps and the removal of any evidence that a meeting had occurred. Sweeping clean the traces was part of the double life. The two men loped to a hollow worn in the lazy incline and crouched among the marram and wire grasses to assess and to confer.

Realm listened for a while. 'No parties appear to search for us.'

'For our enemy does not suspect.' The Catholic guide allowed a trace of satisfaction to his words. 'We are the wolf in the night, the beast that outruns the governor and his hounds.'

'Mistaken confidence may kill the predator.'

'I reach this destination and will deliver you to yours, brother. It is my obligation and my vow.'

'Such fellowship is welcome. Such steadfastness is to be commended.'

'We share common devotion and a sacred cause.'

'This is true.' Instinctively, Realm grasped a powdering handful of rock and trickled it through his fist. 'That I once more should feel our treasured earth is a miracle which fills me with hope.'

'Within short bound we shall find the mainland, brother.

After it, a journey to Lyndhurst and collection of the horses. Then on to Winchester and London.'

'You will accompany me?'

'Each step and to the glory of God. The Protestants array themselves here to the east to thwart Spanish intrusion. We shall slip by and will not be challenged.'

'All endeavour must be taken to prevent discovery.'

'Rest assured, brother.' A fraternal hand clapped Realm on his shoulder.

Lonely exile was in the past. Years spent in Madrid and Lisbon, the training of the Janissaries, the murder of captives in St George's Castle, the evolution of a plan. Delay and setback had tested his resolve. Yet he endured, had survived even confrontation with intelligencers sent by Walsingham from England. They had discovered little. While they were aware of neither his intrigue nor identity, he had learned the name of their young commander, of the transient lover of Constança Menezes, of the agile duellist who had placed a scar upon his cheek. Christian Hardy would rue the night in the Alfama he had lunged with a drawn blade. His countrymen would equally regret another night-time, when the wind was slack and the moon cowled and a galleass came calling on the shore.

~

In the morning light, immobilized by the lack of wind, the two contesting fleets bobbed listless to the south of Dunnose Head. With its cliffs and underwater ledges and its fast-flowing currents, the coastline of the Isle of Wight could prove a hazardous location. Each rival preferred to keep his distance, neither wanting to commit. Better to eye the opposition and perform repairs. A wary respite of sorts. There was no telling what Medina Sidonia might attempt, no foolproof prediction of where his forces were headed. Occasionally a warning shot was fired or rowing-boats deployed to edge a ship around. It was a time to gather strength and an environment in which miscalculation could mean disaster.

Not all were content to accept inertia and the status quo. Two Armada ships had loosened from their formation and fallen behind: the galleon *San Luis* and the armed hulk *Castillo Negro* – red meat for English seafarers hungry and so far denied their prize. Becalmed he may have been, yet the veteran John Hawkins had every intent to claim a kill and lead his centre squadron into decisive contact. He gave his orders. Longboats were launched, their crews heaving on oars and towing the *Victory* behind. She was moving near, would be swung into position and unleash her broadside to devastating effect. But the enemy replied.

Musket-fire peppered the small boats, spattering the works and felling the unprotected rowers. It was a rout. As miniature spouts of water plumed about them, as limbs tangled and sudden wounds gaped wide, the survivors bent to their retreat in a flurried splash of oars. Their enemy were not finished. The *Victory* was forward and exposed, unsupported by the rest and presented for the seizing. It provoked a rush. Spanish galleons and galleasses spread towards her, absorbing their own stragglers and pinching close on the defiant Hawkins. He was fortunate other craft were in the water, rowing-boats that frantically aligned the *Ark Royal* and the *Golden Lion* for the massed delivery of their shot. A fluid situation, the give and take of battle. Through the rolling banks of powder-smoke, Hawkins left the scene.

Distress-cannon sounded and a warning ensign raced to a masthead. It signalled a change, a resumption of the southerly breeze and the imminent snaring of an English ship caught in the lee and shadow of the enemy formations. The tide pushed the vessel further within their reach. Frobisher and his *Triumph* were again in difficulty.

'*El Draque! El Draque! El Draque!*'

It was a familiar cry and the worst of news, a violent puncturing of any Spanish belief that they controlled events or might ever gain the upper hand. The nightmare scourge was returned. From seaward, attacking from the quarter he valued most, Drake brought his squadron to bear. There would be no let-up now, no opportunity for the Armada to curve gracefully and in unhurried order into the opening of the Solent. The dismal tidings volleyed inbound on a swarm of black and screaming cannonballs.

'Would you conceive of it?' The cupped hand to the face of the English vice admiral did little to disguise his pleasure. '*Triumph* becomes a ship named *Ruin*. Frobisher is once more in the throes of trouble.'

Hardy shared in the joke. 'You will ever come to set him free him, sir.'

'I am at times persuaded to watch him turn.'

'Is this such occasion?'

'Sadly, it is not. Our Yorkshireman does us favour, puts himself in danger and thus swallows in the foe. They are made ragged and undefended.'

A brutal overview of conditions that played out in a hundred fights and offered possibility to a master gamesman. The scrapping melee whirled on the current past Bordwood Ledge and Luccombe Bay, a flux of punches thrown and thrusts deflected, each side scratching for the lead. Frobisher had crawled from danger, the *Triumph* towed awkwardly by her eleven-strong team of rowing-boats. He would not be thanking Drake for his intervention. Nor would Medina Sidonia. The Spanish captain-general had committed the *San Martin* to a desperate rearguard charge, had held the centre and seen his mainstay

286

shot away as his other ships jostled to escape. Winds, current and *El Draque* had conspired to ruin everything.

On board the *Revenge*, the cannon rippled an emphatic *feu de joie* and the Irish dog Fearnot chased through the smoke in barking ferocity from the fo'c's'le to the stern.

Drake gripped a halyard and raised himself for a better view. 'Recall this day, Christian. The twenty-fifth of July in the year of 1588. How we broke the Spaniard and chased him past St Catherine's Point. How we shattered his spirit and ended his dream.'

'I do not see him destroyed, sir.'

'You observe the wrong signs.' Sir Francis breathed as though tasting the air and testing its form. 'Our job is near done and nature succeeds us to take her course.'

'Our shot scarce harms the enemy, sir.'

'Yet our sorcery and witchcraft shall. We crowd the foe, Christian. We harry his flock. We herd him ever onward.'

'Is this the same as victory?'

'It is akin to our salvation.'

'You jest, sir?'

'What scarce faith for one who stood with me in the furnace of Cadiz.' Drake winked amused at his junior. 'The Spaniard may no longer enter the Solent, no longer find anchor or succour on our shore. The wind and tide are our closest allies, and the shoals become our dear friend.'

That was it, the clue, the answer. Ahead of the Armada, where it was driven north-eastward by the wind and the flank-ing raids of Drake, lay Selsey Bill projecting from the mainland. In itself it posed a hazard. But below it, churning and breaking the water, was a more menacing threat: the trailing shoals and infamous shallows of the Owers Banks. Their four-mile spine of ragged boulders would rip the hulls and heart from any fleet. Medina Sidonia saw the risk. He could not manoeuvre

287

freely, could not negotiate a passage through. His sole chance and only choice was to veer south-south-east on an outward tack. The Armada put about and headed to sea.

At the extreme right of the force, stationed on board the *San Mateo* and watching the prows of vessels plunge and buck against the waves, the eighteen-year-old Salvador sensed the plight of his fellow pilgrims. How ridiculous they seemed, and how superfluous their actions. As the once-proud Armada creaked on to its easterly setting, coaxing its ships like the dragging of its entrails, the Isle of Wight disappeared astern. Another waypoint reached and gone and an opportunity missed. The young Portuguese noble had already completed his grieving. For the wasted hope, the wasted lives, the wasted mission. There was nothing that could be done.

He was back among his countrymen, and he did not much care for them. Accompanied by the Catholic agent, Realm ascended the steep dirt track that bisected the coastal town of Lymington. Its folk smiled at him as if wishing to share glad tidings, as though he were one of them. He would never be one of them. Yet he was pleasant in his response, mirrored with gusto their optimism and zeal. After all, Drake had roundly beaten off attack and chased the Spanish from the Isle of Wight and out to sea, was already the toast of every Hampshire tavern. So the English renegade and his associate joined in the self-congratulation. A welcome here and a knowing chuckle there. Just comrades-in-arms passing through.

They walked on towards the old church, leaving behind the bustling quayside and its surrounding clusters of whitewashed cottages. On the green outside an inn, men and women were drinking and dancing, liberated from immediate danger and stood down from their duties. Trust-filled eyes scarcely noticed the strangers. Realm was content to belong. Beside him, his collaborator strolled and perspired, plainly feeling the strain. There was little to worry about, scant reason to expect discovery, and many an excuse should it arise. Lucky these fools could not read his heart or view his soul; fortunate too they remained unaware that the sword at his belt, with its spiral guards and straight two-edged blade, was made of Spanish steel. The damage he would inflict.

Close by the church, fields opened up and the smell of earth and farmyards replaced the salt air of the waterfront. The two companions were moving inland. There were plentiful wagons on which to hitch a ride, the transport of choice for armed irregulars paralleling the seaborne action. The recent influx of conscripts and volunteers would soon become an exodus. It was nice to be part of a crowd, to sit at the rear of a cart lurching on its journey. Realm lifted his hand and waved to a passer-by. People were so cheery and grateful.

Over one hundred and forty English men-of-war had gathered off the Sussex coast, a vast assembly of naval power never before encountered at a home mooring. There were the four divisions of Howard, Drake, Hawkins and Frobisher, the squadrons of Sir Henry Seymour and Sir William Winter, the individual commands of young gallants flocking from London to pursue the kill. It seemed they would be disappointed. The Armada had escaped across the Channel for Calais, while its would-be nemesis sprawled uneasily at anchor and foraged for supply. Shot was spent and powder low, reserves of drink and biscuit nearly gone. Still worse, sickness was spreading through the crews. Sunday 28 July 1588, nine days since first sighting of the Spanish and two since last engagement off the Isle of Wight. A gulf existed between intention and reality, a stretch of water separated the English from enacting a decisive blow.

At the table of Lord Admiral Howard on his flagship *Ark Royal*, the mood was one infected with recrimination and rancour. Drake was there, his friends attending. But so also was Martin Frobisher, and he was no ally. Strain of battle and frustration at the chase, a natural envy and abiding hate, each fed the irascibility of the gruff Yorkshireman towards Sir Francis. An incendiary combination. The calm indifference of the legendary vice admiral was unlikely to improve affairs.

Frobisher jabbed an accusatory finger. 'You steal from us, Drake. You enrich yourself at our expense. You pillage from us all.'

'I supposed the *Rosario* to be a ship of the Armada.'

'Do not goad me, Drake. You douse your stern-lantern, turn your ship and show your back, abandon your position by night to plunder for yourself.'

'It is no crime of which I know.'

'Some would deem it treason. Some would claim you endangered our fleet.'

'While others may say I perceived a threat to our south and discharged my duty as would any loyal servant.'

'What would your pirate sensibility know of duty?'

Frobisher glared, his wrath inflamed by the dismissive civility of his adversary. The little corsair had no conscience or integrity, clearly did not plan to share in his good fortune.

The Yorkshireman tried again. 'Fifty thousand ducats or more, Drake. Such sweet accident of fate, and so fine a profit for your coffers.'

'God and providence bless me.'

'As mere men are apt to curse.' A nerve flickered below the eye as Frobisher leaned to force his point. 'We who made same effort sit about you. We, your brother captains who meet equal perils of campaign, are denied a single penny.'

'I judged you to be busied, Frobisher. I deemed you

cornered, as is your way, by a host of Spanish galleons.' There was laughter, but it went unshared by the commander of the inner squadron.

'Is this all you offer, Drake?'

'I recall saving your ship and neck on several occasion. Find your prize and you shall earn.'

A fist slammed hard on wood. 'Answer me, Drake. By what right have you higher claim than we to Spanish gold?'

'Possession.'

'You wrong us. You deceive us.'

'Not by the law of this land nor custom of the sea.' Drake tilted his head in sly and affable condescension. 'Such choleric spleen, Frobisher. Recent knighthood scarce improves your humour or distemper.'

'I shall give you distemper, will proffer you duel.'

Antipathy had reached its natural zenith. In the pandemonium of roared insult and rowdy exchange, Frobisher had jumped to his feet but was tussled to a standstill. Through the confusion, his bewhiskered and colour-flooded face gaped in wild belligerence. Captains jostled and took sides. Mariners were unafraid to voice opinion.

A semblance of order was reinstated, Lord Admiral Howard imposing his will with a tired smile and a refusal to notice. Energies were bound to flow into confrontation which generally subsided when new challenge presented.

'An army lies across the water, gentlemen. Close to it sits the Armada in the roads of Calais. Neither is yet vanquished.'

A senior captain spoke up. 'It will remain so until the Queen and her council see way to provision us with fresh shot and powder.'

'I will swear to it.' Another commander added his complaint. 'There is not a ship among us with full resource to prosecute an action.'

From the far end, a third voice intervened. 'What are we to do, my lord? Pick stones from the beach and hurl them at the foe?'

'At last, a plan.' The joke was bitter and fell away unloved.

Conversation swung back down the table. 'My men have no food, my lord. They are wearied and grow sick, lose stomach for the fight.'

'And yet.' The Lord Admiral propped his chin on his hand and surveyed them all. 'Without renewed vigour and devotion to the hunt, we leave England abandoned. More damnable yet, we surrender defence of our Queen and nation to the Earl of Leicester and his army in Essex.'

Muttered derision and disgruntled snorts greeted the short summary. There was no love and limited respect for the ageing courtier and incompetent soldier Leicester. But the comments of the Lord Admiral directed thoughts and focused ambition.

Smarting from his earlier quarrel, Frobisher slumped hostile in his chair. 'No doubt Sir Francis will tempt us with response.'

'Fireships.'

'Of course. He plucks it like a magician does a trick from his sleeve.'

Drake aimed his gaze at Howard. 'I give you stratagem and no trick, my lord. It achieved before, and will succeed again.'

'Speak on, Sir Francis.'

'We must break up the Spaniard, disperse him to the wind and waves. There is no finer chance or more pressing need.'

'The weather is with us.'

'Moment too.' The Vice Admiral stared around the table. 'Already I prepare vessels and urge you to the same. Our fight with Spain is not complete.'

In the aftermath of conference, the commanders hurried to descend to their skiffs and longboats and take passage to their ships. Alone, Drake strode along the deck of the *Ark Royal* and sought out his messenger. The man was expecting him.

'Send word to Christian Hardy. The hell-burners sail.'

~

'It is over.'

There was a dread finality to the words of Medina Sidonia. In the cabin of his flagship *San Martin*, his admirals had gathered to hear the contents of the letter held taut in his fingers. It was a message from the Duke of Parma, communication from the general for whose army they had travelled far and weathered storms and braved the fury of the English. The previous night they had made it to Calais, had slunk by the light of a full moon to find anchorage in the roadstead current. To listen to this. Some trembled, some paled, some wiped a glistening tear from the corner of their eye. Dejection registered on every face.

Well it might, for the promise of a landing force ready for embarkation had proved illusory. Invasion would not come to pass. The once vaunted band of hardened veterans some thirty thousand strong was diminished by malaria and dysentery to a shadow of sixteen thousand men. Those left were going nowhere. To confound the Netherlands enemy and protect against counter-attack, Parma had not brought his troops up to the coast. There his trials would only begin. The shallow-draught barges were unprepared and their havens blockaded by prowling Dutch fleets of armed and agile flyboats. Move from their sanctuaries and the Spanish regiments faced massacre. Stalemate was an ugly place.

'Dunkirk, Antwerp, Sluys and Nieuport.' Medina Sidonia spoke with the slow delivery of the condemned. 'The chosen points for embarkation. Each is assailed and invested by enemy craft, none may load or release barges without fear of tragedy.'

'May we not aid them, your grace?' A half-hearted suggestion for a desperate measure.

The Captain-General appraised the speaker. 'How?'

'Send our pinnaces and offer fight, your grace.'

'Our force is too few and they are too many. Therein is the truth of our dilemma. Through threat of shoals and bars, the Armada is obliged to stand off at least ten miles. A distance Parma and his army dare not cross by open barge for fear of being butchered.'

'Why must we lend effort to an army that scarce exists, an army reduced by ague and the flux?'

Another voice backed the previous. 'If Parma wishes to proceed, he alone should force the pace.'

'Is it not the task of soldiers to try, your grace?'

'It is not the role of their commanders to squander them in vain.' The Captain-General placed down the letter and smoothed it flat. 'Six days it will take for Parma to muster and arrange his force. Meantime we sit and wait and gather our resolve.'

'All the while, the English fleet is undefeated.'

Medina Sidonia nodded. 'Thus we must guard our position and resource.'

'Shall the English lessen their endeavour, your grace? Will they hesitate to inflict on us their spite?'

'We are safe as we may ever be.'

'Yet you say yourself it is over.' It was Admiral Recalde who broke his own silence. 'No Armada is created to stay idle at anchor, no fleet secure until it puts to sea.'

'Would you have us brave the winds of the northern waters, Admiral?'

'I would brave anything but long sojourn at Calais.'

Medina Sidonia sensed disunity. 'While we are here we persuade and influence event, may yet gain advantage in negotiation with the heretic queen Elizabeth.'

'If she does not seek parley, your grace?'

Admiral Leiva had joined in debate, a senior figure as distraught as any at the grim unfolding of dispatches. He and Recalde had defended first the flanks and then the rear of the Armada, had experienced the increased vehemence and ferocity of the English attacks.

His gaze was unwavering. '*El Draque* will not let matters lie, your grace. As we rest, he will plan. As we speak, he will send hell-burners to wreak havoc in our midst.'

'I am aware of his appetites.' Medina Sidonia distractedly waved his hand. 'We have all precaution against eventuality.'

Yet it was still over.

Preparing a fireship was both alchemy and an art. It took the mind of a brigand and the tactics of Drake to bring it to conclusion and apply it with effect. Combustibles needed to be placed and illusion created, a trick of light and size produced that would provoke terror and a mindless impulse to flee. None wished to be caught in its path. A single spark could set rigging ablaze, a travelling flame could start inferno. Mariners had every reason to fear conflagration at sea. In a compacted fleet of wooden hulls, each of which contained a powder magazine, anxieties would be multiplied. As they worked to fit out the two-hundred-ton barque abutting a jetty at Dover, Hardy and his companions understood the import of what they did. One success could alter irrevocably the outcome of war; one mistake would see them die. They applied themselves to their task with care.

There was not much in the way of talk, not even the altercations that so often flared when Luqa and Hawkhead combined their effort. This morning they laboured apart. Swinging in a makeshift harness, the dour little English sailor engaged himself in smearing the masts and rigging with thick coatings of tar and pitch. A pinch of saltpetre, a sprinkling of gunpowder, and there would be a display to remember. The Maltese islander was occupied elsewhere. He knelt on the main deck, hunched over with a chisel and mallet, was scoring a channel in the planking to ease the powder run. About him were a scattering of tools and earthen jars, the resins and naphtha, the spirits and linseed, essentials for the execution. Attention to detail was part of the craft. Nothing would be overlooked.

Hardy clambered from below and surveyed with expert eye the progress of their toil. They were on schedule. In the hold he had placed kindling and bales of straw-soaked in rum, had laid powder-kegs and pots of brimstone topped with canvas fuses. All were connected, everything garlanded by hanging twists of oil-steeped oakum that climbed to the upper works. At the key moment and with a slow-match, when the wind was fair and the rudder set, the process would start and the magic begin. Across the Channel, the galleons and transports of the Armada were nestling. It would challenge decorum to make them wait, would confound expectation to avoid deploying every weapon in the English arsenal.

The priming was complete. They came ashore for the last time, using the minutes to cough out the fumes and breathe fresh air, to check firearms and charts and bid farewell to watching crews. Escorting ships would take them so far, would wait at sea as darkness fell and the current turned and the principal mission went in. That was for later. Hardy splashed his face from a pail of water, Hawkhead chewed baccy and stropped his knives, Luqa held Fearnot and reassured his canine he would return. None observed the muted trembling of the Maltese islander. Departure was imminent.

How distant it all seemed, and how quiet the city. From the marbled balcony of her Lisbon palace, Constança looked out upon the Tagus and tried to imagine the river filled once more with ships. The Armada had been gone these two months past. It was as though it had never been, as though sacred conflict was never declared, as though Inquisitor Garza had never learned of her subterfuge and treachery. Yet the death sentence over her remained. She could live with it, at some unspecified future moment would surely die from it. The Inquisition rarely forgave.

Loneliness crept in, a dull emptiness that came of abandoned love and warmth and happier times. She wondered if Christian Hardy ever thought of her, if he was far from threat and wrapped content in the safe embrace of his family. Men such as he seldom found solace without a blade in their hand. She had been dazzled by him, intrigued by him, drawn and discarded by him; in another time she would repeat it all. Then there was Salvador, the beloved brother she had deceived and whose loyalties were once so different. In a letter sent from Corunna, he had forgiven her and asked in turn for absolution. Their father had been right, the Spanish wrong, the lives of good Catholics and patriots frittered on a careless war. The eighteen-year-old was now embarked on that campaign. She crossed herself and prayed for him, for Christian, for every sailor and soldier and soul committed by others to the fight. God hear her, and God help them.

Chapter 16

Night provided the illusion of concealment and safe haven, allowing the wounded Armada to rest if not to sleep. Lookouts watched and small boats patrolled, the men ever vigilant for the next move and malign trickery of the foe. A neutral port was no reason for complacency. Summer tides, a westerly breeze, and Flemish shoals to the lee ensured a precarious existence. It helped that the governor of Calais was a Frenchman and Catholic with a grudge, an ageing soldier who had lost a leg some thirty years before in hostile engagement with the English. The sentries and gunners on his fort would provide an early warning. So the ships sat in the open roads, anchored fore and aft and sheltering from uncertainty and the wider sea.

Somewhere a bell clanged, its tone dampened but insistent in the squalling gusts of rain. Shouts followed, feet thudding on decks as a cannon bellowed and mortar-flares popped to cast a brief and dazzling brilliance across the crowded scene. In an instant, nervousness had transformed to high alert. From the maintops and rails, from every different vantage, crewmen stared. They had detected movement, a hint that developed to a glow and blossomed into stronger light. Fireships were inbound. Through their own sulphurous mist they came, shadow-vessels glimmering and sparking and spread out on the wind. Eight of them. Flames were taking hold, leaping to the rigging, streaming up their masts, igniting fireworks and powder-barrels and cannon packed with double-shot. The Devil himself had sent them.

'*They will explode! They will consume us all!*'

'*Cut the anchors! In the name of God, do it quick!*'

'*We are finished!*'

'*Jesus Christ have mercy! Blessed Virgin save us!*'

A collective groan seemed to crawl from the throats of men too anguished and dumbstruck to articulate terror. Before them was the spectacle of impending inferno, around them a maelstrom of fright and haste. Escape had never been this chaotic. Hawsers were cut and anchors abandoned, sails tumbling and flapping for air, crews racing in blind confusion. Anything but to be caught in the path of the travelling pyres. If ships could carve through the hulls of others to assist in breakout, they would have tried. Savage disorder reigned. It was everything the English had hoped for, the confluence of skill and good fortune and a one-off investment. For some five thousand pounds, the treasury of England was forcing the pace and creating the rout of the entire Spanish Armada.

'They lie defenceless, Christian.' Hawkhead scanned ahead and put his foot up on the prow. 'Is it not time to light our fuse and take to the open boat?'

'When we are close and when I am sure.'

'Sure your breeches are alight? Sure we are well trapped among the Spaniard?'

'Pace and occasion are all, Hawkhead.'

'I merely observe that seven craft are ablaze and we are not; their crews depart and we do not.'

'A shilling for your insight.' Hardy laughed and called back to Luqa. 'Lash the wheel, brother.'

The deep report of cannon sounded to starboard, more theatre and deception heaped on the event. Each detonation increased the hustle and the torment, every spray of flame reflecting on the waters reminded that true hell-burners could explode. They might erupt at any moment. It explained why Spanish longboats stationed to head off such calamity were themselves pulling away at speed; it played on the fears of a military often bloodied by Dutch irregulars employing similar schemes. Hardy could almost smell the urgency.

'A boat remains, Hawkhead. You see it?'

'It turns on us, Christian. A brave act.'

'Or a foolhardy one.' Another shout to Luqa. 'Put the match to the fuse.'

There was a silent query from aft, a reluctance that carried in the brief hesitation. But Luqa trusted his commander and friend. The young Englishman applied the same method and battle-madness as his father to place himself in danger and by shrewd calculation of risk extract himself in time. A balancing-act. It was why Drake feted him. Yet it was Luqa who as a boy had knelt beside the corpse of the earlier Christian Hardy, who had witnessed the gunshot wounds and leaned to kiss the cooling forehead, who had lifted a small silver crucifix from the tilted throat and hung it about his own. With a shrug and without comment, the Mediterranean islander touched the glowing tip of the slow-match to the trail.

Events shifted, appearing to slow and accelerate in conflicting measure. A single flame moved fast along a canvas tube, splitting and evolving until its fiery offspring were darting through the barque on countless guided tangents. All pathways had their ending, were intended for a flashpoint. The fireship deserved its reputation. As barrels of pitch burned and the sheets and sails rippled with light, Hardy and Hawkhead discharged their arquebuses and sought to drive off the enemy. It counted little that their vessel was ablaze, mattered less that flaming debris was beginning to blanket them from above.

Hardy tightened the kerchief about his nose and mouth and rodded home another round. 'They did not expect a hell-burner to offer battle.'

'My surprise is equal.' Hawkhead loosed a shot, his features ever unsmiling.

'You lament joining me in comradely exploit? Sitting with Black Jack before my window and calling me out on quest?'

'Each day, Christian. Every hour of each day.'

'I value such truthfulness.'

'As I cherish my skin unburned.' Hawkhead blew excess powder from the breech and again raised his gun. 'You will yet be the death of me.'

With a forewarning crack, a spar dislodged and crashed alight to the deck in an angry riot of embers. The smoke was thickening now, the heat mounting and buckling the planks. The roaring of the fire had long succeeded the damp grumbling of the wind. It was almost time to leave.

Hardy stooped to plunge a length of canvas into a waiting pail of seawater. 'We fell enough of them, Hawkhead. They will little disturb us.'

'It is not their fire which diverts me.' The sailor shielded his face and peered upward. We are no safer than hogs at their own roast, Christian.'

'These hogs may still run. To my count, make ready.'

He emptied the pail over the head and clothing of his accomplice, crouched as incendiary fragments billowed and the cannon cooked off below. Three, two, one. The race began, the pair leaping up and hurtling for the stern. Through the fissures in the deck, heated tongues of orange lapped at their pounding feet; from all sides the frenzied bursts of incandescence created a pulsing and airless tunnel. Welcome darkness sat at its finish. Hawkhead stumbled, was dragged along.

Choking and their clothes asmoulder, they coursed over the edge, throwing themselves down the rope and landing disarrayed in the skiff. Luqa cast off. From the well of the boat, Hardy lay on his back and painfully sucked in oxygen.

'Measuring the moment is a skill, brothers.'

Hawkhead examined the charred border of his waistcoat. 'Possessing judgement is another.'

'We escaped, Hawkhead.'

'Not for want of placing ourselves in the claws of hell.'

'See what we achieve.' Hardy hauled himself up to study the glowing result of their handiwork. 'All about is turmoil. The Spaniard will not recover.'

'Nor shall I, Christian.' Hawkhead rasped up a ball of blackened phlegm and coughed it overboard.

'We are the three of us together, our task complete.'

'And I and the Maltese reunited as brothers.'

Luqa ignored the jibe. He attended to the tiller and remained oddly silent, perhaps awed by events and the consequence of the action. Navigating passage to the forward English ships was no simple undertaking. Hawkhead rose to pick his way to the bow, swaying as the boat rocked close to the wind.

A plume of flame burst from the fireship, illuminating its surroundings and catching the skiff in the brief intensity of its radiance. It was sufficient. The defensive screen of Spanish longboats might have dispersed, but random vessels prowled and the previous target of Hardy and Hawkhead had not entirely retreated. Aligning a musket and discharging a shot towards the elusive raiders was easier than offering pursuit. The round struck. Hawkhead flexed and grunted, appearing to shudder, clutching for support at the boom before crumpling hard against Luqa.

'My back is shot away.' The words trickled out on a growl. 'I am done for, Christian.'

'Not until I give command.'

They lifted him gently, propping him in the careful embrace of Hardy. The small man was trembling, his lungs drowning in arterial blood, his breathing liquid and shallow. There could be only a single outcome. His young commander kept him still, tried to whisper comfort in his ear.

The body spasmed to the pain as Hawkhead fought it down. 'You outlast me, Maltese. Such mean fate.'

'Rest now, friend.' Luqa murmured soft and low.

'I am near death and prefer to jest.'

Hardy rested his hand on the jerking head. 'We are beside you as we have ever been.'

'Beside me in an open boat on a turbulent sea and with enemy in strength about us.' His voice was guttural and weak. 'It is your nature to bring me to woe, Christian.'

'Yours to find pride in the quarrel you create.'

'There is no regret.'

Breathing laboured on and the skiff reared and fell through the oncoming waves. Hardy struggled to cushion the dying man, cradled him from the swell as though he were a child. There was nothing else to be done. Far off, the sporadic rumble of chaos reached them in dim sequence.

It gained approval from Hawkhead. 'Hark to it. My funeral oration, or the sound of angels.'

'A noise we played some part in.'

'Who would suppose it when we stood on Plymouth Hoe, Christian? Who would presume it would end at this hour?'

'You were worthy comrade.'

'And now it is settled.' Words bubbled to a higher pitch and abruptly subsided. 'You weep for me, Maltese?'

'I would shed tears for any brother.'

'Such instant is here.'

Breath and speech fluttered into deeper silence, and

unconsciousness strayed towards conclusion. Hardy and Luqa did not speak. They listened to the rattle in the throat and the moaning wind on the sail, hunkered down in their own thoughts and grief. The abrasive and irascible Hawkhead was departing, their warlike companion who over years had shared in trial and argument and expedition. It had been a strong bond. By the time they reached the first reconnoitring English pinnace, Hawkhead was dead.

Behind them they had abandoned a collage of howled prayer and consuming panic, of galleons and hulks recoiling from the fireships, of Spanish commanders throwing caution and their vessels to the wind. Only Medina Sidonia and a smattering of his closest escorts held their nerve and kept their anchors. The rest were in blind and stricken exit, driving north-east for the treacherous banks and waters off Zeeland. There was no turning back, no pause to deliberate or gather courage, to snatch advantage from the eye of despair. Fire could do that to seafarers.

Through collision, and in his haste to plot a course from danger, the commander of the galleasses ran aground his rudderless flagship *San Lorenzo* on the sands below Calais fort. It was the culmination to a series of inglorious episodes involving the oared goliaths. Becoming stranded on a beach was almost to be expected. As the vast hull rolled and was forced higher on the shore and the late hour made way to the early morning of Monday 29 July 1588, the Armada wallowed fretfully and waited for the close.

~

It was at dawn that Lord Admiral Howard led his squadron in attack. But avarice and competition, the promise of an easy prize, deflected him from giving chase to the scurrying Spanish formations and directed him to the Calais roads. There the *San Lorenzo* heeled in the shallows, her underside tilting and her cannon pointing useless to the sky. The English launched their small boats. Without much effort, the raiding parties could swamp the defence and take the foundering galleass, could apply the rude and brutal skills learned through previous experience. A cheer went up and the boats went in. Standing off, their commanders impatient for result, the *Ark Royal* and twenty major ships of war maintained their position and watch.

The Spaniard did not quietly submit. Amid volleys of musket-shot and the clash of blades, Hugo de Moncada led the counter-charge. Clambering over the hull, he stood and roared his defiance, urging his men to fight and spitting insult at the encroaching foe. He was proud to be holding them at bay, and happy he at last could inflict true punishment on the heretics. If only they knew what he had done; if only they realized he had put ashore a renegade who promised to wipe the satisfaction from their faces. His own expression altered to the crushing impact of a heavy lead ball between his eyes.

Skirmish changed and fortune varied, the crew of the galleass jumping from their posts and floundering ashore in untidy retreat. The governor of Calais would not stand idly by. He too wished for reward and sought as prize the *San Lorenzo*; he also loathed the English and embraced the opportunity to do them harm. Anything to deny Queen Elizabeth and her servants. From the ramparts of his castle, his artillery opened up and drove the enemy back. Lord Howard and his brother thieves would hurt to lose their trophy, would regret wasting several hours of campaign. The Armada was at sea, and it was left to Drake to complete outstanding business.

'*Cowards! Protestant whores! Lutheran chickens!*'
Never before had the English sailed so close, and never had

the taunts of the Spanish crews borne such rage and misery. At point-blank range, the squadrons of Drake, Hawkins, Frobisher and Seymour sidled in to deliver their broadsides and manoeuvre to leeward. Everywhere was smoke, and everything was commotion. In the centre, the *San Martin* of Medina Sidonia sacrificed herself to the pummelling shot, the Captain-General placing his flagship to draw fire away from the regrouping Spanish fleet. It was a valiant and thankless task. With him were others, a few brave outriders to the storm, Admiral Recalde on the *Santa Ana*, Leiva on his *Santa María*, and three Portuguese galleons, turning to wind in support of their chief. Loyal to the end.

Grapples flew and missed as another English warship skittered by and released its ordnance to concussive effect. The vessels juddered in the aftershock, one giving and the other collecting, the English crews steadying their guns for the reload and their Spanish opposites already dead. Enemies were a mere fifteen feet apart. More smoke swelled in the space between them, obscuring the broken timbers and crumpled gun-cradles and the trauma wounds to a hull now dressed with human remains. A second English galleon lined up.

'Surrender to us and we shall spare you.'

An English officer, his sword drawn, leaned from the maintop and shouted his opening bid to the rearing deck across from him. Maybe the Spanish had endured enough, would prefer the certainties of an honourable defeat to the horrors of further combat. From his vantage, and where the wind scraped hollows in the whitening mist, he could view the piteously maimed and dismembered strewn about the upper surface.

He called again. 'Your duty is done. Prevent this needless slaughter. Lay down your arms and strike your flags.'

His offer was considered and rejected, the answer arriving in a patter of shots that burst the doublet of the Englishman in a vulgar spray of crimson. He sagged and fell ungainly from the mast. The deal was off. Below, the matches were put to powder-fuses and the muzzles flung their solid shot. It was an incident repeated in a hundred actions, a single episode lost within the maelstrom whole.

Two adversaries scraped sides, a pursuing ship playing too close and grazing the *San Mateo*. A fleeting kiss between rivals. In the blood-fury of that instant, an English sailor found he had leaped aggressive and alone to the Spanish vessel and was abandoned to his fate. It took a while for him to absorb his mistake, his gaze flitting bug-eyed from his receding home to his existing predicament, his eagerness decaying through uncertainty into fright. Around him, his new hosts were gathering.

'*El Draque* throws us a bone to gnaw on.'

'See how the bastard quakes.'

'He has reason to.' The tip of a blade rose and circled. 'Shall we flay him or dice him?'

'Whichever brings the louder scream.'

'Let him run to give us sport.'

'We shall have our game, my brothers. A veritable chase.'

The cornered man spoke no Spanish, yet understood the malice and intent. He stared wildly, shifting and backing in the narrowed confines, his stammered distress faint against the wider murmur. His challengers advanced. Horror-stricken, he darted for escape and chose instinctively to climb. In the rigging he had options, could grope for height and cling to hope, would clamber and jump and confound the pursuit. After all, it was the environment he knew. Perchance these foreign Catholics would tire and show mercy, might prove themselves gentle ambassadors of their nation. He scrambled faster, aware of the futility.

Swords jabbed and drew blood and shrieks, the lone quarry slipping and regaining his hold. He would not give up. Resourcefulness must count. Figures spider-crawled towards him, swinging near, responding to the alarm-vibrations of their web. With care they could sustain their pleasure and extend the outcome. There were whoops and laughter, the petrified appeals of the man, the yipping and competing taunts of Spaniards in search of retribution. Another step, a further thrust. A hamstring had been sliced through. Gasping in his weakness and unable to move, the English sailor hooked an elbow through the netting and watched the enemy cluster.

Without announcement, the short quarrel of a crossbow caught him in a shoulder and knocked him from his hold. He went down, his foot entangling, his body pitching helpless and inverted and tethered for the onslaught. It became an open contest. Additional arrow-bolts travelled in and burrowed, each collision disabling and jerking the target and earning fresh applause. Arquebusiers joined in, the crackle of their shot enthusing the mob, their marksmanship transforming the carcass to bloody and unrecognized form. A hand hung limp and twitching. That too was shot away.

'Stay your deeds!' Salvador had hauled himself beside the corpse and was bellowing at the crew. 'You would besmirch yourselves by dishonouring the dead?'

'Heretic dead. Climb away, boy.'

'One further strike and it shall be through me.' The young noble edged sideways to hitch a cloak over the remains.

'Our dealings are not finished.'

'You may deal then with me.' Ferocious resolve burned in the eighteen-year-old. 'What gallantry lies in your sport? Where is the righteousness to your cause?'

A voice called back. 'We seek only for an easy aim.'

'In doing so you find damnation.'

'Why do you care so, pup? Is he not a hated Englishman, a vile Protestant, an apostate and false Christian?'

Salvador nodded. 'All these things and a seafarer besides. He is a brother sailor who suffers a fate we each of us may meet.'

'Look about you from your lofty height. Our own lie strewn and broken. Yet you would have us revere a worthless carcass of the foe.'

The young man did not flinch. 'In death we are rendered equal.'

'Allow us at him, boy.' A musket lifted.

'Fire on him and you let fly at me. Kill me and you will burn in hell.'

They wavered, their impulse and unity no match for his commitment. Confrontation was past. In sullen acquiescence, two of their number scaled the rigging to dislodge the cadaver and return it to the deck. Without ceremony and with the token mumbling of a prayer, it was dumped overboard. Where the *San Mateo* and her cohorts were headed, no passengers were required.

Warfronts assumed many guises and came no quieter than this. In a secluded glade beyond the New Forest village of Lyndhurst, Realm and his companion broke bread and shared wine. They had left their hostelry before dawn, eager to make progress and avoid undue contact with others. At the centre of the forest, and the hub of its arterial routes, the hamlet offered a conduit for the passage of gossip and goods to Winchester and London. It was gratifying to be joining them. All were consumed with news of the Armada, postulating on this, worrying about that. The people of England were following the wrong event.

Realm chewed on his meagre rations and watched the sunlight break and scatter between the trees. He wondered briefly how his galleass the *San Lorenzo* fared, if the Spanish fleet had reached Calais and the army of the Duke of Parma was embarked. They had their concerns and he had his. At some impending moment Queen Elizabeth would leave the shelter of her Richmond palace to embark on fateful journey into London, would travel east to review the preparedness of her army based in Essex. Catholic spies had predicted it. Her Majesty understood the imperative of leadership and grand gesture. It was why his Janissary sharpshooters would be cleaning their arquebuses and conducting final rehearsal aboard their vessels on the Thames; it was why he himself voyaged to the capital.

He tore off a crust. 'Simple fare for pilgrims.'

'As manna to the Israelites, the smallest morsel will sustain us.' The Catholic agent took a drink from his leather bottle. 'With you landed and our task afoot, I would go hungry for a month and not protest.'

'You endure much already.'

'No more than any other true believer, brother. No more than the people of the West Country slain by the mercenaries of heretic King Edward or the citizens of the North murdered by Elizabeth.'

'Vengeance returns to haunt her.' Realm placed the bread in his mouth.

'That it does, brother. And when she is dead, ten thousand upon ten thousand will rise up and clamour to reclaim the Religion.'

'I am glad to be part of it.'

'While I am honoured to have you with me, brother.'

Realm studied the man. 'I cannot work miracles. I can do no more than pursue a course to the best of my mortal purpose.'

'Our Lord is beside us. It will suffice.'

'Amen to it. Yet fortune may turn in ways we do not foresee.'

'To try is to find salvation. To try is to break the fragile tenure of the Protestants.'

'Let it be so.' Realm floated his gaze to their horses drinking at the stream. 'Are you readied for the danger ahead?'

'My mind is strong and my mace of steel, brother.'

Realm stood and stretched. 'At any turn and in every nook lurk those who desire us ill, men who by dint of their suspicion would deliver us to Walsingham.'

'We will not permit it.'

'Nor should we allow his Searchers to pick up our scent.'

The Catholic agent nodded his agreement. 'Each step we take we shall cover well.'

'With regret, I must be certain.'

In a single turning move, Realm fetched his scabbard, drew his sword, and bent to the attack. His erstwhile guide offered no resistance or sound, had not been quite so ready as he boasted. And then there was one. The next stage could proceed.

'Be Englishmen, boys! Be English!' Drake called from the fighting-tops of the *Revenge* to his crew scampering invisible below. 'Remember the fate of the French Huguenots! Remember the seventeen martyrs of Lewes!'

Beside him on his narrow eyrie set high above the smoke-line, Hardy glimpsed the brutal dismantling of a holy crusade. Every English ship appeared to be in action, and each Spanish vessel seemed to be sinking or aflame. He heard the hubbub of battle and felt the tremor of broadsides conducted up the mast, saw the blighted forests of shredded sails and fractured spars. Hawkhead would have approved. There would be no recovery for the Armada, no chance it might turn and link with the stranded army of the Duke of Parma. The English Vice Admiral deserved his satisfaction.

He clamped a hand on the shoulder of his young lieutenant. 'Our fireships began this overthrow, Christian. Here now off Gravelines it is near concluded.'

'Such ending is a wretched thing.'

'It is the contest for which we prayed, which even our esteemed Lord Admiral deigns eventually to join. The Spaniard is for the dark, and we, by the grace of God the victor, are destined for a happier place.'

'What path is left to the enemy, sir?'

'A troubled one, should the wind gather and the waves rise. We shall encourage them north and see how they fare.' It was not said with charity.

Hiatus came with the slap of a musket-ball that split wood and ricocheted singing between them. A marksman on the Portuguese galleon *São Felipe* had almost found his aim. Unpertubed, Drake continued to study the changing vista.

'We have beaten the stuff and fight from them, Christian. Observe Recalde and his *Santa Ana*.' The Vice Admiral pointed.

'She puts up a bold fight.'

'Do I not know it? My own bedcot is pierced through with shot.' His attention switched. 'There a transport lies in its wreckage. There too a Spaniard rudderless. And there a galleon without bowsprit or foremast.'

'I have not in my life witnessed such ruin.'

'We are not without loss.' Drake glanced at the young soldier. 'Yet we enjoy a good day, and the hour advances when the light fades and we must quit assault.'

That assault was lessening regardless, faltering into random volleys and occasional bouts as the English expended their final stores of shot. Ships were holed and their crews exhausted, the men lacking sleep and food and the energy to persist. Drake leaned on the platform-rail and blew three times on a brass whistle. The action was concluded.

They descended wearily and swung themselves to a deck blackened and littered with the debris of war. Close encounter with the Spanish had left the *Revenge* in a parlous state, her guns cracked and her sailors hollow-eyed and depleted. She had escaped the worst. Yet there was sickness on board, the smell and sound of a company beset by poisoning and dysentery and the onset of disease.

Hardy caught sight of Fearnot, the Irish dog and mascot that had been ferried out on command of Drake to rejoin his ship. The canine was not in routinely boisterous mood. He whined, prowling anxiously, fretting to paw and nuzzle at a shape slumped prone against a bulkhead. Luqa was down.

'Do you hear me, Luqa? Do you suffer a wound, brother?'

The eyes of his friend were glazed in uncomprehending stupor, the brow hot and the body shivering. But there was no sign of injury or trace of blood. Hardy shouted for water, for the surgeon, for a blanket to provide comfort and to ease the chill. He had lost two of his comrades, and was ill-prepared to bid farewell to a third. A sound brought him back. The islander was in convulsion, his knees brought up, his fists balled against his head and his mouth contorted to emit a wailing scream. *We enjoy a good day*, Drake had observed. Not now, not here. The front of the shirt gaped, and Hardy reached to loosen its drawstrings. In an instant he saw the rose-red marks that spread on the chest, the betraying rash that foretold of decline and mortality. He rose slowly, his breath and heartbeat uneven and his focus unchanged. Typhus fever had struck.

Cruelly mauled, the Armada lurched on in the aftermath of combat as the English shortened sail and shadowed from windward. The Spanish chaplains were busy taking confession, administering last rites, committing bodies to the water. There was much to occupy them. Around their proceedings, crews toiled to patch ships and render them seaworthy, to clear toppled masts and apply canvas plugs to the leaking undersides of hulls. Some vessels were past saving. The Biscayan *La María Juan* had sunk with all hands bar one. At least it freed the small boats to duties elsewhere, allowed them to traverse the fleet and scavenge for flotsam. The seamen tried to ignore the hundreds of corpses pitching in the swell.

Aboard the *San Mateo*, Salvador held a water-gourd to the lips of a dying man. Only time divided him from this unfortunate. Tomorrow or the next day they all would be dead, would be shot to pieces or dashed on rocks, would be as nameless and faceless as every other victim cast into the deep. He wondered if he would be as frightened as this poor soul.

In the darkened seclusion of his cabin on the great transport *Gran Grin*, Inquisitor Garza too made preparation. Closing out the exterior sounds of salvage and restoration, surrounded by the artefacts of his vocation, he knelt in quiet contemplation and prayer. Whatever transpired, God would look favourably upon all he had done. By now his English renegade would be heading for London and his Janissaries would be enacting their final plans. There were matters to be grateful for, things to look forward to. The English might celebrate a perceived victory; the Armada might fail in its immediate quest; the invasion of Albion might never arise. Yet he was content. He gazed in the brooding candlelight at the perfection of the Giorgione, at the oil-rendering of the Crucifixion and the centurion knelt at the foot of the Cross. In desolation there was ever hope. It was not over until he decreed it.

From the poop-deck of the *San Martin*, Medina Sidonia watched as the crew heaved on a windlass and another grease-covered diver was raised from the sea by a rope attached to his ankle. Cosmetic repairs made no difference to the outcome, could not alter the horrors that awaited. He was under no illusion. The smoke of battle still stung his eyes, the jostling images of defeat still seared his mind. No excuse would placate the King or expression of regret properly reflect his despair; no explanation could do justice to the scale of disaster. His leadership had brought them to this. It was a sobering and terrifying consideration, a thought that paralysed and filled him with dread. For the while, the Armada had crawled back to the defensive structure it knew best, had reformed into a semblance of its crescent-moon formation. A mockery, a waste, a sham. The old mariner Santa Cruz, Admiral of the Ocean, would be laughing or weeping from his marble tomb. *Your ambition will see you undone*, he had vowed, and realization of his prescience was a bitter thing. If the English did not take them, the rising winds would finish the task.

A ship brushed close, the shaven head and belligerent stance of the Guipúzcoan commander visible at its stern. Some would refuse to give in. The Captain-General waved to him and shouted.

'*Qué hacemos?*' What are we to do?

The answer cut back. '*Lucha y muere con las botas puestas!*' Fight and die like a man!

~

To the regal accompaniment of drums and horns, and with the feathering rise and fall of gilded oars, the procession of barges made stately passage downriver. Tuesday 30 July 1588. Eleven days since first sighting of the Armada off the English coast, Queen Elizabeth was heading for temporary residence at the Palace of St James. Her advisers had counselled her to make the journey. In her new quarters she would be protected by

315

high walls and the troop emplacements of her personal guard, would be situated closer to her army mustered at Tilbury. As commander-in-chief, it was imperative she was both near to the front and sheltered from prevailing danger. The threat was not yet extinguished, and her ministers fussed and argued. Rumour spread through London. Her Majesty had arrived, *Gloriana* was come – a sovereign queen willing and ready to lead her forces against the feared battle-squares of the Duke of Parma. Protestantism and the people of England waited.

Out at sea, a violent storm was starting to blow.

Chapter 17

This was how hope and glory ended: with shipwreck and capture and a forced march through the malarial swamplands of the Scheldt. Salvador kept his head down and his pace steady. He heard the shuffling tramp of the feet about him, sensed the defeat and misery in his fellow prisoners. They were all of them headed for the same destination, all of them stripped naked, all of them reduced to an indistinguishable mass. The easier to kill. He was under no misapprehension, only surprised to have endured so long. Even the flies by their ceaseless intrusion treated them as corpses. It was a matter of time, and that time was drawing close.

Damn the Dutch. He would not go weak and cringing to his end. The eighteen-year-old lifted his face and stared ahead, observed the locals gathering mute for the event. Their very silence conveyed hostility; their lacklustre eyes possessed the desensitized glaze of those who now passed judgement on their persecutors. Spain would pay for her maltreatment of the Protestants. A bystander doffed his hat in mock salutation. It was headwear taken as trophy, a single item among hundreds torn from the captives and donned by prowling inhabitants. A symbol of everything that had gone awry for the Armada. Salvador reflected on the final moments of the *San Mateo*, on the howling gale and the foaming surf, on the crashing timbers and the animal-shrieks of drowning men. At least the dead did not have to suffer a parade.

A walled town appeared, and a shudder spread through the disordered ranks. Every journey had its start and conclusion. For the surviving crews of the *San Mateo* and the *São Felipe* the voyage had begun in Lisbon and carried them on to Corunna, had fed them along the Channel and through English fire to false haven in Calais and the sandbanks off Nieuport and Sluys. Quite a ride. Salvador had learned much, had gained insight through adversity, had discovered for himself and too late the folly of the mission. He had wanted to find honour and restore the family name. Instead he was sacrificed to the imperial whim and ambition of King Philip II. Every man and boy of them was to disappear. Sick and gaunt-faced, leaking the diseased contents of their bowels and lacking all hope, they were marshalled into Flushing.

'Did I not say I would stand with you when judgement came?'

He recognized the voice and turned to see the bearded old sailor at his side. The man winked as he had done in the work-detail on the beach at Corunna.

Salvador smiled. 'I doubted you. I deemed our cause just and myself invincible.'

'And now?'

'At this hour I believe you to be right and that I was wrong.' He nodded to the veteran. 'You claimed then I would need my brothers.'

'You have them.'

'For it, I am thankful.'

'A young noble with humility is truly a man. And as men and brothers we stride for oblivion.'

'Will they not ransom us? Are they not open to parley?'

'Look in their faces and you will find no appetite to

converse.' The older man spat disdainfully in the dust. 'Give ear to the sound, boy. It is the murmur of an execution.'

Salvador listened, could distinguish the low and insistent hum of townsfolk spilling on to streets to give them full welcome. He blinked, taking in a church spire, knowing that each recorded sight was for the present only. Their God was as severe and unforgiving as his own.

A young seaman gripped his arm. 'Will they burn us? Tell me they will not burn us.'

'Be of faith and courage, brother. It is the facing of death and not the manner that counts for our salvation.'

'I have no wish to die.' The words were part whispered and half sobbed.

Salvador placed an arm about the thin shoulders of the boy. 'If we are to enter heaven or hell, we shall do so together.'

They passed through the gates, appeared to stagger and recover beneath the directed weight of hatred. Women hissed and children jeered, men hurled threat and insult. A stone flew and struck the head of a prisoner, drawing blood, causing his eyes to roll and his legs to sag. The man was borne along upright in the shambling throng. Salvador tightened his hold on the crying boy, wanted to give strength and avoid his own frailties. How alike they were to the poor victims of the auto-da-fé in Lisbon, he thought. The same gauntlet of expectant faces to run, the same stumbling progress, the same twilight pause between life and eternity. Behind them, the portcullis dropped and the great doors swung shut. No going back.

He gasped a question to the old sailor. 'You have a wife?'

'A love in every port from Corunna to Cadiz and on to the Azores.' Greybeard chuckled at the memory. 'They will not much lament for me.'

'Who may tell of those who would mourn?'

'Trust me, young brother. They are damsels who would rather drink and dance.'

'I am drawn by such thoughts.'

'Grasp them and do not let go. For they are women to amaze, women to awe, women to bring a smile and stiffness to the most limp of men.'

'You experience much.'

'In India I saw elephants, and in the Indies a spider that devours birds. There is no strange event nor outlandish sight I do not witness in my life.' The gnarled mariner grimaced at the spectacle about him. 'Yet this I have not before encountered.'

'Then we are all of us novices.'

A rolling barrage of shouts drowned their speech, the heightened excitement pointing to an ending and paving the way. Salvador crossed himself. The narrowed vista was opening into a square, one side of it bounded by a towering wall. There were pikes and muskets and stolen Armada garb, the herded and helpless nudity of the prisoners, the howled obscenities of the spectating mob. And the young noble felt calm. He had expected and prepared for this, welcomed it as the deserved outcome to his earlier mistake. Maybe his beloved sister Constança would comprehend. In standing tall, in challenging fate as his father once did, he had won the right to his title and found his redemption.

First the musket-volleys and then the charge. The locals would spare no one. It was their sport and their revenge, the chance to gouge and behead and immerse themselves in the splashed insanity of a cull. Blades worked and spear-points furrowed. Some captives prayed and others pleaded; some resisted and grappled hard. They were all of them cut down. In their midst, as the waves of Zeelanders closed, Salvador linked arms with his older and younger brethren. He started to sing, the words patriotic and his voice defiant. Bodies fell around him. Nothing compared to this, to the mystery of death and the magic of being unafraid, to hearing his comrades join him in chorus. Tomorrow and tomorrow and tomorrow. Let it be done.

~

They carried Luqa ashore at Margate, another casualty to the malign fever that swept the English fleet. A fortnight since the Armada was sighted off the Lizard, and the world had changed. The Spanish were in full and clumsy flight, driven northward on the wind, pursued towards the Firth of Forth by the squadrons of their foe. Defenders had become aggressors. Yet here in the sheltered harbour where he had previously come in haste and escape from Newgate jail, where he had boarded the spy-vessel *Black Crow* for furtive excursion into Lisbon, the Maltese islander made his return.

Hardy watched and followed, Fearnot anxious at his side, as two sailors bore the litter into the cramped interior of a whitewashed cottage. He had paid in silver to allay the unease and procure the kindness of its occupants. Few liked to care for those brought sick to them by boat. He did not blame them, was too battle-fatigued to summon emotion of any kind. Black Jack was dead and Hawkhead also, and now it was the turn of Luqa to lie stricken and wasted at the threshold. Luqa, the boy who had fought in the Great Siege beside his father; Luqa, his roguish mentor and loyal bodyguard; Luqa, who had served as errant brother and uncle and comrade-in-arms. His bridge to the past. The young Englishman dared not think too deep on it. He would focus on the present to avoid grim prospect of the future, would embrace faint hope and cling to the possibility that this was no more than rehearsal for a burial. It was both the least and most he could do for his friend.

Wringing water from a cloth, he reached to wipe the sweat from the pallid features and bring some relief.

Luqa shivered, his tongue heavy and his breathing slow. 'I should have remained a horse-thief, Christian.'

'To be hanged for your trouble? To let pass the sweep of history, our sortie to Lisbon, the great chase of the Armada?'

'See where it has ended me.'

'Do not speak of ending, brother.'

'It is the truth which we each know well.' The head lolled against the straw-filled mattress. 'Once it was I who nurse-maided you, Christian. You remember?'

'In every detail, I do.'

'How I taught you to swim and fish, instructed you in the rougher arts of fighting.'

Hardy smiled in solemn reminiscence. 'You tutored me too in theft and deceit, in sharp trick and all kind of conspiracy, in corruption and subterfuge and every form of devilment.'

'It has stood you well, Christian.'

'I owe my life to it. To you.'

'Though I have imperilled it enough.'

'And saved it more.'

'How to measure debt when we share in all our dangers?' Luqa paused to catch his breath and summon his strength. 'You are more than mere son of your father, Christian. You are my pride, my young brother, my warrior-boy.'

'While I will set aside opinion until you stand with me to welcome home our fleet.'

It might have been a shake of the head or the ghost of a grin that crossed the face of the islander. Luqa was not a reflective man, preferred the simplicities of gambling, stealing and brawling to mawkish word and thought. Illness had changed him in so many ways. His teeth chattered, and Hardy leaned to draw the blanket higher.

A hand clamped cold on his and pressed it tight. 'Where is Drake?'

'Still chasing and baiting the Spaniard.'

'That most favoured English pursuit.' The words of Luqa coagulated with a sigh. 'Would that I lived to see him prick Frobisher with steel.'

'Stay with me and I shall arrange it.'

The Maltese sailor grunted. 'We made fair profit with the little corsair. Did we not, Christian?'

'Most every penny I have.'

'From here on, you have more. My money is yours.'

'I will not hear it, brother.'

'You will take it as you will heed my counsel. I am tended and content in Margate, so go to your duties and let me rest.'

'Am I not your chief?'

'I give thanks you are not my physician.'

With the lethargy of despair, Hardy stepped from the room to the outside light. He wanted air, wanted to sink to his knees, wanted to shout oath and obscenity at the sky. The gaped muzzle of a pistol aimed at his head prevented him. Behind the trigger was Isaiah Payne, his plumage vibrant, his eyes and body restless, and gun-hand perfectly steady. The gargoyle was visiting, had an armed posse and unlimited remit.

'A prodigal seafarer restored as intelligencer. Welcome ashore.'

Hardy squinted against the August rays. 'What brings a Searcher to this door, Payne? The smell of carrion?'

'Hunting is my nature and my pleasure.'

'You will find no recusant in Margate, no Jesuit priest, no popish threat or treachery.'

'Yet what of those who would hide or harbour such?' The smile and firearm were unwavering. 'There exists the small matter of concealment, of masquerade by one who would play the hero, the soldier returned, the loyal aide to Drake.'

'Do I not prove myself?'

'Proof is flimsy and unpersuasive where hazard to England is great. None is above suspicion.'

'That his honour Walsingham directs you to these Kentish parts is worthy illustration.'

The gaze had hardened. 'Where is the list of English papists, the book you carried from Portugal aboard the *Black Crow* in which are placed the names of Catholics?'

'It is a wondrous thing you are mended since last we met.'

'You may not so swift recover.' Knuckles tightened on the pistol-grip. 'Inform me, Hardy.'

'How should I inform of an object I do not possess?'

'You dissemble.'

'As you suppose.' Hardy bent and put his forehead to the gun-muzzle. 'Are my words enough to have me killed? Do I give such offence his honour Walsingham would wish me dead?'

'Many a slip and mishap arise when a gun is mated to a tired finger.'

'One you could explain? One you care convey to Drake, to Walsingham, to the Queen and her council?'

He thought not. Yet it was rewarding to provoke and test, to chance everything on casual defiance. Isaiah Payne was an abomination. His affectation and menace, his record of citizens brutalized and oppressed, served as a cautionary symbol. Hardy would not bow to it. He peered at his adversary, stared down the barrel of a loaded weapon.

The danger lifted, Payne tilting the pistol upward and discharging it in a violent report that startled his own men. Still Hardy did not flinch.

Payne studied him. 'Lamentably, it is often wives and their brood who are mauled in the savage crossfire of our age.'

'Venture near my Emma or Adam and you will enter hell screaming.'

The lips retracted in a smirk. 'My task is merely to cut out malignancy and contain the disease.'

'You kill by your cure.'

'At some later day, I shall arrange to kill you.'

Such warning slid from the mind as Hardy watched them leave. The pistol-shot had roused other thoughts, had snapped him back to the shot fired by an English renegade in the darkened streets of the Alfama. He had not dwelt on the incident for a time, had not in his imagination revisited Constança or his mother or the house of Inquisitor Garza in which existed a painting snatched from his childhood. The maritime campaign was over, and he was thrust again into the world of Walsingham and the dangers it presented. Luqa suffered, and yet he would need to leave this blood-friend behind. It was the price of his vocation. He must travel to London to ensure the safety of his wife and son and banish the crowding demons. The enemy was not finished.

In the warm orchard behind the house off Fetter Lane, Emma strolled with a basket and picked cherries from the weighted boughs. It would not be long before Christian returned. All talked of how the Armada was put to flight, traded gossip and account of fireships and daring action, of storms and Spanish woe. She had read every handbill and listened to every crier, believing in half and hoping it entirely true. Wise heads counselled that the Duke of Parma remained poised with his army to strike across the narrow sea. Yet wisdom counted for nothing when faith and optimism were in the air.

She paused while reaching to pluck the fruit, and laughed at the sight of little Adam attempting to peel a fig. He was as tenacious as his father. What relief it was her worries would soon be ended, the clinging dread of potential widowhood and the dark sense of feeling watched be for ever banished. No more the call of Drake or the draw of Walsingham; no more her soldier-husband leaping to join in raid and foreign affray; no more the creeping fingers of spies rummaging through her life and dwelling. She would hold on to Christian and never let him go. Around these parts the malformed Isaiah Payne had prowled and hired assassins had been slain. It would unnerve the stoutest of hearts. Her concern was to protect her child and be a loving wife. A simple wish in a complex world. Within days or even hours, a beloved figure would appear at the doorway and enfold her in his arms, would kiss her with the intensity of a man soiled by war and starved of human kindness. Her Christian was homeward bound, and for it she felt blessed.

There were reasons for searching out this half-timbered house in the crowded alleyways abutting the cathedral. Winchester was a fine city, a waypoint on the route to London. Realm could be satisfied with his progress. Somewhere in the New Forest he had buried the corpse of his Catholic guide, had sent the head on a different journey stowed among flour-sacks on a passing cart. Retaining a sense of humour helped alleviate the tension. Killing was so much a way of life, he was uncertain if he did it as habit or best practice. With a fresh horse arranged, there was time to while; with the need to escape the tittle-tattle of the street, there was guilty pleasure to obtain. People talked of nothing save the doomed Armada and the fading prospect of invasion. It could grow irksome, could drive a man to what he would do next.

She cocked her head, a harlot with few teeth and no scruple, a woman aged by drink and coarsened by her trade. Realm loathed her as much as he despised his own complicity. Her false smile, her greedy eyes, her rough features so crudely painted, her inconsequential chat. All grated. He would pay now as she would most surely pay later.

'A soldier.' She regarded him, did little to disguise her indifference. 'I believed all action was at sea.'

'For such reason I seek my action elsewhere.'

'You visit the right lodgings, sir. We shall soon have your sword unsheathed.'

'What price?'

'A penny, before you so much as touch.' Her palm opened to receive.

He paid her, a simple transaction conducted without formality or delay. Each party knew the rules of the engagement. She started to unfasten the ties of her shift, performed the act with minimum of show.

'How far do you travel, sir?'

'Further than any may imagine or where most men would seek to go.'

'For myself, I have never left this town.'

'Perchance you never shall.'

The dress slipped to reveal a bruised shoulder and the chapped and melting globe of a breast. 'What fighting do you see, my soldier? What wars do you inhabit?'

For a whore she was full of questions, trespassed by dull accident on the reasons for his being. Yet he was content to answer, to pile his clothing in the far corner of the room. In stripping off, he could lose himself; through carnality, he could sate his passion and free his inclinations. A renegade and a punchable nun, and their paths had collided. Odd bedfellows. The prospect was hazardous for one of them.

'Such war I conduct will save the nation.' He felt himself stiffen, his ache and need swell. 'My journey is long, sister.'

'I vouch it is hard.' She stepped from her dress and sidled towards him.

He gasped as she stroked him and slid her body close, bit his lip as the pleasure outweighed the burning pain of his disgust.

Christ forgive him. It was no straightforward endeavour to voyage back through a country he had fled. If this unfortunate creature was to bear the brunt of his anger, so be it.

She nuzzled and whispered at his ear. 'Why, you are wounded my brave soldier. I must be kind with you.'

'There are ever scars we carry, ever retribution which we seek.'

'A skirmish? A great battle? A sword? A knife?' Her fingers touched the mutilated tissue.

His hand caught her wrist and squeezed it to withdrawal. 'Concern yourself to the here.' She winced at the pressure and complied.

Pleasantries were over and transaction could begin, the woman clambering to her knees for a different head-to-head. It allowed Realm to scan the room and plot his moves, to interpret in the squalid sparseness every trick and turn of her existence. Not much of a life. It would go as unmissed as that of his former colleague and greeter. He let his eyelids close. The doxy was working hard for her commission, her tongue flicking and her mouth engaged and pumping fast. Everyone was good at something. His brain descended to his balls, his senses directed, his contentment deepening. Small wonder man was cast out of Eden.

They moved to the thin mattress of horsehair, its cloth worn and patched and stained with the history of loveless encounter. Without protest, she rolled on her belly and pushed her fleshy buttocks high, with a shallow intake of breath allowed him to mount. The most unoriginal of sins performed in the most mechanical of styles. He found his rhythm, slapping her to the beat, feeling her give and sway as her pelvis tipped and her breasts shuddered. There was no telling what she thought, and no need to know. For these undulating minutes he was just another nameless client on just another shabby day.

A wasp was trapped confused behind the shutters, its efforts to reach the outside sunlight filling the chamber with a furious drone. What wasted energy. The English renegade panted, pressing down and riding the hips, conscious he would be the last to purchase entry to her favour. She seemed unaware of her destiny.

'You are too forceful.' She hissed a caution over her shoulder. 'Slacken your effort.'

'A lively wench.' He tightened his hold and intensified his thrusts.

She squealed. 'You hurt me.'

'It is my training as a soldier.'

'Here is no battle and I am no foe.' She attempted to scuttle forward, to break the lock. 'We are done, sir.'

'We are far from done.'

'Are you a fool? A madman?'

'Some would deem it so. I would claim to be a servant of God.'

She was becoming agitated and quite irrational, was acquiring the passion she had earlier lacked. It would increase his sense of reward. At some point he would confide in her, would tell her of his mission and objective. He doubted she would respond kindly to the news. That was a Hampshire prostitute for you. First he would finish off, would come for his investment. He pondered idly on the whereabouts of Garza, whether the Inquisitor was having as rough a time of it as the mewling bitch beneath him. The Armada was cut loose to the winds and he, an adherent to the old cause, was deep within the corrupted nation of Walsingham and Drake and Christian Hardy.

The woman was bucking and weeping, and Realm mused whether to employ the dagger, the sword or the flanged mace, and where he would dispatch her severed head.

~

'Sinners pray and repent at the hour of your death. The Lord is with you, even in the shadow of darkness . . .'

Another wave struck the *Gran Grin*, and the ship recoiled as though its back was about to break. More timbers fell, further crewmen were swept flailing from the yards, and the bow nosed and porpoised to greet the next crashing impact. Garza steadied himself against the rearing poop-deck and screamed his exhortations.

'Open your hearts to the Lord! Be comforted and still in the midst of tempest! Rejoice in His work!'

But there was little celebration. Medina Sidonia had ordered his tattered squadrons homeward, and his storm-scattered force was crawling spent into the cold greyness of the North Sea. Ahead lay an outlook more dismal and foreboding than anything they had yet encountered. No fireships or English broadside, no pursuing enemy, could match the horrors of the untamed ocean. As they steered round the craggy north of Scotland and down the western Irish coast, they would meet the Atlantic and all that it implied. Already weakened by campaign and exhaustion, half starved and crazed by lack of food and water, not a single man on board could escape the coming travails. They would have a bad time of it. Scarcely the Devil himself could have invented so bleak a trick.

Garza raised his arms in blessing above the crew. They were deserving of his benediction, would require spirit and sinew if they were to ever reach the shores of Spain. It would be the loneliest and most forbidding of voyages. In past days they had glimpsed the shadow of a distant nao, had heard the faint echo of distress-guns. Everyone was for himself, and every vessel in a battle for its survival. Fortune could turn on a freak gust of wind or a chance wave breaking at an inconvenient moment.

He knew all about the agony of disappointment, about the

sour realization he was unlikely to become Inquisitor General of England. Not this year. God sorely tested him, plainly wished him for other purpose. He would accept as any penitent, would go forward with a crusading fire in his belly still burning and in a state of grace. After all, his renegade was alive and ashore and making for London. The Janissaries too were in place. It must count for something.

In ecstatic fervour, he shouted out. 'I am the Word, sayeth the Lord. I am Alpha and Omega, the beginning and the end. Trust in me. Tremble and bow down.'

'Enough of this, Jesuit.'

He swivelled to catch sight of the captain approaching. The man had the wild eyes of the condemned, his hands reaching to grasp Garza at the throat and thrust him against the rail.

'You would strike a priest, Captain? You would challenge a holy brother, an Inquisitor appointed by the Suprema and the King?'

'Your position does not sway me, Garza.'

'I am a soldier of Christ.'

'My men are the true soldiers.' The grip on his cassock tightened. 'They die as you preach, labour and suffer in the storm while you pass verdict on their souls.'

'My calling is to serve, to save my fellow man from the pernicious fires of hell.'

'Mine is to cast you with the corpses overboard.'

Garza sought dignity from his humiliation. 'Forget not who I am, Captain.'

'How may I forget? The tribunals you chaired from Valencia to Grenada, the bloodshed you brought, the fires you kindled in Seville and Saragossa. I forget nothing.'

'Then heed my words.'

'You shall heed mine.' The Jesuit was pinned by the weight, his head forced round by unyielding fingers. 'Regard my crew, Inquisitor. You will not find among them Lutherans or Moriscos, will not discover in their breasts treason or foul heresies.'

'What would I determine?'

'Loyal men. Good men. God-fearing men.' Each utterance was accompanied by a violent shake of the priest.

'I am with them, Captain.'

'Is it not you who condemns them? Is it not you and your zealous kind who consign them to the hellfire of which you speak?'

Garza struggled for manoeuvre and breath. 'I say again, I am with them.'

'Prove it and you shall keep your place. Work among them and you will earn your keep.'

The hull dipped and the Inquisitor was sent sprawling. It provoked a laugh from the captain and a cheer from his sailors. There was ever a scapegoat in an emergency. Garza wiped blood from his lip and climbed slowly up, his authority punctured and his self-control gone. From a Jesuit to a fallen priest, from Inquisitor to a thin and trembling man garbed in a sodden black cassock, in the space of a single voyage.

He pointed at the commander. 'You will be damned.'

'Are we not already so?' The captain nodded to his bosun advancing with a lash. 'Scale the rigging, Inquisitor. Climb as though your life depends on it.'

Garza was under few illusions that it did.

~

He had been briefed well and had rehearsed in Lisbon for the day he would reach the English capital and saunter with insouciance down its crowded lanes. At the top of Fleet Street, Realm paused. There was gaiety in the air, the cheeriness of people emerging from dread and daring to embrace a future

332

devoid of Spanish occupation. Maybe they were being too hasty. The renegade stood insignificant at the periphery of the scene. He wanted to absorb the sounds and images and the now so foreign dialects, wished to appreciate the irony of his visit. No sentimental fondness dwelt in his heart. These chattering citizens were naive, would be as surprised and overwhelmed as had been his late Catholic accomplice and an impoverished Winchester whore. Against belief, righteousness and a small army of hostile marksmen, Walsingham was powerless. The sightseer pushed on.

An argument blazed, a punch was thrown, and Realm shifted to the opposite side. He had no intention of becoming embroiled by default. His priorities were different, his instinct taking him past the windows of bawdy-houses and the open doorways of taverns and on through the milling host. He had reached the gallows and the turning into Fetter Lane.

'Fair day to you, mistress.'

Emma gazed at the stranger, her hopefulness it might be Christian fading soft in her throat and eyes. She was more uncertain than afraid. The man might be a messenger, a bearer of tidings from the coast, an aide to Drake or a servant of Walsingham. It was hard to tell. He seemed polite enough, stood unthreatening at her door with a slight smile and his head tilted as though to appraise.

She responded with shy formality, her glance noting the sword and leather jerkin. A soldier of sorts, his face scarred by combat, a visitor with the earthy openness of a friend. He was no Searcher, no acolyte of the dreadful Isaiah Payne.

'You come armed, good sir.'

'When peril is so great, I would be careless to venture forth without my blade.'

'Is the danger not passed?'

'There is ever a papist in the shadow, a malcontent waiting

to do wrong.' He offered a crooked grin. 'Christian would not pardon me should I appear ill-equipped and unable.'

'You know him? You have seen him?' Her words almost caught in their eagerness.

'We have fought together.'

'How does he fare? Is he soon to return? Does he achieve much on board the *Revenge*?'

'From Lisbon to Plymouth, he is quite the brave hero.'

'Forgive my caution and discourtesies, sir. A brother to Christian is welcome to our home.'

She moved aside, wanting to hear more, excited at the prospect of further news. It was a pity her maid was on outside errand. Entertainment would not be lavish. But she could feed the man and offer wine or ale, would listen rapt to his legion of stories.

'Tell me of Christian and of yourself, sir. You have a name?'

'Realm.'

She was momentarily puzzled. 'I cannot say he has spoken of you.'

'Yet I vouch he thinks of me often.' The stranger cast his slow stare about the room. 'What idyll and refuge you create, mistress.'

'We are content and happy here.'

'Happiness, as life, may be fleeting.'

He turned to face her, and she took an involuntary step back. There was something opaque in his manner, a falseness that hid secrets, a feigned interest disguising his aims. She cursed herself for being a fool. The sweat pooled in the small of her back, and faith and temperature fell like mercury in her spine.

'What is it you would have of me, sir?'

'An instant of pleasure. An occasion for revenge.' His sword rasped harsh in its unsheathing.

334

She would not scream, could not take the chance that Adam might awake from his young slumber in the garden and come searching for his mother. It was her duty to stay silent, to protect him, to endure. If she could eke out her last minutes, she was providing some hope. That was her gift and her final thought.

In the dark confines of a vessel moored close to London Bridge, Janissaries had gathered for a simple meal of rice and salted fish. It was their custom to sit around the cauldron, to converse and laugh within a bond of martial brotherhood. They were chosen, the finest sharpshooters of their age, and they would not disappoint their paymaster Garza. The target had been chosen and the target would be killed. So they put their cares aside and ate. Their time was approaching.

Chapter 18

Even the buildings seemed to sweat in the close heat of late summer, vapour lifting from the marsh banks of the Thames and feeding the London stench. Yet the citizens went about their business as they always did. They were confident at last the immediate danger was over and the Armada gone, certain the English army would deliver a mortal blow to any massed phalanxes of the Duke of Parma. It was an open secret the Queen herself would shortly visit her loyal forces at Tilbury. Whether as stately gesture or propagandist trick, whether to celebrate deliverance or to lead her troops in battle, her presence was welcome and her people would gather to cheer. Everyone wished to believe the worst was flown; all were eager to catch a glimpse of history and the river progress of *Gloriana*.

At the watergate to Whitehall Palace, the joy of two of her senior ministers was somewhat more restrained. Sir Francis Walsingham and Lord Chancellor Burghley had come both to discuss matters of security and state and to evade the listening recesses and panelled walls of court.

Burghley peered downriver and frowned. 'All parts are bedecked with flags and London Bridge arrayed in finery. And yet I do not feel in festive mood.'

'Could it be you begrudge the Earl of Leicester playing host to Her Majesty in his camp at Tilbury?'

'Begrudge, Sir Francis? I despise him, curse him, damn him

unto death.' There was the petulant slap of a fist in his palm. 'He was out of favour, banished from court, disgraced by costly and frivolous expedition to the Netherlands. Now he resurrects himself, by pomp and display reclaims his place in the affections of the Queen.'

'He was ever one for conceit and theatre, my lord.'

'If only it were mere theatre. Mark my words, Sir Francis. Robert Dudley, Earl of Leicester, rekindles his ambition and seeks anew to cut us from our influence.'

'Will he succeed?'

Walsingham was cool as Burghley was heated, his unruffled reply suggesting a man with differing concerns. The Earl of Leicester would keep, could enjoy for the while his military tableaux and fetching pageants. The real threat and future battle lay elsewhere.

The Lord Chancellor regarded his ally. 'You deem me an old and fearful pantaloon, Sir Francis.'

'I judge you the wisest of counsellors and most astute of friends, my lord.' Walsingham summoned a half-smile. 'Yet Leicester is no real danger. He sickens grievously to the cancer as I, will be dead before year-end. We race each other for the grave.'

'Meantime he makes mischief. Meantime he positions his stepson the Earl of Essex to gain power in our midst.'

The spy-chief rested himself against a marble balustrade. 'Worry not, my lord. The young noble is a heedless dreamer and a reckless soul.'

'Is he not also commander of the cavalry, a handsome and flame-haired gallant who catches the eye and kindness of the Queen?'

'While tomorrow?' Walsingham had turned to gaze towards the Lambeth foreshore. 'His tempestuous nature and unruly spirit will surely make him overreach. Then will you see us push other pretty favourites closer to the Queen. Then shall you witness his chin rested on the block.'

They were words spoken with the quiet conviction of an expert, of one who could foretell what others did not see. Burghley could be reassured. His colleague the Secretary of State was match for any in the land, was guaranteed to outwit an enemy before the foe had even thought to move. In this one courtier dressed soberly in black was a presence, a force, a controller, a hunter, an essential element in the defence of England. Woe betide those who plotted.

Burghley tugged contemplatively on his gown. 'I am the aged wolf and you the sly and sloping fox.'

'The wiliest of foxes may yet be trapped.'

'You are vexed, Sir Francis.' It was a statement in place of a question.

'Is it not our purpose to be weighed down by doubt? To seek truth where it is hid? To find hazard in the celebration?' Walsingham was still as he spoke. 'Do not look to the Earl of Leicester or the distant Duke of Parma for menace, my lord. It rests closer.'

'Your puzzles confound me.'

'Let me enlighten. Where is the Queen most secure, my lord?'

'At the Palace of St James, when removed and surrounded by two thousand guards posted by Lord Hunsdon.'

'When does she lose such protection?'

'During royal progress and while travelling by barge.'

'And when are we the more passive and blind, my lord? When are all unwary and content?'

Burghley grunted. 'In carousing and merriment, in diversion and sport.'

'Then will there be attempt on the life of Elizabeth.'

His verdict deepened the furrow on the brow of the Lord

Chancellor. The older statesman was accustomed to the ritual paranoia of espionage. He had been told of the warning given by a Scots agent in Lisbon, had been alerted to the encrypted and intercepted message smuggled by the Spanish to their supporters in England. Yet there was no proof of an assassin or confirmation that a vague intent had solidified into action.

'What is it you say, Sir Francis?'

'That should the Queen journey beyond this watergate, we may send her to her murder.'

'A quandary.' Burghley nodded in recognition. 'The mind of Her Majesty is set. She would scarce countenance delay. She would interpret our counsel as petty malice against Leicester, as sure proof of our jealousy in his new-won position.'

'It is our duty to warn and protect, my lord.'

'Not at the risk of misinterpretation and at expense of our standing. Nor if we are to suffer the indignity of banishment.'

'Yet the Queen might die.'

'Speculation and sparse theory, Sir Francis.' Burghley clasped his hands behind his back and paced fretfully within a narrow radius. 'Have you facts I may present the Queen? Have you something which may defend us from her ire or being laughed from court?'

'My reputation and my instinct.'

'Though immeasurable, in this knotted bind they are insufficient.'

Walsingham raised his arm and pointed to the west. 'Outside our haven here there are men who would do our nation and sovereign lady harm. The Armada is gone, but its residue still lingers. I taste it in my mouth.'

'And what are we to do, Sir Francis? How should we chase myths and phantoms, sift the London streets, perceive the base and solitary worm amid the barrel of apples?'

'The phantom is armed, my lord.'

'Every young blood bears a sword, each wildfowler a gun.'

Burghley paused, aware that Walsingham was suddenly transported and focused on another place. The expression of the spy-chief was unchanged. But his concentration had switched, his stare retreating to an inner aspect in which he could assess, compute, resolve. Something engrossed the Secretary of State.

'When the blood-red light of a sickle moon casts deadly spell upon the river waters.' Walsingham murmured each word in careful monotone, repeated part of the deciphered Spanish communiqué.

'More riddle and mystery, Sir Francis?'

The reply came in Latin. '*Donec repleat orbem.*' Until it fills the world.

It was the ancient motto of Othman, a previous sultan of Constantinople, who had added the legend beneath his personal standard of the crescent moon. Connections were being made. As Burghley had observed, every wildfowler possessed a gun. Indeed, a wretched hunter had once discharged his weapon from a riverbank close to the passing royal barge and injured one of its oarsmen. The miscreant had almost hanged for his offence. Now that royal barge was to travel again, was to ferry Queen Elizabeth not past wildfowlers but near boats in the Pool of London crewed by Ottoman Turks.

Until it fills the world. Walsingham closed his eyes, wanting to preserve the fragile skein of thought, trying to strengthen its intricate threads. He recalled Isaiah Payne reporting to him in Richmond, informing him of the cornered Turk who had cut his own throat with a spring-blade. On the Armada too he dwelt, and his original belief that the crescent moon and river waters of the encoded Spanish letter had referred to the enemy fleet and its approach towards the Solent. What a dull-witted fool. He had been wrong – glaringly so. The crescent was not one formed by the ships of Medina Sidonia; the river was not the expanse of water sliding by the Isle of Wight. Ottomans were on the Thames. Ottomans were present to do business and bear war materiel home to Constantinople. Ottomans were in London to assassinate the Queen.

His eyes opened at the revelation. 'Inquisitor Garza almost outwits us, my lord.'

'Almost?' Burghley waited patiently for disclosure.

'I have been insensitive to the signs, abstracted as the Inquisitor desired by the noise and lightning of their navy.'

'Should I suppose you are no longer?'

'Assume it well, my lord.' Within the calmness of the spy-chief there was a building energy. 'There is not one killer loosed, but many. There is not a plan based on random chance, but a plot conceived with dreadful and audacious intent.'

'How shall we fight it?'

'Through the skill and illusion of a conjurer and with the assent of Her Majesty.'

'She cannot be put in the way of harm, Sir Francis.'

'Nor may we insist she abandon her progress.' Determination shone dark in the hooded eyes. 'Our enemy sought to bend us from our task, my lord. It is our turn to divert him from his own.'

A messenger approached on foot, hastening with an urgency that brought a halt to the discourse. Walsingham studied the man. Much could be read from the speed and gait, from the tilt of a head or a frown, from hesitancy or forcefulness of manner. Breathless, the envoy bowed. Bad news generally arrived with a flourish.

~

Hardy had smelled the city from a distance, had drawn near almost as a stranger. Partaking in sea-battles and commanding a fireship divided him from the populace that snaked about in celebration. He was happy for them. Yet they would never have the odour of pitch and gunpowder burning in their nostrils, would never climb the sheer sides of an enemy hull, would never hold a mortally wounded comrade or see a blood-brother prone with the typhus. At least he had helped to purchase time for these people. They could drink and make merry, fornicate and fight, pray to a Protestant god, because of Walsingham and Drake, because of Black Jack and Hawkhead and Luqa.

He crossed Fleet Street and strode up Fetter Lane, eager to be home. Emma would radiate the warmth and quiet delight of their reunion, and Adam would bound and dance with laughing glee. The thought quickened his pace, added to the panting beat of anticipation. He could shed all doubt, cast off the past, immerse himself in the exuberance of a hard-earned peace. That was his wish.

But in an instant he understood that existence was frozen and all had changed. He had wanted to tell Emma of the magnificent sight of the Armada when first he spied it, of its billowing sails and colourful pennants, of its roaring cannon and pattering musket-shot. She would not be hearing of it. At the edge of his land he stopped, the familiar replaced by an alien scene, the comfort of a homecoming usurped by a terror that dried his mouth and constricted his throat. The men of Walsingham were stationed at the entrance to his house. He recognized their silent purposefulness and watchful stares. They would kill for their master or spy for their master, were part of his private army. Their presence announced calamity.

Movement and speech had stilled in him. But he had no reason to question or call out, no need for explanation. The hero was returned, a husband and Judas enriched by the prize of the *Rosario*, but instead of heralding his arrival he had unwittingly sent ahead death. By the very blankness in their faces, the servants of the spy-chief revealed what lay within.

They parted as he moved forward, made no attempt to restrain him as instinct rather than strength pulled him towards discovery. He pushed wide the door and stepped through as the killer must have stepped, shuffled into a space redolent with blood. For a second, he imagined he had entered the wrong dwelling, by hypnosis or strange chance had strayed to the domain of madness. Everything was altered. Yet Emma was here, had remained behind for him. Slowly he knelt beside her body; slowly he bent over her; slowly he put his fingers to her cheek, her lips, her eyes, her hair.

'My Emma. My sweet Emma.'

The past could throw a forward shadow. Murder had been no mere afterthought, was performed with the careful savagery of reprisal. Hardy cradled the head, heard himself whisper meaningless things. In this corpse was a greeting from Lisbon, a reminder of his infidelity and betrayal, of Constança and the English traitor, of a thousand moves that converged on a single point. Splayed limbs and a shattered face were the result. He mumbled in wonderment and strange tongues, again said her name. It could not be, was not his Emma. For his Emma was alive, had warm eyes and a tender heart, possessed the tranquil spirit and soft laugh of a wife and love he knew. This cadaver was alien.

Confused, he stood and steadied himself on the embroidered back of a chair. Her needlework, her industry, her hand. Already there were too many memories of her. He tried to avert his eyes, but was transfixed. She was not at rest, could never find peace or consolation in a death like that. Somehow the man with whom he had duelled in the darkness of a Portuguese night had made his way to London to exact a particular revenge. A sideshow to the higher goal of regicide.

Hardy continued to stare, his head bowed and his eyes wide and dried with shock. Anguish and rage, despair and misery, pity and regret, all had boiled away to leave grey and enveloping cold. He was a twenty-two-year-old soldier, a prize-hunter and fortune-seeker, who had visited destruction upon those he cherished. And he had a son.

'Where is he? Where is my Adam?'

At first the maid did not answer. She sat on the rough-hewn bench in the orchard and hugged herself close in a dream-like state. It was as though she had neither courage nor energy to crawl from her refuge.

He crouched before her and took her shoulders. 'You must tell me, Alice. All that you know.'

'They kill my mistress. They kill my mistress.' She swayed entranced to her own words.

'Be of strength, Alice.'

'They murder her, master.'

'What is done with Adam?' His grip tightened. 'The boy, Alice? What of my son?'

Her gaze was unfocused. 'Why, he is saved. The officers took him, the men who questioned me, the strangers who invested your home.'

'Walsingham has him?'

'They ignored my protest. They threatened me. They said young Adam with them is protected.' She blinked. 'Yet my mistress is dead.'

'You found her?'

There was a nod, or a shudder. 'The door was open on my return, master. Not a sound until I heard the cries of Adam from this garden. Thus I entered.' She would say no more.

Perhaps he should have comforted her, could have unearthed a fragment of solace in shared embrace and mourning. Such emotion was for a different time. He kissed her on the cheek

344

and left her to her dazed sorrow and the ripening fruits, ignored the other sights that might catch on his feelings and break him. A wooden toy he had fashioned for his son, a discarded cloth of white muslin, a basket filled with dried lavender. The signs of a previous life.

When he emerged from his home, he had exchanged his rapier for the Katzbalger and his seafaring jacket for the velvet-fronted armour of his blue brigantine. There were many ways to fight a war.

The leader of the posse sent by Walsingham inclined his head in grave acknowledgement. 'Our thoughts may bring some comfort, sir.'

'You little comprehend what would bring me comfort.'

'No soldier as you deserves such homecoming. No man alive should merit such loss.'

'Yet it happens.' Hardy viewed the man from a hard inner landscape. 'My son vanishes, is seized by your henchmen.'

'Would you have him left to the designs and mercy of the predatory assassin? Would you have him guarded by any save his honour the Secretary of State?'

'It balances on the motive.'

'Sir Francis proffers nothing but his shoulder and solicitude.'

'Or does he with my stolen Adam seek means to bind me closer to his further purpose?'

It produced no wrinkle in the groomed and urbane act. 'Is it not for you to measure when you go to him, sir?'

A horse was already saddled and waiting. The spymaster was always ahead, ever predicting, judging foe and friend alike. Hardy would accept the invitation. He could not run or hide, abandon his son, ignore his calling. That was fate, and that was Walsingham. The figure in black who stalked his life had sent him on a mission that was left unfinished. Now he would see it to the end, would track and slay the killer of his wife. Walsingham would lay out the plans.

Hardy breathed slow, shook the dullness from his head. 'My destination?'

'Ride for Seething Lane, sir. His honour there expects you.'

'What of Emma?'

'We shall guard and honour her, will see her mortal remains respected and prepared and carried to a chapel of rest. You have my word and the pledge of the realm.'

Realm: a powerful word, an entity for which he fought and in whose care his beloved had been butchered. It seemed an unequal compact: on one side the master and on the other a sacrificial fool. He had arrived home as a husband, joyous at his return, and was departing it a widower. Yet this officer promised to convey the body of his wife to a chapel, and for it he was grateful.

In the midst of dread reverie, he headed through the gathering to take the reins of the chestnut steed. From somewhere filtered the murmur of onlookers, the occasional sob, the subdued remarks of the concerned and the curious. He did not hear them. One day he would grieve, would join others in sentiment and weeping. For the present he was revisiting the field of espionage and soldiering, would take the life of a blood-stained traitor. Two could play at retribution.

'It is good to see you, *Reino*.'

At the rented house on London Bridge, the commander of the Janissaries welcomed the Englishman with understated pleasure. That either of them had come so far and survived was close to a miracle; that all aspects were in place boded well for their venture. In this quiet corner of this busy crossing, they

346

could converse in Spanish and plot to change the lives of every man, woman and child passing only feet away.

Realm allowed himself to share in the satisfaction. 'We each of us has made long journey. Now we are here and the grand design begins.'

'Cheerless news reaches London, *Reino*. There is nowhere a person who does not speak of Drake and his victory, no face which is not wreathed in smile.'

'I have seen for myself the captured Armada banners they already hoist upon this bridge.' Realm tilted his head towards the ceiling. 'Our celebration will far outlive their own.'

'Yet there is danger, *Reino*. Even as they dance and sing, their eyes may notice and their tongues wag.'

'More is the reason for patience and a steady nerve.'

The Janissary flared. 'Doubt not our strength. Question not we are ready.'

'My faith in you is constant, my confidence in the mission entire. It is I who chose and tutored you.'

He reflected on the secluded months spent in the Castle of St George, the rigours and repetition, the drill and exercise. Through the smoke and flame and the crackle of arquebus-shot had sounded the fading screams of victims tethered or running in the final seconds of their lives. Many had died for the pursuit of excellence, in the quest to reach this stage. The wife of Christian Hardy was simply the latest in this line. She had not been quite so meek as he expected, had bitten and clawed with the ferocity of a cornered vixen. A pity he had not stayed to savour the kill, to hunt down any of her cubs. Duty drew him on.

'Have you report of the Inquisitor, *Reino*?'

Realm shook his head. 'Garza is in the hands of God, must pursue his course as we. If a Jesuit cannot find favour with the Lord, the rest of us are damned.'

'I would rather be damned than confined to a ship riding through the storm.'

'Let us perceive what hurricane you will create.' The renegade walked to the rear of the chamber and opened the shutters. 'Outstretched below us is an innocent scene, a picture of commerce, a Pool of London we intend shall turn to lake of blood.'

The Janissary stepped alongside. 'Our vessels are placed to either side, our arquebusiers stationed on each. The English queen will not pass by unscathed.'

'If her oarsmen should attempt escape?'

'Shock and confusion will prevent it.' He pointed. 'To her front, our boats will move to bar her progress and our fusillades will lighten her crew.'

'And behind?'

'This very house will be a fortress, will rake their retreat with fire and shot. At our feet are trapdoors through which grenades of wildfire and splinter may be dropped. Above us is the *hautpas*, an overhead passage to other buildings from which we may press home attack.'

'Then all is done that may be done.'

Realm watched the dragonfly circuit of the wherries, the insect labour of boatmen and fishwives, and felt nothing. From the heart of revels and a bridge spanning nine hundred feet, he was looking out upon the future. Neither Walsingham nor his trusted Christian Hardy could deflect the aim of the sharpshooters or the nature of the outcome. It was akin to being God. He wished his mother and father were alive to witness the event, to marvel at how the bastard usurper who had put her seal to their death warrant was herself finally undone. That would be immortality and a job completed.

It was some while later when Realm left the house and headed for the south bank of the Thames. He had earlier found lodgings for himself and stabling for his horse, would sit and drink among the loud and bawdy company of a roadside tavern. A cockfight, a game of cards or dice, an impromptu bout of bare-knuckle pugilism: all could fill the hours before the reckoning. Strangers provided anonymity, permitted him to hide and keep watch for those who had a different beat, those who might search, those employed by Walsingham. He would pace himself for the coming outrage.

As the London hub of English counter-espionage, the mansion of Sir Francis Walsingham on Seething Lane had a life and dark energy of its own. Civilian guards patrolled unobtrusively, at any hour messengers came and went, and private secretaries and officers of state made journeys of a few hundred yards to hear in the Tower the howled confessions of recusant priests. A place of study and intrigue, a receptacle for secrets and statements gained by ungentle persuasion. It was where the spymaster had laid bare some of the most deadly plots against the kingdom and where he had masterminded the ruin of Mary, Queen of Scots. Hardy had visited several times.

'Papa! Papa! Papa!'

His two-year-old rushed for him, and he swept the boy into his arms, lifting and holding him and burying his face against the small body. Adam pulsated with joy. He did not know what his father had witnessed. It deepened the void. Hardy caressed and kissed him, wanting to comfort him for a grief the youngster did not share, needing to protect him against a world he could not yet understand. Maybe his son would one day forgive him.

'I thank God you are safe.' He stroked the beaming face. 'Your papa is with you, Adam.'

'Where is Mama?' An innocent question with the bite of a viper.

Hardy smiled and stared in his eyes. 'She is on a journey and wishes you to be strong and brave and good.'

'Yes, Papa.'

'There are things I must do. Matters I must go to, Adam.'

'Things?' The eyes of the child dipped towards the sword.

'I will not leave you long.' Hardy pressed the small back to reassure. 'You understand?' He let the fingers of his son curl around his own.

Finally, a nod.

Surrendering possession of his son to the nurse in Seething Lane added ache to the existing loss. Yet in a world without reason it made sense. The Secretary of State expected him. He was beckoned through by a silent aide to a large chamber with windows looking out towards the Tower. Walsingham liked to have his workshop close.

The spy-chief seemed apparition-grey above his collar-ruff. 'Would that my greeting came in happier circumstance and my words could bring some consolation.'

'We are rarely blessed with what we desire, your honour.'

'The Queen hears of your suffering and bids me tell you of her sorrow.'

'Her Majesty is kind.' But her sympathy would not restore a wife to him, or a mother to their son.

Walsingham appraised him with shrewd eyes. 'Elizabeth is your sovereign lady and you her avenging sword, Mr Hardy.'

'Have I not served her? Do I not prove my obedience?'

'In contest between good and evil, the work of intelligencers and warriors is rarely complete.'

'You will find mine done, your honour.'

'Yet you wear your sword.' The Secretary of State would not give precedence to compassion. 'Our enemy is here in London, Mr Hardy. The foe who killed your wife I am certain has intent to slay the Queen.'

'There are other dutiful servants of the Crown, further lieutenants you may call to the search.'

'None as you.'

Three words that were either an accusation or an order. With Walsingham, it was difficult to gauge. Hardy stood neutral, observing from afar as a spy and soldier he once knew as himself was directed by a dark and artful prince. Emma was dead. He had relinquished all right to protest, could not feign a lack of interest.

Sir Francis sat back in his chair, spoke with the calm forcefulness of the decided. 'Anger may create or destroy, Mr Hardy. Put it to use. Apply it as a tool. Guide it to the purpose of countering the threat.'

'See where it has ended me and led my son.'

'Would you rather dwell as guest within the glittering misery of the court? Would you prefer to sit and regard the inner torment of your soul? Would you lie passive and let others do your work?' Walsingham fixed Hardy with the directness of his stare. 'Or will you take arms against a perfidious rebel who inflicts such loss, whom first you met in Lisbon?'

'Have you knowledge of his situation, your honour?'

'Merely that he is alive and loosed, that he has an appetite for causing woe and chaos. I suspect he mingles among the public throng, will venture soon to the army camp established by the Earl of Leicester.'

'Shall the Queen be there?'

'She will, Mr Hardy. And you besides.'

The young soldier hesitated. 'What powers have I that others do not possess? Do four thousand men-at-arms not own wit or resource to guard Her Majesty and detect the traitor?'

'A herd makes for a poor rat-catcher.' Hard insistence

permeated the measured delivery. 'Should Leicester learn of our participation, there will be uproar. Be cautious, Mr Hardy. Tread with politic feet and wary eye. Let your blade strike true.'

'There is no certainty I will find this man.'

'Trust my instinct as I trust yours.'

Will and argument grappled in the silent space between them. He had been chosen before by Walsingham, commanded to endanger himself for the sake of the nation. The most poisoned of chalices. *Trust my instinct as I trust yours.* There was no irony behind the words. Yet the spymaster had sent Isaiah Payne to pick over his existence, had commissioned him to an enterprise in Portugal that had taken lives and changed his own. Belief was not so easy.

Walsingham looked to the window and the blank edifice of the White Tower beyond. 'Should harm befall the Queen, there will be civil war. Brother will fight brother, families will be rent, many thousands will be dragged by horse and hurdle to their deaths upon the burning pyre.'

'I will submit to your bidding, your honour.' Hardy inclined his head, his body stiff with self-control.

'Then it is settled.'

Things were far from settled. Shortly after Hardy had departed the house, Sir Francis Walsingham took a horse-drawn litter the short distance to the Tower of London.

~

'It is the royal barge! The Queen approaches!'

'*Gloriana* is here!'

'Hark to the trumpets! Listen to the drum!'

'Hail to Her Majesty!'

'God bless and preserve you! The Lord bear witness to our victory!'

People scrambled and people cheered, onlookers to great event, wanting to pay homage in a tidal surge of adulation. This was their moment and their triumph, a time to weep with relief, to embrace, to sing, to gawp at the travelling splendour and the deity in its midst. None could remember such spectacle. Some knelt as the royal barge passed, others doffed their hats and bowed or curtsied. Thursday 8 August 1588. Excitement was everywhere.

'Her eye glimpses us! I tell you, she sees us!'

She goes to lead her army, and yet we all of us are in her heart!'

'What courage! What love! What majesty!'

Elizabeth was indeed an imposing sight, a figure shimmering in cloth of gold and seated beneath a silken canopy, a queen at the centre of procession and the focus of all eyes. On other vessels minstrels and trumpeters played, royal guards stood proud, and nobles and pages clustered in attendance. Gilded and garlanded, the royal barge swept on. It was a craft some seventy feet in length, manned by sixteen oarsmen, linked by cable to a forward boat in which a further dozen rowers were placed. They were nothing more than stage-hands, a means to propel the moving theatre on its voyage down to Tilbury. Goodwill and the warm cries of the masses went with them.

Slack water. The timing was everything, the approach to London Bridge made when the current turned indecisive and safe navigation could be achieved. It would not be a simple manoeuvre. On many an occasion, river-craft had collided or capsized, had foundered on the support-starlings or been pushed through at breakneck speed on the foaming torrent. Not this day. Professionals were at work, aligning the steering-boat and the barge behind, steadying and coaxing their onward passage. The most delicate of undertakings. Regal and unmoved on her dais, Queen Elizabeth of England was carried beneath the span.

Chapter 19

A spell could be broken suddenly, an instant altered with shattering violence. The tow-boat and barge had negotiated the widest opening to the bridge, the oars descending from the vertical to dip and pull once more against the water, the royal presence remote and resplendent on its travelling throne. All was according to plan. Yet arrangements could change. A shot cracked, a second, a third, a gust of fire sputtering into fusillades that swept and repainted the open decks. Order was replaced by chaos.

The tillerman on the lead boat dropped, was joined by an oarsman. Another slumped, motionless and hunched, his tunic ripped and leaking red. Oars flailed. In the fury of retreat and haste to find shelter, hulls collided. More confusion, more shouts and conflicting orders, more random and futile beats of the wood blades. Behind them, smoke-pots dropped from London Bridge to obscure the point of entry and withdrawal, arquebus volleys from the overhead perches limiting decision and keeping help at bay. Progress had faltered and magnificence vanished, and the vessels were going nowhere.

'A trap! We must escape!'

'Pull harder! Bend to it!'

'I am hit! I am hit!'

'Sever the cable and cut us loose!'

'We must save Her Majesty!'

She was beyond saving. While shouts rose and fell erratic as the splashing oars, she was framed beneath her canopy. Few could miss and more than a few were aiming for her. State regalia and the stiffness of her gown would keep her upright and still. An easy mark. A round struck her in the temple and rocked her slightly to the side, a further headshot exiting her skull in crude eruption and carrying off a portion of her wig. It was merely a precursor. Her jaw, her neck, her back, her arm, her abdomen, there was scarcely a part of her bejewelled and pitching figure that was not rent and coloured by the encounter. Some shots went wide, others ricocheted or splintered on the gemstones. Most reached and found their target. Yet even in death, when disfigured and torn within her smoking robes, Elizabeth retained a semblance of her grace and bearing. She was authority, an icon, an example. She was a decoy.

Consumed in their murderous task, grasping for arquebuses loaded by others, the marksmen aimed and fired with relentless efficiency. It was what they had trained and travelled for. Through the powder-smoke, beyond the kick of the gun-barrel and the ringing deafness of the fray, they glimpsed the foreign queen die and her attendants holler and panic in useless momentum. A feeble response to a flawless execution. Inquisitor Garza would be proud, would hail them for rewarding his trust, for carrying his sacred project to fruition, for bringing low the Beast. The barge and its passenger were stalled.

'*Each position is spied! Take them!*'

Unwittingly, in achieving their goal and through the very act of sniping, the Janissaries had revealed their places of concealment. Wherrymen transformed to armed musketeers, lighters became raiding craft, eel-boats were suddenly populated not by resting fishermen but with soldiers of the Crown intent on giving fight. A battle was in train and the melee now two-sided.

'*We have the Ottoman bastards! Show no mercy!*'

None would be shown. As two fishing-boats pulled alongside a Turkish vessel that had swung midstream to block the royal advance, English soldiers leaped to meet the Janissaries. The best of Walsingham pitted against the finest of Garza. Scimitars were drawn and crossbow-quarrels flew, muskets and pistols improvised as clubs as confrontation went close and hand to hand. Brutality was assured. Blows were traded and shots exchanged, each inch of the deck contested and cleared as the boarders pushed in. They had surprise in their favour, would use it to effect. A cornered Janissary managed to parry several thrusts, but was lost beneath the surge; a comrade took down a pair of adversaries with his axe before slipping on blood and succumbing to a single rapier lunge; a marksman in his haste discharged an arquebus ramrod direct into the belly of an opponent and died at the same instant. Everywhere, carnage and commotion.

'*A shot to your right . . .*'

'*I see him! I have him!*'

'*More are below deck! Smoke out the dogs!*'

It was hard and bloody going. Around the Pool of London, the scene had disintegrated into a hundred skirmishes and fire-fights, the hunters and the pursued hacking, firing, moving, darting between masts and spars to seek temporary refuge or precarious foothold. Combat and its outcome swayed back and forth. The river seemed swollen with the violence, spectators crowding to make sense of the tumult. Not quite the event they had gathered to witness.

At the house on London Bridge, an armed assault was under way. From adjoining buildings, from the water, from every quarter, the troops of the spymaster were flocking to ensure any Ottoman stand would be the last. A battering-ram was employed from the street, members of its party culled with bursts of well-laid shot. Reinforcements quickly took their place. Entry was forced and the teams went in, stabbing-blades and pistols in hand and their chests protected by heavy cuirasses. To the outside, the clash of arms was left to the imagination and hearing; within, it was gladiatorial slaughter. A window broke and a body fell through, arquebus balls yipped and snapped, and the yells of dying or charging men sounded dully from the walls.

'Curse them! Another appears!'

The young officer raised his arm, his voice constricting with alarm. He need not have worried. An English bowman had noted the threat, responded with the easy draw of a string, the bending of yew, and the rapid flight of a goose-feathered arrow. Pierced, the Janissary fumbled his weapon and sank awkward over the sill. It had earned the archer extra pay and the plaudits of his comrades. Traditional skills were plainly not redundant. In the *hautpas* corridor running overhead, they were also put to use. Janissaries had created barricades of furniture and wares, were employing every device, any delay, to blunt the ingress of the foe. Pockmarked plaster and smears of blood encircled their retreat.

'You must end your resistance.' An English officer called out to the besieged Ottomans from behind the piled safety of rolled mattresses. 'We shall treat you well.'

'I care not for your treatment.'

'Surrender to us and none shall be harmed.'

'Are we to take the word of an Englishman? An Englishman whose queen we kill?'

'It is either my word or my sword.'

Laughter came back. 'Know that we are Janissaries, the chosen, the Invincible Ones. We shall ever prefer the sword.'

'Your brothers are slain and your mission failed. There is nothing left for which to fight.'

'Save our honour and our name.'

'Where is honour in futility? What is a name when it is forgotten?'

'Forgotten?' The Janissary leader snorted his response. 'With my own eye I see your ruler dead, my men loose havoc upon your kingdom. It cannot go unnoticed.'

'Yet it shall lapse from memory as any drama of no consequence. Queen Elizabeth is hale and well and receives no wound, proceeds on to rendezvous.'

'You lie, Englishman.'

'My pledge you are to suffer death is no deceit. Submit to us, foreigner.'

'Our path is chosen.'

Conclusion was sealed and engagement completed in a brief and furious action thundering along the passageway. Lives and journeys that had begun as Christian children given up to the Ottoman Empire, which had led through military training-schools, through campaigning and capture to obedience beneath a Spanish flag, were erased in a loud and smoke-filled chamber.

Standing at the Tower, Walsingham observed the petering close to the event. He waited as the royal barge moved slow to his location, watched silently the offloading of its dead. It had been the most brilliant of ruses. In short measure he had arranged his forces and identified the hostiles, had visited the dungeons and selected his bait. The victim had come willingly. As a recusant, the young priest was offered chance of redemption and liberty, had eagerly agreed to participate in exchange for full pardon. A simple trade. To don the wig and female finery of *Gloriana*, to be tied immobile to a throne, to travel in state and style and woo the crowd with a fleeting vision. That was not too arduous an endeavour. Or so this papist knave from the College in Rome had believed.

Walsingham surveyed the damaged features of the counterfeit Elizabeth, the eyes and mouth set rigid in shock, the skin daubed thick with cosmetic. A disguise that had outlived both its purpose and its owner. Perchance the cadaver smiled, found black humour in its fate. There was certainly a grim irony in deploying a Catholic priest to counter a Catholic plot. The spymaster wondered what Inquisitor Garza would make of it.

More bodies were landed, each provoking in Walsingham a twinge of pity and regret and a hollow sadness. Risk was part of the covenant, human loss the price of serving God and preserving the integrity of the Protestant Crown. Each of these dead men had volunteered, every one of them placing himself in danger without hesitation and aware of what the voyage might bring. Heroism was a noble conceit and a harrowing sight.

Across the river, screened by people at first perplexed and then anxious to celebrate, Realm quietly considered the result. There was ever a fallback. He had to commend his foes for their cunning, could find no fault with the bold stroke of Walsingham. The wily demon had lost none of his aptitude. So be it. There was still chance, still a plan, still ways to outwit and to kill. He had not trained and martyred his disciples in order to flee. Conditions as these existed to test him. With a parting glance, he tugged at the bridle of his horse and walked it from the south bank. Ahead lay the ride to Tilbury.

Several hours later and some twenty miles downstream, a separate procession of boats was making its landing. It had been an uneventful trip from the palace at Greenwich. To the throb of drums and fanfare of horns, Queen Elizabeth stepped ashore and was welcomed into a receiving-tent; to the applause of thousands, she emerged adorned in silver armour and mounted on a magnificent white gelding. Drawn up before her was her army, its backdrop a tented encampment lavished with banners and pennants. A moment to stir the heart, a patriotic gathering rich in symbolism and heavy with spectacle. The sun flashed and glinted on the breastplate of the Queen. She was an angel, a warrior-leader, a holy presence called among her followers.

The Earl of Leicester, dourly grey with illness, bent his knee to her and bowed his head. 'We, your unworthy yet most loyal of subjects, desire to serve Your Majesty unto death.'

'As your queen and commander in turn desires to serve you.' Elizabeth peered at her general, gentle concern in her eyes. 'You are stricken, my lord.'

'Your visit imbues in me new life, Majesty.'

She cast her gaze above the assembled. 'How many are we here?'

'Four thousand strong, and a further six thousand Kentish men readied at Sandwich.'

'So few.' A comment delivered as a murmur.

'Each day our numbers swell, Majesty. By the hour added force of over fifteen thousand heads I am told with resolve from the shires.'

'Do we have these days? Are we granted such hours?'

'By the grace of the Lord, we shall attain victory, whatever our condition.'

'Amen to it, my lord.'

'Rumour has it Parma already embarks with his troops, will strike for us this day or the morrow.'

'It is as well I am present to offer him battle.'

Preceded by her chaplains, earls and pages bearing her gleaming helmet, her Bible, her personal standard and sword of state, and led by Leicester, himself bare-headed and on foot, the Queen paraded along the lines. If these men were to waver, she would give them strength; if these men were to die, she would be beside them. They and the nation depended on it.

'I thank you! God bless you all!' She lifted her hand and cried out again. 'God bless you all!'

And they replied, some weeping, many kneeling, their pikes and ensigns lowered in salute. The most extraordinary of sights. As the waves parted, she moved through the coloured sea, an enchantress and Amazon at the height of her power. Pipes sounded and the drumbeat continued, marking progress, reflecting the tread of her steed and the plumed and nodding tempo of her cavalry escort. A transfiguration.

'*We are with you, Majesty! May the Lord guide you! Let Christ stand at our shoulder and smite the Spaniard! Pray God, preserve our Queen!*'

They shouted their adulation, caught up in occasion and the infection of mass worship. Nothing could defeat them now. There would be a service of intercession, displays and a march-past, feasting and solemn prayer. The sovereign was arrived, and her soldiers were ready.

In the late afternoon, Elizabeth rode to the nearby manor of Saffron Garden, home to Edward Ritchie, a landowner and local worthy. She would lodge there for the night, return in the morning to the camp at Tilbury for more example of martial show and prowess. The eighth of August 1588 had proved a proud day to be an Englishman.

～

Celebration or crisis invariably favoured the insurgent. It meant flux, the toing and froing of strangers and the press of numbers. Pigs also could help in the subterfuge. Realm wandered through the camp with two dead sucklings in his grasp, a small investment that offered future dividend. Troops required feeding, sat around their fires, welcomed with raucous cheer any who approached bearing victuals or sour beer. He would provide. The Queen might enjoy a fine banquet and masque, would sleep no doubt on a bed of feather-down, but her soldiers were resigned to humbler pursuits. For one night only, an English renegade had bought his way in.

A musketeer called to him. 'What have you there, brother?'

'Simple repast I am eager to share.' He raised his offering towards the man. 'Too much for one alone to eat.'

'There are mouths aplenty here. Be seated with us, friend.'

'Your words are answered prayer after such long journey.'

'As are your hogs to greedy scoundrels.'

Space was made and jokes exchanged, Realm ensuring the brim of his hat stayed low as he kept to the outer shadows of the firelight. It served no purpose to get too close. He had already found in this band the cover he needed, could sit and laugh and while the hours, would feel his way and determine his course. His eyes appraised and measured. The soldiers were diverted by their appetites, were spearing the carcasses on to improvised spits. Hard to tell who was the most skewered.

Another musketeer proffered the liquor bottle. 'From whence do you hail, brother?'

'The New Forest.' Realm pretended to drink. 'My feet are blistered and my throat raw for it.'

'You shall forget such ills when the Duke of Parma lands.'

A third soldier joined in. 'That he will. Yet we shall crack the Spaniard, will splinter and spoil his force as I hear tell we did this day at London Bridge.'

'No base or bastard Catholic may touch our Queen.' The

first of the group thrust a stick angrily in the flames. 'All about, these papist fiends probe to find our weakness.'

'They will discover none.'

'What they shall encounter is our musket-shot and spear-tips, an army that is ready.' Hearty agreement swelled upward.

Realm passed on the bottle. 'Our good Queen Bess at least will lead us.'

'Lead us? She will carry us to victory, brother.' More fighting talk. 'She came before us as a vision, spoke to us as divine messenger.'

'*God bless you all*, she cried.'

'*We are with you*, we shouted as one.'

A hand tapped Realm on the arm, a musketeer leaning drunk to make his point. 'Tomorrow the Queen is once more at our head. There is no foe on earth great enough to resist or strong enough to vanquish us.'

Straightforward folk with uncomplicated tasks, Realm mused. He could not condemn their enthusiasm. They were easily led, manipulated by propaganda and parade. The failure and death of his Janissaries had merely added to the English sense of destiny. How misguided and illusory it would prove. It was not Elizabeth afforded the part of divine messenger, but himself.

Hours drew in and the campfires dwindled, soldiers bedding down on blankets and sacks to slumber through till dawn. Coastal patrols and forward pickets would rouse them if attack should come. Realm stayed awake. He watched the huddled and dormant forms, the occasional glimmer of firebrands and lanterns marking the shuffling passage of men destined for the shit-barrels and pit latrines. England had no standing army.

A musketeer grunted, broke wind and fumbled drowsily to light a rush torch in the glowing embers of the fire. Nature and the drop-pits had called. The man rose and stumbled from the group, his progress spotted with angry complaint and his own muttered apology. Realm trailed him as he moved downwind. Population thinned at this end of the camp. It was unfortunate for the intended victim that he was not a sergeant and thus was barred from resting in a tent, worse for him that he remembered his musket and wore clothes of acceptable fit. Destination was reached. As the soldier planted the sputtering brand, placed down his gun and busied himself with unfastening his breeches, the English renegade slid forward. The cord ligature was looped and readied in his hand.

Twenty days since the Armada was first sighted off the coast of Cornwall, twenty days in which the enemy fleet had been defeated and his Emma slain. There was seldom a tidy ending to things. Hardy crouched silent in the deeper groom beside a canvas pavilion, stared into the glimmering night vista. The traitor might be anywhere or nowhere, could pose as an infantryman or cook, as a royal servant or camp follower. His commitment was not in question. Hardy rubbed his eyes and blinked the sleep away. He had to keep awake, had to think, had to walk himself through the imagination of his enemy. If only he could restore lost time, return to the Alfama and punch his Katzbalger a hundred times into the gut of the demon. That demon prowled new territory. A grieving twenty-two-year-old would be waiting for him, would find comfort in the killing. He would never allow Inquisitor Garza to win.

The captain of the *Gran Grin* had finally relented, had ordered the Jesuit and the rest of the crew to return below deck. In the face of worsening storm, there was little else to do but shorten sail and batten down and cry plaintively to the Lord. They had entered the Pentland Firth. It was the worst of times and most terrible of conditions, a careering progress into the ravaged waters north of Scotland where the Atlantic slammed into the North Sea to create a churning world of giant troughs, peaks and whirlpools. These were stout-hearted men, sailors accustomed to hard journey and the trade routes of the Spanish Main. Yet nothing had prepared them for what they now encountered.

God in heaven! The hull vibrated and the timbers cracked as the vessel climbed another wall and pitched into the next trough. Garza steadied himself against a bulkhead and resumed with his lantern his crawl about the ship. Others did the same, yet they were hunting for rats and roaches, while he collected the souls of men. Their mortal flesh might be condemned, their bodies made skeletal by starvation and disease; he was more interested in salvation.

'Cleanse your heart, my son.' The Inquisitor reached and placed his hand across the forehead of a slumped crewman. 'Confess your sins and seek forgiveness and everlasting light.'

A different voice intruded. 'He is gone, as are most of us here.'

Whoever spoke was right. The *Gran Grin* was a ship of either the dead or the damned, a haunted place, a tossed and leaking wreck populated by ghosts. A rage stirred in Garza. It was not anger at the human cost and misery, nor ire at their likely end: it was the chill fury of one betrayed, of a believer whose mission was undermined by the weakness found in others. As Christ was tested in the wilderness, so would he be challenged and would yet prevail. He pushed himself onward.

Above the shuttered darkness and oppressive stench of the hold, sailors lay in rapt attention. Hunger had driven them to unconventional pursuits. They were using as bait the blooming remains of a crewmate, were waiting until the rodents were immersed to their tails before dropping their net and counting their haul. The first catch of the day. Garza left them to it. Around him were groans and whimpers, occasional conversations transmitted through parched lips with swollen tongues. Madness, horror and decay abounded.

Somewhere there was the faint sound of weeping, the near-silent expression of consuming despair. Curled foetal in his own filth beside a gun-cradle, a boy scarce out of childhood whispered to his mother and the Blessed Virgin.

Garza raised his lamp. 'You cry, boy.'

'Have I not cause?'

'Tears are for those who are condemned and not saved.'

'Am I saved?'

'Open yourself to Christ and you shall be.' Garza leaned closer. 'Raise yourself up and you will be counted.'

'My brothers are dead.'

The Inquisitor shook his head. 'They are alive, for they enter heaven as the sacred fallen, as crusaders in the holy quest.'

'Look about you, Inquisitor.' The youngster did not move, was almost speaking to himself. 'There is no crusade on a plague ship, no sacredness in a pile of bones.'

'You blaspheme.'

'Am I alone in it? Do I speak what others do not say?'

'Take care, boy.'

The eyes of the youth opened, turning to look at the priest. 'I fear the sea more than I could ever fear you.'

'The King grants me supreme authority.'

'And the King commits us to my grave.' The eyelids closed. 'It is over.'

Garza struck the face hard, had his hands about the throat, pulled the boy upright and thrust his ragged frame against the culverin. The youngster had not the energy to resist.

'Sinner. Deceiver. Apostate.' The body shook to each word. 'You seek to abominate the cause? You choose execution above absolution?'

There was no answer. The youth had already strayed into unconsciousness, his head dipping and his arms hanging limp. Garza released his grip. His power was reduced to this: to skulking in the twilight of a rolling hulk and menacing the afflicted. He had better things to do. The crew might surrender themselves to dismay, could abandon their faith and ignore all hope. It was not over as the boy had claimed; purpose was not discarded while he was Inquisitor, while the imperative stood, while Elizabeth ruled and his renegade trod the tainted earth of England.

The *Gran Grin* lurched and another spar fell crashing. Ahead was Cape Wrath.

~

'Cavalry of the Queen, advance to the gallop . . .'

With a flourish of his sword the Earl of Essex commanded his squadrons into a sweeping charge, the lances lowered and locked and the caparisoned horses moving from trot to canter and on to headlong stampede. A thrilling event of wagging plumes and gleaming armour, of churning hooves and dust and trembling ground. It was 9 August 1588 and the Queen was returned from her overnight sojourn. Today would witness parade and mock battles, a fine banquet for the sovereign and climactic finale for the whole. However his maladies, the Earl of Leicester could congratulate himself. His ruler was content, his standing was secure, his exercise in propaganda and self-aggrandizement had surpassed in its success even his grand expectation. Now his stepson Essex, current favourite to Her Majesty, swept by in mighty show. Burghley and Walsingham would not be pleased.

Again mounted on her white charger, adorned in her cuirass and a virgin-white robe, Elizabeth raised the gilded baton in her hand in acknowledgement and salute. Applause swelled. She inclined her head, gravely accepted the approbation of her troops. It was her army, her day, her destiny. Acclamation grew to a roar.

She steadied the horse and bent towards Leicester, who held the bridle. 'Tumult is such, I fear I am already in the din and heat of battle.'

'They are devoted to Your Majesty.'

'As my love for them is multiplied a hundredfold. What honour indeed it is to lead them.'

'Your presence alone is worth a thousand English armies, Majesty.'

'A boon I shall have no need to pay them all.' She lowered the baton to her side. 'I bid you lead me forward, for I would speak to them now.'

'Is there not risk, Majesty?'

Elizabeth glanced down. 'If a queen cannot address or trust her men, she is unworthy of their reverence.'

'Majesty, I must counsel vigilance and care.'

'While I, your commander, enjoin you to obey.'

Dutifully, Leicester walked the horse into the no–man's-land before her. It was as though a measureless force was cowed by a single presence. Murmur faded to a hush, to a quiver of expectation that carried in a wave throughout the throng. She eyed them, waited still upon her mount.

'My loving people. We have been persuaded by some that are careful of our safety to take heed how we commit ourselves to armed multitudes for fear of treachery.' She paused, continuing to regard the faces, fearless in their midst. 'But I do assure you I do not desire to live to distrust my faithful and loving people.'

Her words rang clear, cut loud and uncompromising into the stillness. The line of succession had brought her to the throne, divine right kept her there, and she would yield to none without a fight. Hardy barely heard her. He was scanning the captivated crowd, reaching to detect any change in pattern or jarring movement, any deviation or darker focus. An impossible task. But Walsingham had faith in him, believed he would be able where others would fail. He studied his subjects, perused their reaction to the oratory of their queen. Her Majesty was wrong, should have maintained her distance from her faithful and loving people. Someone in the multitude worked as an assassin; someone was hidden deep.

'And therefore I am come amongst you, as you see at this time, not for my recreation and disport, but being resolved in the midst and heat of the battle to live or die amongst you all . . .'

They cheered and Hardy watched. Their leader understood them, cared for them and touched their hearts, held them in her palm. Silence descended, the pikes and muskets resting. And Hardy saw. A flicker, a suggestion, a near-imperceptible shift in energy and direction. The image was lost. He strained to part the haze of colour, to distinguish one soldier among thousands, to differentiate a musketeer whose fleeting profile bore a strange and troubling intensity. There had been no affection present.

Part obscured by a cap, the bearded features wavered into view. This time the musket appeared different in its elevation, a wheel-lock tilted from its sloped position on the shoulder and readying to track downwards and rest upon a pintle. The hands that grasped it were not resting. Hardy gauged the distance between himself and the suspect, from the suspect to Elizabeth. A triangle of unequal lengths, an immediate threat demanding instant decision. He had to be sure.

370

'I know I have the body of a weak and feeble woman. But I have the heart and stomach of a king, and of a king of England too . . .'

Simply words. In a puff of smoke they could end; with a single report of a musket *Gloriana* would be spun from her horse and her oration replaced by rushing crisis and appeals for calm. There was no opportunity to shout a warning, no opening to challenge the foe with a blade. Hardy would be cut down as soon as he made to move. It was the price of being an armed intruder, of pushing through with a sword drawn, of accosting the Queen with fiery and unknown intent. Solution was essential, might yet be found in disturbance of another kind. The gun barrel angled forward.

'I myself will take up arms, I myself will be your general . . .'

He barged, striking hard, displacing the weight of his neighbour to send him sprawling into the man beyond. Knock-on was immediate and widespread. Soldiers tumbled, their curses loud and their weapons dropped, arms and legs flailing in the confused throes of collapse. An entire section was affected. Through it came Hardy, vaulting obstacles, flowing into breaches, worming his way fast for the point of last sighting. He glimpsed the traitor. The face had turned towards his own, the musket jostled from its aim, the body endeavouring to steady itself against the unexpected force. Recognition occurred in the commotion and closing divide. One Englishman to another. The mutilated ear and the trace of a scar beneath the beard, the later scratches caused by Emma, the eyes that narrowed and did not stray. A renegade who betrayed himself. Hardy pressed forward, hunching his shoulders, ignoring the complaints and the angry clutching at his arm.

His quarry fled. It was more a stealthy withdrawal, the employment of cover and ruse to disguise a tactical disengagement. Hardy altered course, broke through to the rear, stopped to take his bearings. The traitor was darting into a painted tent, and chase resumed. Elizabeth continued to speak of important things. *We shall shortly have a famous victory over those enemies of God, of my kingdom, and of my people.* Conflict was more immediate than she pictured.

'You fail.'

Pursuit had ended in the kitchen tent, with a renegade near cornered by his adversary. There was to be a royal banquet at noon, and the trestles were laden with heaped platters and sides of meat. Roasted hog lay glazed and opulently decorated; venison sat with gilded antlers; pies and pastry towers rose beaded and bejewelled. The richest of feasts and the most unlikely of battlegrounds. Each man had unsheathed his sword.

Hardy gathered air into his lungs, let the Katzbalger balance in his hand. He wanted to observe and understand, wanted to touch the scars left by Emma, wanted to drive home his verdict. The traitor occupied a particular place in his soul. He was the turncoat who had violated and murdered his wife, who had trespassed from the neutral ground of espionage to break all law of humanity. The young soldier was in unforgiving mood.

'Could it be Christian Hardy?' Realm offered him a cool stare. 'You near took me in Lisbon.'

'I have you now.'

'A vow you will find hard to keep.'

'It is you not I this time on enemy soil. You not I who will suffer injury.'

The pale eyes of the renegade were untroubled. 'Are not your wounds the more profound?'

'You snatch from me my beloved, and for it you will pay.' Hardy stood poised.

372

'Fiery talk from a handsome buck. I cannot blame Constança Menezes for her devotion.'

'Constança?'

'She speaks in high praise of you, is another condemned by your ill-chosen acts.'

'Let us see who is condemned.'

Fight began, flowed with a commitment and savagery that saw tables toppled and onlookers run. Thrusts were parried and feints made, attack and defence trampling and rebounding across the scattered wreckage of previous delight. Steel clattered, canvas tore, cooked meats and dainties were slashed aside in the ferocity of encounter. Realm dodged behind a cauldron, warded off the blows with a wooden stool, circled as Hardy jabbed with his sword and a requisitioned fire-iron. The fencing-master was adept at improvisation. His opponent should have checked the pot. With a booted foot Hardy tipped its contents, releasing a scalding broth across the lower limbs of his nimble rival. Realm screeched and backed away.

More food was dashed aside as Hardy advanced. 'Is this all you may do, traitor? Is it the best you may summon?'

'I am not finished, Hardy.'

'Yet I soon will be.' He kicked an obstacle from his path. 'Each of us when called can brawl and fight foul.'

'You embrace a heretic creed, accept employ with the wrong master.'

'As you lecture the wrong man.' Hardy slashed with his blade, brought down an array of copper pans.

Realm leaped to retreat and reposition. 'All which you touch turns to ash, Hardy. Your mother screamed at the stake, her struggle tortured and akin to the protests of your wife.'

Sweat and blood smeared on the panting face of the renegade. But there was also the hint of a smile, the quiet acknowledgement he had scored a small victory.

'Maria, my mother, is slain? You burn her?' There was a disbelief that conveyed full knowledge.

'Inquisitor Garza insisted. I myself chose to visit your home.' The smile broadened. 'Proud and defiant women, I can attest.'

'They were precious to me.'

'Of no consequence to myself.'

'You are wrong.'

Hardy drove forward, beating back resistance and repulsing the counter-strokes. He would not let up until the job was complete, till the creature was dismembered and he scooped its entrails with the point of his sword. The man was weakening beneath the assault, his eyes wide and breathing agonized, his bravado, grip and dexterity faltering. Within seconds, a traitor would be dead.

Then a concussive impact to the head and Hardy felt himself falling, sensed the ground swell upward and the blackness draw in. From a deep pit he heard voices, a rumour, comprehended his adversary was gone.

Chapter 20

'It seems it is I who hold both sword and upper hand.'
He was still alive and remained in the tent, gazed upward at the point of a battle-rapier and the leering countenance of the Earl of Essex. Not the most comfortable of occasions. Hardy attempted to rise, but the steel pushed him back. The favourite of the Queen was not about to relinquish his prize, might have no intention to let his prisoner live. There was an audience too, armed servants of the Earl, silent men who could be relied upon to keep his secrets and do his bidding. That was the power of patronage.

Hardy lay still, felt the dull ache from the blow to his head. The rapier was circling over him. Dangerous triumphalism flickered in the eyes behind. Essex had not forgiven him the beating meted out on the winter night in London, had not forgotten their exchange of words in a chamber of Richmond Palace. Two men of equal age, of wholly unequal station.

There were means to test agenda. 'Nobility does not afford you manners, Essex.'

'Though it grants me power of life and death.' The sword-tip pressed into the velvet front of the brigantine jacket, could pierce its plated armour with a single committed thrust. 'Did you not once declare any site would do for sport and blood-letting?'

'I jested.'

'Like the cur you are, you lie prone. And, as a dog, you shall come to lick your balls, when I cut them from your body.'

'I save the Queen from certain death, Essex. I protect her from the musket-shot of an assassin.'

'Reward may disappoint.'

'It exceeds my contempt for your lack of honour.'

The handsome face of Essex turned in pleasure to his following. 'Hark how the beast makes sound.' Again the rapier prodded. 'Perchance we should take his noise to a higher level.'

'You wrong me, Essex.'

'Can a noble do wrong to a useless wretch?'

'A wretch who serves loyally the Crown. A wretch who does more in battle than you ever shall.'

Anger reared behind the smile. 'Careful how you speak, Hardy.'

'Does it imperil me the more?' Hardy stared at his rival. 'The Queen would not permit your act.'

'Would she not?' A booted foot slammed into the ribs of the prisoner.

'Cowardice sits ill with your rank, Essex.'

The rapier was poised. 'You measure me a coward?'

'None but a weakling would delight in simple murder. None but a callow fool would blacken his repute.'

'My standing is assured, with the people and my Queen. For I chance upon an impostor, an embittered rebel who lurks with his blade close to the royal presence. He menaces, commits foul offence, creates affray and all manner of destruction. It is I, through providence and judgement, who corners and overwhelms the devil.'

'So concludes your glorious military career.'

Hardy kept his eyes open, viewed the changing humours and wrestling thought in the features of the Earl. A passionate man, a proud man, a poetical man, a man raised sensitive to a mere jibe or slight. He had reached a decision. The intended victim waited for the moment, understood that negotiation was through and the next step unavoidable. Such fleeting periods could be restful. Emma was dead and he would join her, after spell in purgatory would have occasion to state his case and make amends. He feared death no more than he feared life. Each was to be accepted with elan.

The pause extended. Attention had been jolted, the eyes and focus of the group shifting to a different axis, to parted curtains and raised musket-barrels, to the dejected ingress of sentries who themselves appeared under armed guard. Essex waited for explanation, stood inscrutable before the bank of guns. His creative play was rudely disrupted.

'*You will desist, my lord.*'

His lordship failed to put up his sword. 'On whose command, sir?'

'By order of Lord Burghley and Sir Francis Walsingham.'

'They have no authority to trespass in the affairs of a military camp.'

'As you have no right to commit an act of treason.'

'Treason?' Essex frowned.

'I say it as it will be seen, my lord.'

The nobleman peered inquisitive at the officer. 'You enter at late stage of the proceedings, stranger. I disarm this knave and betrayer, prevent foul mischief against the Queen.'

'Then you will welcome Her Majesty adjudging your fine and righteous stand.'

It did not appear Essex would. His fury glowed, his face flaming baleful. No man enjoyed being tripped at the finish; no self-regarding courtier appreciated humiliation and limitation on his conduct. The insult was near-unbearable, and the sarcasm of the visitor worthy of armed contest.

Resentment stung in the voice. 'I cannot hazard how Walsingham places his agents and lickspittles in the breast of our formations.'

'Is it not his role as Secretary of State, his commitment to protect the person of Elizabeth?'

'Yet he sends his force to confront me.'

'Force he bids me set loose should you disregard my warning.'

'Disregard your warning.' A line repeated as if held and turned for examination. Essex nodded, aware that he had overreached, miscalculated, had lost that particular round. The muskets remained trained on him and his lieutenants. Neither bluff nor clever footwork would extract him from the situation, nor jest nor ill grace change it.

He looked down at Hardy. 'For a mean and lowly villain, your influence spreads as far as court.'

'His honour Walsingham graces me with his shelter.'

'It will not always suffice.' The noble toyed with his sword, reluctant to accept defeat. 'There shall come occasion when these attentive stewards are too slow to your aid.'

'I await such time, Essex.'

Rehousing his rapier, and with a brusque wave of his head, the young aristocrat stalked from the tent. His henchmen fell in behind. In their absence, Hardy clambered slowly to his feet and picked the fragments of food from his clothing.

'I thank you for your intervention, sirs.'

The newcomer smiled. 'You are a better intelligencer than cook, Mr Hardy.'

'There is ample reminder of it.' He regarded the devastation and shook hands with his rescuer.

Of the assassin, little would be found. Discovery had driven him away, would send him along the Catholic underground of bolt-holes and dank cellars until passage and sail could be

arranged for the Continent. Like thwarted earls, renegades followed the path of least resistance; like chafing nightmares, bad
things tended to return. It was the way of the Elizabethan
world.

On 10 August 1588 the Queen led a great victory parade into
London. Church bells rang out, cannon saluted and the crowds
roared in joyous tumult as Elizabeth and her army passed by.
She had left for Tilbury with intent to do battle, returned as
heroine of the age and of history. Even Catholics would champion her as the saviour of England; even the Pope and the
princes of Europe would pay admiring tribute to their avowed
opponent. She was invincible, all-conquering *Gloriana*.

Yet peace would not bring peace of mind. Defence of the
realm had cost the nation dear, had seen taxes raised and loans
forced from town halls and city merchants. Everyone suffered.
In the weeks that followed, the army would be disbanded and
the navy decommissioned. Men who had stood firm, who had
fought at sea or formed up at Tilbury to serve unto death,
would find themselves cast out and forgotten. Many already
succumbed to disease and malnutrition. Her Majesty had few
regrets.

'Long live the Queen!'

'God preserves us and smites the papists!'

'We are your loyal servants, Majesty! We are the true
believers of England!'

Faces radiated happiness and the drunken pleasure of relief.
These were her people. Elizabeth graciously inclined her
head, humble in the storm of adulation, a monarch supreme
and riding immortal into the texts and annals. King Philip II
of Spain would be heading ceremonies of a very different
kind.

★

Drake continued to patrol off Gravelines, baiting the Duke of Parma, ensuring the Spanish general would remain unable to embark and his cherished dream sour and fade to dull memory. The little corsair of Elizabeth was ever vigilant and prepared.

~

A fortnight and more had elapsed, a time of bonfires and festivity, of prayers and thanksgiving. Hardy did not participate. There was Emma to mourn and Adam to care for, the absence of his friends to fill with restless wandering and thought. Walsingham had yet to discharge him from his duties. Once an intelligencer, always at the call of the Secretary of State. By night he would take a wherry to the south bank of the Thames, retracing his route and revisiting his haunts, losing himself among the brothels and taverns, reprising his act as showman and fencer. It was more rewarding than being a soldier or spy. Sometimes he would pick a fight; at other instants the fight would choose him. He never lost.

Another day arrived, 26 August 1588, and at the Palace of Whitehall the Earl of Essex staged a grand military review. He and his stepfather Leicester were not about to mislay the royal favour or political advantage they had gained. The court marvelled at the event, buried its collective envy and malevolent spite beneath generous and open remark. It was how the Queen desired it.

To a blast of trumpets and proclamation by heralds, the joust began. It was Essex who rode as champion to the Queen, Leicester who stood beside his sovereign at a window and admired the spirit and virtuosity. And, in the milling crowd of nobles and gentry, Hardy watched the lance of his enemy lower and the mounted charge proceed. Essex was for ever the darling of the ladies, the dashing romantic, the perfect knight in unblemished armour who drew gasps and applause with his soldierly skill. He knew nothing of real war, Hardy mused.

'Spectating poor fits you, Mr Hardy.'

Walsingham emerged discreet from the surroundings and acknowledged his junior with a transitory glance. Through judicious intervention, the former had saved the life of the latter; with quick wits and daring, the latter had preserved the reputation of the former and shielded the person of the Queen. The higher the stakes, the less need for extravagant gesture.

The spy-chief followed the galloping trajectory of the horses, the clash and recover, the rearming, the wheeling and return. 'A rare and noble sight, is it not?'

'For some the joust is all, your honour.'

'Essex believes it so.'

'He sits firm in the saddle, runs the ring well, carries his lance proud and the hopes of many with him.'

'And yet he is the most callow and conceited of fools, Mr Hardy.' Contempt was delivered as bland observation. 'It is said the heart of Her Majesty would break should harm befall him.'

'As her devoted subject I then must wish him health.'

'A selfless gesture, Mr Hardy.'

Forces met and hurtled on, the Earl of Cumberland unseated from his steed sent crashing to the ground. Mannered persons yelled their delight. Along the line of the tilt-fence, the winner trotted and danced his horse in merry dressage and dipped his lance towards Elizabeth.

Response from Walsingham was muted. 'Fate may not always deliver what we ask.'

'I know it too well, your honour.'

'So let us accept our lot and embrace good things.' The Secretary of State withdrew a letter from a pouch hidden beneath his cloak and passed it to Hardy. 'Read it, for it comes from Drake aboard his *Revenge*. He speaks of you in warmth and esteem.'

'My regard for him is yet higher.'

The younger man unfolded and studied the page, suddenly drawn by the bold hand and familiar style, conveyed by his imagination to the cramped cabin of the Vice Admiral and the noise and choking smog of combat. His throat constricted. Perhaps it reacted to the memory or dredged up past and sad emotion.

Hardy returned the letter. 'I am undeserving of his praise.'

'I deem our friend the better arbiter.' Walsingham conjured the epistle away. 'He is less flattering of ministers than I, rebukes the council for its meanness, accuses us of betraying the fleet and denying it necessaries and resource.'

'Is there truth in his charge?'

'Where is reality that it may not be changed? Where is fact where it may not be challenged?' The world of politics, the realm of Walsingham, of Burghley, of Elizabeth, of government.

Hardy surveyed the courtly swarm about them. 'We are surely at peace when blame is traded as readily as shot.'

'At least it will be in the English tongue and with Protestant and not Catholic oaths.' The eyes of Walsingham were as dark and indecipherable as ever. 'Our council will respond to Drake, will refute his allegation, will declare the captains wanting and lacklustre in their Armada chase.'

'You would peddle a lie, your honour?'

'I will do the bidding of my Queen.'

'And while insult is heaped and letters sent, brave and loyal seamen will fall to pestilence and dearth of food.'

'All must die of something, Mr Hardy.'

Most of those he loved already had. Hardy turned away, anxious to free himself from the enquiring mind and probing demands of his chief. It was not his place to have opinion, not the company he was accustomed to keep. So much had been sacrificed, and in the barren aftermath they held a joust.

Walsingham had not finished. 'What am I to do with a soldier of Drake who is yet an agent of mine?'

'Release him from your employ.'

'Battle continues, Mr Hardy. Threat remains.'

'Neither holds curiosity for me.'

'They sit in your heart, infest your soul.'

'Like the renegade at Tilbury, they are vanished.'

'Vanished maybe.' The voice was as dry and caustic as quicklime. 'But the stray round of a musket, the couched stiletto in a hand, may with single event change the path of history.'

Hardy swivelled slowly on his heel and stared into the closed countenance. 'Have I not done my part, your honour?'

'Has any actor in our theatre of campaign?'

'My beloved wife would be alive save for the course I chose. My service to you, my journey to Lisbon, my meeting with a traitor – each step brought the Reaper closer to my door.'

'Foresight and divination is rare granted, and hindsight has no value.'

'Your honour, my value is spent.'

He offered the faintest of bows, a minimum courtesy to avoid offence. The gesture was a farewell to Walsingham, to espionage and arms, to an existence removed from the ordered normality of others. He wanted to raise his son. He wanted to throw his Katzbalger blade deep into a lake. He wanted to sit at the grave of his dead wife.

'You shall come back, Mr Hardy.'

As he pushed his way through the jewelled and pomandered throng, minions were ferrying off the downed and unconscious Cumberland. Fresh challengers would be found, further aristocratic pursuits called up to divert the onlookers. Hardy paused. A spectre had intruded, in a snatched instant the face of the English renegade transposing with another. The image slid away. In its stead was Isaiah Payne accompanied by his Searchers, a band of men paid to shadow, to suspect, to discover all secrets. Hardy quickened his pace.

Margate had spawned a shanty town, a dismal settlement of hovels and shelters thrown up in haphazard array. It stank of death. Behind sparse walls of driftwood, or beneath torn scraps of canvas, former sailors of the English fleet coughed and groaned and breathed their last. This was their reward and their resting place. For sickness had taken hold, was winnowing the men who had manned the tops and fired the cannon in the squadrons of Howard, Drake, Hawkins and Frobisher. Occasionally a burial party would move through to kick down the pitiful structures upon the dead and create a new swathe of temporary graves. But mostly the inhabitants were left alone. The beach colony had become a cemetery.

In the limewashed house where he had last seen him, Hardy found Luqa teetering in the borderland. The Maltese islander was closer to extinction than life. Yet he had clung on with the tenacity of his nature, with a will that challenged the clawing appetite of his disease. It would not be long now. By the light of his lamp the English soldier smelled the gangrene canker of damaged lungs, glimpsed the swollen face and bloodied spittle, heard the high and fading whisper of the breath.

His friend stirred. 'Fearnot is loath to approach me, Christian. He knows I die.' The voice was forced and ragged.'

'He sits as sentinel at your door.'

'Ever my faithful guardian.' Luqa exhaled a sigh. 'And you, my brother? What returns you to this plague-pit?'

'Fine company and old acquaintance.'

'I cannot stand with you to welcome home the fleet, Christian. The ships are gone, and I with them.'

'To sit and talk is sufficient.'

'My talk is as poor as the fight in me.' Luqa heaved breathless on a paroxysm, struggled to contain the spasm. 'Tell me of London, brother.'

'It is full of sound and carousing, of knaves and nobles laying claim to having vanquished the Spaniard.'

'How quick they forget us.'

'Yet how easily they seize our victory for themselves.'

Humour crept into the swollen features. 'Would you wish them beside us in war, brother? Would you care to smell the stench in their silken hose?'

Conversation ebbed as energy drained from the dying man. Lucidity could end and delirium encroach, the body convulse and writhe with shuddering force. Typhus tended to kill its prisoners. Hardy sat quiet, attentive, waiting, swallowing the misery that ached in his throat.

The question came. 'How fare Emma and Adam?'

'They are well.'

It was the briefest of statements and the greatest of lies, an attempt to conceal the truth and ensure Luqa went unburdened to the other side. He did not need informing. There was enough at present to dwell upon, ample suffering contained within the chamber and spread out on the soiled pallet of straw.

Hardy deflected attention elsewhere. 'The Queen led in service of thanksgiving at St Paul's. She descended from her carriage, kissed the earth, proclaimed out loud at our deliverance.'

'My rejoicing is more subdued, brother.' The eyes glowed dim. 'Tell me of Queen Elizabeth.'

'She survives all manner of threat which Garza sent against her. You recall your visit with Black Jack to the Castle of St George?'

'I do, Christian.'

'You remember the cracked and emptied rice-cauldron lying abandoned near a gate?'

'It too, brother.'

'Such vessel belonged to the old enemy, Luqa. To those you fought with my father. To Janissaries.'

'Janissaries?'

There was a wistfulness in the croaked response, a reaching for memory and a yearning for campaign. Luqa was still the boy with slingshot and deadly aim, still the boy who had jumped up on the saddle of a soldier-adventurer named Christian Hardy, still the boy who swam between the besieged harbour forts of the heroic Knights of St John on that blood rock of Malta. The circle was closed.

'Did you find once more your traitor, Christian?'

'He remains alive in spite of my endeavour. We skirmished and wrestled hard, broke sweat and every kind of object, near brought down a kitchen tent upon our heads.'

The rough laugh of the islander dissolved into choking, Luqa vomiting and struggling before subsiding gradually to calm. Hardy leaned to wipe the blood-foam from his lips.

'Take my hand, Christian.' Luqa grasped for contact and pressed his silver crucifix into the receiving palm. 'This cross I have worn at my throat since a child. I once guarded it for your father, lifted it from about his neck when he was lying slain. He told me it belonged with the living.'

Possession was passed and the talisman stayed with the living. No more words were required, no more tales or goodbyes needed to be traded. Understanding went deeper than vocabulary. In simple respect, and as final salute, Hardy stood and stooped to kiss the blistered forehead of his friend.

On the way from the room, he turned and whistled for Fearnot, and the dog followed.

Shepherds were playing cricket, the batsman stationed against a wicket-gate and lofting high the wool-and-leather ball with a curving sweep of his crook. Hardy left them to their game. He had ridden deep into the weald of Kent, through the orchards and smallholdings, past the apple-barns and barley-stores, and up on to the higher ground. None would disturb him here. It offered the seclusion he craved, provided a space and freedom in which to think or ignore thought, allowed him to shed tears for that which was done and those who were lost.

His mother Maria, his wife Emma, his friends Black Jack, Hawkhead and Luqa, the brave Scotsman and merchant mariner Mr Hunter – all were dead. Undoubtedly the English traitor had told the truth in their encounter at Tilbury, had laid bare the consequence of his life. Everyone he touched indeed turned to ash. He had thought he was doing his duty to the Queen, had believed he was living by the code of his father, but his boldness, his adventure, his selfishness had only injured or consumed each person he held dear. The wounds gave him identity.

He eased Fearnot from his saddle-berth and himself dis-mounted, tethering the horse to a beech and busying himself with fetching wood. The fire was soon built. Kindling, naphtha and the strike of steel on pyrite, and the sparks flew and flames caught. He coaxed them higher. When darkness gathered he remained crouched before the blaze, permitting time to coast and emotions to settle, pulling a cloak about his shoulders against the early autumnal chill. There were outstanding issues to address.

Carefully, he eased from his saddlebag a leather-bound volume of modest appearance. A Flemish agent employed in the Lisbon household of the Marquis of Santa Cruz, then Admiral of the Ocean, had thought it pertinent to his task and removed it from Spanish ownership. Hardy was the beneficiary. He opened and scanned it now, running a finger over the inscriptions, turning the pages and studying their contents. Luqa had protected it well for him. Each English man or woman named within, every Catholic identified as potential friend to a Spanish occupation, was condemned by supposition and the scratch and loop of a quill to the rack, the stake, the saw, the noose.

Hardy tore out the first sheet and fed it in to burn, repeated with another. He had denied to Walsingham the existence of such a ledger and stayed ahead of the Searchers. Because enough innocents had perished for their belief; because it was better for a person to consign a book to the flames than for the book to consign a person; because, by some perversity of nature, mankind had sufficient religion to hate and insufficient faith to love. And for the reason that his own mother had been paraded to immolation in an auto-da-fé on groundless charges of treason and heresy.

Eventually he committed the final fragments to burn, watched them ignite and curl and blacken. Throughout England vast bonfires were lit and people danced in boundless celebration. But his more modest construction represented the true defeat of tyranny. In this small hollow and with a simple act he defied Walsingham and the established order, challenged the cruel fervour of zealots as Isaiah Payne and Garza, found redemption and reawakened hope. A magical location. The light of the embers glowed blood-red, shimmered on the silver crucifix at his throat, glanced from the warm eyes of Fearnot. With total certainty, Hardy comprehended his father would have done the same.

~

'*The ship is lost . . . Throw yourselves to the sea . . .*'

Words were snatched away in the torrent, the misted shapes of men and timbers pluming and vanishing against the backdrop. The *Gran Grin* was foundering. She had done well to reach so far, had plunged down the west side of Ireland with the doggedness of the condemned, had remained afloat when other ships of the Armada were strewn as wreckage or swallowed whole. Luck of any kind was ended. In a dawn blackened by tempest, she heeled in the surf. The jettisoning of canvas and snapped masts, the application of roped barrels and sea-anchors and desperate pumping of the bilges had merely prolonged the agony and not prevented the inevitable. The vessel, like her crew, was to be abandoned to the fates.

Grasping for purchase, blinded by the salt sting, Inquisitor Garza crawled on to the main deck. He would not submit, would never accept circumstance was anything more than a supreme test of his faith. As the tumult roared, he would think upon the five wounds of Christ; as the company about him drowned, he would cast himself to the waves and by dint of prayer and the blessing of God would make it to the shore.

He stumbled and recovered, inching his way, dodging a loosened cannon, clutching the Giorgione painting of the Crucifixion tight beneath his arm. The object was a symbol of everything he had worked for, of all he had achieved. As Inquisitor in Lisbon or Inquisitor General of England, he would see himself and his keepsake to safety.

Terrified at the brink, a sailor clung to fallen rigging and shrank from the heaving abyss. He blocked the progress of

Garza. The Inquisitor did not wait for consultation, would not have heard the pleas. Self-preservation and holy mission commanded him to action. He raised his foot and kicked hard into the face, feeling the teeth give and nose break, again struck until the head recoiled and the body shifted. Yet the victim was stubborn. He continued to grip, immune to the blows, sliding away with a long and silent scream only when Garza broke his hands.

The Jesuit took his place, clambering down until the hull tipped, the sea peaked mountainous, and he was enveloped into a tumbling and frozen world and raced towards death. Not even faith could prepare him. Every sense was swamped, every bone compressed, every particle of air squeezed from his lungs. There was a moment at which he reached for oblivion, when his body closed down and the pressure-pain of unrelenting immersion carried him to an altered state. He floated, he sank, he drowned. Thanks be to God.

Reprieve was unexpected. Only the retching of seawater from his mouth, the pulsing agony in his chest and head, convinced him that he lived. Death would not sow such confusion. Christ, how cold he was. He felt the rough sand between his fingers, shuddered to the chill, sobbed and snivelled mystified at the numbing realization. His task endured. Gradually he raised his head, noted the figures tending to the scattered bodies or straining to pull random survivors from the breakers. Miracles still occurred. A rescuer bent to aid a mariner fighting for his breath and life, a pair of stalwarts dragged an injured man higher up the beach, a kindred soul administered to a stricken sailor whose entrails had burst through. These Samaritans were so merciful.

Tentatively the Inquisitor climbed to his feet, swaying to the effort and almost collapsing at his weakness. He must thank the strangers, bless them for their generosity. Not all were barbarians as he had imagined. He lifted his hand to draw their attention, was pleased to see eyes turn and smiles widen. They approached with their open and guileless faces, and he stepped to greet them. Maybe they were of the Church of Rome.

It was the blow through his chest from a boat-spike that changed things, which disabused him of his notions. In the dying instant before he toppled he appreciated the gravity of his error. They were not arranging a rescue, but supervising mass murder. Sailors were being butchered about him, were having their throats cut and their clothes and possessions taken, were begging for life and given no chance. The pirates of Clare Island were of a different faith. Their gods of the sea demanded feeding, the onset of autumn required they pre-serve their food stocks and limit ravenous mouths. There was little room for sentiment.

Whispering a short prayer, Inquisitor Garza expired. His prized Giorgione rolled close by in the shallows, its face scoured clean of any image and its gilt surround fading to the tide. Like the Armada itself, it was become so much driftwood and memory.

End

At least encroaching death allowed him finally to rest. Sir Francis Walsingham lay on his back in the darkness, listened dispassionately to the fluttering of his pulse and the ebbing of his breath. He was close to the moment of infinite mystery. There were few regrets, nothing he would have changed or could have done in any other manner. It was a life full-lived in humble service to his Saviour and to *Gloriana*, a calling and career spent fighting the enemies of both. What a conflict it had been. And he had won if through less than fair means, had outwitted them all, had preserved the Crown and defended his faith. God save Queen Elizabeth, and God bless England.

His thoughts drifted, rolling and surging, navigating the plots and intrigue, the countries and battlegrounds of his past. Men killed, loyalties purchased, lives wrecked or saved. Almost single-handed, his endeavour often despised by his sovereign, he had laboured ceaselessly in the sewer labyrinth of espionage to defend the realm. This was his reward and his luxury: to die in his own bed, as his own man, with the comforting words of his own religion on his lips. The nation hailed Drake, applauded him as deliverer of great victory. But the nation had only partial sight.

Agents in Lisbon and Madrid had delivered the final tally. Of some one hundred and twenty-five ships of the Armada, half had failed ever to return. Of the mighty host that had embarked, almost twenty thousand were lost. King Philip was right to grieve. For Spain, it had been the most catastrophic of disasters. Many of those who were shipwrecked, most of the bedraggled survivors who had hauled themselves to land, lived long enough to regret not going down with their ships. They were hunted and pursued, attacked by the Irish and hanged by the English, fell prey to bounty-hunters and crusading zealots and the lethal search-posses of the Lord Deputy of Ireland Sir William Fitzwilliam. Some had escaped, fleeing to Scotland and finding their way home. They were in a minority.

Walsingham saw a distant light, felt its pull and did not resist. His ravaged body would make for poor viewing. He preferred to slip away, to bid farewell in the private and understated manner of a spy-chief. True fighters had few vanities. Ceremony was for dolts such as Leicester, an earl who had beaten him to the casket, a man finished off by the cancer in his stomach within a fortnight of the parade and revels in Whitehall. How the Queen had mourned. She would scarcely be moved by the demise of her Principal Secretary of State.

Opiates crawled in his brain, unlocking compartments and releasing ghosts. He studied their faces – identified the recusants he had interrogated and sent to the hangman; stumbled upon Mary, Queen of Scots; observed the Spanish sailors whose corpses had washed ashore in their thousands off the Giant's Causeway, Blasker Sound, Donegal Bay and Tralee Bay. Fugitives from the past. Everyone made sacrifices. He had beggared himself in his efforts, had sold estates to pay off debt, had spent every shilling combating the parsimony of his queen and constructing the most effective spy apparatus in history. For the greater good and the glory of the Lord. Catholics had no right to haunt him now.

He counted down, eased his head against the pillow. It was appropriate he should die in Seething Lane, lay in the chamber where so often he had dreamed his most audacious plans. Those plans had spawned result; those dreams had provided the foundation for a free and Protestant land. Almost two years had elapsed since the fleet of Medina Sidonia appeared in the waters of the Channel. Time in which tumours and carnosity in a wearied body could grow. Walsingham sensed the coldness pressing at his heart. His life was run, his will written, his grave prepared. Nothing more needed to be done. Calmly, he folded his hands across his chest and headed for perpetual sleep. He was unafraid of judgement.

In the early hours of 6 April 1590, Sir Francis Walsingham died. The following night, with few mourners and in secret, he was buried in a crypt beneath the choir of St Paul's. By holding his funeral in darkness, his family could evade both the attention of his creditors and the expense of dressing buildings in black along the route. The head of English espionage remained covert to the end.

~

The satisfaction of a homecoming. Realm breathed deep, could almost smile at the stench of Lisbon and summon enthusiasm for the sewage and effluvia that ran freely in the streets. It meant the culmination of his journey, sanctuary after so long spent hiding in the squalid wynds and rookeries of Edinburgh, in the teeming slums of Paris, in the festering and fly-blown waypoints that marked his passage down to Portugal. It was the sweetest of things to be back.

He strolled through the Baixa, taking in familiar sights and listening to the chatter, watching the inhabitants flow among the taverns and churches. The mood had changed since last

394

he was here. Then there had been optimism and the promise of conquest, the high fervour of holy war. Results had proved indifferent, and disappointment ever awkward to expunge or explain away. They must have gawped at the sick and dying being offloaded from the listing Armada hulls, must have stared dumbfounded as the once-proud admirals and captains were carried like aged invalids to the shore. Religious conflict had certainly exacted a toll. After a while, the citizens would have abandoned their hope of seeing further vessels return, would have lit their candles and said their prayers and whispered dark opinion of the Spanish. Hardly his problem.

With confident tread, he reached his lodgings and ascended the narrow stairs. Soon he would find new quarters, would direct his earnings and deserved reward towards a residence fit for a hero. Whatever the outcome of his venture to England, however failure or success was measured, he merited the applause and gratitude of the Catholic world. He had come closer than any to killing Elizabeth, and by the grace of God and divine intervention would one day try again.

'You seem well after your journeys, *Reino*.'

It was not a Jesuit he recognized. The priest was short and stooped from learning, his eyes questing, his hands soft as those of any lawyer. An Inquisitor, an occupant of the Estaus Palace.

Realm was motionless. 'I did not suppose such early greeting.'

'What is it you supposed, *Reino*?' The Inquisitor stood in the doorway mild-mannered and unthreatening. 'You are the talk of the Suprema.'

'My humble service does not warrant its acclaim.'

'Though it is demanding of close scrutiny. You fail, *Reino*.'

The renegade was suddenly wary. 'Then I am no different to Medina Sidonia and his admirals, inseparable from the wider fortunes of our Armada.'

'One was dispersed by fireships and storm. The other . . .' Words tailed off into inference.

'You would make accusation of me?'

'I would raise matters which of late have come to our concern.'

Realm bridled, his consternation and sense of outrage growing. 'Base tales and foul rumour spread by malcontents will not touch me, brother.'

'Men have been put to the rack for less.'

'Regard me, brother. I have suffered, travelled, outwitted capture, shed my blood and that of others.'

'Yet you have not prevailed.'

'None may challenge me for want of my enterprise.'

'You stand condemned on account of your treason.' The Inquisitor regarded him with kindly concern. 'We have evidence, *Reino*.'

Uncomprehending, Realm shook his head. 'Sole proof is of your mistake. Was it not I who came within a shallow breath of killing Elizabeth? Was it not I who trained the Janissaries, toiled to unseat the Protestant heresy, strove to further our sacred cause?'

'Mere ruse and concealment for your blacker purpose.'

'I have no purpose but to serve King Philip.'

'Your master is Albion, your aim to subvert and to sit as the double-faced serpent at our heart.'

'Inquisitor Garza is a friend to me. He would ill presume to make such shameful claim'

'Garza is dead and his office vested in me.'

Realm noticed the glint of armour behind the priest, half turned and saw other soldiers moving up behind. An

396

impossible situation. He was the victim of lies and mis-judgement, the scapegoat in a scenario he did not understand. Surely there was room for negotiation and agreement.

The Jesuit seemed not to concur. 'We find codes and secret inks in your chambers, Reino. We uncover letters from England, instructions to you, vile messages confirming your misdeeds.'

'They are forgeries.'

'As you are an enemy intelligencer of the most dishonour-able kind. A man who abused our trust and weakened our cherished plans, a common murderer who at behest of London slew with poison our Admiral of the Ocean the Marquis of Santa Cruz.'

A chill dawning projected sweat on the face of the renegade. 'I am innocent.'

'Guilt is decided and protest futile, your confession to be drawn by branding and torture.' The Inquisitor offered him the sign of the Cross. 'May the Lord have mercy upon you.'

The Inquisition would be less forgiving. Verdict was given and sentence handed down.

Across the street, masked by the heavy drapes on the windows of her carriage, Constança watched the party appear, the guards drag their struggling prisoner towards *El Papa Negro*, the black pope, collecting-coach of the Inquisition. The loud complaint of the Englishman rose in pitch. It was quickly stifled as he was thrown inside and the door slammed fast. Constança waited until the cavalcade drew away and the drama passed from view before ordering her coachman to drive on. Even from the grave Sir Francis Walsingham, spy-master and Secretary of State, enjoyed the final word.

★

397

Flavit Deus et dissipati sunt
God blew and they were scattered

Historical Note

While there is no direct evidence of involvement by Walsingham in the death on 9 February 1588 of the Marquis of Santa Cruz, original commander of the Armada, it is worth noting that the English spymaster had (through his intelligencer Anthony Standen, alias Pompeo Pelligrini, based in Tuscany) recruited a long-term Flemish agent in the private household of the Spanish grand admiral.

Agents of Walsingham had previously encountered Santa Cruz when in 1582 the Spanish commander was tasked by King Philip II with leading a flotilla to the Azores and putting down residual Portuguese opposition to his rule. Although fronted by Dom António, Prior of Crato, a Portuguese pretender to the throne, resistance was organized and a multinational force of adventurers and privateers co-ordinated by Philip Strozzi, a trusted Florentine in the pay of the English spy-chief. Santa Cruz defeated the motley naval formation of his enemy at the Battle of Ponta Delgada off Terceira island, and the Prior and his allies fled. The rebellion was yet another example of Walsingham fighting Spain and thwarting its ambition by proxy.

Attempts by Walsingham to deflect or subvert the Armada were comprehensive and far-reaching. Even as the Spanish fleet scattered and sailed around the north of Scotland, his efforts continued. In October 1588, as she sheltered from the weather in Tobermory Bay in the Sound of Mull, the galleon *Florencia* was blown apart by explosion in the powder magazine and sank. John Smollett, an agent of Walsingham, is implicated in the action. A Scots merchant-mariner named Hunter did exist and was betrayed to the Spanish authorities while using his ships to spy on the build-up of the Armada. His fate is unknown.

A number of English renegades and 'Hispaniolated' Catholics did serve with the Armada. One, a certain Francis Limbrecke (alias Francisco Lembri), acted as pilot to the Spanish fleet as it sailed up the Channel. He survived the catastrophe and was later captured by the English after having spied for the Spanish between 1611 and 1615 on the newly established Virginia settlement of Jamestown. Brought back in chains by the High Marshal of the colony, Sir John Dale, on board the ship *Treasurer*, Limbrecke was tried, convicted and hanged from the yardarm within sight of the English coast. Also on the vessel were the native-American princess Pocahontas and her child.

Countless attempts on the life of Elizabeth either occurred or were mooted. Plots ranged from schemes to poison her bedclothes to plans for mass attack by armed horsemen while she was out riding. All were uncovered and foiled by Walsingham. An incident did arise in which a wildfowler accidentally discharged his gun as the Queen passed by on her royal barge.

Even at slack tide, London Bridge was a fearsome and treacherous structure to navigate by river-craft. Anecdotal evidence suggests Elizabeth traversed it by royal barge only once – an experience which so dismayed her she vowed never to repeat the manoeuvre.

★

It is believed that as few as sixty English sailors died in action during the entire Armada campaign. Yet many hundreds more succumbed to pestilence and typhus in its immediate aftermath, the diseases exacerbated by malnutrition, food-poisoning and inadequate clothing and shelter. Both Drake and Howard petitioned the court, but neither the Queen nor her advisers were persuaded to release funds. Several government ministers even considered the fatalities a means of cutting costs, for crews went unpaid until formal discharge after conflict. So appalled were they by such parsimony and callousness, several admirals (including Drake, Howard and Hawkins) later established the world's first naval charity.

Conflict between England and Spain did not end with the Armada. In the spring of 1589, Elizabeth sanctioned Sir Francis Drake, Sir John Norris and Sir Walter Raleigh to mount a large expedition to Portugal in order to destroy the remnants of the Spanish fleet and place the Portuguese pretender Dom António on the throne. Some one hundred and fifty English ships and twenty thousand men were involved. The mission was a fiasco. Driven off by the Portuguese, and against the express orders of the Queen, the English made for the Azores. By the time the depleted force returned to England, in early summer, the venture had cost the privy purse almost fifty thousand pounds and caused the death of eleven thousand Englishmen. Not content with his earlier misjudgement, King Philip II mounted a further excursion against England. It too was dispersed by storm.

Ignoring the wishes of Elizabeth, the Earl of Essex accompanied the failed 'English Armada' expedition to Lisbon. His chequered military career was to culminate with his involvement as Lord Lieutenant in the Nine Years War in Ireland.

This too was a disaster. Ostracized by the Queen, stripped of his privileges and outmanoeuvred by Principal Secretary Robert Cecil, he eventually led an armed and ill-fated insurrection against his sovereign. He was beheaded on Tower Green on 25 February 1601.

Drake was to die from sickness aboard his flagship *Defiance* on 27 January 1596 while raiding Spanish possessions and sailing off the island of Buena Ventura near Panama. His crew buried him at sea.

Acknowledgements

M y profound thanks are owed to the following for contributing in so many ways to the writing of this book: Lizzy, Jamie and Joe for accompanying and steering me in my research both at home and abroad; Carolina Peralta, Hugh Dickson, Alan Gray and Jane Dymock for their invaluable local knowledge; Miles Ashley for poring over his sailing charts and offering his nautical insights; Eugenie Furniss, my agent, and Kate Parkin, my editor, for their friendship and faultless instinct; the armed forces of the United Kingdom for their enduring professionalism and devotion to duty. *Realm* draws much on that spirit. Finally, I must salute the memory of Sir Francis Walsingham and Sir Francis Drake, two genuine English heroes without whose character, ruthlessness, skill and daring there would have been no story.

KT-433-320

COMPLETELY AWESOME!

RIPLEY
PUBLISHING

a Jim Pattison Company

PUBLISHING

Publisher Anne Marshall
Editorial Director Rebecca Miles
Project Editor Charlotte Howell
Text Geoff Tibballs
Proofreader Judy Barratt
Researchers Charlotte Howell, Dominic Lill, James Proud
Indexer Hilary Bird
Art Director Sam South
Project Design Rocket Design (East Anglia) Ltd
Cover Design Michelle Foster
Reprographics Juice Creative
Executive Vice President Norm Deska
Vice President, Archives and Exhibits Edward Meyer

PUBLISHER'S NOTE

While every effort has been made to verify the accuracy of the entries in this book, the Publishers cannot be held responsible for any errors contained in the work. They would be glad to receive any information from readers.

WARNING

Some of the stunts and activities in this book are undertaken by experts and should not be attempted by anyone without adequate training and supervision.

Cover image: Peg man, Kelvin Mercado, pinned 161 pegs to his face, more than anyone has ever done before.

Published by Ripley Publishing 2014

Ripley Publishing, Suite 188, 7576 Kingspointe Parkway, Orlando, Florida 32819, USA

2 4 6 8 10 9 7 5 3 1

Copyright © 2014 by Ripley Entertainment Inc.

All rights reserved. Ripley's, Believe It or Not!, and Ripley's Believe It or Not! are registered trademarks of Ripley Entertainment Inc.

ISBN 978-1-60991-101-0

Some of this material first appeared in *Ripley's Believe It or Not! Strikingly True!*

Library of Congress Control Number: 2013037047

Manufactured in China in November/2013
1st printing

First published in Great Britain in 2014 by Random House Books, Random House, 20 Vauxhall Bridge Road, London SW1V 2SA
www.rbooks.co.uk

Addresses for companies within The Random House Group Limited can be found at
www.randomhouse.co.uk/offices/htm

The Random House Group Limited Reg. No. 954009

A CIP catalogue record for this book is available from the British Library

ISBN 9780099568223 (UK)

No part of this publication may be reproduced in whole or in part, or stored in a retrieval system, or transmitted in any form or by any means, electronic, mechanical, photocopying, recording, or otherwise, without written permission from the publisher. For information regarding permission, write to VPIntellectual Property, Ripley Entertainment Inc., Suite 188, 7576 Kingspointe Parkway, Orlando, Florida 32819
email publishing@ripleys.com
www.ripleybooks.com

Contents

Ripley's World

Marco Polo, Christopher Columbus, Neil Armstrong... there are few true adventurers that can be compared to such great men—but Robert Ripley just might be one of them! In 1918, considering the limited forms of travel, Ripley's determination to visit countries barely known back home showed a pioneering spirit no less extraordinary than those intrepid explorers.

With style, in bow tie and spats, Ripley traveled to Papua New Guinea, Armenia, Tibet and beyond—his aim was to uncover the world's wonders and weird-ities, miracles and monstrosities and feature them in the Believe It or Not! cartoon he drew daily for *The New York Globe*.

Americans couldn't get enough of Ripley and he rocketed into radio and television—broadcasting from places such as the bottom of a shark tank. Soon he was said to be more popular than the U.S. President!

By 1933, Ripley had opened an Odditorium (museum) in Chicago to display the artifacts he'd collected. Today, Ripley's is a global empire with 32 Odditoriums, three aquariums, a warehouse packed with artifacts, and an archive of more than 25,000 photos and 100,000 cartoons.

Ripley's Believe It or Not! daily cartoon was an instant success and the phrase "believe it or not" soon entered everyday speech.

During a NBC 1936 live broadcast from Silver Springs, Florida, Ripley and his co-host Ross Allen entered into a pit full of poisonous snakes.

Robert Ripley with Arjan Desur Dangar, one of the performers at Ripley's Odditorium exhibition at the 1933 Chicago World's Fair.

"MILKING" A RATTLE
Ripley's
BELIEVE IT or NOT PROG
Sunday — May 17, 1936
NBC
BLU
NI
WO

ALLEN

RIPLEY

Ripley enlisted the help of yaks to pull his car out of a snowdrift when it got stuck in a snowy mountain pass in Georgia in 1934. By 1940, Ripley had visited no fewer than 201 countries.

Available now! The first ever biography of Robert Ripley, *A Curious Man.* Visit www.ripleys.com for details.

UK

US

Ripley's Legacy Lives On

Here at Ripley's, we're inquisitive. Every second of every day, we've got our ears to the ground, eyes peeled and fingers flicking through files and every kind of social media—only stopping short of sniffer dogs—in the pursuit of a barely believable truth, or a person with a life more extraordinary—continuing the legacy of Robert Ripley.

We have researchers, curators, archivists and model-makers, as well as editors and correspondents, who compile articles and write for the Ripley's Believe It or Not! books. Dedicated and passionate about what we do, we never tire in our mission to uncover and preserve the unbelievable side of life.

Robert Ripley always encouraged his dedicated readers to submit material and photographs—a tradition that exists to this day. With a huge database of incredible stories, a massive photo archive, and a warehouse stuffed with exhibits, Ripley's celebrates our amazing world, without ever passing judgment.

Daily cartoons are still produced and printed to this day, and appear online and in a number of newspapers around the world. Ripley's Believe It or Not! is the longest running syndicated cartoon in the world.

We've been out and about!

Ripley's archivist Edward Meyer bought this bike made from road kill bones by artist Rasha "Reese" Moore from Florida. Rasha brought his creations to the Ripley's St. Augustine "Bizarre Buying Bazaar" in July 2013, an event that encouraged people to bring along their "Believe It or Nots!"

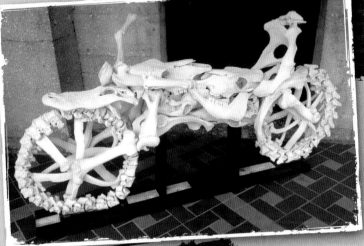

There have been lots of changes going on at the Mrytle Beach Odditorium in South Carolina (below)—with over 40 new exhibits! This Captain America Superhero collage (right) was made by Cristiam Ramos, and represents comic book characters—both Marvel and DC, hero and villain. Cristiam made the entire sculpture by hand.

Ripley's Aquarium of Canada

Over 15,000 marine and freshwater fish, including some of the most amazing underwater creatures on the planet, have taken up residence in Ripley's new aquarium in downtown Toronto, Canada.

A total of 450 species enjoy 1½ million gallons (5.7 million liters) of water in 45 different habitats, ranging from the majestic kelp forests of Canada's Pacific Northwest to the spectacular color of a tropical Indo-Pacific reef. The aquarium features the longest underwater moving walkway of its kind in North America, which takes visitors through Dangerous Lagoon where turtles, sawfish, stingrays and sharks—including 9-ft-long (2.7 m) sand tigers—swim overhead.

Ripley's — Believe It or Not!

Download the Ripley's Believe It or Not! app and access Ripley's content wherever you are. Head to the app store now to download and experience the world of Ripley's!

This is your one-stop portal into the incredible world of Ripley's. Download the world's weirdest phenomena onto your mobile device, including the latest Believe It or Not! photos, videos, stories and facts. This app features Ripley's image recognition technology, oddSCAN™, giving you the ability to scan real-world targets in Ripley's Odditoriums and some Ripley's books with your phone camera to unlock exclusive hidden content. It also offers live feeds, a guide to Ripley's attractions worldwide, Ripleyzines and more!

Unlock exclusive videos, photos and more using your smartphone.

ODDSCAN

POINT - SCAN - REVEAL
IT'S THAT EASY!

Some of the amazing features in our new app

cartoons

Ripleyzines

▲ Why not also download Ripley iSword on the app store now! The world's first ever sword swallowing app!

facebook   twitter   Odditoriums

SEND US YOUR BELIEVE IT OR NOT!

Contribute via our website: www.ripleybooks.com

Send your stories to www.ripleys.com/submit

Send an email to bionresearch@ripleys.com

Or write to us: BION Research, Ripley Entertainment Inc., 7576 Kingspointe Parkway, 188, Orlando, Florida 32819, U.S.A.

BELIEVE IT!

The Great Inferno

Tim Cockerill, aka The Great Inferno, happily gargles hot molten lead until it cools and hardens into solid metal in his mouth. During the day, Tim is a zoologist at Cambridge University in the U.K.

When he is not working in the lab, or trekking through a jungle to study insects, Tim wows audiences with such stunts as hammering nails into his head, heating his tongue with a blowtorch and swallowing fire. The Great Inferno has been amazing audiences for more than 15 years with his extremely painful-looking acts.

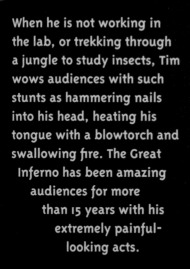

TIM ON CHEWING MOLTEN LEAD

"Fire-eaters have been doing this stunt for over 200 years, and the technique is still a closely guarded secret. Just like fire-eating, it takes years of practice before you can be ready to perform, and even then it is still highly dangerous. First, the metal is melted in a small furnace, and then a small amount (about a tablespoon) is transferred to a spoon. I then take this into my mouth and keep it there until it solidifies completely. After about 30 seconds I spit the nugget out onto a tray or catch it with a pair of thick gloves."

TIM ON THE BLOCKHEAD STUNT

"The Human Blockhead was invented in the 1930s by sideshow performer Melvin Burkhart, 'The Anatomical Wonder.' What you see is what you get with this stunt— a solid steel nail is hammered all the way into the face. This is not something to be tried by anyone—get the angle wrong and the nail would go straight through the skull and into the brain!"

High Horse

From the 1880s through to the 1970s, one of the most popular shows on the Steel Pier in Atlantic City, New Jersey, was the horse high dive. Highly trained horses, usually ridden by girls, would leap from heights of up to 60 ft (18 m) into a pool 10 ft (3 m) deep. Riders asserted at the time that the horses enjoyed diving, were excellent swimmers, and were never forced to jump. However, owing to public pressure, diving horse shows died out in the 1970s and only one show remains—in a scaled-down form—in New York, where a riderless horse named Lightning will jump 10 ft (3 m) into water for a bucket of oats.

Lottery Luck

Since 1993, Joan Ginther of Las Vegas, Nevada, has won the Texas Lottery four times, each time scooping at least $1 million, with total prize money of more than $20 million. She bought two of her winning tickets at the same store in Bishop, Texas, while visiting her father. Her chances of winning four lottery jackpots were put at more than 200-million-to-one.

Roar Deal

A thief in Germany stole a circus trailer unaware that there was a five-year-old lion in the back. The vehicle was later abandoned with its engine running after crashing into a road sign. Police believe the driver may have panicked on hearing the lion—named Caesar—let out a hungry roar.

Dump Dig

Sanitation workers in Parsippany, New Jersey, dug through 10 tons of trash at a city dump to successfully recover a wedding ring that had been accidentally thrown away by a couple. Bridget Pericolo had placed the ring in a cup, but her husband of 55 years, Angelo, mistakenly threw it out with the garbage before leaving for work.

Spelling Mistake

The general manager of the Chilean mint was fired after the country's name was spelt incorrectly on thousands of coins. The 2008 batch of 50-peso coins bore the stamp CHIIE, but amazingly no one spotted the spelling mistake until late 2009.

Classroom Relic

In June 2010, while cleaning up her classroom before a move, schoolteacher Michelle Eugenio of Peabody, Massachusetts, discovered a colonial-era document dating back to April 1792 among a pile of old books and scraps of paper.

Mistaken Identity

The dead body of a 75-year-old man slumped over a chair on the balcony of his third-floor Los Angeles, California, apartment was left undisturbed for several days one October as his neighbors thought it was a Halloween dummy.

Incriminating Evidence

An 18-year-old from Philadelphia, Pennsylvania, turned himself in to police in December 2009 for stealing a cell phone—after he took a photo of himself with it and it automatically sent a copy to the owner's e-mail!

Double Take

When Helen MacGregor was sent a 21-year-old postcard of the town in Yorkshire, England, where she grew up, she was amazed to see herself in the center of the photo as a toddler. A friend had sent her the postcard of Otley, unaware that the child pictured in the street scene was Miss MacGregor, then aged three.

Close Relatives

Adopted by different families at a young age, biological brothers Stephen Goosney and Tommy Larkin finally found each other nearly 30 years later—and discovered that for the past seven months they had been living almost directly across the street from each other in Corner Brook, Newfoundland, Canada.

Unexpected Mourner

Brazilian bricklayer Ademir Jorge Goncalves gave friends and family a surprise in November 2009 by turning up at his own funeral. Relatives had identified him as the disfigured victim of a car crash in Parana state, but actually he had been out on a drinking spree and did not hear about his death until his funeral was already underway.

Party Bug

Bug-eating parties are all the rage in Tokyo, Japan, where guests chow down on dishes such as grilled cockroaches, fried grasshoppers, cricket pie, and this red moth larvae soup.

Giant Pumpkin

Christy Harp of Jackson Township, Ohio, took first place at the 2009 Ohio Valley Giant Pumpkin Growers' annual weigh-off with a pumpkin that weighed 1,725 lb (783 kg)—nearly ten times the weight of an average man. At one point her prizewinning pumpkin grew at a rate of 33 lb (15 kg) per day.

Curry Favor

Feeding curry to sheep could help save the planet by lowering methane emissions. The spices used in curry kill the "bad" bacteria in a sheep's gut, reducing the amount of methane the sheep produce by up to 40 percent.

Salsa Bowl

During the 2010 Jacksonville Tomato Fest in Texas, a team of 20 volunteers made a 2,672-lb (1,212-kg) bowl of salsa.

Chocolate Landmark

A team of Chinese confectioners built a 33-ft-long (10-m) replica of the Great Wall of China entirely out of chocolate. The wall was made of dark-chocolate bricks held together with layers of white chocolate. It was unveiled at the 2010 World Chocolate Wonderland exhibition, which also featured 560 chocolate replicas of China's 2,200-year-old famous Terracotta Army.

Earthy Taste

Thuli Malindzi, 22, of Cape Town, South Africa, is addicted to eating soil and consumes a chunk every day. She has been eating earth for more than ten years. Although she has tried to give up, she cannot resist hard lumps of clay, which she says to her taste like fudge.

Chocolate Wall

To mark the 20th anniversary of the fall of the Berlin Wall, French chocolate-maker Patrick Roger constructed a 49-ft-long (15-m) replica of the landmark in chocolate. Over a period of three weeks, he used 1,980 lb (900 kg) of chocolate to build the wall, and even added graffiti and artwork to the surface by spraying it with cocoa butter mixed with food coloring.

Scorpion Snack

Li Liuqun of Hunan Province, China, is addicted to eating live scorpions and estimates he has eaten more than 10,000 of them over the last 30 years. Stung by a huge scorpion one day, he angrily bit off its head and enjoyed the taste so much that he now eats up to 30 in a single sitting. Luckily, he appears immune to the venom, which can paralyze and even kill.

1821 Bun

A hot-cross bun baked on Good Friday, 1821, has been kept in a Lincolnshire, England, family for 190 years—and still shows no sign of mold. The fruity bun, which has the date March 1821 on its base, was made by Nancy Titman's great- great-great-grandfather, William Skinner, who owned a bakery in London. It was not eaten at the time and has been preserved in a box ever since, passed down through generations of the family as an unusual heirloom. The bun is now rock hard and the currants have disintegrated, but the shape of the cross is still visible.

Creative Cakes

Debbie Goard of Oakland, California, has created hundreds of incredibly lifelike custom-made cakes in the shape of animals, foodstuffs and everyday objects. Her cake designs include dogs, a scorpion, a warthog, a burger, popcorn, spaghetti, sneakers, a Blackberry, a camera and a baby giraffe that was nearly 2 ft (60 cm) tall. Her life-sized Chihuahua cake was so realistic that restaurant patrons were concerned there was a real dog on the table!

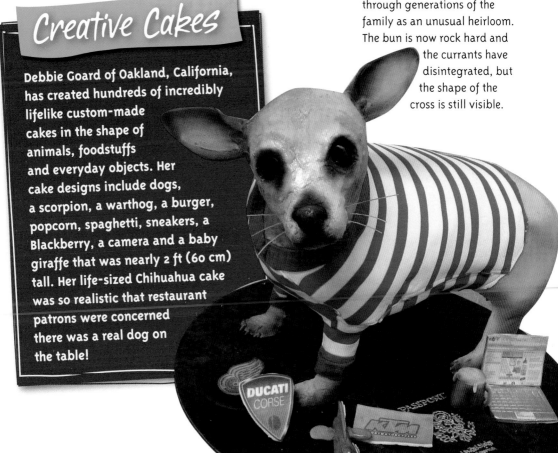

Buoyancy Castle

Three men from London, England, invented a bizarre new water sport when they fulfilled an ambition to ride a full-sized bouncy castle across Lake Garda in Italy. After drifting into the path of a sailing regatta and being redirected by a police launch, adventurers Jack Watkins, Chris Hayes, and Dave Sibley completed the 5-mi (8-km) voyage in two hours.

Yoga Queen

At the age of 87, Bette Calman of Williamstown, Victoria, Australia, still teaches up to 11 yoga classes per week. She can perform headstands and "bridges," and, from lying on her front, can raise her whole body off the ground using only her arms.

Mighty Pen

Three men in Hyderabad, India, have created a pen that is not only mightier than a sword but is the size of a giraffe! The brass pen, which cost more than $5,000 to make, stands 16 ft (4.9 m) tall, 1 ft (30 cm) wide, weighs 88 lb (40 kg), and is embossed with Indian cultural illustrations.

Remote Patrol

Burglars who broke into a man's apartment in Midwest City, Oklahoma, were caught via webcam by the man's wife more than 8,000 mi (12,875 km) away in the Philippines. Jim and Maribel Chouinard used the webcam to communicate face-to-face when they were apart.

Bike Jump

At Reno, Nevada, in 2009, U.S. motorcyclist Ryan Capes soared an astonishing 316 ft (96.3 m) through the air from one ramp to another.

Maggot Transfer

In May 2009, Charlie Bell of London, England, moved 37½ lb (17 kg) of live maggots from one container to another—in his mouth. He practiced at home with rice for months before finally replacing the grains with the "revolting" maggots.

Late Appointment

Reynolds Smith Jr. was appointed by the Alabama Democratic Party to sit on a party panel in October 2009—even though he had in fact died 11 months earlier!

Secret Stash

Calin Tarescu of Alba Iulia, Romania, discovered that his wife had thrown away a pair of his old shoes in which he had stashed $64,000. Police helped him to recover the majority of the money.

Hand Stolen

The mummified hand of a cheating gambler was stolen from a locked cabinet at a pub in Wiltshire, England, in March 2010. The hand, said to have been cut off a gambler caught cheating at the card game whist, was clutching a pack of 18th-century playing cards and is rumored to be cursed.

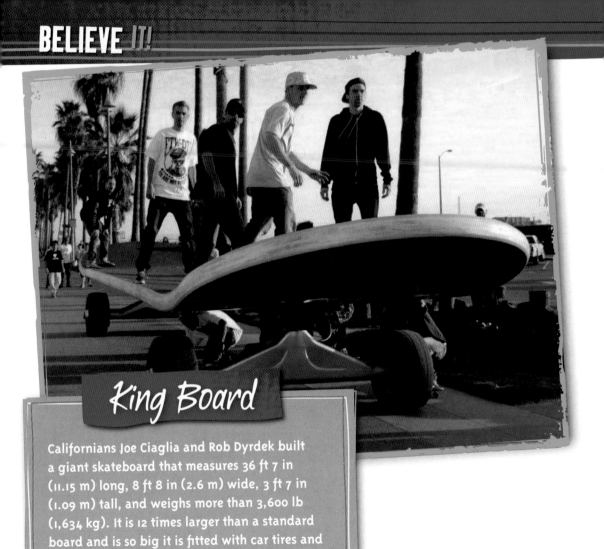

King Board

Californians Joe Ciaglia and Rob Dyrdek built a giant skateboard that measures 36 ft 7 in (11.15 m) long, 8 ft 8 in (2.6 m) wide, 3 ft 7 in (1.09 m) tall, and weighs more than 3,600 lb (1,634 kg). It is 12 times larger than a standard board and is so big it is fitted with car tires and has to be transported on a flatbed truck.

Edible Plates

To save on washing up after school dinners, catering boss Tiziano Vicentini from Milan, Italy, has devised a range of edible plates made from a kind of dough that is tough enough to last a lunchtime, but tasty enough to eat afterward.

Big Dipper

Students from Miami-Dade, Florida, filled a 13-gal (49-l) bucket with homemade guacamole. The dip weighed 4,114 lb (1,866 kg) and was made from 3,500 lb (1,588 kg) of avocados, 500 lb (227 kg) of tomatoes, 100 lb (45 kg) of mayonnaise, and 500 limes.

Triple Yolker

Bob Harrop from Devon, England, beat odds of 25 million to one when he found a triple-yolk egg while preparing his breakfast. The former hotelier has fried more than 155,000 eggs over the years and has seen hundreds of double yolkers, but this was the first time he had ever come across an egg with three yolks.

Chocolate Fashion

At the 15th Paris Salon du Chocolat in Shanghai, China, chefs and clothes designers from across the world combined their talents to create dresses, jackets, shoes and handbags all made from chocolate.

Expensive Bottle

In London, England, in 2009, jeweler Donald Edge unveiled a gold, pearl and diamond-encrusted bottle of Chambord raspberry liqueur that was valued at more than $2 million. The bottle featured 1,100 individual diamonds.

Pizza Chain

A chain of 2,200 pizzas stretching 1,630 ft (496 m) was laid out in 14 rows at Bucharest, Romania, in 2009. The pizza chain required 1,320 lb (600 kg) of flour, 880 lb (400 kg) of mozzarella, 440 lb (200 kg) of tomato sauce, 4 gal (15 l) of olive oil, and 6 lb 10 oz (3 kg) of yeast.

Moon Beer

In its thirst to create even better beer, the family-owned Brewery Caulier in Péruwelz, Belgium, has begun producing beer made by the light of a full moon. The full moon speeds up the fermentation process, shortening it from seven days to five, which can add extra punch to the beer, giving it a stronger flavor.

Frog's Heart

Customers in Japan who order Frog Sashimi eat the still-beating heart of a freshly killed American bullfrog. The rest of the frog is eaten as a raw dish, with any leftovers, including the feet, turned into soup.

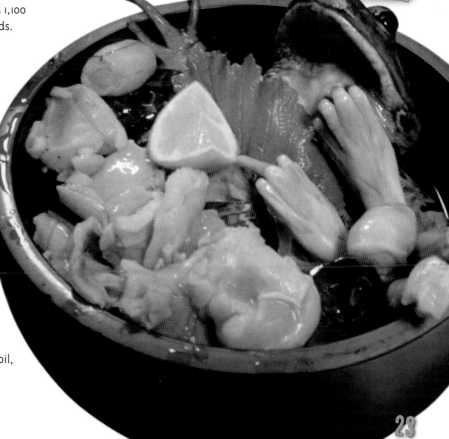

23

Mummies

EGYPTIAN CAT

The ancient Egyptians, who practiced mummification on royal personages, also mummified animals. These underwent the same elaborate treatment as human corpses, with cloth wraps, a large amount of salt, and resin. This Egyptian cat is more than 2,000 years old.

ANCIENT TATTOOS

In 2006, a 1,500-year-old, heavily tattooed, and very well-preserved female mummy was discovered in a mud-brick pyramid in northern Peru. She was buried with many weapons, leading experts to believe that she could have been a rare warrior queen of the warlike Moche people.

THE ICE MAIDEN OF AMPATO

The frozen, mummified body of a teenage Inca girl was discovered near the 20,700-ft (6,310-m) summit of Mount Ampato, Peru, in 1995. It is thought that she was ritually sacrificed more than 500 years ago. Other mummified children have also been found on the mountain. The "Ice Maiden," as she is known, was removed from the site and is kept under controlled conditions in a Peruvian museum.

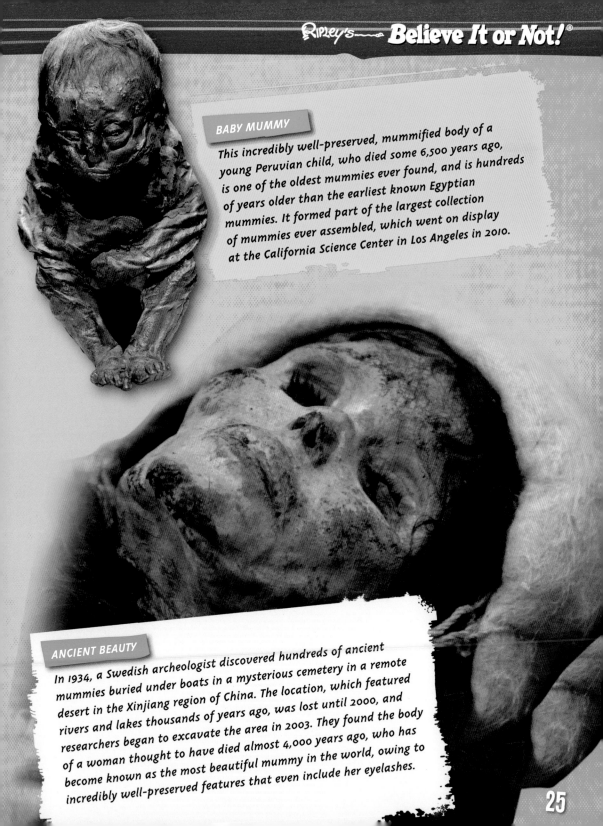

BABY MUMMY

This incredibly well-preserved, mummified body of a young Peruvian child, who died some 6,500 years ago, is one of the oldest mummies ever found, and is hundreds of years older than the earliest known Egyptian mummies. It formed part of the largest collection of mummies ever assembled, which went on display at the California Science Center in Los Angeles in 2010.

ANCIENT BEAUTY

In 1934, a Swedish archeologist discovered hundreds of ancient mummies buried under boats in a mysterious cemetery in a remote desert in the Xinjiang region of China. The location, which featured rivers and lakes thousands of years ago, was lost until 2000, and researchers began to excavate the area in 2003. They found the body of a woman thought to have died almost 4,000 years ago, who has become known as the most beautiful mummy in the world, owing to incredibly well-preserved features that even include her eyelashes.

25

BELIEVE IT!

Ant Arsonists

A house fire in Daytona Beach, Florida, was started by ants. Dozens of carpenter ants had built their nest around an electrical box and, when the insects came in contact with the live wiring, they ignited. The resulting flames burst out of the box, set fire to an adjacent desk, and then spread to the rest of the house.

Dead Candidate

Carl Robin Geary Sr. was elected mayor of Tracy City, Tennessee, on April 13, 2010, several weeks after he had died.

Parallel Lives

Identical twins Jim Lewis and Jim Springer from Ohio were separated a month after birth, then reunited at age 39. Both had divorced a Linda, married a Betty, had sons named James, driven blue Chevrolets, and owned dogs named Toy.

Lennon's Toilet

A toilet once owned by Beatle John Lennon was sold for the grand sum of $14,740. The builder who had removed the lavatory from Lennon's Berkshire, England, home in 1971 kept it in his shed for almost 40 years.

Granny Auction

Ten-year-old Zoe Pemberton of Essex, England, put her grandmother Marion Goodall up for sale on eBay in 2009, describing her as "cuddly" but "annoying." Although the listing was meant as a joke, bidding for the granny reached $30,000 before the auction website took it down.

Lot of Dough

Using a secret 1950s sourdough recipe involving Somerset flour, Cotswolds spring water, and Cornish sea salt, baker Tom Herbert from Gloucestershire, England, creates loaves of bread that cost more than $30 per loaf. Each 4½-lb (2-kg) hand-crafted shepherd loaf takes him two days to make from start to finish.

Unique Stamp

The one-of-a-kind Treskilling Yellow postage stamp is worth about $7.4 million. First issued in Sweden in 1855, it owes its value to the fact that it was printed in yellow by mistake, when the rest of the batch was green. It survives today thanks only to a 14-year-old Swedish schoolboy who rescued it from his grandmother's garbage bin in 1885 and sold it to a dealer for about $1.

Soap Drama

A wife from Pune, Maharashtra, India, divorced her husband on the grounds that his refusal to allow her to watch her favorite soap operas on TV amounted to a form of domestic cruelty.

Ear Wig

Radhakant Bajpai has a striking claim to fame: magnificent ear tufts that are longer than the hair on most men's heads, and probably the longest ear hair in the world. When Radhakant's hair was officially measured last, it stretched 5.2 in (13.2 cm), but since then it has more than doubled to a reported 11 in (28 cm). Although some think that his extreme ear hair is odd, Radhakant is very proud of his achievement.

Completely Hooked

Massachusetts stuntman Ses Carny, "the American Madman," entertains audiences by inserting two stainless-steel fishing hooks into his eyes. With the sharp hooks resting on the orbital bones at the base of the eyes, he then pulls down on the hooks to reveal what it looks like under his eyeballs!

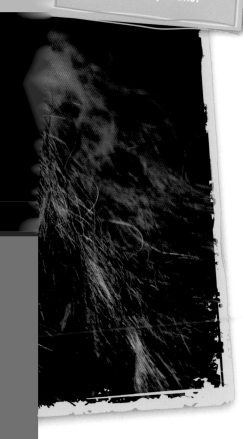

Top of the World

Jordan Romero of Big Bear Lake, California, reached the summit of Mount Everest—at the age of just 13. He climbed with his father and three Sherpa guides, and on getting to the peak of the world's highest mountain he telephoned his mother and said: "Mom, I'm calling you from the top of the world." Jordan has conquered many of the world's highest mountains, and climbed Africa's Mount Kilimanjaro when he was only ten.

Limbo Queen

Shemika Charles from Buffalo, New York State, weighs 140 lb (63.5 kg) and stands 5 ft 9 in (1.75 m) tall, but can limbo under a bar just 8½ in (22 cm) off the ground—while carrying a tray with three fuel canisters in each hand.

Happy Meals

Kelvin Baines of Devon, England, began his collection of McDonald's Happy Meal toys in the 1980s and he now has more than 7,500.

Rubber Bands

Allison Coach, 11, from Chesterfield Township, Michigan, has created a rubber band chain that measures more than 1.3 mi (2.1 km) long. She keeps the chain, which consists of more than 22,000 rubber bands, wrapped around a wooden stand made by her grandfather.

Clog Dance

More than 2,500 people in Pella, Iowa, took part in a mass clog dance in May 2010. To ease the discomfort of the wooden shoes they were wearing, many of the dancers put on extra-thick socks or stuffed their clogs with sponges.

Blind Speedster

Turkish pop singer Metin Senturk drove a car at 182 mph (292.9 km/h)—even though he is blind. He drove a Ferrari F430 unaccompanied along the runway at Urfa airport, with a co-driver giving him instructions through an earpiece in his helmet from a car following behind.

Tower Leap

In May 2010, Algerian-born rollerblader Taig Khris leaped from the 131-ft-high (40-m) first floor of Paris's Eiffel Tower and landed safely onto a 98-ft-high (30-m) ramp.

Serpent Queen

While working for Ringling Bros. Circus in the 1880s, petite American Millie Betra, billed as the "Serpent Queen," regularly handled dozens of huge pythons that were almost twice her size, even wrapping many of the snakes around her body simultaneously.

Lucky Numbers

Beating astronomical odds, Ernest Pullen of Bonne Terre, Missouri, won $3 million in two separate lotteries in the space of three months. After picking up $1 million in June 2010, he won another $2 million in September, combining his lucky numbers with numbers he had dreamed about six years earlier when foreseeing that he would one day win a lot of money.

Mattress Mishap

After accidentally throwing away a mattress that her mother had stuffed with $1 million, a Tel Aviv woman searched in vain through Israeli landfill sites containing thousands of tons of garbage. She had bought her mother a new mattress as a surprise.

Own Phone

After his cell phone was stolen, a Californian man bought a new one on classifieds website Craigslist, choosing it because it looked just like his old phone. When it arrived, it actually was his old phone and still had his numbers stored. Luckily for the police, the thief had put his return address on the package.

Battle Dead

In 2010, Brian Freeman, a former Australian army captain, uncovered the forgotten site of a World-War-II battle in Papua New Guinea, with the bodies of three Japanese soldiers still lying where they fell in 1942. Local villagers led him to Eora Creek—the biggest single battle of the Kokoda campaign—where he found the remains of the soldiers, along with their weapons and equipment.

Balloon Daredevils

Early balloonists used highly flammable hydrogen gas instead of hot air or helium. In 1785, the French inventor Jean-Pierre Blanchard and American John Jeffries used an early hydrogen gas balloon to fly across the English Channel between England and France. When Jean-François Pilâtre de Rozier attempted to do the same, his balloon exploded and he became the first person to die in an air accident.

Delayed Delivery

Gill Smeathers of Northamptonshire, England, received a package in February 2010 that was postmarked November 4, 1982.

Inflated Numbers

During World War II, the 1,100 men of the U.S. Army's 23rd Headquarters Special Troops used inflatable vehicles, sound recordings, and fake radio broadcasts to deceive the enemy into thinking they were an army of 30,000 soldiers.

High Tea

Waiters serve lunch to two steel workers perched on a girder high above New York City in 1930. The men were working on the construction of the 47-story, 625-ft-high (190-m) Waldorf-Astoria Hotel on Park Avenue.

Faithful Feet

Hua Chi, a monk at a monastery near Tongren, China, has been coming to exactly the same spot to kowtow at the temple for so many years that perfect footprints have been worn into the wooden floor. For nearly 20 years he has carefully placed his feet to bend down, and lie prostrate, 2,000–3,000 times a day, although now that he's over 70 years old, he can manage only a thousand!

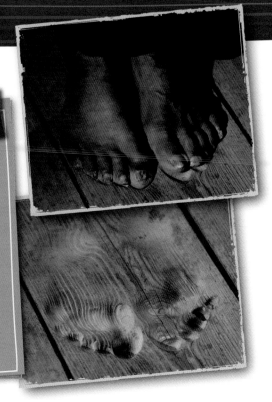

Four Babies

Four sisters from one family each gave birth within four days in 2010. The same obstetrician delivered the babies of Lilian Sepulveda, Saby Pazos and Leslie Pazos at the same Chicago, Illinois, hospital on August 6 and 7, and a fourth sister, Heidi Lopez, gave birth in California on August 9.

200 Grandkids

During her life, Yitta Schwartz (1917–2010) of Kiryas Joel, New York, had 15 children, more than 200 grandchildren, and a staggering total of more than 2,000 living descendants.

Cash Bonfire

Infamous Colombian drug baron Pablo Escobar once burned more than $1.5 million in cash to keep his daughter Manuela warm during a single night on the run. When he realized she was suffering from hypothermia at his mountain hideout, he lit a bonfire using wads of U.S. dollars.

Document Leak

A 2,400-page restricted document from the U.K.'s Ministry of Defence giving advice on how to stop documents leaking onto the Internet was itself leaked onto the Internet in 2009.

Fake Workers

After adding biometric scanning to record employee attendance, the city of Delhi, India, discovered 22,853 fake workers on its payroll.

Extra Time

A Thai man spent three extra years behind bars in an Indonesian prison because of a typo in his paperwork. Kamjai Khong Thavorn should have been released in 2007 after serving a 20-year sentence for possessing heroin, but a clerical error wrongly stated his first year in prison as 1997 instead of 1987. No one spotted the error until 2010.

End of War

Although fighting in World War I finished in 1918, the war did not officially end until October 3, 2010—92 years later—when Germany finally settled its war debt by paying $90 million, which was the last instalment of the reparations imposed on it by the Allies. Germany was forced to pay compensation toward the cost of the war by the 1919 Treaty of Versailles—the bill would have been settled much earlier but Adolf Hitler had reneged on the agreement.

Croc Monsieur

After receiving reports of a 12-ft-long (3.6-m) crocodile circling boats in the English Channel, French authorities banned swimming near Boulogne and broadcast warnings to vacationers in both French and English—only to discover that the reptile was nothing more dangerous than a floating piece of wood.

What Fire?

A man in Pittsburgh, Pennsylvania, slept while his house caught fire and part of the roof collapsed. It was not until fire crews did a walk-through of the house more than two hours later that he woke up.

Working Flat Out

Hurrying to impose new parking restrictions ahead of the 2010 Tall Ships sailing races, council workers in Hartlepool, England, painted yellow lines right over a squashed, dead hedgehog in the road rather than move the animal.

Slice of Luck

A restaurant in Hankou, China, selected from 15 applicants for the post of chef by asking the candidates to slice a melon on a woman's stomach. The successful candidate, Hu Gua, chopped up his melon in less than a minute without hurting the woman who was protected from the blade by just a thin sheet of plastic.

Taste Test

As a designer and tester with Fox's Biscuits, Simon Pope of West Yorkshire, England, is paid to eat more than 7,000 cookies every year.

Chicken Feast

At the 2010 Canoefest in Brookville, Indiana, 1,654 lb (750 kg) of fried chicken was served up in a donated canoe. Up to 200 volunteers had cooked the 2,700 lb (1,225 kg) of raw meat.

Lime Pie

During the Key West, Florida, 2010 Conch Republic independence celebration, locals used 1,080 Key limes to prepare a 450-lb (204-kg), 7-ft-wide (2.1-m) Key lime pie.

Margarine Marge

Restaurant owner Simon Smith of Staffordshire, England, celebrated the 20th birthday of *The Simpsons* by making a 4-ft-high (1.2-m) bust of his favorite character, Marge, out of margarine. He used 26 lb (12 kg) of special heat-resistant puff pastry margarine on the sculpture and achieved the shape by wrapping it around chicken wire.

Headless Chickens

In parts of Asia, no part of the chicken goes to waste. In Bangkok, the capital of Thailand, barbecued chicken-head kebabs are available to buy as fast food. Once cooked, the brain and soft tissue can be eaten. Roasted, boiled and deep-fried chicken heads are also popular.

Fiery Sauce

Eight teenagers in Augsburg, Germany, were treated in a hospital after a test of courage in which they drank chili sauce that was more than 200 times hotter than Tabasco sauce. The sauce reached 535,000 on the Scoville scale, which measures the hotness of sauce, compared to 2,500 for regular Tabasco sauce.

Haute Dog

New York City restaurant Serendipity 3 introduced a $69 hot dog in 2010. The Haute Dog comes with white truffle oil, a salted pretzel bed, truffle butter, duck foie gras, Dijon mustard, Vidalia onions and ketchup.

Locust Topping

When a plague of millions of locusts hit the town of Mildura, Victoria, Australia, pizza café owner Joe Carrazza put dozens of the dead insects on his pizzas as a topping.

A Bug's Life

Artist Chris Trueman of Claremont, California, came up with an unusual way to make this portrait of his younger brother dressed up as a cowboy look like an old, yellowed photograph—he used 200,000 dead ants.

At first Chris tried to catch the harvester ants himself, but he soon realized that it would take him years to catch enough for the painting. So, he bought the ants live over the Internet and, after killing them, incorporated their bodies into the painting with tweezers and a resin called Galkyd, which has a yellowish color. It took him about two weeks to apply each batch of 40,000 ants to the portrait. The painting was first exhibited at the Alexander Salazar gallery in San Diego, but is now owned by Ripley's and is on display in Ripley's Odditorium in Baltimore.

RIPLEY'S ASK

What is the story behind the original photograph?
I staged and photographed my youngest brother Bryce when he was six or seven. I had him dress up in my old cowboy outfit and hold my father's unloaded rifle. He was in my parents' suburban backyard. It was a menacing image, as he pretended to be a cowboy, but was holding a real gun.

Why did you decide to use ants for the image?
I was revisiting a specific experience from my childhood. When I was five years old, my younger brother and I attacked an anthill and were bitten by red ants. That was the first time I intentionally tried to harm intelligent life and, more than 25 years later, I decided to return to that experience. Ants ride the line of what we consider intelligent life—if we see them in the kitchen, many of us think little of killing them all. But if we take the time to look at them closely, they are in fact remarkable creatures.

How long did it take to complete?
It took several years, not because of the actual labor, but because at one point I started to feel bad about killing all of the ants and I stopped the project for over a year. Then I decided that because I was most of the way done, the first ants would have died in vain if I didn't finish the work, so I decided to continue. It was also quite an expensive work to produce as each shipment of ants would cost $500.

Red harvester ants are native to the southwestern U.S.A. and are relatively large, measuring ½ in (1.3 cm) long. They are venomous and will give a painful bite!

37

Nose for Trouble

Surprise Visit

After nine-year-old Beatrice Delap wrote to Captain Jack Sparrow—Johnny Depp's character in the *Pirates of the Caribbean* movies—asking for help with an uprising against teachers at her school in Greenwich, London, Depp responded by turning up at the school in full pirate costume. The Hollywood star was in the area filming the fourth movie in the series and gave the school 10 minutes' notice that he was on his way.

Sold Soul

More than 7,000 online shoppers unwittingly agreed to sell their souls in 2010, thanks to a clause in the terms and conditions of a British computer-game retailer. As an April Fool's Day joke to highlight the fact that online shoppers do not read the small print, GameStation added a clause to its contract granting it a "non transferable option to claim, for now and for ever more, your immortal soul."

An anti-landmine organization based in Belgium uses African giant pouched rats to sniff out deadly landmines in Mozambique and Tanzania. The rats' relatively light weight means they are unlikely to explode the mines, even when scratching at the ground to indicate their whereabouts. These super rats, trained with food rewards, are also able to smell the life-threatening disease tuberculosis, analyzing samples more than 50 times quicker than a laboratory scientist.

Unlucky Number

Superstitious phone company bosses in Bulgaria suspended a jinxed cell phone number—0888 888 888—after all three customers to whom it had been assigned over the previous ten years suffered untimely deaths.

Identical Couples

Identical twin brothers married identical twin sisters in a joint wedding ceremony in China. Grooms Yang Kang and Yang Jian sported different haircuts for the ceremony so that people could tell them apart, while brides Zhang Lanxiang and Jiang Juxiang wore differently colored wedding dresses.

Ghostly Sale

Two vials said to contain the spirits of ghosts exorcised from a house in Christchurch, New Zealand, were sold on an online auction site for more than $1,500 in March 2010. The sales pitch claimed that the "holy water" in the vials had dulled the spirits' energy and put them to sleep. To revive them, the buyer would need to pour the contents into a dish and let them "evaporate into your house." The seller, Avie Woodbury, said that once an exorcist's fee had been deducted, the proceeds of the spirit sale would go to an animal welfare group.

Dead Ringer

Biker David Morales Colón of San Juan, Puerto Rico, became a dead ringer for his idol Meat Loaf by attending his own funeral in 2010 on the back of his beloved Honda motorcycle. So that friends could pay their respects at his wake, undertakers mounted his embalmed body carefully on the machine, hiding a series of body braces beneath his clothes and covering his eyes with wraparound sunglasses.

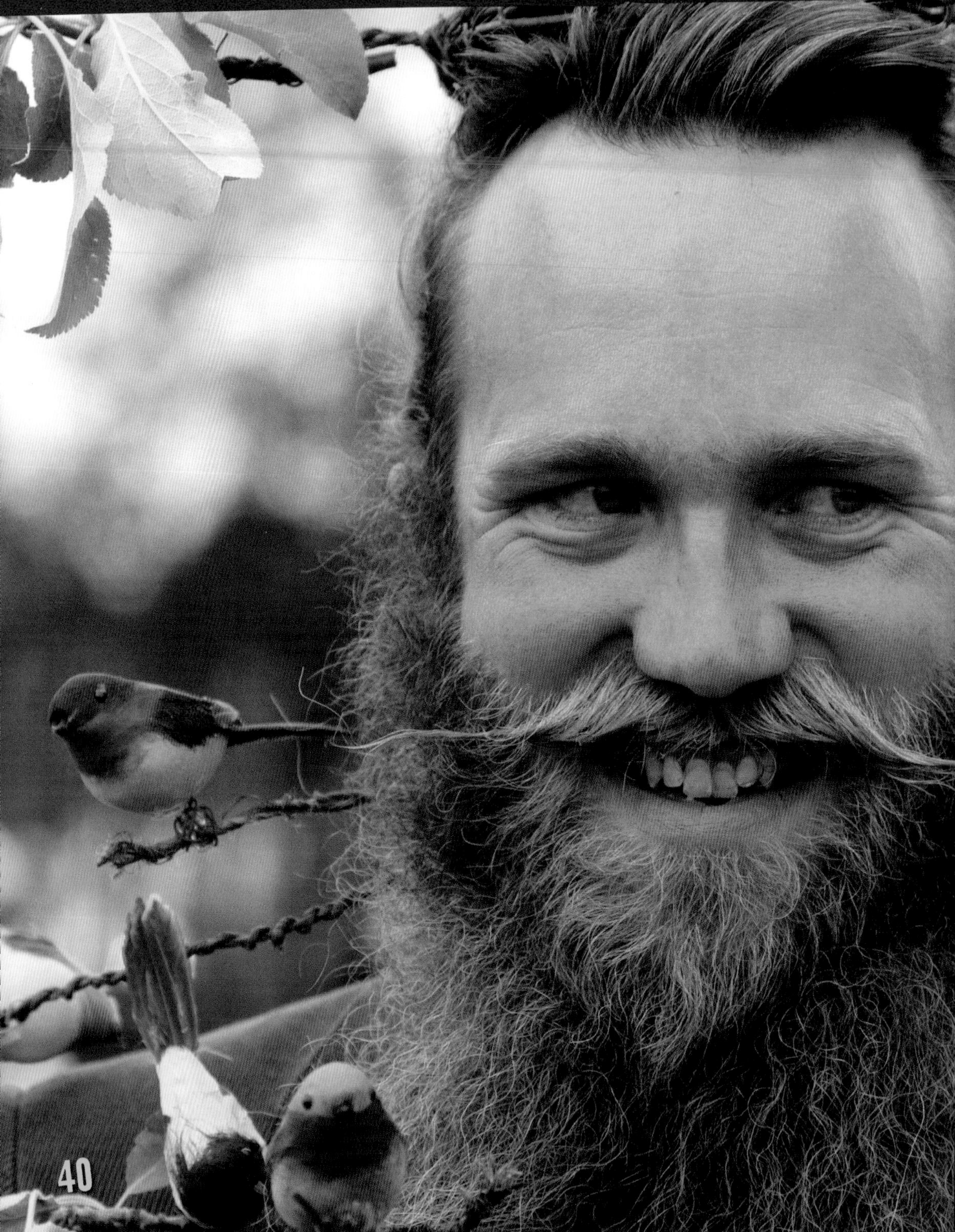

Watch the Beardie

Charles Earnshaw of Anchorage, Alaska, displays his "Beards of a Feather" facial hair sculpture at the 2010 U.S. National Beard and Mustache Championships in Bend, Oregon. There were over 200 entrants, and this creation earned him a prize in the freestyle section.

Satan Image

A family in Budapest, Hungary, abandoned their new-look bathroom after an image of Satan appeared overnight in a tile. Emerging from her first shower in the freshly decorated room, Andrea Csrefko fled in horror when she noticed the horned head of the devil in one of the tiles. The spooky image had not been there when husband Laszlo had put the tiles up and no cleaning detergent was able to remove it.

Long Fry

John Benbenek of Buffalo, New York, was eating lunch at Taffy's Hot Dog Stand when he found a massive 34-in-long (85-cm) French fry in his meal.

Go Slow

Road safety campaigners in Canada encouraged motorists to reduce their speed by painting a large 3-D image of a child on to the road outside an elementary school in West Vancouver, British Columbia. The picture of a girl chasing after a ball appeared to come alive when drivers were 100 ft (30 m) away, giving them time to slow down.

Dummy Guard

In July 2010, two prisoners escaped from a jail in Argentina that, because of a lack of resources, was using a dummy to man one of its guard towers. Staff had put a prison officer's cap on a football to try to fool the convicts into thinking they were being watched from the tower by a real person.

Frozen Assets

In May 2010, the Iowa Court of Appeals ordered the family of Orville Richardson, who died in February 2009 at age 81, to exhume his body so that his head could be cut off and frozen. In 2004, he had signed a contract with an Arizona company and paid $53,500 to have his head placed in cryogenic suspension after his death, but his siblings had buried him instead.

Gold Rush

A huge 220-lb (100-kg) Canadian gold coin was sold at auction to a Spanish company for $4 million. One of only five $1 million Maple Leaf coins ever produced by the Royal Canadian Mint, it measures 21 in (53 cm) in diameter and is 1¼ in (3 cm) thick.

Changing Fortunes

Brothers Zsolt and Geza Peladi were homeless and living in a cave outside Budapest, Hungary, when they discovered in December 2009 that they were due to inherit part of their grandmother's multi-billion euro fortune.

Blood Match

Eight years after breaking into a house in rural Tasmania, Australia, Peter Cannon was convicted of armed robbery because his DNA matched that of blood found inside a leech at the scene of the crime.

Picture Perfect

When Royal Dutch Navy sergeant Dick de Bruin lost his camera while scuba diving off the Caribbean island of Aruba, he thought he would never see it again. However, seven months later the camera was found 1,130 mi (1,800 km) away by a coastguard at Key West, Florida—and although it was covered in crusty sea growth, it still worked.

Old Student

A woman in China became an elementary school pupil at age 102. Ma Xiuxian from Jinan, Shandong Province, started work in a cotton mill at age 13, but had always longed for a proper education. Eighty-nine years after leaving school, the grandmother went back, joining the grade one class at Weishan Road Elementary School. She used hearing aids to make sure she could hear the teacher and a magnifying glass to help read text books.

All the Nines

Henry Michael Berendes of Wisconsin was born at 9.09 a.m. on 9-9-09 and weighed 9 lb 9 oz (4.3 kg).

Piglet Bank

An Internet site is selling a piggy bank made from a real piglet! The brainchild of designer Colin Hart from Belfast, Northern Ireland, the taxidermied pig with a slot in its back costs $4,000 and must be ordered 12 months in advance.

Tattooed Ladies

The tattooed lady was an astonishing and beautiful addition to the circus sideshows, dime museums, and carnivals that were found in North America and Europe in the late 19th century.

They featured in such shows for around a hundred years, when the last tattooed lady retired, aged 80, in 1995.

DISOWNED

Betty was born in 1909. During a girls' weekend in Atlantic City, New Jersey, she got a small tattoo and, as a result, her family disowned her. She claimed she had no other choice but to get more tattoos and make a career out of them. Betty worked with many circuses and was an attraction at the 1939 New York World's Fair with the "John Hix Strange as it Seems" sideshow.

INK REPELLANT

One of the first Western women to be significantly tattooed was Irene Woodward. On her debut in 1882, she scandalized the public with her tattoos—until then tattoos had previously only been seen on sailors. Inked by her father, Irene maintained (probably not truthfully) that he did it to protect her from being captured by American Indians. Described on one show billboard as "A pretty picturesque specimen of punctured purity," Irene was a shy and dignified performer.

SHOCKING STORY

Every great tattooed lady had a sensational story, and Nora Hildebrandt dramatically claimed that she'd been forcibly tattooed by American Indians while tied to a tree for a year. She even said that Sitting Bull was involved in the murky affair. The truth was a little less scandalous—Nora's father tattooed soldiers fighting in the Civil War and used to practice his designs on his daughter. By the time she began to exhibit herself in 1882, she had 365 tattoos.

45

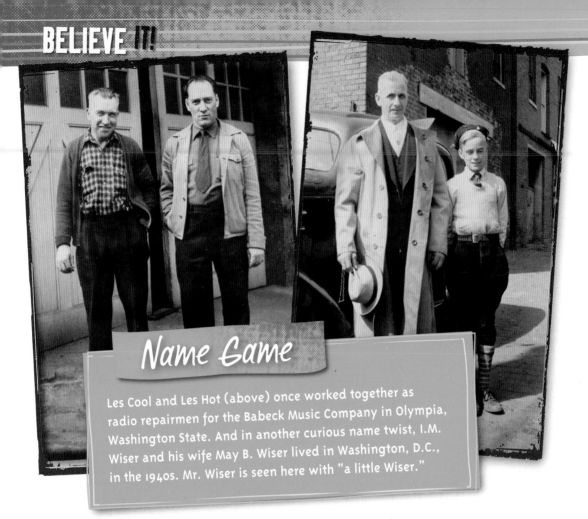

Name Game

Les Cool and Les Hot (above) once worked together as radio repairmen for the Babeck Music Company in Olympia, Washington State. And in another curious name twist, I.M. Wiser and his wife May B. Wiser lived in Washington, D.C., in the 1940s. Mr. Wiser is seen here with "a little Wiser."

Last Post

A postcard bringing holiday news to a couple in West Yorkshire, England, was delivered 40 years after it was posted.

Thumb Find

When fisherman Blake Robinson caught a 6½-lb (2.9-kg) lake trout at Flaming Gorge Reservoir, Wyoming, he discovered a human thumb inside it.

Small World

In 1980, when Alex and Donna Voutsinas lived in different countries and long before they met and married, they were captured in the same photo at Walt Disney World, Orlando, Florida. Five-year-old Donna was photographed at the same moment as three-year-old Alex, who then lived in Montreal, Canada, was being pushed down Main Street in a stroller by his father.

Shoe Thief

A second-hand shoe store owner stole more than 1,200 pairs of designer shoes by posing as a mourner at hospitals and funeral homes in South Korea. His victims were genuine friends and relatives of the deceased, who had slipped off their shoes in a traditional demonstration of respect. The thief would remove his own footwear, pay his respects, then put on a more expensive pair and walk off.

Force Farce

The entire police force in a Hungarian town quit after winning more than $15 million on the lottery in 2009. The 15-strong squad in Budaörs resigned immediately after scooping the jackpot.

Short Journey

Six-year-old Heidi Kay Werstler tossed a message in a bottle into the sea at Ocean City, New Jersey, in 1985 and it washed ashore 24 years later at Duck, North Carolina—less than 300 mi (480 km) away.

Swing the Lizard

As a change from roaming the grassland at India's Corbett National Park, an Indian elephant named Madhuri picked up a passing monitor lizard and played with it for several days. With the lizard's tail firmly grasped in her trunk, she carried it with her wherever she went, swinging it around in the air over and over again, sometimes tossing it high and even dropping it before finally letting the dazed reptile go.

Money to Burn

A German snowboarder stranded in the Austrian Alps for six hours in February 2010 was rescued after attracting attention by setting fire to his money. Stuck 33 ft (10 m) above ground after the ski lift was switched off at dusk, Dominik Podolsky was finally spotted by cleaners as he burned the last of his euros.

Buried Alive

After spending hours digging a 10-ft-deep (3-m) tunnel at a beach on Tenerife in Spain's Canary Islands, a 23-year-old German tourist had to be rescued when the sand collapsed and buried him up to his head. He was trapped on the beach for nearly two hours before 15 firefighters were able to free him.

Bridge Picnic

More than 6,000 people sat down to breakfast on Sydney's famous Harbour Bridge in October 2009 after it was closed to traffic and carpeted with grass for a giant picnic.

Bacon Envelopes

U.S. company J & D's Foods, whose motto is "Everything should taste like bacon," have created "Mmmvelopes," envelopes that have a bacon flavor when you lick them.

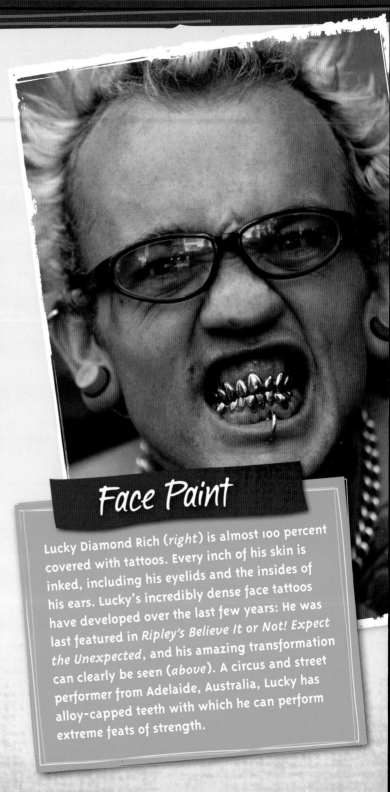

Face Paint

Lucky Diamond Rich (*right*) is almost 100 percent covered with tattoos. Every inch of his skin is inked, including his eyelids and the insides of his ears. Lucky's incredibly dense face tattoos have developed over the last few years: He was last featured in *Ripley's Believe It or Not! Expect the Unexpected*, and his amazing transformation can clearly be seen (*above*). A circus and street performer from Adelaide, Australia, Lucky has alloy-capped teeth with which he can perform extreme feats of strength.

Double Yolks

Fiona Exon from Cumbria, England, beat odds of more than a trillion to one when she discovered that all six eggs she had bought in a single carton from her local grocery store had double yolks.

Lucky Seven

On March 31, 2010, the four-number state lottery in Pennsylvania came up 7-7-7-7 and had a $7.77 million payout!

49

Bearded Mother

Richard Lorenc of Kansas finally tracked down his birth mother in 2010—and discovered that she is a famous bearded lady who as a young girl worked in a circus sideshow. Vivian Wheeler boasts an 11-in-long (28-cm) beard, as a result of inheriting the condition hypertrichosis, also known as werewolf syndrome, which causes the growth of excessive facial hair from an early age.

Lung Stolen

Organizers offered $2,000 for the return of a left lung that was stolen from a traveling exhibition of human cadavers in Peru in 2009.

Kept Corpses

Jean Stevens of Bradford County, Pennsylvania, lived with the corpse of her dead husband for ten years and with the body of her dead twin sister for almost a year. After her family members died, Jean had their embalmed bodies dug up and stored at her house. She maintained the immaculately dressed corpses as best she could, spraying sister June with expensive perfume and keeping her on a couch in a spare room while husband James rested on a couch in the garage.

Frustrated Caller

A woman from Clarksville, Tennessee, was arrested after she kept calling 911 to complain that a man refused to marry her.

Confused Clergy

Two female clerics at the same church in Cambridgeshire, England, share the same three names—Rhiannon Elizabeth Jones. Both are also graduates of the same college.

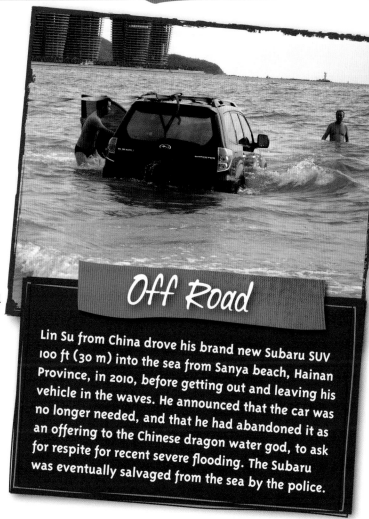

Off Road

Lin Su from China drove his brand new Subaru SUV 100 ft (30 m) into the sea from Sanya beach, Hainan Province, in 2010, before getting out and leaving his vehicle in the waves. He announced that the car was no longer needed, and that he had abandoned it as an offering to the Chinese dragon water god, to ask for respite for recent severe flooding. The Subaru was eventually salvaged from the sea by the police.

Cash Stash

Four children aged between ten and 13 who found $20,000 stuffed in a brown envelope on their way to school in Frankfurt, Germany, shared it out among their friends in the playground. After teachers were alerted, police managed to recoup most of the cash.

Antique Gown

When three-month-old George Parfitt was baptized in Devon, England, he wore the same antique christening gown that had been used by 20 members of his family since it was made by his great-great-great-grandmother in 1884.

Cheating Death

GREAT BALL OF FIRE

Pilot Captain Brian Bews parachuted to safety seconds before his $30-million CF-18 fighter jet crashed and exploded in a devastating ball of fire at Lethbridge County Airport, Alberta, Canada. Having completed his practice routine for the 2010 Alberta International Air Show, he was returning to the airport when the plane suddenly nose-dived on approach. Just 100 ft (30 m) from the ground, he managed to escape using the plane's rocket-powered ejector seat. Moments later, the plane smashed into the ground and was engulfed in smoke and flames, but Captain Bews survived with only minor injuries.

CHEATED DEATH

Stunt pilot Dino Moline cheated death by a split second by deploying his built-in parachute after a wing of his plane fell off at an air show in Santa Fe, Argentina. After performing a series of daring, acrobatic maneuvers, Moline was flying upside down when he felt an explosion and saw the shadow of the detached wing pass the cockpit. As the plane spiraled out of control, he instantly activated its parachute, which slowed the aircraft's descent and allowed it to float gently to the ground where it caught fire. Moline escaped with only one small injury— a burned foot.

GLIDER CRASH

Former racing-car driver Mike Newman escaped unharmed except for three broken vertebrae after the glider he was piloting crashed at high speed into the runway in front of 15,000 spectators at an air show in West Sussex, England. After performing his routine, he prepared to land but a malfunction caused the glider to plunge almost vertically to the ground, striking its wing first. The nose section crumpled around him and the cockpit burst open, leaving him dangerously exposed. He lay stunned amid the wreckage for a minute before managing to stumble out onto the runway.

Sundae Lunch

A London ice-cream parlor offered a new twist on the traditional British Sunday roast, with each course being a frozen dessert. The "Sundae Lunch," designed by Italian mixologist Roberto Lobrano, comprised a starter of fresh pea sorbet with mint, followed by a main course of beef bouillon and horseradish sorbet topped with a Yorkshire pudding wafer. The final course was an apple-and-blackberry-crumble gelato.

Chocolate Coin

Chocolatiers Gary Mitchell, Jess Nolasco, and Rita Craig, from Purdy's Chocolates, Vancouver, Canada, spent more than eight hours making a 25-lb (11.3-kg) chocolate coin, measuring 24 in (60 cm) wide and 1½ in (4 cm) thick, and valued at $625.

Fast Food

"Humble" Bob Shoudt from Royersford, Pennsylvania, won first prize of $2,500 for eating 7 lb 14½ oz (3.58 kg) of French fries in ten minutes at the Curley's Fries Eating Championship at Morey's Piers, Wildwood, New Jersey, in May 2010.

Fat Dragon

Japanese-born pastry chef Naoko Sukegawa created a sculpture of a dragon made from margarine. The dragon, built over a steel and mesh frame, stood 29 in (74 cm) high, weighed 35 lb (16 kg), and took four months to make.

Mice Lunch

While making sandwiches for his family, a father from Oxfordshire, England, found an unwelcome ingredient in the bread he had bought from a local grocery store— a dead mouse baked into the half-eaten loaf. To make matters worse, the unfortunate rodent was missing its tail, leading Stephen Forse to wonder whether his family had already eaten it.

Super Potato

Amateur gardener Peter Glazebrook of Northampton, England, grew a potato that weighed 8 lb 4 oz (3.74 kg)— the weight of a newborn baby and 25 times more than the weight of an average potato. The supersized potato would make 66 bags of potato chips, 33 portions of fries, 80 roast potatoes, or 44 portions of mashed potato.

Status Symbols

Pineapples were status symbols in 17th-century Britain, and wealthy people would rent them by the day to place on their dinner table and impress their friends.

Vintage Cognac

A French entrepreneur bought a bottle of Cognac dating back to 1788—the year before the French Revolution—for nearly $37,000 at a Paris wine auction in December 2009.

Sushi Roll

In November 2009, hundreds of students at the University of California, Berkeley, assembled a 330-ft-long (100-m) sushi roll. They used 200 lb (90 kg) of rice, 180 lb (82 kg) of fish, 80 lb (36 kg) of avocado and 80 lb (36 kg) of cucumber. To cater for vegetarians, the final 15 ft (4.5 m) contained tofu instead of seafood.

Banana Bonanza

Banana peels make up more than half of the trash collected on Scotland's Ben Nevis mountain. During a September 2009 survey, more than 1,000 discarded banana skins were found on the summit plateau.

CRAZY WORLD

March of the Lava

Run! These scientists got a little too close when the eruption began in 1983.

The active volcano of Kilauea in Hawaii has been constantly erupting since 1983, and its unstoppable flow of burning lava has devastated hundreds of homes and businesses in its vicinity. Incredibly, it has also gradually extended Hawaii's coastline by an area the size of Washington, D.C.

In 1990, the entire town of Kaimù and part of the town of Kalapana were buried under 50 ft (15 m) of slow-moving lava from Kilauea. Despite the constant threat from the volcano, there are a few Kalapana residents who still choose to live alongside the lava.

As the lava builds in height, road signs are lifted out of the ground before the lava cools to solid rock.

The building finally succumbs to the heat.

Molten lava oozes toward the house.

59

Down the Drain

This giant chasm in Lake Berryessa, California, is the biggest drain hole in the world, at 30 ft (9 m) in diameter. When the lake reaches capacity, water tips over the lip of the drain and surges down a 700-ft-long (213-m) concrete pipe to exit through the Monticello Dam some 300 ft (91 m) below. Swimming or even boating near the hole is strongly discouraged; in 1997, a swimmer strayed too close and was sucked into the powerful drain. Water gushes through the "glory hole," as locals have named it, at a rate of 362,057 gal (1,370,534 l) every second—that's enough to fill 15,000 bathtubs. When the lake's level is low, local skateboarders and BMX bikers ride the giant exit pipe.

King Carbone

Former flower grower Giorgio Carbone spent nearly 50 years championing the independence of the Italian village of Seborga, which he claimed should be recognized as a separate nation because it had never been formally included in the 19th-century unification of Italy. Proclaiming himself His Tremendousness Giorgio I, he ruled over 360 subjects until his death in 2009. He gave the principality its own currency, stamps, flag and even a Latin motto—*Sub Umbra Sede* ("Sit in the Shade").

Inaccessible Inn

Built in the middle of the 17th century, the Old Forge pub on the Knoydart peninsula in Northern Scotland can be reached only by boat or by walking 18 mi (29 km) from the nearest road over hills that rise to 3,500 ft (1,067 m).

Acid Drip

Snottites are colonies of bacteria that hang from the ceilings of caves and are similar to stalactites. The bacteria derive their energy from volcanic sulfur compounds and drip sulfuric acid that is as corrosive as battery acid.

Dam Cops

Nevada's Hoover Dam has its own police department whose duties include protecting the dam and safeguarding the lives of visitors and employees.

Sewer Fat

In a huge underground cleanup of central London in 2010, more than 1,000 tons of putrid fat were removed from sewers—enough fat to fill nine double-decker buses.

Moon Lake

Lake Titan, on the north of Saturn's moon, is 39,000 sq mi (101,000 sq km), bigger than Lake Superior. The lake is most likely filled with liquid methane and ethane.

Limestone Forest

Water erosion has turned parts of Madagascar's Tsingy de Bemaraha National Park into forests of giant limestone spikes made of fossils and shellfish that died in the sea 200 million years ago.

Desert Snow

China's largest desert, the Taklamakan, covers approximately 125,000 sq mi (325,000 sq km) and, in January 2008, snow blanketed the entire area for the first time ever.

Jesus Image

While looking for holiday destinations on the mapping website Google Earth, Zach Evans from Southampton, England, spotted an outline of the face of Jesus Christ in satellite pictures of a field near Puspokladany, Hungary.

Hanging Coffins

The Bo people, an ethnic group from China's Sichuan Province that disappeared hundreds of years ago, hung the coffins of their dead on the sides of cliffs. The coffins were lowered on ropes from above to rest on precipices or wooden stakes. Some were hung as high as 425 ft (130 m) above ground, as the belief was that the higher the coffin was placed, the more propitious it was for the dead. The earliest hanging coffins found in the region date back 2,500 years.

Great Hedge

The Great Hedge of India was planted across the country by the British in the mid-19th century to prevent salt smuggling. The barrier of living impenetrable thorny hedge was 2,000 mi long (3,200 km) and was patrolled by up to 14,000 attendants.

CRAZY WORLD

Last Speaker

An ancient dialect called Bo, thought to date back 65,000 years, became extinct in 2010 after Boa Sr., the last person to speak it, died on a remote Indian island. At 85, Boa Sr. was the oldest member of the Great Andamanese Bo tribe before her death in Port Blair, the capital of Andaman and Nicobar Islands.

Burning River

The Cuyahoga River in Ohio was so polluted in the 20th century that it caught fire more than half a dozen times.

Volcano Video

In May 2009, U.S. scientists videotaped an undersea volcanic eruption off the coast of Samoa, 4,000 ft (1,220 m) beneath the surface—the first time a sea-floor eruption had been filmed.

Rabbit Island

It cost more than one million dollars to rid the tiny Scottish island of Canna of rats in 2006, and now, less than four years later, it has been overrun with thousands of rabbits—because there are no rats to keep their numbers down! The island's only restaurant has responded by adding a number of rabbit dishes to its menu.

Mail Boat

Since 1916, a boat has been delivering mail to dozens of homes on Lake Geneva, Wisconsin—and because it never stops, teenage carriers are hired to jump off the moving boat, put the mail in mailboxes on the dock, then scurry back on board, hopefully without falling into the lake.

Watery Grave

As drought conditions dried up a pond in Aligarh, Uttar Pradesh, India, in May 2009, 98 human skulls were found at the bottom.

Sparsely Populated

The state of Nevada covers an area about the size of the U.K. and Ireland combined, but has only 70 towns, whereas the British Isles has more than 40,000.

Shifting City

The Chilean earthquake of February 27, 2010, moved the city of Concepción about 10 ft (3 m) to the west. The quake was so powerful that it shortened the length of the day by 1.26 microseconds, and even Buenos Aires—840 mi (1,350 km) from Concepción—shifted by 1.5 in (3.8 cm).

Dual Rule

The U.S. city of Bristol straddles the borders of Virginia and Tennessee and has two governments, one for each side.

Huge Hailstone

A giant hailstone that fell in Vivian, South Dakota, on the night of July 23, 2010, measured 8 in (20 cm) in diameter, 18½ in (47 cm) in circumference, and weighed 1 lb 15 oz (900 g)! This and other ice missiles were so large that some punched holes into roofs big enough for householders to put their arm through, while other hailstones gouged holes in the ground more than an inch (2.5 cm) deep.

Bone Décor

The Sedlec Ossuary in Sedlec, Czech Republic, is a Roman Catholic chapel containing more than 40,000 human skeletons, the bones of which have been arranged to form the chapel's decorations and furnishings.

Tough Tree

A Sabal palm tree with a 6-in-wide (15-cm) hole through its trunk has survived several hurricanes in Estero, Florida.

Taking a Liberty

At 8.45 p.m. on the night of September 22, 2010, New York City photographer Jay Fine took this incredible photo of lightning striking the Statue of Liberty. He spent two hours braving the storm and took more than 80 shots before finally striking lucky. The iconic statue attracts more than 600 bolts of lightning each year.

Poop Light

In 2010, a park in Cambridge, Massachusetts, had a street light that was powered by dog poop. Created by artist Matthew Mazzotta, the "Park Spark" project encouraged dog walkers to collect their pets' poop in biodegradable bags and drop it into one of two 500-gal (1,900-l) steel tanks. Microbes in the waste gave off methane gas, which was fed through a second tank to the lamp and burned off.

School Mascot

The mascot of Yuma Union High School in Yuma, Arizona, is a criminal dressed in a prison uniform. It was adopted nearly a century ago after classes were held in a prison building when the original school burned down.

Railroad Room

The Washington Hotel in Tokyo, Japan, has created a special room for model railway enthusiasts to sleep in. It includes a grand model of the local area, complete with working railroads. Train lovers can bring their own models or, alternatively, the hotel will happily provide some.

Tunnel Vision

Over a period of four weeks, sculptors Dan Havel and Dean Ruck from Houston, Texas, transformed two connected properties to create a large, tunnel-like vortex, making it look as if the interior of the buildings had exploded. The outer skin of the two houses—made from planks of pine—was peeled off and used to create a 60-ft-long (18-m) spiral, which narrowed to a width of about 2 ft (60 cm) at the far end.

Cigarettte House

A house in Hangzhou, Zhejiang Province, China, is brightly decorated throughout with more than 30,000 empty cigarette packets. The occupant collected them over a period of six years and has even created seats and tables from the empty packs.

Mecca Clock

The Royal Mecca Clock, located on a skyscraper in Mecca, Saudi Arabia, has four amazing faces each measuring 151 ft (46 m) in diameter—that's more than six times larger than the faces of London's Big Ben clock. Over 90 million pieces of colored glass mosaic decorate the sides of the clock, which is visible from every part of the city. On special occasions, 16 bands of vertical lights shoot from the clock 6 mi (10 km) into the sky.

Home Wrecker

In February 2010, a man bulldozed his $350,000 Moscow, Ohio, home when a bank claimed it as collateral for outstanding debt.

Lost Language

The writing on the back of a letter discovered in 2008 by archeologists at a 17th-century dig site reveals a previously unknown language spoken by indigenous peoples in northern Peru. The letter, found under a pile of clay bricks in a collapsed church near Trujillo, shows a column of numbers written in Spanish and translated into a mysterious language that has been extinct for at least 400 years.

Vast Collection

The British Museum in London has 80,000 objects on display—but that is only one percent of its total collection.

Rotating House

A rotating house north of Sydney, Australia, guarantees Luke Everingham and his family a different view every time they wake up. The octagonal-shaped house sits on a turntable powered by a small electric motor and controlled by a computer, which allows it to move on demand, completing a full rotation in half an hour.

Whistle Blowers

Officials in Alor Setar, Malaysia, blow whistles loudly at litterbugs in the hope of shaming them into never littering again.

Buried Lake

At 155 mi (250 km) long and 31 mi (50 km) wide, Lake Vostok is about the same size as Lake Ontario—but lies beneath 2.5 mi (4 km) of Antarctic ice.

Ginkgo Stink

The ginkgo tree species, native to Asia, is so resilient that several trees survived the atomic bomb blast in Hiroshima, Japan. However, their smell is becoming a problem in Iowa City, U.S.A. When the tree eventually drops its seed shells, it produces a sticky mess that smells of rotten eggs, creating a very smelly city.

River Logjam

Over several centuries, a natural logjam in North America's Red River grew to a length of more than 160 mi (256 km). When people began clearing it in the early 1800s, it took 40 years to complete the task.

Lightning Storm

In just one hour on September 9, 2010, Hong Kong was hit by 13,102 lightning strikes. The violent electrical storm contained wind gusts of 62 mph (100 km/h) and caused power cuts that left people trapped in elevators.

Pink Lake

Lake Retba (the Rose Lake), situated 25 mi (40 km) north of Dakar in Senegal, has pink water, which can even turn purple in strong sunshine. The 1-sq-mi (3-sq-km) lake gets its unusual color from unique cyan bacteria in the water and also from its very high salt content.

Widespread Snow

On February 12, 2010, all of the states in the U.S.A. except Hawaii received some snow.

Asteroid Blast

A 33-ft-wide (10-m) asteroid exploded with the energy of three Hiroshima atom bombs in the atmosphere above Indonesia on October 8, 2009. The asteroid hit the atmosphere at about 45,000 mph (72,000 km/h), causing a blast that was estimated by NASA to be equivalent to 55,000 tons of TNT, and which was heard by monitoring stations 10,000 mi (16,000 km) away. There was no damage on the ground, however, because it occurred at least 9.3 mi (15 km) above the Earth's surface.

Life on Mars?

Huge plumes of methane—a gas that can indicate the presence of living organisms—have been found on the northern side of Mars. The methane may come from live organisms or from the decomposing remains of dead ones.

Hot Water

At the bottom of shallow bodies of very salty water, temperatures can reach 176°F (80°C) and stay that way 24 hours a day.

Unconquered Peak

Gangkhar Puensum, a mountain in Bhutan standing 24,836 ft (7,570 m) tall, is the highest unclimbed mountain on the planet.

Floating Stump

The Old Man of the Lake, a 30-ft-tall (9-m) tree stump, has floated around Crater Lake, Oregon, for more than 100 years. During that time, high winds and waves have caused it to move great distances—in one three-month period of observation in 1938 it traveled more than 62 mi (100 km).

Fog Nets

Communities in Chile's Atacama Desert use nets to catch the morning fog—the only accessible fresh water in the region. One of the driest places on Earth, it gets significant rainfall only two to four times a century, and in some parts of the desert no rain has ever been recorded.

Starling Flock

Thousands of starlings in the sky above Taunton in Somerset, England, formed the shape of one giant starling! These acrobatic birds have created many different patterns in the sky, including a rabbit, a rubber duck and a turtle.

Storm Hole

A Guatemala City clothing factory and an entire traffic intersection were swallowed by a cavernous sinkhole, which suddenly opened up during a tropical storm in 2010. The sinkhole was almost perfectly round and measured 65 ft (20 m) wide and 100 ft (30 m) deep.

Jet Power

The Dubai Fountain, located beside the Burj Khalifa skyscraper in Dubai, is almost 900 ft (275 m) long and can fire jets of water 500 ft (150 m) into the air.

Souvenir Snowball

For more than 30 years, Prena Thomas of Lakeland, Florida, has kept a snowball in her freezer—the souvenir of a rare Florida snowfall. When 2 in (5 cm) of snow fell on the normally balmy state on January 19, 1977, she was so surprised that she collected some of the snow and put it in her freezer.

Cave Man

After living in a 7-ft-wide (2.1-m) cave for 16 years, officials evicted Hilaire Purbrick of Brighton, England, in 2009 because his underground home lacked a second fire exit.

No Flow

When astronauts cry in space, their tears stay in a ball against their eyes until they are wiped away, because there is no gravity to make them fall naturally.

Violent Quake

On February 7, 1812, a massive earthquake struck near New Madrid, Missouri, and shook so violently that the Mississippi River flowed backward for several hours.

Windy Planet

Wind speeds of 4,350 mph (7,000 km/h) were measured in 2010 in the atmosphere of planet HD209458b, which orbits a star in the constellation Pegasus, some 150 light years from Earth. The planet has a temperature of about 1,800°F (1,000°C) on its hot side.

Space Smash

A 4.6-billion-year-old meteorite smashed through the windshield of a truck in Grimsby, Ontario, Canada, in September 2009. Minutes beforehand, local astronomers had witnessed a "brilliant fireball," 100 times brighter than a full moon, streaking across the night sky.

Fish Rain

For two days in February 2010, the remote desert town of Lajamanu in Australia's Northern Territory was bombarded with hundreds of small fish falling from rain clouds in the sky—even though it is 326 mi (525 km) from the nearest river.

Disappearing Island

An island that was at the center of a 30-year dispute between India and Bangladesh disappeared beneath rising seas in 2010. Measuring 2.2 mi (3.5 km) long and 1.9 mi (3 km) wide, uninhabited New Moore Island in the Bay of Bengal had been claimed by both countries—however, environmental experts said that global warming had finally resolved the matter of ownership.

Deadly Icicles

In the winter of 2009 to 2010, Russia's coldest in 30 years, five people were killed and over 150 injured by icicles falling from the rooftops of buildings in St. Petersburg.

Snowball Payment

For hundreds of years, Scotland's Clan MacIntyre delivered a single snowball in the summer to Clan Campbell as part of a long-standing debt.

Freeze that Fire!

When water was used to put out a burning building in Montreal, Quebec, Canada, in the late 19th century, the air temperature was so cold that the water quickly turned to ice.

St. James Street Fire, Montreal.

CRAZY WORLD

Haunted House

Josh Bond of Cuchillo, New Mexico, put his 130-year-old haunted house up for sale on the Internet auction site eBay. The listing offered 1,250 sq ft (115 sq m) of space spread over three bedrooms, an antique wood-burning stove, and the spirits of the restless dead.

New Ocean

A 2005 volcanic eruption caused a 35-mi-long (56-km) rift, 20 ft (6 m) wide in places, to open up in the Ethiopian desert in just days. In 2010, geologists predicted that the rift would slowly become a new ocean, as Africa begins to split in two.

Cursing Festival

Every February, youngsters in the neighboring South Nepalese villages of Parsawa and Laxmipur hurl insults at each other and passersby in a ten-day cursing festival. On the final day of the festival, they set heaps of straw ablaze and celebrate the Hindu festival of Holi, which is marked by raucous "play" fights using powdered colored paints and water. Villagers say the best thing about the tradition is there are no bad feelings after the festival.

More Singapore

Thanks to numerous land reclamation projects, the island city-state of Singapore has 20 percent more land than it did four decades ago.

Cargo Cult

For more than 60 years, villagers on the island of Tanna, Vanuatu, have worshiped "John Frum," an American they believe will one day return with a bounty of cargo. Clan leaders first saw the mysterious figure in the late 1930s and he is said to have appeared before them again during World War II, dressed in white like a Navy seaman. In his honor, the islanders celebrate John Frum Day every February 15.

Crystal Clouds

Noctilucent clouds are formed by ice crystals 50 mi (80 km) above the Earth, on the very edge of space. They reflect sunlight at night, so that they glow.

Tree Dwellers

Members of the Korowai tribe of Papua New Guinea live in tree houses that are built as high as 150 ft (46 m) off the ground. They reach them by climbing vines or stairs carved into the trunks.

Starfish Graveyard

More than 10,000 starfish died on a beach in Norfolk, England, in December 2009 after being washed ashore during a storm. The creatures had gathered in the shallows to feed on mussels, but were swept on to the beach during high tide and quickly perished once they were out of water.

Shrinking Storm

Jupiter's giant storm, the Great Red Spot, shrank by more than 0.6 mi (1 km) per day between 1996 and 2006.

Passion Play

The village of Oberammergau, Bavaria, Germany, has held a Passion play, depicting the Crucifixion of Jesus, every ten years with few exceptions since 1633, when villagers swore an oath to perform the play every decade after their town was spared from the plague.

High Cloud

Morning Glory clouds, which appear regularly over Northern Australia each spring, stand 1 mile (1.6 km) high and can stretch for hundreds of miles. The clouds are often accompanied by sudden wind squalls and can move at speeds of up to 37 mph (60 km/h).

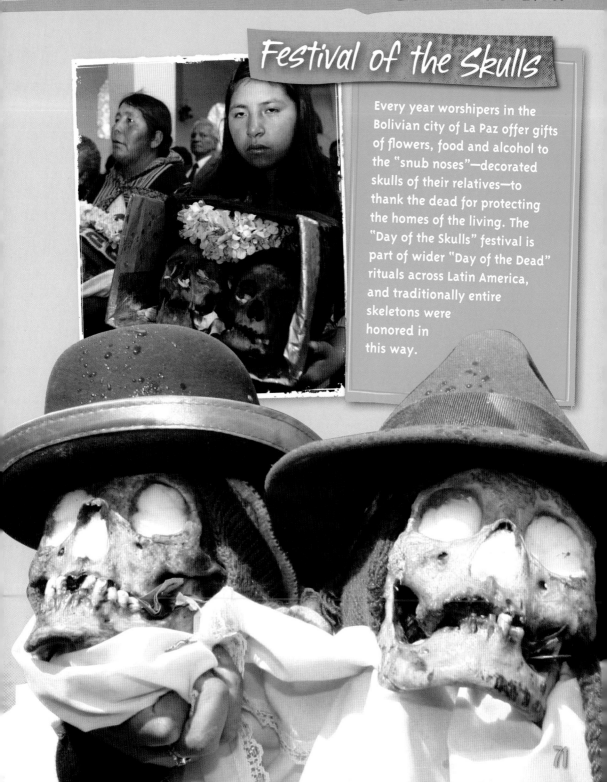

Festival of the Skulls

Every year worshipers in the Bolivian city of La Paz offer gifts of flowers, food and alcohol to the "snub noses"—decorated skulls of their relatives—to thank the dead for protecting the homes of the living. The "Day of the Skulls" festival is part of wider "Day of the Dead" rituals across Latin America, and traditionally entire skeletons were honored in this way.

71

All the Fun of the Fair

Between 1933 and 1934, about 48 million people visited the Chicago World's Fair—a showcase of thousands of exhibits including the latest scientific, architectural and transport innovations.

The Century of Progress Exposition, as the Fair was known, was held to commemorate Chicago's 100th anniversary and to illustrate the amazing technological developments that had taken place worldwide in that time. It was staged on an area of 427 acres (173 ha) along the shoreline of Lake Michigan, and opened on May 27, 1933. It closed on November 12, but had proved so popular that it was re-opened the following May, and ran until the end of October 1934.

SKY RIDE, CHICAGO WORLD'S FAIR

36A29

3A-H8

HAVOLINE THERMOMETER *Century of Progress International Exposition* CHICAGO 1933

ROCKET TRAVEL

The most recognizable symbol of the Fair was the Sky Ride, an aerial tramway that visitors used to travel from one side of the Fair to the other. It had a span of 1,850 ft (564 m) and two towers 628 ft (191 m) tall. Visitors could travel to the top of the towers using high-speed elevators that ascended at a rate of 700 ft (213 m) per minute, and from the top, four different states were visible on a clear day. Suspended from the tramway 220 ft (67 m) above ground were rocket-shaped cars, each carrying 36 passengers across the Fair.

HIGH-RISE TEMPERATURE

Another principal landmark of the Fair was the 218-ft-high (67-m), 21-story thermometer that was sponsored by the motor oil manufacturer Havoline. The air temperature was shown by means of neon light tubes on the outside of the building.

Fair Facts

- The electric lighting for the 1934 Fair came from 250,000 incandescent bulbs and totaled 30,000,000,000 candlepower—enough electricity to supply the needs of a town of 10,000 people.

- More than six million people rode in the Sky Ride elevators in the first 5½ months of the Fair.

- If all the steel cable in the Sky Ride had been stretched out in a single cable, it would have been more than 100 mi (160 km) long.

- The fountain at the 1934 Fair shot water 45 ft (14 m) into the air, pouring out 68,000 gal (260,000 l) a minute.

- A restaurant seating 3,500 people was a replica of the Old Heidelberg Inn, Germany.

- On October 26, 1933, the 776-ft-long (238-m) German airship Graf Zeppelin visited the Fair.

- The 1933 Fair employed 350 painters to create a "carnival of color" by using 25 different exterior colors and 36 interior colors of more than 25,000 gal (113,500 l) of paint to cover 10,500,000 sq ft (975,500 sq m) of surface area.

Ripley's Odditorium

Also appearing at the Fair was the first-ever Ripley's Odditorium, which was one of the most popular crowd-pullers, attracting over two million visitors. Show-business agent Clint Finney had been assigned by Robert Ripley to find the best performers to appear at this Odditorium, and Finney managed the show in 1933 and 1934 with C.C. Pyle. With their help, Ripley scoured the world for unusual performers, his "human rarities and oddities." Ripley's many international contacts also sent him photographs and telegrams suggesting possible people to include.

...TICE TO KULI ALI BEI, FAKIR
CEKANAVICIUS AND OTHERS

People with peculiar characteristics or peculiar ...physical built (freaks), are wanted for worlds ...air in Chicago, from June 1 to November 1, 1934. ...certain firm will pay a round trip passage fare ...d living expenses such as meals, board etc. to ...such exponents that will be demonstrated at ...fair. The firm will cover all expenses and ...ages to guides who will accompany non English ...eaking exponents. It will also furnish all documentary ...needs and formalities for the entrance into the United

Postal Telegraph
THE INTERNATIONAL SYSTEM

New York   Aug. 21, 1933

...aptain Gois
      Imperial Hotel
            Dubrovnik   Jugo Slavia
...range to bring small man and father to America at on...
...l pay all expenses and reasonable salari...
...tos immediately

Postal Telegraph
THE INTERNATIONAL SYSTEM

19 54 WIRELESS COLLECT VIA MACKAYRADIO=N MANILA 1048A MAR 7 1934

RIPLEY KINGSYN=

:NEWYORKNY (RIPLEY KINGS FEATURES SYNDICATE 235 EAST 45 ST)=

AINABLE TWELVE MALE FEMALE PRIEST MAGNUNUS FIRE WALKERS
IRITUALIST DAGGER CEREMONY PRECEDING WALK STOP OBTAINABLE UP
FIFTY COMPLETE SETS BONTOC IGOROT HEADHUNTERS ARMS WAR
OSTUMES PARAPHERNALIA FOR RITUALS DANCES CORRECTLY EXECUTED
...STI... OUNTAINEERS ALLOTTED TRAVEL NO DIFFERENCE LANGUAGE
APPEARANCE STOP IF INTERESTED CABLE FUNDS=
:LILIUS CABLE ADDRESS AEOLUS.   851P   ...al Telegraph
...one Your Telegra...

Official Post Card of
RIPLEY'S
"BELIEVE-IT-OR-NOT" ODDITORIUM
A CENTURY OF PROGRESS

The name y address sa ...this card was written upside down and ...backwards and at ease. Now seem... you can read this ...just fill in the closed spaces, not the open ones...

WHATS 92 of 12, 14... XII CUT IN HALF VII THIS VII

POST CARD
CENTURY OF PROGRESS
CHICAGO 1933

Robert L. Ripley.
c/o New York American,
South Street,
New York City,
N.Y.

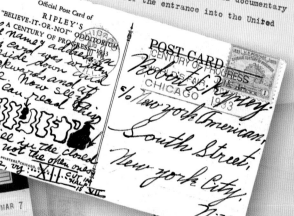

Believe It or Not
ODDITORIUM
Ripley

INTERNATIONAL ODDITIES, INCORPORAT...
666 LAKE SHORE DRIVE
CHICAGO, ILLINOIS

May 8, 1934.

"BELIEVE-IT-OR-NOT" EXHIBITION
CENTURY OF PROGRESS
JUNE 1, TO OCTOBER 31, 1934

Memo for Mr. Simpson:

In regard to the Chin... man that
you believe could be dressed in Korean reli... costume
and ... a good attraction, beg to advise th... ere are
... here w... ...from... to 8½ feet... would...
m... ...ing a ...rat...

FROM
RIPLEY'S
"BELIEVE·IT·OR·NOT" ODDITORIUM
A CENTURY OF PROGRESS—1934
CHICAGO, ILLINOIS

W.A. Cunningh...
817-So-4...
Louisvi...

Bitty Cunningh...
817 So 4...
Louisville...

Ripley
Ripley

Believe It or Not   Believe It or Not

Dear Joe:

NO SWORD SW...
Too Coney Isla...

OBTAIN "PINK MAN" FROM
HAITI. THIS IS GOOD. DON'T ...
STORY ABOUT PILL.

CAN'T GET BORNEO BELLES
"   " CARVED FACE MEN
BUT TRY ALEKO E. LILIUS
P.O. Box 3220 Manila. Cable address
AEOLUS

Mabukay
Steele

OBTAIN WILLIAM D'ANDREA
88 - South Elm St
Waterbury. Conn.
CAN PLACE HIS FOOT IN HIS POCKET

HINDU SITTING ON NAILS - Many of
...m. Try "Cook's" Company - Calcutta
Manager of CLARKS HOTEL
Benares.

At Chicago Exhibit of Believe-It-Or-Nots

Thousands of Americans who have followed the famous
Believe-It-Or-Not Cartoons of Robert Ripley are seeing
the actual Believe-It-Or-Nots housed in the palatial Ripley "Odditorium" at the Chicago Century of Progress.
Included among the exhibits are (left) Singhlee, a Hindu who can grasp a
red-hot metal bar and put it to his mouth; (below left) Albert Nelson
and his one-man mechanical band of thirty instruments; and (below
right) Blystone, the rice writer.

RIPLEY
BELIEVE IT OR NOT

F. L. BLYSTONE
of ARDARA, PA.
WROTE 2871 LEGIBLE LETTERS
... A SINGLE GRAIN OF RICE
PRIZE WINNER
NATIONAL Believe It or Not CONTEST

Ripley's Curiosities

More than two million visitors flocked to the Ripley's Odditorium to see sword-swallowers, fire-eaters, eye-poppers, and many other curiosities. The attraction proved so popular that Ripley's founder, Robert Ripley, went on to open many other Odditoriums across the U.S.A.

Head contortionist Martin Laurello discovered his unusual ability as a child and spent many years mastering his stunt of looking backward while walking forward, baffling scientists and amazing Odditorium audiences.

Habu Koller from Germany could lift more than 100 lb (45 kg) using a hole in his tongue. According to his Ripley backstory, Habu reportedly received the hole as punishment for refusing to bear arms in World War I.

Freda Pushnik from Pennsylvania was born with no arms or legs, but she was determined to master everyday tasks. Aged just ten years old, she wowed audiences at the 1933 World's Fair with her cheerful repartee and demonstrations of writing and sewing. Freda performed in Ripley's Odditoriums for six years, and went on to have a successful sideshow career before retiring from the stage in the 1950s.

Grace McDaniels complained about her early billing as "the ugliest woman in the world," but nevertheless was a popular sideshow draw for many years, later becoming known by her preferred moniker, "The Mule-Faced Woman." After fielding several marriage proposals, she settled down and had a son, Elmer (pictured here), who later became her manager.

Charles Romano, the "Rubber Arm Man," could twist and turn and throw his arms around in such a way that audiences were amazed that he could return his body to its normal shape and position.

Professor A. L. Morrell, the "Jack-Knife King," was billed as the world's greatest whittler. Assisted by his wife, he wowed audiences with his astonishing exhibit of carved objects displayed in a variety of small-necked bottles.

Egyptian Hadji Ali could drink up to 50 glasses of water in quick succession and then return it all to a receptacle in a steady stream, turning himself into a "human fountain." He also swallowed a range of other items before regurgitating them in any order requested.

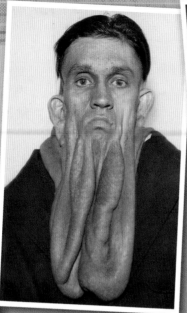

Agnes Schmidt from Hamburg, Germany, was known as the "Rubber Skin Girl." Her skin stretched for 14 in (35 cm) and could be pierced in any place without pain or drawing blood.

Arthur Loos was known as the "Rubber-Skinned Man," because the skin of his neck would hang 18 in (45 cm) down onto his chest.

Captain Ringman Mack—seen here holding two genuine shrunken heads—was a European strongman who could pull cars and suspend heavy weights with hooks through his nipples without any sign of pain. He had performed in sideshows since the early 20th century.

With his unique ability to make his eyes pop out of his head, Leonard "Popeye" Perry from Richmond, Georgia, was an Odditorium sensation. He went on to work in other Ripley's Odditoriums for many years after the Chicago Fair.

Singlee, the "Fireproof Man," belonged to an Indian fire-worshiping sect. He said that fire was part of his religion and as long as he was faithful to his fire god, fire could not harm him.

Known as the "Anatomical Wonder," Anato Hayes could displace his entire abdomen, raising his intestines into his chest. Ladies in the audience were advised to "get a good firm grip on [their] escort's arm" before he appeared!

J. T. Saylors from Georgia had never demonstrated his talent for jaw-dislocation and pulling funny faces professionally, despite offers from show people and motion picture companies, until he appeared at the Odditorium in Chicago.

Kanichka, or "The Man with the Ostrich Stomach," swallowed billiard balls, goldfish, silver dollars, wristwatches, and doorknobs—and would then regurgitate them. As a finale, he would swallow electric lights, visible within his stomach when switched on. He was described as having an ostrich stomach because they swallow stones.

Lydia McPherson of Los Angeles was billed as having the longest red hair in the world, which stretched 7 ft 5 in (2.3 m) in length.

Sword-swallower Joseph Grendol had worked a season for the Ringling Circus before joining Ripley's Odditorium. He would swallow a 20-in (50-cm) bayonet attached to the butt of a rifle and then fire the gun while the bayonet was in his stomach!

A seasoned performer known variously as the "Human Pincushion" or the "Painless Wonder," Leo Kongee would drive pins and nails into his face, and even had a button sewn onto his tongue, and seemingly felt no pain.

Time Tunnel

Ramchandra Das of Bihar, India, spent 14 years cutting a tunnel 33 ft (10 m) long and 13 ft (4 m) wide through a mountain with only a hammer and chisel so that his neighbors could avoid an arduous 4½-mi (7-km) trek around the mountain to work and so that he could park his truck closer to home.

Hidden Home

Sharon Simpson created a luxurious tent home—complete with solar shower and satellite TV—on a busy traffic circle in the center of Derby, England. She lived there unnoticed for five months and moved out only when leaves falling off nearby bushes took away her privacy.

Underwater Meeting

In October 2009, the government of the low-lying islands of the Maldives in the Indian Ocean held an underwater meeting to highlight the dangers of global warming. Dressed in full scuba gear, President Nasheed and ten colleagues took part in the 30-minute meeting at a depth of 20 ft (6 m) off the coast, near the country's capital Malé. Most of the Maldives is barely 3 ft (1 m) above sea level, and scientists fear it could be uninhabitable in fewer than 100 years.

Piping Hot

The sidewalks of Klamath Falls, Oregon, are kept free from snow and ice—and therefore safe for pedestrians—by hot-water pipes that run underneath them.

Brocken Specter

Local climbers in the Polish Tatra Mountains believe that if they witness a Brocken Specter—their own giant shadow projected on thick cloud below them—then they are doomed to die on the mountain. The phenomenon is named after the Brocken Mountain in Germany.

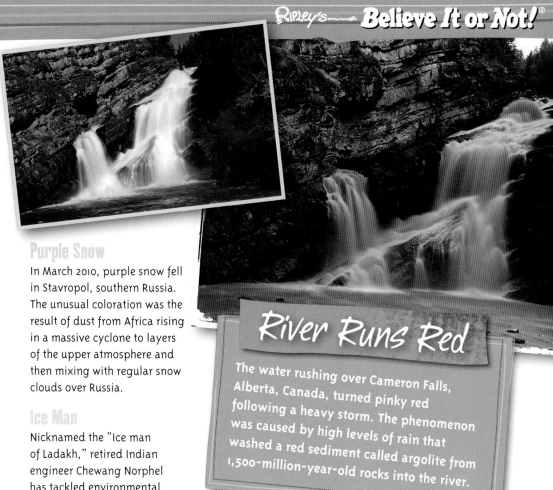

Purple Snow

In March 2010, purple snow fell in Stavropol, southern Russia. The unusual coloration was the result of dust from Africa rising in a massive cyclone to layers of the upper atmosphere and then mixing with regular snow clouds over Russia.

Ice Man

Nicknamed the "Ice man of Ladakh," retired Indian engineer Chewang Norphel has tackled environmental problems by building more than a dozen new glaciers in the Himalayas. He constructs his own glaciers by diverting meltwater through pipes into artificial lakes. Shaded by the mountains and kept in place by dams, the water in the lakes remains frozen until springtime when it melts and feeds the rivers below, which in turn irrigate surrounding farmland. He decided to act after melting glaciers caused floods that destroyed homes and crops.

River Runs Red

The water rushing over Cameron Falls, Alberta, Canada, turned pinky red following a heavy storm. The phenomenon was caused by high levels of rain that washed a red sediment called argolite from 1,500-million-year-old rocks into the river.

New Castle

Since 1997, some 50 workers in central France have been building a new "medieval" castle using only the tools and materials that were available in the 13th century. The brainchild of local landowner Michel Guyot, the Château de Guédelon is being built from sandstone, and when it's finished in around 2022 will boast a main tower more than 90 ft (27 m) tall.

Time Travel

Russia has no fewer than nine different time zones—and the eastern region of Chukotka (just across the Bering Strait from Alaska) is nine hours ahead of Kaliningrad in the extreme west of the country. There were 11 time zones in Russia until two were scrapped in 2010.

81

Leaning Skyscraper

The 530-ft-high (160-m) Capital Gate building in Abu Dhabi leans at an angle of 18 degrees—four times more than Italy's famous Leaning Tower of Pisa. The new 35-story building achieves this angle by using staggered floor plates from the 12th floor up.

Towering Tent

A giant tent 490 ft (150 m) high opened in Astana, Kazakhstan, in 2010. Designed to withstand the nation's extreme variations in temperature, the Khan Shatyr Entertainment Center took four years to build. Made from three layers of transparent plastic, it stands on a 650-ft (200-m) concrete base and houses shops, restaurants, movie theaters and even an artificial beach and a running track.

Security Cage

After being burgled eight times in six months, 80-year-old Chinese grandmother Ling Wan turned her apartment in Changsha into a giant birdcage. She sealed up the stairs and built an iron cage around the apartment so that the only way in and out is via a ladder that is securely locked on her balcony.

Container Store

Shoppers visiting the flagship Freitag bag store in Zurich, Switzerland, certainly need a head for heights, as the building is made from a dizzying stack of used steel shipping containers. It consists of 17 containers of which nine form the 85-ft-high (26-m) tower. The recycling theme of the building mirrors the bags sold inside, which are made from such items as old truck tarpaulins, bicycle inner tubes, and car seat belts.

Capsule Hotels

Japan's capsule hotels have rooms that measure roughly 7 x 4 x 3 ft (2.1 x 1.2 x 0.9 m)—not much bigger than a coffin! They are stacked side by side on two levels, with steps providing access to the upper capsule. Some hotels have more than 700 capsules.

Light Tower

The Eiffel Tower in Paris, France, weighs less than a cylinder of air occupying the same dimensions. The force of the wind causes the top of the lightweight metal tower to sway up to 3 in (7.6 cm).

Sole Occupant

Owing to the recession, for three years Les Harrington was the only resident of a 2.4-acre (1-ha) luxury village in Essex, England, that boasted 58 cottages and apartments.

Luxury Igloo

In January 2010, Jimmy Grey built a luxury, four-room igloo in the yard of his home in Aquilla, Ohio. The igloo had 6-ft-high (1.8-m) ceilings and an entertainment room, complete with cable TV (which was plugged into an outlet in his garage) and surround-sound stereo.

Luminous Beams

A mysterious "rain" of vertical luminous beams appeared for nearly an hour in the night sky above Xiamen, China, in July 2010. At first there were just five beams, hanging low in the sky, but soon the number increased to 50. A local observatory confirmed that it was definitely not a meteor shower.

Hard Wood

Ironwood trees—including the black ironwood species that is native to the U.S.A.—have wood so dense that it won't float in water. It sinks instead.

Glass Elephant

Built on top of an old coalminer's washroom, the Glass Elephant in the Maximillianpark, Hamm, Germany—designed in 1984 by artist and architect Horst Rellecke—stands an amazing 115 ft (35 m) tall.

Mud Volcano

A mud volcano in Sidoarjo, East Java, Indonesia, spews enough scalding mud daily to fill 50 Olympic-size swimming pools. Since its first eruption in 2006, it has buried 12 villages.

Falling Ice

In 2008, a 6-lb (2.7-kg) chunk of ice fell from the sky, crashed through the roof of a home in York Township, Pennsylvania, and hit Mary Ann Foster, who was sleeping, on the head. It turned out to be atmospheric ice, formed when moisture in the atmosphere freezes into small ice balls, which then bump into each other and sometimes attach themselves together to create larger chunks.

Crackers

During the Chinese Lantern Festival celebrations in Taiwan, it's customary for onlookers to launch firecrackers at a shirtless man who represents the god of wealth. The more fireworks that hit their intended target, the more successful the firework thrower will become. This dangerous-looking ritual has been performed in the area for over 50 years.

Underground Home

Unable to afford a bigger house, retired Chinese miner Chen Xinnian tunneled out a one-bedroom apartment measuring 540-sq-ft (50-sq-m) beneath his existing home in Zhengzhou, Henan Province. The apartment is 20 ft (6 m) underground and is so cool that food does not need to be kept in a refrigerator.

River Ritual

More than ten million devotees from all over the country came to Haridwar, India, in February 2010 for the Kumbh Mela Festival, held here once every 12 years, to bathe in the River Ganges.

Royal Shrine

Mehrangarh Fort in Jodhpur, Rajasthan, India, has a shrine bearing carvings of the handprints of royal widows that committed *suttee*—a ceremony in which women were burned alive upon the funeral pyre of their husbands.

Lunar Pit

Photographs of the Moon taken from the Japanese Kaguya spacecraft revealed a giant pit about 427 ft (130 m) in diameter on the lunar surface— that's large enough to swallow an entire football field.

Flaming Festival

Each year the city of Toyohashi in Japan hosts an extreme fire festival. Fearless volunteers launch enormous homemade bamboo fireworks, known as *tezutsu hanabi*, which explode inches from their face. The 300-year-old festival sets off 12,000 fireworks and can draw more than 350 homemade cannons that spew fire up to 65 ft (20 m) into the sky.

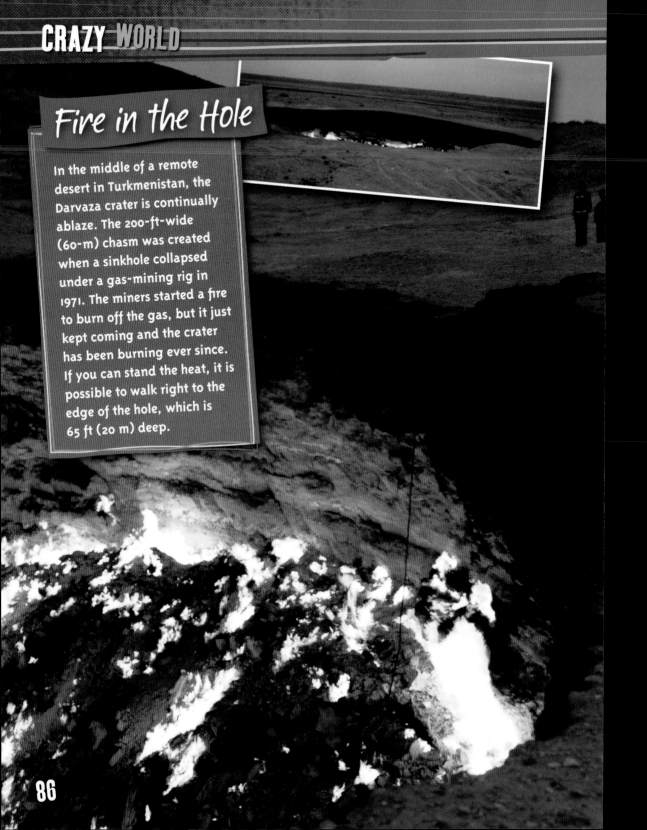

Fire in the Hole

In the middle of a remote desert in Turkmenistan, the Darvaza crater is continually ablaze. The 200-ft-wide (60-m) chasm was created when a sinkhole collapsed under a gas-mining rig in 1971. The miners started a fire to burn off the gas, but it just kept coming and the crater has been burning ever since. If you can stand the heat, it is possible to walk right to the edge of the hole, which is 65 ft (20 m) deep.

The Twitchhiker

Paul Smith traveled around the world for free in 30 days relying solely on the goodwill of people using the social networking site Twitter. By accepting free accommodation and transport from his fellow tweeters, he managed to travel from his home in Newcastle upon Tyne, England, to Stewart Island, New Zealand, via Amsterdam, Paris, Frankfurt, New York, Washington, D.C., Chicago, San Francisco, Los Angeles and Auckland.

Deadly Storm

On April 30, 1888, a violent hailstorm dropped ice balls the size of oranges on the city of Moradabad in India, killing 230 people.

Toilet Tour

German guide Anna Haase runs a different kind of sightseeing tour—instead of showing visitors the traditional sights of Berlin, she takes them on a tour of the city's famous toilets. These range from a historic 19th-century toilet block to a Japanese automatic toilet that costs as much as a small car.

Boy Power

China has 32 million more boys under the age of 20 than it has girls.

Tar Lake

Covering an area of 100 acres (40 ha) and delving to about 250 ft (80 m) deep at the center, Pitch Lake on the island of Trinidad is filled with liquid asphalt, the result of oil being forced up through the faults on which the lake sits. Despite the highly toxic chemicals, the lake is home to bacterial life.

Sewage Symphony

A sewage plant near Berlin, Germany, is breaking down sludge more quickly by playing the music of Mozart to its microbes. The composer's classics are piped in to the plant around the clock via a series of speakers because the sonic patterns of the music help stimulate activity among the tiny organisms, speeding up the breakdown of waste.

Hamster Hotel

In 2009, a hotel in Nantes, France, offered guests the chance to live like a hamster for a day. Architects Frederic Tabary and Yann Falquerho designed the room to resemble the inside of a hamster's cage, and for $130 a night visitors could feast on hamster grain, get a workout by running in a giant hamster wheel, and sleep in piles of hay.

007 Tribute

For a 2009 New Year's Eve party, James Bond fanatics Simon and Angie Mullane spent four months and $4,500 transforming their Dorset, England, home into a 007 movie set. Guests were greeted at a homemade checkpoint manned by dummies dressed in authentic East German border guard uniforms bought on the Internet, while a Sean Connery mannequin dangled from a real hang glider suspended in the garden.

Tunnel Network

During the Vietnam War (1955–75), Viet Cong soldiers using only hand tools dug a single tunnel network all the way from Saigon to the Cambodian border—a distance of over 150 mi (240 km). They created an underground city with living areas, kitchens, weapons factories and field hospitals, installing large air vents (which were disguised as anthills or termite mounds), baffled vents to dissipate cooking smells, and lethal booby traps. Up to 10,000 people lived underground for years, getting married, giving birth, and coming out only at night to tend to their crops under cover of darkness.

Secret City

Believe it or not, hidden directly below the busy streets of Paris, France, there are countless secret tunnels and caverns, and millions of human bones.

The city expanded so quickly in the 18th century that cemeteries and mass graves were soon literally overflowing—it is said that the cellar walls of adjoining buildings would ooze with human remains, and disease was rife. To solve the problem, bodies were removed each night and buried in caves adjoining the Parisian sewers. These catacombs—or underground cemeteries—and the tunnels between them were recycled Roman stone quarries that stretched for 500 mi (805 km). It is thought that the bones of six million Parisians are piled up in the catacombs—over half the current live population. It is still possible to wander through the maze of passages that run 65 ft (20 m) below the city streets.

OSSEMENT S DU
CIMETIERE DES
INNOCENTS
DEPOSES LE
2 JUILLET 1809

Away from the more organized areas of the catacombs, bones lie scattered in forgotten tunnels.

- French resistance troops used the catacombs as a base during World War II, as did occupying German forces. The tunnels also served as air-raid shelters for Parisians seeking refuge from enemy bombing.

- In 1787, the future King Charles X of France held a party in a large cavern deep in the catacombs.

- A gang of thieves was arrested in the catacombs in 1905 after attempting to steal skulls and bones to sell to medical students.

- A team of experts constantly surveys hundreds of miles of the catacombs to prevent any of the caves collapsing, which would potentially cause parts of the city, lying directly above them, to fall into the ground.

- An escaped orangutan perished in the Paris underground tunnels over 200 years ago. Its skeleton is still kept on public display.

THE GATEWAY TO THE CATACOMBS STATES: "ARRETE! C'EST ICI L'EMPIRE DE LA MORT" ("STOP! HERE IS THE EMPIRE OF DEATH.")

Right: This inscription reads: "In the memory of Philibert Aspairt lost in this quarry on November 3rd 1793 found eleven years later and buried at the same place on April 30th 1804."

BURIED ALIVE

In 1793, Philibert Aspairt descended into the catacombs under the hospital where he worked, hoping to steal wine from cellars belonging to monks. His body was found 11 years later, only yards from an exit.

Ice House

The Cleveland Harbor West Pierhead Lighthouse on the shores of Lake Erie, Ohio, looked more like a fairytale castle in December 2010 when it became completely covered in layers of ice. High winds caused waves to crash over the lighthouse, where the water then froze in the bitterly cold temperatures.

Phone Access
Only about one-third of India's population has access to modern sanitation—but nearly half of the population has a cell phone!

Reduced Alphabet
Rotokas, a language spoken on the island of Bougainville, Papua New Guinea, has only 12 letters in its entire alphabet—they are A, E, G, I, K, O, P, R, S, T, U and V.

Lonely Lighthouse
The Stannard Rock lighthouse, Michigan, is the only structure on a large rock 23 mi (37 km) off the coast of Lake Superior. It was staffed for eight decades, until it was finally automated in 1962.

Hot Ash
Volcanic avalanches of hot ash, rock fragments and gas—known as pyroclastic flows—can move at 150 mph (240 km/h) and are capable of knocking down and burning everything in their path.

Narrow House

A three-story house in Brighton, East Sussex, England, is just 6 ft (1.8 m) wide. Owners Iain and Rachel Boyle bought the former donkey-cart shed for just $12,000 in 1998, but have turned it into such a stylish home—complete with a mezzanine bedroom—that they now rent it out.

One-way Traffic

Between 2004 and 2009, nearly 10,000 North Koreans defected to South Korea—while only two people went in the other direction!

Judge Numbers

India has 11 judges for every million people, while the U.S.A. has 110 per million—ten times as many.

Ooh-la-Law!

In 2010, French politicians finally sought to repeal a 1799 law that banned women in Paris from wearing pants except when riding horses or bicycles.

New Ring

In 2009, U.S. astronomers discovered a new ring around Saturn that is so large it could hold a billion Earths. The ring is made up of debris from Saturn's distant moon Phoebe.

Flood Terror

In January 2011, torrential rain in the state of Victoria, Australia, killed over 22,000 sheep and 300,000 poultry and led to the formation of an inland lake of floodwater more than 50 mi (80 km) long. Farther north in Queensland, the floods submerged an area of land the size of France and Germany combined.

Weeping Glacier

A human face, appearing to cry, appeared in a glacier in Svalbard, Norway, in 2009. As the ice cap melted, the water poured into the sea, eroding the ice and creating the mysterious shape.

Crazy Kink

A 7.1-magnitude earthquake near Canterbury, New Zealand, in September 2010 caused rail tracks in the region to buckle alarmingly. A train engineer managed to stop his two engines just 100 ft (30 m) short of this crazy kink. Repairs involved removing the crippled rails and replacing them with new rails that measured about 6½ ft (2 m) shorter than the originals.

Ring of Fire

Three-quarters of the world's active and dormant volcanoes exist within the 25,000-mi (40,000-km) Ring of Fire, situated along the edges of the Pacific Ocean. Among them is Alaska's Mount Redoubt, which erupted in March 2009, sending a plume of smoke nearly 10 mi (16 km) into the air.

Shooting Spores

Pilobolis fungi live in animal dung and are less than ½ in (1 cm) tall, but they shoot packets of spores up to 6 ft (1.8 m) in the air to reproduce.

Meteorite Crater

Max Rocca, an amateur geologist from Buenos Aires, Argentina, found an ancient meteorite crater 31 mi (50 km) across in the Colombian rainforest—by examining satellite pictures. His interest was aroused after he detected a near-perfect semicircular curve in the Vichada River.

Multiple Eclipse

Solar eclipses are a major phenomenon here on Earth, but the planet Jupiter, because it has 50 confirmed moons, can have multiple eclipses happening simultaneously.

School Climb

Erping Village Elementary School in Sichuan Province, China, is built on a platform nearly 10,000 ft (3,050 m) up a remote mountainside. Until 2010, when a new steel stairway was built on the cliff, students could get to school only by climbing a series of rickety, homemade wooden ladders. The school's two teachers had to escort the children up and down the ladders because the journey was so dangerous and exhausting.

Nuclear Reactions

The Sun's core has enough hydrogen to continue fueling its nuclear reactions for another five billion years.

Dry Run

The U.S. side of the mighty Niagara Falls was nearly as dry as a desert for five months in 1969. Engineers stopped the waterfall for the first time in 12,000 years by building a temporary 600-ft-wide (180-m) dam from 27,800 tons of rock and diverting the flow of the Niagara River over the larger Horseshoe Falls on the Canadian side. The work was carried out to remove a large quantity of loose rock from the base of the U.S. side of the Falls, which, if left in place, might eventually prevent the waterfall from flowing at all. To delay the gradual erosion of the U.S. side, faults were also mechanically strengthened. When the task was finished and the dam was blown up, 60,000 gal (227,000 l) of water once again thundered over the U.S. side of the Falls every second.

Young Star

On November 7, 2008, 14-year-old amateur astronomer Caroline Moore of Warwick, New York, discovered a supernova—and the exploding star she found (dubbed SN 2008ha) was about 1,000 times dimmer than a typical supernova.

Black Hole

NASA has found a gigantic black hole 100 million times the mass of the Sun, feeding off gas, dust and stars at the center of a galaxy, 50 million light-years away.

Toxic Lake

Argentina's Lake Diamante, shaped like a diamond, is filled with thriving bacteria despite being oxygen depleted, hyper-saline, spectacularly toxic, and bombarded with ultraviolet radiation.

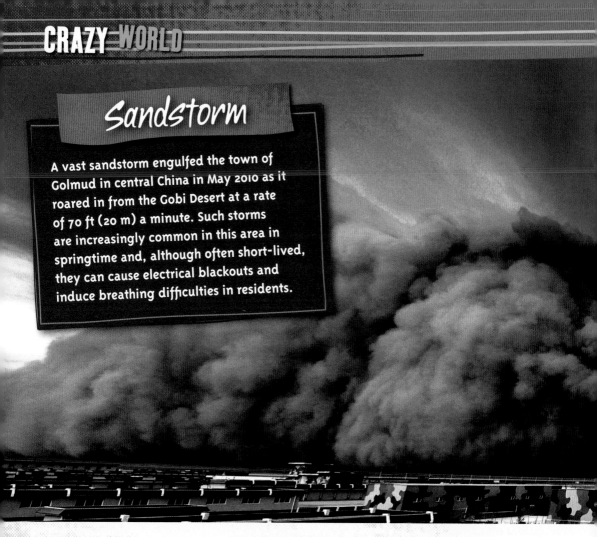

Sandstorm

A vast sandstorm engulfed the town of Golmud in central China in May 2010 as it roared in from the Gobi Desert at a rate of 70 ft (20 m) a minute. Such storms are increasingly common in this area in springtime and, although often short-lived, they can cause electrical blackouts and induce breathing difficulties in residents.

Monster Star

Scientists from the University of Sheffield, England, have discovered a new star that weighs 265 times the mass of our Sun and is almost 10 million times brighter. The monster star—named R136a1—is believed to be around a million years old and is so bright that if it were located where our Sun is, it would completely fry the Earth within minutes.

Painted Peak

Using water jugs to splash an eco-friendly whitewash onto the rocks, a team of workers in Peru have painted the 15,600-ft-high (4,756-m) Chalon Sombrero mountain white. The peak in the Andes was once home to a sprawling glacier and it is hoped that the newly painted mountain will reflect away sunlight and help cool down the slopes to trigger a re-growth of its ice.

Meteorite Attack

The same house in Gornji Lajici, Bosnia, was hit by meteorites six times in three years between 2007 and 2010. The repeated bombardment of white-hot rocks forced owner Radivoje Lajic to reinforce the roof with a steel girder. He says the chances of being hit by a meteorite once are so small that to be hit six times must mean that he is being targeted by aliens.

Glowing Urine

A glowing trail spotted in the night sky above North America in September 2009 was caused by a falling block of astronaut urine. It came from the Space Shuttle Discovery which, unable to unload human waste while it was docked to the International Space Station, had then been forced to dump nearly two weeks' worth of waste in one drop.

In the Dark

A power outage in 2009 left the town of Quipeio, Angola (population 1,000), in the dark for more than two months.

Toxic Island

Owing to the risk of toxic volcanic gases on Miyakejima Island, Japan, residents carry gas masks with them at all times—and sometimes even sleep with them.

Lightning Hotspot

An area near the village of Kifuka, in the Democratic Republic of the Congo, has the greatest number of lightning strikes per square kilometer in the world—about 158 a year.

Black Gold

Beverly Hills High School in California has oil wells beneath its grounds, which earn the school hundreds of thousands of dollars in revenue every year.

Burj Khalifa

The Burj Khalifa, which opened in January 2010, is the tallest structure ever built. At 2,717 ft (828 m) tall, it is more than twice the height of the Empire State Building—the equivalent of 180 giraffes standing on each other's heads. Each of the 160 floors took just three days to build, with the complete tower taking 5½ years to finish, at a cost of $1.5 billion.

Bio Blitz

On a single day in August 2009, a team of 125 scientists and volunteers found more than 1,100 species of life—plants, lichens, mushrooms, bees, bugs, butterflies, worms and bats—in just 2 sq mi (5 sq km) of Yellowstone National Park, including several species that were not known to exist there.

Blown Away

When Cyclone Olivia hit Australia's Barrow Island in 1996, it created a wind gust of 253 mph (407 km/h).

Changing Places

The moons Janus and Epimetheus are in the same orbit around Saturn, with one a little farther out and slower than the other. The faster moon catches up its neighbor every four years and the two moons swap places and the cycle begins again.

New Cloud

Meteorologists believe they have discovered a new type of cloud. The Cloud Appreciation Society has named it asperatus, after the Latin word for "rough," on account of its rough and choppy underside. If the cloud type becomes officially recognized, it will be the first new cloud type since 1951.

Rocky Rain

On the distant planet COROT-7b, which is nearly twice the size of Earth, it rains rocks! Scientists from Washington University in St. Louis, Missouri, found that the planet's atmosphere is made up of vaporized rock, and when a weather front moves in, pebbles condense out of the air and rain down on the surface.

Constant Eruption

Stromboli, off the coast of Italy, aka the "Lighthouse of the Mediterranean," has been erupting for over 20,000 years. The 3,038-ft-high (926-m) volcano emits smoke and lava fragments about every 20 to 40 minutes.

Sun Block

When Tambora, a volcano on the island of Sumbawa, Indonesia, erupted in 1815, the 200 million tons of sulfur dioxide gas that were ejected into the atmosphere reduced the amount of sunlight reaching the ground. This caused temperatures to drop dramatically all over the world, resulting in crop failures throughout Europe, and, in 1816, North America's "year without a summer," snow fell in June and New England experienced severe frosts even as late in the year as August.

Single Bloom

The *Tahina spectabilis* palm tree of Madagascar grows for decades up to a height of more than 50 ft (15 m) before it finally flowers for a single time, then dies.

Rapid Growth

Just a week after it first appeared in a Mexican cornfield in 1943, the volcano Parícutin had reached a height of five stories, and a year later it stood 1,102 ft (336 m) tall.

Deadly River

The 1783 Laki eruption in Iceland sent enough lava spewing from a 15-mi-long (25-km) crack to fill two deep river valleys and cover an area of more than 190 sq mi (500 sq km). The lava river, which was 100 ft (30 m) deep, engulfed villages and released poisonous gases that killed many of those who managed to escape its flow.

Undersea Blast

There are at least 1,500 active volcanoes on the surface of the Earth and an estimated 10,000 volcanoes beneath the ocean. When an underwater volcano off the coast of Iceland erupted in 1963, it did so with such force that it punched through the sea and formed the 1-sq-mi (2.7-sq-km) Surtsey Island.

Pub Crawl

Rather than demolish the 124-year-old Birdcage Tavern to make way for a new road tunnel in Auckland, New Zealand, the country's transport authority decided to move the landmark hostelry 130 ft (40 m) up a hill. After the walls were reinforced by inserting carbon-fiber rods, the three-story building was jacked onto concrete rails lubricated with Teflon and liquid silicon, then painstakingly pushed up the hill by hydraulic ramps. The move took two days.

Time for Change

A giant astronomical clock at Wells Cathedral in Somerset, England, was painstakingly wound by hand for more than 600 years—and from 1919 to 2010 it was operated by five generations of the Fisher family. From 1987, Paul Fisher spent an hour, three times a week, turning the three 550-lb (250-kg) weights about 800 times. The weights were winched up on a pulley system and powered the clock as they descended over the next two days.

Gold Machine

The Emirates Palace Hotel in Abu Dhabi, U.A.E., has a vending machine that dispenses gold bars—with prices updated to correspond to the world markets every 10 minutes.

Gladiator School

The University of Regensburg, Germany, has a summer camp in which students live and train like Roman gladiators.

Beer Crate House

Architect Jörn Bihain used 43,000 plastic beer crates to create what he named the "Pavilion of Temporary Happiness," in the grounds of the Atomium building in Brussels, Belgium, in 2008. The vast temporary structure commemorated 50 years since the Atomium was erected at the 1958 Brussels World Fair.

BRUXELLES
A LA CARTE
LA BELGIQUE
EN RESEAUX
PRENDRE LE TEMPS
DE COMPRENDRE

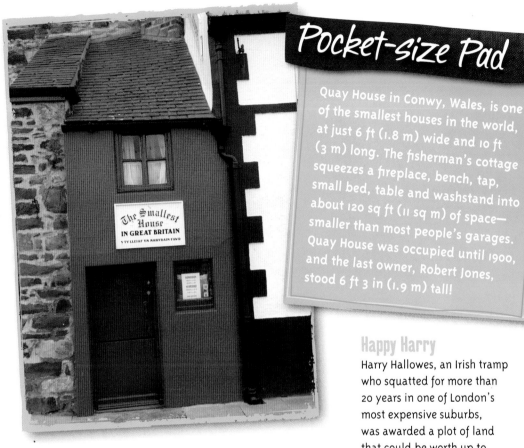

The Smallest House
IN GREAT BRITAIN
Y TY LLEIAF YN NHRYDAIN FAWR

Pocket-size Pad

Quay House in Conwy, Wales, is one of the smallest houses in the world, at just 6 ft (1.8 m) wide and 10 ft (3 m) long. The fisherman's cottage squeezes a fireplace, bench, tap, small bed, table and washstand into about 120 sq ft (11 sq m) of space—smaller than most people's garages. Quay House was occupied until 1900, and the last owner, Robert Jones, stood 6 ft 3 in (1.9 m) tall!

Happy Harry

Harry Hallowes, an Irish tramp who squatted for more than 20 years in one of London's most expensive suburbs, was awarded a plot of land that could be worth up to $6 million. He was given squatters' rights to a patch of land 120 x 60 ft (36 x 18 m) on Hampstead Heath, where he has lived in a tiny shack since 1986.

Tower Highway

The 16-story Gate Tower Building in Osaka, Japan, has a highway running through its middle between the fifth and seventh floors. An exit of the Hanshin Expressway passes through as a bridge, held up by supports next to the building. The office block's elevator moves through the vacant floors in the building without stopping between floor four and floor eight.

4,200 Clocks

The Pentagon, headquarters for the U.S. Department of Defense, has 4,200 wall clocks. Over 200,000 telephone calls are made from the Pentagon every day through phones connected by 100,000 mi (160,000 km) of cable, and although there are 17½ mi (28 km) of corridors, it takes only seven minutes to walk between any two points in the building.

Rat Free

A Japanese shipwreck in 1780 inadvertently introduced rats to Rat Island, Alaska, and the island was heavily infested until 2009, when it finally became free of rats again—229 years later.

AWESOME ANIMALS

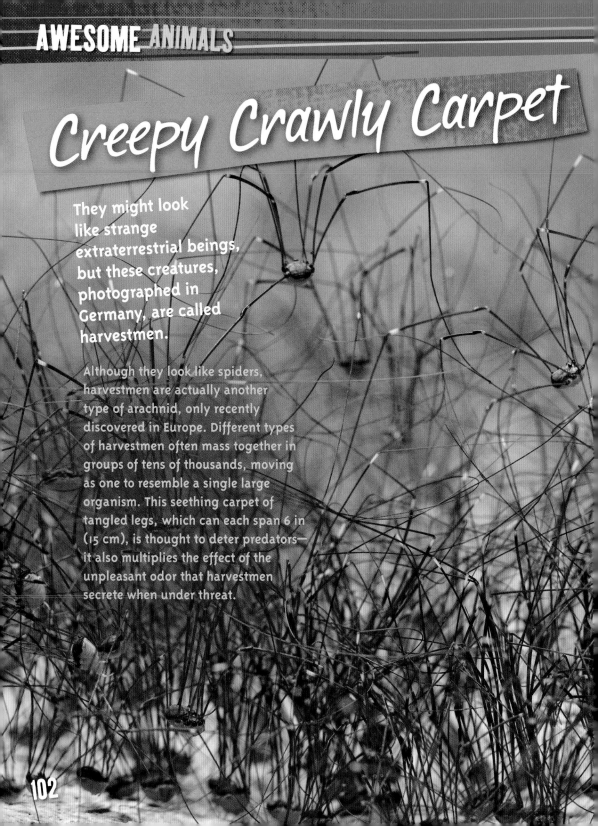

Creepy Crawly Carpet

They might look like strange extraterrestrial beings, but these creatures, photographed in Germany, are called harvestmen.

Although they look like spiders, harvestmen are actually another type of arachnid, only recently discovered in Europe. Different types of harvestmen often mass together in groups of tens of thousands, moving as one to resemble a single large organism. This seething carpet of tangled legs, which can each span 6 in (15 cm), is thought to deter predators— it also multiplies the effect of the unpleasant odor that harvestmen secrete when under threat.

Kamikaze Carpenters

A species of carpenter ant found in Borneo has a gruesome way to defend its colony. Designated soldier ants wait until a predator is close by and then sacrifice themselves by exploding glands that run along their body. These glands contain a sticky poisonous glue that ensnares the would-be invader, but also kills the carpenter ant in the process.

Jack's Journey

A whippet-terrier cross called Jack was reunited with his owners in Sheffield, England, after a marathon 31-hour trek that took him across the M1—one of Britain's busiest expressways—four major roads, and miles of treacherous moorland. The dog, who got separated from his owners on a walk, was especially brave considering he suffers from a fear of traffic, and walks with a limp after being knocked down by a truck in 2005.

Painful Ritual

To prove they are real men, teenage members of the Setere-Mawe people of Brazil subject themselves to being stung repeatedly by bullet ants, the sting of which is so painful it has been compared to a gunshot wound. For the initiation, boys wear a pair of gloves each laced with hundreds of live bullet ants, stingers pointing inward, for ten minutes—and they must go through this agonizing ritual 20 times.

Plunging Parrots

A mystery illness caused hundreds of lorikeets to fall out of the sky over Darwin, Northern Territory, Australia, in 2010. The birds appeared groggy and listless, as if they were suffering from a bad hangover, but recovered over a period of a few weeks.

Living Larders

Some members of honeypot ant colonies eat until they are unable to walk. They then become living food storage containers, regurgitating food for their nest mates as needed.

Adaptable Lungs

Elephant seals collapse their lungs before they dive for food and can stay underwater for up to two hours.

Population Boom

Under ideal conditions, a population of five pregnant female German cockroaches could grow to 45 million—in just a year.

Wasp Stings

A 53-year-old woman from Attleboro, Massachusetts, survived being stung more than 500 times after falling onto a wasp nest outside her home. Firefighters used a carbon dioxide chemical fire extinguisher to blast the aggressive insects off the woman's body.

Faithful Fowl

Of the thousands of pairs of mating swans studied over 40 years at the Wildfowl and Wetlands Trust in Slimbridge, England, only two have ever "divorced" and found themselves new partners.

Air Miles

Arctic terns migrate about 43,000 mi (70,000 km) each year, which, during their lifetime of 30-plus years, works out at a distance equal to three round trips from the Earth to the Moon.

Potty Plant

The mountain treeshrew of Malaysia has a handy place to go to the bathroom. There is a particular type of pitcher plant shaped conveniently like a treeshrew-sized toilet bowl that attracts the small creatures with its sweet nectar. And while the shrew feeds on the pitcher's nectar, the plant has been found to extract food of its own from the shrew droppings.

Bee-stung Lips

The 2010 Clovermead bee beard competition was abuzz with excitement as competitors were loaded with some of the millions of bees kept on the Clovermead farm in Ontario, Canada. A queen bee was attached to each competitor's neck, her smell attracting entire bee colonies. The champion beard belonged to Tibor Szabo, who wore a bee mask that covered his face. He was congratulated by a particularly courageous spectator.

One Big Eye

Although sea urchins don't have actual eyes, they see by using the entire surface of their body as one big eye. They have light-sensitive molecules, mainly in their tube feet and around their spines, and use these to avoid predators or find dark corners to hide in. Therefore, the sea urchins with the most densely packed spines are the ones with the best vision.

Ram Raid

A ram smashed through the glass patio door of a house in Lancashire, England, and ran amok, butting the stove door, knocking over a TV, smashing up furniture, and wrecking carpets. It is believed the animal, which had fled from a nearby field and was agitated because of the breeding season, charged at the patio door after seeing his own reflection in the glass.

Greyhound Wedding

Inseparable greyhounds Pete and Zoe were married in a canine ceremony at an animal shelter in Cambridgeshire, England. The bride wore a specially made dress and afterward she and her spouse devoured a three-tier liver cake. Staff thought a wedding would be a good way to seal the dogs' love for each other and to ensure they would be adopted together.

Open Wide

This fearsome deep-sea creature sports what appear to be humanlike teeth at the center of its tentacles. An unusual species of squid, the Promachoteuthis sulcus was discovered at a depth of 6,560 ft (2,000 m) in the South Atlantic Ocean. In reality it is far less terrifying than it appears—what look like teeth are fleshy lips around its beak, and this specimen is actually only 1 in (2.5 cm) long.

Herd for Heights

These Alpine ibexes think nothing of climbing the near-vertical face of the Cingino Dam in the Italian Alps to lick minerals from the stones. Alpine ibex have incredible agility and balance, which enable them to cling to the rough rock of the 160-ft-high (49-m) dam with their hooves.

Hero Hugo

A cat saved a neighbor's life by rescuing him from his burning home. Andrew Williams was asleep when the fire broke out in his bungalow in Berkshire, England, and he would almost certainly have died but for his neighbor's cat Hugo coming in through a catflap and waking him by clawing at his face. Hugo and his brother Harvey are regular visitors to the home of cat-lover Mr. Williams.

Death Dance

Male Australian redback spiders, which weigh only one percent as much as females, must dance for well over an hour when approaching a female, otherwise they will be eaten before they can finish mating.

Fisherman's Luck?

While fishing 80 ft (25 m) above the water from a cargo ship off the coast of Queensland, Australia, Filipino engineer Algerico Salise was stung by a tentacle from a thimble-sized irukandji jellyfish. The potentially fatal sting happened when the engineer's face was splashed with seawater that contained the jellyfish as he reeled in a fish. Urgent hospital treatment saved his life.

Bird Deodorant

Scientists in New Zealand are seeking a deodorant for some of the country's smelly birds in a bid to make them less attractive to predators. Unlike their overseas counterparts, birds native to New Zealand did not evolve alongside traditional land mammals, and they emit a strong smell when preening themselves to produce the wax needed to protect their feathers. The kiwi emits a mushroom-like scent, while the kakapo parrot smells like a musty violin case—and these odors attract newly introduced foreign predators.

Lost Gator

In 2010, a 5-ft-long (1.5-m) freshwater alligator was found swimming with whales 20 mi (32 km) out to sea in the North Atlantic off the coast of Georgia. It is thought the reptile had been washed out to sea from the mouth of the Altamaha River during heavy rains.

False Legs

Meadow, a calf born in New Mexico who lost her two back hooves to frostbite, was able to walk again after being fitted with a pair of prosthetic legs by veterinarians at Colorado State University.

Thieving Spiders

Rather than build their own webs, dewdrop spiders steal food or eat the leftovers from the webs of larger spiders.

Bifocal Bugs

The principal eyes of the larvae of the sunburst diving beetle have bifocal lenses. The bifocals have been found in four of the larvae's 12 eyes and allow it to switch its vision from up-close to distance— all the better for seeing and catching its favorite prey, mosquito larvae.

Shark Rider

Attacked by a 14-ft-long (4.3-m) tiger shark off the coast of Hawaii, 68-year-old surfer Jim Rawlinson grabbed its fin, pulled himself onto its back so that he was straddling the shark, and then rode it for about ten seconds. Sliding off the beast's back and watching it swim off, Jim returned to what remained of his board (after the shark had bitten a chunk out of it) and fearlessly surfed for another 45 minutes before returning to the beach uninjured.

Boating Otter

Wolfgang Gettmann of Dusseldorf, Germany, has a pet otter that accompanies him on kayaking trips.

Natural Haircut

A manatee living off the coast of Florida receives a natural haircut from dozens of tiny blue gill fish, which crowd around the gentle sea mammal and eat algae, parasites and dead skin off its body.

Draining Experience

Three weeks after disappearing from Susan Garr's home in Salt Lake City, Utah, Millie, a four-year-old Australian shepherd mix, was found stuck in a storm drain. Rescue crews freed the dog, whose weight had dropped from 35 lb (16 kg) to 22 lb (10 kg) during her ordeal.

Stunt Baboon

Moco, a baboon at China's Changzhou Yancheng Wild Animal Park, is such a talented gymnast and daredevil that he has joined a circus. He specializes in the flying rings but can also perform stunts involving the horizontal bars, parallel bars, balance beam, fire hoops and even bike riding!

Turtle Surprise

A monster grouper fish that died after being washed up on a beach in Townsville, Queensland, Australia, was found to have a whole sea turtle inside its stomach. The green turtle had a shell measuring 16 in (40 cm), while the fish, estimated to be 25 years old, weighed a mighty 330 lb (150 kg). Although the cause of the turtle's death was probably the grouper, veterinarians said it was unlikely that the turtle caused the grouper's death.

Spot the Caterpillar

Underground Fish

Stygichthys typhlops, an extremely rare blind fish that lives underground in Brazil, was recently rediscovered almost 50 years after the only known specimen was collected. Biologists believe that the fish may be a living relict that has survived deep below ground while its relatives above ground became extinct.

Lucky by Name...

Lucky, a cat belonging to Keri Hostetler of New York City, survived a 26-story fall from the ledge of her owner's apartment building.

Giant Squid

In July 2009, a 19½-ft-long (6-m) giant squid was caught in the Gulf of Mexico—the first live giant gulf squid captured for more than 50 years.

Doggy Stroller

Jenny, a pug owned by Ellen Zessin of Portland, Oregon, loves to stand on her hind legs and push her soft toy pugs around the garden in a baby stroller.

Long Lives

Splish and Splash, two goldfish won at a funfair in Gloucestershire, England, by Hayley and Matthew Wright in 1977, were amazingly still alive 33 years later.

Bee Careful

Ellie, a Labrador Retriever owned by Robert and Sandra Coe of Santee, California, survived after eating a beehive containing pesticides and thousands of dead bees. The inquisitive dog has also eaten wooden toy train tracks and laptop computer keys.

Believe it or not, there's a hungry caterpillar standing on this leaf! The Baron caterpillar—*Euthalia aconthea gurda*—of Southeast Asia is almost invisible against the background of this mango tree leaf in Kuala Lumpur, Malaysia.

Helpful Marking

In case anyone has any doubt as to what sort of animal she is, Polly, a tabby kitten owned by Garry and Joan Marsh of Staffordshire, England, has the word "cat" clearly spelled out in her fur on her left side.

Four Wings

A guin—a rare hybrid between a chicken and a guinea fowl—was born in Worcestershire, England, with four wings. Although the strange chick had two extra wings at the front, it was unable to fly. Lyn Newman had introduced two guinea fowl into her coop to act as lookouts, unaware that they could in fact breed with her hens.

Hen-pecked

A cockerel and his three hens gained revenge for a series of attacks by killing a young fox that broke into their pen in Essex, England. A table in the corner of the coop had been kicked over, knocking the fox out, allowing Dude the cockerel and hens Izzy, Pongo and Pecky to peck the intruder to death.

Master of Disguise

The blue-striped fangblenny, a reef fish found off the coasts of Australia and Indonesia, can change its color at will to mimic other fish so it can get close enough to take a bite.

Swallowed Soccer Ball

Bracken, a two-year-old Labrador Retriever owned by John Grant of East Dunbartonshire, Scotland, needed emergency surgery after swallowing a whole toy soccer ball. The deflated ball—measuring 5 in (12 cm) long—had become lodged next to his heart, causing him to cough incessantly.

Antarctic Escape

In 2005, a lucky gentoo penguin narrowly escaped a pod of hungry killer whales off the coast of Antarctica when it jumped from the water into an inflatable boat full of tourists that happened to be floating nearby. The penguin then swam away, but quickly returned to the boat to escape the lingering whales for a second time.

Bat Line

More than 130 orphaned bats were wrapped in dust cloths and hung on clotheslines while they recovered after being rescued from the devastating floods that hit Queensland, Australia, in January 2011. Vulnerable after coming to the ground to feed, the baby bats were picked up by the Australian Bat Clinic and then bottle-fed and housed in the cloths to keep warm.

Bat Cave

Bracken Cave, near San Antonio, Texas, is home to 20 million bats that feed on more than 100 tons of insects every night.

Panda Puzzle

Giant pandas possess the genes needed to digest meat, but none of the genes required to digest their only significant food source—bamboo.

Beaver Attack

A large beaver weighing around 42 lb (19 kg) hospitalized fisherman Russ McTindal after launching an unprovoked attack on him. The animal swam across Georgia's Chattahoochee River and launched at him, gnawing at his arm while Russ tried fending it off by hitting it with his fishing rod.

Camel Freed

Fire crews shoveled mud for several hours to free a 1,500-lb (680-kg) camel that had fallen into an 8-ft-deep (2.4-m) sinkhole in Oregon City, Oregon.

Terrible Tusks

Babirusas, the "deer pigs" of the Indonesian archipelago, have a set of tusks that push straight through their nose and can grow long enough to curve back around and poke a hole in their forehead.

Parrot Alarm

Burglars who broke into a house in London's Docklands in July 2010 were scared off when owner Gennadi Kurkul's green Lory parrot, Kuzya, let out a screech that could be heard several streets away.

Crash Landing

A couple on a whale-watching trip off Cape Town, South Africa, got a closer view than they expected when a 40-ton, 33-ft-long (10-m), southern right whale suddenly jumped on to their yacht.

A species with notoriously bad eyesight, the whale navigates by sound, and as the boat had its engine off, this whale probably hadn't realized it was there.

After snapping the mast on impact, the whale thrashed around before sliding back into the water.

INTREPID

Unlucky Puppy

Smokey, a 12-week-old Chihuahua puppy from London, Kentucky, survived a freak accident at a garden party that left him with a barbecue fork stuck in his head. Despite having the 3-in-long (8-cm) fork prongs lodged in his brain for three days, veterinarians were eventually able to operate and save Smokey's life, and he was soon back at home with his owners.

Sixth Sense

A lost cat found her way to an animal rescue center in Fife, Scotland, despite having a can of cat food stuck on her head! The cat was thought to have been scavenging for food when she came across the discarded can. Unable to see where she was going, she somehow managed to avoid being hit by a car and wandered into the Scottish SPCA unit in Dunfermline where the tin headgear was removed.

Vegetarian Spider

Unlike other spiders, *Bagheera kiplingi*, discovered recently in acacia trees in the forests of Central America, is vegetarian. It is almost exclusively herbivorous, only nibbling on ant larvae for an occasional change of diet. The males are also the only spiders that are known to help the females look after their eggs and young.

Run Over Twice

A Utah railway company worker rescued a stray dog that had been run over by a freight train twice on the same day—April 4, 2010. Although hit by the train's snowplow, the small dog survived and was nursed back to health by Fred Krause and his family.

Paws for Thought

Hope, a cat owned by Nicole Kane from County Carlow, Ireland, has 24 digits—six on each paw.

Domesticated Deer

Since being abandoned by her mother five years ago, Dillie the deer has shared the Canal Fulton, Ohio, home of the Butera family, where she has learned to turn lights on and off and fetch one of her favorite meals, ice cream, from the refrigerator.

Car Wash

To raise funds, three African elephants at the Wildlife Safari Park in Winston, Oregon, were taught to wash visitors' cars. For $20 a time, the elephants scrubbed the cars with sponges and rinsed the soap off with their trunks.

High-rise Heifer

A cow was rescued from the 13th floor of an apartment block in Chelyabinsk, Russia, in 2009. No one knows how it got there, but when fire crews arrived they found it trying to get into an elevator. They decided to bring it down the stairs instead.

Sex Change

A cockerel in Tuscany, Italy, changed sex after a fox raid on his enclosure killed all his hens. Within days of the raid, the bird that was previously a rooster suddenly started laying eggs and trying to hatch them.

Determined Diner

Believe it or not, this incredible photograph shows a python attempting to haul a wallaroo out of a watering hole in Kimberly, Western Australia, in order to eat it. The wallaroo is a marsupial related to the kangaroo and can reach a length of 6½ ft (2 m), while the predator is an olive python, examples of which can stretch over 13 ft (4 m)—making it one of the biggest snakes to be found in Australia.

Chimp Chefs

Chimpanzees in the mountain forests of Guinea, Africa, have been observed fashioning their own cutlery to eat food more comfortably. They have been seen using pieces of stone and wood to chop up their food into bite-size portions. This is the first time such behavior has been witnessed in a nonhuman species.

Ticket Seller

A Chinese zoo recruited a baboon to work as a ticket seller. Tianjin Zoo in Tianjin, northeast China, said the baboon, named Chun Chun, accepted money from visitors, handed them their tickets, and gave them their change—but still had to work with a human supervisor because he would only accept 100-yuan banknotes as they are red, his favorite color.

Pig Voter

Pauline Grant took her pig Blossom to her local polling station in East Sussex, England, after the animal was sent a letter by the council asking it to vote at the 2010 general election. Owing to an administrative error, the pig receives several junk letters a month, plus repeated demands for overdue bills.

Joyriding Bear

A bear climbed into an empty car outside a house near Denver, Colorado, honked the horn, and knocked the gear shift on the automatic transmission into neutral, sending the vehicle rolling backward 125 ft (38 m) down the driveway into a thicket. The bear was still inside the car when deputies arrived on the scene. They suggested the bear had been attracted by a peanut butter sandwich left on the back seat.

Guardian Angel

Eleven-year-old Austin Forman of Boston Bar, British Columbia, Canada, was saved from a cougar attack by his 18-month-old Golden Retriever, Angel, who leaped in front of the cougar and blocked its path, giving Austin time to escape. Angel survived, too, despite receiving puncture wounds around her head and neck.

Frozen Journey

In January 2010, a dog was rescued by the crew of a Polish ship after being found huddled on an ice floe 15 mi (24 km) out in the Baltic Sea. The shivering dog had floated at least 75 mi (120 km) down the Vistula River and out into the sea as temperatures dipped to below −4°F (−20°C).

Hunter Hit

In January 2010, a 53-year-old hunter in Los Banos, California, was shot and injured by his own dog when it stepped on the trigger of his loaded gun.

Full House

A 60-year-old woman shared her home in a suburb of Stockholm, Sweden, with her mother, her sister, her son—and 191 cats.

Spider Fossil

Scientists discovered a well-preserved, 165-million-year-old spider fossil in Inner Mongolia, China. It closely resembles a family of modern arachnids.

Artistic Dog

Paintings by Sam, a pet dog owned by Mary Stadelbacher of Eastern Shore, Maryland, sell for up to $1,700. Sam has created more than 20 different works of art, each made by holding a tailor-made paintbrush in his mouth.

Irwin Legacy

A new, rare species of Australian tree snail has been named Crikey steveirwini in honor of the country's famous wildlife advocate, Steve Irwin, who was tragically killed by a stingray barb in 2006.

One Ear

Rabbit breeder Franz-Xaver Noemmer from Egglham, Germany, holds his pet white rabbit born in February 2010 with only one ear.

Heat Alert

A chocolate Labrador trapped in a car in Macungie, Pennsylvania, on a 90°F (32°C) day in July 2010 honked the horn until he was rescued. Max's owner had gone shopping and forgot that the dog was still in the car, but when she heard the sound of the horn she went outside and saw Max sitting in the driver's seat, honking the horn.

Gallant Granny

A 60-year-old grandmother fought off an attack from a 5-ft-long (1.5-m) shark by repeatedly punching and kicking it after it had ripped off chunks of her flesh. Paddy Trumbull suffered deep bite wounds and lost a huge amount of blood in the incident, which occurred while she was snorkeling off the coast of Queensland, Australia.

Four Ears

A four-eared kitten was found living at a gas station in Vladivostok, Russia, in 2010. Named Luntik, his second, smaller pair of ears do not have any canals, however, so his hearing is no better than that of the average cat.

Smoking Viper

Po the viper enjoys two cigarettes a day after picking up on his owner's 20-a-day habit. When Sho Lau of Taipei, Taiwan, casually threw a cigarette butt away, the snake went for it and seemed to enjoy having it in his mouth, subsequently becoming hooked on nicotine.

Diving Dachshund

Sergei Gorbunov, a professional diver from Vladivostok, Russia, has taught his pet Dachshund Boniface to scuba dive in a specially built wetsuit, complete with helmet.

Ankle Biters

A police officer who was escorting a teenager home following a traffic violation was hospitalized after being attacked by a gang of angry Chihuahuas. The five dogs ran from the boy's home in Fremont, California, and rushed the officer, leaving him with a number of injuries, including bites to his ankle.

Rooster Arrested

A rooster was taken into police custody in Benton, Illinois, after it confronted a woman and her child in an aggressive manner. It was the latest in a series of incidents involving the bird, which had been bothering local residents and preventing them from going about their business.

Fish Hospital

Patit Paban Halder runs a hospital for pet fish at his home in Chandannagore, West Bengal, India. The fish doctor does his rounds of the 32 aquariums, takes blood samples, checks the patients for fungus and bacteria, and even gives them tiny injections.

Swallowed Glass

A German Pointer dog had to undergo emergency surgery after downing a shot of Jägermeister liqueur—and the glass—at a party in Australia. Billy made a full recovery following a three-hour operation to remove the glass from his stomach.

Crab Crawl

The 100 million red crabs living on Christmas Island in the Pacific Ocean walk from the inland forest to the island's shoreline and back in an annual breeding migration. Roads are closed and special tunnels dug as the entire island is turned into a creeping crimson carpet.

Pretty Boy

Despite his bug eyes, crooked mouth, and distinctive teeth, Ug, a partially blind two-year-old Pointer cross, proved a big hit with the ladies. April Parker from Doncaster, England, paid £200 ($320) for him—and renamed him Doug—after her two teenaged daughters fell in love with him on an animal sanctuary's website.

121

Escape Bid

A Tokyo Zoo worker dressed as an orangutan pretends to make a bid for freedom from his enclosure as part of the zoo's animal escape drill. Staff practice confronting the escapee, as well as surrounding him with nets, before pretending to shoot him with a tranquilizer dart.

Ace Ape

Following a stint as a painter, where her works fetched up to $3,000, Nonja, an orangutan at Schoenbrunn Zoo, Vienna, Austria, turned her hand to photography. Keepers gave her a digital camera, which issued a fruit treat whenever a picture was taken, and set up a Facebook page for her on which thousands of fans viewed images of her food and her companion, and of the ape herself climbing her rope.

Eight Lives Left

Sandy LaPierre's pet cat Smoka was found alive—after being buried deep in rubble for 26 days. Sandy had assumed that the cat had perished in the fire that destroyed her apartment in Franklin, Ohio, but almost a month later when demolition crews moved in to tear down what remained of the building, they found Smoka's head sticking out from under 16 ft (5 m) of debris.

Breast-fed Calf

After a calf's mother died when it was just three days old, Chouthi Bai of Kilchu, Rajasthan, India, saved the young animal's life by breast-feeding it three or four times a day. As well as giving the calf her own milk, Bai supplemented its diet with chapatis and water. Many people in India consider the cow to be a sacred animal.

Monkey Smuggler

When customs officials at Mexico City International Airport noticed a passenger with a mysterious bulge in his clothing, they discovered that he had 16 live monkeys hidden inside his sweater.

Shrinking Sheep

A breed of Scottish sheep has shrunk in body size by five percent over the last 24 years—because of climate change. The legs of the Soay sheep have got steadily shorter and their body weight has decreased as milder winters help smaller sheep to survive.

Permanently Pregnant

European brown hares are capable of being pregnant twice at the same time—and can therefore potentially be permanently pregnant. Researchers in Berlin, Germany, fertilized female hares in late pregnancy and found they became pregnant again about four days before delivery, a phenomenon known as superconception. Simultaneous pregnancies mean the hares can give birth to up to a third more offspring each reproductive season.

Parachuting Pooches

As part of their training, U.S. Army police dogs make parachute jumps, plummeting 12,500 ft (3,800 m) from a military helicopter at speeds of 120 mph (193 km/h).

Bear-faced Cheek

A 125-lb (57-kg) black bear walked through the automatic doors of a Hayward, Wisconsin, grocery store in October 2009. He climbed 12 ft (3.6 m) onto a shelf in the beer cooler, and sat there for an hour before being tranquilized by wildlife authorities.

Lucky Lamb

A lamb in Shangdong Province, China, gets around well and is steady on his feet despite being born with only two legs. Sheep farmer Cui Jinxin would normally have killed the lamb at birth, but she was so moved by his determination to survive that she spared him and kept him as a pet.

Ripley's Help Ripley

When the My Heart's Desire animal rescue group in Louisiana found this abandoned poodle in a ditch, he was in such an unbelievable condition that they named him Ripley, after Ripley's Believe It or Not! According to shelter co-director Tracy Lapeyrouse, "You would have never believed there was a dog under there. He didn't even look like a dog. He looked like the elephant man. All you could see was his snout." Ripley's fur was so overgrown and twisted that he couldn't see or even get up and walk.

When Ripley's Believe It or Not! heard about Ripley's predicament, they stepped in to help, making a donation to the animal rescue center and pledging to help his new owners cover Ripley's food and grooming expenses. At the shelter, Ripley was shorn of 2 lb 8 oz (1.2 kg) of thick, matted hair, given a wash and a feed, and was soon looking like a dog again, ready for adoption.

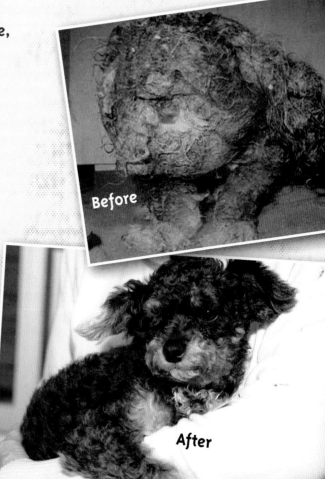

Before

After

125

AWESOME ANIMALS

Pretty in Pink

This rare, bright-pink grasshopper was found in the garden of a house in Havant, England. Grasshoppers are normally green and this one's colorful pigmentation is bad news, as it makes the insect more vulnerable to attack from predators.

Swollen Tongue

Penny, an 18-year-old dog from Paisley, Scotland, nearly suffocated after a freak accident caused her tongue to swell to four times its normal size. She was eating her favorite treat of pig's heart when membrane from the pig's aorta wound itself around the base of her tongue, cutting off the blood supply to the tongue and causing it to swell up. As she tried to paw her tongue free, blood began gushing from her mouth. Luckily, veterinarian Dermot Mullen managed to separate the pig's aorta from her tongue.

Dog on Wheels

Tillman, a five-year-old bulldog owned by Ron Davis of Oxnard, California, can skateboard 325 ft (100 m) in under 20 seconds. The 60-lb (27-kg) dog began skateboarding at just nine months and is now so good that he can do turns and tricks. Tillman can also surf and snowboard. "He's an adrenaline junkie," says Davis.

Mini Horse

Einstein, a horse born in April 2010 in Barnstead, New Hampshire, weighed just 6 lb (2.7 kg) and stood only 14 in (35 cm) tall at birth.

Yoga Bear

Santra, a female brown bear at Ahtari Zoo, Finland, performs a 15-minute yoga routine every morning. Visitors watch in amazement as she calmly stretches both legs before balancing on her bottom and pulling her legs up around her ears.

Too Small

An owl chick had an incredible escape at Paignton Zoo, Devon, England, after it fell from its nest and landed right next to an adult lioness. The tawny owls nest in a tree in the lion enclosure, and this one got lucky because the lioness, Indu, presumably decided it was too small to eat.

126

Chewed Toe

Kiko the Jack Russell terrier saved his owner's life by eating his big toe. After Jerry Douthett of Rockford, Michigan, passed out one day, Kiko sensed an infection festering in his master's right big toe and chewed most of it off. Douthett woke up to find lots of blood and rushed to a nearby hospital where doctors diagnosed him with diabetes, with a dangerously high blood-sugar level. A bone infection meant the toe needed to be amputated.

World Tour

Together with his South African owner Joanne Lefson, Oscar the dog visited five continents and 29 countries in 2009. During their nine-month world tour, Oscar walked on the Great Wall of China, posed beneath the Statue of Liberty, and took in such sights as the Eiffel Tower and the Taj Mahal.

Colorful Cat

Natasha Gregory from Swindon, Wiltshire, England, dyed the white fur of her cat pink with food coloring so that it matched her own pink hair.

Pigs Can Fly

Scarlet, a Hungarian mangalitza pig, loves to bounce around on a trampoline at her home in Shropshire, England. Gwen Howell discovered her pet's hidden talent after leaving her on the family's trampoline in the garden, and soon the pig was spending 45 minutes a day on it.

Swooping Hawk

Canada Post temporarily suspended mail service to 150 homes in a suburb of Calgary, Alberta, in 2010 because a hawk repeatedly swooped down from the sky and attacked the postman. The bird was so aggressive it even broke a bike helmet the mail carrier was wearing for protection.

Seagull Sniper

A seagull was seen flying around the seaside town of Scarborough, England, for more than a month with a crossbow bolt through its head. Local animal rescue officers tried to catch and treat the bird, but to no avail. The victim of a mystery sniper, the seagull was able to survive because the bolt miraculously missed its brain.

Fearsome Furry Family

In the wild, predators Baloo, Shere Khan and Leo would be mortal enemies, but at the Noah's Ark animal center in Georgia, the 1,000-lb (454-kg) American black bear, 350-lb (159-kg) Bengal tiger, and 350-lb (159-kg) African lion live, eat, and sleep together in the same custom-built cabin. The three gentle giants, all male, were rescued as a group of cubs in 2001 and their amazing relationship has developed as they've grown up together.

Bird Slippers

A baby African Crowned Crane was able to walk properly after keepers at a wildlife park in Cornwall, England, fitted its feet with a pair of tiny bright green slippers. The hand-reared chick had been born with a slight defect that left it with curled toes, but the slippers helped to straighten them out.

Happy Reunion

Twelve-year-old Brierley Howard was reunited with her pet Labrador dog Iggy in 2010—nearly five years after he vanished. Amazingly, Iggy turned up 130 mi (209 km) away from the family home in Lancashire, England.

Rare Reptile

A two-headed, albino hognose snake was unveiled at a Venice Beach, California, sideshow in June 2010. Todd Ray paid $20,000 for the bizarre serpent—called Lenny and Squiggy—which he saw on an online reptile message board. Each of the snake's heads is fed twice a week.

Bewildered Bear

An inquisitive black bear in Vermont had a milk can stuck on its head for more than six hours in 2010. After the bear had been seen running around aimlessly, bumping into trees and boulders, rescuers successfully cut the can from the animal's head.

Bravery Medal

In 2010, a nine-year-old black Labrador dog named Treo was given Britain's Dickin medal—the highest military honor an animal can receive—for his work sniffing out explosives in Afghanistan. The medal has been awarded to more than 60 animals since its inception in 1943, including 32 carrier pigeons, three horses and a cat.

Fox's Revenge

A wounded fox turned the tables on a hunter in the Grodno region of Belarus by accidentally putting its paw on the trigger of the hunter's rifle and shooting him. The hunter, who had been trying to finish the animal off with the butt of his rifle, was taken to a hospital with a leg wound while the fox made its escape.

High Hound

Giant George, a blue Great Dane owned by David Nasser of Tucson, Arizona, stands 43 in (1.1 m) tall from paw to shoulder and weighs 245 lb (111 kg). He eats around 110 lb (50 kg) of food each month and is so tall that some children mistake him for a horse!

Muscle Hound

No, this is not trick photography, and this dog has not been pumping iron. Her oversized muscles are perfectly natural, albeit very unusual. Wendy, from Canada, is a "Bully" whippet, a mutation of the breed that causes muscles to grow to double their normal size, meaning Wendy is twice as heavy as a regular whippet.

Close-ups

Dr. Richard Kirby of the University of Plymouth, England, has taken high-magnification photographs of sea angels (*Clione limacina*), microscopic plankton that live in the ocean around the U.K. Despite their size, they anchor the entire marine food chain by providing fish with food and the world with oxygen, and they also play a key role in the global carbon cycle.

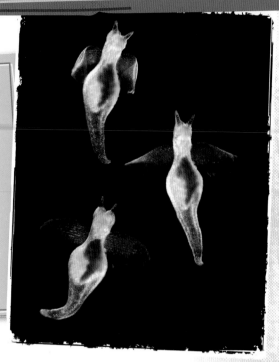

Ice Dive

The dagger-shaped bill of the common kingfisher is so sharp that the bird can dive straight through a thin layer of ice to catch fish.

Zucchini Attack

When a 200-lb (91-kg) bear tried to force its way into a house near Frenchtown, Montana, in September 2010, a woman sent the animal fleeing by pelting it with a large zucchini. As the bear stuck its head through the doorway, the woman grabbed a 14-inch-long (35-cm) zucchini from the kitchen counter and hurled the vegetable at the bear, hitting it on the top of its head and causing it to run off.

Food Sharing

Bonobos—a sister species of chimpanzees—share things just like humans. A scientific study of bonobos in the Democratic Republic of the Congo showed that they voluntarily shared their food with other members of their group, making them the only species known to do this apart from humans.

Cat Nap

A house fire in Port Townsend, Washington State, was started by a cat that managed to depress a toaster lever while sleeping on top of the toaster oven. The cat, which slept there to avoid the family's dog, escaped unharmed.

Clean Kitten

A kitten had an incredible escape after climbing into a washing machine and going through a full wash cycle. Liz Fear's seven-month-old Burmese cat Suki was soaked, rinsed, and then spun dry after climbing in with a load full of dirty clothes at the family home in Melbourne, Australia. Despite her horrible ordeal, Suki was later given a clean bill of health.

Wine Buffs

Baboons invaded the vineyards in South Africa's Franschhoek Valley in early 2010 and ate thousands of bottles' worth of grapes right from the vines.

Monster Bug

Giant isopods are a cousin of the humble pill bug and often measure up to 15 in (38 cm) long. They live 1,000—7,000 ft (300—2,100 m) deep in the ocean and can weigh almost 4 lb (1.8 kg). In April 2010, oil workers in the Gulf of Mexico discovered a giant isopod double this size, measuring 2½ ft (76 cm) long!

Human Mimic

A pet dog in Zhumadian, China, prefers to walk upright on her back legs—just like a human. Owner Zhou Guanshun taught Lu Lu to walk on two legs at the age of four months by holding one of her front paws—and she hasn't stopped since! Even when she rests, Lu Lu chooses to squat on her back legs while keeping her body upright and her front legs off the ground.

Shell Slice

When veterinarians at Brazil's Anhembi Morumbi University discovered that a pregnant tortoise was unable to deliver her eggs naturally, they cut away a small square section of her shell with an electric circular saw and safely retrieved the eggs. They then replaced the piece of shell and left the tortoise to recover.

Purr-fect Day

In an unofficial ceremony, postman Uwe Mitzscherlich, from Possendorf, Germany, "married" his cat Cecilia in May 2010 after being told that the animal did not have long to live. As marrying an animal is illegal in Germany, Uwe paid an actress $395 to officiate at the ceremony.

Royal Lineage

Queen Elizabeth II has owned more than 30 Corgis, nearly all descended from her first dog, Susan, who died in 1959, and was a gift from her parents on her 18th birthday.

Cliff Plunge

Oscar, a five-year-old Cocker Spaniel owned by Rupert and Emma Brown, survived despite running over the edge of a 120-ft-high (37-m) cliff in Dorset, England. He emerged from his death-defying leap with nothing worse than a slight limp after being rescued from the rocks below by a canoeist who had witnessed the accident.

Eggs-hausted

A chicken belonging to Chris Schauerman of Honeoye Falls, New York State, laid a 5-oz (140-g) egg (two-and-a-half times normal size), along with five normal eggs—but the stress was so great that the bird died.

Splash of Color

A beluga whale at the Qingdao Polar Ocean World in China paints pictures that sell for hundreds of dollars. Xiao Qiang paints with the brush in his mouth while his keeper holds the paper. Belugas are able to manipulate a brush because they have more soft tissue around their mouth than other whales, and the turning of the head to paint is a natural movement that they perform in the wild when cleaning sand from their food.

Wire Walk

At a zoo in Fuzhou, Fujian Province, China, visitors flock in their hundreds to see a goat walking a tightrope while being ridden by a small monkey!

Swooping Swan

A motorcyclist in Worcestershire, England, suffered a broken collarbone after being knocked off his bike by a low-flying swan.

Mosquito Killer

In a contest organized by an insect trap company, Huang Yuyen, a pig farmer from Taiwan, killed and caught more than four million mosquitoes in a month. Her haul weighed in at just over 3 lb 5 oz (1.5 kg).

Rabbit Whisperer

Cliff Penrose, of St. Austell, Cornwall, England, has treated hundreds of rabbits with behavioral problems by hypnotizing them. By massaging certain parts of a rabbit's body, particularly the belly, he is able to relax the animal in a matter of seconds. He then "bows" to the rabbit by lowering his head so that it does not feel threatened before shutting its eyelids, leaving it in a trance. He says the rabbit emerges from the trance a happier, more relaxed pet.

Selective Breeding

Researchers at Yale University are working to bring back to life a species of giant Galapagos tortoise that became extinct hundreds of years ago. The selective breeding program, based on the DNA of the tortoises' great-great-great-grandchildren, will take over a century to complete owing to the reptiles' long lifespan and the fact that they don't reproduce until they are between 20 and 30 years old.

Turtle Eggs

In 2006, scientists in Utah discovered a 75-million-year-old fossil of a pregnant turtle, with a clutch of eggs inside.

Regurgitates Fish

A performer with the Great Moscow Circus swallows and regurgitates a live fish. Local authorities banned her act when the circus visited Australia in 2010 for being cruel to the fish.

Sewer Snake

In 2005, a 10-ft-long (3-m) python lived in a neighborhood sewer system in Manchester, England, for three months—moving from toilet to toilet before it was eventually caught.

Replica Romance

Timmy, a 60-year-old tortoise who lives in a sanctuary in Cornwall, England, has fallen in love with a plastic toy tortoise. He never hit it off with other tortoises, but since Tanya the replica was introduced into his enclosure, he has started nuzzling and kissing her and fetching food for her.

Thieving Octopus

Victor Huang was diving off the coast of Wellington, New Zealand, in April 2010 when an octopus suddenly lunged forward and grabbed his bright blue digital camera. The octopus quickly swam off with its booty but, after a five-minute chase, Huang used his speargun to extract the camera from its grasp.

Musical Fish

Diane Rains from Hudson, Wisconsin, owns a goldfish that can play musical instruments, including the glockenspiel and handbells, in perfect time to music playing outside its tank. Jor Jor has been trained to play single notes, chords and four-part harmonies, using its mouth to tug on a string attached to each instrument.

Old Hen

A hen in China is 22 years old—the equivalent of around 400 years in human age. Hens normally live for only seven years, but the bird owned by Yang Shaofu of Yunnan Province has reached three times that age, during which time she has laid more than 5,000 eggs.

Climbing Fish

The climbing perch of Africa and Southeast Asia is a fish that can breathe air and use its spiky gill covers and pectoral fins to "walk" on dry land from one body of water to another. It can live out of water for several days and will actually drown if it is held underwater.

Drink Tears

Three species of worker bee drink human tears. Either singly or in groups of up to seven, the bees were observed in Thailand landing on people's lower eyelashes and sipping lachrymation. It is thought the insects have adapted to drink tears as a means of gaining extra protein.

1

2

Frogs in their Throats

Humans might be divided on eating frog's legs, but eating frogs remains very popular in the natural world.

(1) Tad and Karen Bacon from Maryland discovered this giant bullfrog snacking on another frog after taking a dip in their swimming pool. Bullfrogs can grow to over 12 in (30 cm) long. (2) Luis Fernando Espin from Ecuador came upon an Amazonian whipsnake slowly devouring a large tree frog. The frog has toxic chemicals in its skin but that didn't prevent the snake from eventually swallowing it whole. (3) A burrowing owl in Florida makes short work of a large frog—legs included.

3

Fishing Dog

A dog in China's Hubei Province has become a local celebrity after taking up fishing. Mr. Lin's dog, Ding Ding, had always loved swimming in Donghu Lake, but in 2009 he suddenly started catching live fish. His owner says the dog locates the fish by watching bubbles coming from the water.

Busy Beavers

A beaver dam in Wood Buffalo National Park, Northern Alberta, Canada, is more than 2,800 ft (850 m) long. The construction, which has been worked on by several generations of beavers since the 1970s, is so big that it can be seen on NASA satellite photographs taken from outer space.

Clever Horse

Lukas, a 17-year-old thoroughbred horse owned by Karen Murdock of Chino Hills, California, has mastered 35 feats of intelligence—including counting, spelling and shape sorting. He can spell his own name, Karen's name and that of Karen's husband Doug. Lukas has also learned to nod his head for "yes" and shake it for "no," curtsy and pretend to be lame.

Rodent Infestation

Police who raided an apartment in Aachen, Germany, discovered that it was overrun by 300 guinea pigs—and in some rooms the pile of droppings was 4 in (10 cm) high.

Hero Buddy

Buddy the German Shepherd saved his owner's home by guiding emergency service personnel to the blazing building. The dog was in the Caswell Lakes, Alaska, workshop of his owner, Ben Heinrichs, when a stray spark started a fire. Buddy then ran out, found an Alaskan Trooper at a crossroads and, by running in front of the patrol car, steered him through a series of back roads to the scene of the fire.

Bee Line

A swarm of 20,000 bees attached themselves to colorful socks and underpants that were hanging on a woman's clothesline in Victoria, Australia.

Burpless Sheep

Australian scientists are working on a program to breed sheep that don't burp, in a bid to reduce greenhouse gas emissions. The agriculture sector in Australia produces about 16 percent of the country's total emissions, and two-thirds of that figure comes from livestock, chiefly the result of methane being released from the guts of grazing sheep and cattle.

Balancing Act

A pig in Xincai County, Henan Province, China, can walk despite being born with only its two front legs. Owner Wang Xihai started training the two-legged piglet to walk when it was just a few days old by lifting it up by its tail, and after a month it was able to walk upside down without help. Named by villagers Zhu Jianqiang ("strong-willed pig"), it can balance and move well on its front trotters even though it weighs over 110 lb (50 kg).

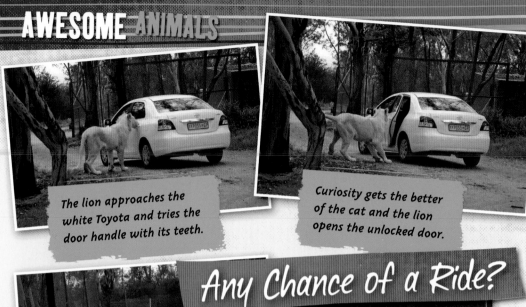

The lion approaches the white Toyota and tries the door handle with its teeth.

Curiosity gets the better of the cat and the lion opens the unlocked door.

Any Chance of a Ride?

The occupants are momentarily frozen in fear before they drive off, the lion looking after them.

A couple visiting Lion Safari Park, Johannesburg, South Africa, had the fright of their lives when a 300-lb (136-kg) lion opened the rear door of their car with its teeth. As they drove off, the lion chased the car to the park gates, where a game warden managed to shoo it back into the enclosure.

Pigeon Spy

A white pigeon that landed in the Indian state of Punjab, close to the border with Pakistan, was taken to a police station where it was held under armed guard and accused of spying. It had a ring around its foot and a Pakistani phone number and address stamped on its body in red ink, but the message it was suspected of carrying was never found.

Secret Growl

Scientists at San Diego Zoo, California, have discovered that, in addition to the familiar trumpeting call, elephants communicate in a secret language that is largely inaudible to humans. They say two-thirds of the elephants' growling sound is at a frequency too low to be picked up by human ears.

Tortoise Masks

Following a fire at Poestlingberg Zoo in Linz, Austria, fire crews saved the lives of six giant tortoises by strapping oxygen masks onto their heads. Although the masks were designed for humans, they fitted the 140-lb (63.5-kg) tortoises and prevented them dying from smoke inhalation.

Pink Hippo

British wildlife photographers Will and Matt Burrard-Lucas were picnicking on the banks of the Mara River in Kenya's Masai Mara game reserve in 2010 when they spotted a pink hippo emerge from the water onto the opposite bank! The animal's rare coloring is a result of leucism, a condition in which pigmentation cells fail to develop properly, causing pale skin color.

Lone Wolverine

Buddy, California's last wolverine, was discovered roaming the Tahoe National Forest in 2008—almost 90 years after the species was declared extinct in the state. He was seen marking his territory to attract a mate—even though the nearest other wolverines are thought to be more than 800 miles (1,290 km) and two states away.

Bear Steals Teddy

A black bear broke into a house in Laconia, New Hampshire, in 2010 and stole a teddy bear! The burglar bear ate a selection of fruit, and drank from the Parkinson family fishbowl, before making off with the stuffed toy after the sound of the garage door being raised scared it.

Tug-of-War

A thirsty baby elephant that ventured to the edge of a waterhole in South Africa's Kruger National Park got the fright of its life when a lurking crocodile suddenly grabbed it by the trunk. As the croc tried to drag its prey into the water, the baby's distress calls alerted the rest of the herd and they managed to scare off the reptile by trumpeting loudly and stamping their feet.

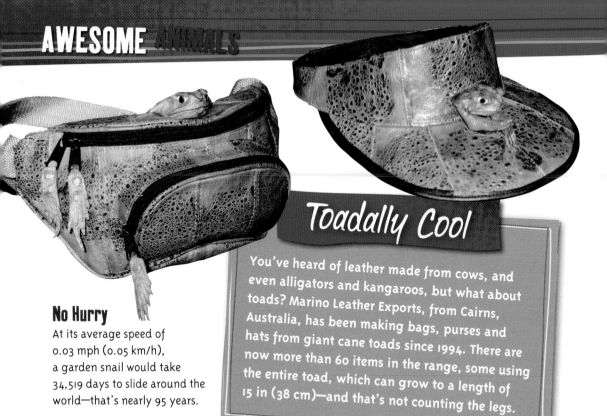

Toadally Cool

You've heard of leather made from cows, and even alligators and kangaroos, but what about toads? Marino Leather Exports, from Cairns, Australia, has been making bags, purses and hats from giant cane toads since 1994. There are now more than 60 items in the range, some using the entire toad, which can grow to a length of 15 in (38 cm)—and that's not counting the legs.

No Hurry

At its average speed of 0.03 mph (0.05 km/h), a garden snail would take 34,519 days to slide around the world—that's nearly 95 years.

Giant Amphibians

The giant salamanders of China and Japan can grow to more than 5 ft (1.5 m) in length and live for as long as 50 years.

Yap Nav

Taxi driver Andrzej Szymcakowi from Lodz, Poland, decided to switch off his GPS after realizing that Bobo, his Yorkshire Terrier, is better at giving him directions. Bobo, who has traveled in the cab since he was a puppy, knows all the routes. He yaps and raises his right paw to indicate a right turn, lifts his left paw for a left turn, and barks and wags his tail for straight on.

Croc House

Shaun Foggett from Oxford, England, shares his semi-detached house with his fiancée, their three children and 24 crocodiles and alligators. He spends $12,000 a year feeding the reptiles.

Clever Collie

Whereas most dogs can recognize about 15 commands, Betsy, a seven-year-old Border Collie in Austria, can recognize more than 340 words. She can also fetch an object after seeing a picture of it.

Gambling Rabbit

Daisy the pet white rabbit has become a regular at the Prince of Wales pub in Malvern, England, where he enjoys a drink of cider while playing the fruit slot machine. His owner says the rabbit loves the flashing lights.

Slippery Surface

A highway in northern Greece was closed for two hours in May 2010 after millions of frogs emerging from a nearby lake caused three drivers to skid off the road.

MATCH	PAUL'S PICK	RESULT	
Germany vs. Australia	Germany	Germany 4	Australia 0
Germany vs. Serbia	Serbia	Serbia 1	Germany 0
Germany vs. Ghana	Germany	Germany 1	Ghana 0
Germany vs. England	Germany	Germany 4	England 1
Germany vs. Argentina	Germany	Germany 4	Argentina 0
Germany vs. Spain	Spain	Spain 1	Germany 0
Germany vs. Uruguay	Germany	Germany 3	Uruguay 2
Netherlands vs. Spain	Spain	Spain 1	Netherlands 0

Insect Velcro

A species of South American ant—*Azteca andreae*—has its own Velcro-like device that enables it to hold on to about 6,000 times its body weight— the equivalent of a domestic cat holding on to a humpback whale. The ant's claws are shaped like hooks and fit neatly into fibrous loops on the undersides of the leaves where it lives, enabling it to trap much bigger insects as prey.

Big Stink

An infestation of stinkbugs hit Brooklyn, New York City, in January 2010. The small brown flying beetles, which are native to the Far East, emit a smell like rotting cheese when they are squashed or even vacuumed.

Psychic Octopus

Paul the Psychic Octopus became a worldwide celebrity after correctly predicting all of the German national soccer team's results at the 2010 World Cup. Before each match, two plastic boxes, one with a German flag and one with the flag of their opponents, were lowered into his tank at the Oberhausen Sea Life Center in Germany. Each box contained a tasty mussel, and the box that Paul opened first was judged to be the predicted winner. After correctly forecasting five German victories, he upset the nation by choosing Spain to win their semifinal clash. Spain duly defeated Germany, and Paul maintained his 100 percent record by predicting that Spain would beat the Netherlands in the final.

Watch Bird

Lorenzo the parrot was arrested in Colombia for trying to tip off a local drug cartel while police officers carried out an undercover raid. Police suspicions were confirmed when Lorenzo spent the whole of his first morning in custody squawking: "Run, run, you are going to get caught."

Quicker by Pigeon

A carrier pigeon proved faster than a rural broadband connection in an English race to determine which was more efficient at sending a video from East Yorkshire to Lincolnshire. Rory the pigeon made the journey carrying the five-minute video loaded onto a computer memory card in 80 minutes, reaching his destination while the computer was still uploading the video.

Tiny Frog

A new species of frog found in Borneo measures a tiny 0.4 in (10.2 mm) long as an adult—that's about the size of a fingertip. The micro species *Microhyla nepenthicola*, which was named after a plant that is also found on the island, had been documented before, but scientists had wrongly assumed it was a juvenile of another species of frog instead of an adult in its own right.

Alien Monster?

Tomas Rak uses macro photography to make tiny, harmless British jumping spiders look like alien monsters from a horror movie. He scours the country in search of the spiders, which measure just 1/4 in (6 mm) long, but can jump six times their own height. Tomas sometimes waits for up to three weeks to get the right shot.

Pet Wash

Animal owners in Japan can wash their cats and dogs in specially designed washing machines at pet supermarkets. The machines, which are claimed to be entirely safe, give the animals a shampoo, a rinse, and a dry in a half-hour cycle for around $10.

Bionic Cat

A cat that lost both of his back paws in an accident can run and jump again after being fitted with two bionic legs. The mechanical implants were drilled into Oscar's ankles by British veterinarian Noel Fitzpatrick, and then treated with a substance that allows bone and skin to grow around them. To give Oscar full movement, fake paws were then fitted on "see-saw" joints at the ends of the prosthetics.

Romantic Stork

A stork named Rodan flies 8,080 mi (13,000 km) each year from South Africa to Brodski Varos, Croatia, to visit his handicapped mate, Malena, who is unable to fly. They have chicks each year and Rodan teaches them to fly. He then takes them with him to South Africa for the winter and returns with them to Malena in the spring.

Ink Intact

Even though it died around 155 million years ago, scientists were still able to extract ink from the fossilized remains of a squid-like creature discovered in a rock in Wiltshire, England. The odds of finding a squid's delicate ink sac intact after so many centuries are put at a billion to one.

UNBELIEVABLE

FEATS

Great Escapes

At 32 years old, Akash Awasthi is already one of the most daring escapologists in India, risking life and limb to escape from a burning haystack, a locked box deep underwater, and a coffin placed in the path of a speeding truck.

He has also ridden a motorbike through the packed city streets of Trivandrum, Kerala, while blindfolded. He is following in the footsteps of his father, Anand Awasthi, one of the most famous magicians in the country.

Akash fights his way out of the burning haystack, which becomes an inferno within seconds.

Akash is hoisted into the air by a 120-ft (37-m) crane.

Famous Escapes

1. Matt the Knife (U.S.A.) took just 11 seconds to free himself from **handcuffs while underwater**.

2. Dorothy Dietrich (U.S.A.) **escaped from a straitjacket while suspended** from a burning rope hundreds of feet in the air.

3. Dean Gunnarson (Canada) **escaped from a straitjacket while hanging upside down** from a trapeze 726 ft (221 m) above the gorge of the Hoover Dam.

4. David Merlini (Hungary) **escaped from a shark-filled pool** while in a straitjacket, weights and restraints.

5. Zdenek Bradac (Czech Republic) **escaped from a pair of real police handcuffs** in 1.6 seconds.

6. David Straitjacket (U.K.) **escaped from a straitjacket while on stilts** in 1 minute 38 seconds.

7. David Blaine (U.S.A.) took 15 minutes to **free himself from shackles and a gyroscope** that had been spinning him around 50 ft (15 m) above Times Square, New York, for 52 hours.

Akash emerges from the flames, unchained, moments before the haystack is completely engulfed. He is tended to by volunteers.

Solo Sailor

At age 16, Jessica Watson of Queensland, Australia, finished a 210-day, 23,000-nautical-mile (42,600-km), solo, nonstop and unassisted voyage around the world. In her 34-ft-long (10-m) yacht *Ella's Pink Lady*, she battled 39-ft (12-m) swells and a ripped sail, and ate 576 chocolate bars.

Jail Jaunt

In June 2009, 194 French inmates made a 1,430-mi (2,300-km) bicycle trip through the country in a prisoners' Tour de France.

Head-to-Head

Croatian tennis player Goran Ivanisevic needed stitches when he tried to head the ball over the net at the 1998 Canadian Open, only to bang heads with his doubles partner Mark Philippoussis, who had tried to do the same thing. Philippoussis got away with only a bruised forehead.

Dodgeball Tournament

In October 2009, more than 235 teams in three divisions competed in a dodgeball tournament in Richmond, Virginia, involving more than 4,000 players.

Novice at 90

Ninety-year-old Mary Tattersall from West Yorkshire, England, hit a hole-in-one at a golf course near Bradford in 2010. She had been playing golf for only two years.

World Cup Miss

Spain's international goalkeeper Santiago Cañizares missed the 2002 soccer World Cup after dropping a bottle of aftershave onto his right foot, severing one of his tendons.

Board Marathon

A team of ten wakeboarders (a cross between waterskiing and surfing) completed 1,448 laps of a Cincinnati, Ohio, cable wakeboard park in 24 hours in June 2010. They traveled just over 506 mi (814 km)—roughly the distance from Cincinnati to Atlanta, Georgia.

Delayed Game

Twenty-one years after a 1989 New Jersey high-school hockey championship game between Delbarton and St. Joseph's was canceled because of a measles outbreak, the players—now in their late thirties—finally took to the ice to play the deciding game for charity.

Mighty Mouth

A man in Lagos, Nigeria, lifts a bar carrying 110 lb (50 kg) of iron weights with his mouth!

Bike Climb

In November 2010, Colombian cyclist Javier Zapata rode up the 649 steps of the Piedra del Peñol monolithic formation in Guatapé, Colombia, in just 43 minutes. Zapata is no stranger to epic climbs. In 2003, he rode his bike up the 1,318 stairs of Mexico City's Torre Mayor, the tallest building in Latin America.

One-legged Wrestler
Michigan-based Zach "Tenacious Z" Gowen, who lost his leg at age eight, made his debut at 19 as a one-legged professional wrestler.

Thrown Away
Jesus Leonardo of Wanaque, New Jersey, earns about $45,000 a year examining discarded horse-racing tickets for winning stubs accidentally thrown away.

Master Jockey
Since 1974, Canadian jockey Russell Baze has won more than 11,000 horse races. In the space of just two days—October 17 and 18, 2007—he won no fewer than 11 races.

Insect Aside
Spotting that an insect had landed on his ball at the 1950 U.S. Open Golf Championship, Lloyd Mangrum of the U.S.A. instinctively picked up the ball and flicked the insect away. However, he was penalized two strokes for his misdemeanor, which ended up costing him the title.

Blind Catch
Sheila Penfold, a legally blind grandmother from London, England, caught a catfish that weighed in at a whopping 214 lb (97 kg) and measured 8 ft 2 in (2.5 m) long on Spain's Ebro River in January 2010. It took Mrs. Penfold, who stands just 5 ft 3 in (1.6 m) tall, 30 minutes to reel in the monster.

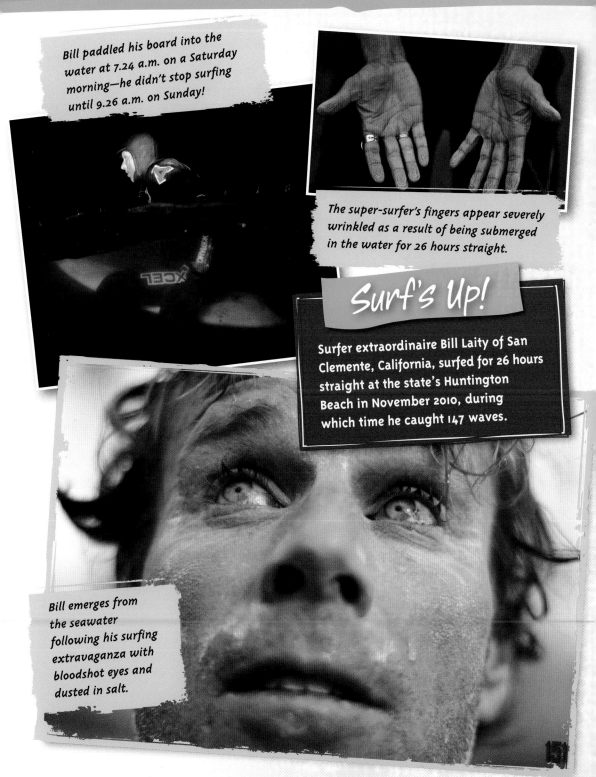

Bill paddled his board into the water at 7.24 a.m. on a Saturday morning—he didn't stop surfing until 9.26 a.m. on Sunday!

The super-surfer's fingers appear severely wrinkled as a result of being submerged in the water for 26 hours straight.

Surf's Up!

Surfer extraordinaire Bill Laity of San Clemente, California, surfed for 26 hours straight at the state's Huntington Beach in November 2010, during which time he caught 147 waves.

Bill emerges from the seawater following his surfing extravaganza with bloodshot eyes and dusted in salt.

Sky Walker

Californian Dean Potter walked across a highline 100 ft (30 m) long and more than 1,000 ft (305 m) above the ground in Yosemite National Park in 2009. He walked barefoot, and unattached. Dean has many years of experience on the highline—if he does slip off, he grabs the line with his arms or legs.

Flying Fish

One of the favorites to win the 2010 Missouri River 340—a grueling 340-mi (550-km) canoe and kayak race—Brad Pennington from Houston, Texas, was forced to quit just hours into the event after a 30-lb (13.6-kg) Asian silver carp leaped out of the water and hit him in the head. He described the blow as like being hit with a brick, and was left with a pounding headache.

Tug of War

Fishing on the Victoria Nile River in Uganda, Tim Smith from Enniskillen, Northern Ireland, landed a 249-lb (113-kg) Nile perch, which at 6 ft (1.8 m) long, was taller than him. He battled for 45 minutes to reel in the monster—and then had to pry his catch from the jaws of a crocodile that launched itself at his tiny boat in a desperate bid to snatch the fish.

Soccer Saints

An executive box at the Hamburg stadium of German soccer club St. Pauli is decorated like a Gothic chapel, complete with stained glass windows, candles, an altar to football, and depictions of the team's players as saints.

Frozen Toe

The U.S.'s Rulon Gardner, the 2000 Olympic Greco-Roman wrestling gold medalist, lost a toe to frostbite in 2002 and kept it in a jar in his refrigerator for years, apparently to remind him of his mortality.

Free Throws

Perry Dissmore, a pastor from Hartford, Illinois, made 1,968 successful basketball free throws in one hour in September 2010—an average of one throw every 1.8 seconds.

Matador Fled

Matador Christian Hernandez quit his job mid-bullfight in Mexico City—by running away from the charging bull, jumping over a wall, and fleeing the stadium to a chorus of boos.

Loyal Fan

Nesan Sinnadurai, a U.S.-based fan of English soccer club Arsenal, has flown more than 6,000,000 mi (9,600,000 km) supporting the club since 1967. Every other weekend during the soccer season, the Sri Lankan I.T. consultant makes the 9,000-mi (14,500-km) round trip from Columbus, Georgia, to London to watch his favorite team.

Blind Abseiler

Blind extreme sports enthusiast Dean Dunbar abseiled down the 658-ft-high (200-m) Eas a' Chual Aluinn waterfall in Scotland. He has also competed in power boating, mountain biking, sea kayaking, and hill running events, bungee jumped from a helicopter, and been hurled through the air as a human catapult.

Super Sprinter

Irish sprinter Jason Smyth can run the 100 meters in 10.32 seconds—even though he is legally blind. He suffers from Stargardt's disease, a disorder that has reduced his vision to about ten percent of that of a fully sighted person, but can run so fast that he competed against able-bodied athletes at the 2010 European Championships.

Too Much Yelling

Manchester United goalkeeper Alex Stepney dislocated his jaw while shouting at his defenders during a 1975 soccer match against Birmingham City.

Bowling Star

Retired high-school principal Allen Meyer of Toronto, Canada, was still bowling twice a week in a league that he ran at the age of 106.

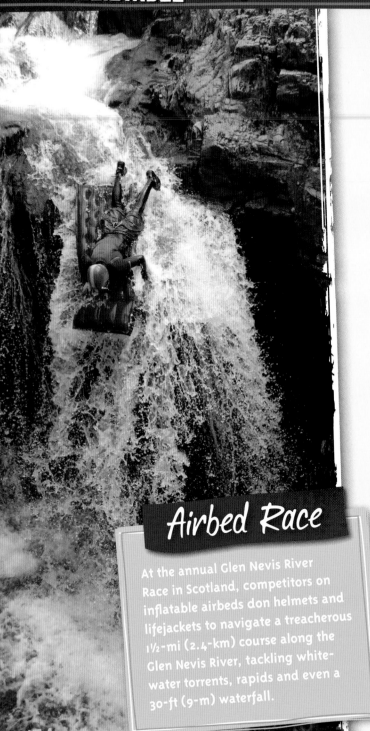

Airbed Race

At the annual Glen Nevis River Race in Scotland, competitors on inflatable airbeds don helmets and lifejackets to navigate a treacherous 1½-mi (2.4-km) course along the Glen Nevis River, tackling whitewater torrents, rapids and even a 30-ft (9-m) waterfall.

Foul Ball

After years of attending Philadelphia Phillies baseball games, Steve Monforto made a great grab to catch his first foul ball. He high-fived his three-year-old daughter Emily and handed her the prize ball... which she then threw back over the railing! The family still went home with a ball after Phillies officials saw what happened and took a ball up to him. What's more, spectators threw back every foul ball caught for the remainder of the game so that Emily didn't feel bad for losing her dad the special ball.

Extreme Hole

The "Extreme 19th" hole at the Legend Golf and Safari Resort in Limpopo, South Africa, has a tee-off on a mountain that is accessible only by helicopter—and sits 1,300 ft (400 m) above a green designed in the shape of the continent of Africa. In 2008, Ireland's Padraig Harrington became the first golfer to make a par-3 at this hole.

Double Faults

In her first-round ladies' singles match at Wimbledon in 1957, Brazilian tennis player Miss M. de Amorim began by serving 17 consecutive double faults.

Solo Row

In her 19-ft-long (5.8-m) rowboat *Liv*, Katie Spotz, 22, from Mentor, Ohio, rowed solo 2,817 mi (4,533 km) across the Atlantic Ocean from Dakar, Senegal, to Georgetown, Guyana, in just over 70 days. Previously she has swum the entire 325-mi (520-km) length of the Allegheny River, run 150 mi (240 km) across the Mojave and Colorado deserts, and cycled 3,300 mi (5,310 km) across the U.S. from Seattle, Washington, to Washington, D.C.

Welly Wanging

Under the British rules of "welly wanging" (or gum-boot throwing), competitors take a maximum run-up of 42 paces before hurling a size 9, non-steel toecap gum boot through the air as far as possible. Finland's Jouni Viljanen has hurled a gum boot more than 208 ft (64 m).

Anvil Blast

In the U.S. sport of competitive anvil shooting, participants use black gunpowder to launch 100-lb (45-kg) anvils up to 200 ft (60 m) into the air. One anvil is placed upside down on the ground, the brick-shaped cavity in its underside is filled with gunpowder, and then a second anvil is placed on top of it. A fuse is lit—and the anvil-shooter runs as fast as he can.

Fiery Bull

In a festival dating back to the 16th century, a Bull of Fire runs through the streets of Medinaceli, Spain. The bull's body is covered in mud to protect it from burns and it wears an iron frame on its horns that bears two torches. The bull is chased through the streets until the torches go out.

155

Milk Man

New Yorker Ashrita Furman once walked more than 80 mi (130 km) around a track in Queens, New York, with a full milk bottle on his head.

Beach Towel

A beach towel covering a whopping 24,110 sq ft (2,240 sq m) of beach was unveiled near Las Palmas on the Canary Islands. A team of 25 people spent 15 days making the towel, and more than 50 people were needed to roll it out on the beach.

Human Dominos

Thousands of people in Ordos, Inner Mongolia, China, formed a human domino chain. Arranged in lines, the 10,267 participants slowly fell backward onto each other in sequence from a sitting position like a line of toppling dominos.

Wheelchair Crossing

Setting off from his home in Lynn, Massachusetts, Matt Eddy crossed the U.S.A. by wheelchair in just over four months. Matt has been confined to a wheelchair since the age of ten and suffers from Duchenne Muscular Dystrophy, as a result of which he is strong enough only to move two fingers and requires a ventilator to breathe. Traveling on the quieter back roads to reach his destination of Long Beach, California, he averaged at least 25 mi (40 km) a day.

Lunge Runner

Jamasen Rodriguez of Modesto, California, is an expert in lunge running, where instead of running, the athlete lunges to his knees, alternating left and right with each step. In August 2010, he completed a lunge mile in 25 minutes 21 seconds, taking 1,370 lunges.

Heavy Suit

U.S. Air Force Staff Sergeant Owen Duff ran a mile (1.6 km) in 9 minutes 22 seconds at Kirkuk Regional Air Base, Iraq, in 2010 while wearing an 80-lb (36-kg) bomb suit.

Balancing Act

One man rode a bicycle 165 ft (50 m) along a tightrope suspended 26 ft (8 m) above a tiger enclosure while another hung below him on a ladder at China's Changzhou Yancheng Zoo in March 2010. The pair, who were part of a stunt that involved a three-year-old girl walking the rope behind them, narrowly avoided tragedy when one of the zoo's Siberian tigers leaped high off the ground and grabbed at the ladder, nearly causing the men to fall into the enclosure.

OLYMPICS

Famous Olympians

Lieutenant George S. Patton (U.S.A.)
A leading general during World War II, he finished fifth in the modern pentathlon at the 1912 Olympics.

Johnny Weissmuller (U.S.A.) He won three gold medals in freestyle swimming at the 1924 Olympics, plus a bronze in the men's water polo, and two more swimming golds in 1928—feats that helped him earn a lucrative Hollywood career playing Tarzan.

Harold Sakata (U.S.A.) He won a weightlifting silver in 1948 before going on to play the evil, super strong Oddjob in the James Bond movie *Goldfinger*.

Philip Noel-Baker (G.B.) He won silver in the 1,500 meters at the 1920 Olympics—and in 1959 was awarded the Nobel Peace Prize.

Crown Prince (later King) Constantine (Greece) He won a sailing gold medal at the 1960 Olympics.

Zara Phillips (G.B.) A grandchild of Queen Elizabeth II, she won silver at the 2012 London Olympics as part of the equestrian team.

Remarkable Torch Relays

Tokyo 1964 This torch relay featured the most torchbearers ever used—101,866—comprising a carrier, two reserve runners, and up to 20 accompanying people for every kilometer of its land journey.

Grenoble 1968 In the later stages of the relay, a diver swam across the French port of Marseilles holding the torch's flame out of the water.

Mexico City 1968 The relay retraced the steps of Christopher Columbus to the New World and featured one of his direct descendants, Cristóbal Colón de Carbajal, as the last runner on Spanish soil before the torch made its way across the Atlantic Ocean.

Montreal 1976 The Canadians organized the transmission of the flame by satellite between Athens and Ottawa by transforming it into a radio signal that was sent by satellite to Canada, where it triggered a laser beam to relight the flame on Canadian soil.

Lillehammer 1994 The flame was transferred between two parachute jumpers—in midair—and then made an impressive entry at the opening ceremony of the Games when it was carried by a ski jumper during his actual jump!

Olympic Oddities

Not Allowed Harvard University refused to give student James B. Connolly eight weeks' leave of absence in order to compete in the 1896 Olympics in Greece. So he resigned from the university, paid for the voyage himself—and went on to win the triple jump.

Wrong Anthem At the medal ceremony for the 1964 Tokyo Olympics marathon, won by Abebe Bikila of Ethiopia, the stadium band did not know the Ethiopian national anthem, so they played the Japanese one instead.

First Gold India has 17 percent of the world's population, but the country did not win its first individual Olympic title until 2008 when Abhinav Bindra won the 10-meter air rifle shooting event.

Bully-off As a reward for winning gold in the women's field hockey tournament at the 1980 Moscow Olympics, every member of the Zimbabwe team was presented with a live ox on their return home.

Walk, Don't Run The three leading competitors in the women's 20-km walk at the 2000 Sydney Olympics were all disqualified for running in the final kilometer, leaving China's Wang Liping to claim an unlikely gold medal.

No Gold Long-Jumper Robert LeGendre, from Washington, D.C., set a new world record of 25 ft 5½ in (7.76 m) at the 1924 Olympics—but he didn't win a gold medal because he was competing in the pentathlon.

Olympic Heroes

Dislocated Arm Konrad von Wangenheim helped Germany's equestrian team to win gold at the 1936 Olympics despite riding with a broken collarbone and his left arm in a sling.

Incredible Double At the 1924 Paris Olympics, Finland's Paavo Nurmi won the men's 1,500 meters final and then just over an hour later he won the 5,000 meters final, setting Olympic records in both events.

Changing Hands Hungarian pistol shooter Károly Takács lost his right hand in 1938 when a grenade that he was holding exploded. So he taught himself to shoot left-handed and won a gold medal at the 1948 London Olympics, successfully defending his title four years later in Helsinki.

Heroic Horsewoman Despite being paralyzed below the knees after contracting polio, Denmark's Lis Hartel, who had to be helped on and off her horse, won silver medals in the individual dressage event at both the 1952 and 1956 Olympics.

Wooden Leg U.S. gymnast George Eyser won six medals in one day at the 1904 Olympics in St. Louis—three of them gold—despite having a wooden leg. His left leg had been amputated after he was run over by a train. He even won gold in the long horse vault, which he jumped without a springboard.

Olympic Howlers

Calendar Chaos After spending over 16 days at sea, the U.S. team arrived in Athens for the first modern Olympic Games in 1896 believing that they still had 12 days to prepare for the competition. In fact, the Games started the very next day—the Americans had forgotten that Greece still used the Julian calendar and was therefore 12 days in advance.

Joined Picnic Exhausted by the heat of the 1912 Olympic marathon in Stockholm, Sweden, Japan's Shizo Kanaguri stumbled into the yard of a family who were enjoying a picnic and stayed with them rather than rejoining the race.

Lost Medal After winning a rowing gold medal at the 1956 Olympics, 18-year-old Russian Vyacheslav Ivanov quickly lost it. He threw the medal into the air in celebration, but it landed in the lake. He dived in but was unable to find it.

Missing Gloves Moments before he was due to fight at the 1992 Barcelona Olympics, Iranian boxer Ali Kazemi was disqualified because he had forgotten his gloves.

Hot Stuff To prepare himself for the heat of Rome, where he won the 50-km walk at the 1960 Olympics, Britain's Don Thompson kept the heat on at all times in his bathroom for 18 months—and ran up a gas bill of over £9,000 ($14,300). He returned home from his triumph to find that the gas had been cut off.

Lost in Translation American athlete Loren Murchison was left at the start of the 1920 Olympic men's 100 meters final in Antwerp, Belgium, because he didn't understand French. When the starter said *prêt* ("get set"), Murchison thought that the crouching runners had been told to stand up and was doing so when the starting gun went off.

Shot in Foot U.S. Lieutenant Sidney Hinds won gold in the free rifle team event at the 1924 Olympics in Paris, shooting a perfect 50—despite having been accidentally shot in the foot partway through the competition when the Belgian rifleman positioned next to him threw his loaded weapon to the ground during an argument with an official.

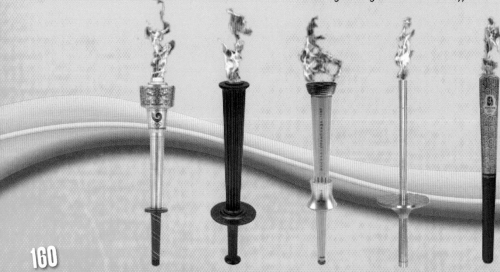

Unusual Olympic Events

Vertical Rope Climb (1896, 1904, 1906, 1924, 1932)
So hard was this event that in 1896 only two of the climbers made it to the top, prompting officials to send the rope back for alterations.

Men's Sailor's 100 Meter Freestyle (1896)
This event was open only to sailors in the Greek Royal Navy. Only three competitors took place in the event. And the winner was from... Greece!

Long Jump for Horses (1900)
A horse named Extra Dry won at the Paris Olympics with a jump of 20 ft ¼ in (6.1 m)—that's shorter than the men's record in 1901.

200 Meter Obstacle Swimming Race (1900)
Held in Paris' River Seine, competitors had to climb over a pole, clamber over a row of boats, and then swim under another row of boats.

Pistol Dueling (1906)
Participants shot over 20 and 30 meters at mannequins that wore fancy frock coats with bull's-eyes embroidered on the chest.

Underwater Swimming Race (1900)
Not the most thrilling visual spectacle, this race was held over 60 meters with competitors being awarded points for each meter swum and time spent underwater.

Pigeon Shooting (1900)
Paris 1900 featured the only Olympic event in history at which animals were deliberately harmed—300 live pigeons. Belgium's Leon de Lunden won gold, bagging himself 21 birds.

Tug of War (1900, 1904, 1908, 1912, 1920)
The Ancient Greeks staged the first tug in 500 BC, but in modern Olympic rules, a team of eight had to pull the opposition 6 ft (1.8 m) to win. London 1908 saw the sport at its most intense, when the United States was beaten in just a few short seconds by Great Britain. The unhappy losers accused the British team—all policemen— of wearing illegal spiked boots, so they were offered a rematch, with the British in their socks. They still lost.

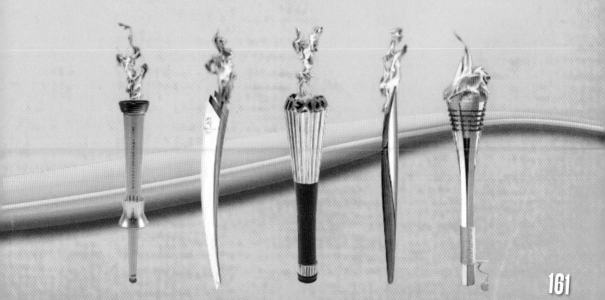

Cold Climb

In February 2010, Andreas Spak from Norway, Christian Pondella from California, and Canadian Will Gadd became the first adventurers to scale the Vøringfossen waterfall in Norway, one of the highest in Europe. In warmer weather, the water surges at 40 ft (12 m) per second, but winter temperatures of 5°F (−15°C) transformed the torrent into a 650-ft (198-m) ice skyscraper.

Surf Club

The Palestinian territory's Gaza Strip has its own surf club, which was founded after a Jewish surfer donated a dozen surfboards to the community.

Fast Match

In October 2009, Jo-Wilfried Tsonga of France and Spain's Fernando Verdasco played a tennis match on board a train traveling at 268 mph (431 km/h). The mini-tennis court was laid out in one of Shanghai's high-speed Maglev trains, so that the players were traveling faster than their serves.

Round-the-World

In 2010, 34-year-old Vin Cox from Cornwall, England, cycled 18,225 mi (29,330 km) around the world in just 163 days. Starting and finishing his journey in London, he took 12 plane and boat transfers, crossed six continents— Europe, (northern) Africa, Asia, Australia, South America, and North America—and cycled through 17 countries.

Big Haul

In August 2010, Jeff Kolodzinski caught 2,160 fish—mostly small bluegills and perch—from Lake Minnetonka, Minnesota, in a 24-hour period.

Liberty Walk

French high-wire walker Didier Pasquette crossed a 150-ft-long (46-m) wire tied between two replicas of the Statue of Liberty on top of the 23-story Liberty Building in Buffalo, New York State, in September 2010. The feat took him about three minutes, and he stopped twice during his walk to wave to the crowds on the ground some 230 ft (70 m) below.

Back Handsprings

At Valmeyer, Illinois, 13-year-old Chelsey Kipping did 32 consecutive back handsprings. She has been doing gymnastics since age four and practices for at least nine hours a week.

Africa Trek

French adventurers Alexandre and Sonia Poussin spent three years walking 8,700 mi (14,000 km) from Cape of Good Hope, South Africa, to Israel, living solely on the hospitality of people they met along the way.

Trapeze Veteran

In his early seventies, Tony Steele still performed as a trapeze artist with the Gamma Phi Circus of Illinois State University, the oldest collegiate circus in the U.S.A.

Karate Kid

Varsha Vinod from Alappuzha, India, became a karate black belt in May 2009—the highest grade in the martial art—at the age of just five. She had been training since she was two and already had more than 15 *katas*, or karate disciplines, to her name.

Manhole Museum

Stefano Bottoni has collected manhole covers from across the world—including from Holland, Finland, Cuba, the Czech Republic, Austria and Romania—for exhibition at his International Manhole Museum in Farrara, Italy.

Ball Control

Twenty-five-year-old schoolteacher Rohit Timilsina of Kathmandu, Nepal, managed to hold 21 standard tennis balls on the palm of his hand for more than 14 seconds in 2008. It took him three years of practice to achieve the feat.

Cat Statues

Winnie Ferring has a collection of more than 1,000 cat statues arranged on every available space inside and outside her home in Lansing, Iowa. She has been collecting them for more than 50 years, and each piece is numbered and documented.

Underwater Juggler

With a single breath, Merlin Cadogan from Devon, England, was able to juggle three objects underwater for 1 minute 20 seconds.

Spinning Yo-Yos

At the 2010 London Toy Fair, Ben McPhee from Australia kept 16 yo-yos spinning simultaneously. He had yo-yos hanging off hooks, his fingers, and even his ears and teeth.

Extra Load

In 2009, British former soldier Kez Dunkley ran the 26.2-mi (42-km) Leicester Marathon in 5 hours 53 minutes with an 84-lb (38-kg) tumble-drier strapped to his back. The previous year he had run the race with a bag of cement on his back.

Harley Jump

California stunt rider Seth Enslow jumped 183 ft 8 in (56 m) on a Harley-Davidson motorcycle near Australia's Sydney Harbour in March 2010. Three years earlier, the bike ace had performed a 200-ft (60-m) jump over a Convair 880 passenger jet airplane.

Young Climber

At just five years old, Sail Chapman of East Yorkshire, England, achieved his ambition of scaling all 214 peaks listed in Alfred Wainwright's famous Lake District guidebooks. He began walking the Cumbrian hills with his family at the age of two and completed the Wainwright peaks when he reached the top of his namesake fell, Sale, which stands at 2,536 ft (773 m).

Tough Granny

Pint-sized Sakinat Khanapiyeva, a 76-year-old grandmother from Dagestan, Russia, can tear through phone books, lift a 52-lb (23.5-kg) dumbbell while standing on a bed of nails, and break iron horseshoes. She first realized how strong she was at the age of ten when she moved a 660-lb (300-kg) box of grain—equal to the weight of four grown men.

Seven Out

In 2009, in his first game as a pitcher for the St. Louis Cardinals, John Smoltz struck out seven hitters in a row—something he had never managed to do in 708 trips to the mound with his previous team, the Atlanta Braves.

Flying Kayak

Miles Daisher of Twin Falls, Idaho, paddles a kayak—across the sky at an altitude of 13,000 ft (4,000 m). The daredevil has invented a new sport, skyaking, a combination of skydiving and kayaking. Sitting in his kayak he jumps from a plane, pulls the chute at about 5,000 ft (1,525 m), and descends at nearly 100 mph (160 km/h), reducing to half that speed as he finally swoops to land spectacularly on water.

Stilt Stunt

In 1891, Sylvain Dornon from Landes, France, walked from Paris to Moscow, Russia, on stilts! He completed the 1,830-mi (2,945-km) journey in 58 days, averaging more than 30 mi (50 km) each day. Earlier in the 19th century, stilts were a fairly common means of getting around marshy terrain in parts of France, especially among shepherds, but, by 1891, Dornon was considered very strange indeed.

Hot Hood

The Russian Extreme Games in Moscow were an opportunity for some of the most daring and crazy stuntmen in Russia to compete against each other in such dangerous events as riding BMX bikes with flaming tires, setting themselves on fire, and riding on the hood of a vehicle as it crashed through an inferno.

Wheelchair Wheelie

Nineteen-year-old Michael Miller of Ellington, Wisconsin, performed a 10-mi (16-km) wheelie in a wheelchair. Michael, who was born with spina bifida, completed 40 laps of a high-school track on two wheels in just under four hours. He performed his first wheelchair wheelie when he was just four years old.

Text Exchange

Nick Andes and Doug Klinger, two friends from central Pennsylvania, exchanged a thumb-numbing 217,033 texts during March 2009. At the end of the month, Andes received an unexpected itemized bill for $26,000—for the 142,000 texts he had sent and the 75,000 he had received from Klinger.

Tea Potty

Over a period of 25 years, Sue Blazye from Kent, England, has built up a collection of more than 6,000 teapots—and they take up so much room that she has converted her home (called Teapot Island) into a museum. Her favorite teapot is in the shape of Princess Diana's head, and was made when Diana got engaged to Prince Charles.

Mayor Moore

Hilmar Moore has served as the mayor of Richmond, Texas, for more than 60 years. He was first appointed in 1949 and has been re-elected every two years since, although the last time he had an opponent was 1996.

Bat Breaker

At the Riverwalk Stadium, Montgomery, Alabama—home of the Montgomery Biscuits Minor League baseball team—Steve Carrier broke 30 baseball bats over his leg in less than a minute. The 6-ft-4-in (1.9-m), 290-lb (131-kg) Carrier, from Dallas, Texas, also bends steel with his teeth.

Happy Hugger

In Las Vegas, Nevada, on Valentine's weekend 2010, 51-year-old Jeff Ondash (a.k.a. Teddy McHuggin) of Canfield, Ohio, gave out 7,777 hugs in just 24 hours—the equivalent of more than five hugs a minute.

RIPLEY'S ASK

Why did you first start balloon flying?
I first became interested in balloon flight as a child—I wondered at a balloon, and how it floated upon the air. Then I thought "If I just get enough of these, couldn't I go into the sky?" As an adult, I left behind the idea that such a thing isn't possible and awakened a dream that had grown quiet.

What inspired you to cross the channel?
The English Channel is a challenge that has called to aviators for generations. There is romance in flying over the famous White Cliffs of Dover and the Lighthouse at Dunkirk.

What was it like when you were in the sky?
A quiet dream. I was 1,000 ft (305 m) above the water and I could hear only the waves. When you're in the air, you move perfectly with the wind, not knowing where you'll land.

Was it a bumpy landing?
The landing was smooth, but after the landing, as I worked to release the helium and take my balloons down, the winds kicked up!

What are your balloon ambitions?
I would like to launch out of California, within sight of the ocean, and then fly inland, above the Sierra Nevada mountains, into the heart of America.

Into the Skies

Aerial adventurer and qualified pilot Jonathan R. Trappe from North Carolina made history in May 2010 by traveling 76 mi (122 km) across the English Channel attached to a bunch of 55 helium balloons. Drifting from Ashford, England, toward France, Jonathan reached speeds of 35 mph (56 km/h) and heights of 7,000 ft (2,135 m). Three hours 22 minutes after taking off, and after a flight adjustment to avoid Belgium, he landed safely in a cabbage field near Dunkirk, France.

Nose-to-Nose

In March 2010, Robert Officer and John Milhiser from the Serious Lunch comedy group touched noses together for 10 hours 34 minutes, with no breaks or interruptions. Robert and John's record-breaking task included a trip on the New York subway and bathroom breaks together before appearing live on the Jimmy Fallon show.

Saddle Sore

Riding 49cc mini-bikes that averaged just 20 mph (32 km/h), Ryan Galbraith and Chris Stinson traveled the 445 mi (716 km) from Denver, Colorado, to Sturgis, South Dakota, in 25 hours 29 minutes in 2009.

Senior Student

Hazel Soares of San Leandro, California, received her college diploma in May 2010—at age 94! "It's taken me quite a long time because I've had a busy life," said the mother-of-six, who has more than 40 grandchildren and great-grandchildren.

Rabbit Jumping

As well as pioneering show jumping, where horses clear obstacles, Sweden established the sport of rabbit jumping, in which domestic rabbits are trained to jump miniature fences without touching them.

Backward Running

Germany's Achim Aretz ran 6 mi (10 km) backward in 41 minutes 26 seconds at the third Retrorunning World Championships in Kapfenberg, Austria, on August 8, 2010.

Ruff Justice

In Athens, Georgia, a woman scared off a would-be burglar by acting like a dog. She got on the floor and began scratching at the door when the intruder tried turning the door knob—he then ran away.

Everest Landing

British skydivers Leo Dickinson and Ralph Mitchell and Indian Air Force officer Ramesh Tripathi successfully landed their parachutes at an altitude of 16,800 ft (5,120 m) on Mount Everest in September 2009. After jumping out of a helicopter at 20,500 ft (6,250 m), they had just five seconds of free fall in which to open their chutes. The trio had to home in on Gorak Shep—a narrow, sand-covered lakebed and the only safe landing spot for miles. "It was pretty hairy," said 62-year-old Dickinson. "If you missed that or overshot it, you were either going to die or end up with something important broken."

First Female

In 2010, Kelly Kulick of the U.S.A. became the first woman to qualify for the Professional Bowlers' Association's Tournament of Champions—and she went on to beat an all-male field of 62 to claim the title.

Pole Balance

David Cain of Liberty Township, Ohio, can balance a 58-ft-long (17.7-m) fiberglass pole on his chin for more than 21 seconds. It took him two years to master the skill.

Sports Survivors

These heroic athletes and fans have the scars to show how sport can be dangerous. Incredibly, all have survived and, believe it or not, returned to the arena for more.

Let's work it out together.

HOCKEY HORROR

Buffalo Sabres' goaltender Clint Malarchuk narrowly escaped death after a collision caused a player's skate to cut the carotid artery in his neck during a 1989 hockey match against the St. Louis Blues. If the skate had hit Malarchuk ⅛ in (3 mm) higher, he would have been dead within two minutes. The injury was so horrific that 11 fans fainted and two had heart attacks, while three players vomited on the ice. Malarchuk needed 300 stitches to fix the wound, but was back playing in goal ten days later.

DANGEROUS RING

Celebrating a goal for Swiss team Servette in 2004, recently married Portuguese soccer player Paulo Diogo jumped on the stadium fence and caught his wedding ring on the top. When he jumped off, he left the ring and half his finger behind. To add insult to injury, the referee showed him a yellow card for time wasting as the doctors searched for the missing finger! Although doctors were unable to reattach the digit, Diogo quickly resumed his career.

MOST DANGEROUS SPORTS IN THE U.S.A.

(Injuries per year)

1. Basketball 512,213

2. Cycling 485,669

3. Football 418,260

4. Soccer 174,686

5. Baseball 155,898

6. Skateboarding 112,544

7. Trampolining 108,029

8. Softball 106,884

9. Swimming/diving 82,354

10. Horseback riding 73,576

UNLUCKY BREAK

Brazilian-born Croatian soccer player Eduardo suffered a horrific broken leg when playing for his club team Arsenal, in England's Premier League in 2008. A tackle by Birmingham City's Martin Taylor left Eduardo's anklebone sticking through his sock and kept him out of the game for almost a year.

DIVING BELLE

Seventeen-year-old Columbus, Ohio, diver Chelsea Davis smashed the bridge of her nose on the diving board while competing at the 2005 World Swimming Championships in Montreal, Canada. She was lifted on to a stretcher, her face covered in blood, but she never lost consciousness and was soon back competing.

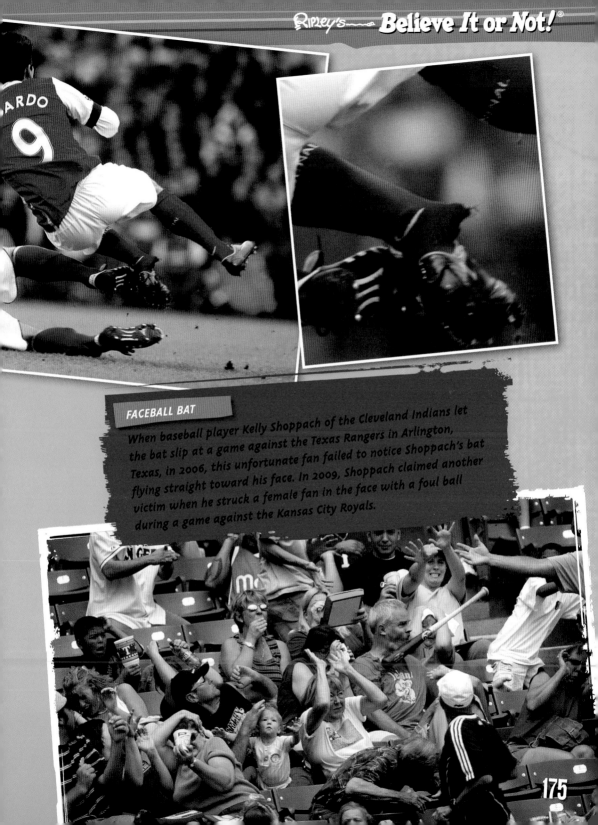

FACEBALL BAT

When baseball player Kelly Shoppach of the Cleveland Indians let the bat slip at a game against the Texas Rangers in Arlington, Texas, in 2006, this unfortunate fan failed to notice Shoppach's bat flying straight toward his face. In 2009, Shoppach claimed another victim when he struck a female fan in the face with a foul ball during a game against the Kansas City Royals.

175

Ice Bath

Wearing only swimming trunks, Jin Songhao and Chen Kecai immersed themselves in ice up to their necks for 120 minutes and 118 minutes, respectively, high up on Tianmen Mountain in China's Hunan Province in January 2011. Jin was even able to write Chinese calligraphy during his ordeal.

California Wingwalk

Traveling at speeds of 100 mph (160 km/h), often in the face of strong winds, Ashley Battles of Tulsa, Oklahoma, stood on the wing of a biplane for more than four hours in June 2010. Her wingwalk took place over San Francisco, California, giving her fabulous views of the Golden Gate Bridge and Alcatraz.

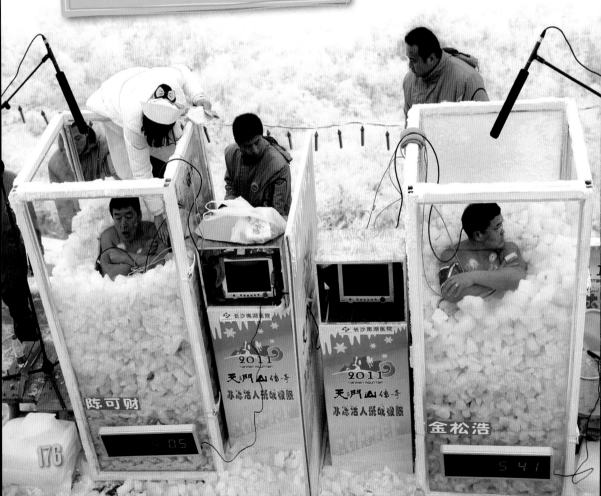

Shark Incentive

Spain's David Calvo solved two Rubik's Cube puzzles one-handed simultaneously in just 76 seconds while inside a tank with six sharks at the Terra Natura Park in Benidorm, Spain.

Tightrope Walk

Chinese tightrope walker Adili Wuxor spent more than five hours a day for 60 days gingerly walking across a 1.3-in-thick (3.3-cm) steel wire strung across Beijing's Bird's Nest stadium at a height of more than 200 ft (60 m) above the ground. He walked about 12 mi (19 km) a day, so that he covered around 700 mi (1,130 km) in total.

Gorilla Run

More than 1,000 people dressed in gorilla suits to take part in the 2009 Denver Gorilla Run, a 3½-mile (5.6-km) charity run/walk through the streets of the city to help raise funds for mountain gorilla conservation.

Poker Session

Professional poker player Phil Laak of Los Angeles, California, played poker for more than 115 hours from June 2 to June 7, 2010, at the Bellagio Hotel in Las Vegas, Nevada. He finished $6,766 up.

Hang Tough

Strapped into special gravity boots and hanging upside down from a frame, Zdenek Bradac from the Czech Republic juggled three balls for 2 minutes 13 seconds, during which time he made 438 consecutive catches.

Speedy Mower

Don Wales drove a lawn mower at a speed of more than 87 mph (140 km/h) at Pendine Sands in Wales, in May 2010. His grandfather, Sir Malcolm Campbell, broke the world land speed record, in a car, at the same venue in 1924.

Stiletto Sprinters

Running along a 263-ft (80-m) course at Circular Quay in Sydney, New South Wales, Australia, a relay team of four women from Canberra—Brittney McGlone, Laura Juliff, Casey Hodges and Jessica Penny—completed the four legs in 1 minute 4 seconds—while wearing 3-in-high (7.5-cm) stiletto heels.

Bulky Wear

Croatia's Kruno Budiselic managed to wear 245 T-shirts—ranging in size from medium to extra large—at the same time. The extra clothing added around 150 lb (68 kg) to his overall weight.

Bathtub Voyage

Rob Dowling of Dublin, Ireland, sailed 500 mi (800 km) down the Amazon River in a motorized bathtub in 2006. The 5-ft-7-in (1.72-m) fiberglass tub was supported by six 36-gal (136-l) steel drums and propelled by a 15-horsepower motor. He had intended to sail from Iquitos in Peru to the Atlantic—2,465 mi (3,967 km)—but his journey ended after just over 500 mi (800 km) when Brazilian authorities told him he didn't have a licence for the bathtub!

Switch Hitters

It took 134 years for the Arizona Diamondbacks' Felipe Lopez to become the first baseball player in history to switch-hit homers from both sides of the plate on Opening Day. It took just one inning, in the same 2009 game, for Tony Clark to become the second.

King Gnome

Andy and Connie Kautza of Wausau, Wisconsin, built a concrete garden gnome that stands 15 ft (4.5 m) tall and weighs more than 3,500 lb (1,590 kg).

Chopper Leap

Defying potentially dangerous turbulence, U.S. daredevil motorcyclist Travis Pastrana successfully backflipped a dirt bike over a helicopter that was hovering off the ground in front of Australia's Sydney Harbour Bridge, clearing the revolving chopper blades by about 13 ft (4 m).

Paper Round

Ted Ingram has been delivering newspapers in Dorset, England, for nearly 70 years. He started his job in 1942 and estimates that he has since delivered more than half a million papers.

Human Wheelbarrow

In Helsinki, Finland, Adrian Rodrigues Buenrostro from Mexico and Sergiy Vetrogonov from Ukraine finished a 131-ft (40-m) human wheelbarrow race in just 17 seconds.

Mass Waltz

More than 1,500 couples—from children to pensioners—danced a waltz in the main square of Tuzla, Bosnia, in 2010. Organizers estimated that as many as 25,000 people danced in the surrounding streets, but the square had to be sealed off so that the couples had room to move.

Free Haircuts

Working round the clock, a team of ten stylists from Pump Salon completed 618 free haircuts in 24 hours in Cincinnati, Ohio, in September 2010.

Car Wash

Students from Bloomington High School South, Indiana, cleaned 1,207 cars in 10 hours in a marathon car-wash.

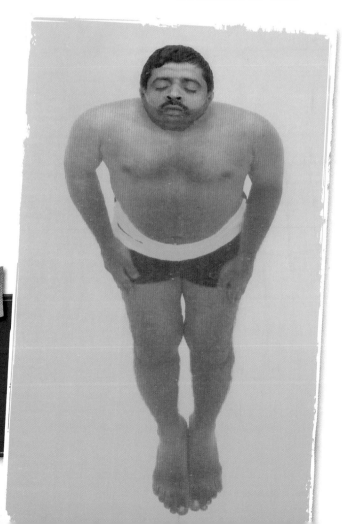

Still Life

S.C. Naganandaswamy of Karnataka, India, can float in 20 ft (6 m) of water for 22 hours continuously without moving any limbs.

Human Sparkler

Dr. Peter Terren of Bunbury, Western Australia, shot more than 200,000 volts of electricity down his body to create a spectacular version of Rodin's *The Thinker*. He turned himself into a human sparkler for 15 seconds by using a homemade Tesla coil, which transforms a feed of domestic electricity into a supercharged bolt of power. He was saved from electrocution by wrapping his torso, arms and legs in builders' insulating foil—the electricity traveled through the foil and out to the earth from his foot. He also wore a tin-foil cap and a wire-mesh mask, and taped steel wool to the bottom of his left shoe to create the shower of sparks from his foot.

Mirror Image

U.S. golfer Phil Mickelson is right-handed in everything but golf. He plays left-handed after mirroring his father's right-handed swing as a child.

One Hand

At 6 ft 10 in (2.1 m) tall, Kevin Laue of Pleasanton, California, received a scholarship to play basketball for Manhattan College despite having only one hand.

Every Ground

In February 2010, Scott Poleykett from Kent, England, completed a 50,000-mi (80,000-km) journey to visit every soccer ground, professional and amateur, in England and Wales. In the course of his ten-year mission, he took photographs of 2,547 soccer fields.

Sand Skis

Germany's Henrik May prefers to ski on sand rather than snow—and in the Namibian Desert he reached a speed of 57.24 mph (92.12 km/h) while skiing down a 246-ft-high (75-m) dune. He has developed a special type of wax that enables the skis he uses to slide over sand.

Tattoo Tribute

Colombian soccer fan Felipe Alvarez has had his upper body tattooed to resemble a jersey of his favorite team, Atletico Nacional. The tattoo is in honor of Andrés Escobar, the Colombian player who was shot dead as a result of scoring an own goal, which lost his side the match, while playing against the U.S.A. at the 1994 World Cup. Seen here with Atletico player Victor Aristizábal, Alvarez now has Escobar's number 2 permanently marked on his back.

Tennis Marathon

At the 2010 Wimbledon Tennis Championships, John Isner of the U.S.A. beat France's Nicolas Mahut in a match that lasted more than 11 hours over three days. The match began at 6.18 p.m. on Tuesday, June 22 and finished at 4.49 p.m. on Thursday, June 24, Isner eventually winning 6-4, 3-6, 6-7, 7-6, 70-68 in a final set that lasted 8 hours 11 minutes.

Flying Shot

In 2010, Tyler Toney, a student from Texas A&M University, made a basketball shot he threw from a low-flying airplane!

Atlantic Crossing

A four-man crew led by Scotsman Leven Brown overcame 40-ft (12-m) waves, two capsizes and an outbreak of food poisoning to row 3,500 mi (5,600 km) across the Atlantic from New York to the Isles of Scilly, which lie off the southwest coast of England, in 43 days in 2010. They were following the route of a Norwegian crew who had made the same crossing in 55 days back in 1896.

Wrestling Champs

In 2010, Blair Academy of Blairstown, New Jersey, won its 30th consecutive National Prep School Wrestling Championship.

Veteran Coach

Soccer coach Ivor Powell finally hung up his boots at age 93. A former Welsh international forward, he went on to train more than 9,000 players during his 53-year coaching career.

Monkey Guards

Organizers at the 2010 Commonwealth Games in New Delhi, India, hired monkeys to work as guards at the athletes' village. They hoped that the special team of 40 gray langur monkeys would chase off the packs of smaller rhesus monkeys that had been breaking into buildings and stealing from the competitors' quarters.

Leap of Faith

Escape artist and evangelist Anthony Martin performed a daring skydive from an airplane flying at 13,500 ft (4,115 m) over Illinois—wearing handcuffs that were locked to a chain around his neck and linked to leather cuffs fastened above each elbow.

To add to the stunt's death-defying nature, the safety device attached to his parachute that automatically deploys the chute at 700 ft (215 m) was turned off. Without this backup, he had just 45 seconds, while spinning to Earth at 180 mph (290 km/h), to free himself from the handcuffs and chains and to reach back to pull the release handle and activate the canopy.

Falling in a sitting-back position, Anthony seemed to struggle with the lock for about 25 seconds before working himself free and safely deploying the chute.

The 45-year-old from Sheboygan, Wisconsin, has been picking locks since he was a child and made his first authenticated escape at age 12, when he managed to work his way out of a regulation police straitjacket. He jokes that he comes from the "School of Hard Locks."

Since childhood he has broken out of a locked box thrown from an airplane, escaped from being buried alive beneath 2,000 lb (907 kg) of sand, and freed himself from a heavily secured coffin submerged underwater. He has even requested permission to break out of Fort Knox—where most of the U.S. gold bullion reserves are stored—but the U.S. Government refused to allow the escape bid.

Underpants Man

Gary Craig from Newcastle, England, also known as the Geordie Pantsman, took 25 minutes to clamber into an incredible 211 pairs of underpants in an unusual charity challenge in April 2010. Gary initially planned to wear 200 underpants, but an Australian rival had achieved this landmark only a few days before, so Gary was forced to set his sights higher and find bigger pairs of pants. This caused problems, as the smaller the underpants the greater the pressure, making it a painful physical challenge.

Beer House

In Schleiden, Germany, Sven Goebel spent three months building a five-room apartment made entirely from 300,000 beer mats. It featured a table, chairs and a fireplace—all made of beer mats. After spending up to eight hours a day, seven days a week, on construction, he then had to knock down the finished building to prove that it had been held together only with static, not adhesive.

Free-fall Solution

After jumping from an airplane at an altitude of 14,000 ft (4,300 m), Ludwig Fichte of Dresden, Germany, flew through the air while sitting in a rubber dinghy and solving a Rubik's Cube puzzle. It took him 31.5 seconds during a free-fall descent of 5,900 ft (1,800 m) to solve the cube, at which point he deployed his parachute.

Stamp Collector

Postman Alan Roy from Dorset, England, spent 70 years painstakingly peeling off two million stamps from envelopes. He soaked each envelope in water and then carefully removed the stamp with tweezers. His collection is so big it fills up 40 packing crates that stack as high as a house.

Old Scout

Reg Hayes, 95, of Oxford, England, retired in 2010 after 87 years as a Boy Scout. He joined the 2nd Oxford Wolf Cub pack in 1923 and moved up to the SS Mary and John 2nd Oxford Scouts in 1930, where he stayed for the next 80 years.

Cucumber Man

Frank Dimmock, 87, from Oxfordshire, England, grew a cucumber 41¼ in (104.8 cm) long in 2010. Known as the "Cucumber Man," he has been growing vegetables since before World War II when he became an apprentice to a gardener.

Pi Chart

Using only a single standard desktop computer costing less than $3,000, French software engineer Fabrice Bellard calculated pi to nearly 2.7 trillion decimal places. The complex calculation took him 131 days.

Plane Pull

In Jilin, China, in 2010, martial-arts expert Dong Changsheng took less than a minute to pull a half-ton airplane for 16 ft (5 m)—by a rope hooked to his eyelids! He had previously pulled a car with his eyelids but this was his first attempt with a plane.

Giant Clock

The family clock-making firm Smith of Derby, England, built a huge mechanical clock 42 ft 8 in (13 m) in diameter with a minute hand 25 ft 7 in (7.8 m) long. The 11-ton clock took a year to design and build and was delivered to its final home—in Ganzhou, China—in 2010 for installation in the 371-ft-high (113-m) Harmony Tower.

Golf Balls

When Chris Morrison from Dunfermline, Scotland, noticed a strange rattling sound coming from the stomach of his black Labrador, Oscar, he took the five-year-old dog to a veterinarian—who removed 13 golf balls from the animal's stomach. One of the balls had been in Oscar's stomach so long that it had turned black and was decomposing.

Commentator's Nightmare

The finish of an August 2010 race at Monmouth Park, New Jersey, was fought out between horses named Mywifeknowseverything and Thewifedoesn'tknow. The two horses were completely unconnected, and had separate trainers and owners.

Human Fly

Jem Stansfield climbed the side of a 30-ft (9-m) wall of a school in Brighton, England, using nothing more than suction from two vacuum cleaners. The 168-lb (76-kg) aeronautics graduate adapted the household appliances' motors into giant suckerpads, which were strong enough to support him and enabled him to cling to the wall.

Flying Lanterns

More than 10,000 twinkling white paper lanterns were released simultaneously into the night sky from a beach in Jakarta, Indonesia, in December 2009. The flying lantern is a Chinese tradition. It is basically a paper bag containing a block of paraffin with a wick suspended by wire across the opening. When the wick is lit, the air inside warms like a hot-air balloon and the lantern lifts off into the sky.

Rubber Bands

Eleven-year-old Allison Coach of Chesterfield Township, Michigan, created a chain of 22,140 rubber bands that stretched nearly 7,000 ft (2,130 m)—or 1.3 mi (2 km)—long.

Champion Plowgirl

Thirteen-year-old schoolgirl Elly Deacon beat experienced farmers for first place in a plowing competition in Hertfordshire, England. Elly, who had driven a tractor for the first time only four days before the event, impressed judges with her straight and smooth plow marks on a 53,000-sq-ft (4,900-sq-m) patch of land, while at the wheel of the six-ton tractor.

Turbo Terry

Terry Burrows from Essex, England, cleaned three windows, each measuring 45 sq in (290 sq cm), and wiped the sills in just 9.14 seconds during a window-cleaning competition in Blackpool, Lancashire. "Turbo Terry" actually finished the task in 8.14 seconds, but was handed a one-second time penalty for leaving two water marks on the glass.

Rain Dance

More than 230 dancers took to the wet streets of Bath in Somerset, England, with umbrellas in May 2010 to perform a five-minute version of Gene Kelly's classic "Singin' in the Rain."

Sand Burial

As part of the 2010 Clogherhead Prawn Festival in County Louth, Ireland, 524 people simultaneously buried themselves up to their necks on a sandy beach.

Cake Tower

Chef Gilles Stassart and architect Jean Bocabeille designed a cake for display in Paris, France, in July 2010 that was nearly 26 ft (7.8 m) tall—that's as high as a two-story house. The "Tower without Hunger" was made from 1,385 lb (628 kg) of flour, 1,120 lb (508 kg) of sugar, 350 eggs, and 40 lb (18 kg) of butter. The towering cake was meant to last four days outdoors but sweltering temperatures made it soft and unstable and it had to be taken down after just 24 hours.

Slow Progress

Lottie the tortoise disappeared from her home in Essex, England, in 2008—and was found safe and well nearly two years later, having traveled just 1½ mi (2.4 km).

Emerald Hunter

Jamie Hill of North Carolina has dug up nearly 18,000 carats of emeralds in his home state since 1998.

Poker Face

Bai Deng from Shandong, China, can hurl a regular playing card so hard and with such accuracy that he can slice a cucumber in two. It's not as impossible as it might seem, given that in 2002 U.S. magician Rick Smith Jr. threw a playing card a distance of 216 ft 4 in (66 m) at a speed of over 90 mph (145 km/h).

BODY
TALES

Major Mite

Clarence C. "Major Mite" Howerton was born in February 1913, and was billed by the press in the 1930s as the smallest man in the world. He stood only 28 in (71 cm) tall and weighed just 20 lb (9 kg). He was so small that he once traveled from New York to Chicago to find a tailor who would make a tuxedo for his diminutive size. He wore custom-made shoes just 2.5 in (6 cm) long.

The Ringling Brothers and Barnum & Bailey Circus signed up Major Mite in 1923, when he was ten years old, and he starred in its sideshow for more than 25 years. As well as being a big draw on the sideshow circuit, Major Mite featured in several Our Gang comedy shorts and played a trumpet-playing munchkin in the 1939 film *The Wizard of Oz*.

After a life in show business, he died in Oregon at the age of 62.

At only 28 in (71 cm) tall when fully grown, Major Mite was no bigger than the average toddler.

Tiny Major Mite being held aloft by his friend, giant Jack Earle.

Major Mite performed with many extreme individuals, such as 700-lb (318-kg) Ruth Pontico.

Reports suggest that Major Mite had a rebellious streak, sometimes dressing in children's clothes and then shocking the public by smoking, shouting—or posing on a motorbike.

What Knife?

Julia Popova of Moscow, Russia, was attacked by a mugger in February 2010 but walked home not aware that she had been stabbed and that the knife was still impaled in her neck.

Skeleton Growth

A person's skeleton continues to grow until around age 25, when the collarbone finally finishes developing.

Miss Plastic

A 2009 beauty contest in Budapest, Hungary, was open only to women who had undergone cosmetic surgery. "Miss Plastic" featured contestants who had enhanced their bodies with everything from new breasts and liposuction to hair transplants.

Secret Bullet

Vasily Simonov of Togliatti, Russia, has lived with a bullet in his lung for 70 years. As a child in 1941, he was playing with a rifle cartridge when he decided to take out the bullet and shove it up his nose. After trying in vain to remove it, he then breathed it in. He forgot all about it and the lodged bullet never caused him any problems, only coming to light during an MRI scan in 2009. Even then, doctors decided it was best to leave the bullet where it was.

Big Baby

At age two, Fan Sijia of Yuncheng City, Shanxi Province, China, was 3 ft 7 in (1.1 m) tall and weighed 100 lb (45 kg)—about four times the average weight for a girl her age.

Strong Boy

Kyle Kane, a 12-year-old schoolboy from the West Midlands, England, lifted a 308-lb (140-kg) weight—more than twice his own body weight—at a junior bodybuilding event in 2010.

Kept "Dying"

Motorcyclist Steven Nixon from Derbyshire, England, suffered a massive heart attack after being in a collision with a car—but he pulled through even though he had technically "died" 28 times over the next few hours when his heart repeatedly stopped beating.

Body Sale

In 2010, anatomist Gunther von Hagens launched a mail-order service for his Plastinarium museum in the German town of Guben, selling human and animal body parts that had been preserved with a special plastic solution. Items for sale included a smoker's lung ($4,440), a chunk of human head ($2,000), a slice of a human hand ($228), and a cross-section of giraffe neck (price unspecified).

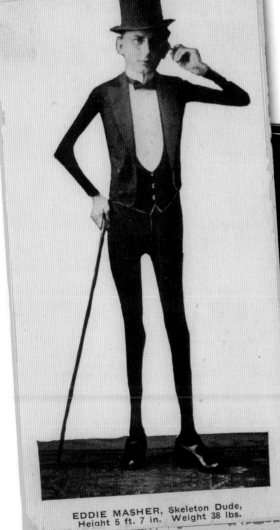

EDDIE MASHER, Skeleton Dude,
Height 5 ft. 7 in. Weight 38 lbs.

Human Skeleton

Billed as the "Skeleton Dude" at Coney Island's Dreamland Circus in 1917, Eddie Masher of Brooklyn, New York, stood 5 ft 7 in (1.7 m) tall, but he declared he weighed just 38 lb (17 kg). Other records have put him at 48 lb (22 kg) or as much as 67 lb (30 kg), but even those weights were astonishingly light for an adult man. He was so skinny that tailors struggled to make a suit that would fit him. He died in 1962 at 70 years old—a good age for a skeleton!

Constantly Seasick

Jane Houghton from Cheshire, England, went on a week-long Mediterranean cruise—and still feels permanently seasick more than nine years later. She suffers from the rare Mal de Debarquement Syndrome, which causes people to feel as though they are constantly bobbing about on a rough sea. She feels so nauseous and wobbly that she has even had to stop buying clothes with stripes or busy patterns because she is unable to focus to iron them.

Busy Brain

The number of neurons in your brain—100 billion—is about the same as the number of stars in our galaxy.

Matching Horns

A Chinese grandmother who grew a 2.4-in (6-cm) horn on the left side of her forehead in 2009 began to develop a similar growth on the right side of her forehead a year later. Zhang Ruifang from Linlou has cutaneous horns—growths made of keratin, the same substance that makes up fingernails. Most cutaneous horns are just a tiny fraction of an inch long, but occasionally they can extend a number of inches from the skin.

Weight Loss

In January 2010, former postman Paul Mason of Suffolk, England, weighed 980 lb (444.5 kg)—but then he instantly lost 294 lb (133.5 kg) after undergoing gastric bypass surgery. The operation involved having part of his stomach stapled off so that all the food he eats goes into a small pouch, vastly restricting the amount he can consume. At his heaviest he ate 20,000 calories a day—eight times the amount needed by an average man.

Coal-powered Bike

Sylvester H. Roper of Roxbury, Massachusetts, built a steam-powered velocipede in the 1860s that drove like a motorcycle but was instead fueled by coal.

Teenage Toddler

Although she is old enough to drive a car, Brooke Greenberg of Reisterstown, Maryland, weighs just 16 lb (7.2 kg), is 30 in (75 cm) tall, and rides around in a stroller pushed by her mother. The teenager has the body and behavior of a tiny toddler, thought to be the result of a mutation in the genes that control her aging and development, and which has apparently left her frozen in time.

Chute Terror

Skydiver Paul Lewis survived after falling 3,000 ft (900 m) onto the roof of a hangar at Tilstock Airfield, Shropshire, England, in August 2009. His main parachute failed to open at 3,000 ft (900 m) and although his reserve chute opened at 2,000 ft (600 m), a problem caused him to spiral out of control from 1,000 ft (300 m) with the canopy only partially opened. Luckily, the parachute became snagged on the hangar roof, preventing him from plunging to the ground and to almost certain death.

Bionic Bottom

After suffering massive internal injuries in a motorcycle crash, a man from South Yorkshire, England, now presses a remote control to open his bowels and go to the toilet. Surgeons rebuilt his bottom by taking a muscle from above his knee, wrapping it around his sphincter, and then attaching electrodes to the nerves. He can operate the electrodes using a handset that he carries in his pocket and switches to on or off to control his bowel movements.

Twisted Tiger

Double contortionists Hassani Mohammed (right) and Lazarus Mwangi of Cirque Mother Africa bend over backward to entertain the audience at a show in Hamilton, New Zealand.

Tooth Test

Scientists can determine the ages of people born after 1943 to within 18 months by examining the amount of radioactive carbon in their teeth, caused by above-ground nuclear weapons testing in the 1950s and 1960s.

195

Iron Man

In 1848, a man working on the Vermont railway survived having an iron rod blasted right through his face and out of the top of his skull. Phineas Gage had been using explosives to clear space for the tracks by packing gunpowder into holes in rock with a heavy iron rod when a spark ignited the powder and the rod shot through his head.

Unbelievably, Gage survived this horrific accident and remained physically able for the rest of his life, although damage to his brain significantly altered his character. His injury became famous in medical circles, and contributed to an understanding of how the brain works. Gage returned to work as a coach driver and died in 1860, 12 years after his accident.

Identified as Gage in 2009, this photo shows him with the same 13-lb (6-kg) temping iron that pierced his brain, which he kept as a gruesome souvenir. He lost the sight in his left eye when the rod passed behind it.

Hair Insured

American football player Troy Polamalu, a defender with the Pittsburgh Steelers, has had his hair insured for $1 million by Lloyd's of London. His 3-ft-long (90-cm) black curls are so famous that he has not cut them since 2000. Although he wears a helmet while playing, his hair is still at risk—in 2006 he was tackled by his ponytail by Larry Johnson of the Kansas City Chiefs after intercepting a pass.

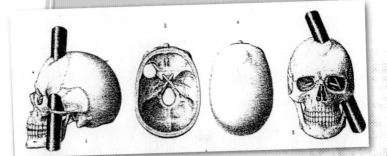

Magnetic Disruption

Placing a magnet on your head can temporarily turn a right-handed person into a left-hander. By positioning a powerful magnet on the left posterior parietal cortex—a region of the brain that deals with planning and working out the relationship between three-dimensional objects—researchers at the University of California, Berkeley, found that normally right-handed volunteers started to use their left hand more frequently for tasks such as picking up a pencil or calling an elevator. This is because the magnet disrupted and confused the volunteers' brains.

Epic Climb

Three U.S. war veterans climbed 19,341-ft (5,895-m) Mount Kilimanjaro in Tanzania in 2010—despite having only one good leg between them. Amputees Dan Nevins, 37, of Jacksonville, Florida, who lost his legs in Iraq; Neil Duncan, 26, of Denver, Colorado, who lost both legs in a roadside bomb attack in Afghanistan; and Kirk Bauer, 62, of Ellicott City, Maryland, who lost a leg in Vietnam in 1969, made the climb on their prosthetic legs in just six days.

Human Heads

When airport workers in Little Rock, Arkansas, noticed a package that was not labeled properly, they checked the contents and found a shipment of 60 human heads. Further investigation revealed the heads were on their way to a company in Fort Worth, Texas, to be used by neurosurgeons for the study of ear, nose and throat procedures.

Face Booked

In 2010, Chang Du from Lishuguo, China, went public with an offer to sell advertising space on his oversized chin. After a small pimple in his mouth swelled massively over a period of five years, Chang made the bizarre proposal in order to raise funds to reduce his chin back to normal size. He confirmed that an $8,000 offer would be enough to secure the space on his face.

Heads of State

Chinese micro-artist Jin Y. Hua has painted the face of every President of the U.S.A. from George Washington to George W. Bush—that's 42 portraits—on a single human hair less than ½ in (1.3 cm) long and just 0.0035 in (0.09 mm) thick. Jin uses a brush made from a single rabbit hair to apply the paint.

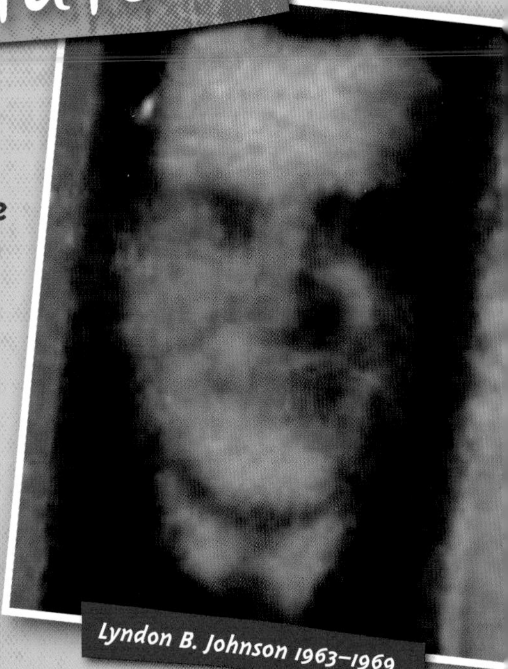

Lyndon B. Johnson 1963–1969

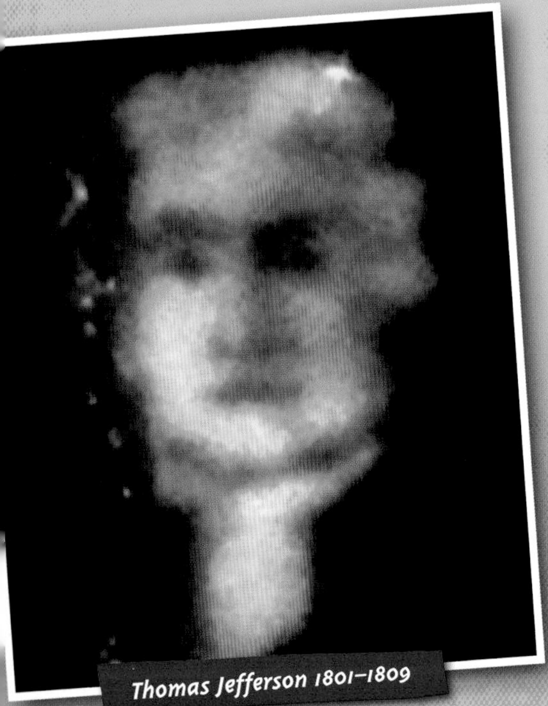

Ronald Reagan 1981–1989

Thomas Jefferson 1801–1809

George Washington 1789–1797

John Adams 1797–1801

Thomas Jefferson 1801–1809

James Madison 1809–1817

James Monroe 1817–1825

John Quincy Adams 1825–1829

Andrew Jackson 1829–1837

Martin Van Buren 1837–1841

William Henry Harrison 1841

John Tyler 1841–1845

James K. Polk 1845–1849

Zachary Taylor 1849–1850

Millard Fillmore 1850–1853

Franklin Pierce 1853–1857

James Buchanan 1857–1861

Abraham Lincoln 1861–1865

Andrew Johnson 1865–1869

Ulysses S. Grant 1869–1877

Rutherford B. Hayes 1877–1881

James A. Garfield 1881

Chester A. Arthur 1881–1885

Grover Cleveland 1885–1889 & 1893–1897

Benjamin Harrison 1889–1893

William McKinley 1897–1901

Theodore Roosevelt 1901–1909

William Howard Taft 1909–1913

Woodrow Wilson 1913–1921

Warren G. Harding 1921–1923

Calvin Coolidge 1923–1929

Herbert Hoover 1929–1933

Franklin D. Roosevelt 1933–1945

Harry S. Truman 1945–1953

Dwight D. Eisenhower 1953–1961

John F. Kennedy 1961–1963

Lyndon B. Johnson 1963–1969

Richard Nixon 1969–1974

Gerald Ford 1974–1977

Jimmy Carter 1977–1981

Ronald Reagan 1981–1989

George H. W. Bush 1989–1993

Bill Clinton 1993–2001

George W. Bush 2001–2009

John F. Kennedy 1961–1963

Richard Nixon 1969–1974

Beautiful Bite

To enhance their beauty, women in the Mentawai Islands of Indonesia have their teeth filed into sharp points. The unusual rite of passage, in which the teeth are chiseled into shape with no anesthetic, conforms to local opinions of beauty rather than any practical purpose. Observers have commented that Mentawai women seem to feel no pain during the process, and that they willingly undergo the ritual.

Worm's-eye View

After John Matthews of Bellevue, Iowa, noticed two spots obscuring the vision in his left eye, doctors diagnosed the cause—a worm had got into his eye. The worm—thought to be either a hookworm or a raccoon roundworm—was then killed by medics who shot a laser into his left eyeball. "I could see it from behind," he said, "moving, trying to dodge the laser."

Free Leg

Needing a $60,000 bionic leg so that he could walk again, David Huckvale of Leicestershire, England, happened to go to his local pub on the same day as surgeon Alistair Gibson, who specializes in fitting the computer-controlled limbs. When the two got talking, Mr. Gibson mentioned he had a spare leg and could fit it for free!

Changing Beard

Sameer Mehta, a businessman from Gujarat, India, makes weekly trips to the barber and has had more than 60 styles of short beard in the last four years. These have included a heart-shaped beard and another trimmed in the design of his country's flag.

Rare Phenomenon

A woman who had been pronounced dead hours earlier at a hospital in Cali, Colombia, following a series of unsuccessful resuscitation attempts, suddenly started breathing again in a funeral home as workers began to apply formaldehyde to her body. Doctors later diagnosed her condition as a case of Lazarus Syndrome, an extremely rare phenomenon in which the body's circulation spontaneously restarts after failed resuscitations.

26 Digits

Heramb Ashok Kumthekar from Goa, India, has six fingers on each hand and seven toes on each foot, giving him a total of 26 digits. He is proud of his condition, called polydactylism, even though he has insufficient nerve endings to feel all his fingers and toes.

Super Schoolgirl

At just 16 years old, schoolgirl Marvadene Anderson stood 6 ft 11 in (2.1 m) tall, making the New Jersey school basketball star 5 in (12.5 cm) taller than her idol, Michael Jordan. Height must run in the family, because the Jamaican-born teenager's older sister, Kimberly, is 6 ft 4 in (1.9 m) tall.

Bullet in Head

After being shot at point-blank range by a German soldier in 1944, Ivan Nikulin of Chita, Russia, lived happily with a bullet lodged in his head for nearly 70 years.

Nose Leech

Tyrannobdella rex, a new species of leech with savage, sawlike teeth, was first discovered in the nose of a nine-year-old Peruvian girl. Named after the most ferocious dinosaur in history, the 2-in (5-cm) bloodsucker came to light after the girl, who regularly swam in tropical rivers and lakes, complained of feeling a sliding sensation in one of her nostrils.

Body Piercing

In April 2010, Ed Bruns of Gillette, Wyoming, had more than 1,500 16-gauge needles inserted into his arms, back, and legs by a body-piercing artist in less than 4½ hours.

Tattoo Proposal

When San Diego, California, tattoo artist Joe Wittenberg decided to propose to his girlfriend, he inked the words "Rachel, will you marry me?" on his own leg.

Dissecting Dad

To help teach anatomy to his students, Dr. Mahantesh Ramannavar dissected the body of his father, Dr. Basavanneppa Ramannavar, which had been embalmed for exactly two years. His father had specified in his will that his body should be donated to the university in Belgaum, India, where his son worked and that his son should perform the dissection, which was shown live on Indian TV.

Serial Sleeper

Claire Allen from Cambridge, England, falls asleep 100 times a day. Her condition—an extreme form of narcolepsy—causes her to fall into a trancelike state where she is unable to see or move. Each episode lasts between 30 seconds and five minutes and is triggered by emotions such as surprise and anger, and especially surfaces when she laughs.

Join the Dots

Inspired by the idea of getting her birthmarks numbered, Colleen A.F. Venable from New York City has a connect-the-dots tattoo that creates the shape of a giraffe on her left leg.

Turning the Screw

After an operation to remove a tumor left a gaping hole in his leg, 14-year-old Simeon Fairburn from Brisbane, Australia, saved the limb by turning surgical screws on a leg brace four times every day for over two years to stretch the bone by 1 ft (30 cm). He initially faced amputation, but after wearing the brace and undergoing 20 operations, he still has a chance of achieving his dream and becoming a basketball player.

Skewered Neck

Twelve-year-old Garret Mullikin from Houston, Texas, survived after a 9-in-long (23-cm) stick skewered his neck. Falling off a dirt bike, he hit the ground and the piece of tree branch, as thick as a broom handle, plunged into his neck and down into his chest, through his lung, and past vital arteries and his heart. Doctors said that if the stick had been pulled out before he was in hospital, he could have bled to death.

Hiccup Cure

After hiccupping an estimated 20 million times over a period of three years, Chris Sands of Lincolnshire, England, finally stopped in 2009 following brain surgery. It is thought that a tumor on his brain stem had been pushing on nerves, causing him to hiccup every two seconds, 24 hours a day.

Diamond Tattoo

South African jeweler Yair Shimansky designed a temporary tattoo made of 612 diamonds and carrying a price tag of $924,000. It took more than eight hours to encrust the ornate floral design on the skin of a model using a special water-based adhesive.

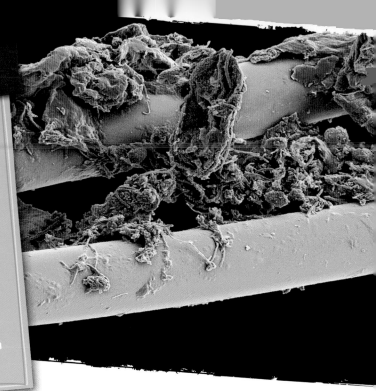

Dental Dirt

This is what your used dental floss looks like when magnified more than 500 times. Dental plaque, formed from bacteria and saliva, is clearly visible on the tiny floss fibers. Photographer Steve Gschmeissner from Bedford, England, used an electron microscope capable of magnifying objects more than 500,000 times to show everyday household items in a completely new light.

Guardian Angel

Angel Alvarez survived despite being shot 23 times by New York City police officers during a disturbance in August 2010. Although he was shot in the arms, legs, abdomen and jaw, all the bullets somehow missed his vital organs.

Deadly Device

U.S. Army Private Channing Moss survived a direct body hit from an anti-vehicular rocket in Afghanistan. Luckily, the explosive head failed to detonate, but he was impaled by the rocket shaft.

Tiny Tot

A premature baby boy born at the University of Goettingen Hospital, Germany, in 2009 survived despite weighing less than 10 oz (283 g) at birth. The tiny tot weighed just 9.7 oz (275 g)—which is 75 g (2.6 oz) below the weight doctors consider the minimum birth weight for a baby to survive.

Canadian Citizen

On December 31, 2008, a Ugandan woman gave birth on an airplane flying over Nova Scotia, Canada. Her newborn daughter was granted Canadian citizenship.

Reading Mystery

On July 31, 2001, Canadian mystery writer Howard Engel awoke from a stroke and discovered he could no longer read—but could still write. He was diagnosed as having alexia sine agraphia, which meant that newspapers and even his own books appeared to be written in indecipherable oriental script.

Supersized Son

At age three, Xiao Hao of Guangzhou, China, weighs a massive 140 lb (63.5 kg)—as much as an adult man. He dwarfs his mom and has been banned by some nurseries as a hazard to other children.

Extreme Survival

Jonathan Metz of West Hartford, Connecticut, saved his own life by partially sawing off his left arm after it had become trapped in his furnace boiler and started to turn gangrenous. Taking a blade from his toolbox, he began sawing through the arm to prevent the infection spreading to the rest of his body. To stem the flow of blood, he used first his shirt and then a telephone cord as a tourniquet. After more than two days—during which his only drink was rust-colored boiler water scooped into his mouth with a flip-flop he had been wearing—he was rescued and taken to hospital where doctors completed the amputation.

Rare Quads

In December 2009, Lisa Kelly of Middlesbrough, England, gave birth to a set of quadruplets made up of two sets of identical twins—a ten-million-to-one chance!

Vulture Tonic

In southern Africa, vultures' brains have become so popular as a traditional medicine that it has contributed to seven of the region's nine vulture species becoming endangered.

Knife Horror

Xiao Wei, a 16-year-old from Jilin, China, had a knife stabbed through his head that went in one side and out the other—but he survived after a two-hour operation to remove the blade.

Lucky Bounce

An 18-month-old boy escaped without a scratch after falling 80 ft (24.4m) from his seventh-floor apartment in Paris, France, bouncing off a café awning and into the arms of a passing doctor. The café was closed for the day and the awning was out only because a mechanism had jammed.

On the Run

Former British Army soldier Mike Buss from Swindon, England, completed 517¼ mi (832.4 km) on a treadmill over seven grueling days. He ran the equivalent of nearly three marathons a day, sleeping for just two hours a day, and lost two toenails in the process.

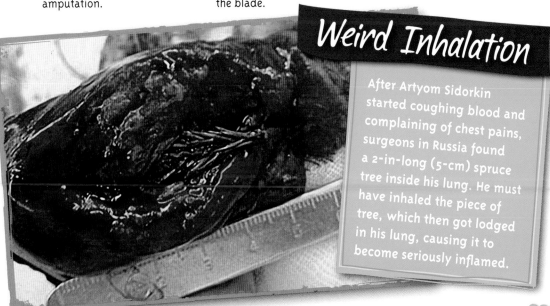

Weird Inhalation

After Artyom Sidorkin started coughing blood and complaining of chest pains, surgeons in Russia found a 2-in-long (5-cm) spruce tree inside his lung. He must have inhaled the piece of tree, which then got lodged in his lung, causing it to become seriously inflamed.

Self-service

After badly cutting his leg in an accident at home, a 32-year-old man became so frustrated at having to wait an hour at Sundsvall Hospital in northern Sweden that he picked up a needle and thread and sewed up the cut himself.

Tugged Off

In June 2009, a man from Shenzhen, China, was competing in a game of tug-of-war when he had his hand pulled off.

Born Twice

Doctors in Texas performed prenatal surgery at 25 weeks to remove a grapefruit-sized tumor from Macie McCartney, while she was still inside her mother's womb. The procedure involved pulling out the uterus of mother Keri and then half of Macie's body. Once free from the tumor, Macie was returned to the womb, where she recovered and grew for another ten weeks before being "born" again.

Snowshoe Beard

David Traver of Anchorage, Alaska, was the winner of the 2009 World Beard and Moustache Championships with his 20½-in-long (52-cm) beard woven to resemble a snowshoe.

Baby Frozen

Sixteen-week-old Finley Burton of County Daurham, England, was put in a hospital "deep freeze" for four days to keep him alive when complications arose after heart surgery. His heart had started to beat alarmingly quickly, so his body was placed in a "cool bag," through which cold air was pumped to keep his temperature down. This slowed his metabolism, which in turn slowed his heart rate.

Large Family

After giving birth to two sets of quadruplets (in 2004 and 2005), Dale Chalk of Sydney, New South Wales, Australia, had twins in 2009, giving her a total of 11 children under the age of seven.

Dangerous Operation

In March 2010, U.S. Army medical staff at Bagram airfield in Afghanistan wore armor in the operating room while removing a live high-explosive round from the scalp of a soldier from the Afghan Army.

Single Handed

Despite being born with just one hand, Kevin Shields from Fort William, Scotland, is an accomplished rock climber and has even mastered treacherous ice climbs.

Baby's Tail

Surgeons in China performed an operation to remove a 5-in-long (13-cm) tail from the body of a four-month-old baby girl. Hong Hong, from China's Anhui Province, was born with the tail, but it quickly doubled in size. X-rays had shown that it was connected to a fatty tumor within her spinal column.

Reverse Walker

Rotating his feet nearly 180 degrees, Bittu Gandhi of Rajkot, Gujarat, India, can walk backward while facing forward!

Parasitic Twin

Eighteen-month-old Kang Mengru of Henan Province, China, had her dead twin removed from her stomach. Her parents were puzzled by her increasingly swollen stomach, which made her look pregnant, until medical scans revealed that she was carrying the parasitic fetus of her unborn twin in her belly. In such rare cases—affecting one in 500,000 births—one twin in the womb grows larger than the other and envelops its smaller sibling. The second fetus never fully develops, but continues to grow within the first baby, feeding off it like a parasite.

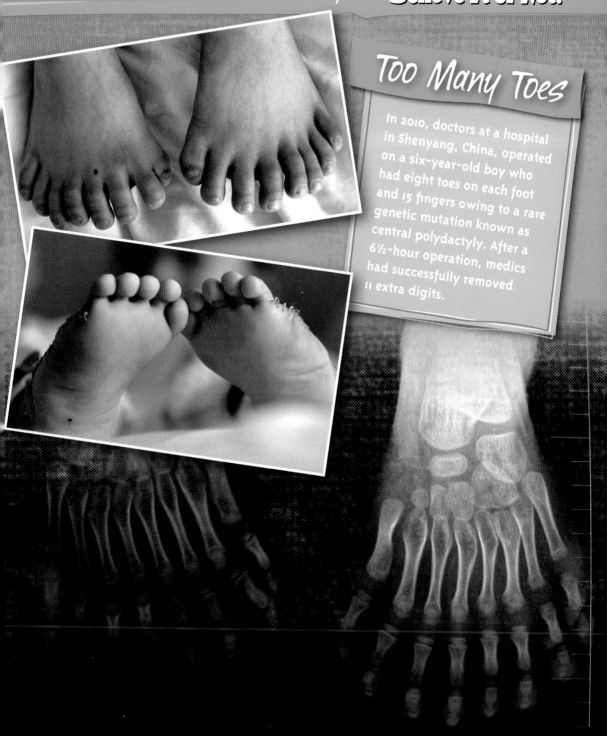

Too Many Toes

In 2010, doctors at a hospital in Shenyang, China, operated on a six-year-old boy who had eight toes on each foot and 15 fingers owing to a rare genetic mutation known as central polydactyly. After a 6½-hour operation, medics had successfully removed 11 extra digits.

A Bicycle Made for Two

Although Charles B. Tripp had no arms and Eli Bowen had no legs, they were able to ride a bicycle—together. Known to circus audiences as "The Armless Wonder" and "The Legless Wonder," they simply combined their physical attributes on a tandem bicycle—Tripp pedaling with his legs and Bowen steering with his arms.

Charles B. Tripp was born without arms in 1855 in Woodstock, Ontario, Canada, but soon learned to dress himself and write using his feet. Remarkably, he made his living as a skilled carpenter until joining Barnum's Circus, which was the start of a 50-year career as a performer. He specialized in penmanship, portrait painting and paper cutting—holding the implements between his toes. Around the turn of the century, he developed an interest in photography and became known as "The Armless Photographer." He died in 1939 in Salisbury, North Carolina, at the grand age of 84.

Eli Bowen was born in Ohio in 1844. He was one of ten children, all of whom were able-bodied except for Eli who had seal limbs, or phocomelia, a condition that left him with no legs and with two feet of different sizes growing from his hips. As a child he walked on his arms, perfecting a technique whereby he held wooden blocks in his hands that enabled him to swing his hips between his arms. The strength he gained from this helped him become a talented acrobat and, at the age of 13, he joined his first circus troupe.

Despite his condition, Eli was considered by many to be the most handsome man in showbusiness and, at age 26, he married Mattie Haight who was ten years his junior. The couple had four healthy sons. Eli continued performing into his eighties, and his death, from pleurisy in 1924, was just days before he was due to appear at The Dreamland Circus at Coney Island, New York.

Eli Bowen with his wife and son.

Charles Tripp having a cup of tea.

Lick Off

Actor Nick Afanasiev from California has an incredible role all to himself—as the owner of America's longest tongue! Stretching to an unbelievable 3.5 in (9 cm), it means that Nick can lick his own nose and even his elbow, a bizarre feat that most people find impossible.

Snake Twins

In June 2009, in Xiaogan, eastern China, Hui Chung gave birth to conjoined twins, who were known as the "snake babies" because they were attached at the waist. The siblings shared one long body with a head at each end, and as they did not have external sexual organs, it was impossible to say what sex they were.

Long Hair

When 79-year-old Tran Van Hay died in Kien Giang, Vietnam, in February 2010, his hair was more than 22 ft (6.7 m) long and weighed 23 lb (10.5 kg). He began to let his hair grow more than 50 years ago, because he often became sick after a haircut. As his hair grew, he balanced it on his head like a basket.

Miracle Escape

A Japanese toddler who wandered onto rail tracks in Suzaka City escaped with only scratches after a train came to a halt on top of her. After spotting the girl, the driver applied the emergency brakes and the train stopped with the girl beneath. She survived because she was trapped in the 20-in (50-cm) gap between the train and the tracks.

Scorched Footprints

For two weeks in 2009, Sikeli Nadiri left a trail of scorched footprints on grassland around his home village in Fiji. There was no explanation as to why the grass had burned away beneath his feet, as he had not stepped on any chemicals or anything else that would cause scorching.

Nickel Allergy

Kim Taylor from Northamptonshire, England, is unable to touch hundreds of everyday items like keys, coins, zippers, scissors, door handles and saucepans because she is severely allergic to nickel. She takes her own wooden-handled cutlery to restaurants and has to cover everything nickel—even her eyeglasses, bra clasp, and buttons—in nail varnish so that her skin doesn't ever come into contact with the metal.

Turtle Boy

Maimaiti Hali from Heping, China, was born with a hard, mutated growth covering most of his back, its shell-like appearance leading bullies to call him "Turtle Boy." The growth was removed from the eight-year-old's back in a two-hour operation in 2010 and replaced with skin grafts from his scalp and legs.

Rope Bed

Gao Yang of Liaoning Province, China, can sleep on a single length of rope tied between two trees for up to seven hours at a time. He was taught special balancing skills at age 12 but it took him nearly a quarter of a century to master this feat by practicing on a 10-ft-high (3-m) rope in his local park every morning.

Cat Boy

A boy in Dahua, China, has bright blue eyes that glow in the dark and enable him to see in the pitch black. Nong Youhui can read perfectly in complete darkness and also has good vision during the day. Medical experts think he was born with a rare condition called leukodermia, which has left his eyes with less protective pigment and made them more sensitive to light.

Sum Girl

A 15-year-old schoolgirl with a love of math was awakened from a coma when her father began asking her simple sums. Vicki Alex of Northamptonshire, England, had been unconscious for three days and had failed to respond to other attempts to stimulate her brain, but after her father's intervention she soon regained full consciousness.

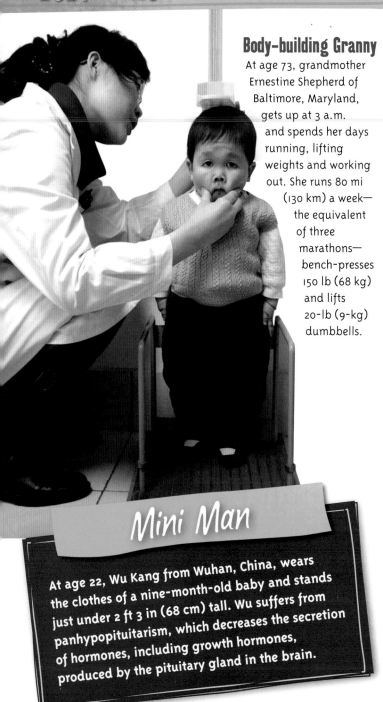

Body-building Granny

At age 73, grandmother Ernestine Shepherd of Baltimore, Maryland, gets up at 3 a.m. and spends her days running, lifting weights and working out. She runs 80 mi (130 km) a week—the equivalent of three marathons—bench-presses 150 lb (68 kg) and lifts 20-lb (9-kg) dumbbells.

Heart Stopped

Joseph Tiralosi of Brooklyn, New York City, miraculously survived after his heart stopped beating for 45 minutes. The 56-year-old father had gone into sudden cardiac arrest inside the emergency room at New York-Presbyterian/Weill Cornell Medical Center, and it was nearly an hour before doctors succeeded in getting his heart going again. Usually if a person cannot be revived within six minutes, they die. Equally incredibly, he came through the whole episode without suffering any form of brain damage.

Sandwich Bag

To keep up the body temperature of a tiny premature baby, medics at Worcestershire Royal Hospital in England used the smallest insulating jacket they could find—a 6-in (15-cm) plastic sandwich bag from the hospital kitchens. The improvised insulator did the trick and saved the life of little Lexi Lacey who had been born 14 weeks early weighing just 14 oz (396 g) and had been given only a ten percent chance of survival.

Mini Man

At age 22, Wu Kang from Wuhan, China, wears the clothes of a nine-month-old baby and stands just under 2 ft 3 in (68 cm) tall. Wu suffers from panhypopituitarism, which decreases the secretion of hormones, including growth hormones, produced by the pituitary gland in the brain.

Breathe In!

Steve McFarlane of South Jordan, Utah, can displace some of his internal organs to suck in his stomach with spectacular effect.

Free Flights

Thirty-one-year-old Liew Siaw Hsia gave birth on an AirAsia flight over Malaysia in October 2009, and as a result the company granted her and her child free flights for life.

Second Face

A baby born in China's Hunan Province has two faces. Kangkang was born in 2009 with a transverse facial cleft that extends nearly all the way up to his ears, making it look as if he is wearing a mask.

Gold Tattoo

A business in Dubai offers temporary body tattoos made of real gold. The 24-carat gold-leaf tattoos are in demand for glitzy parties and weddings and can be bought for as little as $50. The company is also offering tattoos in platinum.

Poke-a-Nut

During a 2009 martial-arts demonstration in Malacca, Malaysia, Ho Eng Hui pierced four coconuts with his index finger in 31.8 seconds.

Making Antivenom

Snake antivenom is commonly produced by injecting horses with snake venom, then collecting the appropriate antibodies from their blood.

Mass Extraction

Between the ages of seven and 12, Chelsea Keysaw of Kinnear, Wyoming, underwent three oral surgeries to remove a total of 13 extra permanent teeth and 15 baby teeth.

Foot Skills

Born without arms, Ren Jiemei from Shandong Province, China, has learned to use her feet to eat, wash, comb her hair, draw pictures and cut paper. She is so skilled with her feet that when she uses them to thread a needle she is always successful on the first attempt—in fact, she is said to be the best embroiderer in her village. In her school days, she often topped the class despite having to write with her feet and use her mouth to turn book pages.

Tattooed Mom

Bishop's daughter and mother-of-three Jinxi Boo, from southern California, has almost her entire body covered in tattoos. She has a tattoo of a black-and-white dairy cow (because she's vegan), portraits of her family, and her favorite musicians (Gwen Stefani, Björk, Cyndi Lauper and Meg White), plus a spectacular octopus tattoo across her throat and chest that took 26 hours to complete. A trip to Disneyland as a teenager inspired her love of tattoos, but she did not have her first design—a small cherry on her ankle—until she was 30.

Route 66

Ron Jones of Bartlesville, Oklahoma, gets his kicks out of having Route 66 tattoos all over his body. He has more than 80 tattoos dedicated to destinations along the 2,448-mi (3,940-km) highway, including the Ariston Café in Litchfield, Illinois, and the arch on the Santa Monica Pier in California, which marks the end of the road.

Einstein Scan

An X-ray of Albert Einstein's skull fetched more than $35,000 at a 2010 auction in Beverly Hills, California. The genius scientist had the scan in 1945, ten years before his death at age 76.

Caught Toddler

Two-year-old Zhang Fangyu survived a 100-ft (30-m) fall in Hangzhou, Zhejiang Province, China, in June 2011 after she climbed out of a 10th-floor window and was caught by a woman walking in the street below. Her rescuer, Wu Juping, suffered multiple fractures to her arm.

Skydiving Champ

Despite losing both his legs in a bomb explosion in Northern Ireland in 1992, former paratrooper Alistair Hodgson of Cumbria, England, is a freestyle skydiving champion and has made more than 5,000 jumps.

Arm Wrestler

Joby Mathew from Kerala, India, may be only 3 ft 5 in (1.05 m) tall but he is a champion arm wrestler. Despite having severely underdeveloped legs, he is able to defeat able-bodied opponents who are twice his height. He can also jump up steps using only his hands and perform push-ups on just one hand.

Miracle Boy

Seventeen-month-old Jessiah Jackson of Leland, North Carolina, fell from a chair in July 2010 and a metal hook pierced his skull. It penetrated 2 in (5 cm) into his brain, but he survived.

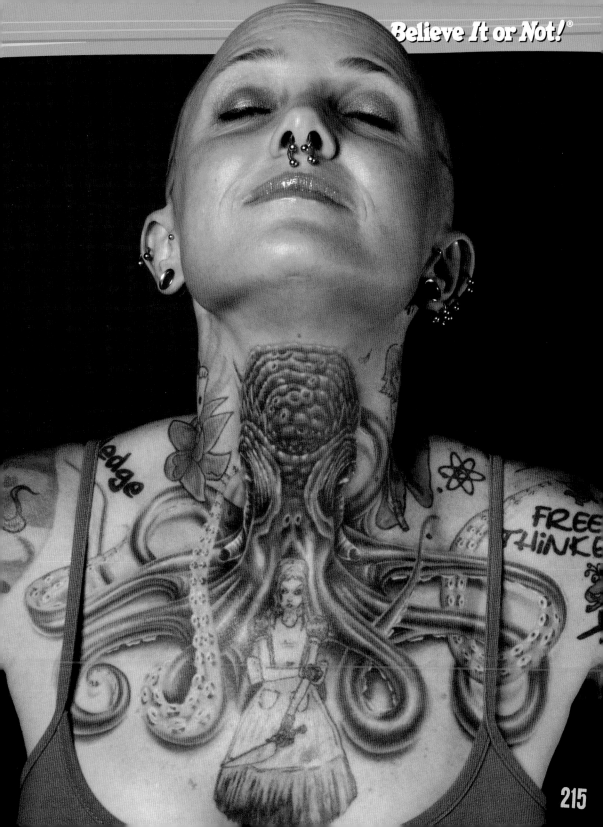

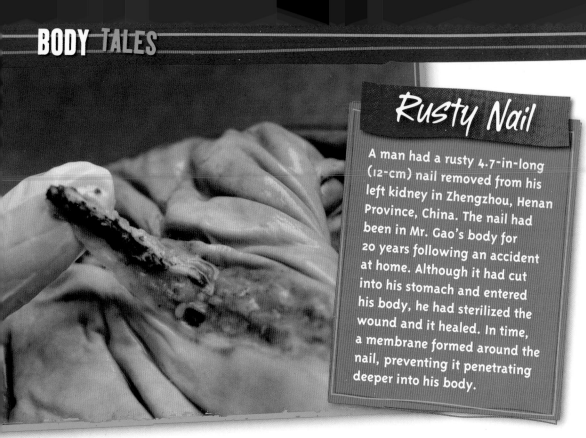

Rusty Nail

A man had a rusty 4.7-in-long (12-cm) nail removed from his left kidney in Zhengzhou, Henan Province, China. The nail had been in Mr. Gao's body for 20 years following an accident at home. Although it had cut into his stomach and entered his body, he had sterilized the wound and it healed. In time, a membrane formed around the nail, preventing it penetrating deeper into his body.

Glass Eater

Wang Xianjun of Sichuan Province, China, has eaten more than 1,500 lightbulbs. He started snacking on broken glass when he was 12 because it was "crispy and delicious," and now regularly eats a bulb for breakfast. He smashes the bulb and swallows it piece by piece while sipping from a glass of water. Although his bizarre diet has apparently not affected his health, it did cost him his marriage. He had kept his glass munching a secret from his wife, but when she caught him, she thought it was too weird and they separated.

Blood Camp

The Indian political party Shiv Sena collected 24,200 bottles of human blood in a single day at a blood donation camp in Goregaon.

Saved by Implants

When a gunman opened fire with a semiautomatic assault rifle in a dentist's office in Beverly Hills, California, Lydia Carranza's life was saved by her size-D breast implants, which took the force of the blow and stopped bullet fragments from reaching her vital organs.

Impaled by Tree

A 13-in-long (33-cm) tree limb crashed through the windshield as Michelle Childers of Kamiah, Idaho, and her husband were driving down the road, impaling her through the neck. Amazingly, she survived.

Sticky Situation

Irmgard Holm, 70, of Phoenix, Arizona, sealed her eye shut after mistakenly using quick-drying glue instead of eye drops. She had confused the two products' similar-looking bottles. Doctors cut off the glue covering her eye and washed out the remainder to prevent serious damage.

Titanic Tumor

Doctors in Buenos Aires, Argentina, removed a tumor weighing 50 lb 11 oz (23 kg) from the womb of a 54-year-old woman in 2010. It had been growing inside her body for 18 months. She entered a hospital for the operation weighing 308 lb (140 kg), but after the removal of the tumor she was discharged weighing just 231 lb (105 kg).

Head Returned

Lewis Powell, a conspirator in the assassination of U.S. President Abraham Lincoln, was hanged in 1865 and was buried headless. His skull had been missing for 127 years when it was found in storage in the Smithsonian Museum and returned to the body.

Tongue Typist

Legally blind and unable to use his hands, Josh LaRue of New Concord, Ohio, wrote a book by tapping out the words in Morse Code using his tongue.

Bee Therapy

Bed-ridden multiple sclerosis sufferer Sami Chugg from Bristol, England, was able to get back on her feet after being stung 1,500 times by bees. The Bee Venom Therapy, carried out over a period of 18 months, involved holding a bee in a pair of tweezers and deliberately stinging an area of skin around her spine.

Chinese Accent

After suffering a severe migraine headache in March 2010, Sarah Colwill of Plymouth, Devon, England, suddenly started speaking with a Chinese accent—despite never having been to that country. Doctors say she has Foreign Accent Syndrome, a rare condition that damages the part of the brain that controls our speech and word formation.

Monster Stone

A kidney stone the size of a coconut was removed by surgeons in Hungary from the stomach of Sandor Sarkadi. Whereas even the largest kidney stones are seldom bigger than a golf ball, this one measured a whopping 6¾ in (17 cm) in diameter and weighed 2½ lb (1.1 kg).

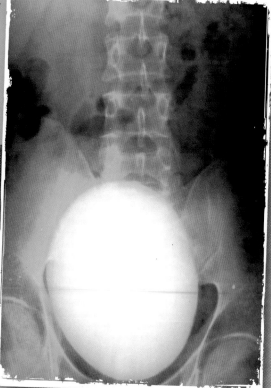

Accidents Happen

SHARP REMINDER

X-rays were first observed in 1895 by German physicist Wilhelm Roentgen, who found them accidentally while experimenting with vacuum tubes. A form of electromagnetic radiation, they have gone on to become one of the most useful tools in medical practice, employed for identifying everything from broken bones to accidentally swallowed toothbrushes.

KEY LOCATION

SAFETY PIN

Bumpy Landing

In June 2009, window cleaner Alex Clay from Eau Claire, Wisconsin, fell six floors, bounced off a concrete first-floor roof, and landed on the ground—surviving with nothing worse than a broken foot bone and a cut on his leg.

Botox Cure

A stroke victim who had been paralyzed for more than 20 years was able to walk again after being injected with Botox, a substance usually associated with smoothing wrinkles. Having been told by doctors that he would never regain his mobility, Russell McPhee of Victoria, Australia, was able to stand up and walk a few yards just a month after his first Botox injection.

Chopstick Removal

A Chinese man had a chopstick removed from his stomach 28 years after swallowing it. Mr. Zhang had swallowed the chopstick in 1982, but thought it had been digested until he started suffering stomach pains. X-rays revealed that the remains of the chopstick were still lodged inside him. Surgeons in Shanghai extricated it by making a small incision in his stomach.

Chance Discovery

An X-ray of a 35-year-old woman from Para, Brazil, who complained of earache revealed that she had over 20 steel needles in her body. She had inserted the needles into herself as a child.

Fatal Pick

In September 2008, a man from Manchester, England, died from a nosebleed caused by his aggressive nose picking.

Horned Man

Jesse Thornhill of Tulsa, Oklahoma, has two devil horns on his head, created by surgically implanting Teflon lumps under the skin to stretch the scalp. The heavy-metal fan also boasts tattooed eyebrows, lengthened earlobes, and implant earrings on his head.

Echo Location

A blind English boy has learned to "see" again after adopting a technique used by dolphins and bats to detect where objects are. Jamie Aspland from Ashford, Kent, navigates his way around obstacles by means of echolocation, whereby he utters high-pitch clicks and then interprets the sound that rebounds off the surfaces around him.

Tortoise Woman

For nearly 30 years, Sun Fengqin from Inner Mongolia carried a 55-lb (25-kg) tumor on her back, which resulted in her being nicknamed "Tortoise Woman." The tumor started as a yellow birthmark but grew so large that in the end she struggled to walk upright.

Rubber Man

Vijay Sharma of Rajasthan, India, is so flexible that he can pass his body through a tennis racket, wind his arms around his back so that his hands grip each other at the front of his waist, wrap his legs over his head, and drink from bottles that he has gripped between his toes.

Souvenir Finger

After losing part of his small finger, Matthew Tipler of Bend, Oregon, took the tip, encased it in clear plastic, and made a keychain out of it.

Amnesia Victim

In 2009, a man later identified as Edward Lighthart walked out of a park in Seattle, Washington, with $600 in his sock but with no idea of who he was and how he got there—the victim of a rare form of dissociative amnesia.

Tall Teen

At age 14, Brazilian teenager Elisany Silva towers over her sisters because she is already 6 ft 9 in (2.06 m) tall. She is so tall that she had to stop going to school because she could not fit on the bus. Medical experts believe she could be suffering from gigantism, a condition in which the body produces excessive amounts of growth hormones. If left untreated she could continue to grow up to 6 in (15 cm) more a year.

Hidden Needle

Doctors in China's Henan Province removed a needle from a man's brain that may have been there for 50 years. Following a seizure, Lin Yaohui, 51, was rushed to hospital where X-rays revealed the 2-in-long (5-cm) metal needle embedded in his skull. As an adult's skull is hard, surgeons believe the needle must have penetrated his head before he was 18 months old.

Bearded Lady

When she suddenly started to grow facial hair in the 1920s, Mrs. Baker B. Twyman of Peoria, Illinois, supported her family by joining the circus as a bearded lady. She later had the surplus hair surgically removed.

Name Jinx

The parents of a boy who has failed to grow since being born on Dwarf Street claim the name has jinxed their child. Four-year-old Liu Chengrui from Wuhan, China, still weighs just 11 lb (5 kg) and stands only 2 ft (60 cm) tall.

Eye Twitch

Barbara Watkins of Halifax, England, suffers from a rare and bizarre condition that causes her to wink thousands of times a day. She has blepharospasm, an incurable condition that causes frequent muscle contractions around the eyes and affects just a handful of people in every million.

High Life

Husband and wife Wayne and Laurie Hallquist of Stockton, California, measure a combined height of 13 ft 4 in (4.07 m). He stands 6 ft 10 in (2.1 m) and she is 6 ft 6 in (1.97 m).

Extra Bones

Dan Aziere of Danbury, Connecticut, suffers from multiple hereditary exostoses, a rare genetic disorder that causes extra bones to keep growing in his body. He estimates that he has about 50 excess bones—some as large as 4 in (10 cm) long—and since the age of five he has had more than a dozen operations to remove them.

Sneezed Bullet

A man who was shot in the head during New Year's Eve celebrations in Naples, Italy, survived after sneezing the bullet out of his nose. The .22 calibre bullet went through the right side of Darco Sangermano's head, behind his eye socket, and lodged in his nasal passage. Bleeding heavily, he was rushed to a hospital but while waiting to be seen by doctors, he sneezed and the bullet flew out of his right nostril.

Tiny Tot

At 21 years old, Hatice Kocaman from Kadirli, Turkey, has the body mass of an eight-month-old baby. She suffers from a rare bone disease and stands just 28 in (70 cm) tall and weighs only 15 lb (6.8 kg).

Belly Button Bears

Artist Rachel Betty Case from Bethlehem, Pennsylvania, turns belly button fluff into tiny bears. She collects the lint from the belly buttons of male friends and sells her cute fluffy creations in small glass jars.

Eight Limbs

Before having an operation to remove them when he was seven years old, Deepak Paswaan of Bihar, India, had four extra limbs—the result of being born with the arms, legs, and buttocks of a parasitic twin protruding from his chest. Although the parasitic twin's arms were small and withered, its legs grew at the same rate as Deepak, meaning the youngster had to carry a heavy weight around.

Talented Toes

Since having both arms amputated at age ten after an accident, Liu Wei of Beijing, China, has learned to do everything with his feet. He uses his toes to eat, dress himself, brush his teeth and surf the Internet. He even plays the piano with his toes and earned a standing ovation when he performed on the TV show *China's Got Talent*, which he then went on to win.

Bullet Surprise

A 35-year-old Polish man who went to a hospital in Bochum, Germany, worried about a small lump on the back of his head, was unaware that he had been shot five years earlier. It was only when doctors removed a .22 caliber bullet from his skull that he remembered receiving a blow to the head around midnight at a New Year's Party.

Metal Muncher

Doctors in Cajamarca, Peru, removed 2 lb 3 oz (1 kg) of metal from a man's stomach, including nails, coins, copper wire and scrap metal. Requelme Abanto Alvarado said he had been eating metal for months and had once swallowed 17 5-in (13-cm) nails in one day.

Not Twins

In 2010, Angie Cromar from Murray, Utah, found herself pregnant with two babies at the same time—but they weren't twins. She was born with a rare condition called didelphys, meaning two uteruses, and she had conceived in both—at odds of one in five million.

New Language

A 13-year-old Croatian girl woke from a 24-hour coma speaking fluent German. The girl was no longer able to speak Croatian but was able to communicate perfectly in German, a language that she had only just started studying at school.

Self-amputation

Ramlan, an 18-year-old construction worker who was trapped by a fallen concrete girder in the rubble of a building that collapsed during a 2009 earthquake in Padang, Indonesia, survived by sawing off his own leg.

Toddler Plunge

Two-year-old Zhu Xinping had a miraculous escape after falling from the 21st floor of an apartment block in Jianyang City, Sichuan Province, China. She escaped with nothing worse than a broken leg after landing on a freshly dug pile of soil that cushioned her fall.

Long Lobes

Jian Tianjin, a farmer from Taiwan, has stretchy earlobes that make his ears 6½ in (16 cm) in length. His lobes are so long and flexible that they reach his shoulders and can be wound around his chin.

Hairy Hands

Since becoming the first American to undergo a double hand transplant, Jeff Kepner from Augusta, Georgia, has noticed that his new hands are considerably hairier than the rest of his body because the donor had more hair than him.

Gall Stones

Doctors in Shenyang, Liaoning Province, China, removed more than 880 stones from the gall bladder of a 67-year-old woman. Mrs. Miao's gall bladder was so full of stones it had swollen to the size of a fist, forcing doctors to remove the whole bladder. They estimated that the stones had been forming inside her for about 20 years.

Sucked Hair

After her car swerved off the road in Colorado, Cynthia Hoover survived for five days in the freezing wilderness of the Rocky Mountains by sucking water from her wet hair into her mouth. She was eventually found because she managed to crawl 450 yd (410 m)—despite having 11 broken ribs, a punctured lung and several broken vertebrae—to where she heard voices coming from a disused mine.

Still Singing

After suffering a stroke, singer Ann Arscott of Birmingham, England, was left unable to speak—but she could still sing. She has aphasia, a condition caused by damage to the areas of the brain responsible for language. It impairs speech, but some people with it can still sing, as music activates a different part of the brain.

Celebrity Tattoos

Steve Porter from Nottingham, England, has 12 autographed pictures of celebrities—including Alice Cooper, Anastacia and Ozzy Osbourne—inked onto his skin as tattoos. In total, he has more than 20 tattoos of actors and rock stars covering his body.

Body Bacteria

There are as many as ten times the number of living bacteria and bugs in and on our bodies as there are human cells. Of the estimated 100 trillion microbes, the most densely populated areas of flesh are the belly button, the bottoms of the feet and between the fingers.

Sneezed Nail

Prax Sanchez, 72, of Colorado Springs, Colorado, had an MRI scan for an ear problem, which dislodged a nail in his head that he then coughed up after the procedure. He had no idea that the nail was there and it could have been decades old.

First-aid App

During the 65 hours that U.S. filmmaker Dan Woolley was trapped following the Haitian earthquake in January 2010, he used an iPhone first-aid application to treat his fractured leg and head wound.

Deep Sleep

A Polish man woke up from a 19-year coma to find the Communist Party no longer in power and food no longer rationed. After being hit by a train in 1988, railway worker Jan Grzebski also slept through the weddings of four of his children and the births of 11 grandchildren.

Facial Transplant

Thirty Spanish doctors at the Vall D'Hebron Hospital in Barcelona worked for 22 hours in March 2010 to perform a full facial transplant on a patient, which included skin, nerves, muscles, nose, lips, cheekbones, teeth and a jawbone. The recipient, a 31-year-old man, is eventually expected to regain up to 90 percent of his facial functions.

Star Wars Tattoos

Star Wars fan Luke Kaye from Wiltshire, England, has undergone more than 100 hours of pain to have his body tattooed. His back, arms and legs are covered with tattoos of over a dozen characters from all six Star Wars movies, including Luke Skywalker, C-3PO and Darth Vader.

Churchill's Chompers

A pair of gold-plated false teeth owned by former British Prime Minister Winston Churchill sold at auction for £15,000 ($24,000) in 2010. Without his dentures, Churchill would never have been able to make his rousing wartime speeches—in fact, they were so valuable to him that he carried a spare set at all times.

Long Locks

Asha Mandela from
Clermont, Florida, has
hair that measures
over 19 ft (6 m),
longer than a pickup
truck. Asha has not
had her hair cut
for an astonishing
25 years.

225

Furry Features

Supatra Sasuphan from Bangkok, Thailand, was born with Ambras Syndrome—or congenital hypertrichosis—a rare genetic disease that causes excessive hair growth on the face and other parts of the body.

It affects one person in a billion, and there are fewer than 40 known cases in the world. There is no permanent cure for the condition, but nine-year-old Supatra doesn't let it affect her life and enjoys the same activities as her schoolfriends. She hopes eventually to become a teacher.

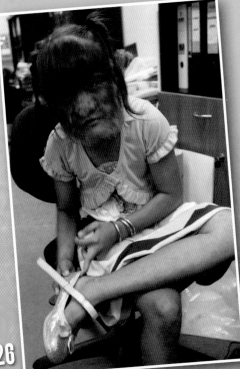

Parachute Plunge

When her parachute became entangled seconds after she exited an airplane above South Africa, skydiver Lareece Butler plunged 3,000 ft (915 m) before hitting the ground—she survived with a broken leg, broken pelvis, bruises and concussion.

Seven-foot Worm

Sailing on board the ship *Elizabeth* from Cork, Ireland, to Quebec, Canada, in June 1825, 12-year-old Ellen McCarthy fell ill and coughed up three intestinal worms, the longest of which measured 7 ft 3 in (2.2 m).

Lightning Strike

Dog-walker Brad Gifford of Kettering, England, had a miraculous escape after he was knocked unconscious, burst both eardrums, and exploded into flames when a 300,000-volt bolt of lightning struck him on the ear. The lightning was traveling at 14,000 mph (22,500 km/h) and had heated the air around it to 54,032°F (30,000°C)—five times hotter than the surface of the Sun.

Illustrated Lady

Julia Gnuse of Foothill Ranch, California, got her first tattoo to cover unsightly blisters on her legs, but she became hooked and now has tattoos over 95 percent of her body, including her face. Known as "The Illustrated Lady," her body drawings include jungle scenes, cartoons, and the cast of *Bewitched*.

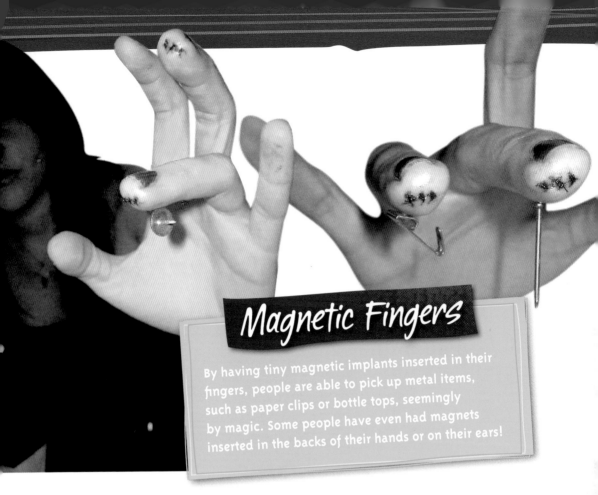

Magnetic Fingers

By having tiny magnetic implants inserted in their fingers, people are able to pick up metal items, such as paper clips or bottle tops, seemingly by magic. Some people have even had magnets inserted in the backs of their hands or on their ears!

Big Baby

At ten months old, Lei Lei, a baby from Hunan Province, China, weighed 44 lb (20 kg)—equivalent to the weight of an average six-year-old.

Back to Life

A 73-year-old woman was brought back to life 30 minutes after her heart stopped beating during a hospital test in Changsha, China. Usually a person dies if they cannot be revived within six minutes.

Ate Finger

In a protest over unpaid wages, a Serbian union official chopped off his finger and ate it. Zoran Bulatovic, a union leader at a textile factory in Novi Pazar, was so angry because some of his fellow workers had not been paid for several years that he used a hacksaw to chop off most of the little finger on his left hand and then ate it to underline the fact that the workers could no longer afford to eat conventional food.

Beatle Tattoo

Beatles fan Rose Ann Belluso of Downington, Pennsylvania, took a sign to Paul McCartney's Philadelphia show in August 2010 asking him to sign her back with a marker pen that she had brought along. After the singer called her up on stage and obliged, she decided to make the inscription permanent the next day by getting a tattoo artist to ink over the signature.

ALES

f... Boom!

ndi Susanto of
lost six of his
a cigarette he
ng mysteriously
in February 2010.

reak

ymond Curry
ed his car near his
Northumberland,
he was rushed to
ital with a fence post
through his chest.
ospital, doctors were
to see that the post
azingly missed all of
organs. They found
eafed clover stuck
ack!

Saving Lives

Ben Kopp, a U.S. Army Ranger
Corporal, was killed while
saving six soldiers in a firefight
and then helped save the lives
of 75 others by donating his
organs and tissues.

Little Miss Dynamite

Dr. Thienna Ho, 5 ft (1.5 m)
tall and weighing barely
95 lb (43 kg), deadlifted
104,846 lb (47,557 kg) in
one hour in San Francisco.
The barbell she lifted weighed
46 lb (21 kg)—nearly half
her body weight. She has
previously completed more
than 5,000 sumo squats in
one hour.

Sprouting Pea

Doctors in Cape Cod,
Massachusetts, investigating
the cause of a patient's
sickness, were stunned to
find that he had a pea plant
growing in his lung. They
believe Ron Sveden, from
nearby Brewster, had eaten
a pea at some time in the
previous couple of months
but that it had gone down
the wrong way, and the
seed had split inside him
and started to sprout,
growing to about
½ in (1 cm) in size.

Self-styled

Etienne Dumont, a journalist from Geneva,
Switzerland, has some of the most stunning body
modifications in the world. He is tattooed from head
to toe with vibrant images including skulls, flowers
and animals, but most striking are the designs
covering his face and a hole stretched in his chin,
held open by a transparent disk through which
you can see his teeth. He also has a synthetic horn
implant protruding from his scalp and has also used
progressively larger disks to stretch his earlobes.

231

EXTRAORDINARY

ART

Body of Work

A closer look at these images reveals that they are all created using the human body. By painting directly onto skin, artist Craig Tracy of New Orleans, Louisiana, manipulates the natural shape of his models against a meticulously designed background, creating mind-blowing illusions without the use of computer trickery.

Craig uses photographs to plan the image and then models often sit for hours at a time as he applies the paint, with each painting taking on average one day to complete.

IMMACULATE

Immaculate *features a hand-painted and airbrushed background. Once the models are in position, Craig adds the final paint to their body.*

BUTTERFLY

Named after the butterfly shape visible on the nose of the panther, Craig completed Butterfly in one mammoth 24-hour session, with only one hour of sleep for both him and his model.

Crochet Lions

English "crochetdermist" Shauna Richardson spent two years hand-crocheting three huge lions, each measuring 25 ft (7.5 m) long and 10 ft (3 m) high. She crocheted the skins in wool, accurately tracing the animals' muscular contours, over a polystyrene and steel framework. Shauna also crochets life-size pieces, which have included wild boars, bears and baboons.

New York Bears

Joshua Allen Harris placed inflatable polar bears made from discarded plastic bags above ventilation grates in the New York City subway so that the animals inflated and deflated with the passing of underground trains.

Traveling Bible

A unique 1,500-page traveling Bible, written in 66 languages—one language for each book of the Old and New Testament—has toured more than 150 countries. The huge 15-lb (7-kg) book, which measures 18 x 12 in (45 x 30 cm), set off on its tour from the Philippines in October 2008.

Baseball Mementos

Mitch Poole, clubhouse manager with the Los Angeles Dodgers baseball team, turns milestones into mementos by painting significant game balls with details of the achievement. It is traditional for a clubhouse manager to retrieve the ball when an important hit, run, steal or win takes place, and for more than 20 years Mitch has decorated hundreds of balls. Using acrylic paint, he writes the player's name, opponent, accomplishment, date, box score and other information on the ball.

A New Leaf

Victor Liu collects dried old leaves from the streets around his home in Hebei Province, China, and very painstakingly carves into them beautiful images of subjects such as Barack Obama, Marilyn Monroe, the *Mona Lisa* and the Statue of Liberty.

Original Nintendo

In February 2010, a video-game collector paid $13,105 for an original Nintendo entertainment system and five game cartridges.

Painting with Wheels

Ian Cook of Birmingham, England, created an artwork of a racing car 33 x 16½ ft (10 x 5 m)—painted with the wheels of remote-control cars, go-karts, a racing car, a sports car, a motorbike and a six-ton truck. He took a huge canvas, applied paint and then drove across it, creating the image with the different sizes and patterns of the tires. He said painting with the truck was a challenge because the back wheels were twice as wide as the front ones so it was difficult to see what he was doing.

Sand Sculpture

A group of 30 artists took 75 days to create a 73-ft-tall (22-m) sand sculpture at the Zhoushan Sand Sculpture Festival in China. The sculpture depicted a Nigerian story of how a hummingbird managed to become king of all animals.

Daily Grind

Instead of paint or ink, Bend, Oregon, artist Karen Eland creates replicas of famous artworks with coffee. Since her first espresso painting in 1998, she has completed more than 90 illustrations—many of which incorporate coffee drinking—including Leonardo da Vinci's *Mona Latte*, *Whistler's Mocha*, and *Rodin's The Drinker*.

Stage Epic

German producer Franz Abraham has created a stage version of the Roman epic *Ben-Hur* featuring 400 actors, 900 costumes, 50 scene designs, 46 horses, 120 doves, five chariots, two eagles and two vultures. The action takes place in a 26,000-sq-ft (2,415-sq-m) arena covered with 10 in (25 cm) of sand, and uses 30 mi (48 km) of cable, 250 moving lights and 25 tons of sound equipment.

Big Business

In Minneapolis, Minnesota, in 2009, entrepreneur Lief Larson presented a work contact with a giant business card that measured a noticeable 60 x 34 in (150 x 85 cm).

BB-ball Gaga

Sculptor and artist John O'Hearn of Gainesville, Florida, makes colorful mosaics from thousands of Airsoft BBs—the ¼-in (6-mm) plastic balls used in a BB gun. Among his designs are a portrait of Florida Gators quarterback Tim Tebow from 46,308 BBs, which measures 4 x 6 ft (1.2 x 1.8 m), and this mosaic of singer Lady Gaga that is 4 x 8 ft (1.2 x 2.4 m) and contains 61,509 BBs.

Splendid Sari

A team of weavers in Chennai, India, spent 4,680 hours making a $100,000 sari that was woven with precious metals and gems.

Big Monet

At the 2010 Normandy Impressionist Festival, 1,250 fans of 19th-century French artist Claude Monet gathered in Rouen and held painted panels above their heads to create a giant, 6,460-sq-ft (600-sq-m) replica of his 1894 work *Rouen Cathedral at the End of the Day*. The result was captured by cameras perched 90 ft (27 m) above the city hall.

Bone Images

Swiss-born artist and photographer François Robert, who is now based in the U.S.A., produces works of art from real human bones. He spent hours arranging bones into striking shapes for his photographic collection *Stop the Violence*, which featured bone images of a gun, a tank, a bomb, a grenade, a Kalashnikov rifle and a knife. He hit upon the idea after trading a wired-together human skeleton, found inside some school lockers he had bought, for a box of 206 human bones.

High Horse

Tony Dew from York, England, hand-carved a wooden rocking horse that stands 11 ft 10 in (3.6 m) high and 16 ft (4.9 m) long—more than twice the size of most real horses.

Cart Art

Ptolemy Elrington trawls rivers and lakes near his studio in Brighton, England, for abandoned metal shopping carts and turns them into enchanting sculptures of animals, insects and birds. By breaking up the carts and welding them into the desired shapes, he has created such designs as a heron, a frog (with bulging eyes from the cart's wheels), a dragonfly with a 6-ft (1.8-m) wingspan, and this kingfisher eating a fish.

Pothole Scenes

Urban artists Claudia Ficca and Davide Luciano from Montreal, Canada, travel North America transforming unsightly street potholes into works of art. They have been photographed in the guise of a woman washing her clothes in a pothole, a priest baptizing a baby in another, and a scuba diver taking a dip.

Same Glass

For more than 35 years on an almost daily basis, Peter Dreher of Wittnau, Germany, has painted a portrait of the same drinking glass in the same position in his studio. He has so far completed more than 4,000 paintings of the glass.

Lego Repairs

German artist Jan Vormann travels the world fixing crumbling walls and monuments with LEGO®. Among areas he has brightened up with the toy bricks are the old quarter of Tel Aviv in Israel and New York's Bryant Park.

Midnight Knitter

Under the cover of darkness in early 2010, an unknown person dubbed the "Midnight Knitter" draped tree branches and lampposts in West Cape May, New Jersey, with small, brightly colored woolen sweaters.

Movie Veteran

Aachi Manorama, a veteran of India's Tamil film industry, has appeared in more than 1,500 movies and 1,000 stage performances.

Gum Dog

Gareth Williams of the U.K. created this sculpture of a dog, which was exhibited at London's Royal College of Art in 2009, with hair clippings from his own head stuck together with pieces of used chewing gum.

Sitting in Silence

Over a period of nearly three months in 2010, Serbian performance artist Marina Abramović spent 700 hours simply sitting and staring across a table at members of the public at New York's Museum of Modern Art. She sat on a chair for seven hours a day, six days a week, for her installation *The Artist Is Present*. Around 1,400 people—including singer Björk and model Isabella Rossellini—sat opposite her and returned her silent gaze. Some managed an entire day; others lasted just a few minutes.

Cool Music

Norwegian composer Terje Isungset has recorded several albums with instruments made entirely of ice, including percussion, horns and trumpets.

Early Watch

In 2009, art experts discovered a 450-year-old painting that featured an image of a watch. The portrait, painted by Italian Renaissance artist Maso da San Friano around 1560, shows Cosimo I de' Medici, Duke of Florence, holding a golden timepiece. Watches first appeared shortly after 1500, making this one of the oldest paintings to depict a true watch.

Tower Cozy

Robyn Love of New York City crocheted a yarn cozy for a wooden water tower on Broadway. Over a period of three weeks, she and six assistants used 60 balls of yellow and black yarn to transform the tower into a huge yellow pencil, complete with point.

Expensive Doll

A French doll designed by Paris artist Albert Marque in 1915 was sold at auction in Atlanta, Georgia, for $263,000 in 2009. Only 100 examples of the doll were ever made and each was individually costumed, in styles ranging from 18th-century French court to traditional Russian folklore.

Holiday Snaps

A series of 19th-century watercolor paintings of European beauty spots by an unknown female British holidaymaker was sold in London for more than $5,000 in 2010. The paintings of such picturesque locations as Bavaria, the Swiss Alps, and the Belgian city of Bruges were made in journals as holiday snaps by the woman following vacations she took with her husband in 1850 and 1853.

241

Living Dolls

When British artist Boo Ritson tells her subjects she wants to paint them, she means it literally. Boo covers her human volunteers in layers of water-based paint to create giant action figures, which she then photographs. She specializes in American symbols, which means that as well as painting subjects such as cheerleader and cowboy living dolls, she has also applied the technique to donuts.

Tattooed Pigs

Belgian artist Wim Delvoye tattooed pigs with Louis Vuitton designer logos for an exhibit called *Art Farm*. He tattooed the LV logos on the animals when they were piglets and watched the designs increase in size as the pigs' bodies grew.

Some Yarn!

Over the period of a week, Austin, Texas, artist Magda Sayeg covered a Mexico City bus from front to back with brightly colored knitted yarn. She has also knitted woolen coverings for trees, car antennas, and signs in the U.S.A., as well as for the Louvre Museum in Paris.

Typed Portraits

Keira Rathbone of Dorset, England, uses manual typewriters—some up to 70 years old—as her paintbrushes to create portraits of famous people, including Barack Obama, Marilyn Monroe and supermodel Kate Moss. After deciding which of her collection of 30 typewriters she wants to use, she turns the roller and selects different characters— numbers, letters and punctuation—to make the required shapes.

Sound your Horn!

A giant, working vuvuzela horn 115 ft (35 m) long and 18 ft (5.5 m) in diameter was placed above a highway in Cape Town, South Africa, in 2010.

$11 Million Book

A copy of the book *Birds of America*, written and illustrated by Haitian-born John James Audubon in the early 19th century, was sold for more than $11 million in December 2010. Only 119 complete copies of the large-format book, which has foldout pages measuring 39½ x 29½ in (100 x 75 cm), are in existence, and all but 11 of those are in museums and libraries. To obtain such accurate likenesses of birds, Audubon stalked his subjects across the U.S.A. and shot them before hanging them from wires and painting them.

Behind the Smile

Dr. Vito Franco of the University of Palermo, Sicily, Italy, believes the enigmatic smile on the face of Leonardo da Vinci's *Mona Lisa* was the result of very high levels of cholesterol. After studying the painting closely, the doctor says he can detect a build up of fatty acids around her left eye.

Tan Art

James Titterton of London, England, endured a full body wax and eight sunbed sessions to have a fish, a cockerel and a ship's anchor bronzed onto his flesh. He masked off parts of his chest, arms and legs with vinyl stickers of the various images before having the outlines tanned on to his skin. Dressed in only underpants, he then exhibited his tanned artwork at a gallery in Sussex.

Hay Castle

In January 2010, visitors flocked to Rob Marshall's sheep farm in West Victoria, Australia, to see a castle measuring 100 x 20 ft (30 x 6 m) that he had built out of hundreds of bales of hay. The castle remained in situ for six weeks until Rob dismantled it and used the bales to feed his sheep.

Tree Sculpture

Inspired by a silver birch tree, Swedish furniture chain IKEA created a huge tree sculpture made only from white kitchen appliances—including a washing machine, a dishwasher and a microwave oven—that was erected outside London's Barbican Centre in 2010.

Guitar Windmills

Mimicking The Who guitarist Pete Townshend's windmill actions, Spencer Borbon of San Francisco whirled his arm around 79 times in 30 seconds at the 2009 San Francisco Treasure Island Music Festival.

Tracker Bob

Bob "Tracker Bob" Hiemenz of Flora, Illinois, has a collection of more than 60,000 eight-track audio tapes. Since acquiring his first tapes in 1985, he has spent about $7,000 on his passion, which covers everyone from Abba to ZZ Top.

Bard Boost

Performing William Shakespeare plays to cows can help boost milk production. After the Changeling Theatre Company entertained Friesian cows at a farm in Kent, England, with *The Merry Wives of Windsor*, milk yields increased by four percent.

Finger Portraits

U.K.-based artist Kyle Lambert creates amazingly lifelike portraits of celebrities, including Jennifer Aniston and Beyoncé, using an iPad.

Curiouser Creation

Los Angeles art group L.A. Pop Art wrote out every word from the first 11 chapters of Lewis Carroll's novel, *Alice In Wonderland*, to create an illustration from the story. From a distance it appears to be solid color, but almost every inch of the artwork is formed from Lewis Carroll's own words, written clearly in felt-tip pens. The text was written upside down so that the artists didn't smudge the ink.

Inflated Animals

Chinese artist Yang Maoyuan creates animal sculptures with a difference—he takes the skins of dead animals and inflates them to monstrous sizes, often dyeing them in lurid colors.

Beijing-based Yang travels to Hebei in northern China to buy horse, goat and sheep skins. He then stitches and processes the skins before blowing them up so that their bodies become bloated and round. He chooses animals from his Mongolian ancestry, making them larger than life to reflect his oldest dream symbols, and gives them a round shape that represents harmony in China. To make his sculptures even more grotesque, he gives some of the sheep two or three heads.

Yang's bright blue, three-headed, many-legged goat.

Yang's art has been a hit in galleries worldwide.

247

Plastic Fantastic

Sayaka Ganz creates amazing wildlife sculptures from items of discarded plastic found in garbage cans and thrift shops, or donated by friends—and her finished works sell for more than $12,000.

Sayaka, who was born in Japan but now lives in Fort Wayne, Indiana, has made models of penguins, an eagle, a horse, a cheetah and a fish, varying in length from 18 in (45 cm) to 8 ft (2.4 m) and incorporating plastic sunglasses, cutlery, baskets and cooking utensils. The biggest sculptures contain up to 500 pieces of junk and take nine months to make. She sorts all her plastic into 20 color groups in her basement and then ties the chosen items onto a wire frame to create each sculpture. Sayaka studies photographs showing her animal subjects from different angles so that she can perfect the lines of motion. She says, "I get great satisfaction from fitting these objects together to create a beautiful form that seems alive."

Chocolate Train

In October 2010, London, England, food artist Carl Warner unveiled the *Chocolate Express*, a 6-ft (1.8-m) train sculpture made from chocolate, and running on chocolate tracks. It took ten days to build and also incorporated chocolate rolls, Wagon Wheels, Crunchie bars and Dime bars.

Toast Portrait

Laura Hadland from Leicester, England, created a portrait of her mother-in-law, Sandra Whitfield, from 9,852 slices of toast. Laura and 40 friends used nine toasters to brown the slices from 600 loaves of bread to varying degrees before arranging them to make a lifelike mosaic measuring 32 ft 8 in x 42 ft 3 in (10 x 13 m).

Girl Gucci

At just 13 years old, Cecilia Cassini of Encino, California, is already an accomplished fashion designer. After receiving a sewing machine for her sixth birthday, she went on to design clothes for children and adults, and a number of celebrities have worn her designs.

Photographic Memories

Munish Bansal of Kent, England, has taken pictures of his children every day for 13 years. He has filled more than 600 albums with over 8,500 digital images of his daughter Suman, 12, and her 10-year-old brother, Jay, since the day they were born.

Lord of the Sticks

Patrick Acton of Gladbrook, Iowa, spent three years building a replica of the *Lord of the Rings* city Minas Tirith from 420,000 matchsticks.

Part Art

Artist Franco Recchia from Florence, Italy, constructs models of cityscapes from the discarded parts of old computers. He uses circuit boards, casings, processing chips and various other computer components as his building blocks.

Golden Monopoly

San Francisco jewelry designer Sidney Mobell has created a Monopoly set made with solid gold and jewels. The dice are encrusted with diamonds and these alone cost $10,000.

Porcelain Seeds

In 2010, London's Tate Modern gallery staged a work called *Sunflower Seeds* by Chinese artist Ai Weiwei. The piece consisted of more than 100 million individually handmade porcelain replicas of seeds.

249

The Candy Man

Mexican artist Cristiam Ramos makes amazing candy portraits of celebrities. Instead of paint, he uses Gummi Bears, licorice, M&M's®, and after-dinner mints as his artistic materials. His works include likenesses of Elvis and Michael Jackson from hundreds of M&M's®, and a portrait of Lady Gaga from gumdrops, M&M's®, and yellow licorice.

Monster Mona

A giant version of Leonardo da Vinci's *Mona Lisa* went on display in a shopping mall in Wales in 2009—50 times bigger than the 16th-century original. It covered a massive 2,600 sq ft (240 sq m) and was big enough to fit 22 buses inside. A total of 245 people worked on the project under artist Katy Webster, and it took them 987 hours to create, using 23 gal (86 l) of paint.

Couscous City

French-Algerian artist Kader Attia built a scale model of the ancient city of Ghardaia, Algeria, entirely out of cooked couscous.

Wicker Men

In Romania, a team of 16 craftsmen created a huge wicker basket that was large enough to hold one million loaves of homemade bread. It took nine days to make, measured 59 x 33 ft (18 x 10 m) and was 31 ft (9.5 m) tall.

Celebrity Pumpkins

Gardener David Finkle carves impressive portraits of famous people—including Barack Obama, Michael Jackson and Simon Cowell—out of pumpkins that grow on his small farm at Chelmsford in Essex, England.

Concert For Dogs

Australia's Sydney Opera House staged a concert for dogs in 2010. More than a thousand dogs turned up for the 20-minute Music For Dogs event, which was organized by U.S. musician Laurie Anderson and her rock-star husband Lou Reed. It featured a concerto of high-pitch whistles, whale calls, synthesizers and strings—some inaudible to human ears.

Dental Display

To entertain and relax his patients, dentist Ian Davis from London, England, has created a series of sculptures featuring miniature men scrubbing, cleaning, and repairing teeth. The men can be seen digging out fillings with tiny pickaxes and polishing and scaling teeth with the help of scaffolding—and all the teeth he uses are taken from the casts of real patients' mouths.

Marilyn with Wings

Mexican artist Enrique Ramos created his portrait of Hollywood icon Marilyn Monroe from hundreds of rainforest butterflies. Enrique has also created an image of U.S. President John F. Kennedy in the same way. Both insect portraits are on display at the Ripley's Believe It or Not! Odditorium in London, England.

Mini Me

Indonesian photographer Ari Mahardika has "cloned" himself dozens of times for a series of intricate montages. Using a self-timer to take photos of himself in different poses against a white background, he then shrinks the portraits into mini-me characters, positioning them so that it looks as though he is interacting with himself.

Lost Movie

A lost Charlie Chaplin film valued at $60,000 was bought on eBay for $5.68 by a British collector in 2009. Morace Park of Essex, England, purchased the battered olive green film canister listed as "an old film" and was amazed to discover that the movie in question was *Zepped*, a 1916 Chaplin propaganda film poking fun at the zeppelin, the German instrument of terror during World War I. As recently as 2006, a movie expert stated that the seven-minute movie had almost certainly been lost forever.

First Exhibition

When Leo Haines was born with cerebral palsy and a terminal condition affecting his lungs and heart, he was given only six months to live. However, in 2010 the five-year-old from Somerset, England, stunned doctors by opening his first art exhibition. He began painting alongside his grandmother and has since completed more than 40 works, which are said to be reminiscent of famous U.S. abstract artist Jackson Pollock.

Bean Mosaic

A candy shop in Brighton, England, displayed a colorful mosaic of Queen Elizabeth II made from 10,000 jelly beans.

Dollar Mosaics

A Latvian artist creates mosaics made entirely out of U.S. dollar bills. Irina Truhanova sketches an outline of her subject before filling it in with snippets of the bills. Her creations include the Statue of Liberty, a Bentley car, and Russian President Vladimir Putin.

Urban Dancers

As part of its 2009 "Bodies in Urban Spaces" project, Dance Umbrella, choreographed by Willi Dorner, placed its performers in unlikely locations around the center of London, England. Passersby stumbled across dancers squeezed between pillars, wrapped around lampposts, folded into a bicycle rack, and clinging to a wall like Spider-Man.

Junior Drummer

At just three years of age, Howard Wong's rock drumming has attracted nearly ten million hits on YouTube even though he can barely see over the top of his drum kit. Howard from Penang, Malaysia, first started playing at the age of 18 months and now performs regularly with his father's band.

Typewriter Art

Cerebral-palsy sufferer Paul Smith of Roseburg, Oregon, who died in 2007, became a world-famous artist by creating masterpieces using manual typewriters. He achieved his amazing images by pressing the symbols at the tops of the number keys, and as his mastery of the typewriter grew, he developed techniques to create shadings, colors, and textures that made his work resemble pencil or charcoal drawings. Over the years, he created hundreds of artworks—each one taking him up to three months— including landscapes, animals and portraits.

Underwater Gallery

Diving enthusiasts in Lithuania have opened the country's first underwater picture gallery. Twenty large-format photographs by local artists were put on display beneath the surface of Lake Plateliai, and the organizers hope to expand the project to include sculptures, stained glass and watercolor paintings. The idea originated after a couple from a diving club put their wedding picture underwater so that they could enjoy it every time they dived.

Mosaic Mural

More than 130 artists and 500 children worked for three years to create a ceramic mosaic mural in Hanoi, Vietnam, that measures nearly 2½ mi (4 km) long. The brainchild of artist Nguyen Thu Thuy, the mosaic depicts images of Vietnam's history, life and culture.

Poo Shoes

British artist INSA created a pair of 10-in-high (25-cm) stiletto shoes with platforms made from elephant dung. He sourced the waste from the same family of elephants that provided the material for a famous series of elephant-dung collage paintings by Turner Prize-winning British artist Chris Ofili in the 1990s.

Glass Holograms

Using special pencils, multiple layers of painted glass, and between 14 and 30 glass panes, artist Xia Xiao Wan from Beijing, China, is able to transform ordinary 2-D glass into stunning 3-D holographic images.

Bargain Buy

A decade after buying 65 photographic plates at a garage sale in California for just $45, Rick Norsigian found that they could be the work of celebrated U.S. nature photographer Ansel Adams and therefore be worth around $200 million.

Playing with Food

Brazilian artist and photographer Vanessa Dualib creates cartoon animals from misshapen food and then takes pictures of them against appropriate backdrops before they go rotten. Among her 70 characters are radish mice, blowfruit fish, a potato dinosaur and Pepe the pepper.

27-hour Concert

Gonzales, a Canadian musician, played a 27-hour concert in Paris, France, in 2009. His 300-song set ranged from Britney Spears to Beethoven.

Whistle-stop Tour

German guitarist Vicente Patiz drove more than 600 mi (960 km) to give concerts in eight countries—Germany, Belgium, the Netherlands, France, Luxembourg, Switzerland, Lichtenstein and Austria—in just 24 hours.

Bamboo Dance

More than 10,700 people assembled on March 12, 2010, to perform the Cheraw dance together in Aizawl, Mizoram, India. They spread out over an area of about 1¾ mi (3 km) to dance an eight-minute routine with bamboo sticks.

Roadkill Hats

Fashion designer James Faulkner of Edinburgh, Scotland, has created a range of hats from roadkill. Inspired by the idea of using a dead magpie he found by the roadside to complement a friend's black-and-white dress, he has developed a range of 36 animal hats, using the wings, feathers and fur of squashed pigeons, rabbits, foxes, pheasants and crows.

Miscellaneous Mosaic

Kris Kuksi, a sculptor and painter from Kansas, creates macabre yet beautiful sculptures assembled from hundreds, sometimes thousands, of discarded toys, figurines and general trash. His work has been bought by celebrities and exhibited around the world.

Kris explains how *Lies and Persuasion* came together: "My pieces are a collection of many different things. I started out by gathering miscellaneous figurines, small rocks, jewelry—anything I could incorporate. After I found some essential "supplies" that I felt were important for the individuality of the piece, I built a foundation, and everything after that is just assemblage. When it's all finished, the piece gets various coats of paint.

"*Lies and Persuasion* has so many little things in it and, interestingly enough, the skull forms in the piece are actually the same skull split in half. I'll buy anything, anywhere, if I feel it's needed for a piece. I'd say that the whole assemblage, that is, the creation itself—withholding the mental preparation and shopping—lasted about a month."

Sticky Sculpture

When a popular adhesive tape company challenged people to come up with the best sculpture made entirely from sticky tape, it received some incredible entries. Artist Annie K. stuck together this giant jellyfish that appears to be floating in the air and ensnaring a bicycle in its tentacles. Some of the entries included an office desk made from 36 rolls of tape and a drum kit made from 48 rolls—that's over 7,770 ft (2,368 m), or enough tape to wrap around an aircraft carrier seven times.

Microbial Art

Dr. T. Ryan Gregory of the University of Guelph, Canada, is a pioneer of microbial art, where scientists design patterns by brushing fungi, deadly bacteria, and dye around a petri dish. He creates images by using a small paintbrush and E. coli in liquid medium. These are then allowed to grow in a laboratory incubator, but the "living paint" soon dies, so the pictures are only temporary.

Noncontact Instrument

The theremin is an electronic musical instrument that is played without any contact from the player! Named after Russian professor Léon Theremin, who invented it in 1919, it consists of two metal antennae that sense the position of the player's hands and send corresponding electric signals to a loudspeaker.

Cardboard Scream

Artist Mark Langan from Cleveland, Ohio, re-created Edvard Munch's haunting painting *The Scream* using discarded cardboard boxes. He spent 90 hours cutting up five old boxes with a craft knife and layering them to create a 3-D picture that measured 2.2 in (5.5 cm) deep. His creation sold for $2,500.

Ant Invasion

Dutch artist Henk Hofstra painted some 500 giant red ants over the town of Drachten for his work *Invasion of the Ants*. The ants each measured 10 x 6½ ft (3 x 2 m) and were created over three nights in May 2010. They were placed so that they appeared to be invading the De Lawei Theater, which was celebrating its 50th anniversary.

Quick on the Draw

Singaporean artist Peter Zhou, aka Peter Draw, drew nearly 1,000 people nonstop, without food, for 24 hours.

Rubber Beasts

Artist Ji Yong-Ho from Seoul, South Korea, makes animal sculptures from old tires. Using the flexibility of the rubber to imitate skin and muscles, he has created powerful lions, dogs, rhinos and this 10-ft-long (3-m) shark, each work taking three months to make and selling for up to $75,000. To vary the skin texture, he uses different kinds of tread. For example, the neck and forehead of his rhinoceros are made from broad-treaded tractor tires layered beneath a rough outer skin of motorcycle tires.

Giant Chair

Furniture craftsman Radoslav Russev carved a wooden chair that was almost 15 ft (4.5 m) high and weighed more than 770 lb (350 kg). He made the oversized chair, which was placed in the main square of Razgrad, Bulgaria, from 70 cubic ft (2 cubic m) of pinewood.

Leather Portraits

Welsh artist Mark Evans creates huge portraits of famous people—in leather. Using knives as his "brushes," he has scraped impressions of Muhammad Ali, Sir Winston Churchill and model Naomi Campbell into leather hides. He discovered his talent by accident after spilling blood on a new leather jacket. He tried to repair it with a palette knife but scratched too hard and ended up etching a portrait of Jimi Hendrix onto the back of the jacket.

Dead Flies

Magnus Muhr collects dead flies from windows and lamps around his house in Sweden, places them on white paper, draws in legs and a crazy background, and then photographs them. The photos show the insects appearing to dance, sunbathe, dive, ride horses and perform acrobatic circus routines.

Many Parts

Bollywood actress Priyanka Chopra played all 12 characters in the 2009 movie *What's Your Rashee?* Each character was one of the 12 zodiac signs.

Board Game

In 2009, board-game fanatic Luanga Nuwame created a 900-sq-ft (84-sq-m) wooden board game based on the city of Mississauga, Ontario, Canada... with real people as the pieces. He also built a huge dice with which to play it.

Washington's Fine

New York Society Library says George Washington owes it $300,000 in library fines. Its ledgers show that the first U.S. President borrowed two books that he should have returned on November 2, 1789, but are now over 220 years overdue.

French Anthem

Claude-Joseph Rouget de Lisle composed "The Marseillaise" in 1792 in return for a bottle of wine. The tune became the anthem of French Revolutionaries and was later adopted as the French national anthem. Ironically, Rouget de Lisle was a royalist who was thrown into prison during the Revolution and narrowly escaped being guillotined.

Serenading Sharks

Andy Brandy Casagrande IV, an American wildlife cinematographer, strummed a waterproof guitar and played a song underwater to sharks off the coast of Mexico—without a cage. He penned "The Great White Shark Song" to raise awareness of shark conservation and decided the best way to make his point was to don scuba gear and play his tune in shark-infested waters.

Cereal-ism

With the help of 150 students, high-school teacher Doyle Geddes of Smithfield, Utah, used 2 tons of breakfast cereal to create a massive reproduction of Vincent van Gogh's painting *Starry Night* measuring 72 x 90 ft (22 x 27 m).

Costly Comic

A copy of the 1938 edition of *Action Comics No. 1* sold in March 2010 for $1.5 million on an auction website. The issue, which features Superman's debut, originally sold for 10 cents.

Decorative Recycling

Florida-based artists Alain Guerra and Neraldo de la Paz create stunning sculptures from discarded clothing. They drape old garments over a wire frame to form colorful designs including a rainbow, a snake and a series of clothing trees that represent all four seasons of the year.

Last Suppers

For his *Last Suppers* series, British artist James Reynolds re-created the final meals requested by American Death Row prisoners. He filled a succession of orange prison-issue trays with their genuine last meals, which included a single black olive; an onion, a packet of chewing gum and two bottles of Coke; and six raw eggs.

Dirt Shirts

Remembering how they always used to end up with manure on their clothes when they helped on the family farm as kids, Patti Froman Maine of Corry, Pennsylvania, and her brother Sonny Froman designed a range of T-shirts that are deliberately coated in the stuff. Their CowChipShirts don't smell and come in colors such as Udder Rose and Silage Brown.

Gold Painting

Russian artist Elena Zolotaya created a 10-ft-wide (3-m) picture painted entirely with 14-carat gold.

Tall Order

For a wager, Norway's Ola Helland collected over one million giraffe pictures in 440 days. He was backpacking through South America when, as a keepsake to remember all the new friends he had met, he asked each to draw him a giraffe. When a friend bet him he couldn't collect a million, Ola set up a website and was soon deluged with giraffe pictures from 106 countries, including a giraffe made from a banana, and another made out of bread.

New Books

Each year, in the U.S.A. alone, about 30 million trees are used to make paper to print new books.

Many Hands

At the 2010 Baltimore Book Festival in Maryland, 512 people contributed to a single piece of art. Local author K. Michael Crawford erected an easel with a blank canvas and invited passersby to add to the picture.

Turning Heads

After going bald in his twenties, Philip Levine of London, England, began using his scalp as a canvas for art. Every week, body painter Kat Sinclair transformed Philip's designs into a different piece of head art. He turned his head into a disco ball covered with 1,000 crystals, had it painted with flowers, cartoon characters and smiley faces, and even had acupuncture needles inserted into his scalp in the shape of a butterfly.

Morten Viskum, The Hand with the Golden Ring II, 2010.

Helping Hand

For his painting *The Hand with the Golden Ring*, Norwegian artist Morten Viskum said he used the hand of a human corpse as a paintbrush. He claims that he's been working with a severed hand as a brush for over a decade, and uses it to apply animal blood, acrylic paints and sometimes glitter to his canvases.

Deep Drawings

Chilean artist Fredo creates mind-boggling 3-D pencil drawings that appear to rise out of the page. Despite its 3-D appearance, all his work is pencil on flat paper. At only 17 years old, Fredo is already exhibiting his work in Chile.

Strand of Beads

In October 2009, the city of Providence, Rhode Island, created a strand of red-and-white beads that measured 1,349 ft (411 m) long!

Late Returns

In 2009, a former student at Camelback High School, Phoenix, Arizona, returned two library books that had been checked out half a century earlier, and enclosed a $1,000 money order for the fines. The books had been taken out in 1959, but the borrower's family moved to another state and the books were mistakenly packed away.

Toothpick City

Scott Weaver of Rohnert Park, California, spent thousands of hours during a 34-year period building a toothpick model of every major landmark in San Francisco, using more than 100,000 toothpicks. The construction, titled *Rolling Through the Bay*, stands 9 ft (2.7 m) tall, 7 ft (2.1 m) wide and 2 ft (60 cm) deep. It has survived four house relocations, an earthquake, and Trooper—one of Weaver's four Great Danes—who once obliterated Fisherman's Wharf and about 100 hours' work with a careless wag of his tail.

Human Hoover

Artist Paul Hazelton of Kent, England, has made a model of a complete bedroom—including a TV, armchairs, and a wardrobe—out of dust! Known as the "Human Hoover," he collects dust from furniture, pictures and window sills, and then transforms the bunches of tiny particles into 3-D sculptures by wetting, shaping and drying them. Some of his dust models—which also include a briefcase, a moth and a humanoid—are 20 in (50 cm) high.

Hot Lips

Makeup artist Rick DiCecca applied lipstick to more than 300 women in one hour at Macy's Department Store, Chicago, Illinois.

Lego Ship

For nearly a week, 3,500 children used 513,000 LEGO® bricks to build a 25-ft-long (7.6-m) model of a container ship in Wilhelmshaven, Germany.

Pistol Puzzle

GarE Maxton, a machinist-artist from Michigan, created a 125-piece metal puzzle sculpture that can be assembled into a working, muzzle-loading pistol.

Observation Test

To help improve their powers of deductive observation, a group of New York City police officers visited the Metropolitan Museum of Art to discuss with an expert what conclusions they could draw from the contents of pictures by the likes of Caravaggio and Guercino.

Party Pooper

With the help of local schoolchildren from Sichuan Province, China, sculptor Zhu Cheng made a replica of the famous *Venus de Milo* statue—from panda dung. The poop statue later sold for $45,000.

Intrepid Builder

Using 250,000 pieces of LEGO®, Ed Diment took nine months to build a 22-ft-long (6.7-m) replica of the World-War-II aircraft carrier U.S.S. *Intrepid* in the conservatory of his home in Portsmouth, England. The finished model weighed more than 500 lb (227 kg).

Underground Music

Norwegian singer Unni Lovlid staged two sell-out 2010 concerts in a Victorian drain 20 ft (6 m) underground in Brighton, England. The sewer could accommodate 25 audience members wearing hard hats.

Tabletop Landscapes

New Jersey photographer and artist Matthew Albanese devises spectacular images of windswept tropical islands, tornadoes and volcanoes by building models from everyday items.

The azure sea in his tabletop *D.I.Y. Paradise* is actually melted sugar and tin foil, and the island is made from salt. He carefully arranged cotton balls over the scene to create clouds, and even the palm trees are not as they seem—the leaves are formed from feathers.

Matthew has also made convincing icebergs from sugar and waterfalls from salt, and re-created the surface of Mars with paprika, cinnamon, nutmeg, and chili powder. His tornadoes are made from steel wool and he has created an impressive Aurora Borealis using a shower curtain, a corkboard and strobe lighting. His photographs of these homemade natural phenomena sell for over $900 each.

Ticket Tower

British artist Robert Bradford created scale models of three U.K. landmarks—St. Paul's Cathedral, Edinburgh Castle and Blackpool Tower—from a total of 115,000 used train tickets.

Moon Scent

Printers in Edinburgh, Scotland, have created a scratch 'n' sniff artwork that smells like the Moon. They developed it by talking to former NASA astronaut Charlie Duke, who was a member of the Apollo 16 mission in 1972, and who described the Moon's surface as smelling like spent gunpowder.

Victory at Last

Using an original wooden beam from the H.M.S. *Victory*, sculptor Ian Brennan from Hampshire, England, spent 17 years carving a 47-in-long (1.2-m) model of Admiral Horatio Nelson's 18th-century flagship. The model contains 200 ft (60 m) of rope, 104 miniature guns and 37 sails.

Cow Maze

In a field near Berlin, Germany, workers cut corn and hemp into the shape of a giant cow. The maze depicted the bovine digestive system and was designed by the country's Federal Institute of Risk Assessment to promote healthy eating habits.

Apple Killer

Together with photographer Paul Fairchild, San Francisco artist Michael Tompert staged an exhibition of butchered and mangled Apple products. Tompert has shot, burned, hammered and sawed his way through a range of merchandise and even ran over seven iPods with a diesel locomotive. His greatest challenge was an iPad, which survived a series of blows from a sledgehammer, before finally exploding after its insides were heated with a soldering torch. He says he's trying to make people think about their relationship with these highly popular items.

Human Ashes

Dutch artist Wieki Somers makes 3-D printed sculptures of common household appliances—including bathroom scales, a vacuum cleaner and a toaster—out of human ashes.

Gallery Blunder

Polish experimental artist Leon Tarasewicz sued a gallery for $30,000 after it ripped up one of his paintings and threw it in a trash can in the mistaken belief that it was a large bunch of scrap paper used for getting excess paint off brushes. The 25-ft-high (7.6-m) exhibit had been on display in the gallery in Katowice, but staff thought that it had been left behind by decorators.

Microscopic Models

Origami artist Mui-Ling Teh of Thornhill, Ontario, Canada, makes paper models so tiny—as small as 0.08 in (2 mm) long—that they look like a speck to the naked eye. She makes her microscopic models of objects such as birds, flowers and airplanes with scissors and tweezers. She first began to experiment with origami at age ten when she made small models out of candy wrappers.

Auto Robot

A 33-ft-tall (10-m) version of Transformer Optimus Prime made from the bodies and tires of old cars and motorcycles was unveiled at Beijing's Green Dream Park in 2010. The *Autobot* sculpture weighed six tons and was assembled from five truckloads of recycled parts.

Huge Hammock

Hansy Better Barraza, a professor at Rhode Island School of Design, created a 33-ft-long (10-m) hammock, covering an area of 264 sq ft (24.5 sq m) in Boston, Massachusetts, in 2010. The sculpture consisted of 4,278 ft (1,304 m)—that's nearly a mile—of "rope" made from recycled bottles woven over curved steel pipes.

Smelly Issue

Issue No. 23 of the German magazine *mono.kultur* was infused with 12 smells suggested by Norwegian scientist, artist and odor expert Sissel Tolaas. Using a technique called microencapsulation, the smells were printed into the pages of the magazine, with the reader rubbing the paper to release them.

Beef Bikini

For the September 2010 cover shot of Japanese magazine *Vogue Hommes Japan*, U.S. singer Lady Gaga wore a bikini made of raw meat.

Screw Mosaic

Saimir Strati spent two weeks creating a mosaic of a U.S. banknote 8 ft (2.4 m) high and 16 ft 1 in (4.9 m) long from 300,000 industrial screws. The giant bill features a portrait of the ancient Greek poet Homer in the center.

Natural Sculptures

Peter Riedel, an artist and photographer from Toronto, Canada, spent five hours creating 42 temporary outdoor sculptures in the city's Humber River by balancing rocks and boulders on top of each other. He never uses glue in his works but arranges the rocks so that they don't fall.

Tasty Shoes

Israel's Kobi Levi has designed shoes in the shapes of bananas, cats, shopping baskets, dogs, rocking chairs—and one pair with a pink stiletto heel that makes it look as though the wearer has stepped in a piece of chewing gum.

Illusion Confusion

There is a lot more to this portrait of legendary artist Salvador Dalí than meets the eye. It is in fact a large 3-D illusion, consisting of a shark, a bull's head and a seal, among many other objects. These bizarre items appear to be randomly piled up but are actually meticulously placed to complete the image from just one perspective. Bernard Pras, the artist from Belgium, has been re-creating famous pictures out of junk for more than 30 years.

Man-made Monsters

Using only man-made materials, Californian artist Doug Higley makes monsters for showmen to display at flea markets and fairs across the world. He has created fake mummified and petrified creatures, bogus mermaids, shrunken heads, chupacabras, freaky jungle pygmies and atomic death worms. His work has been exhibited in 34 countries and one of his mermaids appeared at Buckingham Palace, London. He also once created 42 mermaids for a car-dealer promotion in the U.S.A. and Canada, whereby potential customers were invited to see the "strange creature" found in the trunk of a trade-in vehicle and take a test drive. The gimmick sold thousands of cars!

Still Famous

In the year following his death on June 25, 2009, Michael Jackson's estate earned one billion dollars.

Small Portions

Using acrylic paints and a magnifying glass, French artist Stephanie Kilgast creates miniature clay models of food in 1:12 scale. She painstakingly molds the clay with scalpels, blades, art knives and toothpicks, and has made more than 600 cakes, pastries, fruit and full meals, including a full English breakfast with baked beans, bacon, sausages and fried eggs.

Ancient Shoe

Archeologists in Armenia have found a leather shoe more than 5,500 years old. The shoe, which was stuffed with grass, was discovered in a mountain cave where it had been kept in excellent condition thanks to a thick layer of sheep excrement that acted as a protective seal.

Corn Maze

Bob Connors cut images of Stewie and Brian, two of the characters from the animated TV comedy *Family Guy*, into a seven-acre cornfield maze at his farm in Danvers, Massachusetts.

Fashion Ferrari

A full-size replica of a Ferrari Formula-1 car was made out of $60,000 worth of designer clothing. Eight people worked for five hours at a store in London's Carnaby Street to turn 1,999 items of clothing—including 1,682 red T-shirts, 88 pairs of jeans, 64 pairs of shoes and 31 belts—into a 14-ft-long (4.3-m) model car. The wheels were made from water bottles, the wing mirrors from sunglasses and the tires from black jeans.

Avid Reader

Nonagenarian Louise Brown from Dumfries and Galloway, Scotland, has borrowed 25,000 library books in her lifetime. She has read up to a dozen books a week since 1946 without incurring a single fine for late returns.

Poem Boxing

Japan hosts the National Poem Boxing Championships where contestants fight it out with words in three-minute rounds. The poets step into a boxing ring and read out verses on a wide range of subjects, hoping to secure a win. In the final round, the last two combatants still standing must improvise a poem incorporating a random word that the judges tell them to use.

Same Shot

Except for the years of World War II, Ria van Dijk had a photograph taken of herself at the same shooting gallery in Tilburg, the Netherlands, every year for 74 years. The first picture was taken in 1936 when she was 16.

Phone Dress

A London fashion company has introduced the M-Dress, a little black dress that also serves as a cell phone. The dress, which has a tiny antenna in its hem, allows wearers to make and receive calls by putting their SIM card under the label. To take a call, they raise their hand to their ear; to end it they let it fall to their side.

Tentacle Terror

In 2008, artists Filthy Luker and Pedro Estrellas positioned huge inflatable green octopus tentacles through the windows of an unnamed building in France.

Wooden Chain

Markley Noel of Hickory Corners, Michigan, carved a 480-ft-long (146-m) wooden chain from a single 25-ft-long (7.6-m) maple plank. The chain, which has 1,993 links, each 4 in (10 cm) long, took him seven years to make.

Pencil Tips

Dalton Ghetti of Bridgeport, Connecticut, has been creating miniature graphite masterpieces from the tips of pencils for more than 25 years, including a sculpture of Elvis wearing shades, carved from a single pencil tip. He uses three tools—a razor blade, a sewing needle and a sculpting knife—but no magnifying glass. He digs into the graphite with the needle, then scratches and creates lines, turning the pencil slowly in his hand. One piece—a pencil with interlinking chains—took him two-and-a-half years. He has made more than 100 pencil-tip shapes in total, such as a saw, a screw, a key on a chain, a boot, a chair and all 26 letters of the alphabet.

Roll the Dice

Ari Krupnik, a software engineer from Silicon Valley, California, builds mosaics of famous people from hundreds of dice, achieving different shades of gray according to which face is up. He created a portrait of revolutionary leader Che Guevara from 400 dice and one of George Orwell, author of *Animal Farm*, from 1,925 dice. He has also made a 3-D image of actress Uma Thurman from hundreds of M&M's®.

Pretty Paddies

Each year, the farmers of Inakadate Village, Aomori Prefecture, Japan, use different-colored varieties of rice to create works of art spanning entire rice paddies.

Blind Draft

U.S. novelist Kent Haruf writes the first draft of each of his books blind! He takes off his glasses, pulls a stocking cap down over his eyes, and types his words in darkness.

Rubik's Replica

Five artists in Toronto, Canada, spent two months making a replica of Leonardo da Vinci's *The Last Supper* measuring 8½ x 17 ft (2.6 x 5.2 m), using 4,050 Rubik's Cubes.

Vast Violin

In 2010, a dozen workers in Markneukirchen, Germany, created a playable violin that measured 13 ft 11 in (4.3 m) tall, 4½ ft (1.4 m) wide, and weighed more than 220 lb (100 kg).

Gum-wrapper Dress

Elizabeth Rasmuson of Garner, Iowa, made her 2010 high-school prom dress out of hundreds of gum wrappers that she and her boyfriend, Jordan Weaver, had been collecting for six months. She also made him a matching vest out of blue-and-white gum wrappers.

In the Dark

London's Tate Modern gallery unveiled a giant installation in 2009—40 ft (12 m) of pitch darkness. It was created by Polish artist Miroslaw Balka who said that the darkness was a metaphor for life.

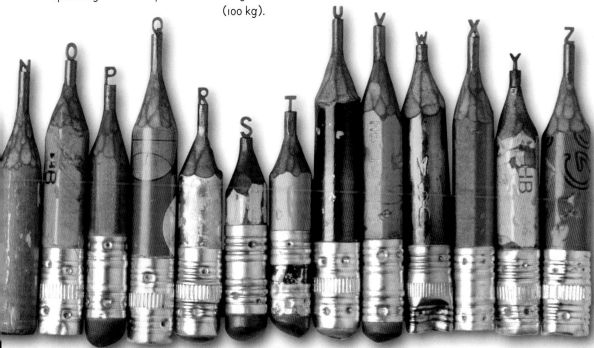

Party Poopers

U.S. rock band Kings of Leon had to abandon a concert at the Verizon Amphitheater, St. Louis, Missouri, in July 2010 after they were bombarded with pigeon droppings. An infestation of birds in the rafters above the stage led to bassist Jared Followill being hit several times during the band's first two songs, including in the face.

Tiny Tiger

A Taiwanese artist has created a painted tiger sculpture that is smaller than a grain of rice. Chen Forng-Shean spent three months carving the 0.04-in-high (1-mm) tiger from resin. He has also made delicate miniature sculptures from sand, dental floss, rice, ant heads and fly wings.

Garbage Pictures

Richard Broom of Lincolnshire, England, spent hours photographing litter along Britain's roadsides and posting them on an Internet blog in an attempt to get the government to tidy up the country—but his photos, including discarded paper cups, old cans, a broken toilet, and bottles of urine, proved so popular that they have turned into highly collectable art.

Mini Mansion

Peter Riches of Hove, England, spent nearly 15 years creating an elaborately decorated doll house and sold it for $80,000—that's enough to buy a real home in some places. His miniature 23-room mansion boasted a music room with grand piano, a hand-crafted games room with snooker table, and a library with more than 1,000 individually bound books. He made the shell of the house from plaster and hand-etched 32,000 bricks on its walls. He cut the 5,000 roof tiles from cardboard. The finished house measured 4 ft (1.2 m) wide, 3 ft 3 in (1 m) high and 2 ft 7 in (80 cm) deep.

Cloud Graffiti

U.S. pop artist Ron English created cloud graffiti in the skies above New York City in September 2009. He hired a skywriting plane and got it to spell the word "cloud" in puffy white dots several times over the city.

Chalk Drawing

Head of a Muse, a simple black chalk drawing on paper by Renaissance painter Raphael, sold at an auction in London, England, for $47.9 million in December 2009.

Pinhead Nativity

In 2009, Italian craftsman Aldo Caliro sculpted a nativity scene—featuring hand-carved figures of the Virgin Mary, Joseph, and an angel, plus a tiny baby Jesus in his crib—on the head of a pin! He painted the figures with a single paintbrush hair. He had previously carved tiny nativity scenes on a lentil and a coffee bean.

Long Story

It will be nearly 1,000 years before the cover of the May 2009 issue of *Opium* magazine can be read in its entirety. It will take that long for the successive layers of ink to degrade—at the rate of one word per century—thereby revealing a nine-word tale created by U.S. conceptual artist Jonathan Keats.

Lego® Plane

LEGO® enthusiast Ryan McNaught built a $5,500 replica of the world's biggest passenger plane—the Airbus A380—with more than 35,000 bricks. It took him more than eight months to build the model, which is 7 ft (2.1 m) long and 6 ft (1.8 m) wide, in the garage of his home in Melbourne, Victoria, Australia.

Blood Painter

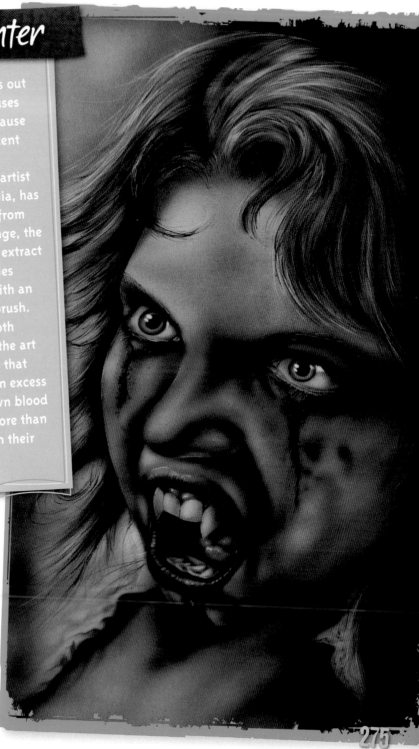

Rev Mayers never runs out of the unique ink he uses for his paintings, because it's one hundred percent his own blood on the canvas. The extreme artist from Sydney, Australia, has the blood extracted from his arm using a syringe, the way a doctor would extract blood. He then applies the precious fluid with an airbrush or a paintbrush. More detail and depth becomes visible as the art ages. Rev estimates that he has so far used in excess of 12 pints of his own blood in his paintings, more than most adults have in their entire body.

Precise Worker

U.S. bestselling horror writer Stephen King, originally from Portland, Maine, writes exactly ten pages (around 2,000 words) a day, whether he's in a creative mood or not.

STRANGE STORIES

Head Stand

Kris Sleeman of the Dallas extreme performance group Traumatic Stress Discipline appears to feel no pain.

At the grand opening of the Ripley's Believe It or Not! Odditorium in San Antonio, Texas, he lay face down in a pile of freshly broken glass bottles, and then invited Ripley employee Viviana Ray to stand on his head. Kris's pain-defying feats also included having a concrete block on his chest shattered by a sledgehammer while lying on a bed of nails.

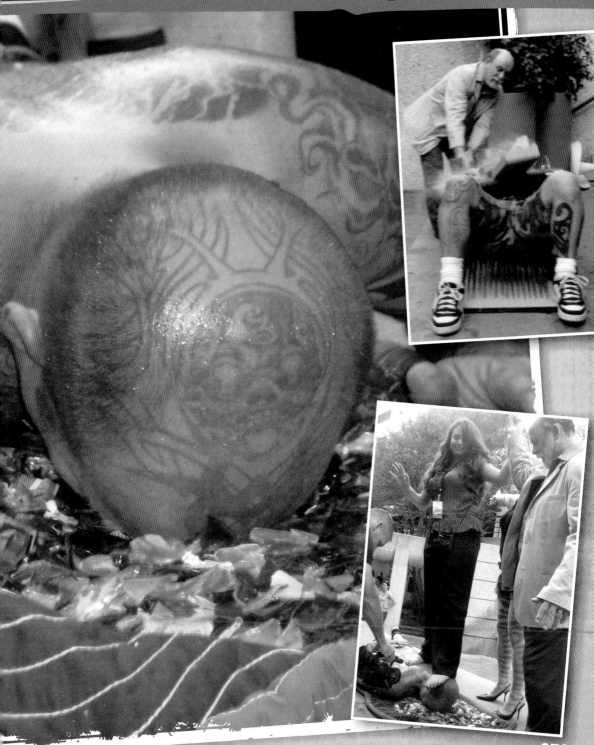

Florida Monster

Two boys playing on the beach near St. Augustine, Florida, in 1896 spotted the carcass of a huge creature half buried in the sand. It seemed to have a number of tentacles, some up to 30 ft (9 m) long, prompting the belief that it was some kind of giant octopus. However, a similar blob washed up in Chile in 2003 turned out to be a decomposing sperm whale. When some marine creatures decay, their form changes so much that they can look like unidentified sea monsters.

Wonder Well

Chand Baori, a stepped well 100 ft deep (30 m) in the village of Abhaneri, Rajasthan, India, was built more than a thousand years ago with 13 stories and 3,500 steps.

Missing Belt

For reasons unknown, Jupiter loses or regains one of its two belts every ten to 15 years. The planet usually has two dark bands in its atmosphere—one in its northern hemisphere and one in its southern hemisphere—but pictures taken by astronomers in April 2010 showed that the Southern Equatorial Belt had disappeared. The dark belts are clouds created from chemicals such as sulfur and phosphorus, which are blown into bands by 350-mph (560-km/h) winds.

Human Punchbag

Xiao Lin, a fitness coach from Shenyang, China, rents himself out as a punchbag for stressed women who want to let off steam. The women pay $15 for a 30-minute session during which they can hit him as hard and as often as they like.

Traffic Calming

City transportation officials in Cambridge, Massachusetts, tried to calm drivers annoyed at receiving parking tickets by putting instructions on the reverse side about how to relax by bending the body into simple yoga positions.

Metal Spheres

Over recent decades, miners in Klerksdorp, South Africa, have dug up hundreds of ancient metal spheres that look entirely man-made. However, they were found in Precambrian rock dating back 2.8 billion years—that's over 2.79 billion years before Neanderthal man! The mysterious spheres measure about 1 in (2.5 cm) in diameter and some are etched with three parallel grooves running around the middle.

Unique Stone

The Mystery Stone of Lake Winnipesaukee, New Hampshire, has distinctive markings that make it unique. The egg-shaped stone—found encased in a lump of clay in 1872—has intricate man-made carvings and a hole bored through both ends, but its origins and purpose remain unknown and no matching stones have ever been discovered.

Baghdad Battery

An ancient clay vessel was an early example of a battery—even though batteries were not rediscovered for another 1,800 years. The 2,000-year-old Baghdad Battery contained a copper cylinder and an oxidized iron rod, both held in place by asphalt. When filled with an acid or alkaline liquid, it was capable of producing an electric charge.

Ape Man

On an expedition to Venezuela in 1920, Swiss geologist François de Loys claimed to have stumbled across a 5-ft-tall (1.5-m), red-haired, tailless ape that walked upright like a human. He shot the animal and photographed it, using a long stick to prop up its head, but the corpse went missing before it could be examined. If genuine, it would have been the first ape ever discovered in the Americas, thereby rewriting the theory of primate evolution, but scientists decided that the photo was merely a common spider monkey whose tail was conveniently hidden or chopped off.

Super Sub

Cyril Howarth from Lancashire, England, spent $75,000 on converting a 70-ft-long (21-m) canal narrow boat into a replica of a World-War-II German U-boat. Unlike other submarines, this vessel stays strictly on the surface.

Own Juror

William Woods was about to stand trial in Ottawa, Ontario, Canada, in 1999 on charges of dangerous driving, but the trial had to be postponed because Woods was summoned for jury duty—for his own case.

Political Clown

A professional clown was elected to represent São Paulo in Congress after picking up 1.3 million votes in the 2010 Brazilian general elections. Tiririca (real name Francisco Oliveira) received the highest number of votes for any federal deputy across the country with his catchy TV slogans including: "What does a federal deputy do? I have no idea, but vote for me and I'll let you know."

Too Close for Comfort

Two people found themselves in an unbelievable predicament after being thrown from their motorcycle in Hubei Province, China, in 2010. They flew headfirst into the mouth of a drainpipe just 1 ft 8 in (50 cm) wide and were stuck fast. Fortunately, passersby saw their feet protruding from the polluted water pipe and notified firefighters, who dug the couple free in just ten minutes.

Head for Heights

A six-year-old boy slipped through window bars of an eighth-floor apartment in Hubei Province, China, but ended up dangling by his ears 60 ft (18 m) above the ground after they got trapped in the bars because the rest of his head was too wide to pass through.

Bottleneck Mystery

A 60-mi (96-km) traffic jam trapped thousands of vehicles on the Beijing–Tibet expressway for 11 days in August 2010—but then it completely disappeared overnight without any apparent explanation.

Dancing Cop

Dressed in police blues, white gloves, and an officer's cap, Tony Lepore dances while directing the traffic at an intersection in Providence, Rhode Island. He began his dance routine in the 1980s through boredom and although he retired from the police department in 1988, he returns each year for two weeks to entertain passersby.

Mother Cat

Peter Keonig, a Buddhist bank robber serving five years for armed robberies in Germany, had his request for his cat to be granted visiting rights to him in jail rejected by a court—despite his plea that the animal is the reincarnation of his mother.

Cesspit Hell

A Chinese man was rescued in 2010 after spending two days stuck up to his neck in a toilet cesspit. The man had slipped while using an outhouse toilet in Wuyuan, Inner Mongolia, and had fallen into the pit below. Unsurprisingly, as soon as he was freed, he ran to a nearby pond to have a wash!

Lost Letters

While on a 2010 field trip to the Alps, Freya Cowan, a geography student from the University of Dundee, Scotland, stumbled across a U.S.-bound mailbag from the Malabar Princess, an Air India plane that crashed near the summit of Mont Blanc while en route to London in 1950, killing all 40 passengers and eight crew on board. Some of the correspondence inside the mailbag was still in such good condition that she set about sending 75 letters and birthday cards on to their intended recipients 60 years late.

Alien Autopsy

A display at the U.F.O. Museum at Roswell, New Mexico, re-creates the alleged autopsy of a dead alien killed when his spacecraft crashed in the area in 1947. The dummy extraterrestrial was originally made for the 1994 movie *Roswell*.

Aliens Welcome

Bob Tohak has believed in U.F.O.s since he was a kid. He is so eager to make contact with aliens that he has put a 42-ft-high (13-m) U.F.O. landing port on his property in Poland, Wisconsin. "I'm just hoping that something will show up," he says.

Ambulance Stolen

An Illinois man was arrested for stealing an ambulance in Mount Horeb, Wisconsin—with a patient and paramedics still inside it.

Ashes Live On

For $3,000, U.K.-based firm And Vinyly will press a person's ashes or those of their pet into a playable record featuring their favorite music, a personal message or their last will and testament. The ashes are sprinkled onto a raw piece of vinyl and then pressed by plates. When the plates exert pressure on the vinyl to create the grooves, the ashes are pressed into the record. Customers can also have their own album-cover portrait, created by mixing their ashes into the paint.

Band of Holes

Nearly 7,000 man-made holes are located on a plain near Peru's Pisco Valley—but their origins and purpose remain unknown. The Band of Holes stretches for 1 mi (1.6 km) and some of the holes are up to 7 ft (2.1 m) deep.

They're Here!

A 2010 April Fool's report in a Jordanian newspaper wreaked havoc in one town. Its front-page article described a U.F.O. landing near Jafr, 185 mi (300 km) from Amman. Residents panicked, keeping their children home from school; and Jafr's mayor even sent security forces in search of the aliens. He was about to empty the town of its 13,000 residents when newspaper journalists came clean.

Straight Line

Four ancient historical sites—
Easter Island in the Pacific
Ocean, the Nazca lines in
southern Peru, the Inca city
of Ollantaytambo, also in
southern Peru, and the Great
Pyramid of Giza, Egypt—are
all exactly aligned along a
straight line. Other world
wonders that are within just
one-tenth of a degree of this
alignment include Persepolis,
the capital of ancient Persia;
Mohenjo Daro, the ancient
capital of the Indus Valley;
and the lost city of Petra in
modern-day Jordan.

Near Miss

Pilot David Hastings from
Norwich, U.K., revealed a close
encounter with a U.F.O. when
flying over the Mojave Desert
in the U.S.A. in 1987. He said
a mysterious black shape
came at his plane head-
on, then flashed overhead.
Seconds later the object was
moving at high speed at the
plane's side. Hastings took
photos and showed them to
U.S. Navy officers, but they
refused to comment.

Ghost Ship

Carrying a shipment of coal,
the Carroll A. Deering was
found run aground off the
coast of North Carolina on
January 31, 1921—but its 11-man
crew had vanished. There
was no sign of the crew's
belongings or the ship's
navigating instruments, log
or clock, yet evidence in the
galley indicated that food
was being prepared for the
following day's meals.

Fire Starter

A ghostly young girl was pictured
in a building on fire in the town of
Wem, England, in 1995. Many were
convinced that the photograph
captured the ghost of a girl that
died after accidentally setting
the same building alight in
the 17th century. In 2010, after
the photographer had died, it
was suggested that the 1995
photograph was a fake. The
ghostly girl in the fire had
been copied from a 1922 Wem
postcard, which was spotted
in the local newspaper by an
eagle-eyed reader.

Cow Suit

Milkman Tony Fowler from Leicestershire, England, wore a black-and-white cow suit to receive his M.B.E. from Queen Elizabeth II at Buckingham Palace in June 2010. The Friesian outfit should have had a tail at the back, but Fowler's dog chewed it off.

Unwanted Coins

A stockpile of dollar coins worth more than $1.1 billion is languishing in storage because Americans prefer dollar bills. If stacked, the pile of coins would reach seven times higher than the altitude of the International Space Station.

Royal Residence

Janet and Philip Williams have turned their four-bedroom home in Woonona, New South Wales, Australia, into a royal museum, attracting thousands of visitors each year. They have more than 12,000 items of House of Windsor memorabilia, ranging from a life-size model of Queen Elizabeth II to a pair of Prince Charles and Princess Diana slippers. Even the toilet is decorated like a royal throne, complete with purple velvet trim.

$9,000 Toothpick

In December 2009, a toothpick that once belonged to British author Charles Dickens sold for $9,150 at an auction in New York City.

Lint Leonardo

Laura Bell of Roscommon, Michigan, has made a replica of Leonardo da Vinci's painting *The Last Supper* out of laundry lint that measures 13 ft 8 in x 4 ft 4 in (4 x 1.3 m). She bought towels in the colors she wanted, laundering them separately to achieve the right shades. To obtain the amount of lint she needed to make the picture, she had to do about 800 hours of laundry and it then took her another 200 hours to re-create the famous Renaissance masterpiece.

Same Sneakers

As part of a bet he made with his Spanish teacher, high-school freshman Ben Hedblom of Tampa, Florida, wore the same pair of sneakers every day for four years until he graduated—even though they wore away so that his toes eventually stuck out the front and he had to encase the shoes in plastic bags on rainy days.

Reptilian Row

A row over loud music between two South Carolina motel guests ended with one being accused of slapping the other in the face with the head of a 4-ft (1.2-m) python. The suspect was charged with assault and the weapon—the python—was handed over to his family for safe keeping.

Manure Message

To celebrate his wife Carole's 67th birthday, farmer Dick Kleis used a manure spreader to spell out HAP B DAY LUV U in a field visible from the living room of the couple's home in Zwingle, Iowa. It took him three hours and four loads of liquid manure to create the message—he was going to add a heart, too, but he ran out of manure.

Jesus Lives

When a 50-year-old man was taken to a hospital with minor facial injuries after being hit by a car in Northampton, Massachusetts, in May 2010, he gave his name as Lord Jesus Christ. Police officers checked his I.D. and confirmed that it was indeed his legal name.

Bogus Tycoon

Echoing the real-life escapades of Frank Abagnale Jr. in the movie *Catch Me If You Can*, a 17-year-old boy from Yorkshire, England, posed as an aviation tycoon for six months. He tricked British companies into believing he was about to launch his own airline and that he had a fleet of jets. When the ruse was uncovered, the boy was found to be suffering from a form of autism, which enabled him to recall the exact detail of every airline's flight schedule.

Just the Job

Jason Sadler of Ponte Vedra Beach, Florida, earned more than $85,000 in 2009, promoting different businesses by wearing their T-shirts.

Magic Gel

"Aerogel" was created in 1931 by U.S. scientist Samuel Stephens Kistler following a bet with a colleague over who could replace the liquid in gel with a gas without causing shrinkage. Even though it is 99.8 percent air, the unique substance aerogel can withstand temperatures of up to 2,550°F (1,400°C) and is strong enough to support 2,000 times its own weight.

Lost Army

Twin brothers Angelo and Alfredo Castiglioni believe they have found the remains of a 50,000-strong Persian army, said to have been drowned in the sands of the Sahara Desert 2,500 years ago. The Italian archeologists have discovered bronze weapons, a silver bracelet, an earring and hundreds of human bones that are thought to have belonged to the lost army of Persian King Cambyses II, whose men were reportedly buried in a terrible sandstorm in 525 BC.

Toy Parts

Dr. William H. Sewell invented an artificial heart pump prototype with parts from an Erector set toy while at Yale Medical School.

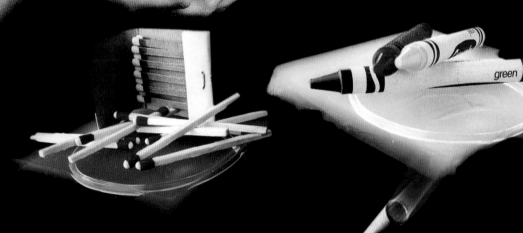

Invisible Man

Scientists at Tokyo University have developed camouflage technology that makes people disappear. A coat made of a high-tech reflective material has a video camera placed in it, which sends film to a projector. This, in turn, bounces the moving image off the front of the coat, making the wearer appear transparent, even when the fabric is creased.

Stench Busters

The city of Beijing, China, has installed 100 high-pressure deodorant guns, which can spray dozens of liters of fragrance per minute, to combat the stench from one of the city's many overflowing landfill sites. Beijing's 17 million people generate nearly 20,000 tons of waste every day—7,700 tons more than the capacity of municipal disposal plants.

Solar Slug

Elysia chlorotica, a green sea slug that lives along the Atlantic seaboard of the U.S.A., runs on solar power. Scientists at the University of Maine have discovered that it photosynthesizes using genes "stolen" from the algae it eats.

Magnetic Lift

Scientists have successfully levitated fruit, insects, frogs and mice by applying a repelling effect on the water molecules in their bodies with powerful magnets.

Quake-proof Bed

Wang Wenxi from Shijiazhuang, China, has invented an earthquake-proof bed. When an earthquake strikes, a strong board automatically slides into place, protecting the person from falling debris. His secure bed has cupboards at both ends with water, canned food, a hammer, and a megaphone to help the occupant survive for several days beneath rubble.

Strad Beaten

A violin made of wood that had been treated with fungus for nine months was judged better than a $2-million 1711 Stradivarius in a sound test conducted in Germany before an audience of 180 people. Scientists say a fungal attack changes the cell structure of the wood, giving it a warmer, more rounded sound.

Perfect Fit

In Peru, the ancient site of Sacsayhuaman features three huge stone walls built so expertly that it is impossible to insert a piece of paper between the different-shaped stones, some of which are 9 ft 10 in (3 m) high and weigh 200 tons.

Ectoplasm

Communicating with the dead was a popular pursuit in the early 20th century, and mediums who went into a trancelike state were often seen to produce a peculiar white substance called ectoplasm from their mouth, ears, nose or navel.

Participants at seances would then watch in amazement as the ectoplasm was apparently transformed into spiritual faces, fully functional arms and even entire bodies. It also appeared to give mediums the power to perform astonishing feats of telekinesis, such as raising tables and chairs without any physical contact. But was it all genuine or just an elaborate hoax?

BEYOND DOUBT?

German physician Baron Albert von Schrenck-Notzing always imposed strict conditions to ensure that mediums could not fake ectoplasm. For this experiment, noted Polish medium, Stanislawa P., was sewn into a special fraud-proof coat, but still appeared to create ectoplasm from her mouth.

While in a trance in Winnipeg, Canada, in 1929, Scottish medium Mary Marshall produced nasal ectoplasm. At the center of it was a face that her spirit guide—Walter—claimed was that of Sherlock Holmes creator Sir Arthur Conan Doyle, himself a confirmed believer in spiritualism. The necklace worn by Mary in the photograph is an "apport"— an object that materialized during the seance, but was not there before or after the event.

GHOSTLY FACE

At a 1912 seance, ectoplasm from French medium Eva C. (Eva Carrière) formed into the shape of a man's head, which, according to an observer, then made bowing movements. Eva C. was renowned for being able to produce ectoplasm, but skeptics said it was nothing more than chewed paper or fabric that had been regurgitated. Once, after the flow of ectoplasm had been reabsorbed into her mouth, she was given a powerful emetic and when she failed to vomit, the doubters were satisfied that she had not swallowed anything to fake the ectoplasm.

Solar Detector

The Super-Kamiokande Detector is a gigantic cylindrical stainless steel tank, measuring 136 ft (41 m) high and 129 ft (39 m) in diameter, located more than half a mile (0.8 km) underground in Japan. Holding 50,000 tons of water, it is lined with 11,146 ultra-sensitive light detectors and serves as a scientific observatory to monitor solar neutrinos—particles that are produced in the Sun by nuclear fusion. This will help us understand what goes on inside the Sun and how matter was created in the early Universe. The Detector is located underground to shield the experiments from cosmic rays and background radiation.

Renewed Vows

Margaret and John Beauvoisin of Hampshire, England, celebrated their diamond wedding anniversary by taking their vows again. The couple got married in 1948 and have renewed their vows every year since 1950, only missing out in 1949 because John was stationed in Bermuda with the Royal Navy.

Doll House

Bettina Dorfmann from Dusseldorf, Germany, owns more than 6,000 Barbie dolls—and some are worth up to $10,000. An entire room of her house is devoted to displaying 1,500 of them while another 3,000 Barbies from her collection are on show at exhibitions and museums around the world.

Pink Lady

Los Angeles actress Kitten Kay Sera has worn nothing but pink for over 25 years. "The Pink Lady," as she is known, even wears pink to funerals and once dumped a boyfriend because he was colorblind and therefore unable to appreciate the joy of pink. She dyes her Maltese dog, Kisses, in her favorite color using beetroot-juice baths.

Snake Smuggler

After customs officers in Kristiansand, Norway, discovered a tarantula in the bag of a ferry passenger who had traveled from Denmark, they decided to conduct a full body search. On investigation, they also found 14 royal pythons and ten albino leopard geckos taped to the man's torso and legs.

Cash Flow

A 47-year-old Ukrainian man got his arm stuck in a public toilet in Chernigov for three hours after trying to retrieve $24 that he had dropped. With the man trapped up to his elbow, rescuers had to use hydraulic shears to cut him free. He emerged unharmed but $24 poorer, while the toilet itself was completely destroyed.

Subway Hideaway

A 13-year-old boy who thought he was in trouble at school spent 11 days hiding on the New York City subway in 2009. Francisco Hernandez Jr. hid on the D train he normally rides during his short commute from his Brooklyn home to school. He slept on trains and survived on junk food he bought from newsstands along the route.

Pillow Talk

In a special ceremony in March 2010, Korean Lee Jin-gyu married a large pillow adorned with a picture of female Japanese animated character, Fate Testarossa. He put the pillow in a wedding dress for the service, which was conducted before a priest. He takes the pillow everywhere—and when he and his pillow bride go to a restaurant, the pillow gets its own seat and its own meal.

Upside-down House

A totally upside-down house opened as a tourist attraction in the grounds of a zoo in Gettorf, Germany, in 2010. Standing on a pointed roof and supported by steel beams in the attic, the 23-ft (7-m) house boasts an upside-down kitchen, as well as a completely inverted bathroom, living room and bedroom. Workers screwed 50 separate pieces into the "floor" (actually the ceiling), including beds, tables and a microwave oven. Needle and thread were used to keep bed linen in place.

Bearly Believable!

A 2010 survey showed that more than one-third of British adults still take a childhood teddy bear to bed with them at night.

Leisurely Stroll

Paul Railton was fined $100 in 2010 for taking his dog for a walk while driving alongside in his car. He was spotted driving at low speed along a country lane in County Durham, England, holding his Lurcher's leash through the car window as the dog trotted next to him.

Upside Down

Wang Xiaoyu, a barber from Changsha, Hunan Province, China, gives haircuts while standing on his head. A trained martial artist, he performs his headstands on a table to achieve the right height for cutting customers' hair.

Blamed Vampire

A Fruita, Colorado, woman who drove her car into a canal in June 2010 blamed the accident on a vampire. She said she was driving on a dirt road late at night, when she spotted a vampire in the middle of the road and hastily put the car in reverse. When troopers arrived, they found the woman's car in the canal, but there was no sign of the vampire.

Concrete Breaker

Kung fu champion Chris Roper from Suffolk, England, can break a 26-in-thick (66-cm) block of concrete with his foot, a 20-in (51-cm) block with his elbow, and a 12-in (30-cm) block with his bare hand.

Car Coffins

Automobile fan Danny Mendez of Winchester, California, has designed a range of $1,500 fiberglass coffins in the shapes of classic cars. Each Cruisin' Casket features motorcycle headlights, alloy wheels from golf carts, and extending side exhausts that serve as handles for pallbearers. In the absence of a death in the family, the coffins can also double as ice coolers.

Guardian Angel

Police in Fribourg, Switzerland, hired a roadside angel to stop motorists driving too fast. Dressed all in white, the angel, played by a bearded actor, stood at different locations and flapped his wings at speeding drivers.

Sailing in Circles

A nautical novice who thought he was sailing around the coast of Britain in a counterclockwise direction ended up circling a small island off Kent instead. He was rescued by a lifeboat after running out of fuel off the 8-mi-wide (13-km) Isle of Sheppey, whose shore he had been hugging day and night on the principle of keeping the land to his right. He had not realized that Sheppey was an island.

Road Hogs

A section of road near Eureka, Missouri, is covered with asphalt made from recycled pig manure, courtesy of a nearby hog farm.

Mayo Misery

A consignment of mayonnaise fell off the back of a truck in Hyogo, Japan, causing an eight-vehicle pileup as cars and motorcycles skidded wildly on the crushed sauce. The highway had to be closed for five hours.

Strong Hair

In November 2009, Manjit Singh from Leicester, England, pulled a double-decker London bus 70 ft (21 m)—using only his hair. By attaching a clamp to his thick ponytail, he managed to pull the seven-ton bus through Battersea Park. The feat made up for his disappointment in 2007, when he had been unable to pull a similar bus with his ears.

Wake Up!

An Australian mining company has invented a hat that wakes up sleepy truck drivers. The hi-tech SmartCap is fitted with brain monitoring sensors, and if the driver seems to be drifting off, the cap sends a message to a computer screen in the truck cab, which then flashes a warning.

Facebook Phenomenon

People across the world spend more than 700 billion minutes a month surfing through the website of Facebook, the Palo Alto, California-based social networking site. Since Facebook was launched in 2004, more than 500 million people have joined the site— that's around eight percent of the world's population.

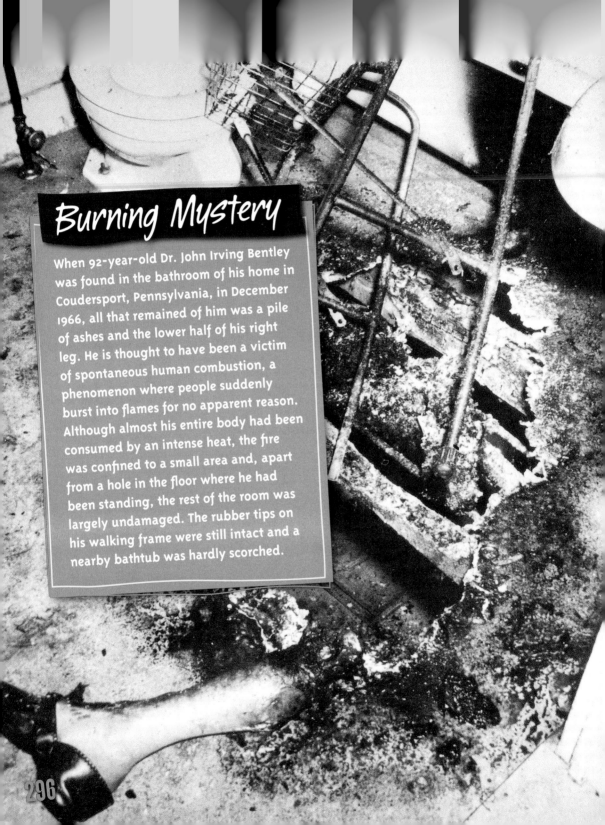

Burning Mystery

When 92-year-old Dr. John Irving Bentley was found in the bathroom of his home in Coudersport, Pennsylvania, in December 1966, all that remained of him was a pile of ashes and the lower half of his right leg. He is thought to have been a victim of spontaneous human combustion, a phenomenon where people suddenly burst into flames for no apparent reason. Although almost his entire body had been consumed by an intense heat, the fire was confined to a small area and, apart from a hole in the floor where he had been standing, the rest of the room was largely undamaged. The rubber tips on his walking frame were still intact and a nearby bathtub was hardly scorched.

Auto Inferno

Jeanna Winchester was riding in a car with a friend in Jacksonville, Florida, in 1980 when she was mysteriously engulfed in bright yellow flames. There was no spilled gas, she had not been smoking, and the car window was up. Jeanna survived, although she suffered severe burns. The car interior, however, was virtually undamaged, with just a slight browning on Jeanna's white leather seat.

Charred Remains

In March 1997, the charred remains of 76-year-old John O'Connor were found in a chair some distance from the hearth of his living room in County Kerry, Ireland. Only his head, upper torso, and feet remained unburned, yet there was little smoke damage to the room or the furniture.

Fatal Fire

Mrs. Olga Worth Stephens, 75, of Dallas, Texas, suddenly burst into flames while waiting in her parked car in 1964 and died before anyone could rescue her. The car was undamaged and firemen concluded that nothing in the vehicle could have started the fatal blaze.

Paper Puzzle

Anna Martin of West Philadelphia, Pennsylvania, was found incinerated at home in 1957, her body totally consumed by fire except for a piece of her torso and her shoes. The medical examiner estimated that temperatures must have reached at least 1,700°F (925°C)—far too hot for anything in the room to remain uncharred, yet newspapers lying just 2 ft (60 cm) away were found intact.

Subway Pushers

Human "pushers" are hired to work on Tokyo's subway system to help cram more people into the overcrowded train cars.

Burning Dress

A dress being worn by Mrs. Charles Williamson of Bladenboro, North Carolina, unaccountably burst into flames in 1932. Her husband and daughter ripped off the blazing dress with their bare hands yet none of the three suffered any burns. Over the next four days, various items in the house suddenly caught fire, but each time the flames, which had neither smoke nor smell, vanished after the article had burned itself out.

Vaporized Flesh

At Blackwood, Wales, in 1980, a man's body was found burned beyond recognition in his living room. The armchair that he was sitting in was hardly damaged—neither were some plastic objects nearby—but the fire was so intense that it left a coating of vaporized flesh on the ceiling.

Versatile Performer

Yang Guanghe, from China's Guizhou Province, can perform more than 30 different stunts—including standing on lit lightbulbs, lifting buckets of water with his eyelids, using an electric drill on his nose, standing on upturned knives, pulling a car with his eyelids, and inserting a live snake into one of his nostrils then pulling it out from his mouth.

Crystal Tears

Between March and November 1996, a 12-year-old Lebanese girl, Hasnah Mohamed Meselmani, produced glass crystal tears from her eyes. She wept tiny crystals at an average rate of seven a day, and although they were razor-sharp, she felt no pain. Physicians were mystified by her condition, which stopped as suddenly as it had started.

Mystic Cat

Oscar the cat has correctly predicted the deaths of over 50 patients at the Steere House Nursing and Rehabilitation Center in Providence, Rhode Island, by curling up next to them some two hours before they die. For more than two years, he was present at every death in the home—except one when relatives asked him to leave the room. Nurses once placed Oscar on the bed of a patient they thought was close to death, but he immediately went to sit beside someone in another room. The cat's judgment proved better than that of the medics, because while the second patient died that evening, the first lived for two more days.

House of Cards

Bryan Berg of Santa Fe, New Mexico, built a model of the Venetian Macao Resort-Hotel in Las Vegas from 218,792 playing cards, without using glue or tape. It took 44 days and 4,051 decks of cards to complete the model that measured 33 x 10 ft (10 x 3 m) and weighed 600 lb (272 kg).

Great Shakes

Dorena Young of Wallsburg, Utah, has a collection of more than 3,600 salt-and-pepper shakers. She has been collecting them for more than 60 years and has ones shaped like boats, cats, dogs, deer, vegetables, hats, lighthouses and sea horses. She even has a pair of J.F.K. and Jackie Onassis salt-and-pepper shakers.

Sneaker Line

Collecting more than 10,500 sneakers sent in by readers, *National Geographic Kids* magazine unveiled a 1.65-mi (2.65-km) line of shoes, tied together by their laces, at Washington, D.C.

Ringing Rocks

Ringing Rocks Park in Upper Black Eddy, Pennsylvania, is home to a field of boulders, which, when hit with a solid object such as a hammer, produce melodious bell-like tones.

Daring Plunge

Amateur kayaker Christie Glissmeyer from Hood River, Oregon, paddled down the 82-ft-high (25.2-m) Metlako Falls at Eagle Creek, Oregon, in May 2010—a plunge that was nearly twice the height of any waterfall she had previously run.

Dust Bunnies

These cuddly looking bunnies are actually composed of household detritus, including Christmas tree needles, discarded toddler toy parts, dryer lint, toenail clippings, and human hair. Suzanne Proulx, from Erie, Pennsylvania, took 2½ years to collect enough dirt and dust to make 16 of her *Dust Bunnies*. Suzanne's first bunnies were a humorous comment on the dust and dirt that seemed to invade her house and multiply like wild rabbits. They are also about rebirth and renewal, taking what has been thrown away and creating something new.

Skeleton Staff

When the Post-Mortem Club held its annual breakfast in Chicago in 1934, the guest of honor was the skeleton of its late founder, Mr. J. M. McAdou of Florida, who had died the previous year. The club was an organization of naprapaths (practitioners of a manual medical technique similar to osteopathy) and had a rule that stated each member should leave them his skeleton so that it could attend future meetings... although probably not vote.

Bacterial Rain

Over a three-week period in August 1994, gelatinous blobs rained down over Oakville, Washington State, leaving animals dead and people with flu-like symptoms. The blobs contained human white blood cells and two types of bacteria, one of which is found in our digestive system, but no one knows exactly where the blobs came from.

Slimy Cure

According to the African religion of Ifa Orisha, drinking the juices and mucus of Giant African snails can cure the sick.

Fish Deaths

In December 2010, more than 80,000 drum fish were found dead along a 20-mile (32-km) stretch of the Arkansas River and 10,000 red drum fish were mysteriously washed up dead in Chesapeake Bay, Maryland.

Hairy Journey

In 2007–8, German adventurer Christoph Rehage walked nearly 2,887 mi (4,646 km) across China from Beijing to Urumqi and took a picture of himself every day—so that he could document the growth of his beard.

Plain of Jars

Hundreds of ancient stone jars, some weighing up to 6 tons, can be found scattered across several square miles in northern Laos. Their purpose remains a mystery, but they may have been used to house the bodies of dead people until decomposition, after which the remains would have been removed for burial or cremation.

Polar Riddle

When video footage showed a large, white beast lying on the shore, British TV presenter Naomi Lloyd excitedly told viewers that a polar bear from the Arctic had been washed up in Bude, Cornwall. It subsequently emerged that the animal was actually a cow that had been bleached white by seawater.

Game Proposal

A New York City video-game fan proposed to his girlfriend with gold coins in a specially designed level of Super Mario World. Having persuaded her to play the game, he used a level-editing program called Lunar Magic to spell out "Lisa will you marry me?" on screen. He then recorded her delighted reaction in a video posted on YouTube.

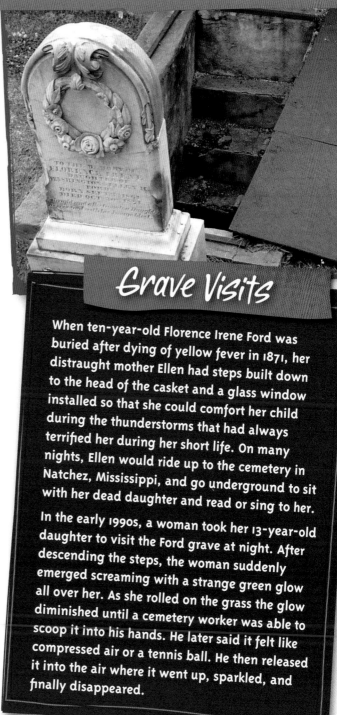

Grave Visits

When ten-year-old Florence Irene Ford was buried after dying of yellow fever in 1871, her distraught mother Ellen had steps built down to the head of the casket and a glass window installed so that she could comfort her child during the thunderstorms that had always terrified her during her short life. On many nights, Ellen would ride up to the cemetery in Natchez, Mississippi, and go underground to sit with her dead daughter and read or sing to her.

In the early 1990s, a woman took her 13-year-old daughter to visit the Ford grave at night. After descending the steps, the woman suddenly emerged screaming with a strange green glow all over her. As she rolled on the grass the glow diminished until a cemetery worker was able to scoop it into his hands. He later said it felt like compressed air or a tennis ball. He then released it into the air where it went up, sparkled, and finally disappeared.

Raining Birds

More than 5,000 dead red-winged blackbirds rained from the sky over Beebe, Arkansas, on January 1, 2011, littering the streets with corpses. Three days later, another 500 birds—dead or dying—fell onto the Louisiana Highway in Pointe Coupee Parish. Scientists say the birds, disturbed by New Year's Eve fireworks or a passing train, may have died after flying at night and crashing into trees, houses and power lines.

Marfa Lights

For over a century, witnesses have been spooked by the Marfa Lights, a strange light phenomenon occurring around the Mitchell Flats, outside Marfa, Texas. Descriptions range from small dancing lights in the sky to a single, stationary bright light that changes color. In a failed attempt to solve the mystery, a former World-War-II pilot even chased the lights in an airplane.

Ghost Yacht

A 40-ft-long (12-m) yacht, the Kaz II, was found drifting off the coast of Queensland, Australia, in 2007, with its engine running and a table laid for dinner but no sign of its three-man crew. The radio was working, the computers were running, and the lifejackets were still on board, but there was no evidence of foul play and no bodies were ever found.

Garden Fairies

Phyllis Bacon believes a fairy fluttered into her life and out again one evening in her garden in London, England. She wasn't even looking through the camera when she held it at arm's length and clicked the button to take a picture of her backyard. She spent months scouring the Internet for butterflies, beetles and moths that might match the image, but came up with nothing.

Real Fairies?

As reported in *Ripley's Believe It or Not! Enter If You Dare*, two cousins, Frances Griffiths and Elsie Wright, rocked the world in 1917 when they said they had photographed fairies in a leafy glen near Elsie's home in Cottingley, England. The five photographs were highly convincing and were published by Arthur Conan Doyle, author of the Sherlock Holmes novels, with an accompanying article. Many experts in photography and psychic research, who examined the pictures and questioned the girls, came to the conclusion that the images were genuine. It was only in the 1980s the girls admitted to faking the pictures with cardboard cutouts and hatpins. However, when Frances Griffiths' daughter appeared on the BBC TV show *The Antiques Roadshow* on January 4, 2009, with a camera given to her by Conan Doyle, she revealed that her mother claimed right up to her death that the fifth and final photograph, taken on a separate occasion and shown here, was genuine.

Rat Supper

By using a special scanning technique, scientists Henrik Lauridsen and Kasper Hansen from Aarhus, Denmark, were able to take X-rays of a python digesting a rat. The rat can be seen gradually disappearing during the course of 132 hours (5½ days) after the snake had swallowed it.

Shrinking Coins

A powerful electromagnetic field can shrink a coin to half its diameter. The technique is known as high-velocity metal forming, a process that creates an invisible, pulsed magnetic field that batters the coin with a strong shock wave, forcing it to change its physical shape in the blink of an eye.

Bullet Blocker

Colombian tailor Miguel Caballero runs a boutique in Mexico City where jackets and shirts are not stacked by size but by how well they will stop a bullet. He uses secret materials, the most expensive of which, called Black, is so light that it can be scrunched up like paper but will protect the wearer from a bullet fired at point-blank range.

Black Hole

Scientists at the Southeast University in Nanjing, China, have created a pocket-size black hole—an 8½-in-wide (21.5-cm) disk that absorbs all the electromagnetic radiation thrown at it. The metal disk has 60 concentric rings that affect the magnetic properties of passing light, bending the beams into the center of the disk and trapping them in a maze of etched grooves.

Speed of Sound

Sound travels 4.3 times faster in water than it does in air. When something vibrates, it causes molecules to bump into each other. As water molecules are closer together, the vibrations transfer faster between themselves.

Robot Olympics

At the 2010 International Robot Olympics held in Harbin, China, humanoid robots from 19 countries competed in 17 disciplines, including running, walking, boxing, kung fu and dancing. All robots had to be less than 2 ft (60 cm) tall and be built with a head, two arms and two legs. The opening event, the 5-m (5-yd) sprint, was won in a time of 20 seconds.

Yellow Deposit

An unexplained greenish-yellow goo fell from the skies and splattered houses and streets in Snyder, New York State, on January 18, 2011. As temperatures dropped, homes were coated in yellow or green icicles.

Resuscitating Roadkill

A 55-year-old man was arrested on a remote highway northeast of Pittsburgh, Pennsylvania, after he was seen performing mouth-to-mouth resuscitation on roadkill. Witnesses said the possum in question was not just playing dead, it had been deceased for some time.

Frozen with Heat

Water can be frozen solid—by applying heat! Supercooled water, which can stay liquid down to −40°F (−40°C), will freeze as it is being heated, as long as the temperature also changes the electrical charge of the surface with which the water is in contact.

Wee Folk

Two tree pods shaped like fairies are kept in a glass box at the Wat Phrapangmuni Temple near Sing Buri, Thailand. According to popular belief, these Naree Pons (or pod people) appeared to the Buddha as beautiful women while he meditated in a secluded area. They then vanished and left behind a miniature humanoid pod form on a nearby tree.

Ghostly Pleas

Sightings of the ghosts of tormented slaves from the 1830s have been reported at Lalaurie House, New Orleans. Servants who begged the assistance of outsiders when the house was burning are seen running back inside, slamming doors, shouting repeatedly. Several people have seen ghostly faces of the dead peering from upper windows.

Flaming Fireball

A massive fireball lit up the sky over five U.S. states—Missouri, Iowa, Wisconsin, Illinois and Indiana—on the night of April 14, 2010. Puzzled scientists say it could have been a meteor, a chunk from an asteroid, or rocket debris.

Eerie Face

The image of a child's face dating back over 100 years was found burned onto an old oven door at a restaurant in Saint John, New Brunswick, Canada, in the 1980s. A lady visitor to the property at 31 Leinster Street had gone into the cellar to inspect the original brick oven, but when the dirt was cleaned away the smiling face of a young girl became visible in the iron door. It is believed the family living there in the late 19th century had used the oven as a crematorium to dispose of their dead daughter. The image on the door was caused by carbons given off by the body during burning, the bright light of the fire having acted as a lens.

Advanced Mechanism

When the Antikythera Mechanism was recovered from a shipwreck near Crete in 1900, the writing on its case indicated that it was made around 80 BC—but an X-ray revealed a system of differential gears not known to have existed until AD 1575. It is believed to be an ancient mechanical computer designed to calculate astronomical positions, but its sophistication is in fact comparable to a 19th-century Swiss clock.

Ghostly Vision

When Kevin Horkin downloaded this photo and saw a pale young woman peering from a window on the first floor of Gwrych Castle in Abergele, he knew something spooky was afoot. The huge Welsh castle has been derelict since 1985 and the floor crumbled away years ago, so no one could possibly have been standing there. Countless sightings, orbs, cold spots and cases of objects moving have been recorded at Gwrych, said to be the most haunted building in Wales.

Mary, the Hanged Elephant

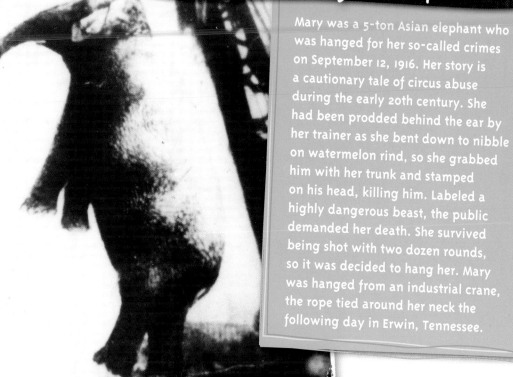

Mary was a 5-ton Asian elephant who was hanged for her so-called crimes on September 12, 1916. Her story is a cautionary tale of circus abuse during the early 20th century. She had been prodded behind the ear by her trainer as she bent down to nibble on watermelon rind, so she grabbed him with her trunk and stamped on his head, killing him. Labeled a highly dangerous beast, the public demanded her death. She survived being shot with two dozen rounds, so it was decided to hang her. Mary was hanged from an industrial crane, the rope tied around her neck the following day in Erwin, Tennessee.

Phone Home

A man has spent two years living in a cramped phone booth in Dalian City, Liaoning Province, China. He sleeps by curling up into a ball on top of cushions and hangs his spare clothes from the roof.

Elephant Collision

Driving home from church in Enid, Oklahoma, a couple collided with an elephant that ran across the highway after escaping from a nearby circus. The elephant was unharmed apart from a broken tusk.

Stone Balls

In the Costa Rican jungle in the 1930s, workmen found more than 300 man-made stone balls, many perfectly spherical and varying in size from as small as a tennis ball to huge boulders 8 ft (2.4 m) in diameter and weighing 15 tons. The stones date back at least 500 years, but nobody knows who made them and how they achieved such perfect spheres.

Paid Piper

Tourism bosses in Vienna, Austria, found a way to frighten off rats from the city's sewers—by playing the bagpipes. *The Third Man* tours, which walk the sewers made famous by Orson Welles' cult 1949 movie, were closed down when health chiefs ruled that the risk of rat bites was too great, but now they're back in business after hiring a bagpiper whose shrill sounds remarkably send the rodents running for cover.

Quiet Companion

Alan Derrick of Somerset, England, lived in a house with the dead body of his friend hidden behind a sofa from 1998 to 2008.

Dam Coincidence

J.G. Tierney drowned in 1922 while surveying the future site of the Hoover Dam. In 1935, his son Patrick became the last person to die in the dam's construction when he fell from an intake tower.

Milk Miracle

For several hours on September 21, 1995, Hindu religious statues all over the world drank milk. When a worshiper at a temple in New Delhi, India, offered milk to the trunk of a statue of the elephant-headed deity Ganesha, the liquid was seen to disappear. Soon Hindu temples in the U.K., Canada, Dubai and Nepal were reporting similar occurrences. Scientists were baffled by the phenomenon, which stopped before the end of the day when statues suddenly refused the milk.

Elephant Electrocution

In an attempt to prove the dangers of Nikola Tesla's alternating current (AC) and the safety of his competing direct current (DC) for use in the home, Thomas Edison electrocuted an elephant in 1903. Topsy was an elephant with Forepaugh Circus at Coney Island's Luna Park, New York City, who had killed three men in three years, and her owners wanted her destroyed. Edison suggested electrocution, a method that had been used for human executions since 1890. Topsy was fed carrots containing potassium cyanide before a current of 6,600 volts was sent through her body, killing her in seconds. A crowd of 1,500 witnessed the event, which Edison also filmed.

Robotic Jellyfish

Scientists in Germany have developed a range of biologically inspired robotic jellyfish that can swim. The battery-powered jellyfish are propelled through the water by eight electrically driven tentacles, the construction of which is based on the anatomy of fish fins. With the help of sensors and control software, the jellyfish steer themselves and can communicate by means of 11 infrared light-emitting diodes, enabling them to work together as a team and to avoid bumping into each other.

Robot Wedding

A wedding that took place in a Tokyo, Japan, restaurant in May 2010 was conducted by a robot. Bride Satoko Inoue and groom Tomohiro Shibata were directed through the ceremony by I-Fairy, a 4-ft (1.2-m) robot, who wore a wreath of flowers and a set of wires that led to a human controller who was sitting at a nearby computer.

Who Goes Hare!

In 1971, a rabbit was shot by Jasper Barrett near his home in Jefferson, South Carolina. On being prepared for the pot by his wife and a friend, the outline in black of a woman's face was found on the skinned flesh of one foreleg. It was about an inch (2.5 cm) across and had a rosebud mouth, curly hair and long lashes. Within a week, 4,000 people had trekked to see the face and police were called to control the crowds.

Healing Hand

Surgeons in China saved a young girl's hand by grafting it on to her leg for three months. Nine-year-old Ming Li lost her left hand when she was run over by a tractor on her way to school in Zhengzhou, Henan Province. Her arm was too badly crushed to reattach the hand to her wrist so doctors grafted it on to her right calf instead, before transplanting it back on to her arm once it had healed.

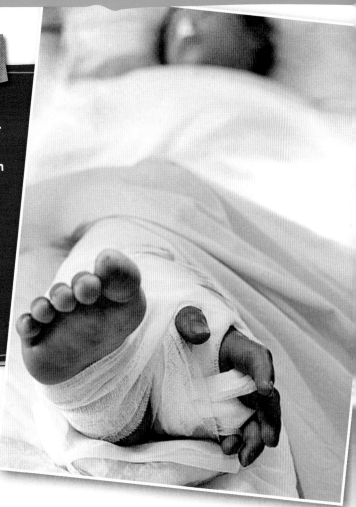

Iceman's Relatives

Nearly 20 years after discovering the mummified body of a 5,300-year-old man—known as Oetzi the iceman—in a melting Alpine glacier, scientists have extracted DNA from a bone in his pelvis with a view to tracking down his living descendants.

Strong Stomach

Julika Faciu from Piatra Neamt, Romania, allowed 50 motorbikes and a 3-ton jeep to ride over his stomach, one by one.

Underground City

A series of streets, houses and tombs belonging to an Egyptian city dating back more than 3,500 years has been located by radar. Austrian archeologists used radar imaging to show the outlines of Avaris, the ancient capital of the Hyksos people, beneath fields and modern buildings in the Nile Delta.

Clean Teen

As a teenager, James Brown from Nottinghamshire, England, had a collection of 50 vacuum cleaners—and his love for them has led to him opening Britain's first vacuum cleaner museum. He can identify different brands of vacuum cleaners in his collection simply by the sound they make.

Dried Shark

A seafront store in Taiwan offers whole dried sharks for sale at a price of 6,500 Hong Kong dollars (U.S. $844) per 1 lb 5 oz (600 g). Shark fins are a popular delicacy in Chinese soup, while other parts of the shark are considered to have beneficial medicinal properties.

Homemade Reactor

Mark Suppes, a 32-year-old web designer for fashion house Gucci, has built his own homemade nuclear fusion reactor on the third floor of a Brooklyn, New York City, warehouse. He took two years to build it, using $35,000 worth of parts he bought on eBay.

Unfinished City

Having spent years constructing 30-ft-high (9-m) walls from perfectly hewn basalt, the inhabitants of the ancient city of Nan Madol, in the Micronesia region of the Pacific, mysteriously abandoned it, leaving some of the walls unfinished.

Homemade Plane

In July 2010, 82-year-old Arnold Ebneter of Woodinville, Washington State, flew his homemade lightweight airplane, the E-1, nonstop from Everett, Washington State, to Fredericksburg, Virginia—a journey of 2,327 mi (3,746 km) —in 18 hours 27 minutes.

King Charles

Charles Wesley Mumbere worked as a nurses' aide for years in the U.S.A., but on October 19, 2009, he reclaimed his crown as head of the mountainous kingdom of Rwenzururu in Uganda, ruling over about 300,000 people.

Rolling, Rolling, Rolling...

Lotan Baba, the "Rolling Saint" of India, spreads his message of peace by rolling on the ground from town to town across the country. He rolls 6–8 mi (10–12 km) a day and estimates that over the years he has rolled about 18,650 mi (30,000 km). His enthusiasm for rolling may be partly explained by the fact that as penance he once spent seven years standing upright, in the same place.

Fire Trim

Italian-American hairdresser Pietro Santoro cuts hair using a naked flame at his barber shop in Washington, D.C. He says that cutting hair with fire gives it more body.

Debt Unpaid

Former British Prime Minister Winston Churchill (1874–1965) died owing 13 rupees to the Bangalore Club of Bangalore, India. The club has maintained the ledger showing that debt and displays it—but refuses to allow anyone to pay his tab.

Ripley's Hero

Daring Thai snake charmer Khum Chaibuddee, also known as the "King of Cobras," was honored as a Ripley's Ambassador by the Ripley's Believe It or Not museum in Pattaya, Thailand, in 2010. He celebrated by performing with his deadly cobras and even kissing them, his signature trick. In *Ripley's Believe It or Not! The Remarkable Revealed*, we reported that a fearless Khum had kissed 19 highly poisonous cobras one by one on the head without being bitten.

Lively Landings

Giant 300-ton Boeing 747s coming in to land at Princess Juliana Airport on the Caribbean island of Saint Martin fly just 60 ft (18.4 m) above the heads of vacationers on Maho Beach.

They fly so low that they blow sand into the faces of plane spotters gathered below. The beach is right next to the runway, which, at 7,054 ft (2,170 m), is the shortest in the world to regularly accommodate 747s.

Over the autobahn Leipzig Hall Airport, Germany.

JADE CARGO

Low tide Barra Airport, Scotland.

Smoothed ice and snow ice runway in Antarctica.

Crossing the highway Gibraltar Airport.

Beige World

After examining the amounts of light emitted by galaxies, scientists at NASA have concluded that the Universe is not really black at all—more a dull beige. They say that the shade is constantly changing and has become much less blue over the past ten billion years because redder stars are now more dominant.

First Computer

Unveiled in 1946 at the University of Pennsylvania, ENIAC (short for Electronic Numerical Integrator and Computer) was the world's first general-purpose computer. It weighed 30 tons and occupied an entire room. Amazingly, its computing ability can be re-created today on a silicon chip smaller than your thumbnail.

Anti-flu Suit

A Japanese menswear company has developed a suit that it claims protects the wearer from the deadly H1N1 strain of influenza. The $550 suit, produced by the Haruyama Trading Company, is coated with the chemical titanium dioxide—an ingredient of toothpaste and cosmetics—that reacts with light to break down and kill the virus on contact.

Oh, Crumbs!

The Swiss-based Large Hadron Collider, the world's most powerful particle accelerator and probably the most complex machine ever built, was shut down in 2009 after a bird passing overhead dropped a piece of bread on a section of machinery, which caused parts of the accelerator to overheat.

Skiing Robot

A skiing robot that can navigate slalom courses has been developed by researchers at the Jozef Stefan Institute in Slovenia. The robot, which is about the size of an eight-year-old child and uses regular skis, has a pair of computer systems. One of them is attached to cameras to help plot the robot's course down the slope, the other is attached to gyroscopes and force sensors to keep it stable.

Plasma Knife

To help stem the loss of blood from serious wounds, the U.S. military has been testing a plasma knife, with a blade consisting of heated, ionized gas, which can cut through flesh just as easily as a steel scalpel. The plasma knife seals off the damaged flesh, stopping the bleeding and protecting against infection.

Phone Control

The iDriver app enables motorists to drive a car using their cell phone. Devised by researchers from Berlin, Germany, the app has a steering wheel, separate buttons for accelerating and braking, and is capable of directing a 2-ton minivan.

Large Dish

The Large Zenith Telescope at the University of British Columbia in Canada uses a mirror made from a spinning dish of liquid mercury nearly 20 ft (6.1 m) in diameter.

Bell Tribute

On August 4, 1922—the day of the funeral of Alexander Graham Bell—all telephone services in the U.S.A. and Canada were shut down for one minute as a tribute to the inventor, who, in the 1870s, had invented the world's first workable telephone.

Rotten Eggs

As part of a safety campaign in 2010, Puget Sound Energy, a utility company in Washington State, added the stench of rotten eggs to its gas bills. Natural gas is odorless, but providers add a chemical with a sulfurlike aroma to the gas so that leaks can be detected.

Smells good

Body Art

Hong Kong radiologist Kai-Hung Fung has created stunning images of the human body that look like works of art. Dr. Fung scans the patient using a conventional computer topography (CT) scan, generally used for diagnosing brain and cardiac problems, before feeding the information into a computer and adding vivid color.

Bite Size

Say what?

317

Wrong Funeral

After reading a death notice in her local paper in Merthyr Tydfil, Wales, stating that upholsterer Ron Jones had passed away, Margaret Griffiths sat through the funeral service for her old friend—only to discover later that she had got the wrong Ron Jones. The confusion arose because there were two men named Ron Jones of similar age in the town and both had worked as upholsterers.

Strange Venue

Jason and Rachael Storm decided to start their life together in 2008 by getting married at a place where it usually comes to an end—a funeral home in St. Joseph Township, Michigan, where the groom was a director.

Mobile Chapel

A 1942 firetruck owned by Rev. Darrell Best, of Shelbyville, Illinois, has been converted into a mobile wedding chapel called "Best Man." It has stained glass windows, an altar, two wooden pews and a fully working pipe organ.

Huge Hole

A 66-ft-wide (20-m) sinkhole opened up overnight in the yard of the Zhang family home in Leshan, China. Several fruit trees disappeared down the hole, which was more than 130 ft (40 m) deep and stopped less than 3 ft (1 m) from the house.

Crab Dispenser

A food vending machine in Nanjing, China, sells live crabs. Designed by Shi Tuanjie, the machine offers live hairy crabs and accompanying bottles of vinegar. The crustaceans vary in price from $2 to $7, according to size. The crabs, a tasty delicacy in the region, are packed into plastic boxes and chilled to 40°F (5°C), leaving them sedated but still alive. An average of 200 crabs a day are sold, and customers are promised compensation of three live crabs should their purchase happen to be dead.

Snow Palace

To create a fairy-tale setting for his ultimately successful marriage proposal to Christi Lombardo in February 2010, Ryan Knotek built a snow castle near his home in Parma, Ohio. Using blocks of snow, he constructed a one-room, one-story palace topped with roof spires and furnished inside with a portable heater to keep the winter chill away.

Flamboyant Funeral

Flamboyant Hong-Kong lawyer Kai-bong Chau, 75, was buried in March 2010 with paper replicas of his gold and pink Rolls-Royce cars and a selection of his most colorful outfits. Paper models of cars, homes and money are traditionally burned at Chinese funerals to provide the dead with comfort and luxuries in the afterlife.

Young Undertaker

In September 2010, George Simnett set up his own funeral business in Leicestershire, England—at age 17.

Blessed Computers

To attract bankers and financiers from the City of London to his church, the Rev. Canon David Parrott performed a service in which he blessed their cell phones and laptop computers.

INCREDIBLY
STRANGE

Fast Food

Patrick "Deep Dish" Bertoletti from Chicago is one of the world's most successful competitive eaters. In 2008, he became an official pizza-eating world champion, devouring 47 slices of 16-in (41-cm) deep dish in 10 minutes. Most people might not finish even half of one large pizza in that time.

Highlights of Patrick's career include finishing off more than 10 lb (4.5 kg) of Key lime pie in 8 minutes and 275 pickled peppers in 10 minutes. These and many more appetite-busting achievements mean that Patrick is ranked in the top five eaters in the world by the sport's Major League Eating organization. In 2010, in Black Hawk, Colorado, Patrick swallowed 3 lb 11¾ oz (1.7 kg) of deep-fried bull's testicles in 10 minutes.

You don't need to be extremely heavy to be an eating champion; in fact many eating champions are in good shape. Culinary-school graduate Patrick weighs in at 190 lb (86 kg), relatively lightweight given his 6-ft-2-in (1.88-m) frame and the vast amounts of food he consumes at eating competitions—

regularly gulping down more than 10,000 calories in a few minutes. Fittingly, Patrick works as a chef and hopes to open his own restaurant—serving regular-sized portions.

Patrick's Menu		
Food	Amount	Time
Blueberry pie	9 lb (4 kg)	8 minutes
Slushie	22 fl oz (650 ml)	9 seconds
Hotdogs	55	10 minutes
Pizza (16 in/41 cm)	47 slices	10 minutes
Hamburgers	94	8 minutes
Chicken wings	227	30 minutes
Chili spaghetti	11½ lb (5.2 kg)	10 minutes
Ribs	8½ lb (3.8 kg)	12 minutes
Subs (8 in/20 cm)	14	10 minutes

All at Sea

American sailor Reid Stowe returned to shore in June 2010 after spending more than three years at sea without touching dry land. He set off from New Jersey in his 70-ft (21-m) schooner Anne in April 2007 and docked in Manhattan at the end of a 1,152-day voyage, to be greeted by his girlfriend, who had joined him on part of the voyage, and their 23-month-old son, whom he had never seen before.

Bullion Bugatti

Made from solid 24-carat gold and platinum and featuring a large, flawless diamond on the front grille, the Bugatti Veyron Diamond must be the most expensive toy car ever made. It may be only toy-sized, weighing 15 lb (7 kg) and measuring 10 in (25 cm) in length, but it costs a cool $2 million to buy—that's almost twice as expensive as a real, regular-sized Bugatti Veyron! Jewelry designer Stuart Hughes from Liverpool, England, and Swiss model expert Robert Gulpen spent two months creating this intricate replica, which also features functional steering and a detailed engine.

Hang Time

An Oklahoma driver escaped disaster after reversing his Mercedes sedan through the exterior wall of a parking garage—seven floors up! The driver's foot had become stuck on the gas pedal, but luckily the vehicle lodged itself halfway through the exterior wall. Falling debris damaged several cars, but no one was injured and the driver exited his vehicle safely.

High Security

The $400-million yacht, 557 ft (170 m) long, owned by Russian billionaire Roman Abramovich, is equipped with a swimming pool, two helipads, a mini-submarine and a missile defense system.

Highway Party

Some 20,000 tables were set up along a 37-mile (60-km) section of a German autobahn between Dortmund and Duisberg for a street party with a difference. The high-speed road was closed to motorists and turned over to cyclists, skaters, and picnickers in an event attended by more than three million people.

Bacon Kevin Bacon

J & D's Foods in Seattle commissioned Pennsylvania artist Mike Lahue to create a sculpture of actor Kevin Bacon, from crispy bacon bits! The tasty Hollywood head took three months to complete, but unfortunately it is inedible owing to a protective lacquer coating.

A bacon-obsessed food company from Seattle, J & D's Foods produce bacon soda, "baconnaise" mayonnaise, bacon popcorn, envelopes that taste of bacon when you lick the seal and even bacon lip balm. Their company slogan is "Everything should taste like bacon."

Curry Boom

In 1950, there were only six Indian restaurants in the whole of Great Britain, but by 2004 their number had grown to around 9,000.

Persistent Offender

A Saudi-Arabian student racked up $97,000 in driving fines—the result of 400 traffic violations in Dubai over a period of less than two years.

Slow Getaway

A burglary suspect in Hillsborough County, Florida, was quickly captured after trying to evade arrest by escaping on a lawn mower.

Spoon Fed

Surgeons in Rotterdam, the Netherlands, removed 78 different items of cutlery from the stomach of 52-year-old Margaret Daalmans after she had gone to the hospital complaining of stomach pains. X-rays showed she had swallowed dozens of forks and spoons as a result of her insatiable appetite for cutlery.

Field Day

James Field from Sheffield, England, made 42 bungee jumps in one hour—that's nearly one jump a minute—from a crane that was raised 160 ft (49 m) in the air near Tower Bridge, London.

Lucky Leap

During a traffic accident in August 2009, Carl Brewer of Canton, Ohio, saved himself by leaping from his motorcycle onto the back of a moving pickup truck.

Ship Found

In 2010, archeologists excavating the World Trade Center site in New York City discovered the remains of a wooden ship believed to have been buried there more than 200 years ago.

The Lost Squadron

A World-War-II fighter plane was rescued and restored to flying condition after spending 50 years buried beneath 268 ft (82 m) of solid snow and ice in Greenland.

The Lockheed P-38F Lightning, since nicknamed "Glacier Girl," was part of an eight-strong squadron making its way across the Atlantic to fight in Europe in June 1942. Bad weather forced the squadron to crash-land on a remote ice cap in Greenland. The crews were rescued after ten days on the ice, but the planes had to be sacrificed.

Later attempts to recover the aircraft proved unsuccessful because decades of snowstorms and shifting ice had carried them 2 mi (3.2 km) from their original location, and buried them so deep no one could find them. Then, in 1988, Glacier Girl was tracked down by a combination of magnetometers (to detect underground magnetic fields) and radar. A daring rescue and restoration project then swung into action.

Glacier Girl flying above Nevada in 2006. More than 80 percent of the new aircraft was built from original parts retrieved from deep beneath Greenland's ice and snow. In October 2002, before a crowd of 20,000 spectators, Glacier Girl took to the skies once again—60 years after her fateful crash in the Arctic. Now the plane can be seen at air shows across the U.S.A.

Sparkling Blades

War correspondent Michael Yon captured an unusual phenomenon while working in Afghanistan. When U.S. Air Force helicopters come in to land, the dust in the air reacts with the spinning blades to create static electricity that throws out bright sparks around the chopper. Michael named this the Kopp-Etchells effect, after U.S. soldier Benjamin Kopp and British soldier Joseph Etchells, both of whom Yon knew and whom died in the conflict.

Back to Life

A 1929 Austin 12/4 car that had been languishing idly in a garage in Lincolnshire, England, instantly roared into life in 2010 when its starter handle was turned for the first time in nearly 50 years. The car had been owned by Roger Bulled's late father, Leslie, who had last driven it in 1961.

Hypersonic Flight

Flying off the coast of southern California in May 2010, an unmanned X-51A Waverider aircraft flew for more than three minutes at Mach 5—that's five times the speed of sound and more than 3,800 mph (6,115 km/h).

Wrong Nuts

In May 2009, a car traveling down a Swiss highway lost all four of its wheels at the same time. The owner had used the wrong nuts to secure them.

Police Tractor

To combat crime in rural areas of Lincolnshire, England, a farm tractor has been converted into a police vehicle, complete with a flashing blue light.

Off the Rails

One of the most bizarre rail accidents in history occurred in 1895, when a steam locomotive thundered into the Montparnasse station in Paris, France, at full speed. The engine plowed through the platform and then the station wall, crashing into the street 30 ft (9 m) below and killing a pedestrian. The train had been 2 mi (3.2 km) from the station and traveling at 55 mph (90 km/h) when the driver realized that the brakes had failed. Despite the driver's best efforts, the locomotive hit the station at 35 mph (55 km/h). All those aboard escaped serious injury.

Helicopter Rescue

A Swiss van driver and his vehicle had to be rescued by helicopter after his GPS sent him up a remote mountain footpath near Bergun. Robert Ziegler found himself stranded on the narrow track, unable to go forward or turn around.

Lost Torpedo

The Taiwanese navy offered a reward of nearly $1,000 in 2010 after sailors aboard the submarine Sea Dragon lost a torpedo during a routine training exercise.

INCREDIBLY STRANGE

Flame Thrower

Fed up with car drivers cutting him off on the road, James Bond fan Colin Furze from Lincolnshire, England, designed the ultimate revenge—a gadget that fires 15-ft-long (4.5-m) flames out the back of his moped.

Toilet Car

Dave Hersch of Lakewood, Colorado, spent four years designing a twin-bowl motorized toilet capable of reaching speeds of 30 mph (48 km/h). His "toilet car" has a 6.5 horsepower motor, can seat two people, and features six toilet rolls and a magazine rack.

Busy Airport

London's Heathrow Airport is six times the size of the country of Monaco and has three chaplains—Anglican, Catholic, Free Church—and representatives for the Jewish, Muslim, Hindu, Buddhist and Sikh faiths. Nearly 70 million passengers pass through the airport each year, and 10 percent of Britain's perfume sales take place there.

Ejector Scare

A civilian passenger in a South African Air Force display plane accidentally activated the ejector seat while reaching for something to steady himself during a spectacular midair maneuver. The startled passenger instantly shot through the jet's Perspex canopy and was blasted 300 ft (90 m) into the sky by the rocket-powered emergency chair. He subsequently floated down to the ground on a parachute that opened automatically.

Barbie Ban

Forty-year-old Paul Hutton of Essex, England, was banned from the road after being caught drunk driving in a toy Barbie car that had a top speed of 4 mph (6 km/h). The electric car was designed for three-to-five-year-olds.

Much Traveled

German police who stopped a double-decker Latvian tour bus in Berlin in 2010 found that it had 1.1 million mi (1.8 million km) on the clock—enough to take passengers to the Moon and back twice.

Jet Bus

It wouldn't take long to get to school in Paul Stender's jet-powered school bus. School Time is equipped with a massive Phantom jet-fighter engine with the power of more than 250 family automobiles, propelling the 35-ft (10.5-m) bus to speeds of more than 350 mph (560 km/h). Paul has also built a 10,000-horsepower Dodge pickup that can reach up to 400 mph (645 km/h), and a jet-powered outhouse featured in *Ripley's Believe It or Not! Seeing is Believing*.

Sausage Drama

A cleaner was taken to hospital in May 2010 after his head and shoulders were sucked into a sausage machine at a factory in Danvers, Massachusetts. The victim, who was not seriously hurt, was cleaning the inside of a cylinder that draws marinade into the meat, when the machine was accidentally switched on.

Gigantic Grill

Jack Henriques, an engineer from Gloucestershire, England, has built a giant barbecue that can cook 1,000 sausages or grill 500 burgers at once. He spent three months welding together the steel grill, which weighs 2 tons and measures 16 ft (5 m) long, 6 ft 3 in (1.9 m) wide, and 11½ ft (3.5 m) tall. The $15,000 barbecue, which requires 14 bags of coal to fill fully, is so big it can cook seven whole lambs, three whole pigs, or two whole cows at the same time.

Super Salami

A monster salami measuring 7 ft 3 in (2.2 m) long and weighing 143 lb (65 kg) went on show at the Agricultural Trading Exhibition in Anhui, China, in February 2010.

Volcano Barbecue

When Iceland's Fimmvörðuháls volcano erupted in April 2010, Reykjavik chef Fridgeir Eiriksson cooked soup, flaming lobster, monkfish, and shallots using the volcano's 390°F (200°C) lava as an oven. Two customers paid $1,000 to enjoy the special Champagne dinner on the bubbling volcano.

Flying Car

A company from Massachusetts has devised a road car that can convert into an airplane in just 30 seconds. The Terrafugia Transition, which has four wheels, two folding wings, and a propeller at the rear, can reach speeds of 80 mph (130 km/h) on the ground and 115 mph (185 km/h) in the air. It can be stored in a conventional garage, yet has a flight range of more than 490 mi (790 km).

Wall of Death

The crowd peers over the Wall of Death as the powerful motorbikes roll into the ring. The sound inside the track grows deafening as the motorbikes accelerate, tires rumbling. As they pick up speed, the bikes climb the steep, wooden walls until the riders flash inches past the faces in the audience.

Tubular tracks with steep walls, Walls of Death, or Motordromes, evolved in the early 20th century. Riders would start at the bottom of the circular track, increasing their speed and the angle, until they were racing at just over 55 mph (88 km/h) at right angles to the wooden wall. One slip could spell disaster—early Wall of Death riders had little or no safety equipment, often neglecting to wear helmets because the force of gravity would make it hard to keep their head straight. Soon riders started to increase the risk, racing two or three abreast, crossing each other. Eventually, the races introduced motorcars, too. Optimum speed was essential. If the bikes went slower than 55 mph (88 km/h), they would drop off the wall; too much faster and the riders were in danger of blacking out as the centrifugal force could drain blood from the brain. Motordromes are now rare—few exist in North America and Europe, but they are still popular in Asia.

Cookie Crum, still riding motorbikes and now living in Oregon, was one of the few female Motordrome riders. She first started to ride the Wall of Death in 1949, at only 17 years old, and she toured the U.S.A. for eight years. Cookie also rode in what became known as "liondromes." To thrill the crowd even further, fully grown lions were let loose on the boards, the idea being that they would chase the rider around the ring. Incredibly, they were also trained to sit in vehicles as they tore around the Motordrome (see far left).

Stuntmen perform death-defying feats on motorbikes and in cars whizzing around the walls of "Wells of Death" at fairs across India. A modern twist on the original Walls of Death, these dromes attract large crowds wherever they spring up.

Yellow Lines

Sally Baker left her Peugeot 206 on a street in Manchester, England, because the road had unrestricted parking—but when she returned she found the vehicle was facing the other way, had double yellow lines painted underneath, and had a parking ticket on the windshield. In her absence, council workmen had hoisted her car into the air so that they could paint double yellow "no parking" lines beneath it.

Bike Burial

When Harry "The Horse" Flamburis, a Hells' Angels motorcycle club leader from Daly City, California, died, he was buried with his motorbike.

Lamborghini Replica

Truck driver Chen Jinmiao of Hunan Province, China, built a replica Lamborghini supercar—complete with the famous wing doors—for just $3,000. He downloaded the drawings from the Internet and bought materials from markets and bargain stores to construct a working car with a top speed of 50 mph (80 km/h)—compared to a real Lamborghini's 200 mph (320 km/h).

Personal Potholes

In an attempt to finance the repair of its crumbling roads, the village of Niederzimmern, Germany, put its many potholes up for sale in 2010. For $68, people could buy a hole in the road, and in return the authorities repaired it and put a personal message on top. TV channels and newspapers soon bought some of the potholes for advertising.

Melon-coly Motorists

A busy motorway near Basel, Switzerland, was closed for two hours after a Spanish truck carrying melons lost its load and splattered fruit all over the road. Drivers in the 3-mi-long (5-km) traffic jam eased the pain of their delay by getting out of their cars and helping themselves to the melons.

Homemade Sub

In October 2009, Tao Xiangli, a farmer from Beijing, China, made a successful maiden voyage in his homemade submarine. Without any expert advice, he spent 18 months building the 4-ft-10-in-high (1.5-m), 21-ft-long (6.5-m), one-man, battery-powered sub from used scrap. The body is made out of five oil drums, the sonar is improvised from a stethoscope, and the periscope is an old camera. He tested the vessel by taking it down to the bottom of a local river and staying on the riverbed for nearly five minutes.

Gatorbike

Jim Jablon from Florida has made a wild custom motorbike from a real-life alligator. Each year a number of wild alligators in the state are culled to control the population, and Jim decided to put one to good use. The reptilian chopper, named the GatorBike, took over a year to build, and features the full skull and skin of an alligator. Worth $80,000, the bike was created to raise funds for Jablon's wildlife rehabilitation park, which has its own rescued alligators alongside other animals, such as Arctic, the large albino Burmese python pictured around Jim's neck.

Built to Last

School caretaker Owen Hook of Cambridgeshire, England, has ridden the same bicycle for nearly 60 years. He bought the top-of-the-line three-speed Raleigh cycle in 1953 and still rides it half a mile (0.8 km) to and from work every day.

Sound Asleep

A French teenager who fell asleep between rail tracks escaped injury when a high-speed train passed right over him. The driver of the TGV train between Paris and Quimper noticed the 19-year-old lying stretched out on his stomach between the rails, but the train was traveling so fast that it continued for another 900 yd (820 m) before it was brought to a halt, passing right over the man who remained sound asleep throughout.

Maiden Flight

After six years of design and construction, a Chinese cobbler, who left school with only a basic education, completed a maiden flight in his homemade airplane. Huang Jianjun of Hunan Province spent more than $15,000 on the project—and in June 2010 his plane soared to a height of over 1,640 ft (500 m) before safely landing.

Emergency Landing

Pilot Matt Conway was forced to make an emergency landing on a busy Atlanta, Georgia, highway after his plane experienced engine problems. He touched down on Interstate 85, a few miles from Peachtree DeKalb Airport, and skidded to a halt without hitting any cars. However, the plane did block four lanes, causing a long traffic jam until it was hauled away a few hours later.

Modern Sailing

To cut fuel costs by 20 percent and reduce greenhouse emissions, the 10,000-ton German cargo ship MV *Beluga Skysails* is partially powered by a huge kite. In a throwback to old sailing ships, the 433-ft-long (132-m) vessel is pulled by a computer-guided 1,720-sq-ft (160-sq-m) kite, which is tethered to a 49-ft-high (15-m) mast.

Viking Land Boat

Matt Norris of Austin, Texas, spent two years building a 45-ft-long (14-m) human-powered road vehicle in the style of a Viking longboat. Made of steel and corrugated plastic, it glides on trailer tires, has the axle of a golf cart, and is propelled by its crew of 13 people who "row" a system of pulleys and cables.

Banana Ketchup

Made from mashed banana, sugar, vinegar and spices, banana ketchup is a popular Filipino condiment that is often colored red to resemble tomato ketchup. It was first produced during World War II when there was a shortage of tomato ketchup but an abundance of bananas.

Long-life Burger

Wellness consultant Karen Hanrahan of Chicago, Illinois, has kept a burger for more than 14 years—without doing anything to preserve it—and it still looks as fresh as the day she bought it!

Bottle Track

Li Guiwen, a military driver from Beijing, China, gently steered a car along a track made up of two rows of upright bottles for more than 195 ft (60 m). His journey along the 1,798 bottles of beer took 8 minutes 28 seconds.

Taos Hum

For years, people in and around the town of Taos, New Mexico, have been able to hear a curious low-frequency noise known as the Taos Hum. Not audible to everyone, it has been described as sounding like a distant diesel engine, but its source has never been traced.

Inflatable Weapons

Russian balloon manufacturer Rusbal has created a range of full-size inflatable weapons—including fighter planes and tanks (see above)—that look realistic to the enemy from as near as 330 ft (100 m). The country's defense department commissioned the models as decoys in order to protect real combat units from strikes.

Such inflatables are not a new invention. During World War II, the British army used blow-up rubber tanks as decoys. Designed to look just like a U.S. Sherman tank—and easily carried by four men—they were deployed before the Normandy Landings in 1944 in an attempt to deceive the German Army.

Fake Porsche

Austrian artist Hannes Langeder spent six months building a life-size Porsche sports car from plastic pipes, tape, and cardboard. The aluminum-foil-covered Ferdinand GT3-RS has no engine, but is powered by a hidden bicycle, which is why it has handlebars instead of a steering wheel.

Waterfall Diver

A former chauffeur, Di Huanran now makes his living by diving from waterfalls at Jingpo Lake, Heilongjiang Province, China. It was there, in 1983, that he first plunged nearly 75 ft (23 m) down the Diaoshuilou Waterfall into the fast-flowing waters below, and he has since made thousands of dives.

Bridge of Bottles

Jack Waterfall who comes from Cambridgeshire, England, designed a 118-ft-long (36-m) bridge made from 14,100 plastic milk bottles. The bridge represented the amount of plastic that people in Cambridgeshire use each day by lunchtime.

Holy Boy

An 11-year-old boy decided not to go back to school in Boston, Massachusetts, in 2009 after he was declared the reincarnation of a Buddhist holy man who first died in 1250. Instead, Jigme Wangchuk has moved to Darjeeling, India, where as the head of a Buddhist sect he will spend ten years in virtual seclusion. His parents say they realized he was not like other children when he went into trances and talked about his "past life," giving vivid descriptions of a temple he had never visited.

Base Jump

Two days after the official opening of the 2,720-ft-high (828-m) Burj Kalifa tower in Dubai, BASE jumpers Al Neyadi and Omar Alhegelan, who have made more than 17,000 skydives between them, plunged 2,204 ft (672 m) from the structure. After free falling for 10 seconds, they unfurled parachutes to sail another 30 seconds to the ground.

Cone Fall

Shortly after takeoff, a 20-lb (9-kg) engine tailcone, measuring 4 ft (1.2 m) long and 3 ft (90 cm) in diameter, plummeted thousands of feet from a Delta Air Lines jet and landed on the lawn of a home in Roosevelt, New York. None of the crew noticed that the part had fallen off, and the plane—a Boeing 777—was able to complete its journey from Kennedy Airport to Tokyo, Japan.

Lion Burger

To mark the 2010 soccer World Cup in South Africa, a restaurant in Mesa, Arizona, added lion burgers to its menu. Cameron Selogie's Il Vinaio restaurant offered the burger (from farm-raised lion) at $21, served with spicy homemade fries and roast corn on the cob.

Ring Recovery

A man who promised his wife of three months that he would find his wedding ring after it fell into Wellington Harbour, New Zealand, in 2008 finally recovered it 16 months later. Ecologist Aleki Taumoepeau was checking the harbor for invasive plant species when the ring fell into 10 ft (3 m) of water. He threw an anchor overboard to mark the spot and although initial searches failed, his persistence eventually paid off.

Pier Pressure

Over a period of two years, Hazel Costin and Jay Preller of Somerset, England, kissed at the end of all 55 British piers before getting married on Brighton Pier. They had originally met on the Grand Pier at Weston-super-Mare.

Steel Suit

During World War I, the U.S.A. developed the Brewster Body Shield, a suit of armor designed to protect soldiers from bullets. It consisted of a breastplate and headpiece and was made from steel plates to repel machine gun fire at 2,700 ft per second (820 m per second). It weighed a heavy 40 lb (18 kg).

School Flight

When a ferry service was stopped in late 2009, the school children of Papa Westray in Scotland's Orkney Islands were forced to take a 96-second air flight to school each day.

Mini Motorbike

Santosh Kumar of Mysore, India, built an electric motorcycle less than 18 in (45 cm) long and less than 1 ft (30 cm) tall, but capable of carrying a person.

Long Leak

The World-War-II ruin of the battleship U.S.S. *Arizona* is still leaking oil into the ocean nearly 70 years after it was sunk in Pearl Harbor, Hawaii.

Monster Limo

The Midnight Rider, a giant tractor-trailer limo, is 70 ft (21 m) long, 13 ft 8 in (4.2 m) high, has 22 wheels, weighs about 50,560 lb (22,930 kg) and has room for 40 passengers. Owned by Pamela Bartholomew Machado from California, the monster vehicle, which costs $1,000 an hour to hire, boasts three lounges, a bar and a bathroom. A full tank of gas costs about $700 and a full oil change costs around $1,000.

Treasure Hoax

When Patty Henken bought an old rocking chair at an auction in 2008, she found in the stuffing a typewritten note describing a lead chestcontaining $250 in U.S. gold coins that was supposedly buried 15 ft (4.5 m) underground in a vacant lot in Springfield, Illinois. She dug unsuccessfully for the treasure, only to discover later that the note's signatory, "Chauncey Wolcott," was the pen name of a prolific prankster, John "Jay" Slaven, who died in 1976.

Horse-drawn Hummer

Jeremy Dean of New York City spent $15,000 on his Hummer H2 sport utility vehicle, and then turned it into a horse-drawn carriage.

Warthog Alert

In November 2009, an Air Zimbabwe plane made an emergency stop after hitting a warthog on the runway in Harare, Zimbabwe.

Wheelie Wizard

Tyler Shepard, the "Wheelie Wizard" of Middletown, Ohio, rides near-vertical wheelies on a Honda XR 50 motorbike without a front wheel. His wheelie shows include such incredible feats as riding his one-wheeled bike in a wheelie while blindfolded, and maintaining a wheelie for 1 hour 30 minutes nonstop during a parade.

Bottle Boat

Four months after leaving San Francisco, California, the Plastiki, a 60-ft (18-m) catamaran built from 12,500 recycled plastic bottles, reached Sydney, Australia, in July 2010 at the end of a 9,550-mi (15,370-km) voyage across the Pacific Ocean. The boat's bottles were lashed to pontoons and held together with glue made from cashew nut husks and sugar cane. Even the sails were made from recycled plastic.

Lucky Escape

A driving lesson on Good Luck Road, Lanham, Maryland, ended with a large family car crashing through the wall of a ground-floor apartment and finishing up on a bed where the homeowner had been lying just minutes earlier.

Last Orders

Matthias Krankl of Maulburg, Germany, was banned from driving by police after converting a beer crate into a motorized mini quad bike.

Versatile Vehicle

Dave March of the Californian company WaterCar has created the Python, a $220,000 amphibious supercar that can reach speeds of 125 mph (200 km/h) on land and 60 mph (96 km/h)—faster than many speedboats—on water. All the driver has to do before entering the water is put the gears into neutral, engage the jet drive, then push a button to raise the wheels.

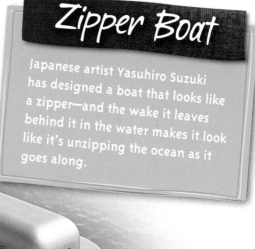

Zipper Boat

Japanese artist Yasuhiro Suzuki has designed a boat that looks like a zipper—and the wake it leaves behind it in the water makes it look like it's unzipping the ocean as it goes along.

Kicking the Bucket

Gaetano Di Furia's coffin was carried to his funeral in Lincolnshire, England, in the bucket of a JCB digger. His family chose it instead of a traditional hearse because he had always enjoyed driving JCBs at work.

Floating Palace

At 1,187 ft (362 m) long, the Finnish-built liner *Oasis of the Seas* is four times the length of a football field and, at 236 ft (72 m) high, it is taller than Nelson's Column in London. Over 3,300 mi (5,310 km) of electrical cabling and 150 mi (240 km) of pipework run through the ship, which took 8,000 man years to build (three years in actual time). Around 160,000 gal (600,000 l) of paint were used to decorate the luxury vessel, which boasts every conceivable facility, including basketball courts, ice rinks, a hospital, a landscaped park, and a wedding chapel. Some 55 tons of ice are produced onboard every day to supply the ship's 37 bars and 20 cafés and restaurants, and no fewer than 50,000 pieces of cutlery are housed in the main dining room.

Backward Driver

Indian taxi driver Harpreet Dev drives everywhere in reverse. His backward driving skills have become so famous in his hometown of Bhatinda that he has even been given a special government license allowing him to drive in reverse anywhere in the state of Punjab. His enthusiasm for driving backward at speeds of up to 50 mph (80 km/h) began one night in 2003 as he was returning home from a party. He discovered that, owing to a mechanical fault, only the reverse gear of his Fiat Padmini worked. He has since redesigned the car's gearbox so that it has four reverse gears and just one forward one.

Super Model

Tony Nijhuis of East Sussex, England, has built a balsa wood and plywood model airplane that weighs more than 100 lb (45 kg) and, with a 20-ft (6-m) wingspan, is as wide as a house. The model is so large it is classed as a light aircraft and has to be licensed by the Civil Aviation Authority. He spent two years and £8,000 ($12,900) constructing the 1:7 scale version of a 1950s U.S. Air Force Boeing B-50 Superfortress bomber, which has four electric motors, 96 batteries, and can reach a speed of 40 mph (64 km/h).

347

Extreme Devotion

These religious devotees are masters of mind over matter, performing totally unbelievable feats that require intense physical and mental discipline and endurance.

Sadhus, sometimes known as fakirs by people in the West, are predominantly Hindu mystics from India. Following an ancient practice of spiritual devotion, sadhus remove themselves from normal life and dedicate themselves to extreme physical feats, often for their entire lifetime. They often claim to be able to control pain using the power of thought, and some have demonstrated this by walking on razor-sharp blades, or piercing their flesh with metal pins. Some go for years without sitting down—or standing up.

HAND HELD HIGH

Many Hindu sadhus make a pilgrimage every four years to the Kumbh Mela festival at the Ganges River, India. This man claimed to have held one of his arms aloft, and not cut his nails, for more than 20 years.

HEAD IN THE SAND

Some Hindu sadhus—such as this gentleman photographed in the 1970s—will bury their head in the ground for extended periods of time.

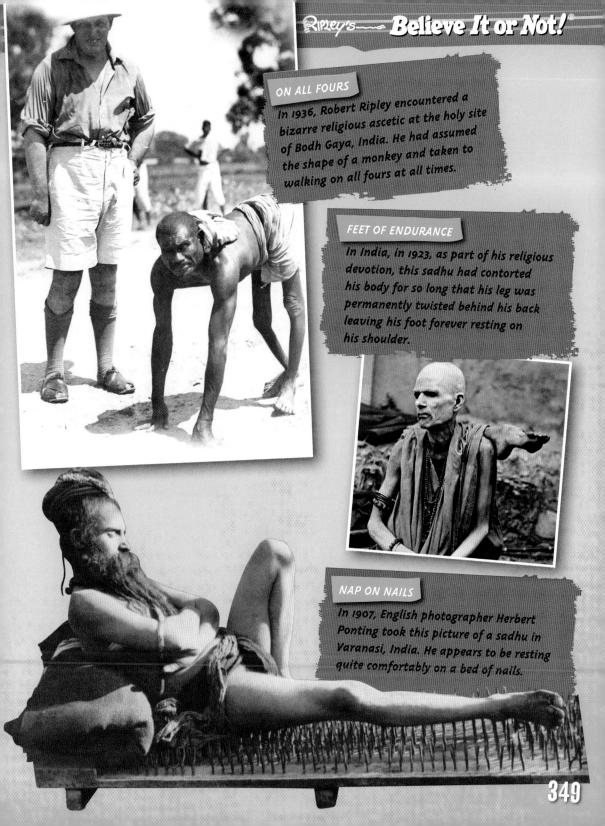

Believe It or Not!*

ON ALL FOURS

In 1936, Robert Ripley encountered a bizarre religious ascetic at the holy site of Bodh Gaya, India. He had assumed the shape of a monkey and taken to walking on all fours at all times.

FEET OF ENDURANCE

In India, in 1923, as part of his religious devotion, this sadhu had contorted his body for so long that his leg was permanently twisted behind his back leaving his foot forever resting on his shoulder.

NAP ON NAILS

In 1907, English photographer Herbert Ponting took this picture of a sadhu in Varanasi, India. He appears to be resting quite comfortably on a bed of nails.

349

Ash Man

Artist Daniel Roberto Ortega from San Diego, California, turns the ashes of dead people and pets into cherished works of art. His first human cremation piece included the ashes of his late father. Bereaved relatives or pet owners send the former mortician's assistant ashes and bone fragments, together with a photograph and biography. He mixes the cremated remains into a paste, adds artifacts representing aspects of the subject's life, and then paints the resulting pattern. He dries it, then applies an acrylic finish.

Same Name

Even though he had no connection with the town, Eric Gordon Douglas, of Edinburgh, Scotland, left more than $17,000 in his will to Douglas, Isle of Man, simply because it shared his surname.

Family Church

When Daryl McClure married Dean Sutcliffe at St. Michael's and All Angels' Church in Ashton-under-Lyne, Greater Manchester, England, she became the seventh generation of her family to marry at that church. At least 11 members of her family have been married there since 1825, but the connection could date back as far as the 17th century.

Long Dead

Tokyo officials trying to update their list of centenarians in preparation for Japan's Respect for the Elderly Day in September 2010 discovered that the city's "oldest man" had actually died more than 30 years earlier. Police said Sogen Kato, who was born in July 1899 and would therefore have been 111, was in fact discovered lying in his bed in a mummified state, wearing pajamas and covered with a blanket.

You Can't Hurry Love

A couple with a combined age of 184 married in England in July 2010. After a four-year courtship, Henry Kerr, 97, tied the knot with Valerie Berkowitz, 87, in North London.

Body Snatchers

An illegally parked funeral van—with a corpse inside—was once towed away by the New York Police Department. Funeral director Paul DeNigris had parked his 2002 Dodge minivan outside the funeral home while he went inside on business, but he returned to find the vehicle—and the body in the back—had been towed to the city pound. He had to rush there to reclaim the corpse and put it on a flight to Miami, where it was headed for cremation.

Faint Pulse

Pronounced dead three hours after suffering a suspected heart attack, Jozef Guzy of Katowice, Poland, was about to be sealed up in a coffin when a funeral director detected a faint pulse. Mr Guzy, 76, was taken to hospital where mystified doctors could find nothing wrong with him, and a few days later he was allowed to go home.

Video Girlfriend

In 2009, a man in Tokyo, Japan, married his animated video-game girlfriend—who exists only in a Nintendo DS game—in a public ceremony complete with a priest, a D.J., and speeches made by friends and family.

Macabre Marriage

To mark the end of his bachelor days bridegroom Pat Vincent arrived for his wedding in London, England, in a coffin. After marrying Jacqueline Brick, he climbed back into the wooden box and was carried on a train to the wedding reception.

Age Gap

A couple who married in Guriceel, Somalia, in 2009 had an age difference of 95 years. Ahmed Muhamed Dore, who claimed to be 112, wed Safia Abdulleh, 17, making him old enough to be her great-great-great grandfather.

Grass Diet

Fifty-year-old Li Sanju of Guangdong Province, China, spent more than two years eating only leaves and grass. He said he enjoyed his unusual diet but admitted that he did smell strongly of grass.

Humongous Hummus

Chefs in Beirut, Lebanon, prepared a massive plate of hummus weighing more than 2 tons. They used 2,976 lb (1,350 kg) of mashed chickpeas, 106 gal (400 l) of lemon juice and 57 lb (26 kg) of salt to make the dish that weighed 4,532 lb (2,056 kg).

Deep-fried Beer

Texas chef Mark Zable has created a recipe for deep-fried beer. The beer is placed inside a pocket of salty, pretzel-like dough and dunked in oil heated to 375°F (190°C) for about 20 seconds. When customers take a bite, the hot beer mixes with the dough to give an alcoholic taste.

Hot Chocolate

In 2009, scientists at Warwick University, England, unveiled an environmentally friendly racing car, built partly from vegetables and powered by chocolate. The bodywork of the WorldFirst car was made from plastic bottles and scraps from airplanes, the seat from flax and soy, and the steering wheel from the waste of juiced carrots. The car, which reached speeds of 135 mph (217 km/h), used plant-oil based lubricants and could run on biodiesel made from chocolate-factory waste and stale wine.

Zebra Pizza

A pizza takeout store in Burnley, England, sells pizzas topped with the meat of zebras, crocodiles, kangaroos and buffalo, alongside more familiar flavors. Owner Arash Fard sells around 20 of his exotic pizzas every week.

Burger Candle

Columbus, Ohio-based fast-food chain White Castle offered customers a new way to sniff its produce by introducing candles that smell like its oniony Slider hamburgers.

Mega Meatball

In 2009, Nonni's Italian Eatery in New Hampshire created a meatball that weighed a colossal 222 lb 8 oz (101 kg). The giant ball of minced meat took three days to cook.

Rich Dish

A 513-lb (233-kg) tuna sold for $177,000 at an auction in January 2010 in Tokyo's Tsukiji fish market. That works out to $345 a pound.

Exotic Tea

Made from older leaves, Puer tea is renowned in China for its exotic taste and healing properties, and is so coveted that just one third of an ounce (10 g) of century-old tea can sell for $10,000.

Still Bubbly

Divers exploring the wreck of a sailing vessel 180 ft (55 m) below the surface of the Baltic Sea off the coast of Finland found 30 bottles of Champagne some 230 years old. As the bottles had been preserved in the ideal conditions of cold and darkness for so many years, experts said the Champagne tasted remarkably good despite having lost some of its fizz.

Wrap Artists

In Lewisburg, Pennsylvania, cooks used 15 lb (6.8 kg) of bacon and 175 wraps held together with about 1,200 toothpicks to create a sandwich wrap 102 ft long (31 m).

Tasty Spider

To raise funds for his school in Kent, England, headteacher Aydin Onac ate a baked Cambodian tarantula spider in front of a packed assembly. He said it tasted like burned chicken.

Jellyfish Candy

In response to an invasion of 6-ft-wide (1.8-m), 440-lb (200-kg) jellyfish, students at Obama Fisheries High School, Japan, harvested the creatures and then turned them into caramel candies.

Dig In

Some people eat the strangest things—wood, glass, metal, clothing, stones, hair, and even excrement. The Glore Psychiatric Museum in St. Joseph, Missouri, has a display of 1,446 unusual items swallowed by a patient and removed from her intestines and stomach—including 453 nails, 42 screws, and assorted safety pins, spoons, and salt-and-pepper shaker tops. She died during surgery from bleeding caused by her weird diet.

DIET OF BUGS

Mr. Zhu from Sichuan Province, China, has eaten live centipedes since he was a child. In just one month, he and his friends consumed more than 3,000 bugs and worms.

SHE'S CRACKED IT

Zhou Yuqin from Chongqing, China, says she has cured all her ailments by eating up to 50 eggshells every day for 13 years. She has even persuaded her children to copy her. When eggshells aren't enough to satisfy her appetite for the unusual, she also nibbles on sand and cullet (broken glass).

DIRT DISH

Fan Qianrong from China's Hebei Province has stayed healthy by eating soil and mud for more than 40 years. Millions of people around the world consume soil, a practice known as geophagy.

Wooden Bicycles

Max Samuelson of Cape May, New Jersey, builds functional bicycles out of wood, using as many as 120 pieces of wood in a single bike.

Motorized Unicycle

In 2009, Japanese auto manufacturer Honda unveiled a motorized unicycle designed mainly for the country's aging population. It has a series of smaller, motor-controlled wheels inside the main wheel, so that to steer the 22-lb (10-kg) battery-powered device on a busy sidewalk all you have to do is lean in the direction you want to go.

Welcome Tip

Taxi driver Don Pratt from Cornwall, England, retired from work after a grateful passenger left him a $375,000 tip in her will. Don had spent 20 years ferrying pensioner Mary Watson to and from her local stores.

Extended Journey

Given permission to drive the family pickup truck to the end of the driveway to unload trash at their home in Damascus, Oregon, a 12-year-old boy kept going for nearly 100 mi (160 km) until police eventually stopped him.

Electric Bullet

In August 2010, the Buckeye Bullet 2.5, an electric car designed by a team of students from Ohio State University, clocked an average speed of 307.7 mph (495.2 km/h) on Utah's Bonneville Salt Flats. The Bullet is powered by nearly 1,600 compact lithium-ion batteries, the kind that are used to power laptops.

Sole Owner

In 2012, 93-year-old Rachel Veitch of Orlando, Florida, finally parted with the Mercury Comet Caliente that she had bought new in 1964 and has since driven nearly 600,000 mi (965,500 km).

When is a Stratoliner airplane not an airplane?

Parking Space
An uncovered, outdoor parking space in Boston, Massachusetts, was sold for $300,000 in June 2009.

Close Encounter
A motorist in London, England, tried to avoid a fine for driving in a bus lane by claiming aliens had forced him into it.

Out to Launch
Having spent nearly 30 years building a boat in his mother's back garden in Hampshire, England, Owen Warboys finally launched the 40-ft-long (12-m) sloop in 2010. He got the 20-ton vessel out of the garden by hiring a crane that lifted it 40 ft (12 m) into the air over the house and onto a truck.

Plane Sailing

Is it a boat? Is it a plane? Actually, it's a bit of both—a plane-boat. Visitors to Fort Lauderdale, Florida, can charter Dave Drimmer's *Cosmic Muffin*, a boat recycled from movie-producer Howard Hughes' old Boeing B-307 airplane. The historic Stratoliner plane was rescued from landfill in 1969 by pilot Ken London, who bought it for $69 and spent four years removing the wings and converting it into a luxury boat. The cockpit of the original plane still houses the controls that steer the craft.

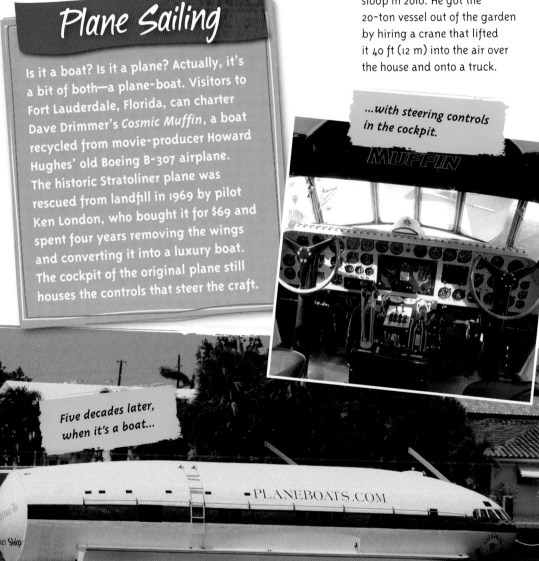

...with steering controls in the cockpit.

Five decades later, when it's a boat...

-PLANEBOATS.COM

Jumbomania

Jumbo was an African elephant of monumental proportions, and he enjoyed fame on both sides of the Atlantic every bit as huge as his stature.

Jumbomania, as it was called, began in 1861 when the elephant was captured in the French Sudan and then exported to the Jardins des Plantes Zoo in Paris, France. He then moved on to London Zoo, where he became famous for giving rides to visitors. Placed under such unnatural restraints, Jumbo's patience wore thin. The elephant, whose name was based on *jumbe*, the Swahili word for "chief," became too hot to handle and he was sold to "The Greatest Show on Earth"—the Barnum & Bailey Circus based in the U.S.A. The whole British nation rose up to protest. Crowds converged on the zoo, legal proceedings against the decision began, and Queen Victoria, herself a huge fan, received 100,000 letters appealing for her to intervene. American P.T. Barnum was offered £100,000 ($160,000) in exchange for the precious elephant, but in a moment of huge showbiz drama, he refused the offer. Jumbo was to be shipped out of London for good.

WHAT HAPPENED TO JUMBO?

After Jumbo's death, the New York Times *reported that taxidermists had removed the elephant's hide—which weighed 1,600 lb (726 kg) and needed 100 tons of salt and 100 lb (45 kg) of elm bark to cure it—and bones. His skeleton was given to New York's Museum of Natural History, and his heart was bought by Cornell University. The rest of his body was cremated. His stuffed hide traveled with the circus until Barnum donated it to Tufts University, near Boston (left), where Jumbo became the official mascot. He was displayed there until destroyed by a fire in 1975.*

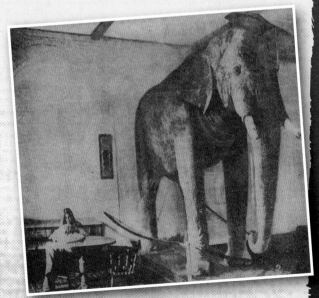

Sweet Skulls

Marina Malvada, an artist from Montreal, Canada, uses genuine human skulls—borrowed from a tribal art collector who specializes in collecting cannibal skulls—to cast life-sized skulls in chocolate. Each head is solid chocolate, takes four days to complete and is entirely edible—although at a weight of 5½ lb (2.5 kg) each, one is enough.

Barter System

In 2010, a bar owner on Estonia's Hiiumaa Island in the Baltic Sea revived the age-old barter system to allow customers to pay for drinks with goods. Tarvo Nomm agreed to sell beer in return for bundles of firewood and catches of fish to help the locals beat economic hardship.

Banana Boxers

Australian company AussieBum has unveiled a range of men's underwear made from bananas. The eco-friendly range incorporates 27 percent banana fiber, making the garments lightweight and absorbent without actually smelling of bananas.

Half-mile Pizza

In August 2010, chefs in Krakow, Poland, used 3.5 tons of flour to make a pizza measuring 3,280 ft (1,000 m) in length—that's more than half a mile (0.8 km) long!

Chocolate Shoes

Confectioner Frances Cooley from Bristol, England, sells shoes and handbags made of chocolate. She has developed a line of individual, high-heeled shoes—including zebra-striped and polka-dot versions—which she makes by hand in her own kitchen. The largest shoe is 6¾ in (17 cm) long and made from two 3½-oz (100-g) bars of Belgian chocolate.

Scott's Butter

Two blocks of New Zealand butter nearly a century old were found intact in 2009 in an Antarctic hut used by British explorer Robert Falcon Scott on his doomed 1910–12 expedition.

Nacho Tray

At Northstar Church, Frisco, Texas, more than 300 volunteers built a 3,555-lb (1,613-kg), 48-ft-long (14.6-m) tray of nachos, loaded with 2,200 lb (998 kg) of tortilla chips, 600 lb (272 kg) of nacho cheese and 250 lb (113 kg) of sour cream, as well as an extra 250 lb (113 kg) of jalapenos, 200 lb (90 kg) of shredded Cheddar cheese and 200 lb (90 kg) of sauce.

Dogs' Dinner

An ice-cream van exclusively for dogs attended a 2010 pet festival in London, England. Created by a team of scientists, the canine-friendly, K99 ice cream comes in two flavors— Dog Eat Hog World, a gammon and chicken sorbet topped with a biscuit bone and served in a cone, and Canine Cookie Crunch, dog biscuits and ice cream topped with a biscuit bone.

Soluble Gum

Scientists at Bristol University, England, have devised a nonstick chewing gum. Rev7 has the same taste and texture as normal gum, but it disintegrates over time and can be removed from shoes, hair, and other surfaces with just soap and water.

Tea Nation

Britons drink 165 million cups of tea every day—around three cups a day per person. Although Great Britain accounts for less than 1 percent of the world's population, it is responsible for about 4 percent of its tea consumption.

Testicle Cooking

At the 2010 Testicle Cooking World Championship in Ozrem, Serbia, chefs produced dishes made from the testicles of animals including bulls, wild boar, horses, sharks, ostriches, kangaroos, donkeys, turkeys, goats, reindeer and elk.

$1,000 Burger

Joe El-Ajouz's restaurant in Sydney, Australia, has a burger on the menu that costs $1,000. It weighs 210 lb (95 kg), requires 178 lb (81 kg) of minced meat, 120 eggs, 120 cheese slices, 4½ lb (2 kg) of lettuce, 16 tomatoes, 46 lb (21 kg) of bread, and 1.1 lb (500 g) of barbecue sauce. It takes over 12 hours to cook and serves more than 100 people.

Double Banana

Having bought a bunch of bananas at a grocery store in Somerset, England, Cedric Hooper got home and found that one skin in fact contained two bananas!

Fast Grub

Eating insects is so popular in Thailand that the country even has its own insect fast-food chain. Insects Inter has more than 30 outlets selling fried, crunchy grasshoppers, crickets, grubs and silkworms in 70-cent pots with ketchup or hot chili dips.

Pub Crawl

Since 1984, Stuart Ashby of West Sussex, England, has drunk more than 8,500 pints of beer in over 17,000 British pubs, from Cornwall to the Shetland Islands, in the process traveling some 25,000 mi (40,000 km).

Long Lunch

In September 2010, chefs in Italy served lunch on a table that was more than a mile (1.6 km) long. The 5,775-ft-long (1,760-m) spread was laid out for 2,700 diners and stretched from Bosco to nearby Borzano. The organizers' biggest problem was that the table required a 5,905-ft long (1,800-m) tablecloth.

Wee Dram

London-based designer James Gilpin has created whisky made from the high-sugar urine of elderly diabetic patients, including his own grandmother. Gilpin, who is himself diabetic, filters the urine by the same processes used to purify water, and in doing so removes the sugars, which are then used in fermentation. The drink, named Gilpin Family Whisky, is not for sale.

Safe Breakfast

Scientists in the U.K. have developed a breakfast that won't make you sick if you go on a roller coaster shortly afterward. It consists of yogurt mixed with blueberries and grilled bacon in a wholemeal bun with tomato. It is served with a drink of celery and carrot juice with ginger. U.K. theme park Alton Towers was so confident in the product that it offered to refund anyone who was sick on a ride after eating the breakfast.

Beers and Spirits

For more than nine months in 2009, a ghost apparently kept topping up drinkers' glasses at the Apsley House pub in Southsea, Hampshire, England. Landlady Janice McCormack complained that the specter was costing her a fortune because it was giving away her beer.

Vegetable Phobia

Vicki Larrieux of Portsmouth, England, suffers from lachanophobia, a fear of vegetables. The only vegetables she can bear to eat, touch or see are potatoes. The sight of a carrot or a pea, not just on her plate but even on grocery-store shelves, leaves her sweating and stricken with panic attacks.

Giant Cupcake

Chefs in Boca Raton, Florida, unveiled a 1,500-lb (680-kg) chocolate cupcake. It stood 4½ ft (1.4 m) high, 6 ft (1.8 m) wide, and was topped with pink frosting, handmade 5-in (12.5-cm) sprinkles, and a cherry with a circumference of 12 in (30 cm). It was baked in an oven measuring 10 x 10 ft (3 x 3 m).

Golden Curry

Restaurateurs Padma Prasad and Bhagat Saxena of Hyderabad, India, added finely ground flakes of gold and silver to create a chicken curry that costs $300 a serving.

Molto Macaroni

Chef John Folse cooked 2,469 lb (1,120 kg) of macaroni and cheese—enough for 6,500 servings—in New Orleans, Louisiana, in September 2010.

Full O Bull

The Cowtown Diner in Fort Worth, Texas, serves a chicken fried steak that weighs about 10 lb (4.5 kg) and packs a fattening 10,000 calories. The "Full O Bull," which comes complete with 6 lb (2.7 kg) of mashed potatoes and 10 slices of toast, normally costs $70—but if you can eat it solo, it's free!

Squirrel Ale

In 2010, a Scottish brewery packaged bottles of its new beer, "The End of History," inside the bodies of dead animals. BrewDog sold bottles of its strong, limited-edition Belgian ale—made with juniper berries and containing a staggering 55 percent alcohol—for $1,000 if housed inside a dead squirrel and $750 for bottles encased in a dead stoat. The limited edition 12 dead-animal bottles were hand-crafted by a Yorkshire taxidermist using only creatures that had died of natural causes.

INDEX

ACKNOWLEDGMENTS

12 Chin Boon Leng; 14–15 Alex Smith - www.as-images.com; 16 Getty Images; 18 Richard Jones/Sinopix/Rex Features; 19 Debbie Does Cakes/Rex Features; 20 Honda Motor Europe Ltd; 22 Californiaskateparks.com; 23 Kevin Le; 24 (t/r) National Geographic/Getty Images, (t/l) SSPL via Getty Images, (t/r) Stephen L. Alvarez/National Geographic/Getty Images; 25 (b) Jae C. Hong/AP/Press Association Images, (b/r) Robyn Beck/AFP/Getty Images; 27 Barcroft Media; 28 Jayna Sullivan Photography; 30 Charles Eisenmann Collection/University of Syracuse; 31 Getty Images; 32 Reuters/Reinhard Krause; 33 Collect/PA Wire/Press Association Images; 34–35 Paul Christoforou; 37 Chris Trueman/Alexander Salazar Gallery; 38 APOPO; 39 © EuroPics[CEN]; 40–41 Theo Stroomer / Demotix; 42 Wenn.com; 43 The Cheeky/Rex Features; 44 Getty Images; 45 Charles Eisenmann Collection/University of Syracuse; 47 Jagdeep Rajput/Solent; 48 Reuters/Will Burgess; 49 Chin Boon Leng; 50 KeystoneUSA-ZUMA/Rex Features; 51 © EuroPics[CEN]; 52 (t) AP Photo, The Canadian Press, Lethbridge Herald, Ian Martens, (b/l, b/r) Gabriel Luque/Rex Features; 53 (t/l) AP Photo, The Canadian Press, Lethbridge Herald, Ian Martens, (t/r) Polaris/eyevine, (b/l) Rob Yuill/Albanpix Ltd/Rex Features, (b/r) Rob Yuill/Albanpix Ltd/Rex Features; 54 Eddie Mitchell/Rex Features; 55 INS News Agency Ltd./Rex Features; 56 Photo by Havel Ruck Projects, "Inversion". 2005, (demolished), Dan Havel & Dean Ruck, Site-specific sculptural installation, Art League Houston, Houston, Texas; 58 (b) J.D. Griggs/US Geological Survey/Rex Features, (t) David Jordan AP/Press Association Images; 59 (c/l) Ethel Davies/Robert Harding/Rex Features, (b/l, b/r) EPA/Photoshot; 60 (b/r) John Terning, (b/l) Carl McCabe; 63 Jay Fine/Caters News; 64 Photo by Havel Ruck Projects, "Inversion". 2005, (demolished), Dan Havel & Dean Ruck, Site-specific sculptural installation, Art League Houston, Houston, Texas; 65 Imagine China; 66–67 Massimo Brega, The Lighthouse/Science Photo Library; 67 Apex; 69 © Hulton-Deutsch Collection/Corbis; 71 LatinContent/Getty Images; 72 © Swim Ink 2, LLC/Corbis; 73 (l) Rykoff Collection/Corbis, (r) © Blue Lantern Studio/Corbis; 77–79 Library of Congress; 80 EPA/Photoshot; 81 Solent News/Rex Features; 83 www.Freitag.ch; 84 Tsuzuki Minako; 85 Reuters; 86 Dmitry Dudin; 88–89 Will Hunt; 90 (l) Mark Duncan/AP/Press Association Images, (r) U.S. Coast Guard photo by Petty Officer 2nd Class Lauren Jorgensen; 91 Barcroft Media via Getty Images; 92 Malcolm Teasdale/KiwiRail; 93 (t) Barcroft Media via Getty Images, (c) © Vladone/istockphoto.com; 94–95 ChinaFotoPress via Getty Images; 96 Bloomberg via Getty Images; 98 Alain Van de Maele; 99 Rex/Wendy Connett/Robert Harding; 100 Diane Smith/www.noahs-ark.org; 102–103 Ingo Arndt/Nature Picture Library; 104 Mark Moffett/Minden Pictures/FLPA; 105 © Ch'ien C. Lee; 106 Tibo Szabo, Sue Lees, Photographer Michael Orescanin; 107 Richard Young; 108 Caters News; 110 Caters News; 111 Conny Sandland/Rex Features; 112 R. Roscoe (photovolcanica.com); 113 Luke Marsden/Newspix/Rex Features; 114–115 James Dagmore / Polaris / eyevine; 116 Caters News; 117 Nicole Kane; 118 Wenn; 120 Armin Weigel/DPA/Press Association Images; 121 Rossparry.co.uk/syndication/Doncaster Free Press; 122 Reuters/Michael Caronna; 123 © Europics; 126 M & Y Agency Ltd/Rex Features; 127 Jonathan Pow/Ross Parry Agency; 128 Diane Smith/www.noahs-ark.org; 129 © Stuart Isett / Anzenberger represented by: eyevine; 130 DR Richard Kirby/BNPS; 131 Image courtesy of Expedition to the Deep Slope 2006 Exploration, NOAA Vents Program; 132 Quirky China News/Rex Features; 135 (c) Luis Fernando Espin/Rex Features, (t) Karen Bacon/Solent News/Rex Features, (b) Michael Cenci/Solent News/Rex Features; 137 Quirky China News/Rex Features; 138 www.sell-my-photo.co.uk; 139 © Johann Opperman/solentnews.co.uk; 140 www.toadfactory.com; 141 Reuters/Wolfgang Rattay; 143 Tomas Rak/Solent News/Rex Features; 144 www.tesladownunder.com; 146–147 Akash Awasthi; 149 © Akinunde Akinleye/Reuters/Corbis; 150 AP Photo/Luis Benavides; 151 Swell.com; 152 Jeffrey Cunningham; 154 Iain Ferguson, The Write Image; 155 © Wifredo Garcia Alvaro/epa/Corbis; 156 Dan Callister/Rex Features; 157 Quirky China News/Rex Features; 158 © -M-I-S-H-A-/iStockphoto.com; © dtimiraos/iStockphoto.com; 162 Christian Pondella/Caters News; 164 Getty Images; 166–167 EPA/Photoshot; 169 Nick Obank/Barcroft Media LT; 170–171 Edmond Hawkins; 172 Harry Scull Jr./AP/Press Association Images; 173 Eric Lafargue /www.LPS.ch/; 174–175 (t) Stephen Pond/Empics Sport; 174 Ryan Remiorz/AP/Press Association Images; 175 Ron Jenkins/Fort Worth Star-Telegram/Polaris; 176 Rex/Imagine China; 178 Nagananda Swamy; 179 www.tesladownunder.com; 180 Henrik May/ski-namibia.com; 181 AFP/Getty Images; 182–183 anthonyescapes.com; 184 The Shields Gazette; 190 ChinaFotoPress via Getty Images; 191 (t/c) NY Daily News via Getty Images, (t/r) Getty Images; 192 Xinhua/Photoshot; 193 Charles Eisenmann Collection/University of Syracuse; 194 Christine Cornege/AP/Press Association Images; 196 Collection of Jack and Beverly Wilgus; 198 © Europics; 198–199 Sinopix/Rex Features; 200 (t) Chad Grochowski, (b) Bob Huberman; 202 KPN; 203 Joey Miller; 204 Steve Gschmeissner/Science Photo Library; 205 Atlas Press/eyevine; 206 Reuters/China Daily Information Corp – CDIC; 208 Circus World Museum, Baraboo, Wisconsin; 210 Nick Afanasiev; 212 © Europics [CEN]; 213 Pictures courtesy of Steve McFarlane; 214 Mario Rosenau/Bizarre archive/Dennis Publishing; 216 Quirky China News/Rex Features; 217 EPA/Photoshot; 218 (t/r) Science Photo Library, (b/c) Scott Camazine/Science Photo Library, (b/l) Kaj R. Svensson/Science Photo Library; 220 Reuters/Paulo Santos; 221 Getty Images; 222 Chuck Nyce; 225 Asha Mandela; 228 Dennis Van Tine/ABACA USA/Empics Entertainment; 229 Anders (The Piercing Guy) Allinger www.phatpiercings.com; 230–231 Alan Humerose/Rezo.ch; 232 Yang Maoyuan; 234–235 Pictures courtesy of Craig Tracy; 236 Images courtesy of Shauna Richardson; 237 Victor Liu/Solent News/Rex Features; 239 Drew Gardner/eyevine; 240–241 Getty Images; 242 Caters News; 244–245 L.A. Pop Art www.lapopart.com; 246–247 Yang Maoyuan; 248–249 Solent News/Rex Features; 252 Ari Mahardhika/Solent News/Rex Features; 254 Insaland.com; 255 Xia Xiao Wan; 256–257 Kris Kuksi; 258 Solent News/Rex Features; 259 Ji Yong-Ho/Solent/Rex Features; 260–216 Geoffrey Robinson/Rex Features; 262 Guerra de la Paz; 263 Images courtesy of Morten Viskum and VEGAS gallery, London; 264 Fredo; 266 (t/l) Matthew Albanese, (t/r, c/r) matthewalbanese.com/Solent News/Rex Features; 267 Michael Tompert/Paul Fairchild/Rex Features; 269 Bernard Pras; 270 www.grindshow.com; 272–273 Solent News/Rex Features; 275 Dr Rev Bloodpainter; 280 DeWitt Webb/www.cfz.org.uk; 281 Fortean Picture Library; 282 Quirky China News/Rex Features; 283 Quirky China News/Rex Features; 284 Fortean Picture Library; 285 Tony O'Rahilly/Rex Features; 288 JPL/NASA; 289 Shizuo Kambayashi/AP/Press Association Images; 290–291 Fortean Picture Library; 292 Kamioka Observatory, ICRR (Institute for Cosmic Ray Research), The University of Tokyo; 294 Andy Willsheer/Rex Features; 295 © Europics; 296 Fortean Picture Library; 298 Stew Milne/AP/Press Association Images; 299 www.suzanneproulx.com; 300 © Bettmann/Corbis; 301 Pictures courtesy of Donald Estes/Natchez Cemetery; 302 www.sell-my-photo.co.uk; 303 SSPL via Getty Images; 304–305 Henrik Lauridsen, Kasper Hansen, Michael Pedersen and Tobias Wang; 306 Leon Shadeberg/Rex Features; 307 Courtesy of Caz Housey; 309 © Illustrated London News Ltd/Mary Evans; 310 © 2009 Heiner Muller-Elsner/Focus/Eyevine; 311 Quirky China News/Rex Features; 312 Claire Carter; 314 Fabi Fliervoet/Solent News/Rex Features; 315 (t) Flughafen Leipzig/Halle GmbH/DPA/Press Association Images, (b/l) Cover/Getty Images, (c/r) James D. Morgan/Rex Features, (b/r) Getty Images; 317 Barcroft Media via Getty Images; 318 Quirky China News/Rex Features; 319 Reuters/Sean Yong; 320 Pictures courtesy of Tyler Shepard sponsored by Dreyer Honda of Indianapolis, IN; 322–323 © Edward A. Ornelas/San Antonio Express-News/Zuma/Eyevine; 323 (c/r) © Val Horvath/Shreveport Times/Zuma/Eyevine; 324 Rex Features; 325 KPA/Zuma/Rex Features; 326 Annie B. Brady; 327 © Europics; 328–329 Lou Sapienza/Polaris/eyevine; 329 (b/l) Philip Makanna/Polaris/eyevine; 330 Michael Yon; 331 Roger Viollet/Getty Images; 332–333 Indy Boys Inc; 334 Wenn; 335 Kristjan Logason / Demotix; 336 Getty Images; 337 (t) Courtesy of Cookie Crum, (b/r) Reuters/Amit Gupta, (b/l) Reuters/Fayaz Kabli; 338–339 Barry Bland/Barcroft USA; 341 (t/r, t/l) East News/Rex Features, (b) Roger-Viollet/Rex Features; 342 (t) Hannes Langeder/Rex Features, (b) Manfred lang/Rex Features; 344 www.themidnightrider.com; 345 Pictures courtesy of Tyler Shepard sponsored by Dreyer Honda of Indianapolis, IN; 346 Wenn.com; 347 Ross Parry Agency; 348 (b/r) Raghu Rai/Rex Features, (b/l) Rajesh Kumar Singh/AP/Press Association Images; 349 (b) Herbert Ponting; 350 Daniel Ortega; 354–355 ChinaFotoPress via Getty Images; 356 Collection of the John and Mable Ringling Museum of Art Archives; 357 From the John and Mable Ringling Museum of Art Tibbals Digital Collection; 358 Marina Malvada/Rex Features; 360–361 AFP/Getty Images; 363 David Branfield www.davebranfield.com

Key: t = top, b = bottom, c = center, l = left, r = right, sp = single page, dp = double page
All other photos are from Ripley Entertainment Inc.
Every attempt has been made to acknowledge correctly and contact copyright holders and we apologize in advance for any unintentional errors or omissions, which will be corrected in future editions.